PHOENIX RISING

THE COMPLETE SERIES

ANNIE ANDERSON

PHOENIX RISING
The Complete Series

International Bestselling Author
Annie Anderson

Edited by Angela Sanders
Cover Design by Tattered Quill Designs

www.annieande.com

Dear Reader,

This book is intended for readers aged 18 and older. Within these pages are situations containing effluent cursing, torture, blood, guts, gore, sex, love, despair, war, heartbreak, corruption, and death. If you are unable to handle these situations, I would advise putting this book down immediately.

Because shit's about to get real.

All jokes aside, if you would like a full list of CW in this book, please find them here:
annieande.com/content-warnings

FLAME KISSED

PHOENIX RISING BOOK ONE

ANNIE ANDERSON

PROLOGUE

AURELIA—1855

FATES, HELP ME. THEY ARE GOING TO KILL EACH OTHER.

Breath saws through my lungs as I whip my head, searching. The colors of the withering leaves tumble and writhe together as I stumble through the forest. I can't see them, but I know they're out there. Just like I know something is wrong.

I can't find him. I can't. I can't.

But what's more, I don't *want* to find him—or rather *them.* I do not want to see another reality of a vision I will never change. I don't want to confirm the truth that is painfully etching its way into my soul.

Dead leaves crunch beneath my feet as I scramble through the bedrock and crest the first foothill toward the outlook cliff.

Stupid skirt. Stupid slippery shoes.

I'm not moving quickly enough, but in my state, I'm surprised I can move at all. Cradling the swell of my belly, I try to climb faster, the stitch in my side nearly bringing me to my knees.

Where are they?

I stop and search the sky for them—for their flames, for their wings, but I know it's too late. It is rapidly darkening to the inky black of evening of the early Autumn, and without the light from the moon tonight, I'll never see as properly as I should.

A vision slams into my consciousness once more: my husband and his childhood friend, Rhys, locked in the heat of battle. I want to shout, but I'm lost to the depths of their conflict, and as my husband rains down a blow upon his friend, my eyes snap open. I'm overcome with disillusion at first, the phantom pains from the vision ripping through my flesh. Then I see the very real blood dripping down my arm.

But I'm alone. How can this be happening?

I hear and see no one, only the large gaping gash that has torn open my arm from wrist to elbow. The coppery bite of blood turns my stomach as the warm, sticky stream seeps past my fingers and drips onto the dirt.

Blackness clouds my vision for a moment, but I force myself to forget the constant pulse of my injury and pull myself together. Ripping a swath from my billowing skirt, I use the fabric to bind my arm in an effort to stem the bleeding. The navy-blue patterned fabric turns indigo from the blood quickly oozing from my wound.

I should already be healing, but I'm not.

Dread fills my gut as the nausea returns.

This is not good.

Picking myself up from the gritty forest floor, I rethink the panicked pace of before and plod forward at a more sedate pace. Running with this injury just isn't possible. I'm already pushing it with this silly corset and dress, especially in my delicate condition.

As if impending motherhood was anything but delicate.

There.

The sound of Rhys and Lucien clashing together somewhere in the distance rings through my ears. If I don't get there in time, I am certain they'll kill each other. The chilling growl of an angry man drifts through the trees, and my feet carry me faster as if they have a mind of their own.

But when I get there, I realize I should never have stopped to catch my breath.

I should never have bound my wound.

I shouldn't have waited.

"Lucien?" The whisper of his name falls from my lips on a sob.

My husband is on the ground, and all it takes is one look at his still form to know he's dead. I know, just as I knew I was with child long before my cycle refused to come. How I knew so many things that I wished I didn't.

"Lucien?"

His cool blue eyes fail to move. They simply stare at the rapidly darkening sky, his body still and cold.

Lucien's not breathing, and Rhys is just standing there bleeding, holding the blade he used to kill my husband. Holding that same blasted knife that I saw in my vision.

No. No. No.

I haven't a clue as to what made me do it. And looking back, it's still a mystery to me as to how the blade moved from Rhys' loose grip and into my hand, or how exactly I knew where to pierce his flesh to hurt him the most.

Driving the blade home in his flesh, blood instantly pours from my own belly, down my bodice, and through my skirt. Shock and bitter anguish tears through me as realization dawns.

I knew then that when my arm had been sliced, it had actually been Rhys who had gotten cut first—it had been Rhys who had bled first.

I stabbed him, but we both bled.

Bound, my mind screams. *We are bound.*

Then the contractions start.

And I will forever blame Rhys for two deaths that day.

I

AURELIA

IT STARTS JUST LIKE THEY ALWAYS DO, FROM THE BLACKNESS OF a sleep so deep, the fabric of what is real and what is dream weaves together to make what would be.

An entryway or vestibule, the room seemed small. A little girl had opened the door, a lovely walnut wood, inlaid with a stained-glass window. The mother's heels clicked against the cream-colored marble floor with an urgent gait as she hurried toward her daughter, her pink skirt suit swishing against her legs as she fiddled with the simple strand of understated pearls at her neck.

"I thought I told you not to—"

The girl's white-blonde hair practically gleamed against her skin as her mouth formed an "O" of surprise. She was young, maybe six or seven, and deeply tan, as only children could be with their terminable immunity to the heat and sun.

Moving behind the girl, the shock on the mother's face morphed into fear so quickly her features seemed to warp, like a piece of untreated wood that had been left to the elements to rot.

She gripped her daughter's shoulders, shaking her violently in an attempt to get the poor girl to move, to back away from the looming shadow. Clearly male, the figure was backlit by the rising sun. The woman recognized the man, however. She didn't need to see his face to know what danger lay before them—she could easily see the large caliber handgun gripped in his meaty palm.

Shrieking for her daughter to run, the mother roughly tugged the poor girl behind her back. But her daughter was either in shock or too scared to move because she stayed rooted to the spot, clutching the hem of her mother's designer suit.

Slowly, calmly, the man raised his gun as if he had all the time in the world to take his shot. The muzzle fired once, and a tiny hole appeared in the woman's chest. A small trickle of blood bloomed over the heart of her blouse. She went down slowly, dropping first to her knees, sliding to her bottom, and then to her side. Even in death, she was careful not to fall on her child. Again, the muzzle fired, and this time, the daughter collapsed, her wound considerably less pretty, given the caliber of the gun and her small size.

And in that tiny little vestibule, in what was surely a beautiful home of a nice family, the mother and daughter were left to cool in their drying lifeblood.

I SHOULD WAKE UP SCREAMING, BUT I DON'T. AFTER THESE many years, dreaming night after night of the horrors people inflict on one another, I stopped screaming several decades ago. As per usual, though, I sit bolt upright in my bed, sheets tangled around my legs, damp with cold sweat.

My best friend Evan would call me a psychic, but I tell her on the regular she's full of shit. Psychics know things before they happen, and I do. On occasion.

But not enough for me to actually make a difference.

Not enough to save the people who need saving.

And just once? I'd really like to be wrong.

For curiosity's sake, I pull my laptop onto the bed, praying I don't blow up this beautiful piece of equipment. I have a bad habit of frying electrical devices when I'm upset, and watching a mom and daughter get gunned down in their home definitely puts me in the "agitated" column. In fact, this is my fourth laptop this year.

Closing my eyes, I take a deep breath. Once marginally centered, I type the local news site into the browser. Sure enough, the breaking news story is of Victoria Ness, thirty-four, and Vivian Ness, seven, who were gunned down in their University Park home two hours ago. The shooter, Victoria's estranged husband, then turned the gun on himself.

Figures.

What kind of psychic am I? Well, evidently, I'm the shitty kind. I *maybe* see ten percent of what I should, and I can't alter a single second of it. I see what I see, and then I brace myself because it's going to happen. There's nothing I can do.

Believe me, I've tried.

Just once I'd like to have a vision I could change.

Just once I'd like to see something other than how *and* when someone will die.

But I know my fate, and sanity just isn't in the cards for me.

Staring out the huge picture window, I take in the view of the mountain range beyond. The craggy rocks and giant boulders are so vastly different from where I started my life. There are fewer trees here in the subalpine Rockies than in the Pacific Northwest, and the sun shines more days throughout the year. The heat, the sun, the smell of dry earth —all these differences help me breathe when I wake from a new vision.

A new death.

Seeing that blue sky goes a long way to calm me down when I should be rocking in a corner.

Getting out of bed, I immediately rip off the sweat-soaked sheets. It's a ritual of sorts. A fresh start. A means of washing away a death I can't change, and the helplessness of another life gone. Snapping the clean sheets on the bed, I begin bracing myself for the total freaking production tonight will be.

I have an art show this evening, and though it's July in Denver, I'll be covered from neck to ankles to hide the ink on my skin, wear contacts to cloak the eyes that mark me as what I am, and pray that no one finds me. Yes, it's Denver, and yes, even grandmothers are inked these days, but it's the eyes that get people.

As a seer, I was born with the ability to observe events that will come to pass in vivid Technicolor right inside my little noggin. And my eyes? They marked me before I ever had my first vision. My irises are an extraordinarily pale, milky green. Like in old westerns where the elderly guy is blind, and he has those freaky eyes where the iris and pupil nearly blend into the sclera? Yep, that's what I've got going on here.

But my sight is better than most humans. Likely better than most Ethereals, too. But the Ethereal community prefers not to remember we even exist—our presence reminding them that there's no such thing as a true immortal. Everything dies. Witch or warlock, wraith, or even a meager human, they all perish in the end. And when they do, flames and wings are what you better hope you see.

It's better than the alternative.

And let's not get into the fact that sometimes I randomly electrocute people without meaning to. If people weren't already looking at me funny before—*which they are, because my eyes freak people way the hell out*—they would after I randomly zapped them.

So I wear contacts when I leave my home, because if I don't, people assume I'm blind, for one, and they act all awkward and try to help me do stuff or get around. Or *numero dos*: their faces say they are skeeved way the hell out. Also, when I'm pissed, they kind of, well, glow.

Like an incandescent bulb, *glow*.

So the fact that I'm different is really fucking obvious and that doesn't even touch on the flames.

Or the wings.

Hello, my name is Aurelia Constantine, and I am a phoenix.

No offense to Greek mythology, but I'm not a damn bird. I'm a person. I just so happen—on occasion—to burst into flames, have visions, and electrocute people with a shield that I can't seem to control. Oh, and those wings? Very, very real.

And they're persnickety little bitches to boot.

My last phase totally ruined my favorite leather jacket. I've had that jacket for the past twenty years. They just don't make leather like they used to. Replacing it was a pain in the ass, and in the end, I had to have it custom made.

Also, I don't age. Or die. Wait. I take that back. I've died. *A lot.* I just don't *stay* dead.

I've looked thirty-ish for the last one hundred and fifty years or so. Since I was born about thirty years prior to the aging halt, I'm assuming my kind ages at a normal rate until we reach our bodies' maturity. Then we stop aging altogether.

Or it could just be me.

I *should* know all these details for sure, *should* be knowledgeable about the basic facets of my species, but escaping my Legion at twenty means I was never taught several important aspects of being what I am.

What I do know is that when you're a seer in my culture and reach maturity, you get permanently blinded so your visions will be "pure"— whatever the hell that means—transforming a lowly seer into an oracle.

Our visions are important. Seers and oracles alike foresee visions of death, and in predicting death, we can direct the gentry to the dead or dying to send the souls on to be reborn. Seers cannot change the outcome of their visions. Oracles, however, have enough advanced warning and the power to change the future.

In my mind, it is the only advantage for the price they paid when they gave away their eyes.

One hundred and eighty years I've been alive, and for nearly all of them, I've been running. Hiding amongst the humans so ignorant of our existence. Trying so hard to blend in, not get caught again by the people I once called family. Doing my best to make sure I don't lose what little autonomy I have left.

But all it takes is one person to put two and two together and realize I'm not human.

All it takes is one person to notice my differences or see me change into what I really am.

All it takes is one person to remember me, and I'll be fucked.

Truth be told, I'd prefer not to go to the show at all and just get the check for any of my work that's sold. I'd rather change into fresh pajamas, order takeout, and binge *Supernatural* for the five-zillionth time. But Evan, who does double duty as the curator for the James Gallery and the poor soul who calls herself my best friend, has decided I'm a shut-in long enough three hundred or so days a year.

Every single opening, she makes me go and pretend to look at my art like a real live person, who breathes and speaks and shit. It's utterly exhausting. Personally, I think she's overexaggerating. I go out.

Occasionally. To get tattoos and groceries—but so what? That counts as out, dammit.

Why she's my friend, I'll never know.

I say that, but I know why. She's my friend, because when I was at my lowest, when I thought I couldn't go on another day, she crashed into my life and gave me someone to look after. She is the yin to my yang, the Disco to my Heavy Metal.

In reality, she's a wraith princess, the only child of John Black, the Wraith King. Phoenixes and wraiths are supposed to hate each other, but I couldn't hate that girl if someone paid me. Other wraiths are a bit sketchy, but Evan, she is the light in the darkness.

I just wish she'd let me stay home and avoid this whole mess.

So far, I've managed to maintain my anonymity. That's what Evan is for—because she can be in the spotlight when I can't. She has the freedom to move from city to city, selling, curating, being an all-around wonderkid where I cannot.

All because of my stupid Legion.

So tonight, I'll be hiding in plain sight, eating finger food and drinking cheap wine like any other art-consuming hipster, pretending I'm not the one who painted the pretty pictures.

Suddenly, "Shake Your Groove Thing" blasts from the speakers of my phone. Why Evan thought Peaches & Herb was an appropriate ringtone, I'll never know.

"What?" I answer, knowing she is T-minus three seconds from an Opening Day meltdown of Chernobyl proportions.

"Where in the blue fuck are you? You were supposed to be down the mountain already and driving into Denver, and your ass is probably still sitting in bed! You do this to me *every* single *time*. Dammit, *Ari*, get your *ass* in gear."

"I'm getting a very bad feeling about tonight," I whisper, but I say this each and every time.

This time, though, it's the whisper that catches her attention.

"You see anything?" she breathes.

Evan knows too much. Well, Evan knows pretty much everything. I know she feeds most of the information to Rhys, but I can't muster up the courage to tell her to stop. Evan is like a dog with a bone.

"Nothing but a murder this morning. You know the Ness family?"

"Yeah, I do," is all that comes through the line on a broken gasp. "They're huge patrons. They're supposed to be here tonight."

A bone-deep chill races down the length of my spine.

Houston, we have a problem.

"Well, they're not coming. I don't think I am, either."

"We've been through this." She sighs heavily. "You *have* to be here, Ari. You have to see how your work affects people, how it moves them. If anything, I'm begging you to be here for me. Victoria was a friend."

I feel horrible. I'm sad for that family, but only on the periphery. Evan actually knew her.

"I don't have to do anything. Especially since you've been ditching our sparring sessions and avoiding me for the last month."

"But—"

"But, I will...for you. Give me ten and I'll be heading down the mountain."

"Thank you." The relief in her voice hits me square in the chest.

"Yeah, yeah. Don't make me regret it," I say with a roll of my eyes she can't see. "There better be yummy snacks."

"Of *course* there'll be yummy snacks. What kind of operation do you think I'm running here? I have to give the patrons *something* since the artist is conspicuously missing. Again," Evan huffs. "The things I do for you."

"Snacks."

"Yeah, yeah. I got your snacks."

"Thanks. See you in forty-five."

Ending the call, I rush through the disguise prep, but instead of the dowdy outfit I was planning on, I opt to dress in attire that will be easier to fight in. In lieu of the brown suit, whose added fabric will hinder my movement and ease of weapon retrieval, I pick a nice pair of fitted black straight-legged slacks with a good, thick heft to them. I pair it with the matching jacket that helps conceal my tattoos and spine holster.

I choose a blousy, sapphire peplum top to go under the jacket (because I'm a freaking girl and I need the pretty). In the same vein, I pick my black leather, four-inch wedge-heeled booties with the weapon loops sewn into the inner lining. One would think I couldn't run, fight, or walk in these beauties, but they'd be wrong. These are the most comfortable pair of shoes I own, and likely, they're the most functional.

Shakily, I still put in the emerald-green contacts, put my hair in a bun at the back of my head, and throw in a few stainless-steel spikes as hair sticks. I love them because they are as thin as knitting needles, sharp as knives, and hide in plain sight.

Just in case the shiver of fear I feel is the real thing, I slide three thin throwing knives in the holder in my right bootie, and load and stow a Glock 19 in the specialty-made left-handed spine holster.

And Evan wonders why I don't go outside. Wearing enough weapons to satisfy me is a production and a half.

As I head out to the garage, a cool finger of dread prickles at the base of my neck. Just in case, I step back inside and carefully open the gun cabinet disguised as a full-length mirror. Picking up a few extra mags, I stow them in the ammo loops of my left bootie.

Ready as I'll ever be.

Let's just hope I don't die again.

2

AURELIA

Screeching into my parking spot at the gallery, I turn the car off and hop out of the seat like my ass is on fire. I'm late—just as Evan predicted I would be—which is irritating. Somehow, despite my abilities, I still managed to get caught in traffic. Which is just par for the freaking course in my book.

Of course, I have about the worst ability on the planet that only seems to work in fits and spurts.

Did I know I would get caught in traffic? Technically, yes, but I thought I could go around it, having no idea that even the side roads would be backed up, too. Did I know that Rhys was four cars behind me the whole way down the mountain and parked on the street to avoid me spotting him? Yes, I did. I also know he has on mismatched socks and a Morganite knife in his boot.

But none of that information is useful, and all I'm stuck with is a feeling in my gut that I didn't pack enough weapons.

Slipping in the hidden side entrance, I try to skirt the crowd without being noticed as I make my way to the only reason I'm here.

Food.

Assessing the spread on the snack table, I mentally give Evan kudos.

Cubed cheeses, grapes, bruschetta, those cute little cucumber chive cups, pancetta cheese tomato skewers, and a bunch of other yummy snacks decorate one massive table positioned expertly next to the open bar.

I have to give it to her. The little devil really knows how to throw a party.

Speaking of the devil, Evan pops up by my side as if she materialized from thin air. Which isn't too far from what she's actually capable of. The jury's still out on whether she just showed up on her own two feet, or if she appeared in a puff of smoke in front of an entire roomful of people. I'm going with option one solely based on the number of humans in the room.

While it's great my showing is well attended, the room is far too people-y for me. But the crowd isn't the only thing giving me pause. Despite the riot of curls and tiny stature, my pixie of a best friend is typically a little more robust than she is right now. And while I feed her until she busts every time she comes over, I have a feeling she isn't getting sustenance from the other half of her diet—the soul-eating side.

It's not as bad as it sounds. As a wraith, Evan eats damned souls, transporting them on a one-way slide straight to Hell. By the sharpness to her cheekbones, she hasn't consumed a soul in a hot minute.

I want to ask her about it, but this is neither the time nor the place.

"Finally decided to grace us with your presence?" Evan asks with a snarky little smile. "I thought I was going to have to send out a search party. And by search party, I mean your personal guard dog."

Rude. After a century-plus of us being BFFs, Evan has tried to get me to forgive Rhys about three billion and one times. She would love to lock us in a room together and throw away the key. I'd likely end up killing him, which would temporarily end up killing both of us. Wouldn't be the first time.

Phoenix bondings are stupid.

I hate that I wonder if he's okay. I loathe that I worry that he's not happy, if he's in the same Hell as I am. If he regrets what happened to us. But more? I hate that the bond makes me care at all—makes me want to give in to the love of a man I should detest.

Picking up a plate, I slide a few of the cucumber cups onto it before moving to the pancetta.

"Below the belt, Evangeline," I mutter, sending her a healthy dose of side-eye. "Give me time to inhale some of these goodies before you start in on me."

Using her given name makes her eye twitch, which was the intended goal. If she's going to hit me where it hurts, I'll do the same to her. She purses her red-painted lips, undoubtedly deciding if yelling at me in this room full of people would be worth the ass-kicking she'd get later.

"You've sold four already," she offers, diverting from the thorny Rhys talk. "Simone is wheedling with two others for the dollhouse painting. I think that one is going to start a bidding war in a minute."

Nodding, I stuff a morsel in my mouth—whole—and chew. I don't really care how much the paintings sell for—I only want them gone. All of them—every single one—is a depiction of how someone died, an artistic rendering of the deaths that stayed with me long after I opened my eyes. The dollhouse is my least favorite, and I'll be glad to see it go.

"Here," she says, offering me a small cut crystal whiskey glass.

Gratefully, I accept it and take a healthy swig, allowing the burn of the alcohol to warm me. Yeah, it's July, but staring at these paintings make me shiver.

Suddenly, I yank Evan behind the cover of a steel column, pushing her little body in between the edges of the I-beam, unable to articulate the pictures that just rolled across my brain in enough time.

"What—" Evan squawks before the *ping-ping-ping* of bullets hit the metal.

Screams erupt around us, the crowd stampeding to the exits, and I wonder if I have enough cover to get Evan behind the snack table.

"When I say 'go,' you flip that table over and get behind it," I order, staring Evan down.

She nods, pressing her lips together so hard they turn white around the edges.

The images in my brain tell me there are two phoenixes—soldiers to be exact. Great. I slide out from the cover of the I-beam, pull the gun from my spine holster, and yell for Evan to go, before the soldier in front of me even has time to blink. Wasting five shots on his vest, I quickly realize he's wearing body armor before he starts returning fire.

Taking off into a run, I move in between two free-standing walls that wouldn't stop a BB gun, and keep moving to the next I-beam. But I can't stay here much longer. The other soldier skirts around the periphery of the room, ready to corner me. I'm being herded.

Fantastic.

Moans of pain reach my ears, and it's all I can do to swallow down my tears as I attempt to block them out. Focusing on the heavy footfalls, I try to gauge their position. Reaching up, I pull one of my hair sticks from the bun and throw it like a missile. I enjoy the girly scream coming from a man's mouth—more than I can possibly say—as the thin rod of metal embeds into his eye. Grabbing three more, I toss a few into the shoulder of his compatriot before giving him a matching skewer in his other eye.

Above everything—the moans of pain from patrons caught in the crossfire, the sound of a gun being reloaded, the screeching of the phoenix who'll have to regrow his eyes—I hear the whimpers of my best friend.

Shit.

Evan is softer than I am, and not that she can't handle herself—she can—but she hasn't seen the things I have. She hasn't endured. And she can't be around the death coming for us without phasing—something she shouldn't ever do in public.

If I phase, I look like an angel. Evan, however, resembles something out of a nightmare.

Avoiding the perimeter of the room, I manage to circle back to her, practically doing a baseball slide to dodge the bullets aimed for my head as I make it back to cover. After a second of inspection, I realize all too quickly from the hallmarks of blackened eyes and inch-long fangs that Evan is about a nanosecond from losing it.

"Get out of here," I insist, reloading my Glock as I desperately try not to succumb to the fire that begs to explode from my skin.

My best friend isn't like other wraiths, and that fact is made all too apparent when pieces of the floor start abrading away beneath her. I've seen her level an entire city once—by accident—over a century ago. Granted, her control has grown exponentially since then, but I'm not eager to push it.

Evangeline doesn't acknowledge me at all, lost in bloodlust or fear or something I can't name. Despite my unwillingness to hurt her, I can't have a repeat of San Francisco. My free hand cracks across her face, and the inky quality to her wraith eyes slowly bleed back to human.

She sucks in a breath, shaking herself back to sanity.

"Get out of here," I repeat, growling so she knows I mean business.

She scrambles backward, still under cover of the table, cowering at the barest edge. Her fear for me burns, even as necessary as it might be.

"What about you?" she croaks, still worried about me even though I just slapped her.

Her voice shakes even through her fangs as she tries to keep herself in check.

"Rhys is here somewhere. He'll back me up once he finally sacks up and gets out of his truck. I'll be fine. Meet you at the cabin?"

Evan takes two deep breaths, one after the other, before she gives me a hesitant nod.

"Good. Get the hell out of here so I can kill these idiots. Say hi to the parental units for me."

Evan smiles hesitantly before a swirl of black smoke envelopes her and she disappears, traveling to her family's cabin in Grand Lake. Now all I need to do is take out the trash…

What I didn't tell her was that Rhys likely won't get out of his truck. He most likely won't come in at all, and depending on where he parked, he might not see the stream of people flooding out of here like their hair is on fire or hear the shots from these idiots' hand cannons.

That's on me, I suppose. I've made it clear over the last century and a half that I don't want to see him, and I don't need his help. Typically, I don't, and today is probably no different.

Maybe.

I'm pretty sure I can take care of these two jokers on my own, but what if they aren't alone?

What if this is it? What if these are my last free breaths?

A guttural gasp breaks into my thoughts, and I shrug out of my jacket. A man not ten feet from me has a bullet in his gut. I try to keep my eyes closed as the vision of his death on an operating table fills my mind, little details about the man coming with it. I didn't need a vision to tell me he was a goner, but I lay down cover fire as I sneak out of my hidey-hole to drag him to the modicum of safety the table provides.

Pressing my jacket to his wound, I whisper, "Everything is going to be all right, George. Don't you worry. Keep pressure on that, okay? Help is coming."

It's a lie, but he doesn't need to know that. All George wanted was to buy a little art for his college-aged daughter. He didn't ask to be gunned down in the middle of an art show.

A burning-hot prickle to my skin has me sucking in deep breaths for calm. The absolute last thing this poor man needs to see in his final moments is me turning into a smoldering Valkyrie.

He needs vengeance.

And he'll get it as soon as Rhys removes his head from his ass and gets in here.

Whenever that will be.

3

RHYS

GUILT IS SOMETHING I LIVE WITH ON A DAILY BASIS, BUT IT GETS worse on days like today. Today I get to play stalker to a woman I've been in love with every single day for the last century and a half.

A woman I cannot have.

A woman who hates me with every single fiber of her being.

Go me.

As her soldier, I've been bound to Aurelia for nearly one hundred and sixty years. I thought as a young man I knew what love was. The inane notion I assumed was love as a boy is nothing compared to the iron chain tying her to me now.

I'll never love another woman—the bond assures that. It also ensures that as long as she hates me, I'll never be happy. Because that's what a soldier is.

A guardian, a lover, a husband. Not that she'll ever accept me now.

Hell, it's been fifty years since we were even in the same room together. But that's my fault. After I saved her ass from assassins, I got the bright idea to kiss her, and she almost took my fucking head off. Likely didn't because she'd lose hers, too.

The memory of her body in my arms and her lips on mine filters through my brain. The way her eyes glowed white, the way her mouth parted. Then it all came crashing down when she punched me hard enough to bloody her own lip.

"What the fuck?" I growled, reaching for her again. I'd wanted to wipe the blood away, but my kindness just made her angrier.

"Thanks for the assist, but you and I both know you only saved me to save yourself."

Fates, the hate on her face made me want to scream. "You. I saved you, because... You know what? Never mind. It doesn't matter what I say, you'll always believe the worst in me."

Her face twisted for just a moment, an ounce of regret there before her expression hardened once more. "You're right. I will. You killed—"

"I know what I did. And I've paid for it—relived it—every fucking day for a century." In an effort not to touch her, I raked a hand through my hair, careful not to rip it from the roots. "But I can't change the past. What I've done...or how—"

"Don't finish that sentence, Rhys. Don't you fucking dare. We're bonded, yes, but that's it."

That was the last time we spoke—the last time I felt her eyes on me. The last time I felt a glimmer of hope that she might change her mind.

As long as she hates me, I'll never be what I'm meant to be.

But at least I can keep her safe.

Scratching my scruff, I use the rearview mirror to keep an eye on the side door to the gallery. It's an awkward angle, the collar of my shirt digging into my skin as I crane my neck.

Fucking tie.

Loosening the knot, I curse at myself. I don't know why I bothered to put the damn thing on. I never go into the building. Every single time I come to her openings, I hide in the car and watch the door like a damn coward.

Usually, I borrow a car from a friend, but tonight, I'm stuck in my rusted-out shit-box of a truck with no AC in a bullshit suit that she'll never see. I really should trade up, but this old girl's been with me for twenty years. Letting women go has never been my strong suit.

Finally, I sack up and get out of the cab. The slamming of the door results in a nice little rust confetti shower on the gutter and a loud grating shriek of metal.

So much for subterfuge.

I figure if I keep to the shadows, I can prevent Aurelia from freaking out and keep my ass out of hot water. I'd rather not get stabbed, or shot, or worse—fried. The fried thing hurts like a bitch. But I suppose she has a good reason to be sore at me.

I killed her husband. And allowed our bond without her consent. But how was I to know what would happen? How was I to know that in tying us together, she would lose everything?

It never mattered to her that I didn't choose any of this. I killed him. In a way, I even took her child from her. I did it to save her—to keep her from a fate worse than death.

But some part of me—a big part—is glad he's dead. What kind of monster does that make me, huh? Since the day I learned of their marriage, I wanted what he had—wanted the life he'd found for himself. Wanted her.

I killed my best friend to save her life.

And I've been trying to make up for it ever since.

Crossing the street, I make my way to the side entrance. Like always, the door will be propped open, Evan and her ever-present romantic streak constantly offering an in with Aurelia. She knows I'll be close by, and eventually, I'll man up and get my ass in there.

Just as I creak the door open, several gunshots ring out.

What. The. Fuck.

Ducking my head, a century's worth of training kicks in and I move in a low crouch through the hall toward the main gallery. Said gallery that incidentally contains the source of the gunfire. Pausing for a second, I assess my situation, touching each weapon as if they were my own personal worry stones.

Smith & Wesson M&P40 in my right hip holster, backup mags at my left. Ruger SR40c in the left shoulder holster, extra mags in my right. Backup gun in the shoulder holster, thin Morganite blade at my right ankle lead-lined knife sheath. Small .38 Special five-shot at my left ankle.

While I'm loaded for bear, I could probably be covered in every single weapon I own and not be prepared for what I'm about to see.

Peeking past an industrial-looking I-beam, I survey the wreckage of Aurelia's show. The food table has been knocked over, appetizers strewn everywhere. The detritus of cloth napkins and China plates scatter over the concrete floor. Paintings litter the ground or hang haphazardly on the walls, their frames cracked, their canvases gouged with bullets. The crowd is gone, save for a few wounded patrons.

Evan is missing from the melee, but being what she is, it's probably a good thing.

No one wants Evan to lose it. Including me.

I know Aurelia is alive, and she's here, and since I'm not bleeding anywhere, I know she isn't, either. It's one of the few benefits of our screwed-up bond: I'll always know when she's bleeding or injured.

Still, I don't see her.

What I do see is the thickly tattooed arm of an oracle's soldier, and as I peer farther around my cover, I notice he doesn't look so good. He's wearing a bulletproof vest, yes, but it appears shredded from the number of rounds pumped into it. He's covered in blood from what looks like a double-tap headshot, a thick graze to the jugular, and to top it off, the poor bastard has a pair of wicked-looking throwing knives where his eyes should be.

A phoenix can receive a wound that will "kill" us for a few days, but we will regenerate and get back up once we've healed, unless we're injured with Morganite. So wounds that are considered mortal to humans are still mortal wounds, because while we're healing, we are completely inert.

No breathing. No heartbeat. As dead as dead can be.

For a little while, anyway.

I made a medical examiner nearly shit himself when I popped up on a morgue slab after I'd been declared dead two days prior. That took some explaining. Sometimes humans are a nuisance. Though, given the fact that the man provided a pair of scrubs and a turkey sandwich after he got over his shock, it is possible that humans might not be so bad.

With the healing required for the trio of mortal wounds, it will be a long while before he is up again.

His buddy is still standing, though, and in full tactical gear, save the Kevlar helmet. Since he's also a soldier, he seems to have lost his shirt so he can be a douchebag and display his Legion markings. Like the rest of us, they cover his entire right arm, his right pectoral, and right scapula.

He's wounded, too, with a few metal slivers as thin as knitting needles impaled in his left shoulder, thigh, and shin. He has Aurelia pinned down behind another I-beam, peppering gunfire with an awful *ping-ping-ping* against the metal. But my girl? She's far too crafty for him, and he has run out of bullets faster than expected. I raise my weapon, ready to sever the poor bastard's spinal cord.

Before I have a chance to pull the trigger, Aurelia has abandoned her sanctuary of steel and has launched herself at him. Wearing a pair of black slacks that cup her tight ass like the hand of God, she flies from the I-beam, her ink-covered arms pumping as she sprints toward him.

Fury is stamped all over her face as her raven hair streams behind her, her eyes glowing white even behind those stupid contacts she has to wear to blend in. She has the hilt of one throwing knife in her left hand, and her right hand is empty, her fingers pulled into a tight fist.

Three bounds cross the ten yards that separated them and then she's on him, leaping to hook her legs around his shoulders and hauling his carcass to the ground in an MMA maneuver I've forgotten the name of. His guns are history, having skid across the room in the takedown, and Aurelia has him pinned with a knife to his throat. Her right hand is now grasping his jaw, her fingers digging into his flesh.

Knowing she's most likely going to use the electricity that courses under her skin to fry the fuck out of this dude, I scan my surroundings to see if I'm standing on something conductive. While most of the flooring is concrete, steel beams stand like sentries through the whole building like lightning rods. Yeah... *electricity bad,* especially since if I burn, so does she. I need to stop her before she disintegrates this asshole.

Questioning him might be beneficial.

"Aurelia, *stop,*" I shout, but she's not listening.

Of course she's not. When has she ever listened to me?

Never. The answer is never.

As quick as I can, I rush her, hooking my arm around her waist, keeping her from lighting this entire building up like Christmas morning. Flipping her over, I try to keep her hands away from me while also trying to keep from knocking her around. I'm only marginally successful, and now we have matching cuts on our left cheek.

I'm lucky she didn't take my eye out. But we've got bigger problems than some piddly little nick. The soldier has reached his guns, albeit he's hobbling like an old man. It's completely possible she damaged his spine in that MMA move. Only he seems to be having trouble concentrating because he's still trying to chamber a round.

Seriously? Did Iva send the bottom of the barrel, or what?

"Time to go," I say as I try to scoop her compact little body up, but she's having none of it.

"Don't *touch* me, you *abominable* prick," she screams at the same time she realizes it's me, slapping my hands from her waist.

Normally, she'd try to kill me. Again. But I think the soldier is a bigger threat than I am at this point.

"I was trying to keep you from frying me. Don't blame me for attempting to save your life. Again," I growl, irritated I can't even be the good Samaritan with this woman.

"I wasn't in danger of losing my life, you moron. I am perfectly aware of where I am and the simple fact I'm basically in a metal box. I'm also aware of how the laws of conductivity work, as well as a vast number of other laws of fucking physics. I'm not trying to kill anyone else, and there are some wounded people still here. I was just going to slit his throat like a good little girl."

Well, that takes the righteous wind right out of my sails.

"Oh. Well. Sorry?" I shrug just as the soldier finally heals enough to figure out how to work the firearm in his hand.

"You plan on killing this guy, or are you waiting for him to blow my head off with that hand cannon?" she asks, raising her eyebrows at me.

I lift my weapon and fire two rounds into the soldier's shoulder. Glancing back at her, I quip, "I'd planned on questioning him first."

"Oh." She frowns. "That's smart."

"You can be smart on the physics. I'll be smart on the tactics, Gorgeous," I tease, using the nickname I know she hates.

She rolls her eyes at me and flips me off over her shoulder as she strides over to the soldier, hauling his huge body up off the floor with one hand to the collar of his vest like a pissed-off mama cat. She shakes him viciously, the entire two-hundred-plus pounds of him flopping with the movement.

"Want to tell me why you're shooting up my friend's gallery? Or shall I kill you now, hmm?"

His mouth tightens into a grimace, his heavy brow pulling into a frown.

"I don't think he's going to talk to you," I quip, a hard-won expression of earnestness on my face.

Aurelia's gaze moves from the poor bastard dangling from her grip to me, and I wish I hadn't said anything at all.

"Oh, he'll talk to me. Or I'll take out the Morganite knife stuck in your right boot and carve him like a fucking pumpkin."

Skippy pales at the glow of Aurelia's eyes and the slightly sadistic quality to the curve of her lips. He should be worried. Very worried. She drops him to the concrete with a mighty thud.

"How'd you know I had a knife in my right boot?"

She points to her chest and says, "Seer. Duh."

"So you knew I was here?"

"Of course I did. I know every time you're here, what weapons you carry, and even what color your socks are. Navy and black do not match, BTW. It's the important stuff I can't see. Like who sent this dipshit, but I bet I can guess. Let me see," she says as she reaches for his left shoulder to twist the spike, inciting a pained howl. "Wanna tell me your name?"

"Thad," he gasps. "My name is Thad."

"And who sent you, Thad?" she asks sweetly, which is all the more frightening, given the malevolent expression on her face.

To tell you the truth, I'm feeling a little excluded from this interrogation, so when Thad refuses to answer her, I rip out the spike still protruding from his thigh with a vicious jerk. The agonized scream turns my stomach a little, but it does the job because now Thad can't stop talking.

"Iva. Iva sent me," he gasps. "She sent me to stall you because she has more soldiers coming. She's going to capture you this time, and it doesn't matter what he"—He nods at me—"does to save you. He has a price on his head, too." Thad's breathing hard, panting as if his lungs have decided this very minute is the time to work double-time.

Iva. That slippery little bitch. I've been dodging our Primary—our leader—for over a hundred and fifty years. Just her name sends a shudder down my spine.

Aurelia reaches into my shoulder holster and pulls out the Ruger. She chambers a round and pumps it into his head with enough quickness I don't have the chance to stop her.

I'd yell at her, given that we still needed more info, but the expression of pure, unadulterated terror on Aurelia's face is enough to make me shut up and move.

"We have to go. Now," I say as I take the Ruger from her and re-holster it.

Grabbing her ice-cold hand in mine, I head for the back of the gallery toward the rear parking lot while asking, "Where's Evan?"

"She was losing it, so I made her go ahead of me to ready the cabin. She's safe."

A sigh of relief has my shoulders drooping just a little. "Thank you for keeping her safe."

She swallows thickly. "She's a better sister than I ever got. I'd do anything to make sure that little shit stays breathing."

Aurelia's family shit is the stuff of legend. I've never seen a mother as uptight or unrelenting as hers. Nothing was ever good enough. Aurelia wasn't polite enough, proper enough. It didn't help that she didn't want the role she was born into. It didn't matter to her family what kind of daughter they had—they'd rather have her twin. A sister— as time went on—who shunned her just as harshly as her parents did.

We reach the door, and she pulls me toward a slate-gray, new model Dodge Challenger SRT Hellcat. She drops my hand suddenly as if she'd forgotten she hates me for those few minutes and has just remembered. To ease the newly forming ache in my chest, I take a split second to admire the awesomeness of the vehicle before me, holding my hand out for the keys.

She gives me a look of indignation before reaching under the front driver's side wheel well for her spare key. She shakes her head, presses the key fob, and opens the door to slide in behind the wheel.

"Nobody drives my baby but me."

Throwing my hands up in surrender, I slip into the passenger seat. "Can't blame a guy for trying."

She shrugs as if to give me the point while pushing the ignition button. Peeling out of the lot, she weaves into traffic with an ease I've never seen any driver pull off—driving better than even I can, which is irritating to say the very least.

I'd never tell her, though—she'd have to torture it out of me first.

The wail of sirens start just as we reach the third block out, and four squad cars followed by a SWAT bus scream past us in a blur of speed. It's not like in the movies. No one looks at us. No one suspects we had anything to do with the carnage those poor fellows will walk into.

From what I can feel and see, I know she is uninjured, but I need to know she is all right, though.

"We're going to be fine, you know that, right?" I say, trying to reassure her.

Her face is a blank mask, her thoughts and emotions expertly hidden from me. Her only tell is the grayish-white cast to her knuckles as they grip the wheel.

"I know we will. It's the next part that worries me."

"What's that?" I ask, on edge because knowing Aurelia, it could be anything.

"We have to be in the same car. Together. And driver picks the music," she quips with an evil smile.

Fates, please not—

Of course. Taylor Swift comes out of the speakers just to torture me. Aurelia shimmies in her seat as she punches the beautiful beast into fifth gear.

"You're the Devil," I grouse, crossing my arms, doing my damnedest not to stare at her boobs as she laughs in her seat. The brief glimpse of joy on her face is everything to me, though.

"Well, I can't kill you or inflict any wounds without hurting myself, so Tay-Tay is what you get. Suck it up, buttercup." She smiles as she pops the "P" with her lips.

I feel like she's probably going to torture me forever. I hate that she hates me—that she can't see my side of things.

"You could have just left me there, you know," I murmur, the sting of her rejection twisting the knife in my chest.

"I know I could have. But if they caught you, they'd kill you to kill me. It's a no-brainer, really. I'm helping you to save my own ass. And as soon as I figure out how to remove our binding, I'll never see your face again. Sound like a plan?"

She glances my way, but I school my features long enough to nod. That little quip twists the knife again, and I have to grit my teeth against the ache. Removing the binding, even as hard as it is to bear, would be like cutting off a limb—like cutting out my heart.

"Sounds like you've got it all worked out," I croak, staring out the window at the passing traffic, as we head north on I-25 out of town.

I know this for certain: I am going to get this girl to forgive me if it's the last thing I do.

4

AURELIA

AFTER FIVE AND A HALF HOURS OF DRIVING, ONE FUEL STOP, and a circuitous route, we've made it to the safe house in Grand Lake, or the "cabin mountain on steroids" as Evan calls it. The safe house is more her father's vacation cabin than anything else. I've only seen pictures of it, but they didn't do it justice.

The exterior can only be described as a log cabin's hotter, older, manlier brother. Thick logs run the perimeter of the four-story house, only broken up by large picture windows lit up in the gloom of the night sky. Craggy stone columns bookend the porch, solidly constructed of immense limestone slabs and broad vertical logs. The very top floor seems much smaller than the ones below, possibly serving as a loft or crow's nest for surveillance.

Security doesn't appear to be a concern here. The house is alone on the top of a large foothill surrounded on three sides by the Rocky Mountain National Park, with the closest neighbor half a mile out in any direction. The hundred-acre property is solidly enclosed by a rough stone wall tall enough to classify the place as a fortress.

Getting through the gate is easier than I expected, especially since the security panel at the eight-foot, iron entry gate requires my thumbprint. I'm going to have to talk to Evan about her lack-of-privacy shtick.

My thumbprint? Really?

Several cars and trucks dot the cabin's half-mile driveway: a shiny Jaguar interspersed with late model Fords, and a new Audi mixed with a rusted-out Chevy. I park in the only open spot, incidentally only twenty feet from the front door, and roughly punch the button to turn off the ignition after shifting my baby into park.

Man, I miss the days when you could turn a key. Simply pressing a button just doesn't have the same air of purpose.

Groaning, I open the car door and pull my body to standing. I rub my eyes, so happy I ditched the contacts and shake out my legs before going to the trunk to pull out my go-bag. Every vehicle I own has a small duffel bag stashed somewhere inside them. They contain cash, clothes, one day of rations (*beef jerky and a flask of Jameson—don't give me too much credit*), and a shiny new identity.

The identity I probably won't need just yet, but I will need the set of clothes—my suit jacket lost to poor George, my pants and shirt ruined by Thad's interrogation.

I feel guilty for not using the Morganite knife and killing him for real since I know he'll heal in the next couple of days. My only solace is that it will take a few days to regrow his whole fucking head. *Dick.*

I knew I shouldn't have gone to that stupid exhibit. I swear it's the last time I let Evan talk me into anything.

And I mean it this time.

Rhys was quiet most of the drive, a blessing because I had no idea what to say to him. But it's a curse, too, the barbed guilt of my silence running through my veins. I've spent little time with him that hasn't included me trying to rip him limb from limb, so a conversation might've been impossible. Plus, I'm a little disturbed that having him so close for so long hasn't been the hardship I always thought it would be.

He was quiet, considerate, and he pumped the gas when we stopped, because me getting out of the car would have probably gotten the police called on us. He even got me snacks when he went in to pay.

It's tough to be bitchy to a man that brings me foodstuffs.

And for every minute of those five and a half hours, I had to fight the two warring sides of my brain. One side completely ruled by hate and fear, telling me it's all his fault, even though I know it isn't. The other side worries if he's taking care of himself and likes that he came to help—even if I didn't really need it.

Both sides need to shut the hell up.

Rhys and I meet at the back of the car. He reaches past me to lift my duffel out of the trunk, not even letting me carry my own luggage—the bastard. He raises his eyebrows, almost asking permission, and I nearly lose it. If he'd cooperate and be an asshole so I could hate him appropriately, that'd be great.

Grinding my teeth together in an attempt to avoid screaming, I give him a jerky nod and let him take the bag. It requires a bit of effort, but I gently close my trunk, careful not to hurt my baby—even though I want to smash something.

I stride toward the front door behind Rhys, vigilantly trying not to stomp my feet and pout like a toddler. My anger only grows when I notice how spectacular he looks in a suit.

Holy shit balls.

Being away from him so long, I always forget the pull he has on me. Easily six foot three—maybe taller—he towers over me like a fucking monolith. I'm five-three on a good day, so he's at least an entire foot taller than me. The crisp charcoal-gray suit caresses the wideness of his shoulders and the line of his body as it flows from his strong neck to his lean waist and tight ass.

People I hate are not supposed to be this hot in a suit.

He's not hot. It's just the bond, remember? It's bullshit magic clouding your head. You hate him.

I'm pretty sure being pissed at Rhys is all that's holding me together at this point. Flashes of the wounded humans, blood leaking through fingers, gasps of final breaths bombard my brain, and I swallow hard. Screwing my eyes shut, I try to blot out the horror on their faces of the people as they ran past me. The sight of the young woman who fell close to the back entrance and got stomped on by fifteen people before someone was brave enough to haul her up. The expression of unadulterated fear on Evan's face when I slapped the shit out of her, snapping her out of her shock.

Before Rhys can reach the porch, Evan bursts out of the front door like a jack-in-the-box, followed at a more sedate pace by an incredibly large man who seems capable of murder. Evan's long curly blonde hair flies behind her as she sprints toward me, her wide blue eyes set with determination, a frown pulling at her elfin face. She runs right past Rhys, plowing her shoulder into his gut with enough force, he nearly biffs it on the asphalt driveway. He's saved at the last second by the burly dude, who could give Paul Bunyan a run for his money in the height department.

Instead of the fear I expect, she practically climbs me like a tree and attack-hugs me with enough strength to bruise my ribs and squeezes the breath from my lungs. I never knew the little blonde pixie had it in her. And I do mean pixie. If Evan says she's over five feet, she's lying her ass off.

"I'm so sorry, Ari. Please forgive me," she whisper-sobs in my ear, fully latching onto me like a baby koala.

"For what, baby doll?" I murmur, gently rubbing her back, trying to calm her down. "You didn't do anything wrong."

As horrible as I feel for slapping her, Evan can turn into your worst nightmare if she gets pissed off. The power running under her skin rivals even her father's, and she's a baby. Usually, only the old ones have the kind of juice that she has to keep bottled up, and she's barely over a century old. It's supposed to take *several* centuries to hone those types of powers, and she's had to harness them in her little body for barely more than one.

"I–I did. I was scared of you, and you didn't deserve it. You snapped me back when I could have done something stupid, or fully lost it and hurt someone. Fates, I'm such a *freak*."

"Evangeline Marie Black," I growl, full-naming her just like her mother would. "You are not a freak, you little shit, so stop talking like that. You are special in the best way possible. If I hear you talk bad about yourself again, I'll singe all your hair off, so help me."

My quip shakes a laugh from deep in her belly, and she climbs down to the asphalt, returning quickly for a squeeze before wiping her eyes and nose.

"Calm down, I got it. No need to murder my beautiful hair. That would be a crime against nature, or against the Geneva Convention, or something." She gestures to her perfectly tousled blonde ringlets.

"Oh," she says, bouncing right into the next subject, "I meant to tell you, I popped back to the gallery after letting Dad know the skinny of what was going on. I took care of the security cameras in the gallery as well as the surrounding buildings. I don't know if there are backups to the digital footage or not, but the originals should be gone. Also, I made sure no identifying info is at the gallery, and since you go through a shell company for your royalties, I don't think anyone can trace you through there."

Evan has a proficiency for covering shit up. As she should. Puberty rage, plus a girl who can decimate an entire town in minutes? Girlfriend has experience. Her teen years were hell on wheels to say the least. Just don't look too far into the history of the 1906 earthquake in San Francisco.

So *not* an earthquake.

That's where I met Evan. In the middle of all that fire and ruin, half out of her mind with rage and about to burn to death. I had to knock the shit out of her then, too.

"What about you? Shouldn't you be there now? Aren't the cops still there?"

I'm stunned she got so much accomplished so fast.

"I gave my statement hours ago," she answers with a nonchalant wave of her hand. "You took an age getting here. Did you get lost or something? It's on the news already."

"Not all of us can whisper around like freaking smoke, nerd. Some of us have to drive. Some of us have to make sure we weren't followed. Did any of the wounded make it?"

She nods somberly. "The dude with the gut shot died in surgery, but I'm not at all surprised. I'm amazed he lived as long as he did. The chick with the arm graze is stable, no arterial damage, but I think the docs are going to repair the nerve damage after the initial swelling goes down. The guy that passed out near the exit is going to be fine—he just has a concussion. The other two ladies died from blood loss—they were dead before they hit the floor."

I incline my head, agonized at the massacre one little show caused. I can't believe after all these years, after all the life I've sacrificed, I'm here running from that bitch again. One fucking art show. Shame climbs up my throat for every single human that was hurt or killed—the burn of guilty tears stinging my eyes and nose. I feel the heat of a body sliding close to me.

"Can we get inside now that you're done with your little debriefing?" Rhys asks as he grabs my hand and drags me into the house. "I don't want Ari out here, even if it is in the middle of nowhere."

For a second, safety and warmth grip me. Then I remember why holding his hand is a bad thing. I shake off his fingers as if his flames would actually burn me. "I don't like being touched, douchebag. Especially by you."

Heat creeps up my cheeks at the scene I'm making, and I nearly shake my head. I'm blushing like some stupid virgin girl in a historical romance novel *at the mere touch of the duke's hand*. For fuck's sake, I think I hate myself.

Rhys looks back at me with an unreadable expression that slowly morphs into a little upturn of his lips. Now I'm looking at his lips. *Son of a bitch.* Can I be any more transparent?

I have *got* to get out of here.

Directing my attention to Evan and her brute of a companion, I examine him closely, taking in his wide stance, thick thighs, and sturdy motorcycle boots. His dark hair is pulled from his face into a man-bun, making his jade-green eyes pop. He would be considered beautiful, or at least I assume so, if I could see what lay beneath the mountain of a beard taking up residence on his face. His appearance screams "tough guy," with the copious tattoos on his forearms and thick gauges in his ears, or at least it would if I weren't covered in ink myself.

He has a hand on Evan's shoulder as he steers her into the house. Then it dawns on me. This is the guardian that has been lurking in the shadows for the last several decades—since the '20s, I think. Evan has never introduced him to me, but I've always known he was there, looking out for her, making sure she was safe. Where the hell he was today is anyone's guess.

Facing him, I ask, "What's your name?"

I know it already, but hearing him speak will tell me so much more.

"West," he grunts at me, crossing his arms in such a way it discourages further questions.

"Do you have a last name, West?" I ask, arching a perturbed brow. "What do you do here? And more importantly, where the fuck were you today? 'Cause, I gotta say, your absence when she could have gotten killed is not sitting so well with me."

"Don't worry, Ari," Evan assures me. "It's not his fault. He's simply doing what he's told, aren't you, West?" She says this in such an ominous manner, I'm a little scared for the poor guy.

Glancing past the menacing little wraith, I take in the interior of the safe house. An enormous stone fireplace dominates the great room, the open floor plan leaving the kitchen and a library nook in plain view. The walls are log planked, the décor decidedly rustic with chandeliers made from antlers, and buttery tan leather furniture adorned with plaid throw pillows.

There are two winding staircases on each side of the large opening to the kitchen. One staircase—that appears to be constructed solely of pine logs and branches—leads to the upper floors, and the other seems to lead down to the bottom level. Each of the rooms have large, unadorned picture windows looking out to the view below. The night is dark as pitch, but the moonlight reflects like a mirror on the lake at the base of the mountain.

Evan wraps an arm around my waist and steers me down the hall toward the stairs to the bottom level. Coming from the bottom of the staircase is the sound of male laughter and what I'm assuming is a game room if the sound of clacking billiards is any indication.

"Let's go see Dad before we get you settled."

"Aww! Do I have to? Your dad hates me," I complain, dragging my feet, but the little powerhouse pulls me along as if I weigh nothing.

"He doesn't hate you. He's just angry you won the last round of sparring." She shoots me a censuring look over her shoulder. "Did you have to beat him so badly? He practically had to turn in his man card on that one."

A sly smile slides across my face. Yes, I needed to kick his sorry ass for thinking a *poor, weak woman* couldn't knock his ass into next Tuesday. He should have known better.

I hear two deep chuckles behind me and realize I said the last bit aloud.

Oops.

Glancing back, West—whose face seems to be made of granite and frowns—has cracked a smile. I guess old John isn't everyone's favorite person.

Evan's father, John Black, is a hard man, but for better or worse, I respect him. I'd be stupid not to. And while his motives and mind games might be centuries in the making, he loves and protects my best friend.

"He's the one who said no powers." I shrug. "It's not my fault I train every day."

What I don't say—because it can get me killed—is that I didn't go full blast. I didn't even break a sweat, handing the Wraith King his ass without a smidgen of effort. I figure he either rigged it so I would win—the purpose for which I'm not sure—or he's letting me know he's weak.

Either way, I'm positive I'm not going to like the answer.

5

RHYS

WE REACH THE ENTRANCE OF WHAT IS, IN FACT, A GAME ROOM, and the conversation grinds to an immediate halt. One, lone, billiard ball, plunking into its rightful pocket is the last sound to be heard. As I hit the bottom stair behind the girls, I feel the frisson of a threat in the room, the hair on my arms standing on end.

Aurelia might have her visions, but I have a fully developed sense of when shit is about to hit the fan. Before she can move, I drop the duffel and step in front of her. With my body, I block whatever attack may come, my arm reaching back to clutch her to me. If we need to escape, she's coming with me—I don't care if I have to throw her over my shoulder like a fucking caveman.

I've done it before, and I'll do it again.

I manage to refrain from drawing a weapon—not that it would do any good—but it is a near thing. In the presence of a king, drawing a weapon would be a one-way ticket to a death I wouldn't be able to regenerate from.

"Well, well, if it isn't the runaway oracle and her boy toy," a deep voice rumbles, rough as gravel but with a spark of humor.

The man attached to it isn't tall nor is he short. John Black's features are nondescript: medium-brown hair threaded through with silver, medium-brown eyes, slim straight nose, thick straight eyebrows.

Even his name is unremarkable.

To the eye, he's nothing special. But looks can be deceiving.

His daughter and her guardian have been my friends for many, many years, but I have yet to meet John. And while the king still owes me a boon, meeting him hasn't been high up on my to-do list. It may have something to do with the battles I fought against the wraiths when I was still a member of my Legion, still under the thumb of our Primary, Iva. Or it could be that my family—my brother in particular—was tasked with killing John's wife.

Dealer's choice.

My brother failed in his endeavor, and I made sure Olivia Black survived the attack on her home. I sold out my own brother to the enemy because I didn't like the sanctioned murder of an innocent woman. Killing is not a phoenix's purpose. So, I put a stop to it.

Delivering my brother to the wraiths seemed like my only option at the time. Phoenixes are supposed to be good. We're supposed to send souls on to be reborn.

Not change the future.

Not kill the innocent.

Nothing but helping souls move on.

Iva's been changing the game for centuries, twisting it, and us as a species, into something ugly. I threw a wrench in the spokes of her evil wheel by letting Olivia Black live, and in turn, Evan was born.

"John." I offer him an abbreviated nod in deference instead of the full bow expected of me, my arm still clutching Aurelia to my back, keeping her out of the way.

No way in hell am I taking my eyes off him, or the seven men scattered throughout the room like land mines, no matter what Evan said about proper protocol. Each man has the appearance of leisure, lounging on couches, leaning against the pool table, sitting on bar stools with beer bottles in their hands, but I know differently. One, or maybe none of these men are my friends.

Safe house my ass.

Just as I think the dam of tension will break and kill us all, John calmly rises from his stool. Striding over to me, he takes my hand in his firm grip and slaps my shoulder in greeting. His mouth—that had been set in a hard line—turns up into a smile, and each of the seven men in the room relaxes their posture to one of true leisure.

But what's more disconcerting is the gusting breath of relief that wheezes from West's lips. When I was counting threats—like an idiot—I hadn't counted him. While he's been my friend for the better part of a century, I'm not altogether sure which way West would lean if it came to blows between the king and me.

"I'm glad you got out safely," he says with a warm smile, nodding to Aurelia. "Though, I'm not sure it was a question you would with both of you there."

She moves from my grasp, cautiously positioning herself a step behind me. I look back at Aurelia and see her face is carefully blank, her wide full lips slightly parted on an indrawn breath. Her shoulders are relaxed and loose, but after years of observing her, I can tell it's more in preparation to strike rather than a gesture of good will. Her eyes flick from John's to mine, and in the nearly mint-green gaze is a hint of unease.

I know I'm right to be wary right now. Keeping my body relaxed, my mind tenses, my spine burns, and my wings ache to break free.

"All it takes is one lucky shot," she says. "Even I know that."

I think she's referring more to her win over John than Thad's quick demise, deferring to the king.

"Well, either way, it's good you got out of there. From what Evan and West told me, soon after you left, the place was swarming with soldiers. After you've cleaned up, I think we need to have a discussion about how safe you guys are here. Please, make yourselves comfortable and we'll meet back down here when you are ready."

Bowing my head, I realize we're being dismissed. She may hate it, but I take Aurelia's hand, tugging her behind me as we wind our way back up the circular staircase.

The real problem comes when we get to the door to our room. Evan, being the consummate matchmaker, hopeless romantic, and all-around pain in my ass, has decided Aurelia and I are rooming together.

She gestures between the two of us, then to the door we've stopped in front of. "This is you."

While I have zero problems sharing a room with Aurelia, I cringe in preparation of the shouting I'm almost positive is coming.

"You're fucking with me, right?" Aurelia asks in a low voice.

I'm not sure she realizes she's still holding my hand or not, but if she hasn't, I'm not going to be the one to tell her.

"There are only seven rooms in this house, even with the Murphy beds in the office and the pull-out in the game room. There are thirteen people here. I know the house is big, but where in the hell do you think they're all going to sleep? Plus, Dad has a rule about guardians and their charges sleeping in the same room. I'm even bunking with West." Evan shrugs, barely glancing down at our entwined fingers.

"Speaking of the plethora of men—what the fuck are all these people doing here?" Aurelia hisses. "When I said ready the cabin, I did not mean call every warrior and their brother to come guard us. I meant turn the lights and the hot tub on and get some booze. What's going on?" Aurelia's so mad she's almost stammering.

"I'm going to have to tell you about it later. I don't know if you realize this, but you're still covered in blood. Go take a shower, please. When you're done, come find me. I'll be in the loft," Evan quips and flounces away as if Aurelia wouldn't tackle her where she stands.

It takes everything I have not to bust up laughing right there in the hall. Aurelia's head whips to me as she burns me with a glare, releasing my hand to push her way into the room.

And that's when Aurelia sees red. An enormous four-poster bed dominates the room—its ornate posts and top covered in gauzy white fabric. The heavy, baroque side tables hold vases of flowers and glass-bowled lamps. Across from the bed is a stone-faced fireplace with a fire already burning in the grate. Even in July, the mountains are cold in Colorado, especially in the evenings.

What's worse, the lights have been dimmed, and there are candles burning on almost every available surface. It's like the honeymoon suite of a Harlequin romance novel threw up in here. And I'm obviously not the only one who thinks this if Aurelia's low, menacing growl is any indication.

"Are you kidding me?" she grits, her hands curled into fists.

She seems to be working exceptionally hard not to throw sparks or flame up and burn this whole house down. After the day she's had, I have to commend her on the effort. Or I would if the thing she's so pissed about is being in a room with me.

Tossing my hands up in surrender, I heave a sigh. "Don't blame me. I didn't do the room assignments."

"Whatever," she huffs. "She's right: I do need a shower." Aurelia snatches the duffle from my fingers, slamming the attached bathroom door as she goes.

That could have gone worse.

RHYS—1855

I should have said something before now, I thought as I observed Aurelia's rising blush, but it never crossed my mind Lucien would betray me this way.

Aurelia was a tiny slip of a woman—barely over five feet—but her personality made her so much taller than any meager inch she may have possessed. Her golden skin—so much darker than the pale humans in the next town—was still stained a delicate, glowing pink. In all the years I'd known her, I'd never seen her blush, and the thought of Lucien inciting such a reaction from her set my teeth on edge.

In my head, she had always been mine. I knew it was stupid to think that way—about a woman who hadn't paid me even a lick of attention—but I'd loved her for so long.

She'd been promised to me—the bastard knew it, and still...

Lucien and I used to be friends—closer than brothers—almost inseparable.

Before Selection, we were practically family. After Selection, I lost my best friend. It wasn't as if I'd gotten a choice of placement. Lucian had known we could play soldier and dream all we wanted, but in the end, the Primary chose our fate.

Lucien was selected to be a scholar—an honorable profession in our society. But me? I was chosen to be what Lucien had always wanted to be—a soldier. Aurelia's soldier to be exact, and in that decision, one day

I would get what I wanted more than anything on this earth—to be Aurelia's husband.

Not that she knew it.

She wouldn't accept me—that, I knew for certain. In her mind, whomever the Primary chose for her wouldn't be an option. Ever.

She would never bind herself to me—not of her free will.

Aurelia was not the type of woman who liked to be told what to do, and in a matriarchal society such as ours, usually that wasn't a bad thing. But Aurelia hated the life she'd been borne into. Hated what she was destined for. Hated her eyes, which had dictated the course of her life from the first day they fluttered open.

Those pale, pupilless orbs cemented her destiny as an oracle—and her hatred for me.

Lucien had known how much I burned for her. From the very first day I heard her argue with her mother, I was lost.

"I would rather eat a pinecone than wear that silly corset, Mother. There is absolutely no reason to adhere to a societal norm of a society in which I have no interest in participating."

She was ten, and I twelve, and I knew then that I would do anything for her. But that was before I was a soldier. Before Julian lost his mind and his sense of right and wrong. Before I seriously debated committing treason.

Now, my love would come at a price—a price I never wanted her to pay. If I did what I'd set out to do, Aurelia would be in danger.

Lucien crowded her, putting himself in her space much closer than polite society would allow, but Aurelia didn't appear to mind one bit. She gazed up at him, grinning, happy—until she felt my eyes on her. She shifted her gaze to me, her blush paling as her smile fell. An expression of fear passed over her features, and she dropped her head to stare at the vegetables she was purchasing. She thought I'd tell or cause a scene.

Oh, how wrong she was.

To fight the urge to rip his head off, I pivoted from the woman I coveted more than anything on this planet, attempting to school my features into something resembling calm.

I didn't hate Lucien. I envied him. Because he had her love. He had her trust. He had her, and while I could possibly one day have her future, I wouldn't be her first love. I wouldn't be her first anything—except maybe her first hate.

"RHYS, I NEED TO TALK TO YOU," A VOICE CALLED FROM BEHIND me—Lucien's voice.

Of course he needs to talk to me.

I halted my quick clip through the forest on my way to the cliff top—needing to fly, to be free, if only for a little while. So naturally, I would get stopped when I was a meager inch away from losing my mind.

"What do you need, Lucien?" I growled, not turning around. I didn't want to see his smug, gloating smile—otherwise I'd likely punch it right off his stupid face.

"I have a problem. I'm pretty sure you're the only person I can trust."

"You can't trust me." I chuckled darkly. "You shouldn't even talk to me. I sure as hell don't want to talk to you. Congratulations. You won. She loves you. You'd better love her back, and as long as you do, you don't get to ask a damn thing from me."

I'd made up my mind about a few things. I had to fix my brother, Julian—one way or another—and then I had to leave. Watching them together was the worst sort of Hell.

"How long do you think they are going to wait for her to decide, Rhys? She has pushed and pushed as long as she can, but soon enough, they'll stop asking. They'll decide for her. She's... they... she's carrying my child," he admitted, the words gushed past his lips, slicing their way into my heart.

Lucien's youthful face was lined in worry and fear. Had I ever looked that young? Had I ever been that earnest? Did he honestly believe I wouldn't rip him apart?

"We married in secret months ago. We've kept it from everyone, but she will start to show soon enough." He gripped the back of his neck, his frustration and fear evident. "As soon as we can, we're leaving. But I need help..."

He said more about the Aegis, about Aurelia, about malicious leaders. But I didn't pay much attention to him. The only thing that ran through my head was Lucien's voice telling me I'd never have her.

She's carrying my child. We married in secret.

A strange buzzing took over the thoughts in my head as I left him behind me. My phase ripped through me, the burn of my Fireskin chased away his voice, the ache of my wings bursting from my back providing refuge as I soared off the cliff. The wind whipped through my feathers and past my ears, deadening my senses.

If only for a moment.

6

MOTHER BARRED MY ESCAPE, HER FEATURES LINED IN disapproval, bordering on disgust. She didn't understand me. I wasn't even sure she loved me. In fact, I was almost certain she didn't. In all my life, I had never garnered a smile from her, never a kind word or gentle touch. I couldn't remember the last time I'd been hugged or confided in, or anything resembling the families I'd observed in our community. My family shunned me in private and scolded me in public.

Don't run.

Don't speak so loudly.

Remember your manners.

Act like a lady.

Do what you're told.

After a while, I stopped trying to please them. In their eyes, my sister could do no wrong, so I decided to quit trying to make my family something they were not.

It didn't help that I knew what would happen before it did, or that I knew when humans in the next town—or three towns over for that matter—would pass away. I would always be on the outside.

My eyes made me a pariah in my own home. The seer part of the equation was just icing on the cake.

It was close to suppertime, but it didn't matter for me. I ate my meals separately from them, never within touching distance—but still, she stood, barring my exit. I wondered if I tried to touch her if she'd still stand between me and my freedom. If I yelled and screamed and caused a stir, would she still keep me here?

Perhaps she would, but then again, maybe she wouldn't. I doubted she held me any more than she had to when I was a baby—it was unlikely she'd allow me to come within a foot of her now.

"Where do you think you're going?" she asked as if she had the right. She may have given birth to me, she may have fed me, but she had never given me love.

Not ever.

"I'm leaving this house to see my husband, Mother," I said to her stunned face. I would've admitted I was with child, but honestly, given the puce tinge to her features, she might have combusted where she stood.

"Hu-husband? Have you lost your mind, Aurelia? You have no *right* to take a husband. You are to be an oracle. Your soldier has been chosen for you. You know the rules, *child*. How could you be so careless?"

Oracle. As if I would ever willingly subject myself to the horrors of that job title.

"Careless? The oracle position is not my only option, Mother. I can choose exile, which I would *prefer*, since it is the *only Fates-forsaken* choice I will get to *make*. I would rather make my own fate than take the life someone dictates for me. You should know better. You know I'm not very fond of doing what I'm told, now am I, Mother?"

"You think they will just let you go? Silly little girl." She shook her head, pity clearly written all over her face.

"I spoke to Nicola myself. She said I was allowed to choose as long as I did so before maturity."

"Nicola isn't who I'm worried about," she muttered, and then her eyes widened when she realized what she'd said aloud.

So, it isn't Nicola she is worried about. But if not Nicola...

Iva—our leader, our Primary—was not someone I ever wished to tangle with. She was the ultimate reason I didn't want to be an oracle in the first place. She frightened me down to my very bones. An ominous sense of dread washed over me every single time I stepped within three feet of her.

It was as if she carried the weight of a thousand souls—as if she were stained in death.

There was no way I would ever be an oracle with her as my leader, and no way I would willingly hand that woman the knife to cut out my eyes. I still couldn't fathom how we had progressed so much as a society and still followed that barbaric practice.

I liked my eyes where they were, thank you very much.

"Did you ever consider that perhaps I see much more than you give me credit for?"

My mother sighed a deep, shuddering breath. "That, my dear, has always been the problem. You see too much," she whispered and stepped out of my way. "If you are set on going, I would go sooner rather than later. Take your young man and leave this place before it is too late."

Her voice, so heavy with foreboding, sent a chill skittering down my spine. It was the kindest she had ever been to me, and I had no idea what to do with her words.

"We are trying to leave before the week is out. Do you think this is enough time?"

"I hope so," was all she said before leaving me alone to decide.

Choosing between my family who had given me life—but not an ounce of love—and a man, who not only gave me the love and affection I so desperately craved, but the child I carried.

It was no contest. I opened the thick, oak door and walked toward my future.

AURELIA

It takes no time at all to get undressed and in the shower. The bathroom is just as lavish as the rest of the house, conveniently stocked for guests. But Evan knows me better than anyone and has all my favorite stuff. Speedily, I wash the blood off my arms and neck with the super-expensive ginger and orange oil body wash. Shampooing my hair twice

—because Fates know what's in it—I use a handful of conditioner to tame my wavy locks into submission.

Shutting off the water, I towel off and open my duffle. Inside, I've got five bags of beef jerky—chipotle flavor—my favorite "Fuck My Liver" flask full of Irish whiskey, a quarter-million dollars in varied bills, and a manila envelope containing a whole new identity.

I take the time to braid my hair in a long side tail before dressing in a gray T-shirt, and a pair of jeans with frayed holes in both knees. Sliding on sandals, I clasp my favorite sterling silver feather necklace around my neck and slip a stack of bangles on my wrist.

Throwing open the bathroom door, I find all the candles blown out and an empty room. Lit by a lone bedside lamp, the bedspread is depressed on one side where I assume Rhys had rested for a bit. Despite him giving me the space I demanded, I'm disappointed to not see him here. Irrational anger burns in my gut.

I shouldn't care that he didn't wait for me.

But I do.

I don't care. I hate him.

Yeah, bitch. Keep telling yourself that. How's reality working out for you?

Gritting my teeth, I glance at the bedside clock. I'm bone tired, but I need answers now that I'm done pouting in the bathroom. Even though it's after midnight, I leave our shared room and my bullshit feelings, heading up the stairs to the fourth-floor loft, jingling my bangles the whole way.

I'm doing this because I'm trying to let Evan and West know I'm coming so they'll stop making out and put some fucking clothes on.

But just like everything else, I know what I'm going to catch them doing, and I'd rather not see it in person. The vivid imagery in my brain is plenty—trust me. I'm pretty sure those two have been dating a while behind everyone's back. How she kept it from me, though, I'm not so sure. It makes me wonder what else she's hiding—the little shit. She's practically been MIA for the last month.

I jingle the bracelets harder, but my warning goes unheeded, and I see way more of my friend's boob than I ever needed to. On the upside, West has a very nice ass, and I can attest he has tattoos just about everywhere. Resting my shoulder on the doorframe, I'm careful to look anywhere but in their direction, shaking my wrist as hard as I can.

Nothing.

"Did the loud-as-shit jingling not tip you off I was coming?" I gripe as they startle apart and hastily begin pulling on clothes.

I scold West's back as he tucks himself into his low-riding jeans. "I could have been anyone in this house, you know. I could have been her dad. Hell, I could have been the enemy. Stop thinking with your dick and pick a room with a door, you moron."

He growls at me through a good-natured smile, but his gaze swiftly goes to my best friend and the look in them says it all.

He loves her. Deeply.

"The loft? Really, Evan? You knew I was coming, jerk, and while you do have a fabulous rack, I don't swing that way and I don't need to see it."

"Sorry." She shrugs. "The time got away from us."

"Evidently," I grumble. "So you two are together? I take it that's not new."

She shakes her head with a sheepish expression, brushing errant curls off her forehead.

"Mazel tov. Maybe sometime you can talk to me about it, you know, when the threat of death isn't so imminent. Sound like a plan?"

Evan lets her smile answer for her.

"So, while I'd love to scrub out my brain with bleach to erase what I've just seen, it's not an option right now. Two questions. Where's Rhys? And what the hell are all these people doing here? Go."

"I think Rhys is in the game room getting to know the guys, and Dad's personal guard is here because there's been some serious unrest going on in our community. I talked to Dad a little bit before you got here, and there have been attacks on wraith families in the surrounding states. Five families are unaccounted for." She pauses, swallowing hard. "Dad thinks the shit is about to hit the fan here, so as soon as he can get some things handled, we're all leaving. He wanted me to extend the invitation to you and Rhys as well."

She's leaving something out. I know she is, but I'll needle her about it later when her Goliath is not in the room.

"Why didn't he say anything earlier?"

"I think it's just Dad being cautious. Never can be too paranoid when it comes to times of war. You know that."

I do. Even your own family can turn on you if you're not too careful.

We make our way down to the game room, the sounds just as raucous as before. Only this time when I arrive, the conversation doesn't halt like a bad '80s movie record scratch. Each of the men continue what they're doing as if I'm not here. I notice Rhys across the room talking to John—his body held in such a way I know interrupting would be a bad idea. Plopping down on a barstool, I survey each of the men.

Across the pool table, sitting on the smaller of the two couches, are two men slightly removed from the rest of the guards. They are arguing in murmured tones in a Portuguese dialect I don't recognize. The one on the left of the couch has smooth, coppery-brown skin, full, almost pouty lips, a head of unruly black hair. He's dressed casually in a plain navy shirt, ripped jeans, and motorcycle boots.

The one on the right has sharper cheekbones and fuller lips, his eyes and hair black as night. His crisp coal-black suit is at odds with the heavy fall of hair across his eyes. He looks pissed as hell, his voice dropping several decibels as his gestures and words turn sharper.

At the pool table in front of me are two men dueling with trash talk. The one at the head of the table is lining up his shot, the tight red shirt stretching across his impressive back. His rich brown skin almost glows in the overhead table light. He laughs at his friend, a white smile stretching across his full lips as his eyes crinkle at the corners.

His friend stands on the other side of the table, his stance wide, leaning on the cue like a crutch. He's extremely tall, a thick wool beanie half-covering his shaggy, dark hair. A week's worth of scruff adorns his face, and his caramel gaze is filled with mischief.

Two disgruntled-looking men sit on the larger couch to my right, their blackened eyes and split lips seem to speak of a story I'm dying to know about. Their postures are rigid, scolded, almost as if they've been sent to the principal's office. The one closest to John appears to be worse off, his Romanesque nose bloody and dripping onto his white T-shirt. His dark hair is in disarray as if he's tried ripping it out recently.

His couch buddy runs a hand over his shorn light-brown hair, the fingers of his other hand probing the purpling discoloration of his jaw. His knuckles are bruised, the skin broken across his second and third joint. He shoots a steely glare as he tongues his split lip, one side slightly puffed where the flesh has ripped.

West and the last guy are sharing a joke, and from the bits I gather of their conversation, they're quietly discussing my kicking the king's ass a few weeks ago. This guy is the biggest of them all: easily six foot seven or eight, with a full-scale lumberjack beard. He's built wide and sturdy, with thick arms and thighs, black hair, cut close to his nape and left shaggy on top. His deep laugh resonates throughout the room.

A sense of loneliness fills me, even in the throng of people. An unfortunate realization dawns, that with Rhys across the room, I feel more alone than I have in a very long time.

Ain't this a kick in the teeth.

I'm nursing the beer West slung my way when I sat down, contemplating how vile I think hops are, when the hot, suit-wearing, Portuguese-speaking man approaches. His posture is friendly and unassuming, and while he's smiling, I get no hint he's trying to flirt.

"I'm Carver Lee," he introduces himself, thrusting out his hand to shake.

"Aurelia Constantine," I say as I take his palm in a sure grip.

Many years ago, I would turn my fingers in his like the lady my mother wished I'd been. But I've found people take you seriously when you give a good handshake—not too soft or people think you're weak, not too hard or people think you're an asshole. His grip is firm without being rude.

"Pleased to meet you. Have you been introduced to the rest of these bastards, or are you running blind?"

I'm never blind. I fought hard for these eyes.

"Blind as a bat," I say demurely, lying my ass off.

I'm trying exceptionally hard to say the bare minimum. I don't know if these men are my friends or enemies, and given my track record, I have every right to be wary. The only person I can trust completely is myself. My gut says they are on my side, but any one of these gentlemen could be swayed.

It doesn't take much.

My parents taught me that.

"Allow me, then. This is my husband, Javier Cabal." He gestures to his companion on the couch, and Javier salutes with two fingers. "The two jolly bastards playing pool are Aidan Keenan and his brother, Ian Moran. Aidan is the one wearing the beanie like a twenty-year-old hipster." This earns him the finger from the beanie-wearing man himself.

"The two crybabies pouting on the couch are Cameron O'Connor and Asher Crane. Asher won, by the way," he says as an aside behind his hand, but Cameron seems to hear him, his battered face pulling in a distorted frown. "And last but not least, this big son of a bitch is Kyle Brennan." He slaps the giant man on the shoulder.

"You sure are being awfully nice to someone who kicked the crap out of your king. Should I expect an ambush later?" I say more to myself than anything, but he answers me.

"You and I both know you only won because he let you. Games are afoot, my dear, and they don't stop just because you call a timeout. But war's a funny thing—you gotta make friends where you can."

Coyly tilting my head to the side, I ask, "And I'm a friend?"

"No. But you're not an enemy." He taps his lips like he's trying to decide. "Let's call it an acquaintance with the option for friendship."

"How very lawyerly of you," I grouse, rolling my eyes. "I can agree to that. I take it that's your Jag outside."

"Well, it's no fair playing guessing games with a seer." He straightens the knot of his tie before brushing invisible lint from his shoulders. "Did my impeccable fashion sense give me away?"

"Absolutely." *Yeah, we'll go with that.*

He narrows his eyes a smidge, likely irritated by my vague answers. "You don't talk much, do you?"

"The line between intelligence and stupidity is easily crossed with an open mouth." I shoot him my most saccharine smile.

"Too right. Take these poor bastards over here"—He gestures to the pouty men sitting on the couch like scolded children—"filled with piss and vinegar over a mere difference of opinion."

"And that would be?"

Carver pauses, and I see the debate play out behind his eyes before he answers me.

"You know, it's so trivial, I've already forgotten," he lies with a careless flick of his wrist. "Perhaps a bit of nonsense over a girl."

My head tilts to the side without thought, and my eyes glow without anger, their reflected light shining off his cufflinks. Knowledge streams into my brain, confirming that Carver is evading my questions to the point of lying.

I really hate being lied to.

Especially since the fight was about me and Rhys staying here. But why? Are we more of a danger to them than I thought? Am I not amongst friends?

The whole room tenses at the pale light shining from my eyes, and Rhys is already crossing the room. He's in front of me before I can blink, a vicious growl bubbling from his throat, his shoulders tensed and ready to strike.

Gently, I rest my hand on Rhys' back, doing my best to calm him because a Phoenix vs. Wraith cage-match is not what we need right now. He startles as if being touched by a tender hand is a foreign concept. As if he's never felt a soothing gesture in his whole life.

Maybe he hasn't.

"I think it's time for bed," I suggest, forcing him to meet my gaze. "Rhys, walk me to the room, won't you?"

He grabs my hand and tugs me toward the staircase.

"Oh, Carver," I call out sweetly, tilting my head over my shoulder as we reach the third step.

"Yes?" His wary voice is telling. He knows he fucked up.

"That's strike one. You lose your options for friendship when you lie to me."

7

AURELIA

Rhys drops my hand as soon as we top the stairs, leading me to our room, likely for lack of something better to do. Waiting until our door is closed, he asks the question he's probably been dying to ask the entire trek but couldn't.

"What did you see?"

Debating on what to tell him, I fiddle with the bracelets on my wrist. I must stall too long because he puts a hand over the silver to silence them.

"Tell me."

"The two men who look like they beat the shit out of each other? Carver lied to me about what their fight was about. It wasn't anything major, it's just... everyone's on edge. Wraiths have been attacked in the surrounding areas and then the show gets attacked..." I shrug, pulling my hand from his—gently this time. "I'm picking up on everyone's tension. It's probably nothing. We're safe here."

Rhys sighs before dropping to the edge of the bed, clearly surveying the overdone romance shtick. He doesn't meet my eyes, either embarrassed that Evan did this, or something else I can't name.

"I can sleep on the floor if you want," he offers in a gruff whisper.

A part of me hurts that he felt like he had to suggest the option—that being next to me brings him just as much pain as it does to me.

Deciding to be a full-fledged grown up, I answer him: "Don't worry about it. We could both probably starfish on that bed and not touch. Don't suffer on my account."

Don't suffer on my account. That sentence zings through me as I head to the bathroom to get ready for bed.

How long has he been suffering? I wonder. And how much of it is because of me?

I have a sneaking suspicion the answer is "Always" and "All of it."

MY SCREAMS HAVE QUIETED NOW. I LOST MY VOICE WHAT SEEMS like hours ago. The tears have yet to dry, but as long as there is blood in my veins, there will be tears in my eyes. In my throat. On my skin.

Lucien's body is cold in my embrace, long since dead. I adjust my grip on him, wrapping my arms tighter around his shoulders, grasping him to me, trying to hold his soul a little longer. Our blood has mixed and mingled, soaked into the threads of my dress. I tried wiping the blood from his lips, but it only smeared, his skin refusing to come clean.

It's getting harder to hold him now.

Harder to think.

Harder to breathe.

I ache down to my bones. So tired. I need a healer, but the more I think about it, the more I wish no one would come to my rescue. My whole family is dead on this forest floor. The ones who used to call themselves blood turned their backs on us. Lucien and our child were all I had left after my parents' betrayal.

I have nothing now.

Rhys left hours ago. Searching for help maybe? Perhaps he'll die in the forest like I wish I would.

If I were gone from this earth, maybe Lucian, our unborn child, and I would be together on the Otherside. But I know Lucien would hate to see me so weak, giving up on life so soon—even if dying would be a relief.

My beautiful, strong husband. I thought we would have more time.

The leaves beneath us are as dry as kindling, and before the thought can finish its path in my mind, my fingers have already ignited them. I watch the foliage curl, praying the flames would harm instead of heal.

But they don't.

Carefully, I slide Lucien from my lap to the ground, brushing his golden locks from his bloodstained face—the face that once held so much laughter, so much love. Another soundless sob erupts from my throat as I lay my fiery hand upon his chest. I wish I had enough knowledge of the funeral rites to do this the proper way.

But I know enough. Enough to send him on.

I caress his cheek, his shirt, his trousers, his body igniting as I go, turning the forest floor into his funeral pyre. I still cannot stand—the wound at my belly continues to ooze blood. So there I sit next to his burning body, my tears drying in the heat of the flames before they ever reach my cheeks.

This is where they find me. One hand on the knife that·took my husband and child from me, and the other buried in Lucien's ashes.

Phased and flaming, broken and tattered.

Gunning for vengeance and ready for death.

But death...

Death is not what I got.

FOR THE FIRST TIME IN FOREVER, I WAKE UP SCREAMING. THE electricity under my skin is bubbling up and out, flickering to nothing as soon as I realize I'm awake. With the pulse I sent out, I've blown out the lamps and bedside clock, and the television mounted over the fireplace is smoking. The bed curtains are singed, but not on fire, and the linens appear to be unharmed. The only light comes through the open bathroom and hallway doors.

I'm alone until Rhys runs in from the bathroom with a small red cylinder in his hands, squirting white foam on the TV.

A fire extinguisher?

How many years has it been since I've set something on fire in my sleep? Fifty? A hundred?

My vision is wobbly, and I can't stop shaking. With a *thunk*, Rhys drops the extinguisher on the floor by the edge of the bed. His warm hands reach for me, slowly cupping my shoulders. He doesn't say anything, but I can't blame him.

I wouldn't know what to say, either.

"Don't. Don't touch me," I croak, my eyes rolling in my head like a spooked horse.

His hands not only don't go away, but they wrap around me and pull me into a hug. It's soft and warm and comforting, and for a few seconds, I relax in his embrace. But after all I remember, after all the guilt weighing down my soul, the feeling of his chest against my cheek is enough to make me lose my mind.

Instead of comfort, now all I feel are the cold, hard hands that tore at my flesh. The ones who pulled the skin from my bones. The ones who tortured me for what seemed like an eternity. Funny how that eternity had only been three days.

And that's when I start clawing and shrieking like a feral cat.

"Let me go. Let. Me. *Go*," I screech as I scratch, punch, and kick my way free, many of the blows unnecessary since he let me go almost instantly.

Scrambling backward across the bed, I half-step, half-fall off the other side.

I know that time in my life is over. I know it was a long time ago. But I still feel those fucking phantom hands on me even now.

Focus! Focus, dammit!

I clutch my head, my fingers digging into the flesh of my scalp. And while I can't feel the bite of my nails breaking the skin, Rhys can because he hisses in response. He crosses the room, grabbing my wrists, gently pulling them down and away.

"Stop. You have to stop, Aurelia," he murmurs as I try to get my mind back to the here and now.

I must not have been very successful because he's roaring for Evan.

Soon, our room is invaded by one pissed-off baby wraith, her hands black as coal smoke and curled into talons. The iris and sclera of her usually ice-blue eyes have bled to an almost-demonic black, and she's hissing like a snake through a set of impressive fangs.

Holy shit balls.

That's enough to scare anyone straight, or at least shock me enough to get my shit together. Even with bullets flying in the gallery, Evan didn't fully phase. I'd almost forgotten how scary she could be.

"Put the fangs away, baby doll," I croak. "It's just a flashback."

Just as the words leave my mouth, a very relieved Rhys pulls me into a bone-crushing hug. His embrace is tight enough to steal my breath and warm enough to calm me down to almost normal—or as normal as I'm ever going to get.

"Sorry, guys. Where's a straitjacket when you need one, huh?" I say on a self-deprecating chuckle as I gently push away from Rhys.

He lets me go this time, and I realize I'm wearing next to nothing by way of a loose T-shirt and underwear. That, and the door is open to all and motherfucking sundry with nine warriors peering inside this room.

Fuck. My. Life.

Running to the bathroom like my ass is on fire, I shut the door with a hearty slam. And thank the Fates for forethought, because my duffle is on the vanity. Showering for the second time in twenty-four hours, I sluice off the spent adrenaline and fear. It takes time to rub the blood from my scalp, but the small crescent wounds from my nails nearly healed already.

Staring down at my arms, and through the ink, I spot the slight ridges of scars covered by beautiful pictures. Koi-like mermaids swimming toward a lotus flower conceal a few. Beautiful dark-haired women in *Dia de Los Muertos* makeup hide others. There are flowers and sea creatures and quotes from my favorite novels and songs. An intricate butterfly covers a jagged scar on my ribs. No matter how I treated it, it never healed properly. A cherry blossom tree conceals the thin scar on my abdomen Rhys and I most likely share.

I remember every single second of my time in that hell. I remember every single cut Iva and her soldiers sliced into my skin, making them permanent with those stupid knives. And Morganite is supposed to mean true love.

True love my ass.

I took those horrible scars and turned them into something better. My tattoos made something ugly and twisted pretty again. Just like my soul, every prick of the needle healed my flesh, took what was dirty and made it new. I'm better than I was before. I'm stronger. And I won't be defeated by some fucking flashback.

I will not falter.

I refuse.

Dressing in workout clothes, I finish by pulling my hair into a messy knot on top of my head. I grab my phone and earbuds and set my shoulders, praying no one is in the room when I head out.

I should have known that I've never been that lucky.

Rhys is sitting on the bed, much like he did last night—nervous and riled, trying to figure out what to say and failing miserably. He opens his mouth only to close it with a snap as he anxiously runs a hand through his hair.

"Out with it," I bark, because I've been standing here for five full minutes waiting for him to get his shit together enough to spill.

"What was your dream about?" he asks just above a whisper. "Was it a vision? What did you see that made you scream as if you were being tortured?"

I want to feel sorry for him—to comfort him a little—but a bigger, harder part of me wants him to pay for the pain he caused. The gentleness I felt for him last night is long gone.

Why did he have to kill Lucien? We were leaving the Legion. Others got to leave. We weren't the first to choose something different. We were *choosing* exile.

He should feel the same pain—he should know what I endured. The cruelest part of me rears her ugly head—the part that allowed me to survive. The awful part that forced me to trudge forward without them.

Alone.

"It wasn't a dream or a vision. It was a flashback. And I *was* being tortured. I was reliving scattering the ashes of my dead husband. The husband you killed. The husband I was putting to rest when Iva's soldiers caught me. And before that, I got to relive the death of my unborn child. So, you see the flashback itself was torture—those screams were real." I sneer through my tears, but the satisfaction doesn't last.

His expression wounds me more than anything—because I know that look has been on my face more times than I can count. It's the look of misery. Of guilt. Of remorse. And to give that look to someone else?

It tears me up inside.

I'd give anything to take my words back—to have just shut my mouth and never said anything at all. I part my lips to tell him I didn't mean it, but he's already up from the bed and out the door, the slam of the wood ricocheting through my chest.

Gritting my teeth, I swallow down the sob that tries to break free. I'm getting so fucking sick of how much the guilt of hurting him burns.

I didn't kill anyone. *I* didn't ruin his life.

He ruined mine.

So why does hurting him hurt me so badly?

Yes, we're bonded, but I can't remember when I started giving a shit about breaking his heart. How long has it been? And how long have I been fighting myself—fighting him—making us both miserable in the process?

Sniffing back my tears, I rub the wetness from my cheeks as the anger builds. I want to hit something, but the person I want to hit the most is unavailable to me. As pissed as I am, I quickly realize I haven't eaten in at least twelve hours, and I could eat a moose if my palatal inclinations swung that way.

And that bullshit pisses me off, too.

Opening the door, I make sure the coast is clear before heading downstairs to raid the fridge. I know wraiths have some wonky eating habits, but there's bound to be food somewhere in this place.

The kitchen walls are a mix of planked wood and horizontal logs, a hearty stone backsplash that mesh perfectly with the granite countertops. The Viking stove sits directly across from a copper sink big enough to bathe in. I crack open the monster of a refrigerator and hit the motherload.

Leftover steak and potatoes, a huge bowl of salad, and a small vat of mixed fruit all get pulled out and devoured before I can stop myself. I'm still angry, but at least I'm marginally sated. I rinse my dishes and load them into the dishwasher to be a somewhat decent houseguest.

I turn to head back to my room, but before I can make it a step, Evan appears right in front of me in a swirl of black smoke.

"Dick move, dude," I hiss, clutching at my chest. "Quit popping up all over the place. It's a house, not a continent. You can walk, you know."

"Don't sass me, Ari," she gripes, her fists making a home for themselves on her hips. "What the fuck is wrong with you?"

No doubt Rhys tattled on me.

"What's wrong with me? What the fuck is wrong with *you*? I have a fucking flashback, and because you have me roomed with Rhys—and don't think we're not going to have a lengthy, in-depth discussion about that shit—he freaks out watching me recover and starts asking questions. *Of course* I ripped his head off. *Of course* I'm contrary and mean. If you had to relive the worst day of your life, you would be, too. And what was with you appearing in a full-fledged phase? And the dudes just watching me go full monkey shit? I need some privacy. I don't need to be looked at like I'm a freak when I have a breakdown—which I have regularly, or did you forget? I need to hit something that's not going to hurt me when I hit it, and I need to get the *hell* out of *here*."

This is too much for me. I live alone for a reason.

"I had to room you with him—it's Dad's rule," she says remorsefully, but I'm not buying it.

"Oh, whatever," I argue. "You're only using that as an excuse to screw West under your dad's roof. Don't lie to me."

"Yes, that's a perk, but seriously, it's Dad's rule. A guardian can't protect someone he's not with."

"And when the king speaks..." I mutter on a sigh.

"You nod and smile and do what he says. Exactly. I'm sorry this is so hard on you, but you have to cut Rhys some slack. There are things you don't know. Things I can't tell you... things that could change how you see him."

"Cryptic much?" I grunt out with a half-muffled laugh.

"Hey, I tell you what I can, and hold your fucking hand and show you the rest. Just ask him to explain," Evan shoots back. "Have you ever asked him why? He'd answer you."

"I know, but..." I trail off, not ready to hear his side of the story.

"But nothing," she growls, her eyes flashing black for just a moment. "*Ask* him."

"That might take a while, and I need to make someone bleed first. Got anyone in mind?" My mind starts reeling just contemplating a serious conversation with Rhys—one where we don't kill each other.

"You really frighten me sometimes." Evan is smiling now, so score one for me.

"You scare the shit out of me, too, kid," I admit, clapping her on the shoulder. "It's why we're besties."

"Touché." She nods, looping her arm around mine and dragging me to the lowest level of the house—or what I *think* is the lowest level.

Evan heads to the back wall of the game room and leads me behind the bar. She fiddles with an expensive bottle of Scotch and presses a hidden button on the mirror behind an empty decanter. Like an old film noir flick, a secret door opens to reveal a dark staircase.

"What the hell is this?" I stare in awe.

"You said you wanted to hit something. There's a whole training center in the basement full of hot, sweaty men just waiting to get a crack at the girl who kicked their king's ass."

"Wonderful," I deadpan, not too eager to traverse those stairs now that I know what's awaiting me down there.

"Don't say I never did anything for you."

8

AURELIA

SILENTLY, WE MAKE OUR WAY DOWN THREE STEEL FLIGHTS OF stairs, leading to an open room, lit by several industrial pendant lights. The room appears to be used as a sparring and lifting gym and seems to be twice the width and height of the house above it, and maybe three times the length.

In the far-left corner is a boxing ring. Five red ropes surround the elevated platform, and Rhys and West are circling each other on the canvas like rabid dogs. West is shirtless, soaked in sweat, his hair up in a man-bun with stray hairs falling into his eyes. His loose, black Gi pants hang off his hips in such a way that one wrong move could turn this sparring session into a full show. His nose is bloody, his left eye a little swollen, but otherwise, he doesn't look too bad considering how hard Rhys is hitting him.

I cock my head to the side to get a better view of his ass.

"You know, he's not bad looking with the tattoos and gauges and shirtless and sweaty and those pants..." I shift to face Evan in admiration. "You did good, kid."

"I know. He's yummy, isn't he? I guess I'll keep him. Rhys isn't bad looking, either. You could—"

I pinch her lips together to shut her up. "Already angry. Let's not push me over the edge just yet. Let me hit something first."

Suddenly, I taste the tang of blood and my nose starts to drip. I wipe beneath my nostrils, and my fingers come away red. West must have gotten in a hit hard enough to make Rhys bleed.

Rude.

But my gaze strays back to the ring. Rhys is covered neck to wrists in a blue compression workout shirt, paired with loose black workout shorts, his hands covered in lightly padded, fingered sparring gloves. His nose is just as bloody as mine, his upper lip stained red.

Rhys' moves are economical and calculated—for every step West takes, he has a counter. For every strike with a leg, there is a back-fist or an elbow. They aren't playing by any rulebook that I know of—their style is more like "anything goes" mixed with dirty street fighting. Neither seem to want to grapple, and even when one of them is open for a takedown, the other appears unwilling to take the bait, making the sparring session go on and on.

To the right of the ring is a swinging, red heavy bag, hanging from the concrete wall. Javier— his hands in black wraps—is pounding the bag hard enough to make it sway almost off the hook. His hair and skin are damp with sweat, and every once in a while, he picks up the T-shirt draped over a nearby metal folding chair to wipe the salt off his face.

Carver is right next to him on the speed bag—hands in white wraps —hitting the bag faster than my eyes can track. His lean build is cut with diamond-hard muscle, barely covered in a sleeveless workout shirt.

Along the right wall are three sections of lifting platforms. The first one seems to be used for dumbbells and kettlebells, while the second and third belong to the two side-by-side squat racks laden down with enough weights to sink a ship. At the last rack, Kyle is setting up for a lift that would crush a rhinoceros, his damp hair falling into his eyes.

On the near-right wall is a sea of pegboards, and the adjacent surface is covered in the handholds of a climbing wall. Why an indoor climbing wall is necessary with a whole fucking mountain outside, is anyone's guess. Aidan is fifty feet above us—at the top of the board—with a peg in each hand. As he goes to wipe his brow on the sleeve of his compression shirt, his hand slips from its hold on the dowel, and like a fucking moron, he's not tied into the safety ropes hanging intermittently from the ceiling rafters. He begins to fall, but swiftly smokes out from his rapid descent and is back at the top in his original position, no worse for wear.

Okay, maybe he's *not* a moron.

Ian is appropriately tied into a climbing harness hooked up to a self-belay system in the rafters. It occurs to me that the reason he's tied in and Aidan isn't is because Ian can't transport himself like the other wraiths can. How odd. Maybe he's young or doesn't possess that particular ability.

That, I completely understand.

While I might have wings, they are utterly useless. Not only did I *not* learn how to fly—*thanks, Mom*—Iva permanently clipped my wings when she tortured me.

I swear if I ever meet that woman again, I'm going to cut her fucking head off.

In the largest area at the middle of the room is an immense sparring mat. The thick, blue canvas spans approximately fifty feet wide and one hundred feet long, offset by the substantial collection of weapons affixed to the adjacent wall. The "Wall 'O Weapons" includes every bladed instrument I can think of and some I haven't seen in nearly a century.

"So heavy bag, weights, climbing wall, or the mat?" Evan ticks off our options on her fingers.

"Mat," I tell her, but I notice West has stopped messing around with Rhys and is leaning on the ropes.

His body is coiled in such a way, if I suggest sparring with my best friend, he'll launch himself over those ropes before I can blink. I meet his gaze, shaking my head. I won't spar with his little bird, no matter how likely it would be that she'd kick my ass.

It makes me wonder if he even has a clue that we used to spar on the regular. Evan's keeping more secrets than I can count. I hope she knows what she's doing.

"I'm going to do a few training exercises by myself. Katas can be done alone, you know. Go cheer your man on. Tell him to show no mercy."

She quirks a brow. "He's giving you the evil-eye stare down, isn't he?"

"Absolutely." I nod emphatically. "I'm positive if I touch a hair on your beautiful blonde head, he'll try to kill me in a way I won't heal from. No offense, babe, but I really don't want a showdown with your boyfriend. As much as I love you, I think I need a new sparring partner."

She pivots on a heel and sticks her tongue out at the man in question. "*Fun killer.*"

His stoic mask slips for a second, and a wide grin flashes across his face before quickly disappearing.

"Go watch the boys beat the shit out of each other. I'm fine by myself."

"Have fun," she says as she skips toward the ring.

Even from across the room, I notice as West's face softens a fraction before returning to Rhys with renewed fervor brought on by the presence of his girl. Maybe he'll break Rhys' neck, and I'll get a nice dreamless nap.

Pulling out my phone, I choose the perfect song from my "Pissed Off" playlist, stuff my earbuds in my ears, and set my phone on the hard rubber floor. Selecting a short red-oak bokken from the wall, I bow to the mat and begin.

By the time I'm done with my fifth song, "Joker and the Thief" by Wolfmother starts, and I finally look up. I'm sweaty and a little tired, but I notice I've drawn a crowd. A trill of unease races up my spine. I'm still going through the movements, but I'm aware of my surroundings now.

I feel like my ass is in a bear trap—teeth on all sides.

West, Carver, and Javier are at the edge of the mat closest to me, still respectfully off the canvas, their feet bare like mine. Aidan, Ian, and Kyle are in shoes—on the motherfucking mat—and walking closer. With all these weapons, you'd think everyone would have the respect required for *the mat*, but I guess not. Pausing slightly, I flick an earbud from my ear as I wait for the catch in a breath that will telegraph an impending movement.

It comes from Kyle.

The big man moves faster than expected—especially with the bulk he has—but he's not fast enough. I'm three feet away from my original position, and his big fingers clutch only air. Aidan strikes next, smoking out and popping up six inches away from where I used to be, but now he has a stinging ass cheek where my bokken struck him like a naughty child. Ian just stands there with his hands in his pockets—a sign of peace more than anything else—before turning and walking off the mat as he smiles and shakes his head.

I still don't trust him, but he's less of a threat right now. I pivot to face my intruders.

Kyle and Aidan must have some wordless communication down because they move as one—Kyle running and Aidan popping out simultaneously. Aidan reaches me first, but instead, gets the nasty surprise of my bokken upside his skull. He stumbles, landing on his hands and knees, shaking off the strike to his temple. Before Kyle can get within touching distance, I sweep his legs out from under him with my practice sword.

A shuffling of feet at my back ignites my rage. "You have less than a second to stop and get your dirty, disrespectful shoes off this fucking mat. If I have to tell you twice, you'll regret it."

"Aww. But it was just starting to get fun." Ian chuckles as he picks his brother up off the mat.

Aidan appears a little green around the gills as he passes, his arm thrown over Ian's shoulder. Maybe I hit him harder than I thought. *Oops.*

Maybe next time he won't use his abilities in a sparring session.

Kyle's still on his back, looking dazed and confused.

"You all right?" I ask, glancing over at the felled giant.

"Yeah," he groans. "How'd you do that?"

The sheer disbelief in his tone makes me giggle. "What? Kick your ass?"

"Yeah." He chuckles breathlessly. "That."

"Three ways," I reply, ticking off my index finger. "One, I'm really good at reading people, and you telegraph your movements about half a second before you strike. You may wanna work on that."

He cocks his head and squints one eye as he attempts to focus on my face. "So noted. And the second?"

I tick off my middle finger. "I train every. Single. Day."

That raises his eyebrows, and lifts his head as he incredulously asks: "Why?"

"Because a long time ago, I didn't have the luxury. And it cost me. Dearly," I answer as I level my gaze with his, sobering him instantly.

"And the third?" he croaks.

"I'm a fucking psychic, you dumbass," I tell him, rolling my eyes as I shake my head at the sheer stupidity housed in a single person.

"Huh. I didn't know you were an oracle. How come you still have your eyes?"

"I'm not an oracle," I mutter, massaging my temples, praying for patience. "Just a lowly little seer on the run from her Legion. I like my eyes parked exactly where they are—even if they are ugly as sin."

"Valid." He waggles his eyebrows at me. "Wanna help me up?"

"You still planning on pulling me down? 'Cause ground tactics aren't going to work so well for you when I fry your ass from the inside out."

He purses his lips in contemplation. "I think I'll get myself up."

"Good plan," I mutter as the big man slowly pulls himself to standing, hobbling off the mat.

West and Javier bow to the canvas, then to each other, and start sparring on the far end. They are doing a light-touch technique that focuses more on control of movements rather than strikes.

Carver starts clapping slowly, and I use the bokken like a cane, performing a little bow before stowing the sword on its pegs and moving out of the way.

"Enjoy the show?"

"Immensely," he purrs. "You know they were just playing, right? They wouldn't hurt you."

"Because I'm a girl?" I ask incredulously.

"Because their king has offered you his protection. They only wanted to see what you were made of."

"And here I went easy on them. If I had known it was a dog and pony show, I would have shown some of my best tricks."

"Don't be a snot, dear," he derides with a scoff. "It's unbecoming."

"Don't be condescending," I growl. "It's rude."

"Touché. So what happened this morning? I thought we were getting ready for a fight, and it turns out, you blew up your room. People were phased, shit was on fire." He shoots me a bewildered side-eye. "What the fuck, girlie?"

I shrug, trying to think of a way to explain the drama without sounding like a complete fucking nutter. There isn't.

Might as well go with the truth.

"Well. I have dreams. Sometimes they're visions and sometimes they're flashbacks. Either way, they make me completely batshit crazy. On occasion, I wake up screaming my head off and setting shit on fire by accident. Rhys is not familiar with my episodes, so there was a"—I pause, holding up my fingers spaced ever so slightly apart—"*misunderstanding* this morning."

"So, you're telling me he was yelling the house down because he was worried about you?"

Pursing my lips, I nod. "Essentially."

"And this is a problem because…?"

Oh, the can of worms the honesty would open.

Wincing, the crux of the matter ekes past my lips. "We have a history and it's not pleasant."

"Don't we all? Maybe, since he gives a shit and all, you should cut him some slack? Friends are hard to come by."

Sage advice. Too bad it's easier said than done.

"You're not the first person to tell me that today."

"So, if enough people say it to you, you'll actually believe it? Because I've been watching you two, and whatever you're carrying? It's hurting you both."

9

RHYS—1855

HELPLESSLY, I TENSED AS I WATCHED MY BROTHER ARM himself. When he'd first told me of his mission three days ago, I stood there in shock. His face was so animated and joyful as he calmly discussed the planned assassination of a woman who had done nothing wrong.

I'd always thought phoenixes were indestructible. My parents dying so unexpectedly convinced me we were not. The right blade in the wrong hands could steal our lives just as easily as a human's.

We were supposed to be good, meant to keep the balance—to ferry souls on to be reborn.

Never to fight.

Never to steal life.

Where Julian lost his way, I hadn't a clue.

Only ten years my senior, he'd known our parents better than I ever had, but I remembered them well enough. They never would have allowed something like this. I'd been fifteen years old when our parents were killed—the circumstances of which were still a mystery. We never got the full story from Iva or the head families. We never got to put them to rest. One day they were here, and the next we'd become orphans.

Overnight, Julian became my only family, and then he started to change.

It wasn't the metamorphosis of a man losing his loved ones. It was the change of a man losing his mind. Brick by brick, stone by stone, everything that had once been my fun, good-natured brother was lost as soon as he became a soldier.

But tonight was different.

It wasn't until I'd become a soldier myself, that I realized just how wrong everything we'd been told actually was—how wrong Julian was.

Tonight he armed himself—not to protect but to murder. All because our Primary told him to.

Taking everything we stood for and throwing it away like garbage.

I tried talking to him—tried getting him to see reason—until I realized what I had to do as soon as the word "kill" passed his lips.

I only hoped I had the courage to do it.

"Jules?" I called as we walked from our modest house into the neighboring forest, staying on the path that led to a steep cliff.

"What is it, Rhys?" he barked as he adjusted his blades, picking up the pace. "I don't have much time."

It was now or never.

"I want to go with you," I lied, hoping he didn't see through me. "Keep an eye out for you. This isn't what we usually do. I'm worried."

As his little brother, I always tagged along, so my behavior could be attributed to that instead of my real purpose—being a Judas.

His steps stuttered, and he glanced back at me, relief instantly washing over his face. "Sure, little brother. I'd love to have you with me."

His easy agreement was worse than a knife to the gut.

Because the relief I heard in his voice hadn't been because I was coming with him or that I accepted his mission. It was because I was falling in line. He'd been worried he might have to end me because of my behavior.

Because I wouldn't conform.

I forced a tremulous smile as I waited for the ache in my chest to ease. "Jules, did they ever tell you why? I understand following orders, but this is so far out of our norm..." I trailed off as he turned back to me, leveling me with a single venomous glance.

"I don't need to know why, Rhys," he hissed on a harsh whisper, as if someone might hear him on this secluded hilltop. "It is not my place to know. It isn't yours either."

The brother I knew was truly gone. My eyes stung with the tears of a boy who had just lost the last of his family.

"I understand, brother," I whispered, plodding along behind him as my stomach churned.

Managing to keep my emotions at bay, the loss still dug deep into my chest. Julian—the same brother who tended to me when I broke my arm falling from a tree, the one who played with me when our parents were busy with the council, the one who would pick family over his friends at the drop of a hat—was now lost to me.

He felt different. He felt evil. I knew it in my soul—this wasn't the first life he would take, and if I didn't stop him, it wouldn't be the last.

We made it to the edge of the cliff and phased in an instant—Julian much faster than I—spread our wings and soared from the precipice, the wind roaring in our ears and kissing our cheeks.

The freedom I desired never came.

I felt worse than numb—I was dead inside.

Because my brother had to be stopped—he had to. Julian didn't care that he was blithely running off to kill someone. It didn't matter if it was a woman, and he didn't even have the decency to ask why.

He honestly didn't care.

Our destination was remote: a modest log cabin no more than fifty miles north. We landed in the thick of the forest a few miles from the house and waited for the full cover of night.

I wanted to hug him—to reminisce about the good times—but I didn't. If I did, I wouldn't follow through.

When the moon finally made her appearance, Julian stood, marching at a quick clip in the direction of the cabin. He didn't even make it to the trees before a large man formed—seemingly from the darkness—right in his path.

The stranger was tall with midnight hair pulled away from his face in a leather thong. His features seemed worse than deadly, which at that point, was not the best feeling in the world.

He looked past my shocked brother and asked, "You Rhys?"

"Yes. This is Julian, my brother. He plans to kill your queen," I confessed on a whisper, but I had no doubt they heard me.

Julian shifted to face me, betrayal stamped all over his features.

"We are not made to kill innocents, brother," I murmured, my voice laced with the apology I could never give. "I can't let you murder someone."

I couldn't give it because I wasn't sorry. My only regret was losing the very last person I could call family.

"You can choose," the man I knew only as West offered Julian. "Leave with your brother or die here with me. Either way, you aren't getting past me, child. I'll let you go, but if you take another step toward that house, I'll kill you before you can take another breath."

My brother didn't hesitate, moving like a lightning strike toward West, but the wraith was faster. Julian's neck was snapped in an instant, his inert body falling to the dirt.

"That way won't kill us, you know," I croaked. I tried to keep the sorrow from my voice, but I was unsuccessful. "He'll come back."

"Oh, I know," West muttered gently, the compassion in his voice more than I could take. "I just didn't plan on killing your brother in front of you."

"Thank you," I whispered, unable to bring my voice any louder.

"You're doing the right thing, and as soon as you name it, you may call on any favor from the king," West promised, giving me a slight bow of his head before grabbing my brother's hand and disappearing in a swath of black smoke.

I had a feeling I'd be needing that favor very soon.

I HAD NO PLANS TO GO BACK TO MY LEGION, NO PLANS TO SEE Aurelia's face again—to ever be bound to her.

But my life had been one wrong turn after another. Leaving everything and everyone I knew, I headed toward a secluded cabin in the Canadian Rockies I'd set up before my Selection.

After my parents' death, I didn't trust my Legion, Iva, or my species. I wanted to, sure, but I couldn't—not when my inquiries were met with a bunch of "I don't knows" and "Quit asking questions"—none of which inspired much confidence in a man. So, I did the only thing I knew to do and made a plan—trusting that if I waited and played the long game, I would be fine.

Turned out, I was an idiot.

When daylight crested, I was still in the Oregon territory, my travel hindered by poor night vision and the cold, autumn air. I was tired, and I figured that was the only reason they caught me. Well, that and because I was an absolute moron. Let's not forget that little fact.

Honestly, how much of a fool could I have been? Had I really thought an oracle of the highest order—who would demand the death of an innocent—wouldn't be keeping an eye on the man who was too stupid to stop asking questions?

My parents were dead. I didn't know why, but I was fairly certain who'd ripped them from me. Julian was likely gone, too. The guilt was a knife to the gut.

But I would have preferred the knife of guilt to the red-hot Morganite knife that currently protruded from my belly.

"Once again, Mr. Stevens, do you accept the bond or no?" Iva asked me for the hundredth time, her Irish lilt setting my teeth on edge.

Clad in a long white dress, she appeared like a macabre angel with dark-red splotches of my blood splashed all over her. Her white hair matched her dress, at odds with her youthful face. I didn't know how old she was, only that she'd had plenty of time in her life to learn the art of torture.

She was a master of it.

Each time I said no, I received another slash, another cut, another burn. You'd think phoenixes couldn't burn, but you'd be wrong. When you heated a Morganite knife over an open flame and pressed it against our skin, we burned just like everyone else.

"Well?" she asked as she tossed the bloody blade back and forth between her delicate but deadly hands. "I don't have all day, dearie. It is time to decide. Torture? Or the bond. It isn't the worst thing, you know. Come on, Rhys. Tick tock, dear."

"No," I rasped.

I wouldn't win Aurelia that way. If I agreed to Iva's demands, if I said yes to bonding Aurelia to me... I would be begging her to hate me. Soldier or not, it wouldn't matter if my life would be tied to hers.

If I took away her choices, she would hate me forever.

"Now, now, Rhys. That was the wrong answer," she murmured as she ripped that blade from my gut and ran it from my collarbone past my navel, pressing just enough for the blood to well.

And I screamed for maybe the thousandth time.

"Do. You. Accept?"

I couldn't draw a breath large enough to answer her, so I just shook my head. And it went on and on, again and again. Until I couldn't take another cut or stab or slice or burn.

When I finally said yes, it felt worse than when I handed my brother over to the wraiths.

RHYS

The slow burn of the aged Scotch ignites its way down my throat, setting my stomach on fire. It's 11:00 a.m. on a Wednesday, and I'm sitting in the game room bar with a three-hundred-dollar bottle of Scotch, slowly but surely becoming an alcoholic.

It's been a long time since I've been this angry. Angry enough to fuck up and get myself hit. Angry enough to be a dumb-shit and get her nose bloodied as well as mine. At least my drinking won't affect her, but the consolation is slight.

Why did I have to ask questions?

She was finally warming up to me. She was hugging me, for fuck's sake. She practically slept wrapped around me last night—not that I'd tell her that. But no, I had to go and lose what little ground I had by pushing.

I know who she was dreaming about. And I know how bad it must have been for her, wounded and in agony, lighting Lucien's funeral pyre. He was my friend once, so many years ago. Before I became a soldier. Before he fell in love with Aurelia. Before he used her to get back at me for a destiny I could never have changed.

Before Iva made me choose between my old friend and the life of the woman I loved. I'll never regret choosing her—even if killing him put a black stain on my soul.

It wasn't the first black mark to reside there.

Lucien had been a good man. Flawed, surely, but he was honorable. And I knew he loved her. But Iva has her ways. That miserable bitch has enough tricks up her sleeve to turn any self-respecting person into her little puppet.

I tried not to hurt him, but whatever Iva did to him—whatever spell she used—turned my once-mild-mannered friend into a crazed, knife-wielding psychopath. I don't think Lucien had touched a blade since we were children—even then, we'd only practiced with wooden swords, pretending to be soldiers. He preferred books—or at least he pretended to—making the scholar position he so loathed into his hobby.

Spinning the tumbler in the growing condensation pooling on the bar top, I study the amber liquid swirling in the glass as it melts the ice. Suddenly, the wall opens to the staircase beyond, and a freshly showered Aurelia and Carver emerge from the hidden door. Facing her right now would be too much for me to bear, so I rotate on my stool, nabbing the bottle as I leave the room.

I wish I knew how long we were going to stay holed up here. Don't get me wrong, the house is amazing, the food is amazing, the people... *blah, blah, blah.* It's all fucking Jim-dandy, but what are we doing here?

John is stonewalling me, refusing to reveal his sources inside the Legion. Aurelia hates me. I'm ready to dismember Kyle and Aidan for trying to touch her. And if Carver talks to her one more time, I'm going to murder him. I don't give a shit if he *is* gay.

John's waiting for something. What that is, I'm not sure. While the added firepower would be beneficial in keeping Aurelia safe, I'm seriously contemplating kidnapping my charge and getting the fuck out of here.

I take the stairs two at a time, climbing each flight all the way up to the loft. Luckily, it's empty, and I can be pissed off in peace. I have half a mind to steal Aurelia's keys and take her car on a joyride. But she'd figure out a way to torture me without breaking my skin for that infraction.

She's good at that.

Choosing a leather armchair close to the south window, I slump down into it. It's July, but the water is probably still cold from the late season snows and runoff. What I wouldn't give to not be mired down with the anxiety of impending war, and for once, just have a day to breathe easy. Maybe a day on the lake in the middle of summer to go fishing or grill out or anything but be a hamster on this wheel of training to keep busy and waiting for the sky to fall.

Just one damn day.

Footsteps slowly scale the stairs behind me, and I force myself not to react.

"Rhys," Aurelia calls softly.

Sighing through my nose, I shift my gaze from the window in acknowledgment but say nothing. Honestly, I'm afraid whatever comes out of my mouth might set her off, and for the first time, she almost sounds sweet.

"I'm sorry," she whispers.

Leaning back in my chair, the confusion nearly bowls me over. "For what?"

"For blowing up our room. For making you bleed during my PTSD freak-out. For losing my fucking mind. For being a class-A bitch. Pretty much the entire day."

Sipping my drink, I nod. "Apology accepted."

She takes a step back, clearly shocked, and I can't figure out why. Doesn't she know I would do anything for her—even forgive a piddly fire?

"That easy?" she asks, her mouth dropping open. "I don't need to get on my hands and knees and grovel?"

She's joking, but the mental image of Aurelia crawling naked across a messy bed, flashes across my mind. I almost growl aloud at the thought, my jaw tightening as my eyes go half-mast. Hastily, I look out the window to hide my body's response to the seemingly inane comment, praying she doesn't notice my reaction to a simple sentence.

"Nope," I mutter, proud my voice doesn't break like a damn adolescent.

She sighs, wringing her hands. "Well. Thanks. I'll leave you to it," she murmurs before turning to head back down the stairs.

"Aurelia?" I call as she reaches the third step down.

She pauses, her shoulders tightening. "Yeah?"

"I'm sorry, too."

Those words are laced with every bit of regret I've stored in my soul. Regret for saying yes when I should have died before I accepted a bond she didn't want. Remorse for Lucien, for killing him instead of just breaking his neck. Maybe I could have done it different. Maybe I could have saved him.

Maybe then Aurelia wouldn't be mated to someone she couldn't stand, bonded for eternity to the man who took everything from her.

She nods and, Fates help me, her bottom lip begins to tremble.

How many times have I made her cry? A thousand? A million?

"I-it's going to take a little while for me to forgive you. I know you have your side to the story. I know you have things to tell me, and I've been unwilling to listen. I'm sorry I can't give you better than that, but I'm afraid if I forgive you, I'll have to take the burden of all the guilt I've piled on your shoulders. And I can't bear the weight. I have to blame you, because if I don't, I have to start blaming me, and I won't survive the guilt. So, I'm going to have to hate you a little while longer, if you don't mind," she finishes her speech on a whisper, her voice barely reaching my ears.

The tears have broken free of her lashes, running in rivulets down her cheeks as she swiftly makes her way back down the stairs.

Apparently, just one day is too much to ask for.

IO

THEY CAME FOR ME AFTER I SENT LUCIEN ON TO THE Otherside. After Rhys left me alone in that forest. After I called upon my meager knowledge of the funeral rights and sent Lucien to his rest. While I lost the child in my belly and slowly bled more and more lifeblood. I'd wanted to die, but I never wanted this.

Soldiers came, and I fought. I fought so hard, but it wasn't enough. I was beaten and tortured. Iva loved hurting me, loved it when she drew any measure of blood. Realization dawned as to what she was doing.

She was making Rhys bleed through me, torturing us both for something I'd done. For wanting to leave, for wanting my own life. I was to blame. I would have felt sorry for him if he hadn't stolen the life I'd created for myself.

Blood-covered and shackled to a stone table, my body was littered with a hundred tiny cuts, burns, and puncture wounds scored into my skin. I wasn't bleeding anymore, and I supposed that was likely a bad thing.

Nicola had lied. I wouldn't see my daughter free of the Legion. I wouldn't see her breathe or live or smile. I hated her more and more each passing second—even if she wasn't the one who made me bleed. Because she was the one who'd made me hope.

Several times I lost consciousness, so I hadn't a clue how long I'd been stuck in this Hell. It felt like years, decades, centuries of pain, but it was more than likely just days. A commotion echoed outside my cell door, the distinct sound of bones breaking—particularly, a neck snapping. The door opened, and the absolute last person I wanted to see stood at the threshold.

He reached for me, and I scuttled away as far as my shackles would allow. I didn't want his dirty, murdering hands on me.

Rhys' face went from relief to agony as he made his way across the room and gently removed my bonds. His hands were soft, but I didn't want them anywhere near me.

"Don't touch me," I rasped, my breath catching in my lungs.

"As soon as I get you safe, you will never have to see me again."

"Good," I whispered as he picked me up and carried me into the light.

AURELIA

It takes no time at all to get to our room. And when the fuck did I start thinking of it as "our" room? The bedclothes still in shambles, I head to the linen closet in the bathroom for replacement sheets, dashing the tears from my cheeks on the way.

Of course, I *had* to cry in front of him. Why not? I've already been a basket case and a bitch today. Why not add in an emotional train wreck and round out the trifecta? I snap the sheets on the bed and search for a hamper to toss the soiled ones in. I'm finally rid of them when Rhys slams into the room.

"Why do you blame yourself?" he roars. "Why can't you put the blame on Iva where it belongs?"

Why couldn't he just leave it alone? *Push. Push. Push.* I take a deep breath and finally snap.

"Because she didn't stab him," I grind out, balling my hands into fists. "*You* did."

"And where would we be if I hadn't? I didn't go after him. He came after me. We were already bound. If I let him kill me, you would have died, too. If I let him cut me, you would've bled too."

Rhys tunnels his fingers into his hair and pulls as if he's ready to rip the strands out from the roots.

"What else would you have had me do?" he asks roughly on a parting shot as he stares down at the floor. After I fail to answer him, he slams out of the room for the second time today.

Trembling, I fall back the few inches until my spine hits the frame of the bathroom door. *Shit.*

Before I can get myself together, the door opens again, and he's back—his anger filling the room. He slams the damn thing closed behind him as he plants his feet, his hands in fists at his sides.

"Do you think I wanted to kill him? Do you think I wanted to watch you hate me for the last damn century? Do you think I asked for these fucking scars?" he asks me on a shout as he roughly tugs the collar of his shirt away to reveal thick, white scars against his olive skin. "Do you think I wanted to be tortured for days on end until I said yes to the binding? What makes scars like this on us, Ari? Huh? What makes these scars?"

They start at the middle of his thick, corded neck, disappearing below the dark fabric.

The only thing that could have made those scars permanent is a Morganite knife. It's why I have two full sleeves, why I have so much ink covering the wounds of torture inflicted by Iva's hands. The torture Rhys saved me from.

But no one saved him.

No one stopped his torment until Iva got what she wanted. Tears flow freely down my cheeks, dripping from my chin and down to my chest.

Even though I didn't hear them, his screams of agony echo through my mind. Gritting my teeth, I remember my own screams, my pleas for death. I can't open my mouth enough to respond. If I do, the keening cry caged in my throat will be set free, and I can't...

I can't.

My poor Rhys. What did they do to you?

"I did not ask to be bound to you. I did not ask to tie myself to someone else's woman. I did not ask for this," he grits, pleading for me to understand. "And you piling guilt on me, blaming me for his death, is not right. *Yes*, I feel guilty. *Yes*, I'm sorry he's dead. But I'd do it all over again if it meant I didn't have to kill you. I'd live the last century mired in the guilt of killing him. I'd do it all again if it meant you were breathing."

"But why?" I croak, amazed I can form the words.

An expression of comprehension dawns on his face, and suddenly, he's not three feet away, he's right there in front of me with my face in his hands. Why does his touch feel like a warm blanket around my soul? Why do his words—his truth—heal me in a way I've been dying for?

Why do I believe every word out of his mouth?

But most of all, why would he choose my safety, my life, my *everything* over his?

"Why what? Why save you? Because I've loved you since I was twelve years old when you told your mother you'd rather eat a pinecone than wear a corset. I loved you when you didn't love me. I loved you when you were married to someone else, when you were pregnant with another man's child. And I loved you even when you hated me. I loved you before we were bound... and I love you still."

Nodding, for once my head empty of all the trash that brings me down every day. Rhys saved me, doing it the only way he knew how— twice, if memory serves. He pulled me from the flames of Iva's torture. He watched out for me for years, shouldering the blame of something he had no control over.

For the first time, I'm able to put my guilt down, the weight of it all leaving my shoulders like a stack of bricks. No regrets, no recriminations. Nothing but him and the feeling of his rough, callused hands cupping my jaw and the tips of his fingers softly scraping my scalp.

Leaning down, Rhys touches his forehead to mine, the barest hint of breath whispering across my skin. The relief of it makes my shoulders sag. Letting it all go—the deaths of Lucien and my unborn child, a century and a half of agony—all of it.

The regret and guilt were the only things standing in the way of the bond, and now that those obstacles are out of the way, all that's left is my tie to Rhys. And I don't know if it's a spell, or if this is what Fate has destined for us.

I don't know if it's real or manufactured.

I'm not even sure I care.

All I know is, Rhys is here, and safe, and in my arms—something I've wanted in the back of my mind for more than a century but would never allow myself to have.

His lips brush mine, sliding back and forth against them as my mouth parts to breathe him in. His scent fills my nose—it's a faint mix of the Scotch he's been sipping, spice, and something altogether Rhys.

Shuddering at that simple touch of his lips, the iron bands of the bond seal around my heart. I wonder if sheer force of will kept the spell at bay for this long.

Was I just too stubborn to let myself love him?

Did I simply need to forgive him?

To forgive myself?

After all this time?

Then he's kissing me for real, his lips softer than I ever imagined. They cradle mine delicately, and then they turn harder, firmer, fiercer as his hands move from my cheeks to my hips to haul me against his chest.

My hands move, too. They fist in the shirt at his waist, pulling, tugging to get him to me. I need him closer. His tongue strokes into my mouth, and the taste—*Fates*—it's as if I was born to kiss him.

Maybe I was.

His hunger makes my belly dip and knot, my skin flushing as my entire body aches with need. I can't get close enough.

His hands burn against my skin as they climb under my shirt, biting into my flesh in the best possible way. The faint tear of fabric reaches my ears just as a tug jostles my arms—and then my shirt is gone. But *his* shirt is still in the way. The problem is quickly remedied when I rip open his button-up like tissue paper at a birthday party. I pull my mouth from his—but just barely—sharing the crackling air between our scarcely parted lips. Opening my eyes, I peer into the rich coffee color of his.

Those eyes are dancing, his face the happiest, lightest I've ever seen it. I didn't know Rhys could look this free.

But then I glance down, and I'm absolutely horrified. Not because Rhys is ugly—he could never be ugly. He could be missing limbs, his face could be half-gone, and it wouldn't matter—not now, not anymore. I'm appalled at what has been done to this beautiful man.

How much pain he must have endured to keep from breaking my heart.

How could I have blamed him for a century?

How could I have hated him?

He has endured more than his fair share of agony, too.

Scars run the length of his torso, extending into his trousers. Five thick, white lines as wide as a pencil run from his neck down through his pectoral, past his ribs, and through the muscles of his abdomen. Three burns as big as my hand mar his Legion markings on his stomach.

And the last one—that one? I inflicted.

A three-inch scar sits just above his belt, faint compared to the others he's suffered.

He felt the loss of my child. And I never realized…

I've blamed him all this time, and yet, he endured right along with me.

Gasping out a sob, my shaking hand covers the worst of the burns, pressing in as if to heal the ruined flesh. His skin is warm and alive as I rest my forehead against his heart.

"I'm so sorry," I keen. "It's my fault—all my fault."

"Shh, baby," he insists on a gruff whisper, his hands tilting my face to his. "You didn't do this to me. None of this is on you."

He slants his head, and his lips are once again on mine. I clutch him to me, my fingers digging into his shoulders. And then he pulls me up, his wide, strong hands at my ass, my legs wrapping around his back.

My fingers immediately sift into his hair, pulling his head to the side so I can taste the skin of his neck, his shoulder, softly nibbling at the flesh. He growls at the touch and walks us backward toward the bed. Then he turns, half-dropping me, half-laying me on the mattress, reaching for my shoes and yanking them off with a careless tug.

I sit up, my fingers already working the buckle of his belt. Just as I yank the first button of his jeans, he cups my face again, kissing me with a blistering heat. We fall back onto the mattress, and his mouth moves to my neck, licking, biting, sucking as his body moves over mine. I can't contain the low moan that erupts from my throat.

Reaching into his jeans, I bypass the remaining buttons and snake my fingers inside his tight boxer briefs. Wrapping my hand around him, I relish the groan that vibrates from his chest. But before I can give him a good stroke, he grabs my hands, pulling my arms above my head and pressing my wrists into the mattress.

"Don't move," he orders, and the command in his voice causes my breath to hitch.

For once, I do as I'm told, leaving my hands right where they are as he runs his callused finger down my arms, over my breasts, down my stomach, and to my jeans. He quickly works the button and zipper, pulling the denim down my legs, along with my underwear.

My patience runs out—my ability to follow orders flying out the window—and I move from my back to my knees, reaching for his jeans.

They have to come off. Right. Now.

I manage to get the denim pushed past his knees, and before he can stop me, I wrap my hand around his impressive cock. Leaning down, I bring him to my lips, sucking his hard length into my mouth as far as I can. I revel in his scent—in the taste of him.

His feral groan vibrates through my whole body, making the wetness between my legs go from damp to flooded. I get maybe three hard sucks before I'm miraculously on my back again, his wide shoulders between my thighs. His rough hands are under my ass—he's devouring me—his tongue at my opening, his lips on my clit, gently tugging on that bundle of nerves.

I'm about to come, and it's too quick.

It took me one hundred and sixty years to get over our shit. I'm not coming in the first ten minutes, dammit.

"You," I gasp, barely able to breathe. "I wanna come with you." Tugging him up my body, I kiss myself off his lips, loving the taste of my wetness on his tongue. His hands leave my ass and go to his cock, running it up and down my slit before notching it at my opening.

Rhys' fevered gaze practically touches me everywhere.

"You want me?" he rumbles, teasing me until I'm ready to beg.

"Please, honey. Please," I plead, and he gives me what I want, driving his thick shaft into me all the way to the hilt.

My moan is drowned out by his fierce growl, and we nearly freeze at the sensation. Then he's moving, thrusting into me hard enough to steal my breath.

And it's good. *So* good.

I wrap my legs around his thighs, moving my hips in time with his thrusts, meeting him stroke for stroke. His right hand burrows under my back, and the left sifts through my hair. And then we're sitting up, my body on top of his, taking his cock deeper, but sweeter—our mouths barely touching.

He turns us, my back once again pressed into the mattress as my release barrels toward me faster than a freight train. Rhys must feel the same intense pressure I do, because his thrusts become faster, rougher, less controlled. Our gazes meet and lock, the power in them enough to send me over the edge, and I come on a strangled moan. Everything inside me tightens, clamping down hard enough to ache, but in the best way.

Rhys' coffee-colored eyes narrow into slits, and he grits his teeth, coming on a groan, his fingertips digging into my thigh hard enough to bruise, but I don't care. The bite of pain at the end is enough to make my sex spasm around his cock in aftershocks.

His lips find mine again—hard and passionate. He gently pulls out of me and rests his head on my chest, his hard breaths tickling the skin of my breast.

"I love you too, you know," I whisper, confessing this truth for the first time out loud.

Because it's true. I love him, and I'm only just now figuring out that I've loved him for a very long time.

Before Lucien.

Before Rhys saved me.

Before it all went to shit.

I just wouldn't let myself believe it—too stubborn to admit I cared for the man chosen for me.

Well, I'm choosing him now.

"I know. I was just waiting for you to come around," he says with a relieved smile. "I knew you'd get it eventually."

He questioned it, and my declaration moved a weight off his chest. I wonder how many bricks he still had weighing him down.

"Good you know me so well, then," I mutter, rolling my eyes at the gauzy fabric draped over the canopy bed.

"I'm sure there's more to know. It might take me a while—maybe forever—to learn everything. Mind me sticking around?"

It's how he phrased it that kills me—like he's begging for this to be real, praying that what we have isn't just a fluke or a dream or...

I pull his head up and stare him dead in the eye, whispering my demand. "You'd better."

He nods, a hesitant grin pulling at the corners of his mouth.

I won't let him go.

Not ever again.

II

RHYS

THE BEST THING I'VE FELT IN MY LIFETIME IS WAKING UP TO
Aurelia's soft, warm, naked body half on top of me. Her head is resting
on my chest, one hand pressing against the scars on my stomach, and
one leg curled around mine. Even in sleep, she keeps trying to heal the
wounds I've suffered. One of my arms is banded around her back, and
the other is buried in her inky-black hair, massaging her scalp.

My mind is drifting, and for once in my life, I'm not focused on
anything but the girl in my arms and the next time I can get her to moan
for me.

Fates, her sexy, sweet moan.

I want to bottle it—brand it into my brain. I want to get her to make
it a thousand—no, a million—more times. I want to watch her come
apart forever. A smile pulls at my lips, and I tug on the sheet covering
her luscious ass.

Her body is corded in muscle, but she's soft in all the right places,
her beautiful backside being one of them. Carefully rolling us, I get her
on her back without rousing her, and then begin my wake-up call with a
soft nip at her throat. That earns me a sleepy snuffle, so I move lower

and cup her breast with my palm, giving her nipple a gentle tug with my teeth before sucking it into my mouth.

That wins me a squirm. I smile around her breast and move lower.

When I kiss and nip at her ribs and stomach, she gasps awake on a moan. I never knew that was an erogenous zone. Guess you learn something new every day.

"Morning," she grumbles on a husky sigh.

Her lips are swollen from kissing me all night, and she has the epitome of sex hair, but she's never looked more beautiful. Her eyes are half-closed, and that makes me want to do naughty things to fully wake her up.

Maybe when she's slippery and soapy.

"Oh, good. You're awake," I say brightly as if I didn't just rouse her from a dead sleep. "Wanna take a shower? You're awfully sticky."

One lone eyebrow rises. I have a feeling I'm not going to get much further without some incentive.

"If you get out of bed right now and let me do naughty things to you in the shower, I'll make you an entire pot of coffee."

Her eyes narrow.

Hmm. I'll need more than that. "And I'll make you breakfast."

Her eyes taper into slits.

Not enough, I see. Then I pull out the big guns. "That includes bacon."

"Deal," she says, popping out of bed like a cork.

I've been had. This sexy little minx just played me, and I have *zero* problems with that.

She saunters into the bathroom, naked, like she just won a prize, and if my shitty-ass cooking can be called a trophy, I'm not going to dissuade her. She's brushing her teeth at her vanity, which might be a good idea if I plan on tasting her mouth in the shower. Flipping on the taps of my sink, I watch her spit toothpaste into the basin, but she has her hand blocking her mouth so I can't see her.

It's so cute I have to give her shit for it.

"You're such a girl." I laugh around my toothbrush, foam coating my lips.

"I *am* a girl. And excuse me, but I've never brushed my teeth in front of anyone before. I was trying to be polite. I could be totally gross and hock a huge loogie in front of you—would you like that better?"

Gross. "No. You go right on ahead being girly. I'll be over here not giving you an ounce of shit for it."

With a prim nod, she flounces to the shower like she doesn't have a care in the world. The change in her is remarkable. Yesterday, if someone told me I would see Aurelia flounce *anywhere*, I'd call them a fucking liar.

She warms up the water as I finish up, the sexy silhouette of her curves barely obscured by the fogged glass. I pivot to study her movements as she puts on a little show for me. Meeting my gaze through the shower door, she squeezes soap into her palm and then rubs the suds down her breasts, over her taut, flat stomach and down her smooth thighs. I have to reach behind me to grip the counter, or I'm going to *Hulk*-out and break something. My dick is already standing at full attention.

Quickly, she grants me a reprieve, crooking her finger, and I'm in the shower before she can blink. I step in and turn her body so her back is to me, her smooth, wet skin against mine. My hands take over for hers, and I run my fingers over the dips and curves of her flesh. I start at her slim neck, running my hands down her shoulders, over the swell of her breasts, watching over her shoulder as her nipples tighten into sharp peaks. She shudders as I circle her ribs with my palms, before I trail feather-light touches down her stomach and between her legs.

She moans when the pad of my thumb finds her clit, getting louder when two fingers tease her opening. Aurelia's squirming now, having the hardest time standing still, and her ass rubs teasingly against my cock. At the brush of skin against skin, my control breaks. I spin her, yanking her up by her ass cheeks and slamming us against the rough tile wall.

Her lips are on mine, her fingers in my hair, and all I can think of is lining my dick up with her wet heat. The soap that only seconds ago was so sexy slipping over her skin is now a serious hindrance.

Finally, I think *fuck it*, and we tumble out of the shower onto the plush bath rug, clawing and tugging at each other in the best kind of frenzy. I sit her squirmy ass on the cold granite vanity, palm my cock, and thrust into her searing, wet heat.

The half-growl, half-moan I get in response goes straight down my spine to my dick. Banding my arm around her back, I grasp her hip with my other hand and start thrusting hard and fast. Her legs wrap around me tight, her heels digging into my ass. Her fingers pull at my hair as her lips suck at my tongue. I'm not going to last, but dammit, she's going to come before me.

Maneuvering my hand between us, I circle her clit with my thumb. I rub once, twice, and then...

"*Rhys*," she gasps, her pussy clamping around my cock like a vise as she comes.

Thank the Fates.

Picking her up off the vanity, we drop to the bath rug. Then I'm driving into her—harder, faster—listening to her moan, her core trembling with aftershocks.

"Baby," she moans, the blissful sound reverberating through my chest.

She's going to come on my cock again. I slam into her, and as her whole body convulses in another orgasm, I lose myself. Thrusting in once more, I plant my shaft, growling into the skin of her neck.

It takes a while to come down, and I struggle to catch my breath, my smugness rising as she tries to do the same.

"Does that still count as naughty things in the shower?" she wheezes. "'Cause I'm hungry, and you promised breakfast."

Nuzzling her breast, I consider teasing her by dragging out the word, "May-be."

And then we get to the hard part—the part I wanted to put off but don't think I can anymore. This is the make-or-break part, and I really hope she's not going to break me.

"You gonna let me kiss you where people can see?"

She seems to ponder the question for a moment. "Probably," she offers with a half-shrug and a sardonic smile. "If you're good and don't piss me off."

She can say what she wants, but I know she means it.

"You gonna stick with me?" I ask as I stare into her mint-green eyes, gauging her expression. "Be with me for real?"

"Yeah, but I think I'm getting the better end of the deal. You just asked a PTSD-having, batshit-crazy seer to be your girl. I think we need to investigate your sanity a teensy bit."

"There is nothing wrong with you," I tell her, brushing a wayward strand of hair from her face. "You are strong and beautiful, and I'm lucky to have you. I just need to buy stock in fire extinguishers. No big."

"Whatever," she mutters, smiling. "Feed me, Handsome."

Then I pull us both up, and she tugs me into the shower to clean up. We barely make it out of the shower without mauling each other, before throwing on clothes, and heading downstairs to the kitchen hand in hand.

Evan is sitting at the counter shoveling eggs into her mouth fast enough to choke. She nearly does a double take when she sees Aurelia's relaxed shoulders and smile. In all the years I've been around my woman, this is the happiest I've ever seen her. And I've only seen the better parts.

Evan has seen the worst. Or the whatever worst Aurelia would let anyone see.

"You all right there?" she asks Evan, her eyes still wide as she takes Aurelia in.

"Yeah," Evan croaks. "I'm great."

"Is there any more food? I've been promised breakfast, but I'm a little leery of this one's cooking skills."

"Yeah, sure. The eggs should still be warm on the stove, and the bacon is on the counter." She goes to the cabinet, retrieving two plates from the shelf.

"Coffee?" Aurelia asks hopefully as she fills two plates with eggs and bacon.

"Negative, darling. But you have a big strapping man there." Evan winks, smacking me on the shoulder. "Put him to work."

"Yes, I do," she says, shifting to face me. "As per the terms of our agreement, I am cashing in on that full pot of coffee."

"Done, Gorgeous," I say, trying to make sense of the high-tech gadget masquerading as a coffee pot.

Suddenly, Aurelia gasps, the plates slipping from her fingers, splattering eggs all over the floor. Her eyes flash wide, glowing with white light, her body rigid and bowed in pain. An agonized whimper breaks from her lips. I start for her, but before my fingers can even graze hers, Evan tackles me to the hardwood floor.

"Don't *touch* her," she shouts in my face. "Can't you see it? Her Aegis will *kill* you."

I've never seen an adult Aegis. All the young ones I've known died before they reached maturity. And then the dominos fall in my head, piecing the last century and a half together. I've known about Aurelia's little electricity spurts, the shielding she can create—usually by accident. But Evan has kept the level of her abilities secret from me.

A true Aegis—from what I've read—is outside the Primary's control, having autonomy from visions. They're supposed to be our leaders because they are not ruled by their scant glimpses of fate, not ruled by death.

But none of them have ever survived. I have my suspicions as to why.

No wonder. No fucking wonder why she's been running. Iva wanted her, and she's been running, hiding this long to remain free. To remain alive.

"Aegis? She's an Aegis, and you didn't think I needed to know?" I roar. "Why the fuck would you keep this from me?"

"Because I told her not to," John calls from the doorway.

I look up from my spot on the floor, noticing the king standing with a vaguely familiar redhead, while simultaneously trying not to throw Evan through a fucking wall. I need to get to Aurelia, and she's in my way.

"And why's that, John?" I grind out through clenched teeth. "What reason could you *possibly have* for not telling me my mate is a fucking time bomb?"

"Because the Primary would have seen," the redhead utters in a soft melodious voice.

"And who the fuck are you?" I ask angrily as I pick myself up off the floor, my eyes assessing every person in the room, but not landing on anyone in particular.

"Oh, don't tell me you don't remember me, child?"

Then I really look at her: the red hair, the blue, sightless eyes. But it's her faint British accent that causes all the memories to come flooding back.

Nicola, the Primary's second.

"You," I growl, lunging viciously at the woman who conned me into binding Aurelia against her will.

I nearly reach her when I'm struck in the temple by a huge hand. It takes a second for the room to swim into focus again, but when it does, Kyle is in between me and my target, looking like the boogeyman from a nightmare.

What the actual fuck?

His black hair is disheveled, eyes full black, and his thick fingers have curled into talons. Hissing at me through two-inch fangs, the hulking man is standing between Nicola and I, his arms thrown wide to prevent me from getting to her.

Why is he protecting her? Other than Aurelia and me, I've never seen a wraith give two shits about a phoenix in my life, and vice versa.

I'm two seconds away from pulling my Ruger and putting a bullet in his head when Nicola intervenes. She gently places her dainty hand on his shoulder, instantly calming him. His sclera bleeds back to white, and his hands uncurl, the talons retracting into his nail beds. His fangs are the last to go, the dull crunch of bone reforming in his jaw causing my stomach to turn.

I make the mistake of relaxing my posture, and then like the fucking asshole he is, he strikes, tackling me to the ground with his forearm against my neck. Before I can retaliate in kind, Aurelia gasps.

Then she screams.

She screams so loud and so long, I know I'm going to kill whatever monster is haunting her.

No matter what.

12

AURELIA

THE POWER IS OUT, DARKNESS SURROUNDS ME. THE QUICK PAINED breaths of the injured fills my ears. Lightning slashes across the sky outside, swiftly followed by the roar of thunder. In the scant glimpse of light, puddles of blood and water from the sprinkler system appear, pooling on the hardwood floor of the great room. The broken ruins of lamps are strewn across the wood, alongside jagged shards of the largest window.

The safe house wasn't so safe after all.

My feet are bare, the hem of my already-sodden jeans sucking up the watered-down blood from the floor. The shush of feet moving through the water reaches me, quiet as the flutter of a butterfly's wing. In the darkness, I can't tell if the person is friend or foe. My gut goes with foe, and I tighten my grip on the butcher knife in my hand, ready for anything.

I've been searching for Rhys for what seems like hours, but I know it's only been mere minutes since the siege began on the house. Either Rhys has left me to stave off this attack alone, or he's keeping someone else safe.

Either way, he's not with me.

We got separated, and I can't remember the reason, but now I can't find him anywhere in this pitch-black Hell. I remember reading once that Hell was as black as a moonless night, and they—whoever they were—are right. I'm tortured more by fear of the unknown and what I can't see than I am by anything else that has transpired here.

Clearing the great room and the kitchen, I check the pulses of a lifeless Cam and Asher as I go. Judging by the open maw that used to be Asher's neck, he died quickly. Cam's death was slower—his intestines spilled from his belly onto the kitchen floor. But with each person I find—every single one—has lost their life.

I fear that everyone is dead.

I can't find Evan, West, John, or any of the other guards who were here with us. I can't find anyone alive in this blackness. I fear if I set myself aglow, using myself for light, it will give away my location. My shield is pointless as well, since the house is flooded in an inch of water. It would electrocute anyone touching the ground. Maybe they wouldn't die a true death, but in this pit, I fear hurting someone.

What good are powers if you can't use them?

A hard hand grips my hair—the braid used as a handle as my neck is stretched backward. The thick, cold bite of a knife is thrust against my skin, nearly nicking the flesh. My worry of being found is gone, and my whole body ignites, fire racing over my skin, burning whoever's holding me. The pained growl of a man sounds loud in the dim as I'm released.

A phoenix wouldn't be burned by my flames—only a wraith would.

I turn to see Carver's naturally bronze skin red and puckered from the flames, rapidly healing from the burn. He smiles, his hard lips pulling into a cruel smirk, as he removes a blade from his belt, his other hand holding an intricately crafted short sword. The betrayal burns in my chest. I knew we had a traitor in our midst, but I thought better of Carver.

I thought he was a friend.

"Why?" I plead. "Why would you kill your friends? Why would you do this?"

"I didn't kill them. You did," he hisses. "Just by being here, you damned us all. I'm only trying to live. If I give you over, I'll keep breathing, and breathing is my top priority. Your safety and the ideals of your ridiculous war are not."

His eyes flick just to the left of my head and then back to me.

Before I can move, he has disappeared like smoke, reappearing at my left. I step to counter, but I'm not fast enough. The dagger slides between my ribs, stabbing my lung, cutting off my pained cry.

"Quiet, my beauty," he whispers into my ear, his lips soft on my skin. "I will keep him safe for you until we get you out of there." He slows my crumpling body before it can hit the floor, my flames extinguishing as my light goes out.

I SUCK IN A HUGE BREATH AS I EMERGE FROM THE VISION, BUT only in preparation for the scream clawing its way up my throat. It takes a second, but it finally breaks through the barrier of my teeth. My shield comes up hard enough that it cracks the stone island I'm clinging to, the hiss of the stone cleaving into pieces rattling through my chest.

My sight hasn't returned yet, and I don't know where Rhys is. My fingers reluctantly release the rubble of the countertop as I reach out into the darkness to find him.

"Rhys," I shriek, grasping at nothing. "We have to go. We have to go right now. *Rhys.* Where are you? *We have to go right now.*"

Fates, it's never taken so long to get my sight back after a vision. Even after the bad ones, it's usually only taken a few moments.

Where is he? We have to get out of here before they come. Stumbling a little, I plop gracelessly onto the hardwood floor.

The shuffling of feet and the thud of something large—maybe a person—hit the ground, quickly followed by a mumbled curse. *Definitely a person.* And by that curse, I'm going with it being Kyle.

"Baby, I'm here," Rhys murmurs, his hands cupping my face as he smears the wetness there.

"Your eyes are bleeding, baby," he says in gruff concern, his voice low enough to be classified as a whisper.

I realize now that there are many people in this room. I knew Evan was here, but now I sense the signatures of several people—possibly the whole house—are here with us.

"I don't care. We have to go right now," I repeat on a hiss. "Get my keys and go-bag and anything you need. We have to leave this house."

Blinking, the blackness starts to fade as light finally blooms, lifting the pall of blindness. When my eyes focus on his face, he clutches me to him, turning us, so his back is to the gathering crowd.

"Whatever you saw, can it wait a few hours?" he mutters into my hair. "We have a huge fucking problem."

His fingers massage my scalp, trying to calm me I suspect, but even his touch isn't helping right now.

He didn't see.

"I don't know. I know once the rain starts it'll be too late. Soldiers are coming, and people will die here. I was wearing this outfit, meaning it happens today. We. Have. To. Leave. Do you understand? They are coming for us."

"I know," he assures me, "but I need you to stay calm and hang in there a little while longer. We have a hiccup we need to iron out before we go."

Bracing myself for whatever has Rhys in such a twist, I spot a flash of red hair that makes me freeze. Standing behind the protective trunk of Kyle's arm is a bitch I hoped I'd never see again. Before he knows what hit him, I've forced Rhys behind me, my arm thrown back to prevent him from going forward, enveloping us in my shield.

That's new. Didn't know I could do that.

"John. What in the hell is that bitch doing here?" I snarl, my voice distorted from speaking through clenched teeth.

Yeah, I'm steadfastly ignoring the fact I'm doing something that should be impossible.

"I'm only here to help you," Nicola insists, her blind ice-blue eyes trying to meet mine but missing the mark.

She's the only oracle with her eyes still intact since she was born blind. Because of that defect, her visions have been "pure" since birth. She is the only oracle with zero bonds to Iva and probably the only one able to usurp her.

But did that little bitch help me?

No. She didn't.

She betrayed me instead.

"And I should believe that why, exactly?" I growl. "I remember how much your 'help' worked last time."

Nicola sighs, pinching the bridge of her nose like she's trying to gather the patience to talk to a toddler. "I merely told you the rules of the covenant—you chose to do what you wished. I cannot control the actions of the people around me. And I cannot foresee *every* action by *every* person. I'm not omnipotent, and I'm not infallible. And I tried to right my wrong. Who do you think pulled the soldiers from your cell so he could get you out, *hmm*? If you think he did that one on his own, you're sadly mistaken." She nods in the general direction of Rhys.

"You told me my daughter would be beautiful," I croak, tears clogging my throat. "That even though she would have my eyes, she would grow up outside the Legion, never to be mired in the chains of the Primary. You told me she would live. You *lied*."

It kills me to know that I'm more torn up about the baby I lost than the husband I took to the funeral pyre. I had Lucien longer—I knew him, loved him. But the more I think of how much I missed not seeing my child come into the world—not seeing her smile, not hearing her laugh—the more I hate Nicola for giving me that hope.

In my gut, I knew we weren't going to make it—knew something bad was going to happen. I just assumed it would be a complicated birth, not that I wouldn't even get to have her at all.

Or any child for that matter.

"You may think what you wish, but I did not lie," she snarls, her eyes flashing a brilliant blue. "I'm here to help. And you will sit there. And. Let. Me. Speak."

It takes everything I have—every single ounce of restraint I possess —to not jump over the ruined kitchen island and punch her right in the fucking face. The nerve of this bitch.

"*I did not lie.*"

My ass.

Considering I can't have any more children—hell yes, she fucking well lied. I give her a look of death she can't see and mutter, "Fine," under my breath.

I drop my shield, and Kyle's posture immediately relaxes. If I didn't know better, I'd think the brute of a wraith wanted into the Ice Queen's pants.

Good luck there, pal.

Wraiths have some severe mating habits. While phoenixes are a matriarchal society, wraiths are predominantly run by the males. I figure it's mostly due to the wraith male's irrational need to protect their mate.

If Kyle thinks Nicola is his mate, there is no order he will follow, no rule he won't break for her. If that's what is going on here, Nicola just bought herself a six-foot-seven burly-as-fuck shadow.

"I have reason to believe that your visions have been infiltrated by Iva. From what I understand, she is sending them to you—ones you can't change or interpret until the event has come to pass or is too close to be prevented. It's punishment for you both, but more for you, Rhys."

"Why is she punishing Rhys?" I ask, confused. "Because he didn't want to be my soldier? Because that's cracked, even for her crazy ass."

"Oh, child," Nicola tsks. "You don't know?" She tilts her head in Rhys' direction, but her eyes miss the mark again, drifting toward the light of the picture window behind us. "Why haven't you told her?"

"Because I didn't want her to hate me more than she already did, maybe?" Rhys says scathingly. "You've already let the cat out of the bag —might as well tell her the rest. I've had her to myself for less than twenty-four hours, but you go right on ahead and ruin it."

An expression of disapproval flashes across her face, and Nicola's lips screw into a grimace.

"Anyone want to tell me what the fuck is going on?" I gripe, tossing up my hands.

"She is punishing Rhys for betraying the Legion," Nicola confesses. "Rhys' brother, Julian, was to assassinate Olivia Black before the conception of her next child. It was to look like a rival's kill and not lead back to the Legion. Julian told Rhys of his assignment and refused to be dissuaded from his task. In turn, Rhys delivered Julian to the wraiths to prevent Olivia's murder."

"And because you gave your brother over," I muse, "you saved Olivia, and Evan got to be born? And I'd hate you because of that, why?" I tilt my head slightly to the side to see his expression.

His jaw clenches as he grips the back of his neck, refusing to look me in the eye. "Because my actions resulted in us being bound against your consent as punishment? Because I chose a stranger over my own brother? Really? Take your pick."

"So, you think I'm such a heartless cow that I'd approve of the murder of a harmless woman to prevent my own suffering?" I ask incredulously.

"I don't think you're a heartless cow," he murmurs, finally meeting my gaze. "I just thought you wouldn't see my side."

"Even when I hated you, I still saw your side. I'm not going to fault you for things you did to save someone else. That's just not in me."

"I just didn't want you to hate me anymore."

"I won't. Can we discuss this shit another time? Say, when we aren't in a serious time crunch of impending death? Because I gotta say, this 'We're Gonna Die' bullshit is getting old."

Rhys inclines his head in agreement and shifts to face Nicola. "So, are soldiers really coming, or has Iva cracked the lock on Aurelia's head for real?"

Nicola seems to think about it for a moment. "I believe she's still having trouble due to Aurelia being Aegis. Aurelia's visions of herself seem to be on the level, it's just the visions outside herself that appear to be affected. If you tell me what you saw, I could tell you if it is from Iva or from beyond the veil."

"Whoa, whoa, whoa," I bark. "Who said anything about an Aegis? *Who* the fuck is an Aegis? I know it's not me because all the Aegis I know died before maturity because they fucking vaporized themselves, and whatever way they did it, they didn't come back."

I'm half-shouting at Nicola now because the border of ridiculous has just been crossed.

"And what would a power-hungry diabolical bitch of a leader do if she found one that could survive into maturity?" Evan pipes up from the circle of West's arms. "She'd either bind you as an oracle so she could control what you see—or kill you. Since she can't do one, she's damn well going to try the other."

I pinch my brow, my brain on fire. "And by getting into my head she accomplishes *what*?"

"She gets to torture you—make you crazy. She gets to change that strong-willed, beautiful girl I fell in love with into a freaking hermit," Rhys answers, his voice ravaged. "She gets to twist the knife in my gut because I'm the reason she's doing this."

"But if I'm an Aegis—not that I believe you—wouldn't she have come after me, anyway?"

"It is possible," Nicola murmurs with a slight tilt of her head, "but unlikely. Your full potential was not known to us when you left. Or more accurately, I didn't inform Iva of the full scope of your potential. By that time, I had begun to make moves to remove oracles from her numbers."

"Well, aren't you a fucking saint," I snap sarcastically.

"You know, child, I am supremely fed up with your cheek. May I remind you, I am your elder, your Secondary, and your bloody savior. Show me some respect, or I will let your impertinent hide swing in the wind."

"Look, lady. I don't owe you a fucking thing. The way I see it, either Iva wants something from me, or you do. I'm not sure what it is yet, but I gotta tell ya, I'm disinclined to give it to you. Now you can take that savior shit and shove it right next to the stick rammed up your ass."

"Aurelia, dear," John tries to interject, "let's not piss off the only person who can save our collective asses?"

"She's not going to save shit." I scoff, my lip curled into a sneer. "Look, I'm sorry if this screws with your plan, but I'm not about to make a deal with the devil and get fuck-all in return. I'm leaving, and I'm taking Rhys with me. Anyone else staying, I suggest you get ready because soldiers are coming, and as far as I can see, no one but Carver makes it."

Carver's arm is thrown over his husband's shoulder, holding the smaller man in a loose embrace. Javier appears worried, and if the darkening of his eyes is any indication, he's about two steps away from phasing.

"Oh, and Carver?" His eyes cut to me, furious and worried and blackening into an almost-full phase.

"Yes, ma'am?" he hisses through lengthening fangs.

"If you have some grand plan to hand me over to the enemy to save you and your husband's asses?" I lift a brow in challenge. "Don't."

13

RHYS

I'M GOING TO RUIN EVERYTHING.

I don't want to, but I have to stop my woman from doing something stupid out of spite.

Aurelia is furiously packing, shoving articles of clothing and toiletries into her bag with enough force to split the seams of the duffle. She's quick and efficient, and if I don't hurry, she'll be out the door before I can stop her.

As much as it hurts me to admit, we have to hear Nicola out.

"Gorgeous," I call, but she doesn't stop moving—she doesn't even look at me.

She takes a thick stack of bills and throws it in the duffle, and then gathers up the next.

"Aurelia, stop," I murmur, catching her hand as she passes, reeling her into the space between my knees.

My fingers span her denim-clad hips, and I peer into her beautiful pale eyes. Worry and anger wrench her features and I reach up, cupping her jaw, bringing her face to mine. She tries to give me a quick peck, but my tongue sweeps the line of her lips. She opens her mouth, giving me a begrudging moan in response.

Leaning back, I pull her on top of me as I quickly flip us, resting my weight on my forearms between the legs of my reluctant beauty. In a lust-filled haze, I sadly part from her lips, pressing my forehead against hers for a moment before pulling my face away. I've got to get my dick under control, or I'll forget what I was going to say.

"We have to talk before we do something we can't take back," I gently appeal, praying she'll listen to me for once. "I think we need to hear Nicola out. We at least need to find out if she knows whether soldiers are really coming or not. We owe it to them."

"Because you think my visions are unreliable?" she croaks with a rueful twist to her mouth.

"Given what we know now," I murmur as I massage her scalp, "I don't think we can trust them one hundred percent."

"You're probably right," she grumbles, "but it kills me to give that cow the satisfaction."

"I agree, but it's the right thing to do."

"Um-kay," she grouses. "How do you suggest we go about it?"

"I think she's telling the truth about the Aegis. I've seen you. You use an electrified shield, darling. Just because you can't always control it, doesn't mean it's not there. And who's to say that the others wouldn't have lived? I don't put it past Iva to exterminate an entire faction of phoenixes to secure her throne. Do you?"

"No," she admits. "I wouldn't put it past her. How many of those children did she kill?"

"If I'm going with my gut?" The enormity of it all turns my stomach. "All of them."

Fucking genocide.

"*Fates.* How long has she been Primary?" she asks, pressing against my chest and sitting up. "Has she been killing Aegis children this *whole* time? Why hasn't anyone noticed or done anything about it?"

Aurelia gulps back tears, pressing a hand over her heart. "Then she's killed them her entire reign."

"Yeah."

"She's been Primary for the last six hundred years," she breathes, realization dawning on her face. "There have been at least two Aegis deaths a year—sometimes more—so at the bare minimum, twelve hundred children have died. She's a fucking mass murderer."

"So instead of running from this bitch, we should probably fight."

"Probably?" She shoots me a searing glare. "Ya think?"

"Okay, more than probably," I concede. "Definitely. This has gone on too long."

"That, we can agree on," she says, pacing the length of the room. "But I refuse to be nice to that lying sack of shit."

Fair enough.

A knock comes at the door, but before I can open it, Carver pops into our room in a swath of black smoke. I'm positive the expression on my face tells him this intrusion is *not* welcome.

"What?" Carver shrugs. "I knocked first."

"What are you doing here?" Aurelia asks, her hands crackling with electricity.

I'm a little afraid she's going to kill first and worry about the consequences later.

"I need to know what you saw," Carver demands irritably.

"Why?" Aurelia growls. "So you can stab me in the chest sooner? No thanks, dick."

"Look," he placates, holding up his hands in surrender, "I don't know what you saw, but I wouldn't do something like that."

"Sure you wouldn't," Aurelia agrees sarcastically as her eyes begin to glow. "You wouldn't lie to me either, now, would you?"

"Dammit. Am I going to be judged for trying to keep the fucking peace? *Fine.* Yes, I lied when I said I forgot why Asher and Cam were fighting. I wanted you to feel safe here, and I didn't want you to hate Cam, okay?" Carver tosses his hands to the side in frustration. "Cam is a good guy—he's just a little pissed right now. He has family in Cortez, or he *had* family in Cortez. He lost contact with them about a week ago, and when he went to check on them, he found the whole place burned to the fucking ground. Cam doesn't want you here. He doesn't want Iva here. He sure as shit doesn't want any more war. He was rather vocal about it, and Asher shut him down."

"You're right," Aurelia admits. "I wouldn't have felt safe here, and for good reason."

"And there's no way we would have stayed." I interject, finishing Aurelia's thought. "Is there some reason *you* want us here, Carver?"

"Yes, there's a reason. In case you haven't realized this yet, Iva is having us exterminated like we're motherfucking roaches. Like our truce means nothing. And I know what you phoenixes think of us, okay? Most of you believe wraiths are worse than dog shit on the bottom of your boot, but dammit, we're people, too. And we serve a purpose. It might be awful, but it is necessary, and I'm not going to be ashamed of how I was born."

Wraiths are the trash collectors of the supernatural community. They ferry deceased evil souls to Hell—Ethereal and human alike. To do that, they must consume them. It's a nasty process that no one wants to witness—or be a part of—for that matter.

Phoenixes, in turn, are supposed to ferry all other souls to be reborn. There is obviously a rift between the two species when there shouldn't be. Why people give a shit who does what, I can't fathom, but it's common for phoenixes to be snooty elitists with sticks up their asses.

"What the fuck do you mean, 'you phoenixes'?" Aurelia squawks incredulously. "My best friend in the whole world is a wraith. I understand your purpose, and I commend you for it. I couldn't do what you do—consuming that much evil without going crazy. I can't possibly imagine what you must go through to do that job."

"So *not* the point," Carver says, punctuating each word with a clap of his hands. "I want to know what you saw."

"Come with us to talk to Nicola," Aurelia offers. "I'll tell you both at the same time."

"Fine," he agrees and smokes out.

"Why do they do that? It's not that far of a walk." The whole "poofing" thing is fucking annoying.

I grab Aurelia's duffel, and we head down the hallway to the bottom-level game room. John is sitting in his comfortable leather armchair, half-sprawled, with his head in his hands. He seems to be either trying to rip his hair out or squish his own skull.

Cam and Asher are on either side of his chair, standing like sentries. Nicola is perched on his right with a glass of iced tea in her hand. She appears at ease, either because she knew we were coming, or because she has little to fear with Kyle at her side. Kyle is smugly lounging on the couch next to Nicola with his arm thrown over the back near her shoulders.

I make a mental note to kick his ass in the near future.

Aidan and Ian are sitting at the bar, looking worried and spoiling for a fight. Evan and West are sitting on the loveseat next to the pool table. Evan has her hand entwined with West's, squeezing it hard enough I can hear his bones creaking from here.

"Come to ask me for forgiveness?" Nicola asks, and I suppress a growl.

"Fuck, no," Aurelia answers just as Carver emerges from the hidden basement door. "I came to ask you if Iva's been killing the Aegis her entire reign. I also want to know if soldiers are coming tonight during a thunderstorm. And finally, I want to know if old Carver here is going to get the chance to stab me in the fucking lung."

Javier is on his husband's heels and goes from a smiley, good-natured guy to half-phased in less than a second. "Carver wouldn't do something like that."

"Yes, he would," Nicola counters. "If it meant that you would live, he would do anything. You know that." Her eyes drift in our direction. "I am—what's the word you used earlier? Oh, yes. I am disinclined to answer your questions."

"Look, you catty little bitch," Aurelia says with a cruel twist of her mouth. "I've had about enough. I didn't like you one hundred and sixty years ago, and I sure as shit don't like you now. But it's good you're showing your true colors in front of the people who could be killed if you hesitate. I love how you are so reluctant to stop mass murder. I love how fucking cruel you're being right now. Because you can't see the look on their faces, but I can, and it's just dawning on them that you're no better than Iva. You're just wrapped in a different fucking package."

"Do. Not. Compare me to that bloody woman," Nicola snarls, abruptly rising to her feet, the glass in her hand shattering from the force of her grip.

"Then don't act like her," I growl. "What's your problem? You came to us. Just talk to us without the ridiculous hierarchy you've made up in your head. We're not going to bow to you. Get over it."

"Right. Just answer your questions, because that's all I'm bloody well good for. Absolutely," Nicola says bitterly. "I don't know if Iva has killed the Aegis children. She has shielded herself from my abilities, more so over the last year. She is an expert at hiding herself. Based on the atrocities she has committed over the last three centuries I have been with her, it is within her character. I don't know if soldiers are coming here today. My future is unclear to me and has been for the last three weeks. I can see other peoples near future, but the past few days..." She trails off, shaking her head before lowering herself onto the couch. "I don't know. And yes, Carver would stab his best friend in the back to save his husband. But you all knew that already."

"Great," Aurelia quips. "You know exactly dick. Awesome."

"Oh, I know a few things," Nicola insists, her tone ominous. "Your future just isn't one of them. I know Iva is sending soldiers away from their charges to exterminate wraiths, leaving their oracles unprotected. I know she has sequestered the scholars away from their families. I know the oracle population has grown over thirty percent in the last century, and their numbers have increased to the highest our race has ever had. I know she has revoked the exile covenant, and any seer who refuses the transition to oracle is put to death. And the gentry have been called back from their posts. They are no longer sending souls on to be reborn. As I said, I know plenty. I just don't know what happens today."

"Are the head families just letting this happen?" I whisper in utter disbelief.

"Yes. All four of the original families have several oracles under Iva's care," Nicola answers matter-of-factly. "She can do whatever she wants, and their soldiers are not there to protect them."

"Well, fuck. So, we can't leave, and we have to stop the bitch." I direct my attention to the king. "John, how do you want to play this?"

"We have plenty of weapons in the house, and there is a bunker hidden under the basement gym. Those who cannot fight should be taken to safety," John says, likely referring to Nicola and Evan, even though Evan can hold her own.

"John, I think you should leave," Aurelia cautions. "I saw Asher and Cam ripped to shreds in my vision. Can they go as your guard? I don't know who wants to stay, but those two need to get out of here."

"I must go as well. But I won't go far," Nicola says, her face almost appearing sheepish at the confession of her inability. "Without my visions, I am of little use in combat."

"I'll go with you," Kyle says gruffly.

Nicola's head tilts toward the sound of his voice, and she reluctantly nods.

"Okay, who's staying?" I ask as a roaring clap of thunder shakes the house, and the lights flicker out.

"Everyone," Aurelia whispers. "It's too late."

14

"CAN YOU GET HER OUT OF HERE?" I ASK KYLE, JERKING MY chin in Nicola's direction.

"Absolutely," he says as he grabs her up from the couch, surrounding her with his thick arms. "I'll be back as soon as she's safe." He promptly smokes out of the room, leaving faint whisps of blackness in his wake.

Now that I think about it, all the wraiths could abandon us here to die—just up and leave us to Iva's little invasion. The dread growing in my stomach swells so big, I think I'll drown in it. I shift my gaze to Evan, and it's as if she can read my mind. She shakes her head at me.

She won't leave us.

No matter what.

That assurance has a gust of a sigh wheezing from my lips, my anxiety cooling for a second.

Rhys has already drawn his Ruger, his eyes scanning the room for threats. He has positioned his body so he's between me and the glass French doors leading to the bottom deck. A slight hint of ambient light filters through the glass, but it's quickly fading as the storm gathers strength.

"We need weapons," Evan whispers. "Lots and lots of weapons. I'm going downstairs. Papa, I want you with me."

John appears reluctant. Moreover, he seems kind of off. For the first time, I notice the dark circles under his eyes, disheveled hair, and his haggard expression lined with fatigue. Come to think of it, no one has mentioned his wife, Olivia.

We've been here two days, and I haven't seen her once. Bonded wraiths aren't frequently without their other half—the tie to their spouse soul-deep. Suddenly, I realize that I haven't seen Olivia in months. I've talked to Evan about her in passing, but I haven't clapped eyes on her. Even when I sparred with John at their house, I didn't see her.

Have I been such a selfish asshole that I didn't notice?

Yes. Yes, I have.

The pit in my stomach turns into a boulder, and it's hard to keep the shame off my face. I'm an awful friend.

West is hovering at Evan's left and appears as if he's two seconds away from dragging her to the sub-basement bunker and chaining her there. Finally, he breaks and interrupts the father-daughter stare down that's been going on for some time. Grabbing Evan by the waist, he hauls her to the open basement stairwell.

John, Cam, and Asher follow. Cam and Asher are bringing up the rear, both with their guns drawn. I can't see the make or model in the dim, but I do recognize the suppressors attached to the barrels of their handguns. This makes me feel better. Using firearms in this enclosed space will fuck with our hearing. The suppressors will at least lessen that blow. Even so, I'm pretty sure I'm sticking with silent killers.

Evan pops back into the room. In a rush, she shoves a pile of weapons and holsters at me. I inspect the haul and have to hold in my squeal of delight.

So not appropriate.

"Thank you," I whisper as I yank her into a quick hug.

I start arranging my weapons as she pops back out—first by putting my braided hair in a bun with the handful of throwing spikes as hair sticks. Then I swing a back holster over my shoulders, a lovely pair of hatchets fitting in the leather perfectly. Strapping a bandolier filled with throwing knives on my right thigh, I make sure to seat each one. All that's left is to chamber a round in the small Glock 19 before stuffing the extra mags in my pockets.

Evan knows me so well. If we survive this, I'll need to send her a fruit basket or something.

My spritely friend pops back in the room with West begrudgingly in tow. He helps outfit Aidan, Ian, and Rhys with bladed weapons. Carver and Javier have drifted closer to the mouth of the staircase leading to the upper levels, quietly arguing in Portuguese.

But I don't have time to worry about their little spat. Knowledge filters into my brain, and now I'm certain the vision I had in the kitchen is absolutely correct. Twenty or so men are outside, moving through the trees toward the house. They haven't even set off an alarm yet, but I have no doubt in my mind they're out there.

I really, really hate being right.

"I don't give a fuck what Nicola says," I hiss, meeting Evan's gaze. "My visions have always been spot on. Not a single one hasn't come true, but I've never had this much warning before. So, we need a game plan. Now that they've moved in closer, I can sense approximately twenty soldiers out there, but there could be more in another wave."

"That's what you saw?" Carver breathes, pushing back into the room. "No, you're leaving something out. Tell us the rest." He shakes off his husband's hold, barking at him in Portuguese when he tries to pull him back.

"Fine. A brief rundown? They trigger the sprinkler system somehow. I can't find any of you, but I do find Asher with his head almost cut off, and Cam disemboweled." Now I get to the rough part that's going to make Rhys lose his shit. I don't look at him, instead pinning my gaze on the man I'm about to tattle on. "Carver catches me unaware and stabs me in the chest. But he lets me know he's going to keep an eye out for Rhys, and that you guys are going to save me. To date, it is the most changeable, in-advance vision I've ever had."

Just as I expected, a snarl erupts from Rhys' throat, his big body herding me back and away from the group, Carver especially. He chambers a round in threat, his skin flushing with the heat of his Fireskin. If he's not careful, he'll phase right here in the game room.

Carver advances, holding up his hands in surrender, a pleading expression pulling at his brow. "I wouldn't. I won't."

We both know he would if it meant keeping everyone else safe, and I hate to agree with him. If it meant that everyone else in this room would live, I'd do the same to him. I wouldn't like it, but I would do it.

Especially if it kept Rhys safe.

"We can change it," I whisper to Rhys' taught shoulders. "This one doesn't have to come true."

"Then let's change the motherfucker," Rhys growls, slicing a look at me over his shoulder. "No one goes anywhere alone. We stay in pairs. They are coming to find us—to kill us. Let's remind them what real warriors can do."

"Where are they coming in?" West asks, adjusting his weapons.

My eyes lose focus for a second as I allow the knowledge to filter into my brain. "Second- and third-floor picture windows," I answer, jerking my head upward. "They're repelling from the roof."

"Good luck getting through the glass," Evan mutters with a scoff. "It would take a damn cannon to break it. Why aren't they flying in?"

"Because they plan on leaving with a hostage," West replies, clearly referring to me.

He's not wrong. It's the only thing that makes any sense.

"I want you guys to dispatch any soul you feel is evil," Rhys demands. "Glut yourselves if you have to. We need to weed out those motherfuckers—quick."

"It would be my pleasure," Aidan agrees with an evil smile even I can see in the dim. He shares a look with Ian, and together, they silently head up the stairs.

Carver and Javier move to the second floor, Rhys and I go to the first, leaving Evan and West to the bottom floor closest to the hidden basement door.

In some ways, it's fortunate the only entry and exit points are all located on the south side of the house. Since the garage takes up the entire northwest section, the only entry points are security-enhanced doors that close like a vaulted safe when the power is cut.

However, the system *does* have a fail-safe. One that only triggers in the event of a fire.

Fuck. Just as I think this, the sprinkler system goes off, the hiss of the automatic locks disengaging, gusting through the house.

Son of a bitch.

"They are using it as a diversion," I breathe to Rhys from our perch on the staircase leading to the first floor. A shiver rattles through me at the freezing water falling in a torrent around us. "Five are on standby to see where the biggest threat is. Three are coming in the third-floor window, five through the second. Seven are now planning to go through the first-floor window in the great room."

I *see* them in my mind. I can feel them like a jagged nail scratching into my brain—their racing heartbeats, their minds buzzing in preparation for the fight, their smug boasting of who can kill the most wraiths.

Bastards.

"Bottom floor?" he asks, the cold not appearing to affect him at all.

My head gives a faint shake without me telling it to. "None yet."

"Well, let's get to it. I'm warning you—you better stay with me," he demands on a whisper. "Don't you dare leave my side."

Swallowing hard, I give him a tremulous shake of my head. "I won't. I'm sticking with you, remember?"

After one hundred and sixty years of loneliness, I finally have something worth living for. Just the thought of losing what we have makes my chest ache.

Rhys studies my face for a moment before hooking a rough hand around the back of my neck, hauling me to him. His breath whispers across my lips, his fear palpable with every single passing second.

"I love you, Gorgeous," he murmurs before dropping a short, fevered kiss to my lips. "Always."

"Always," I repeat, touching my forehead to his.

I'm going to keep us alive. I am.

I have to.

Before we leave our positions, I silently slide off my leather-bottomed sandals, their slick soles more of a hindrance than a help.

Barefoot.

I don't want to be barefoot. It's too close to my vision.

Rhys takes point. He's up the three steps and in the hallway leading to the great room, before the window breaks. The poor bastards trying to break it didn't anticipate reinforced glass, though, and the compact battering ram they're using isn't quite doing the job.

Then an enormous phoenix shoves past the others, the hulking giant easily the biggest Ethereal I've ever seen in my entire life. He appears to consider the glass for a minute, then lifts his boat-sized boot and simply kicks the window in.

I pause to reconsider my weapon choice. I'm not sure a nine-millimeter bullet is going to cut it with this burly bastard, but I'm going to give it the old college try. Waiting for the next crack of thunder to muffle my shot, I take aim for the only spot on his body not covered in body armor.

Three rapid-fire squeezes of my trigger, and he goes down like a stone.

Rhys uses his lifeless body as a springboard and tears into the next soldier with a curved blade resembling a machete. His target's head goes flying as his body falls, and Rhys is on to the next. I don't stop firing, taking out two more phoenixes before my mag runs out. Tossing the spent pistol, I swiftly draw the hatchets from their sheaths, weighing the weapons in my palms before I strike at the last man left standing.

He seems shocked at the sight of his fallen brethren but snaps out of it as I approach. He barely has enough time to raise his weapon before I'm on him, and he has the business end of my blade embedded into his eye.

It's swiftly dawning on me that this has to be the first wave. There is no way it could be this easy to dispatch seven men.

Other than the pattering of the artificial rain, the rest of the house is silent. No shots fired, no creaks of steps on the hardwood floors. Nothing.

The dread in the pit of my stomach doubles in size.

"This doesn't feel right," I whisper to Rhys. "It shouldn't be this easy. We're missing something."

He nods in agreement, signaling for me to follow him.

We head back downstairs to check on Evan and West. Each step feels like a land mine. Rhys, finally tired of the lack of light, ignites his Fireskin in a controlled burn. The flames don't deviate from his palm as he uses his fingers like a torch.

Evan and West are standing out of the way of the French doors, wary of an attack from all angles.

"You guys good?" Rhys asks, his gaze scanning the room for threats.

West nods in response, and Evan appears simultaneously bored and worried out of her mind.

"Tell me this doesn't feel right," Rhys grouses.

"Nope," West grumbles. "This feels like one big con."

"I can't see anything," I admit, frustrated as hell. "I don't know what's going on, but no one is waiting to get in. No one else is out there. Whatever threat there is, it's already inside."

West suggests we move together to find the others, and we head to the second floor in search of Javier and Carver. We find neither, but we do see a mound of bodies.

"*Fates save us,*" Evan exclaims, stumbling back as she covers her mouth.

She can obviously see something I can't, because the expression of sheer terror in her eyes is enough to chill my blood.

"Revenant," she murmurs, clearly aghast. "Their hearts are missing."

Rhys brings his fist closer to the bodies, the faint flicker of light illuminating the macabre scene. The floor and walls are spattered in scarlet, the lifeless men lying in a heap of blood and gore and bone.

Whatever tore out their organs was strong enough to go through their body armor like tissue paper.

"*What,*" I hiss, shaking, "the *fuck* is a Revenant?"

But it's West who answers me. "It's what happens to wraiths when they go crazy. They start eating the flesh of the dead. But I've never seen one eat from the living or even kill to get a meal."

"And how do you kill one?" I ask, my voice growing even smaller, because *holy fucking shit.*

"Fire," he replies, his gaze still locked on the gruesome pile.

Well, yippee. At least we have that.

In pairs, we move on, Evan and West searching the northwest section of the floor and Rhys and I looking in the southeast. Together, we clear our room, our bathroom, and the next guest room, only finding one body with his heart still intact. His head, though, is another story.

We make our way back to the rally point, where Evan and West hover around an unconscious Aidan and a critically injured Ian. West is working on Ian, trying to staunch the flow of blood from his neck with Evan's thin cardigan. Ian's eyes roll in his head, a gurgling gasp rattling from his throat.

He's so close to death, but his future is an unknown. I suppose that's a good thing.

"There are medical supplies in the bunker," Evan says. "If I can get him there and stop the bleeding, he'll survive."

I pray she's right.

"Take him," West orders, and Evan grabs him, disappearing in a whisp of smoke.

"Can he not heal like the rest of you?" I ask before the answer filters into my brain. Ian isn't like his brother.

"No," West answers, his jaw clenched tight. "Ian's different. He can't travel like us or heal as quickly, but he has our lifespan and our purpose. We think maybe his mother was human, but none of us know for sure."

Rhys and I nod in understanding. It has happened with our species as well when they mate with humans. I can understand the appeal, but I have a serious issue with the logistics. There is no way to extend their human's lifespan.

No spell.

No remedy.

Nothing to stave off the human condition.

"What about Aidan?" I ask. "Is he all right?"

"Not sure," West replies with a shake of his head. "Won't be sure until we get him in the med bay."

"His breathing isn't labored, he's not bleeding from anywhere but his head, and that seems to be closing up. Let's find Carver and Javi and then get the fuck out of here," Rhys suggests. "You stay with him, Gorgeous. West and I'll check upstairs real quick. Don't move, got it?"

If it were any other time, I'd do something cute like flip him off, but all I can do is nod. The loft is small enough they won't be gone too long. Readjusting the grip on my hatchets, I scan the landing and hallway for threats as the boys head upstairs.

As good as my ears are, I don't hear him until he's three feet from me. And as good as my sight is, I don't see him at all. The monster of a man takes another step closer, as silent as the grave, the scent of death the only thing heralding his presence.

By the time I notice him, he's already too close.

"I knew they'd leave you alone eventually," Javier says with a bloody smile, gore coating his hands, mouth, and chest.

Well, I didn't see that coming.

RHYS

West and I swiftly and silently make our way up the short staircase to the loft, West in the lead since his night vision is much better than mine. With my light, I can make out the watered-down blood sitting in puddles on the hardwood floor. The sprinklers have trickled off, no longer pelting us with freezing-cold water.

He moves to check the bathroom while I work on clearing the bedroom. The room appears empty at first, but I'd feel a hell of a lot better if we could find Javier and Carver. That, and figure out who brought a fucking Revenant to the party.

Catching sight of a shoe, I find Carver half-sitting, half-sprawled on the floor behind the club chair in the corner. He's gasping shallowly, doing his best to try and talk, but given the foamy bubbles coming out of his mouth, his lung is punctured.

That doesn't stop his mouth from moving, his eyes wild, desperate.

Or I should say "eye."

His arms and face are deeply slashed, enough to know that unless he can heal from it, Carver is likely going to lose his right eye. Four deep gashes span from his left shoulder to his belly, and in a circle around his heart, he has five distinct puncture wounds. The Revenant must have been interrupted in the process of ripping out his heart.

Lucky bastard.

Letting out a low whistle, I feel West's approach as I yank a throw blanket from the chair and try to stem the flow of blood.

"Ja-Javier. Re... re... re..." Carver gasps but loses consciousness before he can get the words out.

This whole thing is wrong. First the security breach, then the Revenant, and we haven't found Javi. This situation has "fucked" written all over it. By the expression on West's face, he's thinking the exact thing I am.

"Can he even heal from this?" I ask because wraith anatomy is not exactly something I've studied up on.

"Best case, yes, but it'll take several days. Worst case?" He shakes his head.

My jaw clenches. "You find Javi?"

"No."

That is not a good answer—especially since there is only one wraith unaccounted for. It doesn't take a rocket scientist to figure out who did this. "We need to get back to Aidan and Aurelia and get the fuck out of here."

We don't even make it to the first step before I feel the ripping sensation in my chest. Shock has me stumbling as I reach for my ribs, my hands coming away with the warm wetness of fresh blood.

Aurelia, I think as the already-dark world goes black.

15

AURELIA

Gasping awake, the cold instantly seeps into my bones. My clothes are rough against my skin, stiff with dried blood. The bite of the shackles encircle both my wrists and ankles, my arms stretched above my head, already half-numb from the position. I try, but I can't move my hands or feet more than a few inches. The stainless-steel table I'm chained to looks like a morgue slab. The clank of the metal on metal causes a shudder to shake its way up my spine.

Well, I've been here before.

The panic attack barreling its way through me is nothing new, and it takes roughly an age to get under control. Well, and a teeny, tiny nap as I pass out from hyperventilation. But, hey, I'm being held hostage. I get one freebie meltdown, *right*?

Consciousness takes its sweet, merry time coming back. I know this because now the room has people in it. I can't see or hear them, but I *know* they're here. I'm willing to go out on a limb here and say some form of torture is about to start.

At this juncture, I scratch the life goal of never being tortured again at the top of my wish list.

The barren room is decidedly gray with windowless cinderblock and buzzing florescent lights hanging from the ceiling. Moisture crawls up the walls, the scent of mold and death invading my nostrils.

A cell, my brain supplies, slow on the uptake. *Yippee. I've always wanted to die in prison.*

A soldier appears in my line of sight, and it requires a fuck-ton of self-possession to tamp down my fear. Especially since he has a very large Morganite blade in his hand.

Is that big of a blade really necessary?

Apparently so, because he's using it to cut away my clothes, leaving me in the draft—the pervert. He's quick and efficient, removing my shirt and jeans before I can get over the shock of what he's doing. When he gets to the point of the festivities where he tries to cut the middle of my bra—that's where I snap out of it.

Putting an Aegis on a metal table with steal bonds is a very bad plan. I've never been happier to completely fry someone in my life.

I shove the electricity from my chest, coating my flesh, allowing it to travel down and out of me through the table all the way to the hand the idiot rests on the edge. It's as if I'm touching him with a live wire, disrupting the rhythm of his heart, burning him from the inside out.

A dark smile curls my lips when I see the wetness running down his leg before he collapses. The memory of the bastard pissing himself will probably never get old—even if the smell of charred flesh fills my nose.

But letting that bit of myself go free wakes up the aches and pains in my body. I've squandered too much energy, and now I have the added fun of trying to get out of my shackles.

It takes a while to work myself up to it, but I manage to dislocate my right thumb, just barely holding onto my gorge as it rises in my throat. The smell of flambeed soldier and his loose bowels does nothing to me, but dislocating one measly joint, and I'm ready to toss my cookies.

I squeeze my right hand out of the cuff before snapping my thumb back into place.

Don't puke. Don't puke.

Now I've reached a dilemma. I still have three limbs trapped, and the thought of dislocating another thumb—*nope. I'll wait a minute.*

"It took longer than I anticipated for you to dispatch him," a voice calls, and my already-topsy-turvy stomach nearly loses it.

I'd know that voice anywhere.

Iva.

The woman I've feared for more years than I care to count saunters into my line of sight. Outfitted in a pristine white dress that clings to her slender frame, she surveys the fallen guard as if she can actually see him. Once, I'd thought white had been a symbol of purity, but the way she wears it, the color will always remind me of death. It makes sense that everything—even her hair—carries the trademark shade.

Everything but her eyes.

A century ago, she wore dark, green-tinted spectacles to hide the hollow sockets where her eyes used to be. Now, brown prosthetic ones fill the space, their odd ability to follow my movements unnerving.

"Sorry to disappoint. I didn't know we were having a party," I say referring to her gown. "I would have dressed up."

Iva bends to scoop up the Morganite blade, locating it as if the prosthetics were real.

"I think your clothing is the least of your worries, dear," she warns, her Irish lilt setting my teeth on edge. She tosses the blade from one hand to the other, taunting me. "What you should be worried about is that pesky Aegis taint you have in your blood. I've worked very hard to eradicate that irksome little faction. I'll not have it passing down your line. Oh. That's right, there won't be anyone else in your line, now, will there? No matter." She shrugs as the knife's tip touches the skin of my inner thigh.

It doesn't break the skin, only indents the flesh as she glides the blade down my leg. I try my best not to shake, but fear—*fuck*—it makes me lose myself.

"Now, do I bleed it out of you?" Iva muses. "Or do I use other ways to rid you of that blasted power?" Her eyes squint in consideration, her red-painted mouth screwing up to the side.

I'm pretty sure whatever way she chooses, I'm not going to like it.

Being known for tossing spells around like candy, Iva is not the woman I want experimenting on me. She sets the knife down and places her slender hands against the skin of my face.

Nope. Don't like this already.

When the chanting starts, I can't focus on anything else but the pain. It's like being covered in fire ants, or battery acid, or fire—if fire could actually burn me. Iva's fingertips dig into my cheeks, gouging my skin, the bite of it almost pleasurable compared to whatever spell she's casting.

I can't think.

I can't breathe.

All I can do is lay there and pray this agony isn't killing Rhys, too.

I WAKE UP IN THE GRAY, STERILE, ROOM FROM HELL—*AGAIN*— seriously contemplating how many times I'm going to pass out in this hellhole.

At least I'm alone.

My cotton-filled head is blissfully without pain, though. That or those particular receptors in my noggin decided to say, "fuck it" and bailed on me while I was passed out. Either way, I'm counting it as a win.

I take advantage of my numbed state and dislocate my left thumb.

Nothing. No pain at all.

Groggily, I hope Rhys isn't the recipient of it all. That would suck. I shimmy the cuff off and pop my thumb back into place. Bringing my arms down, I shake the blood back into them. While I can't feel pain right now, I do notice the muted, pins-and-needles sensation of the loss of circulation.

Now I have the arduous task of stretching my body off this table to attempt to reach the downed soldier on the floor. He's lying in a lump where he stumbled away near the end of the table, wearing the traditional garb of a steel breastplate held on by straps of leather and leather combat skirt.

That's it. No under clothing, no tunic, nada.

I always thought it was a waste to have the soldiers dressed as eye candy when the oracles were blind.

The key to the shackles is clipped to the leather-studded belt holding his skirt up. I feel the chain pulling on my ankle, but I'm not bleeding, so I figure all's well.

Just. One. More. Inch.

Fumbling the keys, I manage to catch them before they fall. Now I get to do the semi-hilarious half-crab walk back on the table. Out of the shackles within seconds, I stand, getting my first real look at myself. I'm practically a horror movie reject in my blood-covered bra and panties.

If my friends could see me now, I'd likely get laughed at for days. My thoughts go to them, and I hope everyone is okay. I scoop up the blade and quietly pad over to the door, the adrenaline of impending freedom waking me up a little bit.

The door is unlocked, but I shove the keys into my bra for lack of a better place to put them, snatch the Morganite blade from the table, and make my way toward the light. The hallway is at odds with the cell I just vacated. The rich wood paneling is tastefully adorned with paintings older than Iva. Several doors line the corridor, and my biggest fear is someone walking out of one of them, catching me before I can get the fuck out of here.

The silhouette of a figure moving up ahead casts against the wood, but before they see me, I move into the shadow of a doorway. The small inlet in the wood is not quite enough space for me to hide, though. Then he turns the corner, moving down the corridor, shooting a glance over his shoulder. Even with his face half-turned away from me, I recognize him.

It's tough to forget someone stabbing you in the chest—that's for sure.

Javier saunters closer, and blindly, I reach behind me, praying the hinges are silent. My back to the opening, I thank whatever deity I need to that the door was unlocked.

Glancing around in the darkness, I see almost nothing. No movement, no breathing. The smell is awful, though, as if someone or something has died here. I step farther into the gloom but leave the door ajar. Javier is moving toward me, and I'm sure he'll come to investigate either the smell or the cracked door at some point.

Sure enough, he stops at the entrance to this cell. I don't blink—I don't even breathe as I wait for him to cross the threshold. Tightening my grip on the blade, my impending vengeance curls my mouth into a gruesome smile, and I'm still grinning when he walks fully into the room. Keeping the feral pull to my mouth, I efficiently cut off his head before turning him to ash.

Fire, one. Revenant, zero.

Through the dying embers of Javier's corpse, I glimpse a figure on the bed. A woman. She's unmoving, her matted brown hair covering her face. I check her and note she is not true dead. From what I sense, though, she'll be out for a few more days.

Dead weight.

I can't help her now, but I swear to myself when I get out of here, I'm bringing people back with me to free her and anyone else imprisoned here. Guilt floods me as I make my way out of the room and down the rest of the hallway.

Leaving the woman behind feels wrong. Wrong in a way I can't name or quantify.

Sticking to the wall—mostly for support—I come to a large landing. One side leads to a grand staircase, and the opposite side is a service stairwell—the commotion of a kitchen bubbling up the steps. Keeping to the shadows, I skirt the circular space and pad down the servants' stairs.

Of all the places for me to go, a kitchen is probably the last route I should take. It's bustling with people preparing a meal, and a bloody, underwear-clad woman, is going to go over like a fart at High Tea.

I wait in the shadows trying to decide if taking a hostage is necessary for me to get out of here, or if the workers are too busy to notice me. Hoping for the best, I choose option two. Crouching low, I make it fifteen of the twenty feet to the door before a very young gentry woman notices me.

She may look young, but her gaze is haunted. She knows what's chained within these walls. I put my finger to my lips, and she nods, looking away as if she'd seen nothing.

The next five feet are simple, and the door makes nary a squeak as it opens and shuts. I flee the warmth of the house to the cold, damp, darkness of the night. I'm not sure where the hell I am, but the weather and tree line suggest the Pacific Northwest. The house sits atop a lush foothill of a verdant mountain. Somewhere in Oregon, possibly, and I wonder if it's the same village I grew up in.

These woods were my playground so many years ago, and it doesn't take a psychic to foresee a pair of cut-up, dirt-covered, feet in my future.

The forest is far louder than I expect. The trees rustle in the wind, bugs trill and chirp in the fading light, but I'm still the loudest thing here. As carefully as I step, and as slowly as I'm walking, I still make a huge freaking racket. I stop, crouching in the high grass as I attempt to sense if anyone is following me. My head is still filled with cotton, and I feel nothing.

Picking up the pace, I figure if slow is loud, then I might as well go fast.

The descent becomes sharp, and before I know it, the trees are starting to thin. The precipice of a cliff emerges into view, and I scramble to slow down. My fingers scrabble in the dirt before an errant root allows me to skid to a halt at the edge of a fucking mountain.

Breathless, I nearly start giggling at the utter absurdity of it all. Especially since from what I can figure, I'm only left with two choices. I can attempt to climb the steep incline I just skidded down, praying no one from the Legion house is in the forest looking for me, or I can try to phase and coast down this cliff.

This also requires a fair bit of hope—especially since I don't know how to fly.

While I do have wings, my primary feathers were cut by a Morganite blade when I was tortured by Iva so long ago. Those essential feathers— the ones that could have allowed me to soar—will never grow back.

That said, in the last one hundred and sixty years, I've had a lot of time on my hands, and studying bird anatomy is a hobby of mine. A bird can still coast with their secondary feathers, and I have those.

I might as well try it. It's not like the fall will kill me.

The burn of transformation races over my flesh. The fire is first, coating my hands, up my limbs, to my torso. The flame only stings for a second before it starts to heal. The cuts and scrapes on my feet and legs are closing—my thumbs no longer swollen and tight.

The wings are next—bones crunch and crack before the added weight of my feathers rest upon my shoulders. It's been too long. I stretch, shaking them to adjust to their size. They've grown a little in the last ten years or so—as they are known to do—but I don't think they'll get much bigger. Or at least I hope not. The wings hang down my back and reach the forest floor—the tips slightly bent and dragging.

The colors have changed over the years. As a child, they were fluffy and white, with the barest hint of yellow on the coverts. As a teenager, they were bright orange and yellow. Now they're almost blood-red at the tips of the feathers, bleeding from a candy-apple to amber.

I stretch them out, flapping them once to catch the air with the feathers. In theory, this hair-brained idea should work as long as I have enough room to coast.

Shoring my fears, I hurdle myself off the edge of the cliff. The ground rushes at me rapidly, and I'm positive I'm about to go *splat* before the feathers catch a downdraft, and I glide the rest of the way down. I circle my feet in a running motion like skydivers before they land, but I fail miserably and completely biff the landing, eating dirt like a pro.

Well, at least I didn't die.

The loud shuffle of footsteps sounds to my left, and I crack an eyelid to spy my impending fate. I'm still dazed, too busy coughing up forest bracken to even react. Three pairs of black leather motorcycle boots race into my line of sight—two large pairs and one small, dainty pair. The small ones are tapping a single foot as if irritated.

Craning my head, I blearily gaze up at Rhys, Evan, and West—each standing with their arms crossed, their expressions murderous.

It is completely possible I should have waited before jumping off a cliff.

Whoops.

16

RHYS

Pissed-off energy radiates through the SUV, but as mad as I am, the relief warming my chest holds me together. With Aurelia safely in my arms, it's tough to remember just how angry I am that she launched herself off a fucking cliff.

Seven days, I think, pressing a kiss to her hair. *Seven whole days without her.*

How did I survive these last few decades apart when seven days has been the highest form of torture? Maybe it's because I never really had her.

Maybe it's because she was never really mine. The thought of going another day without her by my side has my heart falling to my stomach.

Aurelia had been held for a full week before she escaped—six days of which, she was unconscious. The second she opened her eyes, that knowledge etched its way into my soul.

None of it made any sense.

Typically, when I "die" so does she. When I'm hurt, we both bleed. But this time was different. This time, I got medical care immediately, while she was stuck bleeding and alone in the middle of enemy territory.

That had never happened—not in a century and a half—and the absence of her presence in my mind was like losing a bit of my soul. She'd always been there in my head: the bits and pieces of emotions, her needs, her wants, but it was so much more now—our bond only growing stronger since we finally came together.

I knew where she was the instant she opened her eyes, and the five of us got on a plane—not that our rescue attempt was necessary.

The first day she woke up, she broke out, and I don't know if that's scary or sexy as hell. Preferring to lean toward sexy rather than think of the alternative, I gather her more securely in my arms and stare out the windshield.

The closest airstrip to the Legion compound is in Eugene, and from there we rented a car to get to the isolated property hidden in the middle of the Willamette National Forest. Said vehicle is filled to the brim with a level of unease I have yet to experience in my lifetime.

A wave of irate energy radiates from Aidan and Ian who are stuffed in the cramped third-row seat. The brothers are still kicking themselves because they hadn't realized that Javier had been a traitorous Revenant. Well, that, and the fact that we left them in the SUV in search of my woman.

In the front seats, West and Evan's emotions match the brothers, but according to Evan's grumblings, it's just because we didn't get to kill anyone. And me? I'm trying to forget that I watched Aurelia jump off a fucking cliff on clipped wings.

The palpable silence continues until we reach a bed and breakfast on the way to Eugene. The agreement to stop to let Aurelia get cleaned up and dressed in something other than blood-covered underwear is done mostly with grumbles and truncated grunts.

It's probably fucked in the head that seeing her bloody, half-naked, and armed made my dick stand at attention, but I can't make myself give a shit. I have every intention of utilizing our rented room's full potential and fucking my woman on every available surface until the ache in my chest goes away.

I don't care if we need to get as far away as possible from Iva and her fucking soldiers.

I don't care if we have bigger problems.

I need her.

I need to feel for myself that she's safe—that this isn't all a dream.

Sneaking her in is easy, the bevy of wraiths in attendance giving us plenty of options as to who will ferry her into the sleepy B&B unnoticed. But being out of touching distance of her does something to me. I'm practically shaking by the time I get to our room, the call of the running water pushing my feet toward the cracked bathroom door.

The simple bathroom is decked out in shades of white, the steam from the falling water making the whole space seem almost like a mirage. Behind the waffle-weave shower curtain, Aurelia is wet, naked, and soapy, the draining puddle at her feet tinted pink from the spent blood rinsing from her skin.

The illogical urge to fuck her against the shower wall nearly overtakes me, and when she meets my burning gaze, I know she feels it, too. Not trying to rationalize it, I start stripping off my clothes, and I'm in the shower without saying a word.

Not that words are necessary.

The only essential thing right now is the connection we share—the need. I don't wait—I just lift her against the cold tile, grab my cock, and line it up with her center, thrusting into her to the hilt.

"Yes," she hisses, her fingers roughly threading into my hair and yanking my lips to hers.

Our tongues collide, and I couldn't give a single shit about the rest of the world. It could all come crashing around our ears for all I care. All I need is her body in my arms, her taste on my tongue, and her slick, wet heat enveloping my cock.

She writhes, urging me to fuck her harder, faster, more. The noises she's making—*Fates*—I love those fucking noises. They are one part moan, one part whimper—like she's begging without ever saying a word. Snapping my hips harder, I give her what she's asking for.

Aurelia's breath hitches, her fingernails gouging the flesh on my shoulders, almost breaking the skin. The bite of pain races down my spine, and I can't keep my pace, can't hold in my growl. I pump my hips faster and faster until her wail of a moan signals her orgasm. The squeeze of her inner muscles nearly have me following her over the edge.

But I'm not ready to let her go yet.

Lifting her off my length, I spin her around, pressing her steaming body against the freezing tile as I enter her from behind. Aurelia's tight as a vise this way, and my release races down my spine. Reaching around, I clutch her lush breast in my hand and move my other down to play with her pretty little clit. Pinching her nipple and clit at the same time, I wrench a scream from her as she comes again, ripping my orgasm from me. My groan is muffled when I sink my teeth into the flesh at her shoulder, just shy of breaking the skin, earning me a shuddering whimper.

Gently, I pull out, turning her so I can kiss her soft lips. Then I do what I should have done before and take care of her. Thanking the Fates for giant water heaters, I leisurely help wash her hair and body. It takes all my effort to be gentle, because something is eating at me, and I figure we both know what it is.

Shutting off the water, I step out and pluck the fluffy towel from its hook. I dry her off, wrapping her in the thick cotton like I wish I could have last week.

You should have stayed with her, I scold myself as I roughly yank the other towel from its perch and wrap it around my waist. *She got taken because you left her behind. What kind of soldier are you?*

Who knows what happened to her in those seven days? We found her nearly naked, preferring to launch herself off a cliff than face whatever lay behind her. None of that could be good.

Aurelia was semi-manic after her brief flying episode, and it took nearly an hour to get her to phase back. Maybe it was the trauma, or maybe it was because it's been forever since she'd last phased. In that hour, she told us everything—or what I hoped was everything, given the lack of clothing when she escaped.

As she rambled, she paced, her jittery hands flailing as she spoke, her flames coating her body as she burned the grass beneath her feet. All the while, I got my first good look at her clipped wings, and it took every ounce of strength I possessed to clamp down my rage.

I thought I knew everything there was to know about Aurelia Constantine, but I had no idea how wrong I was—had no idea that something so vital had been ripped from her, too.

And her wings aren't the only thing Iva has stolen from her.

The way she told it, Iva was under the impression she could remove the Aegis side of Aurelia's abilities. The mere mention of this had my blood running cold. Hell, it still does. Because if Iva did remove it, one leg of Aurelia's protection is dust.

And if she didn't?

Aurelia's Aegis could return at any time.

She could hurt someone.

Kill someone.

But more? Neither of us know what it means for her visions.

I'm still working up the courage to talk to her about our next move when she puts a hand on my arm, halting my search for a blow dryer.

"Stop, baby," she says, staying my hands as they raid the last cabinet. She knows something is still bothering me, and it doesn't take a psychic to figure it out since I'm slamming the cabinet doors like an idiot. "If you want to know something, just ask. If you want to tell me something, just tell me. Whatever it is, I can take it."

I can't look at her. I don't want whatever is on my face to make her lie to me.

"Did anything else happen in there?" I croak, not wanting to know but asking all the same. "Anything that you didn't want to say in front of the others? Like why you escaped wearing only your underwear?"

Asking these questions is the most moronic thing I can think of. If her answers are what I fear, I'll be going back to that compound to murder anyone who so much as touched her.

"No, baby," she replies, squeezing my arm so I meet her gaze. "There was a soldier who tried to get frisky, but my last act as an Aegis fried him from the inside out. No one but Iva touched me."

The anger that throbbed through me slides away. "My bloodthirsty wife. I like it."

"It's a part of my charm," she says with a grin. "And wife, huh?"

Latching onto the soft cotton, I rest my hip against the counter as I pull her to me. "We've been bonded for a hundred and sixty years, Gorgeous. Might as well call you what you are to me. After almost losing you, I want it all. I want to call you my wife. I never want us to be apart. I am in it, and I need you there with me." Moving my hands to her face, I cup her jaw and meet those beautifully odd eyes. "If you want the party and pretty dress, you can have it, but it doesn't change the fact you've been my wife for a very long time."

Lucien might have been her husband once upon a time, but our bond eclipses any claims they made to one another. In our world, that marriage was annulled the second I accepted those rites.

It's just taken this long for her to join me.

And yes, it's fast. Of course she might balk at the idea of us moving at warp speed.

But I have to be honest with her.

A tremulous smile stretches her lips, and Aurelia traces a finger down my scars. "I want the party and the pretty dress. And a ring. A big honking, sparkly, competes-with-the-sun-sized ring. But later. Deal?"

The joy that hits me at her easy agreement nearly takes my breath.

"Deal," I growl before taking her mouth in a fierce kiss.

"Anything else?" she asks when we break for a breath.

"How do you want to play this?" I ask, moving to the next facet of my anxiety. "You escaped, yes, but we didn't win. Now you're down a power, and we don't know when or if it's coming back. If *she's* coming back. We need to decide where we're going."

She considers this for about half a second.

"I want to go home," Aurelia admits, her pale gaze no longer meeting mine. "I want to sleep in my own bed. Evan, John, and their entire crew can come with us if they want to. I have the room. My place is secluded, secure, and has my studio. I need to shake this off and think of a new plan to get that bitch." She places her hands against my chest and pushes away. "There were prisoners there, Rhys. Who knows how many there are? We have to stop Iva. And we have to save those people."

Holing up in her house? It's not a bad plan. "I think we can do that. I know the wraiths will help. And you're right—we can't let her take more lives. I'll talk to the others, see if they're onboard."

She nods and moves me aside to grab the dryer, getting to work on her heavy fall of hair as I pull my clothes back on. Then I leave the warmth of the bathroom to collect a fresh set of clothes for her and whatever else Evan has scrounged up in the last hour. Opening the door, I find the manic pixie holding three bulging shopping bags.

"Go talk to the boys," she says, shoving past me into our room. "She wants to go home, right?"

"How'd you know?" I ask over the roar of the hair dryer.

"She hasn't painted in two weeks. That's like cutting off a limb for her," she answers like I'm an idiot, dumping the fresh clothes out of the bags and removing the tags. "Her house is secure—maybe more than Dad's—*and* she has more weapons."

That has me taking a step back. "How could she *possibly* have more weapons?"

A frown mars my friend's face as she stares at me like I'm a special kind of stupid. "She's been dreaming of war and death for almost two centuries, Rhys. That makes a girl mighty paranoid."

She's got me there.

Leaving her to it, I close the door behind me to go talk to the rest of the men. Aidan answers when I knock on their door, barring my way, likely still mad at me for telling him to stay with his brother.

Dumbass.

"Get over it, dude," I grumble, shouldering past him.

West looks up from his perusal of his phone. "She wants to go home?"

How he knows this already, I have no clue, but I nod anyway. "Yep. After what she's been through, I'll give her whatever she wants, so…"

"It's not a bad plan," Ian agrees. "I'm told it's secure and stocked better than an armory. Thoughts?"

"Why not?" Aidan grouses. "No one else has come up with anything. With Javier's betrayal, so many of our safe houses are gone. We have no idea how many locations have been compromised. Her house?" He lifts a shoulder in indifference. "It might be the only place for us."

Then I guess we have a plan.

WHILE AURELIA'S HOUSE IS MODEST COMPARED TO JOHN'S, THE five-bedroom, five-bath home is nothing if not comfortable. Wide picture windows display the mountains beyond, the smooth plastered walls painted a soothing green that reminds me of Aurelia's eyes. The wide French doors lead to a wraparound deck, but it's the vaulted ceilings that are the real showpiece. Peaked at an incredible slope, they're gently broken up by giant wooden beams that constantly pull my gaze upward.

And the pillows.

Dainty lace ones, medium solid ones, and large printed ones reside on every squashy armchair, couch, and side chair. Aurelia's house was made for loafing—each piece selected for maximum comfort.

Lounging on the chocolate-brown leather sectional, to the untrained eye I appear at ease. My head practically drowning in pillows, I watch her work at her easel. I may seem relaxed, but I'm stressed the fuck out on the inside, thinking about all that Evan has told me.

The both of us—hell, even John searched—but we can't find a single person that can help us bring her Aegis power back. The same power that saved her from the insanity of vision after vision, death after death. We thought she was safe.

Oh, how wrong we were.

No matter who we talk to, they don't seem to have enough juice to help, or they refuse to go against Iva. Our Primary's reign of terror has filtered through every species of the Ethereal.

And it shows. Clawing fingers of dread pull at me as I look at her work.

Aurelia sits perched on a bar stool, her withered frame hunched as she feverishly slaps paint on the canvas. I brought it down from the kitchen island two days ago when her legs refused to hold her up.

Too tired to stand but too amped to sleep, she remains on that stool, creating image after image filled with nightmares. Her paintings blend abstract splashes of color with the realism of portraits. When she does talk, she tells me what they mean—which herald of death they portray. But as the days pass, each painting becomes more and more haunting.

Each death more chilling than the last.

Her hand moves blindingly fast as the black and grey and deep purple meld together to make a horrified face. The picture is a close-up of a woman's eyes, the expression in them pleading. The eyes are tearing with purple blood instead of saline. But the blood isn't blood at all. It appears to be morphing into the reflection of the person that killed her.

Honestly, she's scaring the shit out of me.

When she does manage to nod off, she startles awake, screaming, and the longer we're here, the less she sleeps. But the lack of sleep is not the only toll Iva's machinations are taking on her body.

In just a few short days, Aurelia has practically withered under the strain—her cheekbones sharp, her face creased with exhaustion and worry. I can't get her to eat, and her body is shrinking by the minute, dropping weight she can't afford to lose. Purple shadows have taken up residence under her eyes, and her voice has gone from lively and sarcastic to a half-dead monotone.

So here I sit, watching my woman waste away as I try to come up with another way to help.

Problem is, I've called in every favor I have stocked up from every witch, wraith, and warlock I know. No one can help us.

Her Aegis protected her—and now?

I worry there isn't anything anyone can do.

17

AURELIA

A YOUNG MAN AND WOMAN ARE DRIVING A VEHICLE ON A DARK road. It isn't a new car. Duct tape fails to hold the stuffing inside the driver's headrest, errant fluffs of foam spill from a rip in the tape. A faint knocking comes from the weakly chugging engine. The windows are down, most likely because the AC no longer works, the wind from the summer night whipping their hair to and fro.

The young man is thin to the point of starvation with dark blue-black circles under his eyes and a wary, haunted look on his face. He couldn't be more than fifteen at a push, but the few years he's spent on this earth have not been kind. His joints are knobby and pointed, his chin sharp and dotted with acne and scars of abuse. His lip is split, and he has a blooming purple bruise on his left cheek.

The woman is crying, clutching the boy's hand in a vise grip. Her hands are raw, the fingernails bloody and jagged, some even ripped from the nail beds. Her dark hair is matted against her skull—greasy and filthy, clumped with blood and dirt.

Someone has beaten her severely—her left eye black and closing, her nose bloody, swollen and crooked from an obvious break. She is also hugely pregnant—the thinness of her limbs making her burgeoning womb appear larger than it is. Ridges of her ribs peak through the tear at the breast of her dirty blouse.

They erratically drive down a mountain—the switchbacks making the tires skid from the speed. The tires slide over the road, over the double-yellow lines, and into the oncoming lane. The young man overcorrects the trajectory of the puttering car, sliding once again into the gravel of the shoulder. They pass a well-lit diner, the light of the sign casting a yellow, sickly glow upon the woman's face. She cries out in horror, clutching her belly with her mangled fingers.

And then the blood comes.

Gushes of scarlet pour from between her legs, soaking through her tattered skirt and the battered seat below her. Her face goes gray from the blood loss—even the bruises leaching of color—and she loses consciousness within a few seconds.

The boy slams the accelerator down, desperately trying to make it to their destination. His eyes leak frustrated tears, and he begs the woman to wake up, his screams and pleas growing louder and louder as the minutes pass.

He pushes the poor car as fast as it can go, but he's too late. By the time the bright hospital lights have cast their glow on the beat-up rattrap of a car, she's stopped breathing.

He screeches into the emergency bay, the car skidding sideways as it grinds to a stop. He screams for help as he flies out his door, hobbling to the passenger side. He yanks open the door, shaking the woman by the shoulders, before unbuckling her seatbelt and attempting to pull her from the car.

Doctors and nurses flood from the doors, pulling the woman from her seat, shoving her on a gurney, and rushing her inside.

But they are all too late.

No matter how hard the doctors work, they can't save them.

I'M SHAKEN AWAKE FOR THE FOURTH TIME TONIGHT. RHYS engulfs my sweaty, shaking body into a giant bear hug, his warm skin on mine easing me until I notice red on the sheets. Immediately, I jump up to check myself and the bed for blood. There is nothing on my belly or underwear, but my hands are bloody from my fingernails ripping into my palms in my sleep.

Dammit.

Well, at least I'm not screaming this time. I wish I could call that a win, but I can't. I plop back down on the mattress.

"This shit has got to stop. I want you to take the sleeping pills, Gorgeous," he pleads with me as he grabs the full glass I neglected after the second wake-up call tonight.

"I don't want to," I say in a small, feeble voice.

I hate that voice.

I wish I weren't so tired.

I wish I weren't so weak.

I wish I would sleep and see nothing.

My sanity is frayed, unraveling swiftly with each vision, and I don't have the strength to re-braid the ropes.

"This is the fourth time you've woken up tonight," Rhys reminds me, "and it's only midnight. You're not even asleep for more than twenty minutes before the next vision starts. If a pill helps, you need to take it."

His eyes are weary, his dark-brown hair disheveled from his restless night. I'm hurting him—whether it's from my lack of sleep or my fingers ripping into the flesh of my hands.

I'm hurting him. And I don't want to.

"I'm scared," I mutter, my voice wobbling. "What if I get stuck?"

Fucking tears. They slip and slide down my face in pitiful little rivulets. *When did I get so weak?*

"Let's just try it once," he offers, "and if you hate it or if it doesn't work, then we can stop. But we have to do something. I can't watch you in agony and not do something, Gorgeous."

I have to do this. I have to try. For him.

"I'm sorry you're in pain, too. I'll take the pill." I sigh, twisting the sheets in my fingers. "You'll stay with me, though, right?"

"Where else would I want to be?" he replies before dropping a gentle kiss to my shoulder.

"Okay." I nod, taking the tall glass of water and a tiny pink pill.

Here goes nothing.

A YOUNG BOY—NO BIGGER THAN FIVE—JUMPS IN PUDDLES ON A sidewalk. The gray sky beyond him threatens more rain, but the boy is enjoying his reprieve, bouncing from one tiny puddle to the next.

His mother watches him from under the cover of a porch awning—her curly black hair pulled into a messy bun atop her head. She's dressed plainly in jeans and a T-shirt—the pale-gray cardigan covering her slim shoulders matching the overcast sky. The house is modest but not shabby, the lawn groomed, the shutters freshly painted. The window boxes are blooming with summer flowers, trailing pink and purple blossoms over the sides.

The neighborhood is situated at the base of a mountain range—the verdant hills broken up with jutting bedrock, nearly blotting out the light from the cloudy sky.

She's sitting on the first step, waiting for the boy to get his fill of the outdoors. She has a thick book on her lap, and she is shuffling index cards in her hands, furiously studying. She glances up every few seconds, though, checking on her son.

His little face is screwed up in concentration as he considers the next jump. He counts to three, and away he goes, his bright-yellow rain boots splashing in the water. The vinyl of his raincoat squeaks as he flaps his arms, making boom *and* zoom *noises with his loud little boy mouth.*

It has rained so much in the last few weeks. Almost every single day has been filled with constant deluges of falling water.

The boy doesn't feel the rumble, but the mother does. She tosses aside her book and notes, the white index cards fluttering about the lawn like leaves until they're swept away by the roaring tide of a flash flood.

She makes it to her son, but she's too late to save him.

She's too late to save herself.

He clings to her, and she works so hard, kicking her legs and clawing the water with her free hand to try and keep their heads above the surface.

She tires quickly and then fails in her endeavor altogether when they're slammed into a parked SUV. The torrent rushes up and over the vehicle, but the mother and son are pinned beneath the surface, fighting, and clawing for air in the freezing flood.

A YOUNG WOMAN WALKS ALONE DOWN A DARKENED STREET, shivering in rapidly falling temperatures of a summer night in the mountains.

Slight and blonde, she strides with purpose, her shoulders tensed. She's wearing an old diner waitress uniform—said diner is fading in the background as she makes her way to the lit bus stop ahead. The diner's pale-yellow sign is now off, but the blue lettering still reads "Sunflower Café."

She stops and removes the heavy backpack from her shoulders, pulling a lime-green hoodie from the pack. Her bag is stuffed full of clothes and books, a key chain mace canister attached to the zipper.

Her bulging pack is still at her feet when the man approaches her from behind, a pristinely folded white cloth in his hand. He uses it to cover her face, and her struggle is over quickly as she loses consciousness. The man is well-groomed, wearing a starched navy-blue button-up and pressed khakis. His brown hair is carefully combed, and his leather loafers are polished to a high shine. He looks like a deacon of a church, or a dentist, or an insurance salesman.

The man drags her from the street toward a wooded area beyond, snatching up her backpack as he goes, her tired pink Chucks making tiny ruts in the gravel shoulder of the once-busy road.

He takes little care with the woman as he drags her body in the mud and bracken of the forest floor—the limbs scratching at her exposed skin. He stops in a clearing, placing her body just so before heading to a nearby stump. Resting on the dirt is a silver, hard-sided suitcase.

The stranger carefully places the case on the stump and clicks open the locks, pulling a black instrument case from the felt. He then dons a pair of disposable gloves, snapping the rubber for the perfect fit. Slipping a pair of pliers from their loop, he opens her mouth, and begins ripping each and every tooth from her head.

The woman rouses around tooth fifteen, her pitiful protestations dulled to a gurgle as she chokes on the blood running down her throat. The stranger carefully removes the white cloth from his pocket, drowning out her moans with more chloroform.

Finishing his task, he removes the remainder of the woman's teeth. He then drags her to a freshly dug hole in the ground, tossing her unconscious body into the earth. The man removes a small bottle of lighter fluid from *his pocket and drenches her body with it—squeezing the yellow container until every last drop has fallen from the tiny spigot.*

He throws the plastic in with the body along with her backpack before removing a pack of matches from his other pocket, studying them with interest. The script is delicate and flowery, the name of a local inn emblazoned across the front.

The stranger lights the book and tosses it in, the flames igniting with a whoosh.

The unassuming man studies the flames for a long while, observing the woman's body burn to cinders in her roughly hewn grave. When the poor woman's body is reduced to embers, he takes the collapsible shovel from his suitcase, using it to fill the hole with loose earth. With the flat end of the blade, he tamps down the dirt. When he's done, he drags broken tree limbs and fallen brush over the mound, perfectly concealing the shallow grave.

The stranger returns to the stump, pulling a black velvet drawstring from his roll of tools. Carefully, he places each of the woman's teeth in the bag before pulling the string closed and carefully placing it in the front pocket of his khakis.

Walking from the clearing, the stranger heads away from the busy main road to a rough dirt rut where a shiny SUV is parked. He rounds the vehicle with his tools in tow, smiling all the while—patting his pocket as he goes.

My eyes open to sunlight streaming in through the blinds. Rhys is cuddled up to my back, his arm thrown over my hip—the turquoise sheet pulled up to my chest. His warmth would be comforting, maybe, but now I can't find comfort in anything anymore.

I don't move for a full minute, neglecting to speak, gently lifting his hand off me and sliding out of bed. Padding to the master bath, I carefully close the door before turning on the shower taps, and promptly losing the contents of my stomach.

I know those mountains. I drive down them every single time I head into Denver.

I know that motel. It's two miles away from my house.

I know that diner. I've had lunch there more times than I can count.

I know what this is.

This is the death of every good soul around me. These are souls that need to pass on. The souls I would direct a gentry toward.

This is what I would feel if I never had the Aegis in the first place. This is what a seer really is. No wonder seer's just line up to get their eyes cut out. If this is what I saw every night before maturity, I'd do anything to make it stop.

I still might.

Shaking, I brush my teeth, noticing the graying gauntness of my face in the vanity mirror.

I can survive this, I think as I rinse and spit into the sink. Stripping off my underwear, I toss them in the hamper and step under the scalding spray.

On autopilot, I shower, rinsing the horrors from last night off my skin, thinking of nothing as the world swirls away to blackness.

18

RHYS

THE MIDDAY SUN SHINES ACROSS MY FACE, AND I WAKE wrapped around a still-sleeping Aurelia. Her back is to me, her damp hair tickles my nose as I sigh in relief.

She slept. Thank the Fates.

I drop a kiss to her shoulder and the tender skin of her neck, noticing a change to her scent. She smells different somehow, almost like aged parchment and baby powder—the faint cloying scent fills me with unease. I don't like it and wonder how I could politely ask her to switch body washes to whatever she was using when we first made love.

She stirs, but her controlled stillness bores a hole of worry in my gut. I try to brush it off as the effects of the sleeping medication.

Aurelia rouses, rubbing her ass against my morning erection, and I wrap my arms around her middle to bring her closer. She shifts in my embrace and brushes her soft lips against mine.

"How did you sleep?" I mutter, threading my fingers into her hair.

Aurelia nods, rubbing her nose against mine. She rolls me onto my back, kissing the skin of my chest as she moves with me, nipping at the scars at my ribs. She throws a leg over my lap, and I grab her hips, grinding her naked center against my dick. She's warm and wet, and I'd give anything to have sex with my wife.

Give anything to have this hell past us for good.

She brushes her tits against my chest, stretching her arms under my pillow as I rub against her heat. Even her kiss is different—not urgent, but hard like she's trying to hurt me.

With a jerk, I break from her lips, pressing my head further into the pillow.

When she sits up, she has a Morganite dagger in her hand, and I freeze.

Was it something I said?

"If you wanted a divorce, you could have just asked," I offer nervously. "No need to get homicidal."

Her gaze pierces me to the bed as she tosses the blade from one hand to the other. That motion claws at my brain, and the pit of dread in my belly grows.

"What's the matter, dear," she says as her eyes grow cold, an odd accent coloring her words. "Don't like a little pain with your pleasure?"

If I didn't know that something was off before, the thick Irish brogue coming from her mouth would've raised a huge fucking red flag.

My whole body goes cold.

I know that accent, that cadence, that sick fucking voice.

This is not my wife.

"Iva? I gotta say, the body's new. Wanna tell me what the fuck you're doing?" I buck her off me, scrambling from the bed as fast as I can.

I'm positive I've never been *less* happy that I'm buck-ass naked.

"Mmm," she purrs on a smirk, her tongue sweeping her upper lip. "I do so love seeing my handiwork on you."

Bile rises in my throat as her eyes roam my body—examining each thick scar she'd carved into my skin. Even though she has Aurelia's face, I want to rip her fucking head off.

"What do you want?" I demand, surreptitiously searching for something to secure her with before this gets really bad.

So many things could go wrong. And knowing how fucking crazy Iva is...

"I want to take your love from you," she admits, a sick smile curling Aurelia's lips. "I'm going to enjoy making you watch her die."

I save one little life, and it blows my whole world apart. *No good deed goes unpunished.*

"Why? Because I stopped you from murdering an innocent woman? That's not our purpose. It's not our job to judge or change. It is our job to send souls on. Period. The end."

"And who are you to tell me what our purpose is, you impertinent little fledgling?" she snarls, jabbing the air with that deadly blade.

"I became that person when I read the archives," I confess for the first time. "They told me what our role is—the role the head families are keeping secret so you don't kill off their kin. That's the real reason you spelled Lucien, isn't it? He was digging a little too deep? Knew a little too much? Abusing his job title a little too much for your liking?"

She looks almost pleased I've figured out her game. Like I'm a dog that finally figured out how to shit outside. If she weren't wearing Aurelia's face...

"Yes, it was unfortunate Lucien had to die," she simpers, "but making you kill him was just a bonus. It was also a pleasant little perk making Aurelia hate you—taking away what you most wanted. Your girl sure can hold onto a grudge. And now that you have her, I'm going to enjoy making you watch her slit her own throat before you die."

As she reveals her master plan, I notice my jeans at the foot of the bed, my black leather belt still threaded through the loops. Flicking my eyes back to her, I watch as she raises the dagger.

Her movements change from the flowing grace Iva usually possesses, to an uncoordinated jerky shake—the knife trembling in her hand.

My woman is in there, fighting back.

Her face screws up in concentration, sweat popping up on her brow as the battle wages inside my beautiful wife's body. The knife rises again, slowly heading for her slender, perfect neck.

Wasting no time, I snatch the belt from the loops, roughly ripping the knife from her clenched fingers, and binding her wrists with the leather. I shove her face in the duvet as she struggles against the bonds.

I don't bother to dress—I just yell for Evan.

She pops in a moment later, fully phased and snarling. Well, until she sees me buck-ass naked.

"Are you kidding me with this?" she shrieks, covering her eyes. "I'm blind! West is going to kick your ass."

None of this is funny, and despite Evan's dramatics, there are worse problems than her seeing me naked.

"It's Iva, Evan. She's stowed away in Aurelia's brain. You mind taking over here so I can put some fucking pants on?"

"You got it," she shudders, mumbling under her breath that it's like seeing her brother naked as she takes Iva's bonds in her hands.

I throw on my jeans and rip the sheet off the bed to cover my woman.

"Now what?" Evan asks, struggling to hold onto Aurelia's restraints.

I have no fucking clue.

AURELIA

Realizing I'm chained to the bed is not on my list of top-five favorite ways to wake up. I'm a little fuzzy on the details, but I'm pretty sure I didn't sign on for this particular kink.

At least I have clothes on. What the hell happened last night?

I tug on the chain, the links rattling against the wood of the bed frame and rousing Rhys from a fitful sleep. Relegated to the bedside chair, he's barefoot and scruffy, wearing rumpled jeans and a wrinkled T-shirt.

"Umm." I chuckle nervously. "I think I was supposed to pick a safe word before the bonds came into play. Wanna tell me what's going on?"

"Sure," he replies, his voice rough with sleep, "if you can answer one question. What's your favorite weapon?"

"That depends," I say with a half-shrug, the links clanging against the frame with the movement.

"On?" he asks warily, sitting forward in the chair.

"The situation. If I'm going silent, then my hatchets. If I don't care about noise, a Glock 19. If I want to look pretty, a wakizashi because I'm too short for katanas. If I need silence and distance, I prefer throwing knives."

He breathes out a sigh of relief. "Thank the Fates. You're you."

He rips a hand through his hair, tugging on the strands while he studies my face. The hair-ripping thing is a common tick for him when he's stressed.

"Who the fuck else would I be?" I ask, affronted. But the truth of it slaps me in the face.

I've been losing time. A few seconds at first, and then more. I thought I'd just been spacing out, but...

"Iva must have done something to you, Gorgeous," he murmurs, dropping that particular bomb in my lap. "She took over for a little while."

"What do you mean she took over?" I ask, trying unsuccessfully to sit up, my whole body turning to ice. "What did she do?"

The chains aren't too tight, but they aren't loose, either. I'm stuck flat on my back, and the longer he hesitates to tell me what happened, the more I figure just how bad it could have been.

"She attempted to slit your throat," he mutters, his voice gruff and choked. "While I watched."

It's so much worse than I thought.

"You've woken a few times," he rasps, "but she...but she comes through pretty quick."

My brain seems to be stuck on a loop. I keep hearing his broken, hoarse voice say "slit your throat" over and over. I yank on my bonds, knowing I'm not going anywhere, but my limbs are aching to take flight.

"How long have I been like this?"

"Three days," he croaks, raking a hand down his cheek.

Shock makes my body go numb, my mind blank. And then the tears come—great racking sobs ripping through my chest.

She has held me hostage for three fucking days—invaded my mind, my body. Who knows how long she's been squatting in my brain?

The bitch tortured my husband. Again.

Now I'm helpless—*chained*. A monster has taken me over.

"I really want to hug you, Gorgeous. But the last time I did, she bit me in the neck and tore a sizable chunk out before Evan stopped her."

It takes several minutes for the tears to stop, and even longer for the shaking breaths to cease. In that time, I steel myself, shutting off my emotions, shutting my heart down.

Turning myself to stone.

My voice is still hoarse, but my words are steady.

"You need to find someone to remove the binding," I order with a resigned nod. "Remove it, and leave me here. A better plan would be to kill me, but I won't ask that of you. You need to get as far away from me as you can—as fast as you can. She will never stop. She'll keep hunting you."

It doesn't matter if I'm dead. Iva will hunt him to the ends of the earth, chasing him until she's had her bloodthirsty fill.

His face mottles red before he starts yelling, "I'm *not* giving up on you. We are in this together. I'm not going to let you quit now."

But I'm exhausted—mentally and physically. I don't know if I can go on much longer.

He continues to tell me other things—things I can't understand—because the longer he talks, the more his voice starts to garble. I take one last look at him, knowing this may be the last time I get to see his beautiful face.

Knowing that at any second, Iva could take over.

Knowing I could lose hold of myself at any moment.

A forever without Lucien seemed so long, but I know now that the ache of losing Rhys will haunt me even into the next life.

Losing Rhys will haunt me for eternity.

RHYS

I'm still shouting at my unconscious wife when West busts in the room, kicking in the door with his massive boot. The door has practically split in two, and if Aurelia wakes up, she's going to rip him a new one.

When. Not *if.* Never if.

I rack my brain for any solution that makes sense. We've exhausted all my witch contacts. None of them can protect her. All these years when I was exhausting my favor from the king— making sure she was safe and hidden—she was hiding herself.

Somehow, we have to get her Aegis back. She must be able to use her power to protect herself—there's just no other way.

"We've got a huge fucking problem," West growls, adjusting his grip on the katana in his hand.

He looks like John Rambo and Paul Bunyan had a tattooed baby. Two bandoliers crisscross his red flannel shirt like a gunslinger, a backup katana peeks over his shoulder, and a gun rests at both hips.

I notice all this, but it's in the periphery, the world around me scratching at my brain. All I can think of is the last words Aurelia said to me before she passed out.

She's right. Iva won't stop.

But neither will I.

"Yeah? Add it to the list we have already," I yell as my hands rip through my hair. "I've got bigger problems right now. She wants to dissolve the bond. She wants us to fucking leave her here. She wants to die to save us."

I'm ready to yank it out by the roots. I know she wants us safe—wants the best for me and the rest of us—but Fates be damned, I want her. I refuse to give up on Aurelia just because Iva has a grudge.

No, we're doing this together.

"Well, she's not going to have to save us," he informs me, adjusting his grip on the blade in his hand. "We're going to have to save ourselves. We're surrounded."

Well, of course we are, I think. *What else can go wrong?*

And then the power goes out.

I had to ask.

19

THE BLACKNESS FADES TO GRAY AND THEN TO WHITE. WHEN MY eyes finally focus, I realize I'm looking at a white dress. I'd know those skinny-ass hips anywhere.

"Do you like your accommodations?" Iva's Irish brogue stabs through my brain.

I hate that voice.

Given I'm chained to another slab in another gray room when my real body's somewhere else, not so much. She smiles for a second, and suddenly, the bonds are gone. The room seems to melt like candle wax, and now I'm standing on my own two feet in a dimly lit ballroom. The ceiling is vaulted, with a delicate crystal chandelier casting an ethereal glow.

Iva's holding a glass of champagne, gently swaying to a smooth Jazz number on the parquet floor. Her dress is backless and form-fitting, her hair arranged in a neat chignon. Her blood-red lips pull into a smug smile.

"Neat trick." *Bitch.* "Wanna tell me how I got here?"

"You aren't anywhere," she answers with a shrug, still swaying to the music. "You and I are inside your precious little noggin."

I fucking *hate* Jazz, but somehow, I'd be willing to bet she knows that already.

"In my head? I'll buy that. How long have you been squatting inside my brain, you soulless little bitch?"

Her eyebrows rise at the insult, but she seems to let it go. I guess she's having too much fun.

"Well, for the longest time it was impossible to find you," she admits before sipping her drink. "I'd thought I had eliminated all of your kind, but you, darling, you slipped past me. Very tricky, my dear." She raises her glass in a snide mock-toast. "I'd venture a guess Nicola was behind that little coup. Don't you worry. I'll take care of her later."

Iva sashays to a table that seems to have appeared from thin air. Carefully, she peruses the selection of hors d'oeuvres before plucking a canapé from the tray and popping it into her mouth. After taking a fucking age to chew, she shifts to face me.

"I tried finding your Rhys, but he was hidden as well. I blame that infernal Wraith King for that. And then we used your blood. Well, you shed a bit of that for Javier, didn't you? And after I suppressed your Aegis, it was a simple thing to crack your head wide open."

Suppressed not eliminated.

Either she's lying, or Iva has just fucked up.

"Since you're probably going to kill me, could you tell me why? Is it just to secure your throne? For revenge? Or are you just a psychotic bitch on wheels with a God complex? Really, what exactly do you get out of all this?"

For the longest time, I don't think she's going to answer me. Then, she sips from her glass and gently rests the flute on the table. Next to the glass is a sharp-as-sin Morganite knife. She lovingly caresses the blade before wrapping her slender fingers around the hilt, gently picking up the weapon.

"It's a bit of all three, really. But what do I get?" she whispers menacingly as her red lips twist into a cruel smirk. "I get to kill you. I get to rip your mind apart bit by bit, thought by thought, inch by tiny inch."

RHYS

I'm lucky I have friends who can focus during a crisis. While I've been ripping my hair out at Aurelia's bedside, my friends have been raiding her house for weapons.

My wife has weapons tucked away in every nook and cranny of this house. There are knives and handguns inside cabinets disguised as floating shelves, a gun safe hidden behind a wall mirror near the garage door. Every table and bar stool has some kind of weapon affixed to the underside, and that doesn't even include the huge weapons cache hidden in the dojo.

She's like a survivalist or something. If I found a horde of foodstuffs down there, I wouldn't have been surprised. She was prepared—that's for certain. I just wish we'd thought ahead before her mind started to deteriorate.

We should have moved once we realized Aurelia's mind wasn't safe. I should have thought of that. I should have thought of many things—should have anticipated the danger lurking just around the corner.

I should never have left her alone to guard Aidan. Aidan feels it, too—the guilt that she was captured while she watched over him.

And that's where it all went downhill, isn't it?

The house where I lived the best hours of my life is also a place I hate to the very depths of my soul.

I should have realized Javier was a threat. We should have left that house as soon as the first sign of danger skittered down my spine.

Some soldier I turned out to be.

Evan and West drop weapons in a pile just inside the bedroom door, eyeing me warily. After West kicked the door in and the house went black, I may have gone a little batshit.

Okay, that's an understatement.

I turned into a feral, territorial mate and phased—full wingspan, fire, the whole bit. Aurelia is going to need a few new lamps.

And maybe a new mirror.

Her rug is toast, too.

She's going to kick my ass if she wakes up. *When.* When she wakes up.

I managed to tamp down my fire, but the wings seem to be here to stay. Doesn't matter.

I fight better with them, anyway.

My wings are different from Aurelia's. As a soldier, they should match my oracle's, but because of the forced bond, mine are an entirely different color. Whereas Aurelia's fade from blood-red to orange, mine gradually fade from coal-black to burgundy. Though mine are clipped as well, they were cut while I was being tortured prior to the bonding.

That was the only part of her pain I did not feel.

Other than that...I remember every drop of blood spilled.

Every cut.

Every slice.

Iva deserves to pay. She deserves our revenge.

Not only because she tortured my mate—no—but for what she has done to our kind. And for waging this war within our own Legion.

Our people deserve vengeance, too.

And they will have it, I think as I snatch up a Morganite kukri, testing the blade in my grip.

Evan eases into my line of sight again, and her wary expression is almost comical on her fully phased face. Her eyes have bled to black, her talons curled around a gold inlayed sword.

She doesn't try to speak around her fangs because I've heard her try, and that is one sure fire way to get me to laugh my ass off. She sounded like a metal-mouthed teenager with a lisp.

West comes up behind her, his arms encircling her shoulders as he kisses her temple. When he raises his gaze to mine, I know...

That the battle is about to start.

That we're surrounded.

That we probably won't make it out of here alive.

Or at least Aurelia and I won't. I pivot from his hard stare and go back to Aurelia. Leaning over her, my fists sink into the mattress as I press a kiss to her temple.

Her brows furrow even in her fitful slumber, and I close my eyes, breathing in her scent. For the briefest of moments, I let my forehead touch hers before snapping back to standing.

I'll keep them alive.

I'll keep her alive.

Assuming my place just outside the bedroom door, I shield Aurelia as best I can. Evan and West take the second floor with Ian and Aidan as backup. The brothers stick to the shadows, ready to take out any threat that slips past us.

Just keep breathing.

Keep. Breathing.

And with that last thought, soldiers begin storming Aurelia's house, trying to find a breach point.

AURELIA

Her first strike is a tease—a silly feint I easily avoid. The real blow comes when I move to the left, directly into her waiting blade. She makes a shallow slash to the skin of my bicep.

Rooky mistake. I should know better.

As much as it goads me, I have to treat her with the respect she deserves—the cow *did* take over my mind and body.

If I underestimate her, I'm dead.

It's easy to phase here in this dark corner of my brain, the fabric of reality thin. One second, I'm normal, and the next I'm battle-ready. The flames start at my fingertips, catching like a brushfire over the skin of my arms and chest, before coating the skirt of the black dress I only now notice I'm wearing.

What is with this woman and evening dresses? I know I didn't dream this stupid-ass frock on myself.

The wings come next, erupting from my back, and a satisfied smile graces my lips when I hear the fabric of the fancy dress rip. I shudder in relief as the wings fully extend, their blunted tips reaching out to my sides before folding back to resting.

Resting but ready.

I remember so clearly how much I wanted vengeance for Lucien. For my child.

But now, I want it more for myself.

For the life I could have had—with or without Lucien.

For Rhys whose only crime was doing the right thing.

For the wraiths that died in their beds, committing no crime other than being born.

For every Aegis slaughtered.

Testing how the weight affects my balance, I crack my neck and pop my knuckles.

Iva wants my A-game? She'll get it.

Patiently, I wait for her next strike. The whispers of her thoughts buzz like a swarm of wasps, offering me the knowledge she's trying to hide. Strangely, I sense my body on the outside, lying in bed, and here on the inside, coated in the warm fingers of my fire.

How is that possible?

Somehow, I realize if she hurts me here, it will hurt me out there. If she manages to kill me here, I'll be nothing but ashes.

She can't come at me in the real world, so she had to take the coward's way in?

Fuck. That.

Bring it, you fucking hag.

Iva's attack finally comes, but I'm not there. She doesn't appreciate me turning her game on her. She growls at my ingenuity, her perfectly painted lips screwing up as she snarls.

Who's the cat and who's the mouse now, bitch?

Her next assault is interrupted by my fist in her stomach, earning me a gasped groan in response. Before she can retaliate, I've flitted off again, waiting for her next move. She gags at the blow to her stomach before staggering back to standing.

Oh, she's pissed off now, and her Fireskin *whooshes* over her body faster than I can blink.

Aww. I think I made her mad, I think as I chuckle.

And then my chuckle dies.

Slowly, her wings erupt from her back, their mangled form wrenching a gasp from my lips.

Tattered feathers black as her soul, have fallen away in huge patches revealing the raw, red, and bleeding skin underneath.

And then it all becomes clear.

She's dying.

Then the other puzzle pieces in my brain click together.

If there is no one to send you to Hell, then where do you go?

You go nowhere.

20

RHYS

The steel storm shutters on Aurelia's house are something out of a zombie movie.

Evan used the generator in the basement to trigger the failsafe, slamming them shut before soldiers breached the main entrance. But the attic window was missed, and now they've found a way into the house.

They've breached our walls—the battle has begun.

I'm guarding Aurelia's bedroom, praying no one gets past me. Bodies are piled on the dark hardwood floor, scarlet blood pooling under their bulk. My blades are coated in the gore of the fallen. I use my wings to brush off an attacker, and as he flies into the sheetrock, another approaches from my left. His blade's drawn, ready to cut me down like an errant weed, when my dagger breaches the unfortunate gap in the plates of his body armor.

Four soldiers have met the end of my blade before I'm met with real resistance. The phoenix before me is a big bastard, but unlike so many of them, he actually knows what he's doing.

Taking him down won't be as easy.

West and Evan are paired back-to-back, moving to the living room after being herded down the stairs. He goes high as she goes low, spinning and slicing, smoking out and back again, moving as one. Plucking the life from soldier after soldier, they move in tandem as if they'd been fighting together all their lives.

Ian and Aiden stay to the periphery, exterminating any that get past the three of us. Aidan pops in and out of the shadows, slaying soldiers as he passes, while Ian lies in wait in the gloom.

Although we've only fought together in one battle, I miss Aurelia's presence at my back. Especially when a big motherfucker gets a hit in. The hiss of pain that leaves my mouth is not by my consent.

An agonizing sting rends through my shoulder, the familiar bite of Morganite ricocheting through the limb.

Bastards.

Now I'm pissed. I parry my blade against his as he goes for my head, catching him in the throat with my dagger. Twisting the knife, I open his gullet before ripping out my blade and moving onto the next one.

And the next one.

Cutting them all down until I meet one I can't.

I'm dead—*we're dead*—I know it.

My left arm is useless, hanging listlessly at my side. The soldier in front of me has bested every strike and parry, every feint and backhand.

Everything.

He raises his blade, and I realize my defeat. Slipping my eyes closed, I pray someone sends us on. I pray that when Aurelia and I are reborn, we start again.

That we do it better—be smarter—with less hate and more love. I don't regret a second, because if one thing is certain, she is my Heaven.

She is my peace.

And if I get nothing else, I will know my Heaven is out there somewhere.

And I'll find it.

AURELIA

Even in my subconscious, Rhys' cry of agony reaches me. Stuck in my mind like a fly in sap, pinned in this Hell with a psychopath, his pain tugs at my soul. The skin of my shoulder splits, blood running the length of my arm as my heart nearly shrivels in my chest.

Oh, no.

I've had about enough of this shit. I've got somewhere to be.

Iva's not as composed as she was before—her hair disheveled and falling from her chignon. Her lipstick is smeared, bleeding into the skin of her cheek.

She comes for me again, but with renewed vigor, slashing and stabbing wildly. But she's making mistakes.

Mistakes she shouldn't with someone like me.

Someone who can kill her.

If she's in my head, I know I'm in hers, too. If I kill her here, maybe, just maybe it will kill her in the real world.

Stepping to the side, I barely miss a wild slash, before reaching up and latching onto her hair—wrenching her head as I sweep her legs out from under her.

Her blade goes flying, shattering into five smaller pieces, skittering across the parquet floor. I use the distraction to flip her body over and smash her pretty little face into the ground. Satisfaction fills me at the sound of her pert nose crunching against the floor. Scrambling off her back, I tag a shard of the broken blade as Iva staggers her way back to standing.

The front of her white dress is liberally splashed with the crimson running from her nose and mouth. She spits, teeth and blood hitting the floor, and I can't help the gleeful smile that stretches across my face.

Shrieking, she races for me, fingers descended into blunted claws, broken teeth bared. Her scream is cut off to a gurgle as the shard in my hand slides through the smooth skin of her throat.

Bet she didn't see that coming.

Her eyes widen as her lifeblood leeches from her body, running down her chest, soaking into her dress, and pooling onto the floor of my mind. She staggers, collapsing to her back.

She gurgles a gasp once, twice, and then stills.

She's not breathing, but I don't trust it. To be sure, I take the sliver of Morganite in my hand and saw through the remainder of her throat. Undeterred by tissue and bone, I take her head. The jagged, double edge slices into the flesh of my hand, but I don't care.

I'll wear those scars with honor.

RHYS

I wait for a strike that never comes. When I open my eyes, the soldier—who only moments before was ready to take my life—stares, dumbfounded, at the blade as if he has no idea how it got there. The remaining soldiers—at least the ones still standing—have similar expressions on their faces.

It's as if a veil has been lifted, and now they see the truth.

I wonder how many minds Iva controlled to do her bidding. How many poor souls were used to perpetuate a war that no one wanted? It makes me sorry we killed them true dead, but the good ones we'll send on.

And the rest? Good fucking riddance.

Scanning the crowd of confused soldiers, I spot a blood-spattered Evan hugging an equally bloody West. Both seem a little banged up, but no permanent damage. They're all over each other, so I think the relationship cat is out of the bag. Not that it was a surprise to anyone. It was the worst-kept secret in the Black compound.

Neither Ian nor Aidan are within my line of sight, but Ian's booming laugh echoes from the third floor.

A loud clank of a chain sounds from behind me, and the best voice in the whole world starts cussing a blue streak.

"Hello? Ding, dong the bitch is dead, but I've gotta pee! Can a girl get a fucking rescue here?"

That's my girl.

I try to reach across my body to pull the key from my pocket, but it's not really working out.

"A little help?" I ask Evan.

Evan glances at my pocket, then at the territorial West. Shaking her head, she grabs Aurelia's chain, snapping it from the steel subframe with a tiny flick of her fingers.

Well, that's one way to do it.

"Thank the *Fates*." Aurelia sighs as she hightails it to the bathroom, dragging the chain behind her, brushing a quick peck on my cheek on her way out.

She returns a few minutes later looking relieved, even though she's wounded—her left arm a matching bloody mess to mine. We both need stitches, but I can't bring myself to care.

I should ask what happened—it's plain to see that two battles were fought. But I don't care about anything other than kissing my woman.

Reaching out with my good hand, I sift my fingers under her thick mane, hauling her lips to mine, tasting the mint of freshly brushed teeth.

I pull my head back, raising my brows in question.

"What? I multitasked," she protests. "I didn't want to kiss you with three days' worth of funk on my breath. I'm *considerate*, dammit."

"Did you hide your spitting, too?" I joke, needling her just because I can.

"Shaddup," she says as she sweeps her lips against mine, effectively shutting my mouth.

This is what Heaven feels like—my wife in my arms and a wide-open future that no one can steal from us.

But first we need to make sure the bitch is true dead. For real this time.

AURELIA

The raid on the Legion house in Oregon happened as soon as we could make it on a plane without causing a stir. Something about the woman I'd left behind called to me, and I couldn't leave her there to rot one more second than I had to.

Rhys and I got our wounds treated, everyone got a shower, and off we went. I forgot just how much I hate stitches.

There was no resistance at the gate—even with two exiles and four wraiths in tow. The soldiers practically waved us in.

The house buzzed with whispers—more because of the reappearance of Nicola than from our appearance at the gate. Apparently, Nicola had been cast out over a month ago when the gentry were recalled from their posts. But in the few short hours it took us to get there, and with no one able to find Iva, Nicola had taken up the position of Primary.

No one questioned it—the air of relief palpable with each passing minute Iva remained gone.

In a cell or not, these people had been prisoners, too.

It takes hours searching all the rooms in the prisoner hallway, but we still can't find Iva's remains or the woman my conscience is screaming at me to save.

I can't put my finger on it, but something about her is clawing at my mind. Since my mind has been clawed enough, I need to know she's all right.

From what we gathered from the residents, Iva killed most of the prisoners before soldiers were sent to kill us. Their ashes were sent back to their families in a macabre show of power, but their souls were gone.

Irritated at the lack of help or answers, I finally break down and ask Nicola where Iva's personal quarters are located. She's happy to oblige, as long as I say please.

Fates give me patience. Because if you give me strength, I'm going to kill this bitch.

"Please," I grind out, and she accepts my half-assed gesture.

She leads us to the third floor inside an opulent bedroom. All along the east wall are enormous built-in bookcases. Some of the columns are filled with books, but many—*so many*—of the others are filled with gray canisters.

Moving closer, I realize what I'm looking at.

Glass jars.

Glass jars filled with ashes.

Thick, vibrating energy radiates from them. I know that feeling— I've been missing it since Iva suppressed my Aegis.

And then I finally understand...

This is how she had so much power—why she lived so far past the norm for our species.

This is why the Aegis were being slaughtered.

Horror brings bile up my throat.

How many lives is she responsible for? I wonder, trying and failing to count the jars displayed like trophies.

"Hey, come look at this," Ian calls from the other side of the room.

On the wide, king-size sleigh bed are remnants of ashes on the duvet and sheets, but it looks as if someone has hastily scrapped them off the fabric.

Dread sours the feeling of triumph in my belly.

Too easy. All of this was too easy.

Who knows what kind of nut job could have those ashes? And given the number of jars in this room, we might never find her. Those ashes could be anywhere.

My worry practically grows a new head as the realization, that until a wraith sends her to Hell, someone could bring her back.

It takes days to send each of the Aegis souls on. We go through every single jar, the final count over two thousand. Only fifty of those souls were handed over to the wraiths to consume.

Fifty that were evil out of two thousand souls. My mind still refuses to make sense of the carnage.

After we go through the jars on the shelves, we raid every nook and cranny of Iva's room, coming up empty. I plop down on a fragile settee—secretly hoping I break it—and catch a faint noise near my left ear. I stop moving and shush the room, silently waiting for the sound again.

There.

Beyond the thick material on the north wall, a weak moan escapes the tapestry. No one else seems to hear it, but I know someone is behind that wall. West and Rhys work together, ripping the curtain from its rungs to reveal a small wooden door.

West steps back and kicks it in with his wide, heavy boot. The stench wafting from the depths of the black room speaks of death and blood and torture.

Rhys lights up his right hand and steps close to the ailing body of an emaciated, unconscious girl.

This is her—the girl I've searched this whole house for.

Her dark hair covers her face, and when I pull the matted strands back, my world nearly spins off its axis.

My legs refuse to hold me, and I crash to my knees.

"What is it, Gorgeous?" Rhys asks.

But he couldn't know.

Only someone as close as we once were would recognize her now.

"That's Mena," I say on a gasping sob. "That's my sister."

DEATH KISSED

PHOENIX RISING BOOK TWO

ANNIE ANDERSON

PROLOGUE

MENA—1965

My touch is a death sentence.

Growing up, Mama warned me never to use my power. Never, ever. Because using it could get me killed. "Or worse," she would say, because death is not the worst thing that could happen to a person.

Death is just a step in life.

I roll my mother's harsh but honest words over in my mind as I try to move without being touched through the throng of teenagers hell-bent on getting to the movie theater just behind me. Typically, I would have just crossed the street, but on this night, I figured the crowd was safer. But one little shock, one little slip, and it would all be over.

No more disguise. No more hiding. No more normal life—or normal for me, anyway.

But "normal" was such an inane word. It meant a life of lying, of holding myself back. It meant never feeling another person's touch, never revealing my true self. It meant tamping down everything that I was and everything I could be.

It meant being a shell of a woman, a bitter little outcast holding onto a power I had no hope of containing.

Keeping my power leashed is the real problem. Holding it inside for days and days, as I wait until I can get to a secluded spot in the desert to release the pent-up urge. Like the revving of an engine just before the green light, my body thrums, waiting for the press of the pedal. Waiting until I can release the lightning that courses through my veins—the electricity, the energy—that will one day get me killed.

Since maturity, it's gotten harder and harder to hold it, harder to keep inside. That's all I've been doing. Since birth, I've been *playing* normal, while my twin *lives* a normal life. She's never had to bite her tongue or mask her natural reactions. Never had to watch every single step as if one mistake would tip her hand. She's never had to hide, and that's all I've ever done.

We were born of the same womb but couldn't be more different. I'm tall, she's short. I'm quiet, she's loud. I think before I speak, she... *doesn't.*

I'm an Aegis. A freak of nature that can kill with a single touch: a species of phoenix nearly wiped from the face of the earth.

She's a seer. A psychic who knows way more than she should. And her knowledge could get our whole family killed.

I shift my thoughts from my twin, who we shunned so many years ago, and try to tamp down my emotions.

The bulbs in the movie theater marquee are shiny and new, advertising a movie I won't get to see. Adolescents giggle and push as they move past me on the sidewalk, and I wonder if there will ever come a time where I could have something like that. The comradery. Hell, I'd take friends of any kind. But the times change so quickly, and the years fly past. Just ten years ago, the girls were wearing poodle skirts and saddle shoes, now they're wearing miniskirts and tall boots. Strange how fast things can turn on a dime.

I hasten my steps while doing my best to appear calm and unaffected. Like I'm not aware someone is watching me and has been for a while now. I've felt eyes on me for days and knew without a shadow of a doubt there has been someone out there lurking.

I've been good, fulfilling my duties as a gentry with aplomb. Granted, I wasn't a gentry in the first damn place, but I'm pretty sure I don't deserve to be checked up on like a child.

I practically live at the funeral home where I work evenings masquerading as a mortician's apprentice—not even a full-fledged mortician. An *apprentice.* Like I haven't seen more dead bodies than Mr. Hanby ever will in his whole human life. It's not like I have friends, or a lover, or a life. There's too much to risk, and I have too much to hide. Just wake up, go to work, ferry souls to the Otherside, go to bed. Rinse and repeat, on and on forever.

Tugging on the *Peter Pan* collar of my dress, I contemplate what forever might mean for me, and it isn't a pretty sight. Over a century in hiding, and it never gets any easier.

It's still hot here in Phoenix—it doesn't ever get very cool, especially compared to the cold, wet of the Oregon wilderness I used to call home. Every time I think of my city's name, I chuckle a little. A phoenix living in Phoenix. My lips curve into a smile, and I forget the eyes watching me for a moment.

I shouldn't have. I ought to have been paying attention to the alley to my left, but stupid me, I was trying too hard not to shock the kids pushing past.

Hiding in plain sight would only work for so long. I should have left this life a long time ago, but I so foolishly held out hope that, one day, my family would be together again. That one day, my sister would be home, and I wouldn't have to hide who I was from the other half of my soul. That one day, I wouldn't have to hide what I was from my own kind.

I should have remembered that as soon as I made my first squalling wail into this world, I would never get what I wanted. But I forgot for a moment, letting my guard down for a single second. As I passed a darkened alley on a hot Arizona evening, hard, cold hands wrapped around my throat and snapped my neck.

Something that wouldn't kill me, but I'd grow to wish it would.

Because those perfect shiny lights of that brand-new movie theater were the last good things I would see for a very long time.

I

MENA

I DON'T WANT TO OPEN MY EYES. CONSCIOUSNESS AND I AREN'T friends on a good day, but on a bad one? There are things that supersede the word "torture." Every time I wake up, Iva finds a new cruelty, and even though I stopped feeling the pain a long time ago, it's not just the physical pain for her. She likes to break me down, tear at my mind, my soul—hammering the rock to rubble and starting all over again.

I guess I should be proud. I've never broken. Not completely.

Except that once, my mind snidely whispers in a sing-song tone, but I try to ignore it. Losing it just that once was enough to remind me never to break again. But I try not to think about my greatest shame, since dwelling on it is enough to make me lose what's left of my mind.

Keeping sharp is my primary goal right now. Staying alive is a tenuous second.

I press my eyes closed, praying for a reprieve I know will never come.

A moan tears up the ruined column of my throat, the tiniest bit of sound echoing in this broom closet of a cell. Iva moved me here herself just a week ago. To bring me closer and draw the pain out longer and longer until I smashed my head into a stone wall just to catch a break.

If prison taught me anything, it was how easily a skull could be crushed.

Iva. I didn't think it was possible to hate someone as much as I hate her. She was supposed to be our leader. The oldest of us, she was supposed to lead us, teach us. Instead, she is just like any other megalomaniac—she thirsts for more and more power.

Specifically, the power that writhes beneath my skin.

The door to my cell bursts open, but I don't move. I learned a long time ago that reacting is never the best course of action. Instead, I try to relax my muscles into the unforgiving cot someone threw me on. That particular incident happened after I took a little healing nap while my skull pieced itself back together.

I sense two people in my new cell. Even with my eyes closed, I can see the dank, dark stone tomb Iva has me housed in. No windows, no light. Little bigger than a cubbyhole, the rough walls are vastly different from the sterile cinder block ones I've grown so used to. They appear much older than the rest of the house—what little I've seen of it—as though this part was built first and the rest was added on as the decades flew by.

I can imagine the visitor's placement—near the heavy oak and steel door. The people I sense are foreign to me, so Iva must be stepping up her game by bringing in new players.

A rumble of a man's low voice echoes through the room, followed by a pained gasp. Then, a voice I haven't heard in over one hundred years nearly shatters my soul.

"That's Mena. That's my sister."

At her gasping sob, my eyes flash open, and I notice a small blurry hand hesitate before brushing back crusted hair from my cheek. My eyes haven't quite figured out how to focus, still healing from the self-inflicted head injury.

"Mena-girl, can you hear me?" Aurelia asks as she touches my shoulder before yanking it back in surprise.

She doesn't expect me to flinch away from her or scurry in a backward crab walk off the cot, putting my back against the closest wall. But that's what I do even when I tell my mouth to open, and my voice to say hello. Apparently, my body is working independently of my brain on this one.

Especially when, instead of the greeting I mean to say, I start hissing at her. My breaths speed up, and my eyes roll in my head.

Keep it together, Mena. This probably isn't a trick, but even if it is, you have to keep yourself together.

I hear a *thud-thud-thud...* my body moving of its own volition, slamming me into the wall, trying to smash its way through the stone. My body is doing what it used to do in the beginning: flee. And then Aurelia is rushing me. She grips my arms and yanks me away from the wall.

"Stop hurting yourself. Please, Mena-girl. No one is going to harm you," she says soothingly. She cradles me in her warm arms, oblivious to the stink and dirt and dried blood on my skin. She doesn't seem to care that I'm covered in filth and smell like a sewer. She whispers in my ear, soft words I don't really understand, but eventually, my breaths ease and my eyes begin to focus.

My twin knows precisely what torture is like. Iva bragged about ripping the skin from her bones. She told me of every cut she made, every scream she yanked from my sister's lips. Every drop of blood she drew. Other than wielding the blade on me—which is her favorite pastime—telling me of my sister and her mate's torture was a close second.

I know she can feel that terrible ache along with me.

"Mena-girl, I know you're in there, and I know it's hard for you to talk. So you can just listen. Do you remember the yellow flowers we used to pick when we were kids? I can't remember their name, but we would pick them for Mama and put them in that green glass pitcher that sat on the kitchen windowsill. And she would sneeze. Remember?" she asks as she holds me closer, enveloping me into her warm arms.

"She would sneeze the house down since she was allergic to the flowers, but she wouldn't move them because we gave them to her. Remember, little sister?"

That comment seems to be the key to unlocking my lips because I fire back, "You're only fifteen minutes older than me." My voice is awful, hoarse and cracking like I've somehow swallowed glass.

"There she is. You with me, little sister?" Aurelia asks, tilting her head so she can meet my gaze. "It's just you in there, right?"

Most people would shudder at the sight of my twin's pale pupilless eyes, but they are a balm to me. I've dreamt of seeing her for so long, I can't begin to fathom what her actually being here might mean. Her black hair is longer than I remember, the strands wild and loose around her shoulders. Beautiful, bright colors and pictures decorate the skin of her forearms, leading up to her shoulder. "Tattoos," my brain finally supplies, and I wonder when she'll show them to me.

If we have time.

Frowning for a moment, I contemplate her question before I realize she's talking about Iva. I've heard the whispers in the halls. The gentries quiet, fearful whispering of Iva taking over minds, making soldiers into puppets. Bending once-strong phoenixes to her will. I'd hate to inform her that Iva tried—she tried so hard to get into my head.

She couldn't ever manage it, though. That's one victory at least.

"It's just me in here, and my mind is clear. I just can't always control what my body decides to do. No telling when it will choose to go haywire again. I take it this is a rescue?" I say, my voice threaded with hope.

The hope I didn't have the luxury of holding until now.

"Absolutely. How ya doing, Mena?" Rhys asks, his hand on the pommel of a wicked-looking sword hanging from his belt.

Rhys is the same but different. Same tall stature, same dark hair, same dark eyes, but he's lighter than I remember, happier. A feat I didn't think possible after Iva forced the soul bonding on him and Aurelia. Aurelia had never wanted the mating, never wanted someone chosen for her. Never wanted any of the moors that tied her to our kind—that dictated her path.

So many years ago, I tried to talk my sister out of marrying Lucien, but by that time, our relationship had deteriorated long past amicable. While a good man, Lucien was too weak for my brash and strong-willed sister. He was soft and slightly petty. In fact, his infatuation with Aurelia began out of spite. He was simply not enough for my big sister.

Rhys is enough—more than enough.

"I suppose that depends on your definition of crazy. Where is Iva, and how long have I been here?" I ask, getting right to the point. I know I've been here a long time, just how long, though, is unclear.

My sister's eyes go unfocused for a moment, as if she's using that power that she cursed for so long to answer my question. And when they settle back on me, I know I won't like whatever answer she'll give me.

"She's been neutralized for the time being, and it's... It's been fifty years," Aurelia whispers, trying to soften the blow but tightening her body, bracing herself. It must be obvious to her that I've been here for a very long time.

Shuddering, I think of the dark—always in the dark. I hated living in the blackness, but so much more, I hated being in the light. The light was when the pain began—when *she* would come to cut me, drain me dry, and try to break into my mind. She would rip away my flesh and smear dirt in the wound. Then one day, the pain stopped.

A body can only feel so much before the mind turns it off. But she would leave me to my silent oblivion—letting the voices of my regret claw at my brain.

The pull of a snarl yanks at my mouth. I have been here far too long —longer than I ever thought possible.

Who did I have to look for me? My sister? My only sibling had been cast out of our family ages ago.

What friends did I have in my old life? I had no one.

No wonder it took so long to find me. *I'd been a ghost already.*

I am simultaneously relieved that Iva is no longer a threat—no more daily visits, no more soul-sucking agony, no more barbed taunts, no more of that cloyingly sweet voice whispering in my ear—and enraged that I've been here for so long.

Seething, I mutter, "I've been stuck in this hellhole for half a century?"

I may be furious, but my rage is nothing compared to the wall of white-hot fury wafting from Aurelia.

Her pale-green eyes blaze to a blinding white, and she turns to Rhys. She goes from me leaning on her to standing so fast, I almost fall on my face as she dumps me back onto the floor.

"Guard her. I'm going to find that bitch and rip her head off with my bare hands. There is no fucking way she didn't know about this," she hisses as she stomps out of the tiny cupboard of a room.

"Who is she talking about?" I ask Rhys, who lingers at my side.

"Nicola," he says through gritted teeth, his fingers tightening into fists, looking like they're aching to tear into someone.

"Stop her! Nicola is the only reason I'm alive!" I yell as I try to pull myself to standing. My legs crumple beneath me almost instantly.

Rhys tries to catch me, but I shudder back. The electricity rises in me before I can stop it. As his fingers make contact with my shoulder, his body goes rigid, my power pulsing through him as if he'd grabbed onto a downed power line. I try to shut down my shield as fast as I can, but I'm not fast enough to prevent damage. Aurelia's pained scream ricochets through the stone room just beyond my door.

Their bond—the soul bonding Iva bragged so much about—that makes it so if one is injured, they both bleed. It was her big coup, her greatest trick: changing something meant for protection and turning it into a weapon against them both.

Shame steals through me.

"I'm sorry. *I'm sorry, I'm sorry, I'm sorry,*" I mumble as I cover my mouth and nose with my hands. I didn't mean it. It has been a long time since I've shocked someone by accident. Or even on purpose.

Rhys looks a little worse for wear, and his nose is bleeding, but he hasn't lost consciousness, so I didn't shock him too badly. But still.

"You all right, Gorgeous?" he calls to my sister as he recovers from his doubled-over stance and his kind, coffee-colored gaze meets mine. In an instant, understanding dawns on his face, and then his compassion is gone, flipping like a switch. His expression wipes clean of emotion so quickly, it's easy to see he's trying to keep the pity off his face.

He knows. He knows what happened to me, or at least he has a good idea. It's not too hard to guess what can happen to a woman in captivity when torture is the name of the game. I could give him two guesses, but he'd only need one.

"Yeah. Don't touch the Aegis, spaz," Aurelia shouts back. "I said guard her, not *touch* her."

Ice floods my veins. She shouldn't know that. How does she know what I am? Fear threatens to steal my sanity again, but I force myself to focus. Balling my fingers into fists, I try to center myself on what I can sense. The stone under me, the cool air drifting in from the door, the smell of leather from Rhys' boots, the voices just beyond the room.

"So noted," he mumbles, his gaze never wavering from mine as he crouches near me but not touching.

"Don't tell her," I whisper, thinking if I can just clutch one thing, one tiny shred of dignity in this whole mess, I will feel better.

"Don't tell her what?" he hedges, feigning ignorance.

"Whatever you thought that made that look on your face. That's mine. Don't tell her."

"You realize you're asking me to keep a secret from a psychic, right? From my mate? About her twin? You know how that's going to go," he explains softly, and I feel sorry for the guy. I do, but not enough to let *that* cat out of the bag.

"And what right is it of yours? To decide for me when and who I share my life with, share what happened to me?" I spit at him.

"I have no rights, nor am I telling you what to do. What I'm saying is, if she asks me what happened, I will tell her. I will tell her my assumptions, my thoughts, and nothing more. It is your decision when and what you tell her, but it is mine as well," he says diplomatically. "Secrets kept us apart for too long. I won't risk losing her again."

It's tough to fault the guy when he uses facts and logic.

It ticks me off.

"It's difficult to be mad at you when you speak rationally," I grouse. "Stop it."

That makes a deep, rumbling laugh spill from the wide, white smile blooming on his face.

"Get your mate, Rhys. You might hate Nicola, but I owe her my life. Keep her intact, will you?"

"I won't ask about the other, but you will explain Nicola to me?" He levels a stare at me.

After all I've suffered, he doesn't scare me. The Aegis rises in me for the first time in a long time. More than that minuscule blip that made his nose bleed. My hands glow an icy pale blue as electricity crackles across the skin of my palms. Heat warms my chest as light hits my eyes. I know from experience that they bleed from a muddy green to a luminescent amber.

"No," I say, my voice lowering to a growl, "I won't."

Rhys raises his hands in surrender with an expression of utter confusion. My anger may seem irrational, but they would never understand what Nicola did for me. Hell, I wouldn't understand if I hadn't lived it. She saved me. Even if she had to hurt me to do it, she still saved me. Even on the days I was begging for death, I *still* had gratitude for Nicola.

She told me this day would come. I just had to stay strong.

I just never expected it would take this long.

"Okay, Mena. No questions. Can I help you up, or do you think you'll shock me again?" he asks in a soft, soothing voice. He sounds like he's trying to charm a venomous snake. He's not far off.

"Let's stay on the safe side. Get my sister. She can help me."

The last thing I want is to hurt anyone, but that's all I seem to be capable of. The lives I have already taken will stain my soul for the rest of eternity.

"Okay, kiddo. Whatever you need," he murmurs. "Hey, Gorgeous?" he calls.

"What?" she yells back, sounding mighty irritated. We hear a large shuffle and a heavy *thud*.

"Stop trying to kill people and get in here!"

Aurelia stalks back into the room, her clothes ruffled, rubbing the knuckles of her right hand and muttering expletives under her breath.

"I wasn't going to kill anyone, just permanently maim them is all." She shrugs and flashes an evil ghost of a smile.

"Why don't you help your sister get out of here instead?" Rhys suggests.

"Stop being logical. It's annoying," Aurelia says, and she crosses the room to press a kiss on his lips. Her quick peck is foiled when he latches onto her hips and keeps her there so he can kiss her better.

"Dear God, now there are two of you," he mutters against her lips.

"Umm... I hate to break up this little lovefest, but I'd like to get the hell out of here sometime in the next century. Is that possible, or are you guys going to make out some more?" I ask, getting a bit of my snark back.

"Sorry, little sister. You're right, though," she says as she reaches down to haul my whole body up like she's cradling a small child. "Let's blow this popsicle stand."

Emerging from that small, stone room is not the balm to my soul I thought it would be. As we move closer to the light, all my body seems to want to do is crawl back to my cell. I've been in captivity too long.

There is too much space, too much light.

My breathing comes too fast. I can't catch my breath. Even as the light dims and my heart races, a single thread of hope steals through me that I won't wake up back in that tiny stone room. That this isn't a dream. That I'm really free.

At least for a little while.

2

ASHER

I'M RUNNING OUT OF TIME.

I think this as I watch my King gripping the handrail as he shakily makes his way down the stairs to the subbasement medical bay. His white knuckles clutch the banister, and I realize he's weaker today than he was yesterday. He's fading fast.

Too fast.

I feel like an asshole for thinking it, but the further John's health deteriorates, the more I know I'm a dead man.

Gods, I'm a selfish prick.

Here I thought I'd get to die in battle or maybe after I got to watch my children and grandchildren grow up. But that won't happen. I don't get a mate or children. I wasted too much time on my job, and now I get to watch the man I've considered the closest thing I have to a father wither away to nothing. I get to see my life and my future shrivel to a husk and blow away in the wind.

The job I put so much of myself in will kill me as soon as he takes his last breath.

And there's nothing I can do about it. No foe to fight, no sword to clash.

Wraiths are a tricky bunch. So many of our kind are two-faced assholes. Hiding. Scheming. Manipulative.

When you're the gatekeeper to Hell, sometimes the honor system shits the bed a bit.

But the one thing we're completely transparent about is our mate. John is dying because his mate Olivia is—plain and simple. When a wraith mates, it is a lifelong commitment, effectively wrapping two souls with the same thread of life. If one goes, so does the other, and Olivia has been sick—so sick her guardians are scrambling to find a cure for what ails her. Scrambling to save her and their hides as well.

The longer it lasts, the more I know they won't find some magical remedy to knock Olivia off the path she's on. When a guardian's charge dies, the guardian must forfeit their life for failing to save them.

That's the oath we take—an oath we pay for in blood.

I've never regretted taking the vow to serve John, never wanted to change the path of my life, never wanted to be anything else once I was cast out of what was left of my family after my parents' shameful turn.

But now as I look death in the face, I wish I'd lived more, done more, seen more.

Regret, thy name is Asher.

John reaches the med bay and pauses before he opens the heavy steel door. He turns to level his chocolate-brown eyes at me and my hulking dipshit of a cousin standing just to my left.

"I need you two to stay sharp in there. Aurelia says her sister is a full-blown Aegis. And from what I gather, she is remarkably and understandably unstable. Do not touch her. If you think she is about to lose it, you leave the room. Do your best to avoid engagement. She has been locked away as Iva's personal punching bag for the last fifty years. You know how much that woman was a fan of torture."

I hold in my shudder at the thought of someone being in that crazy bitch's clutches for fifty years. I don't care if it seems emasculating, that woman scares the shit out of me. I don't care if she's ashes, phoenixes have a way of coming back. Trusting that Iva is even remotely dead, seems just plain stupid in my book.

"What are they doing here?" Cam growls at our king. "We just got Aurelia's trouble-bringing ass out of our lives, and now she's back? With a sister? Are you kidding me?"

Fucking imbecile.

Cam hasn't always been too bright. As a teenager, he believed all of his parents' hateful rhetoric. Phoenixes are evil. They oppress wraiths. They kill us. And while some of that is true on some levels, phoenixes aren't the only ones who despise what we are, and not all of them do. Every single faction of the Ethereal has their share of members who hate or fear us. As they should. If they fuck up, we're the ones to send them packing straight to Hell when they die.

Cam used to be reasonable, after getting out from under his odious parents. But since their deaths, especially since it was on Iva's orders, hate fills him.

The longer he stews in this horrible malevolence, the more I worry about him turning into a Revenant.

Turning isn't too hard to do. Most wraiths are half out of our minds, anyway. Consuming enough evil to keep us alive can easily taint the soul. Even the most honorable wraith just needs one little push—a paltry little shove—and bloodlust takes over. Clouding our mind, our souls, taking the need to consume evil just that tiny step further, and then we're not just taking in evil souls, we're eating the flesh of the corrupt.

When I shake out of my thoughts, John's silence stretches and grows until his once-brown eyes turn black. His stare seems to shrink my fuckup of a cousin until it's clear by the expression on Cam's face that he feels three feet tall.

"Do we need to have this discussion again?" John's low voice grates in the small space. "We owe her. We owe the *both* of them. A snake was in our midst, and we saw nothing. They took out Javier and Iva. Aurelia's vision saved us all. They defended this house and your King when they could have run. They fought in your stead to save your life. Show them some fucking respect."

It doesn't matter that he is weak. It doesn't matter that his once-dark hair is turning whiter by the day, heralding his death more than any other sign could. He could give Cam a lesson without moving an inch.

"Yes, sir," Cam mutters, eyes downcast. He fakes contrition, but I know he has zero remorse for his hatred. It's evident by the unyielding line of his shoulders and the fixed set of his jaw. He feels nothing but rage.

Fucking moron, I think as I slap him upside the back of his idiot head once John's back is turned.

Cam flinty blue gaze slices to me, but I refuse to back down. One of these days, I won't hold back when I punch him in the face. He nearly signed his own death warrant just two weeks ago. If I hadn't kept him in line, kicked his ass, and practically held his fucking hand the whole damn time, John would have had his head already. Unstable and malignant, I've slept the fewest hours of my life watching out for him.

One of these days, I won't be here to save his ass.

John grunts as he pushes the door open, but I refrain from helping him. I learned very early on—once he started to deteriorate—that letting him do what he could for himself was the only way either of us were going to survive. The room beyond has stark-white walls and gray cement floors, and while it appears pristine, it carries the faint smell of earth and dirt. I suppose being this far underground will taint the air no matter how many air purifiers are running.

Eight hospital-grade beds—four on each side—line the room. Each bay has the required oxygen ports, IV stands, and monitoring devices. Most of the bays have their privacy curtains open, but one in the far-back right is pulled shut.

Carver is still in the med bay and hasn't yet regained consciousness after a vicious attack from his mate, Javier. At this point, I am not certain it is a bad thing. Javier turned Revenant unbeknownst to us all. A puppet for Iva to infiltrate this house, and now that his mate is dead, I dread the day when we have to tell him what happened. While it doesn't appear as if Carver had any knowledge of Javier's deceit, it is a general rule that most people have a hard time looking at someone who ignored the signs of violence. Mass murder, no matter the cause or reason, usually carries a taint that stains the survivors.

The only other occupied bay has the privacy curtains open, and the rest of the members of the house are loosely surrounding the bed, blocking my view of our newest houseguest.

I still can't believe Aurelia is a twin. I hope they aren't identical, because two of her unpredictable asses would most likely be the worst thing I could think of. The last thing we need in this house is more crazy, yet here we are.

Aidan and Ian block my view, but that doesn't matter. I have no interest in the Psychic Wonder's sister. I just hope her presence is more transitory than it seems. The last thing we need is her to hole up here when everything in our lives is about to change.

And it is. Make no mistake.

If John dies without a plan of succession, we are all fucked.

The brothers move to the side out of John's way, and my King introduces himself to the patient.

"Hello, Mena. My name is John Black. Welcome to my home. I'm happy you are with us, and you made it out of there. You and your family are invited to stay here as long as you need."

Oh, great, just lay down the welcome mat, John.

"Anything you need from us, please just let us know."

Out of the corner of my eye, I see a dark-haired head nod hesitantly. She doesn't make a noise, not a sound, not a whisper. How odd.

Finally, she clears her throat, and then a soft, but hoarse voice speaks. "Th-thank you, sir. Thank you for letting me impose on your generous hospitality. I will not forget this kindness."

That voice.

Something about that voice pulls at me, as if there were steel strings around my soul, and they are finally being reeled home. Without thought, my body moves. I gently push Aidan out of my way so I can get closer. He obliges with a grunt of indignation, but I don't care. He takes forever to move.

Finally.

Finally, I can see her. Her bowed head and downcast eyes are in deference to the king. She's rail thin, the shapeless hospital gown billowing around her like a sail. Her wrists and arms are mottled with purple and green bruises.

And the scars...

Faint pink lines crisscross old white ones up and down both arms. A few of her fingers are irreparably disfigured, especially the pinky finger on her right hand. It is crooked and curled, and even though the rest of her fingers are moving, picking at the nonexistent pills on her blanket, that one lone pinky remains still. Her fingernails are cracked and jagged but clean and scrubbed.

I taste the metallic tinge of blood on my tongue, and I realize my fangs have descended and have sliced my lip. I feel the pinch of my talons growing from the tips of my fingers, and I understand that my body has gone into a full phase without my mind ever asking it to. Rage, the likes I have never felt, washes through me, and I realize I want to murder someone for the first time in my long life. I've killed in my three hundred years of service to the king, but never have I relished the deaths.

But right this second, I want to know who did this to her. I want to know if it was just Iva or a host of her soldiers. I want to rip the skin and muscle from their bones as they watch. I want to consume them until they are left writhing in the depths of Hell.

My brain seems to split in two. I want to maim and murder, but I also want to comfort her. I can almost taste the bitterness of her distress, how much she must hate people looking at her, talking to her after so many years of captivity. I want to see her eyes. I want to know what she's thinking. I can't take the waiting, and I move Ian out of the way and then West and then Evan, making my way to the left side of her bed.

I hear faint sounds of protests and shouts beyond the harsh buzzing in my ears, but I don't care. I know my hands are taloned, but I can't think about reining in my phase.

I reach out to touch her fidgeting fingers, and in surprise, her head finally rises so I can see her face. Her eyes are wide and fringed in black lashes that make her beautiful olive-green irises pop. Her forehead and the left side of her face are covered in bruises, and her nose is pert and cute, even if it's a little swollen. Her cheekbones are high and sharp, and as soon as I can, I'm making her eat until she bursts.

Those eyes that only a second ago were startled, swiftly turn from surprised to angry, and in a flash, her irises turn from green to gold. The last thought of consciousness I have before she shocks me stupid is how pretty her eyes are when she's mad.

3

MENA

ONE SECOND, I'M TRYING TO MIND MY MANNERS AND BE AS
invisible as possible, given the circumstances, and the next, some huge,
black-eyed wraith is trying to grab my injured hand. My right hand has
been smashed and snapped and crushed so many times over the years.
And just for kicks, Iva would rub Morganite dust in my open wounds.
Morganite being one of the few things that can permanently scar or
injure a phoenix.

She was a peach, that woman.

I still can't move my pinkie finger. I'm pretty sure I never will, and
seeing the sharp talons of a fully phased wraith trying to grab my
hand... well, sanctuary or not, I'm damn well going to defend myself.

What concerns me the most about this whole situation is that I
haven't been in this house for more than an hour and I've already
shocked someone. Granted, this time it was on purpose, but I'm
genuinely fearful of the next time. It's building under my skin. That itch,
that urge.

I haven't felt it in years, but the burn is coming.

"What in the cold depths of hell was that?" I screech as I look over the edge of my hospital bed to peer at the man I just juiced. Everyone seems to have frozen just before things start moving at hyper speed.

Aurelia appears in front of me, looking murderous. Flames are already licking up her arms, and she looks about three seconds from turning the man who tried to touch me to ash.

The dark-haired guard steps in front of the king, seeming ready to tear my head off if necessary. A low, rumbling growl vibrates from his chest. Evan and West look torn between the king and me, while the brothers, Aidan and Ian, are trying to hold in their snickering. They're failing, though, and the shorter one, Ian, can't seem to help doubling over and letting out a roar of laughter.

"Well, that's a crash and burn if I ever saw one." Ian guffaws, while holding onto his sides.

The taller of the two, Aidan, who was trying not to lose it, tosses his head back and explodes with a booming laugh. That diffuses some of the tension, but Ari is still mad, and the king's large guard is practically grinding his teeth to dust.

"What the fuck, John? I thought Javier was a one-off. Do we need to leave?" Rhys growls from his perch at my left shoulder. He isn't touching me, but his presence here is protective. Like a big brother. It would feel nice if we weren't in the middle of wraith-central with one of the king's guards going all black-eyed on me.

The king appears almost smug as if a plan has come together perfectly. Iva would get that same look when I did something out of character that gave something away.

I don't like that look. It gives me the creeps.

"I believe Mr. Crane's intentions were of a more... 'affectionate' nature than he portrayed." John smiles, faking a cough, clearly masking a chuckle.

"You don't think... *Shit*." Aurelia pauses. "We'll talk about this later. For right now, can you remove this bumbling oaf until Mena is feeling better?" Aurelia asks, but it doesn't exactly sound like a question. More like a thinly veiled threat wrapped in an ass-kicking promise.

I love my sister.

The flames kissing her skin extinguish into nothing just before she reaches down and slaps the fallen guard upside the head. That rouses him, and a long, pained groan escapes his throat.

"Oooooowwwwwww," he moans. "What the hell happened?" he slurs from the floor.

"Jesus fucking Christ, Asher. Are you new? Don't touch the Aegis, numb nuts," Aurelia chastises him.

For some reason, this irks me. I don't shock people willy-nilly. Well, except Rhys, but that was an accident. I can accept a hug from someone. Someone can hold my hand. I'm not a bomb about to go off.

Well, that may not be true. But I'm not a leper. *At least that's true.*

"Don't treat me like a child. I can defend myself. I just demonstrated that fact not ten seconds ago. You are not my keeper or my defender. Now, tell him you're sorry for smacking him. That's adding insult to injury; I already knocked him out. Smacking him is just mean," I scold her before turning my body so I can see around the wall my sister is making.

Who knew someone so small could fill so much space?

When I see him, I'm struck dumb. He is no longer black-eyed or taloned. Fangs no longer tear into his lips, but blood still stains them red. His eyes are the blue of a cold winter morning, and though he's still sprawled on the cement floor, it's obvious he's taller than me, and that's a difficult feat to achieve. His light-brown hair is cropped short and is sticking up in all directions due to the nice jolt of electricity I slammed through his system. When I get a better look at the blood staining his upper lip, a barb of shame pierces me.

I don't like that at all. Something about knowing I'm the one who put the blood there, makes me want to cry. The biting sting of tears hits my nose.

"Are you all right?" he rumbles from the floor, his head cocked to the side. He's frowning, a tight pucker of his brow, and the sheer lunacy of this moment makes me smile.

"I should be asking you that. I'm sorry I shocked you, but you looked hostile," I say ruefully as I shrug a shoulder.

"My apologies, Miss. I mean you no harm," he murmurs, and from his expression, I believe him. His words are like a balm, soothing and cool against my skin. It makes the ache disappear for a moment.

"Got a funny way of showing it, Asher," Rhys says from the foot of the bed.

I didn't even notice him move. I scan the med bay, and the room has been mostly cleared. All that remains are Evan, my sister's tiny best friend, the king's dark-haired, angry-looking guard, Rhys, and Aurelia.

The guard makes me nervous, and a shudder of fear snakes its way up my spine as I shrink back into the bed. His huge, hulking frame stalks toward me, but everyone is looking at Asher and not the pissed-off wraith eyeing me like I'm horse manure on his boot.

But Asher must have noticed the fear on my face before I shrank back, because before the guard can make it to the foot of the bed, Asher is up from the floor and in front of him, snarling. Not just snarling. He is fully phased: eyes the black of a moonless night, long upper and lower fangs descended. His fingers are curled, ready to slash, and the thick talons erupting from his fingertips put a lion to shame.

The thing that is most worrisome is the swirling black mist that surrounds him. I've never seen anything like it. The rest of the occupants of the room are slowly backing away toward the door—even Aurelia.

When the psychic starts to bail, it's time to leave.

I move my legs toward the floor as quickly as I can, without making a noise. My legs likely won't hold my weight, but with the wraith death match about to go down in front of my hospital bed, I'm going to make a concerted effort to try.

"Stop moving," Asher growls, and I have no idea who he's talking to since he is still looking at the other guard, but the guard hasn't moved an inch since Asher stepped in front of him. I freeze anyway just in case he was talking to me, because the less I can piss off the scary man, the better.

The guard tears his gaze from Asher and stares at me. I'm sure I look like a wobbly baby doe, wide-eyed, and scared, but there isn't much I can do about it now. He gives me a nasty superior look before giving Asher his back and heading toward the door.

I have a feeling I'll be seeing him again soon, and not to exchange pot roast recipes.

Super.

Now I have to worry about more than the obvious psychological issues left over from my captivity. I get to worry about how safe I am. At least in my cell, I knew who was trying to hurt me. Here, not so much.

I am still staring at the door when Asher turns around. His face is back to his usual handsome self again, and the swift way he can phase makes me uneasy. It has been so long since I have phased, I'm not sure I can even do it anymore, but the way he does it is absolutely frightening.

His face turns from enraged to contrite in an instant. He must sense my fear of him, and I wish I could tamp it down, but I can't. I hate that my emotions are so palpable to the people around me.

Asher leans over, his fists to the mattress as he looks me in the eyes.

"I am sorry for this, Mena. I promise you this will not happen again. I'll make sure of it," he murmurs as he reaches his hand out and runs a finger along my ruined pinkie clutched in the rumpled bed sheets. He gently holds my hand, eyeing me warily as he brings it to his lips.

"You will be safe here. I swear it," he whispers against the skin of my hand, sending chills along my arm and down my spine.

The softness of his mouth is in direct contrast to the roughness of the stubble on his chin as he rubs his lips in a gentle whispering kiss against my skin. He carefully places my hand back on the bed and then stalks to the door like a man with a purpose. I don't know if I should be turned on, afraid for my life, or seriously concerned for the king's other guard.

"So this has to be the weirdest day of my life, and I have been in prison for the past fifty years at the hands of a mass-murdering psychopath, so that's saying something. Anyone want to explain what just went on here?" I ask, not taking my eyes off the door.

"Anyone?"

"Bueller?" Evan says as she skips back into the room, her mouth quirked in a tiny half-smile, at odds with the pucker of her brow.

"What?" I ask.

"Eighties movie reference. You missed some good decades. I'll catch you up on pop culture soon enough," Aurelia tells me as she straightens the blanket over my legs and smooths the sheet.

"You still aren't telling me what's going on, which I've got to say, does nothing for my stress level."

"I'm positive me telling you isn't going to help much," she hedges.

"Go ahead and give it a whirl," I prompt. "We'll see what happens."

"Umm... Well." She stalls. "Evan? You wanna take this one? Because I've got nothing."

"Did you ever learn how wraiths mate?" Evan asks me, and my brain decides it has learned enough for one day, since her voice is replaced by a heavy ringing in my ears.

"You know, I think I'm good with my ignorance for a few more days. You can quit talking now," I mutter as my head swims and my vision wobbles. I cannot possibly deal with what any of it might mean for me at this particular juncture of my life.

"So noted. No talking about a possible romantic future with a ridiculously hot dude. Got it," Evan quips. She is a little spitfire, that one.

"You are the least subtle person in the known universe, you know that?" Aurelia grouses at her best friend, rolling her eyes.

"How about you get some rest, and we can talk about your fun reentry into society tomorrow? I get to teach you five decades of pop culture. It's going to be awesome." Aurelia smiles at me. "Unless you want me to stay with you, because I can. I can hang here if you want. Are you hungry?" she asks, her expression hopeful. "I make a mean grilled cheese sandwich."

"No. I'm good here, and you stuffed me full in Oregon. My stomach can't handle any more food."

I cannot take one more "Are you okay?" or "Do you need anything?" I know she means well, but I've used my voice more today than I have my whole life.

Honestly, I haven't been around this many people in a long time, and I need my space.

Maybe then I'll breathe easier.

4

ASHER

I'M GOING TO RIP HIS FUCKING HEAD OFF. I AM GOING TO TEAR
his lily-livered, pansy ass to shreds.

"Oh, Cameron. Come out and play!" I shout through the gym,
careful not to yell until after the medical bay door is shut.

I've scared Mena more than I ever planned to. No need to have her
witness this. I scan the open-concept workout area. Unless Cam is
crouching behind the boxing ring, the place is empty, so I move on and
up the stairs.

He's probably hiding from me. As he well should. He knows his
actions are disgraceful. Not just that, but I could legally light his ass on
fire and watch him burn on the front fucking lawn, and no one could do
a thing about it.

Not even John.

As soon as Mena spoke, I knew exactly who she was to me. I've
heard the stories of John and Olivia's mating, of how rare it is to find our
other half. John once told me that all he heard was her voice and he
knew she was his. He felt it like a rope around his heart, pulling him
toward her. It didn't matter that she was the daughter of his enemy.
Didn't matter that they were strangers.

It doesn't matter to me that Mena isn't a wraith. It's as if someone opened a hatch into my brain and rewired it just for her. My instincts scream at me to protect her—to shield her.

And that's what I need to do. Starting with my idiot cousin.

Attacking a mate is the oldest and most sacred of all our laws—not that wraiths have many. I can only think of three off the top of my head. Rule one—don't harm a mate. Rule two—fulfill your duty. Rule three—respect your King. That's it.

So far, Cam has broken two of the three today, and I'm dying to teach him a lesson. I don't even bother wasting the energy to travel. I walk up the stairs at a slow leisurely pace just waiting for that little fuck to make a move.

After everything I have done for him, after every single time I have saved his ass, he goes and does this? Stalking up the cement stairs leading to the game room, I only briefly pause when I see John in his heavy leather chair, tired and exasperated.

Before I can make it out of the room, though, John calls me back.

"Asher," he says, no inflection, not raising his voice at all, but I feel the censure, anyway.

Even after three hundred years, I still don't know if that ache in my gut from hearing his voice is from the oath or if it's just his innate ability to say so much with so few words. I feel scolded, and he only said my name. John is good at that.

"Sir," I murmur, turning around to face my King.

"Teach him a lesson, but don't kill him. And after you're done, make him clean up. Let him know from me that I am considering his dismissal. Be it temporary or permanent is still up in the air. One more toe out of line and I'll have his head." John's brown eyes hold mine.

I feel less like I am looking at my King and rather like I'm looking at a disappointed father. I hate that, and I'm not even the one in trouble. I'm three hundred and nineteen years old, and I feel more like a fuck-up teenager.

Swallowing before I moderate my tone, I say, "Yes, sir, I will be sure to convey that message. I most likely will have to wait for him to regain consciousness to deliver it, but it will be done all the same."

I go to leave, and his low voice stops me again.

"She's a good match for you, but I think it will be difficult to win her.

She is not built like the rest of them. There is a quiet strength to her. You will likely have to wait for her to come to you," he advises. "Be patient."

"So trying to touch her hand when she is vulnerable and scared was a bad plan. Got it. Any more sage advice to give me before I beat my cousin within an inch of his life?"

"Maybe. These next few weeks are going to get harder for us. You may want to think about that before you go and burn a bridge."

The truth of his words hit me like a punch to the gut. John is dying. Olivia is dying.

And my death is coming, too.

"Aww. Why'd you have to go and pull the death card on me? Fine. I'll talk to Cam first. But if he so much as puts a toe out of line near Mena, I will rip his head off without a second thought. Does that make you feel better?" I concede, but it feels like I'm giving Cam too much leeway again.

Coddling that fucker irritates the ever-loving shit out of me. He frightened Mena, made her shrink back into herself just when I was getting her to smile. *Dick.*

"Immensely."

Nodding, I make my way out of the room, slowly scaling the stairs to the main level before the feeling of utter loss threatens to pull me under.

John doesn't have much time left.

I know he is not my father, but I have called John family for over three centuries. I've had John for many more years than the people who bore me. Other than Cam, I have no other blood family, but when John and Olivia go, I will truly feel like an orphan—more than I ever did when my parents' necks met with John's blade.

It was merely chance that brought John into my life. In fact, had John not been out riding that day with Olivia and their guardians, I would have died near the hearth of my childhood home with my mother's fingers wrapped around my heart. I hate thinking of my parents that way. I hate remembering my mother's twisted face, blood dripping from the wide-open maw of her mouth.

Looking back, the bad stuff is sometimes all I can remember, even though it shouldn't be. There were good times with them, I was sure, but those memories faded with the passing centuries.

When I reach the landing, I find Aidan and Ian decimating the contents of the refrigerator. They are the brothers I wish Cam and I were —what I wish we could have been. Aidan and Ian have barely been in each other's lives for fifty years and yet they are closer than Cam and I have ever been.

We should have been like brothers, and maybe if we had more time, we could have been. But that's all gone now.

Moving on to the living room, I'm tackled from behind by someone the size of a Sub-Zero refrigerator. Before my face can slam into the hardwood, I smoke out from underneath him and reappear in my original position to watch Cam land in a face-first slide across the living room floor.

"You know, I was going to be nice. I was going to talk it out, be friends, but now you've pissed me off," I say as I plant my boot in his ribs, hurtling his body across the room like a rag doll.

One would think a man Cam's size wouldn't be so easy to toss across a room, but I'm pissed and highly motivated to make sure my lesson sticks. His body takes out an end table and a lamp before landing in a heap on the raised hearth of the stone fireplace, cracking some of the stone with a *hiss*.

Cam rolls to his side, tossing off broken bricks.

"You'd really pick one of them. Over your own kind?" he groans from the broken grate. "After everything they've done to us?"

Cam picks himself up off the stone, his joints creaking, mortar dust stuck in his hair.

"One, I don't get to pick. You know that. Maybe it's chemistry, maybe it's fate. Whatever it is, it's not up to me. Two, I could do a lot worse than a beautiful woman who has endured and survived when so many would not. Three, get the fuck over your hate. You're not doing yourself any favors."

I know it's strange to just be fine with finding my mate, especially in the middle of this turbulent time. I'm less concerned with the fact that I have a mate and more anxious that Cam could have hurt her. Mating is something I have always hoped for.

"Oh, really? And I guess you are just looking out for me, huh?" Cam says as he turns his head to the side and pops his neck.

"No. I'm not looking out for you anymore. I have better things to do than saving your ass from the fire. And trust me, you're right in the middle of the flames."

"You know, you talk too much," Cam mutters as he lunges for me. I smoke to the side, but he knows my tricks after nearly three hundred years of fighting side by side. He travels himself, catching me by the middle and slamming me into a wooden support column. Despite the fact that the pillar is the size of a tree trunk, I still hear the wood crack.

Now, I'm really pissed off. I spring forward, head-butting him right in his dumb-fuck nose. The sound that accompanies the break is exceptionally satisfying. He starts to retaliate, but he is stunned by the blow to his nose and can't quite catch me before I land a strike to his middle and an uppercut to his jaw.

And that is Cam's biggest problem. For all his posturing, all his confidence, he is just one step slower, one step behind. Then, it goes the way it did only a few weeks ago: the last time he decided he knew more than John. Cam tries to kick my ass, fails, and we completely destroy the living room—fireplace, furniture, and windows included.

Evan is going to kill us. The tiny blonde terror scares the crap out of me.

I think I'll blame Cam.

Once Cam is in a bloody heap on the hardwood floor, I give him John's message.

"You have fucked up one too many times, cousin. John told me to give you a little *warning*. He is considering your dismissal. The permanent kind. The kind where you no longer have a head, and the rest of your body is burned to ashes and given to your family as a reminder of your disgrace. Get your shit together, Cameron. As the only family you have left, I really don't want your ashes on my mantle," I tell him as I walk to the stairs.

"Yes. You are my only family. Mom and Dad are dead. Burned to ash and God knows what else. Our houses burned to the ground. Our families. And who did that?" Cam gruffly shouts his question, his voice clogged with grief.

I feel the agony of our losses just as much as he does, but I refuse to be hateful because of them. I refuse to be blinded by my grief. I refuse to blame all for the actions of a few. And while I hate that our numbers have dwindled to such a stark number, I will not parcel out my soul to hate a dead enemy.

"Oh, and the king said you have to clean this up. Good luck."

"Fuck you, Ash."

"Love you, too, cousin," I say as I walk out of the room.

5

MENA

The stone of the floor bites against the bare skin of my legs, freezing me to the bone. My body has stopped shivering, and even I know that's a bad thing. The flesh of my left ankle is rubbed raw from the cold steel cuff latched around it. I can almost smell the coppery tang of the blood running down my foot, but it has gone cool now, congealing into a puddle on the stone.

My shoes are gone, and so is anything else that could be used as a weapon or a lock pick.

So cold. And dark. I can't see my parents, but I know they're there. I heard my mother whimpering a few minutes ago, but she hasn't regained consciousness yet. My father has been silent as the grave, and I don't know if he's true dead or not. I guess all my time as a gentry didn't pay off as well as I'd hoped. Or maybe I've been without food and water so long I have lost what senses I do have.

So much for all the training my father put me through. He taught me how not to get caught, not what to do once I was. I should have run the first time I felt the eyes on my back. I should have run as far and as fast as I could.

Sorry, Papa.

My parents got here after me. I was alone for a while, and the silence was enough to drive me insane. Just the sound of my mother's breathing eases my nerves, even though I know my nerves should be shot to hell, since I'm stuck in this dank prison cell for God knows what reason.

A man brought them in, one on each shoulder, plopping them down like sacks of grain on the stone floor. It was hard to see his face, the glaring light blinding me long after he left us all alone.

I've been here for days, I think.

There isn't a window in this cell, but I feel the time passing in fits and starts. It has been so long, I think this must be an interrogation tactic. Other than my secret, I'm not sure what else I am supposed to know.

A long groan comes from my father, and I listen to his breathing go from nothing to labored, to panicked.

"Papa?"

"Mena? Baby?"

"Yeah, Papa, Mama is here, too, but she isn't awake yet. I can hear her breathing."

"Do you know why we're here? I didn't see anything coming. I didn't see..." He trails off.

My father's visions aren't always clear, but Aurelia got her seer gene from him. He is the first male seer in over a millennium, a fact he has been able to hide due to his eyes looking perfectly normal, if the palest green I've only seen on one other person—my twin.

It's probably an old wives' tale, but I heard male seers were killed at birth. The longer I'm in this cell, the more I think that the rhetoric and horror stories my parents have told me over the years have been true.

Why else would we be here unless someone found out my family's secrets?

My mother stirs again, whimpering a low, pained moan before gasping an agonized breath. Her chain rattles in a horrible clank before my father calls out to her.

"Rhea, darling, are you all right?"

"Kale? What happened?" my mother groggily asks.

"I don't know. Mena is here with us."

"Mena? Baby? Are you okay?" her voice is shrill now, wide awake.

"I'm fine, Mama. What is this place? I've been here for days, waiting for

the two of you to wake up. Did I do something wrong? I was good, I swear it."

I did everything I was supposed to do. Everything. What did I do wrong?

"I know you were, baby. I don't know why we're here. Kale, do you see anything that could help us?" she whispers her question.

"You know I can't see around Mena, darling," he whispers back.

Of course. If you want to keep a seer as weak as my father from his power, you put them in a room with an Aegis. Someone knows. They know about all of us.

My blood turns to ice because I finally understand that I'm going to die in this room. Maybe once, maybe a thousand times, but death is coming.

And now I know what my mother meant.

Death is not the worst thing. The worst thing is waiting to die.

Time passes, my parents quietly discuss ways to escape, with no new plan sounding better than the last discarded one. They don't consult me, but that seems like a good idea.

I'm the reason we're here in the first place. I'm the reason my sister left brokenhearted. The reason she and I drifted apart before she left us altogether. I'm the reason Mama and Papa shunned her and continue to refuse to speak of her.

You can't trust your secrets to someone who isn't capable of keeping them.

There was no way we could trust her to keep our secrets. As a seer, Iva would be inside her head, inside her memories, practically inside our lives.

Everything had to be kept from Aurelia.

Every day with Aurelia with us was a constant struggle. Don't draw attention. Don't make waves. Don't do this. Only do that. Be nice. Be proper. Do what you're told. I was lauded for being the better sister—the more obedient one, anyway—when I hated every second of it. I hated being alone when I was half of a whole. When shutting my sister out made my soul shrivel and die within me over and over again.

Now, I'll die for real.

My thoughts are interrupted by the ratchet of the lock turning, and that cold, numbness is gone. In its place, I don't feel the hopelessness of impending death.

No, it's the fear of the unknown.

Someone turns on the light, and when the brightness no longer singes my eyes, I realize I knew nothing of the word fear.

A man is standing in front of the closed door. I might find him attractive in other circumstances. He is not overly tall, probably matching my height of five-foot-ten. His hair is long and blond—like the hippies I used to see so much of—tied back from his face with a leather thong. His muscles are thick, and given the soldier's breastplate and combat skirt, it confirms the theory that we are being held by the Primary. His features are blank for the first few moments, and the full force of my terror slams into me when I notice the leer ghost across his expression as he comes for me. Before he makes it to me, I go numb, and for a while, I am thankful.

Thankful I can't feel it, thankful I can't process it. I always thought that if something like this happened to me, I would fight, I would struggle, I would claw and scream and rail.

But I didn't.

I didn't do any of those things. Because I just couldn't believe this was happening to me. I just couldn't believe…

What I did do was cry.

It isn't until he's finished with me, and what was left of my sanity and innocence lies in ruin on that stone floor, that the real horror begins.

That itch, that urge to release my power can't be contained anymore. When the numbness and shock fade, all I'm left with is disgust and pain and revulsion. I am disgusted with my own skin that smells of the man who robbed me of everything, with the dress that hangs in tatters from my shoulders as I kneel on the stone, with the blood that stains my thighs and the gritty floor.

With my father's screams of vengeance and my mother's sobs of horror.

I can't hold it.

I can't keep it inside.

The power builds in a crescendo, starting from my stomach and radiating out through my limbs like brushfire, igniting everything that lies in its path. My pulse races and a buzzing starts—I think it's my mother's voice. In the back of my mind, I know she is trying to talk me down, trying to soothe away a hurt that will be with me for the rest of my short life.

I can't hear her words, though, and I think even she knows it's too late. I look at my parents as the ice-blue light emanating from my hands illuminates the room. I watch them reach across the space between them so the tips of their fingers touch.

That's the last thing I see as I close my eyes and a scream rips from my throat, power wrenching itself from my skin, sending great arcs of electricity through the room.

When I regain consciousness, I wish my body couldn't withstand the power I hold beneath my flesh.

I wish I were blind. Or dead.

Anything but to see the rubble of that stone room and the ashes of my parents.

Anything but to hear that damned door open again.

Anything but to hear the Primary's disgustingly sweet voice congratulating me on killing them for her.

Anything.

IT FEELS LIKE AN EARTHQUAKE, BUT I KNOW IT'S ONLY ME. JUST like on the horrible morning so many years ago, I have blown up a room.

I thought I had more time, but it's been too long since I had this much power coursing through my veins. Iva used to drain me, keeping me weak and docile, practically sucking the marrow from my bones. I'm just shocked it took so little time to build the energy back.

The hospital bed I was on is decimated, blown apart and melted into pieces, flung like shrapnel. I sit crumpled in the wreckage of what's left of it on the remnants of the floor. The solid handrails that once helped steady me are nothing more than a blob among the rubble.

And the floor...

A two-foot-deep crater bowls the ground where my bed used to be, blowing through the flooring straight into the foundation. The scorched walls are burnt in veins of smoldering black, and the sprinklers that once ran in exposed copper pipes along the ceiling have melted into twisted bows of metal. The curtain that briefly gave me privacy disintegrated to nothing, while the ones in the adjacent bays are on fire, along with the beds they used to surround.

It takes me a minute to remember that I wasn't alone down here. Scanning the far end of the room, I sigh a deep breath of relief that those curtains aren't on fire, even though they are blown back to reveal an unconscious man in the hospital bed. His bed has moved from its position, slammed into the nearby wall, but thankfully upright. My deep breath cuts off into a choking cough from the smoke.

Over the sound of my lungs refusing to work, I hear a *boom-boom-booming* coming from the steel door and a squeal of the metal grating on itself.

They won't be able to open it, not with the metal so distorted.

While burning alive is not an option for me, death by asphyxiation is entirely possible. It's not my favorite way to take a dreamless nap, but I've done it before more times than I can count. I worry more about the immobile wraith lying in the bed at the end of the room.

Fire won't kill me, but it will kill him.

A thick swirl of black smoke denser than the fire wafts in front of me, twisting and writhing before coalescing into the shape of a large man. Asher emerges from the smoke, his eyes frantically searching the room until they land on me.

"Mena," he almost whispers when he sees me. "Are you all right?"

Asher jumps down into the pit of debris eyeing me warily as he goes. I don't blame him. I've been here for one day, and I've already ruined the place, injured someone, and set fire to the house. I am a Murphy's Law trifecta of destruction.

"Don't help me," I choke, pointing to the bed at the back of the room. "Help him. The fire won't kill me. Get him first."

Asher's expression twists at my demand, considering it for a few seconds before he growls under his breath. Stalking to the inert man in the bed, he grabs him before smoking out of the room.

He's not gone for too long, though, before he comes back to me.

"You should have brought a fire extinguisher with you. I melted the sprinklers," I say as I gesture to the copper pipes that now resemble spun taffy.

"I don't think a fire extinguisher is going to cut it, Princess," Asher replies, his lips pulling into a half grin. "Ready to get out of here?"

Asher holds out a hand for me to take, but I ignore his outstretched fingers, trying to stand on my own. My legs refuse to do what they're supposed to and balk at holding my weight. I don't want to touch him if I can help it—not if it means hurting him.

Unfortunately, I need his help because the only way I'm getting out of this room is with Asher. My hand trembles as it hesitantly reaches for his. I wince right before our skin touches, praying I don't electrocute him.

My body relaxes marginally when I don't accidentally juice him again. He doesn't wait for me to relax any further and leans down to grab me up into his arms. At first, my body is rigid, my limbs as stiff as petrified wood, but for some reason, as soon as I feel his warmth against my skin, my muscles loosen. Even in this smoldering room, his heat calms me, eases an ache in my chest like my own fire would.

My respite is short-lived. As soon as my muscles relax, Asher's smoke surrounds us, enveloping us in an instant, and then it feels as if my insides are trying to come up my throat. The blackness thickens, swirling around us in ribbons of dense vapor. Asher's arms clutch me tighter, and then it feels as though I'm being blown apart. Every molecule of my body feels like it's being ripped and stretched. It takes only a moment, but that moment has thickened to molasses, straining the concept of time. Then the agony stops as suddenly as it started.

When the pain is over, I realize I've wrapped my arms around his neck, my chest pressed to his, my fingers fisted in the fabric of his shirt.

I'm shaking, and I can't seem to stop. For so long, I've shut out pain and fear from my mind just to survive. It's been ages since I've felt any form of hurt. Since I've felt real fear. So long since my emotions haven't been dialed down to nothing. But they're turned all the way up now, and I can't seem to shut them off.

It has been so long since my brain has been awake and aware while my body just rolled through the motions. Now, my body and mind are one entity, and it can't decide between frightened at the display of my own power and calm now that I'm being held so tightly, so reverently in his arms.

My calm waves goodbye once the shouting starts, and all I'm left with is fear. People surround us, their voices echoing in the open space of the gym. I can't understand what they're saying, but the threat in their tone causes my breaths to speed up.

For a reason I cannot explain, I grab Asher tighter. He feels safer than any place I've ever been, and that feeling only roots deeper in me once his arms clutch me closer to him.

I wish people would just stop shouting.

Asher's chest rumbles against mine, a menacing growl sounds in my ear and the noise dies down almost immediately. I want to ask about the man that was in the room with me, but I can't bear asking anyone else. I don't want Asher to put me down.

And he doesn't. He carries me to a bench and sits down with me in his lap, holding me just as tight as I am him. We are in a large gym, with a boxing ring and weights all around.

"Asher, is the man okay?" I pull my head back just enough to whisper in his ear, without letting him see my face. "I didn't hurt him, did I?"

"I don't know, Princess. I know Carver's alive at least."

Carver. The man I nearly killed has a name, and guilt hits me square in the chest.

"Alive is good. I'm sorry I caused this mess. Umm…" I pause. "Do you think I should apologize to John?"

He draws away, not letting me have that little bit of embarrassed privacy, and studies my face.

"Probably," he rumbles as he rubs his chin and surveys the damage I caused just to the steel door. The metal is bowed into the room like a bubble waiting to burst.

"Do you think you could coach me on how I'm supposed to say sorry for blowing up the house? My people skills haven't been utilized in a little bit, and even then, I'm not sure I knew how to apologize for something like that."

"It's easy, Princess. Just say you didn't mean it. Tell him it was an accident."

"One hell of an accident, huh? I think everyone would be better off if I wasn't here," I say, my voice rough with remorse and the realization that every single person in this house would be safer if I weren't in it.

Hell, this world would be safer if I weren't in it.

"Don't think stuff like that. We'll worry about arrangements later if you decide you don't want to stay here. Now, your sister looks like she's five seconds from ripping my head off. Do you want to talk to her? Because you don't have to talk to anyone if you don't want to. I can take you away from here. I can keep you safe until you heal. Until you fix yourself. Until you get control," he murmurs in my ear as his hand comes up to rest on my exposed cheek.

It's rough and warm, and I feel my muscles ease by degrees, my fingers gradually loosening their vice grip on his shirt. He is offering me a lifeline, a choice, an option other than relying on my sister and her friends—a way to heal without the microscope. And he's doing it discreetly, murmuring in my ear, giving me a tiny bit of privacy back. My eyes prick with tears.

"I don't think I'll ever get control of this," I admit, and that fact shames me to my core. I should have control of such an innate part of me. Captivity or not, torture or not—I should have control of this.

"Don't feel too bad. Your sister blew up a room here just a few weeks ago. You're not the only one. Granted, it wasn't on the same scale, but she still fried the place."

"What do you mean fried the place?"

"He means I'm an Aegis, just like you," Aurelia says, her eyes narrowed to slits, glaring at Asher.

6

ASHER

AURELIA—LIKE MOST SMALL WOMEN—SCARED THE CRAP OUT of me. Call me a pussy if you want to, but you have to watch out for the tiny ones. They are at the perfect height to grab you by the balls and twist.

Plus, I'd seen her wipe the floor with my King. Powers or no, John is over a thousand years old, having succeeded to King almost seven hundred years ago in the fourteenth century. His succession was not by lineage, but by the blood he'd spilled, culling the herd of corrupt wraiths from our numbers. There was infighting in the wraith community, enough that our presence was making itself known in the whole of Europe.

Ever hear of the Black Plague?

Yep, that was us.

Millions of humans died, plucked from the breast of life by bloodthirsty Revenants and a King who turned a blind eye to the corruption that was spread and prevalent in his own house. John put a stop to it. Even if he had to kill every male member of the royal family to do it, he ended the scourge and took the throne.

So to see a man who has won battles against impossible odds, reigned for centuries, and commanded his retinue in relative peace get his ass thoroughly and soundly kicked by a five-foot-three slip of a girl, makes me a little wary. I especially hate it when her pallid, jade-green eyes begin to glow. I'm not sure she realizes how often those pale orbs spark, giving away any and all spikes of her emotions.

Like her sister, Mena's eyes glow when she's upset. I find myself wondering what they would do when she was happy. Or aroused. Or if they would burn like embers when she came.

Do not pop a boner when she's on your lap, moron.

It takes me a while to collect myself, only aware of the conversation in the periphery of my consciousness. Mena's thin body is still in my arms, and even after all the drama of this ridiculously long day, even though she is so painfully thin and injured, I still want her. I see past her wounds, her apparent malnourishment, her scars, her fear, to see the beautiful, strong woman she is. My dick obviously doesn't give a shit about any of it.

Well, at least the two brains are on the same page.

"Granted, Mena's power makes mine look like a rowboat next to an aircraft carrier, but I have the ability all the same." Aurelia's voice breaks through my thoughts, and she crosses her arms over her chest in a threatening manner, glaring at me.

"Was this a secret?" I ask, genuinely confused.

"No, I just hadn't had the chance to go through the laundry list of familial dramas with my sister, and I would have preferred to tell her my shit myself," she says with an exasperated huff, tossing her hands up.

Aurelia turns her body slightly toward her sister, effectively dismissing me, even though Mena's fingers are wrapped around the fabric at my neck.

I look over Mena's shoulder and meet John's eyes. He is weary and doesn't seem even a little bit surprised. He does, however, look worse in just the few hours since I last saw him. I think he has been ducking Cameron and me—not that it's that hard to duck Cam—to go see Olivia. His brow furrows in distress and exhaustion, his shoulders droop.

I shouldn't let Mena get this close to me, shouldn't let this beautiful, fragile woman rely on me when I'll be leaving her. Looking at John again, my fingers ache to hold Mena closer—to clutch her to me until

I'm ripped away from her. My chest feels like someone has torn out my heart.

I won't get to see her happy or well.

I won't get to do anything but leave her.

She's gone through enough. I can't put her through more. Why would John encourage me to pursue Mena if I was just going to die before I could keep her? No one is that cruel.

Bringing my hand to the back of Mena's neck as she calmly talks to her sister, I shift her body closer to mine and brush my lips against her temple before pulling back. Her words stall out for a moment, and she turns her glowing amber eyes to me.

"What was that for?" she murmurs.

"It's time for me to go, Princess. Are you good with Half-Pint over here or do you want me to make other plans?" I ask her, only half-hoping she picks door number two and kicking myself for it. I can't in good conscience let her rely on me. Not when I'll just fail her.

"I think I'm okay for right now, but I do want to know about the man —err—Carver. Could you find out if he's all right?" she asks sheepishly as she ducks her head, a blush spreading up her neck to her cheeks.

"Sure thing, Princess," I say as my hand reaches down to her hips to shift her off me to the bench, and I freeze.

There at her hip is a significant bump, the bone of her femur jutting out of the socket.

"Jesus Christ, Mena. Your hip is dislocated," I rasp in horror. How long has she been like this that she isn't screaming the house down in pain?

"What?"

"Didn't you notice when you walked? *Can* you walk?" I ask in disbelief. How could she endure so much pain and not notice?

She pauses, and then her eyes go wider as she whispers, "I-I don't think I've walked in weeks, Asher."

Well, fuck that.

"Ian!" I bellow, my gaze searching the open expanse of the gym for the one person I know who has the most medical knowledge in this ragtag bunch.

"You rang? I was busy making sure the oxygen was shut off in the med bay. No one needs the house to go boom," he says as he jogs up from my left, already holding his med duffle. I guess after the commotion he was ready for action—and amen for the backup med supplies in the locker room.

"I think her hip is dislocated," I tell him, gently clutching her to me as if she were spun glass. Her body is vibrating with distress, and it kills me to have her so fearful.

Uncharacteristically silent, Ian's eyebrows rise halfway up his forehead in surprise.

"I want to know why no one checked her before now," I demand. "I want to know how this got past everyone. I know she's a phoenix, and they heal from damn near everything, but fuck, man."

Mena sits there on my lap in shock. Her expression of utter confusion would be cute if it didn't piss me off that she's been injured this whole fucking time while we did nothing.

"She didn't say anything, Asher. We were waiting for the morning so she could get used to us before doing a med check," Aurelia murmurs, her tone contrite.

I want to yell at her, but seeing how shaky Mena is, I understand her logic. There is almost nothing that can kill a phoenix true dead, their healing rates remarkable. Unless a wound came into contact with Morganite, a phoenix could heal from a cut in minutes, broken bones in hours—hell, I heard Rhys healed from a decapitation in less than a week.

Aurelia must have assumed if she needed assistance, she would have asked for it, not realizing Mena had been in captivity so long she wouldn't know to ask for help. And I didn't know if Mena would have allowed someone to prod her at all—even if it was her sister doing the prodding.

Ian moves to touch Mena, and she wakes up enough from her dazed stupor to flinch back. She burrows into me, ripping a snarl from my throat before I can think about what I'm doing. I want to comfort Mena, reassure her—tell her it will be fine, that she has nothing to worry about —but I can't get past my dueling emotions to open my mouth to soothe her.

Aurelia shoulders Ian out of the way, and she roughly grabs Mena's face in her hands. I don't like that, but I rein in my growling objection by the skin of my teeth.

"Ian is a good man. He is not going to harm you. He has been to battle with me, fought with me, nearly died with me, and I would risk my life to protect his. You can trust him. I swear it," Aurelia tells her, giving Ian probably the best compliment a wraith can get.

A wraith's honor is determined by how many would fight alongside him. Telling Mena this is probably a better apology than anything she could offer to John. Mena nods as she shudders out a breath, looking at me for a moment before nodding at Ian to proceed. Then I have to brace myself, so I don't rip his arms off as he pokes and prods her to assess her injury.

"You have to tell me if it hurts, Mena," Ian instructs her.

She's clenching her teeth, but it looks like she's straining, not in pain.

"How are you just sitting there?" Ian asks, seeming baffled.

"It doesn't hurt, I'm just t-trying not to shock you."

"Mena, you should be screaming," Ian tells her while Aurelia nods just behind him. Her eyes are wide and worried, her face looking mildly green.

"I don't feel pain anymore," Mena tells him. "I haven't for years."

"So I don't need to dope you up on pain meds before I pop this back in? By the look on Asher's face, if I don't treat you like crystal, he's going to rip my head off."

Ian steps back, leveling me with his physician stare, and I remember that he's seen more than we all give him credit for. Ian isn't a child, and despite his youth and genial nature, Ian would knock me out before he'd let me keep him from helping someone in need.

"I think it would be better if you stepped out for this," he says to me before turning to Aurelia. "You too, Squirt. Beat it. You look like you're about to puke."

"Dislocated joints make me want to hurl, so sue me," she bites back irritably as she turns and walks toward Rhys, who's sitting on the concrete steps leading up to the main house. She curls herself like a cat and sits on his lap, hiding her face in his shoulder as he gently rubs her back. I guess she's staying.

"Why do I have to leave?" I ask, logically knowing the answer, but unable to let that rule my mind. The ruling force in my brain says to stay —to protect—and no amount of logic is going to override it. Pulling me from my woman? I don't think so.

"Because I like my head firmly attached to my body," he says, like any teenager would say "Duh," and I'm reminded once again how young Ian is.

Sure, he may be just over a century old, but he's still the youngest person in the room.

John's grave voice sounds behind Ian, and his tone brooks zero argument. "Your mate has to have another man's hands on her and is most likely going to be in pain. You need to leave this room so she can get the treatment she needs." I wince at John's tone as Mena stiffens. I instantly feel like an asshole for holding Ian up. I don't realize the implications of what John said until Mena sucks in a breath.

"Mate?" Mena breathes in my ear.

Oh, shit.

Glaring at John for a beat, I stand with Mena in my arms and gently set her on the bench.

"We'll talk about it later, Princess," I whisper in her ear before straightening.

"Oh, sure. In between me blowing up rooms and shocking the ever-living fuck out of people, we'll just pencil it in," she snaps, and the quip is laced with enough sarcasm that it startles a laugh out of me.

"Soon. We'll talk about it soon. Yeah?" I say, even though I have zero plans to do so.

How could I possibly explain the mating? That I couldn't seal that bond no matter how much my body, my mind, screamed at me to do so?

Because I had a death sentence looming over me, and no amount of love, or fate, or optimism was going to change that.

And I couldn't pull her down with me.

Searching Mena's eyes, I'm speared with the bitterness of all the things I'll never have. I'll never have her any closer than she is right now, never get to merge our souls into one.

Mena raises an eyebrow at me, suspicion all over her expression before her face falls already wiping it clean of emotion so quickly I almost miss it.

She'll never really be mine, I remind myself.

And that's for the best.

7

MENA

HE'S NOT GOING TO EXPLAIN A FREAKING THING TO ME, I THINK
as Asher's mouth settles into a firm line. His eyes appear half-pissed and
half-sad. Like he's struggling with something but has forbidden himself
from saying anything.

I haven't spent that much time with Asher, but already I can tell
getting words out of him will take some engine grease and quite possibly
a crowbar. Honestly, I'd rather skip the part where he has to let me down
slow.

"Okay. We'll talk about it later," I concede with a shrug, shaking my
head.

In the grand scheme of things, I have a pretty good idea of what he'll
say. I mean, honestly? Who would pick a girl like me? I'm not sure how
this whole wraith mating stuff goes, but if the man has a choice, he has
to prefer a better crop than me.

So what if I felt a connection to the first man probably ever? So what
if I clung to him like a monkey on a tree? So what if I feel safe with him,
a feeling I haven't had in a very long time? So. What.

I don't deserve a man like him. After the lives I've taken... happiness
just isn't in the cards for me.

"I'm fine. It's not going to hurt. I didn't even notice it was dislocated before now. It'll get popped back in, I'll be able to heal and walk. Win-win. You can go," I tell him, my voice sounding almost dead, even to my own ears.

I need to cut this off as soon as possible. His expression is reluctant, but he needs to go.

"Come on, Asher," Evan says at his elbow, as she escorts him from the room, practically dragging him behind her up the stairs.

My eyes linger on the steps long after he disappears behind the door at the top, and in those moments, I take the time to shore up my heart. I don't need to rely on Asher. I shouldn't even lean on Aurelia or Rhys or prey on the hospitality of the wraiths.

I should do the right thing. For once, I should do what I've always needed to.

But I need to be able to walk to do it.

Taking a deep breath, I shift my gaze to Ian, who is patiently waiting for me to get my shit together enough to let him do his job.

"Thank you for helping me. I'll do my very best to rein in my ability. If you feel uncomfortable putting your hands on me, I understand," I say, my words burning me as they haltingly tumble from my mouth.

"Meh." He shrugs. "You haven't killed anyone yet. I'll risk it."

That flippant comment is like an open-handed slap in the face, so sharp I have to close my eyes to the sting. It takes everything I have in me not to cry, but a hole splits wide open in my chest all the same. The blistering ache of regret settles in my belly, and I have to grit my teeth against the burn.

When I open my eyes again, Ian's dark-brown gaze is knowingly compassionate.

"If I could teach you to do it yourself, I would, but this can't be done alone," he whispers, "You'll just have to try your best, okay?"

Nodding, I brace myself more against my abilities than the pain. I center myself, concentrating on Ian's kindness, his happiness. I focus on his light, refusing to let the blight that is my powers affect him.

Gently, he places his right hand on the inside of my knee, his left on the outside of my thigh. He locks eyes with me and inclines his head. Taking a deep breath, I nod for him to continue, and he wrenches my leg, pulling it to him first before letting it go.

The joint makes a horrible squelching noise before I hear a huge *pop* and the bone settles back into place.

And then I promptly empty the contents of my stomach on Ian's boots.

"Well, that hurt," I rasp before passing out right there on the bench.

"You simply cannot rely on your abilities, Mena. What if you are drained or injured? You have to learn how to defend yourself, darling girl," Papa urges, tossing me the blade. I awkwardly catch it, fumbling a little before nearly slipping in the forest bracken beneath my slick shoes. I look at my father's face—Aurelia and I inherited our sharp cheekbones from our father. Aurelia also got the paleness of her eyes from him.

My poor sister. Sometimes I just wish I could hug her. She is so alone in this family.

"Is there some reason I need to train for combat—which is ridiculous in its own right—wearing this silly corset?" I ask, irritated, sorrowful, and marginally confused.

My mother just started making Aurelia and I wear them. She said they were what all respectable young ladies wore, and now that we were becoming women, we needed to dress appropriately. I hate them. They are tight and uncomfortable and completely unnecessary.

"I am only twelve, can't I be a child a bit longer before the world falls on my head?" I only talk this way when no one is around. If my mother or Aurelia heard me be this bold, I would never hear the end of it.

"No. You cannot." Papa's voice rises nearly to a shout.

Appropriately chastened, I duck my head. He's right, my father. I cannot wait for a better time, can't relegate myself to the wishes of a whimsical child.

My abilities have always been evident, even as a baby, just as Aurelia's have, but now that our monthlies have started, we are infinitely more potent. This frightens my parents, I think—to have two children so powerful. To trust this big of a secret to a child.

I don't tell them that it frightens me as well. That I fear myself.

Fear what I'm capable of.

Fear what I've yet to learn.

Fear what the future holds.

I need to stop whining and focus on the lesson my father is trying to teach me.

"I am sorry, Papa. I know you are trying to protect me. I shall focus," I tell him, my eyes downcast.

"Good. You know, you sounded like your sister just then," he says, amused, and it startles me enough to snap my gaze back to him. He seems proud of Aurelia, and I think I love my father just a bit more for that. He so rarely speaks of her to me.

"All right, Papa. Show me how to use this infernal thing," I order in my haughtiest tone.

Giving him a bit of my twin since she can't be here to do it.

***

I WAKE UP NESTLED IN THE SOFTNESS OF A DOWN COMFORTER, the covers pulled up to my chin, remembering that one happy memory of my father.

Before the training started in earnest.

Before Aurelia was shunned.

Before I killed him.

I wish I had known. I'm pretty sure I would have left back then, saved them from the cancer that is my very existence.

A faint sizzle and crack of a fire hisses in the periphery of my consciousness, and I become aware of my body for the first time in a long time and immediately regret it, wishing I could go back to the painless state I was in before.

My first thought is how hungry I am, followed directly by an ache in my joints so fierce my appetite dies a quick and bloody death. A soft rap on the door pulls my focus from my bones to the blonde oak door. The doorknob turns, and Aurelia's head pops around it to check on me. Her expression wary, she shoulders the door open, holding a tray laden with every bland breakfast food imaginable. There is toast and scrambled eggs and small golden-brown cubes of potatoes.

"I figured you'd be hungry, and I brought some over-the-counter painkillers to help with the remnants of the pain," she says. "We had Ian check you over while you were passed out. He didn't find anything else during his exam, and you should be healed up in a few more hours."

Her voice sounds like she's saying she's sorry, but I have no idea what she has to apologize for. As always with my twin, I never have to wait to know what's on her mind. She sets the tray down on a wide mahogany nightstand. She sits next to me in the crook of my hip, handing me two white pills and a glass of water. Gleefully, I pop them into my mouth, taking a swig of water to wash them down.

"I'm sorry I left you to deal with that by yourself. I know it can't be easy being here, and it's my responsibility to make you safe. I didn't see you before. I-I should have seen you in that hell. I should have go-gotten you out," she says, her voice clogged with tears and guilt, the sound giving me a strange ache deep in my chest.

"Why would it have been your responsibility? You didn't shove me in that cell. As far as I can tell, all you've ever wanted from me is to be a sister to you. I'm the one who failed you. More than you know. I have done things... Things that I wish I could take back," I end on a whisper.

Well, isn't that the understatement of the century?

I bite my tongue to avoid blurting out my sins. As hard as our parents were, as much as she went through with all of us, I still have no doubt she would hate me forever for what I've done.

Aurelia grabs my ruined left hand, giving it a gentle squeeze. "I think we've all done things we're not proud of. We've all done things we wish we could take back. My sins are no different from yours. No matter what you think you've done, no matter what sins you think you have on your soul, I'll still love you."

All I can do is nod. Sure, she says that now, but I can't know how she'll react when I tell her. I can't know... And I can't lose her before I'm ready.

I need these last few days.

Studying her face, I memorize what is already burned into my brain. The shape of her eyes, the slope of her nose, the sharp cut of her cheekbones. My eyes drift to the colorful swirls on her arms. The artist who created them makes me almost weep at their beauty. I look closer and notice slight ridges hidden underneath the pictures.

Scars.

"Your tattoos are beautiful," I say as I reach out to touch her arm. It is a testament to how much she trusts me that she doesn't flinch when my fingers make contact. I haven't seen ink like this. As a phoenix, I am no stranger to tribal markings—most of our males have them in some form or another—but these are something else. Realistic pictures mixed with brilliant splashes of color cover every available millimeter of skin from her wrist to the crown of her shoulder.

"Thank you. I drew most of them. My friend Max inked them."

"Do you think I should get my scars covered?" I ask, but I'm not sure I care either way.

I haven't inspected my body in ages, not after the first few scars. I was vain before my incarceration. I knew I was beautiful, and it was a solace to me when my life changed from simply lonely to completely solitary.

Well, I'm not vain now. I haven't seen a mirror in half a century, and I'm not sure I want to. Looking down at the exposed skin of my arms, I run a single finger over the crosshatched raised flesh. My abdomen and legs are worse. There isn't enough ink in the world to cover this much skin.

"I think you should do what feels right. I covered my scars because I needed to, but ink may not be the right answer for you. You'll have to decide for yourself," she tells me, drawing my gaze from my ruined skin to her face.

"When did you get so smart?"

A ghost of a smile crosses her lips. "Fairly recently, if you can believe it. Rhys helped me get my shit together. I wasn't doing so well for a while there. Now that Iva is out of the picture and my Aegis finally came back, I'm doing much better."

"Did you lose it?"

"My Aegis? Yeah. Iva did something to me—suppressing it or draining me—I'm not sure which, and I was in real pain for a while. I was beginning to see why Oracles cut their eyes out, if you catch my drift. When she died, it started coming back. Now, I'm as strong as I was before."

I knew the feeling, only Aurelia's Aegis helped her. Mine didn't do the same for me.

"That's what I'm worried about," I whisper, dropping my gaze.

"We'll figure it out. You're not alone anymore," she says as she reaches for the tray piled with food, placing it on my lap.

"Now eat until you can't fit in another bite. I actually cooked, so be happy. It's a rare occurrence."

I choose a piece of toast, tearing off a corner and popping it into my mouth, relishing the buttery goodness.

"Well, the toast passes inspection," I say around a mouthful of food.

"Good. Eat up, and then you can have a nice Epsom salt bath. It'll help loosen your muscles and ease your joints. Then we get to try walking. It'll be a hoot," she says with a smile and cute scrunch of her nose.

I can't be the cold one anymore, can't be stoic or aloof when this great surge of gratitude steals through me. Lurching forward, I give her a hug hard enough to startle an "Oof" out of her.

"Love you," I murmur.

"Love you back."

I squeeze her for a second before pulling back and stuffing my face, earning me a brilliant smile.

I'm going to miss her so much, I think, vowing to soak in all of this goodness. It will need to tide me over when it's all gone.

When I'm gone.

8

ASHER

I'M LOSING IT.

I'm losing everything, and as much as I claw and scrape and grab, time is slipping through my fingers. John is fading away.

Mena.

She is the one thing I never had ahold of. The one thing I wanted most. But she isn't a thing. She isn't a toy I can't play with, some inanimate object I just can't grasp. She is a person, a woman, probably the strongest person I have ever met. And the one person I will never, ever have.

As soon as Evan dragged me from the gym, I went to my quarters and systematically destroyed every breakable object I could get my hands on. Lamps, tables, mirrors... I even ripped apart the books and smashed my favorite reading chair. I needed to release all my helpless anger, my righteous indignation at the unfairness of this whole mess. I couldn't protect her. I couldn't take her pain away. I couldn't rip her tormentor to shreds. I couldn't do anything.

I need to let her go.

But as much as I have to release her from my heart and mind, my selfish heart refuses to let her go. I gave up on my destruction, and went to the king's chambers, looking for a reason to not crawl in a hole and die, maybe. Looking for a reason to matter. Looking for anything that will keep me from staring death in the face.

I caught John trying to travel—the smoke swirling around him in great churning arcs, but never taking him anywhere. A piece of my heart withered at that moment, and I had to grit my teeth against the burn.

In the beginning, traveling is difficult—almost unbearable for a young one to achieve. It takes so much out of us, but the pain eventually goes away. At the end of our lives... it becomes impossible.

John is at the end.

I knew where he wanted to go, so against my better judgment, I called Cam—who now seems to have a permanent crook to his nose—and we took him to Olivia.

And here we sit, Cam and I, perched on dainty chintz chairs in the sitting room outside the royal suite. Cam looks ravaged, pain stark on his face, and I realize—like me—he is losing a father figure, a mentor, a friend. It's so easy for me to discount Cam, to take the fact that he's a flaming asshole most of the time for granted.

But he's losing his life—just like me.

Unable to take the silence anymore, I gingerly rise from the fragile chair and stalk to the sideboard to partake of the bourbon stash. I'm even nice and pour Cam a healthy measure, handing him the glass without a word. His expression is almost grateful as he accepts the tumbler, but he doesn't sip the amber liquid. Gently, he rolls the glass in his hands, staring into the mouth of the tumbler as if it holds the secrets we've all been searching for.

Studying the silent man for a moment, I realize I missed something big. I wouldn't have known anything were amiss if I hadn't witnessed the drip of tears falling from his chin.

"Cam?"

I've never seen my cousin cry. Not when he broke his arm in three places as a child, not when he had to put his favorite dog to sleep, not after he came back to us covered in soot, informing the king that his parents were dead. Not ever.

Cam opens his mouth to speak and then shuts it again. He takes a swig of the bourbon as if it will give him the courage.

"I don't know if you ever realized this, but my mother was a horrible woman," he begins, his voice sounding like it has been run over broken glass. I'm so shocked that he's talking about his mother that I can't say another word. Cam has always hated talking about his parents.

Struck dumb, I simply nod for him to continue.

"She was violent and mean, and I've never met someone who could be so evil and not be a Revenant at the same time. She drilled it into our heads that phoenixes were a blight on this world, and it only got worse after your parents turned. Father tried so hard to temper her, but... It's the hardest thing in the world to hate someone who is already dead."

Cam brushes away the tears with the back of his hand, pausing his story to take another fortifying sip of bourbon.

"I lied to everyone when I came back. It wasn't the phoenixes who killed my parents. After my cousins were hit, I went to check on them like I said, but when I got there... my mother had turned. She was eating the flesh of children. Children, Ash." Cam covers his mouth with a hand, trying to hold in a sob.

"And my father was letting her. He was just letting her do it. Do you know what it feels like to have to send your mother to Hell because she was just that evil? To know my father stuck by her, even though she was such an awful woman? I took her head." He sniffed, and then took a deep breath.

"I took her head and killed them both and then I set their house on fire. And I blamed them all—every single one of those winged devils, even though it wasn't them. It was me. And I am so *angry* that Olivia is none of that, and I can't figure out what is killing her. Olivia has been nicer to me than my own mother. She has loved me and treated me like I was special even though I am probably the biggest asshole in the known universe. I know we won't live much longer after they go, but it's going to be worse than losing a limb for me. I wanted to tell you I'm sorry for how I've treated you before it's too late. You are my family, and I have been no better to you than the woman who bore me. I am sorry, cousin," he ends on a whisper, the poison he's been holding onto finally pouring out of him.

I say the only thing I can.

"I forgive you," I tell him, amazed he has divulged this much about himself. Cam has always been almost one-dimensional to me, but now I can see he is more than the foul-tempered jerk he presented himself as. This hurts my heart more. I have discounted him as nothing more than a nuisance, and I am soundly ashamed to know he has endured probably more than he will ever say.

"We should have been like brothers, Cam," I murmur. "Better late than never, yeah?"

He nods and sips his bourbon again. We lapse into a comfortable silence for a while before John opens the double doors to the bedroom. His face is destroyed—there is no better word for it.

"I need both of you to get Aurelia for me," he rasps, and Cam and I spring to our feet.

"She's not—" Cam starts, but his voice catches.

"No. Not yet. But I haven't even asked for her help. If she can see what's hurting Olivia, if she can help... we need to utilize her gifts," John explains. "I have kept this under wraps too long."

Why didn't we think of this earlier?

"Is West still with you and Evan?" I ask, making sure John is covered while we are gone, my guardian instincts kicking in even at the end.

"Evan is sacked out on the chaise, and West is passed out on the floor beside her. I'll wake him up if that'll make you feel better."

"If you wish, sir," Cam concedes.

"Oh, please," he counters, leaning heavily on the door. "I've been putting you boys through hell for these last few months. The least I can do is make sure I'm covered."

"Come on, we knew you were an asshole before we signed up," Cam fires back. "Comes with the job."

John inclines his head with a wan smile and turns, heading back into the bedroom. I look at Cam and we both nod, blackness surrounding us as we travel back to the house in Grand Lake. I have traveled this path so many times over the last few months; I don't need to concentrate on getting there. In just a few moments, we appear in the middle of the game room next to John's favorite chair.

"Are you going to be cool?" I ask Cam.

He grimaces in chagrin and gives me a grumbled, "Yeah."

Since the game room is empty, we search the rest of the house, looking for Aurelia. Well, Cam is searching for Aurelia. I am thoroughly failing in my endeavor to keep away from Mena and can't help but search for her instead. My body's clawing need to find her courses through my veins, overriding every other thought.

My resolve to leave her alone lasted all of two hours.

I am a pillar of strength.

It's instinct that helps me find her. Like an ironclad fist wrapped around my heart, it pulls me, tugs me through the house to the pale wooden door of a bedroom. I know she's there. It takes all my strength not to travel to her side, not to break this door in, to calm myself down and politely knock on the rough pine boards that make the handsomely crafted door. I rest my forehead on the cool wood.

My first knock is faint—no one would hear it even in the stillness of the house. My second one a minute later is only marginally louder, but the door opens, and I'm unbalanced for a moment. Not just from the door moving in front of me, but the sight of Mena upright and walking.

She stands tall, only three or so inches shorter than me. Her board-straight, dark mahogany hair is down and long, almost brushing her elbows. Her slender limbs are covered in a thin, open-weave, green sweater with sleeves so long they cover the heels of her palms, and with a collar so wide, it falls off one shoulder, exposing two, thin, delicate black straps, and a scar on her neck I hadn't noticed before. It's a silvery almost blue that looks the most organic of all her scars. It spans the length of the slim column of her throat and has an eerie resemblance to a lightning strike—a single jagged bolt stretching to her collarbone and the forked tines reaching into her hair like fingers.

It takes a minute for my eyes to move from that beautiful, yet haunting scar and take in the rest of her. She is wearing jeans that flatter the gentle swell of her hips and flat open-toed sandals on her feet. She looks casual and relaxed, an ease to her I haven't seen before. It still shocks me how fast phoenixes heal. Half a day ago, she couldn't even walk, and now she stands tall and proud, and so beautiful it blanks my mind and steals my breath.

"Is there something you need, Asher?" she asks softly, her expression worried, but also open and searching.

She's happy to see me, I think, and my heart does a nice little double bass tap against my ribs.

"Uh... are those new clothes?" I ask lamely. Considering she's worn nothing but a hospital gown in my presence, I sound like a fucking moron.

She gives me a look that tells me she agrees and says, "Yes. Evan got them for me in Oregon, evidently. Somehow she knew my sizes," she ends with a slightly uncomfortable shrug.

"Good, good. Do you know where your sister is? John needs her help," I blurt.

Her face falls, looking hurt for a moment before wiping her expression clean. When she speaks, her tone holds just a hint of pain, and I feel like an asshole. She can't think I don't want her. Not when my default mode around her toggles between stalker and possessive asshole.

"She's training with Aidan in the gym," she says, her voice flat.

Jesus. She seriously must think I don't want her. I have to fix this. I have to. I can't let her think... I have to make her see it. I know it is the bond that draws me to her, but it isn't what keeps me here. It's her quiet strength, her worry for a stranger whom she might have hurt, it is the way she seems to have picked herself up and dusted herself off from nearly a lifetime of adversity.

It's all that is her that keeps me. That makes me know that this is what love must feel like.

Less than a day. How can I care for—no, love—someone in less than twenty-four hours? How can I fall this far this fast?

So much for staying away from her.

The knowledge that keeping myself from this woman is no longer an option hits me like a fist, and I struggle to pick the thread of the conversation back up again.

"I guess he's trying to get her back for smacking him on the head with that bokken," I joke, trying to put the smile back on her face.

"She hit him in the head? A wraith? Aren't you guys supposed to be harder to fight?" she asks, the worry for her sister puckering her brow.

"We are. Your sister is deadlier than any wraith I've ever met," I reassure her. "She put our King on his ass the last time they sparred. I'm not worried about Aurelia at all."

Mena wrings her hands. "I didn't realize she was so... adept. The Aurelia I knew so long ago couldn't hurt a fly. Well, she could slay one with her sharp tongue, but a fly could kick her ass."

"Yeah... not so much now. Do you want to come with me to get her?" I ask, even though I think she'll say no. I'm shocked when she steps from the room like she's jumping off a cliff.

"We're just going to walk, right? None of that swirly black smoke stuff. Because that was unpleasant," she says, her nose scrunching into a wince.

"Yeah. Traveling takes some getting used to. We can walk if you want," I concede as I grab her hand. I don't hesitate or flinch, touching her as I would anyone else.

Except I don't want to hold anyone else, don't want to love anyone else.

I'm certain however long I have left on this earth, I'll never love anyone as much as I love this woman.

9

MENA

STARING AT HIM IN SHOCK, I LET HIM LEAD ME DOWN THE HALL, not coming out of it until we take the first steps down the staircase, when I have to watch my footing so I don't slip. It takes until the blood comes rushing to my cheeks and my heart decides it wants to trip out of my chest before I remember I'm staring at him like a moron. Dropping my gaze, I try to remember if I've ever felt anything close to this.

His hand is rough and warm, and I'm so happy I didn't shock him that my knees go rubbery. I never thought this was possible for me. Simply holding his hand, my fingers tangled with his, is farther than I've willfully gone with anyone. I've never dated anyone, never been close to anyone. I'm one hundred and eighty years old, and I've never even had a boyfriend.

How pathetic am I?

My joints quit aching after an incredibly relaxing bath in a tub the size of a small swimming pool. Aurelia spooned in some lavender salts from a giant cork-topped canister and left me to it. Well, she left me to it after I gave her the look of death after she offered to wash my hair like I was a toddler.

After I got out, my hip had finished healing, even most of my bruising was gone, and I could walk around for the first time in a long time. It is amazing how quickly one can heal if they are fed and not repeatedly reinjured. I got to primp and play with the makeup—not that I put much of it on—and brush my hair with something other than my fingers. After the relative metric ton of conditioner I used on my hair—that was possible. I felt pretty for the first time in forever, and I felt better after I saw the outfits Aurelia laid out for me on the bed. I'm not sure how Evan knew my sizes, and I shudder to know how she knew what my bra and undie sizes were.

Now, here I am, holding hands with undoubtedly the most handsome man I've ever met, and I can't trust it. It's too good too soon.

The incredible rush turns sour in my belly, and by the time we get to the gym, I'm cold again. It stings after the warmth and happiness—so much it steals my breath. There is this emptiness growing in my chest—so deep and wide I don't think it'll ever get filled.

I need to enjoy this time. I need to clutch every second to my breast and keep it there for as long as I can. I won't get very many more moments like these, and it doesn't matter if they're real or fake.

They'll need to last me a long while.

My feet reach the final step of the last staircase trailing behind Asher, my hand still twisted in his and I see Aidan and my sister dancing around each other on a blue mat. The pair of them hold wooden sticks shaped like swords—bokken if memory recalls—and my sister looks like a ballerina, spinning and stepping out of Aidan's way as he tries to get in a hit. Rhys sits on a nearby bench, laughing so loud I can barely hear the music blaring from the tiny speakers at his feet. Aurelia is completely unscathed, but Aidan's nose is bloody. He's also listing a little to his right, nursing a broken rib or two by my guess.

Asher whistles and the combatants lower their weapons, but when Aidan tries to leave the mat, Aurelia smacks him on the shoulder with her sword. Aidan rolls his eyes before turning and bowing to my sister and then stows his weapon on a long wall filled with what looks like every knife, gun, and sword ever made.

"What's up?" Aurelia asks, eyeing our joined hands, her face blank.

"John wants you to see Olivia. He thinks maybe you can figure out what's wrong with her," Asher informs her, but he does something strange then. He tightens his grip and puts our joined hands behind his back, taking a step in front of me, positioning his body slightly in front of mine.

"Asher, what are you doing?" I murmur. "She isn't going to hurt me."

He turns his head, casting his gaze back at me, giving me such a look of pain and anxiety, I can't help but be confused.

"No, she's not going to hurt you. She's going to take you away from me, and I don't want to let you go yet," he admits.

My heart tries to beat its way out of my chest before dying a slow, agonizing death. He's going to let me go. I shouldn't care, because at some point I'll be leaving, but... it still burns.

"But you will let me go," I say, sounding almost like an accusation.

"I suppose at some point I'll have to. But it doesn't have to be right now, and it doesn't have to be today." His low voice is almost pleading.

I do the only thing I can. I lie.

"I'm not going anywhere," I murmur, and the expression of relief on his face is almost enough to cure my bleeding heart. And if it weren't bleeding out from the lie that I just told, it probably would have.

"Good," he says.

"Asher," Aurelia calls.

He tears his gaze from mine to study my petite but menacing sister.

"If you hurt my sister in any way, shape, or form, I will set you on fire and smile while you die screaming. Do you understand?"

Rhys pipes in from the bench, leaning his body to the side to be seen around Aurelia. "And I'll help."

Asher nods and smiles, not the least bit scared. I don't like them threatening him—especially when it will most likely be me hurting him—but Asher doesn't seem to mind.

Cam takes that moment to smoke into the room, and I slide a little farther behind Asher. His fingers tighten around mine, and the tension in my chest eases a bit.

"I talked to him. He should be nicer now," Asher says as he steps to the side, bringing me with him.

"Let's go. Maybe if you can find out what's wrong with Olivia... maybe there's still time," Cam chokes out, and Aurelia's eyes start swimming.

"I'll do my best. I'm ready. Let's go," she says, even though she's wearing workout clothes and no shoes.

"Shoes, Gorgeous," Rhys says as he tosses her flip-flops by her feet and grabs her hand as she slips into them.

"Cam, take Aurelia and Rhys. I've got Mena," Asher says as he turns to Aidan. "You coming?"

"Nope," Aidan says. "Holding down the fort. Give Olivia our love."

Asher pulls me closer, wrapping me in his arms.

Wait a minute.

I didn't know I was going.

The feeling of ripping apart is accompanied by the swirling smoke of his traveling from the relative safeness of the Black compound to the unknown. I nearly pass out when we settle on solid ground.

Mother of all that's holy, please let us never do that again, I think as I rest my forehead on Asher's chest, taking deep breaths to ease the pain from the traveling.

"Oh, my God, that is awful. Why do you people do that all the time? Christ on a fucking cracker..." Aurelia says as she puts a hand over her mouth, looking green around the gills. Rhys looks just like he always does, yet his brow is lined with concern for my tiny sister. He leans down and whispers in her ear, and Aurelia nods—taking a deep breath —and rallies.

"It doesn't hurt us. Quit being such a wimp," Cam teases, jostling her with his shoulder good-naturedly.

"Shut up, jerk," she grumbles, rubbing her belly. "Good to see you got the asshole out of your system."

"Anything for you," Cam grouses as he ushers us through a set of mahogany double doors inlaid with an intricate circular carving of a tree of life—well, the doors seem old enough, they *could* be from the tree of life.

The room beyond is dim, only lit by a single glass-bowled lamp on an accent table next to a chaise, loaded down with a sleeping West sprawled across the upholstery—his massive boot-clad feet resting on the floor on either side of the chair. Curled on his lap like a purring cat is Evan, softly snoring with her hair looking like a hurricane hit it—the curly blonde tendrils half-covering West's face.

John and who I'm guessing is Olivia are curled in the huge, beautifully carved walnut king-size sleigh bed, covers all but obscuring a tiny body, playing little spoon to John's big spoon. Two walls of the room appear to be floor-to-ceiling windows, the thick drapes drawn, obscuring the outside view.

Asher releases me for a moment to gently rouse John, but Aurelia's yell startles the room into wakefulness.

"Oh, my God! Every wraith out of this room right now!" she exclaims, her eyes turning a bright blinding white, heralding a vision that will likely steal her sight for several minutes.

"Why did you wait so long, John? Why did you wait to tell me?" she moans, one of her hands in a tight fist and the other gripping Rhys' so tightly it might snap from the strain.

Her back begins to bow like the invisible strings of Fate are pulling her chest to the ceiling so hard her toes start to point, bending her body further and further. Her head makes a slow ticking motion as her eyes stare off into the distance—seeing things that have yet to be. I hope she sees something she can prevent because her expression is more than a little grim.

Grim would be a step up from this.

This is devastated.

This is agony.

This expression is hell.

I have to snap her from whatever hell she's seeing. From the little bits I've gathered, the last few weeks of her life have been awful. She doesn't deserve more. Her Aegis is barely visible, and I find it almost funny that I hadn't noticed it before now. To me, it is very nearly cute in how small it is. How small and faint, it is barely visible to the naked eye. It isn't hurting Rhys, merely coating him in the soft blue netting of electricity, but he looks afraid to move, so I do the only thing I can.

In the chaos of people jumping from their slumbers and John starting to yell in objection, I grab Aurelia's wrist and pull her out of Rhys' grasp, rocking her head a little. Her Aegis pulls mine from my skin, sucking a bit of my energy before her eyes dim and she takes a long slow blink.

"Thank you. That was bad. Oh, no..." she mutters as she puts a hand to her mouth.

Her face is an awful grayish-green and Rhys gives her a nearby trash can just as she plops her butt down on the carpet and loses whatever she had in her stomach.

"You okay, Gorgeous?" Rhys asks as we both kneel down next to her, and in response, she heaves a second time, gripping the trash can like a lifeline.

"Jesus, baby. It's okay, I'll be okay," he murmurs as he rubs her back.

"Poison... She's being poisoned," she gasps in between heaves. "Get all the wraiths out of the room. Don't let them touch her..." she says, the words coming out in halting sobs.

"How? How is she being poisoned, Ari?" Evan asks, and her voice sounds like a car crash—all twisted metal and broken glass.

"I ca-can't tell you. You'll touch it. You'll get sick. You can't get sick. You have to—you have to le-leave. Everyone has to leave," she moans, her eyes squeezed shut, her breaths sounding like they are being ripped from her lungs.

"Clear the room," West says as he grabs Evan by the waist and Asher yanks Cam by his bicep and drags them out. Evan struggles, begging to stay, but West tightens the band across her stomach and hoists her over his shoulder in the last few feet.

Through all this, even with the chaos and her daughter screaming at the top of her lungs, Olivia doesn't rouse. She doesn't move. Beneath the pale-blue down comforter, she looks like she's barely breathing.

"Tell me," John orders. "Tell me what is wrong with my mate!" His face is ravaged, tears clogging his voice and racing their way down his cheeks.

"You can't touch it," she pleads and only begins speaking again when John nods.

"There's Bixbite in the locket, and the locket itself is protected by a spell. It's draining her. I need you to help Olivia to sit up and lean her forward. Try and get the necklace to hang forward. Mena. Shield yourself. Get her locket. Do-don't be gentle, and don't to-touch the pendant. Only the chain. Do you hear me? Even you could die touching that pendant," Aurelia gasps out the last words as she starts shivering.

"I don't know how to do that," I hiss. "What if I kill her?"

"Try," she growls through gritted teeth. "You're the only one of us who can do this and not fucking die. You are the only one of us who can save her life. Just. Do. It."

Closing my eyes, I take in a huge breath trying to steady myself. No one is going to die.

I'm not going to kill anyone. I won't.

I loosen the reins on my Aegis—just a tiny bit—just enough to feel a surging warmth coat my body. It always feels so good in the beginning. But then I have to leash it again, and it's like a shoe that doesn't fit. First, it's just uncomfortable, and then it's blisters and blood and broken bones.

John is so careful with Olivia, and now that the covers aren't concealing her face, I can see just how sick she is. Her skin is a pale unlined alabaster, but her pallor is almost gray, highlighting the fact that her hair is a brilliant white that only blonds get when they age. She is unresponsive, rail-thin—not that I can talk—and her pale-pink nightie hangs from her shoulders in great gaping sweeps of fabric.

Then I see it: an oval, antique silver locket engraved with scrolling leaves and tiny roses. It's so lovely, but I can feel the evil pouring from it —one better, I can see it—a putrid red and swirling black. Staining the locket, staining the skin of her chest, staining her light.

I don't register when the door opens, I'm still watching the necklace like one would eye an angry snake, but when Asher's fearful growl reaches my ears, I know I have to act. Wincing as I reach for the chain, I grip it with my fingers as I rip it down, breaking the clasp. As soon as the clasp breaks, Olivia takes a deep breath.

Relief swamps me until, out of the corner of my eye, I notice Asher move with purpose toward me.

He's not supposed to be here. This thing, whatever evil it holds in its depths, will hurt him. I know it. So I do the only thing I can. I take off running toward the window, tucking my head and shoulder as I hit the drapes, the glass breaking around me.

It takes less than a second to realize that the house sits atop an enormous mountain at the edge of a cliff, and I am free falling to the earth.

Oh. Shit.

IO

ASHER

Trying to hold onto a pissed-off, scared-out-of-his-mind Cam is like trying to grip a wet fish—fucking impossible. West is no help because Evan has gone from the focused, linear-thinking, happy-go-lucky woman I've known all her life to a half-mad she-cat on steroids. Forcing Evan to do anything is like signing your own death warrant, her destructive abilities able to level entire cities. Maybe more now that she's older.

West is attempting to calm her down gently, but he's not making much headway.

I'm more focused on keeping everyone calm, but I feel this pull, this hook in my chest, and I can't stay downstairs playing babysitter. Out of everyone, I should be the staid one. I should be the one that is constant —that follows orders—but it's me who breaks rank first and heads upstairs before anyone can grab me.

Something is wrong. Mena is in danger—I can feel it in my bones.

For some insane reason, I take the stairs instead of traveling, and when I open the doors, I vow to regret that sixty-second trip for the rest of my life.

I don't remember growling or moving, but when Mena looks up at me, I'm already trying to get to her—trying to get her away from that darkness clutched in her fist. I see the decision cross her face as soon as she makes it. She'll do anything to save the people she loves.

Somehow, some way, that now includes me.

No, no, no!

"Mena!" I roar, forgetting my purpose, ignoring my oath to John, only knowing that I'll follow her down to the depths of Hell if I have to.

It takes less than a millisecond to process the room. I see it, but then again, I don't. Everything is on the periphery of my mind. I know John and Olivia are there. I know she's breathing. I know John is alive. I know Aurelia and Rhys are gaping in shock at the broken window. Rhys is standing, moving to help, but I'm not sure what good a phoenix with clipped wings is going to do.

I pass them all like they're standing still and dive out the window behind the woman who holds all that is left of me.

My power rises to my skin like a flash flood—rumbling, rushing, surging through my pores. The blackness of the smoke coating my skin like an oil slick is at odds with the morning sunshine, cutting the shadow of the mountain like a knife. She is falling fast, the fabric of the drapes she took with her floating away on the breeze like a ribbon in the wind. Mena twists and tumbles in her descent, but I don't hear her scream or cry.

And still, she plummets.

I've never felt as helpless in the three hundred years I've walked this earth as I do at this moment. Following her as she falls, I wonder if I should try to catch her or if I should attempt to grab her. If it will kill us both.

As I'm pondering our imminent death like a spineless pussy, she decides to save herself.

The bright-blue light of Mena's Aegis shines like the surface of the sun as she phases midair, her wings sprouting from her back with a great wrenching scream of agony—the first sound I've heard from her through the wind rushing past us—and my stomach twists. Her wings catch the air, buoying her, and I fall past her for a moment before I smoke out from my descent, reappearing at the bottom of the gorge. At the base of the sharp, craggy cliff, a thin ribbon of a stream slowly widens to a small river as it descends over the rest of the mountain.

River rocks of every shade of teal, amber, and magenta cover the shore.

I watch her as she flies. Her wings are beautifully fragile and match her better than I could have imagined. The feathers are a vibrant turquoise at the tips, darkening to rich cobalt, and then to the softest blue-black I have ever seen in my life. I've never seen wings like hers. Most adult phoenix wings are red, orange, or yellow, never blue—and their flames are never this color. And then I understand. Her wings, her fire, they are all the blue of her Aegis.

Mena doesn't fly straight to me. In fact, when she lands several feet away, the frustration on her face tells me she wishes I hadn't followed. If I wasn't sure of her feelings at the moment, when I step closer, she growls at me to get back, her wings fluttering like a bird's in agitation. Her windblown hair flows wildly down her back, and her ripped sweater hangs from her shoulders, exposing the black camisole underneath. She drops the locket to the rocks at her feet, shaking out her hand as if she's trying to get feeling back into a sleeping limb.

I feel the pull again, the need to go to her, but her growl turns feral.

"I told you to. Get. Back. This is poison. I have to destroy it. Now, back up, Asher," she grits out through clenched teeth.

"I don't want to hurt you." This is a whisper she probably didn't mean for me to hear.

I realize now she's barely holding onto her Aegis. I move back another fifty feet, moving slightly behind a large boulder, and even though that might not be enough, I can't make myself move another inch away from her.

The veins of her power trace over her skin, glowing brighter as she focuses. An orb ribboned with the same threads of her power blooms around her, creating a shield of electricity.

Then, white bolts of light surge from her fingertips, hitting the locket with enough heat and energy, I stumble back on a foot, so I'm not knocked over from the strength of the blast. River rocks fly like shrapnel from a bomb as her bolts of energy slam into the ground. The debris falls all around, but nothing gets within five feet of her before it roasts to a cinder from her shield.

"Is it dead yet?" I call from around the rock, but she doesn't answer.

Only when she drops her shield—her body sagging slightly in the process—do I go to her. I don't go slowly—one second, I'm a hundred feet away, and the next, there is barely a foot separating us. The heat from her flames should burn at this distance, but somehow, they don't. Staring into Mena's blazing amber eyes, I realize I need to hold her. Need to kiss her. Need her to know I'm hers.

Her expression grows worried, unsure but slightly relieved at having me near. But she doesn't break her gaze.

I know it then without really realizing how. Her flames won't burn me. Her Aegis won't hurt me. I'm in her heart just as much as she's in mine and that makes all the difference. The Fates put me on her path, and somehow—some way—they're paving our way.

This clawing need fills me, and I can't hold back anymore. Doing my best to go slowly, I cup her face in my hands, grazing the soft skin of her cheeks with my fingertips. Mena's eyes close as I press my lips to hers, her mouth opening with a gasp at just the right moment. When our lips finally collide, I slide my tongue into her mouth to taste her. She tastes like mint and woman, and the longer I kiss her, the more I want her— the more I need her. She moans, and it spears through me, straight down my spine to my dick.

Jesus.

Mena's hands curl into my shirt at my waist, and if my eyes were open, they'd be rolling back into my head. Wrapping my arms around the small of her back, I tug her closer. Our chests collide, pulling a soft gasp from her lips, and I can't fathom a better sound.

Her fingers find their way to my cheeks, and then some wall in her crumbles because the kiss goes wild—all lips and teeth and hot gasping breaths. Our hands start roaming, and before I know it, I've hoisted her up, and her legs are around my waist. I find my hands on her ribs just under her breasts, and I have to fight with myself, so my thumbs don't go rogue and graze her nipples like they're aching to do.

Fuck. This is going too fast. Even though I don't want to, I break the kiss, resting my forehead on hers for a moment to catch my breath.

After several beats of silence, her eyes open, the irises still glowing amber, and it sends a thrill of satisfaction through me. I did that—I made that secret smile on her face, I made her breaths grow heavy, I pulled that moan from her throat.

She brings her thumb to my lips, rubbing the kiss into the lower one.

She seems fascinated with them for a moment before her mouth drops to mine again, but she's the one leading this time. I'd let her set me on fire if she keeps kissing me like this.

When her tongue spears into my mouth, the taste of her wrenches a groan from deep in my belly that seems to urge her on. Her legs tighten around my waist, and I feel the softness of her feathers, the heat of her flames cocooning us. I'm wrapped up like a bow for this girl and it's the best feeling in the world. She gently breaks the kiss, rubbing her lips across mine back and forth.

"I've wanted to kiss you since the second I heard your voice," I murmur against her mouth, and that pulls her gaze to mine again. Disbelief colors them as if she doesn't realize how gone I am for her.

"It was my first," she admits shyly, her head ducking into my shoulder so she doesn't have to say it to my face.

I'm glad she can't see the smug satisfaction on mine. I probably shouldn't be happy she hasn't had the affection she so rightly deserves, but I am. I'm pleased I'm the first person to love her.

Even if I probably won't be the last.

That weak thought sobers me, and my arms band tighter around her back as if someone were about to tear her away. I wish my brain would stop reminding me that I'm dying. That I don't get to keep her. I wish it would just let me have these few moments of peace.

"One hell of a first kiss, Princess," I murmur against the bare skin of her shoulder, doing my best to keep the sadness out of my voice.

"Really?" she asks as she pulls back, searching my face for a hint of deception—vulnerability stark on her face—and I know she finds none. That kiss was the best moment of my life.

I nod, and the smile I get in return steals my breath. Fates, I love this girl. Bond or no, mate or not, I realize at this moment that I'd love her anyway, and I can't seem to keep my lips from hers.

"We should probably stop kissing and let them know I didn't go squish," Mena says against my mouth.

"Probably," I mutter, and even though I don't want to let her go, I hoist her up so she can unwind her legs from my waist, and I notice that when her wings are folded and resting, the tips drag the ground.

"You want to come with me, or on your own?" I ask, and she shudders for a second.

"I'll go on my own. No offense, but traveling makes me want to vomit. I'm not doing it if I don't have to," she admits.

"That seems to be the usual phoenix response."

"I'll meet you up there," she says as she takes off with a giant sweep of her wings, the displaced air causing rocks and dirt to go flying.

She is beautiful as she flies, her spirit free. That is something I've come to crave in our short time together. I want to give her more of that, whatever way I can.

She circles and climbs until she's perched in the now-broken window, and only then do I go back up there, smoking in right beside her.

When I get to that room, I wish we'd never come back.

II

MENA

Fear, resentment, and rage fill the room. Clawing me, choking me, making it hard to breathe, making it hard to think.

Everyone is so angry.

They are angry at me for jumping out of the window. Upset with Asher for following me. Livid that Olivia was poisoned right under their noses, and no one noticed. The room is empty except for my sister and Cam. Olivia is being tended to, and I can't imagine what it would feel like if even one more person was here.

Aurelia is screaming at me, Cam and Asher are at each other's throats like they're three seconds away from having a death match in the middle of the king's bedroom, and I'm finding it difficult to be in a space with so much hostility.

I wish I'd never stepped another toe into this room.

I wish I hadn't phased back.

I wish I hadn't broken that last kiss.

I should have just kept kissing him.

I haven't let go of Asher's hand since he appeared next to me at the broken window, the wind whipping around us in the maelstrom of voices, screaming at the top of their lungs—their words lost as they tumble over each other. I'd already felt lambasted by Aurelia's tongue by the time he got there, and it only got worse when he showed up. My Aegis keeps spiking, and the louder Cam yells at Asher, the more agitated I become. I can't explain why, but someone threatening Asher makes me territorial and so angry, a thick, red film covers my eyes.

I feel my body heating up, and without letting him go, I somehow find myself in front of Asher, my teeth bared, and I can hear an ugly hissing sound—the first real sound to break through the thick buzzing in my ears. It takes me a second to realize the hissing is coming from me.

Cam's expression goes from murderous to wary in a second, and Aurelia's eyebrows shoot up her forehead so hard I think her face will break. In unison, they both take a generous step back.

"Stop. Yelling," I snarl, and they both nod. I turn to Aurelia and growl, "What, exactly, would you have had me do? You said it was poisonous. I took care of it. Stop bitching at me."

"And you," I say focusing on Cam, "stop acting like an asshole. For all anyone else knew, my wings could have been clipped or cut off entirely by Iva. I could have gone splat protecting you all, so excuse me if someone gave a shit about my fucking life. I didn't see anyone else at the bottom of that damn gorge, so if you have a problem with Ash making sure I lived, you can kiss my ass. Now, we all know my abilities are volatile at freaking best. I'm holding on by a thread here so I would appreciate a moderate tone of voice from here on out. Is that understood?"

Aurelia nods, appearing appropriately chastised, and Cam looks like I slapped him across the face.

"I'm sorry, Mena," he says, clearly contrite and the change in his tone is remarkable. "You did us a kindness, and I... I am proud my cousin was brave enough to make sure you were safe."

I nod in acceptance, deciding I've said enough, but it isn't until Asher whispers in my ear that I realize my fingers are sparking like downed power lines.

"Princess," he says as his hands find their way to my waist, "everyone is calm, you can drop your shield."

His warm hands on my body when no one should be able to touch me turns a key in my chest. I have to fight the urge to run my fingertips over my lips. I want to run away with him, I want to get out of this room and this house and just go.

Even if that is the worst plan I've ever had.

I want to get away from all these people and hostility and death. Because I feel death coming, it rises like an ache in my bones that something awful is just around the corner, and I want to grab Asher's hand and run.

"Right," I mumble and try to focus on calming down. Before it drops, though, Aurelia catches my sparking fingers. She's just as immune to my Aegis as Asher is, and it feels strange to have such gentleness after so long without it. I don't know what to do with it.

"I'm sorry I yelled. I was worried and felt useless because I couldn't get to you. You did the right thing, even if I yelled at you for doing it."

"It's okay," I say with a small wan smile and pull my fingers from her hands. "How is Olivia?" I ask, changing the subject from apologies and my shortcomings to something we should actually be worried about.

"She's awake," Aurelia murmurs, but I can see on her face that isn't the good news we were hoping for. Their anger and fear make more sense now, and I can't help but feel an unexplained clawing sadness for this woman I don't know.

"Do you know who poisoned her?"

Aurelia's face screws up as she closes her eyes, reviewing whatever hell she saw. "I see blackness as an entity in my mind, but it keeps changing shape. They flicker and morph into someone else every few seconds—their faces are covered in black smoke. I think it could be several people, but I feel Iva's footprint here in the magic. It might be a group, but Iva was at the helm, and that scares the shit out of me."

That scares the shit out of me, too. A shivering tendril of fear snakes its way down my spine, and I can't stay in that room. I can't be anywhere near here. Bolting through the tree of life door, I hit a warm wall of a chest. When Asher's strong arms wrap around me, it is a war in my body over whether to run from him or relax into his embrace. My brain says "run," but my heart is driving this train, and my shoulders go slack.

"She's dead, Princess. She's not coming for you. You're safe," he murmurs soothingly into my ear, but he doesn't know. He couldn't have any idea what she's like. He's only heard the stories, but he hasn't seen.

"She'll come back. She always comes back. You think she's done, but no. She'll poke and prod and needle. She'll tie you in knots only to unravel you and start all over again. She is the master of torture."

Shaking my head, terror rises in me again. "The worst agony in the world is letting someone think they're free only to steal the rug right out from underneath them. You don't know. You don't. You think you do…" I end on a shriek when I know I started with a whisper. His hands are gently holding my wrists, forcing them away from my face, and it's only now that I realize he's been trying to keep me from gouging my skin with my nails. My chest tightens, and I can't breathe.

I can't breathe.

"Shh, Princess. Breathe, baby," he murmurs, trying to calm me, but all it does is make me want to get as far away as fast as I can.

She'll come. She'll take everything away from me again, and then I'll kill him just like I killed my parents. I can't be with him. I can't stay.

"Let me go. Let me *go!*" I scream, yanking out of his arms, my body vibrating with fear.

"Mena-girl, I need you to calm down," Aurelia says from my left, and I have no idea when she got there. She sidles in next to Asher, and somehow the room is filling up with people again. I'm surrounded, and that flips a switch in me, changing me from terrified to livid.

"I'm leaving this room and this house, and you're not stopping me. Get out of my way, or I'm going through you," I growl, shaking. "All of you."

The circle around me loosens, and I make my escape down a rustic spiral staircase, my feet going so fast I have to grip the railing so I don't bust my ass on the wood. Asher smokes in at the bottom of the staircase, and the growl that erupts from my chest makes him step back.

"I'm not stopping you. I just want to take you back to the lake house," he almost pleads, holding his hands up to stop me. His eyes very nearly beg me, and in their sadness, I can't seem to tell him no.

"Okay," I whisper as I take the last few steps into his arms. He doesn't wait for me to change my mind and cups my face, dropping his mouth to mine, rubbing his soft lips against my mouth, startling a gasp from me. Traveling doesn't hurt this time, and I am uncertain if it is because I'm used to it or if his tongue dancing with mine kills the pain of every ailment I've ever had. It isn't until our mouths part that I realize we're back where we started: at the door to the room I woke up in.

"I know you're thinking about leaving. I feel it. Don't... just don't, okay?" he pleads as his arms band around my back, pulling me into the best hug I've ever had.

I can't help but rest my forehead on his shoulder and breathe him in. He smells like fabric softener and soft leather and the subtle, clean scent of man. The natural scent of his skin makes me want to run my teeth over his pulse point and nibble the skin there. It makes me want to bury my nose in his neck and breathe him in. It makes me forget, and forgetting is a luxury I've never had.

"Leave this house and this fight if you have to, but... please don't leave without me. I'll go with you. I'll make sure you're safe," he murmurs against my temple, his fingers burrow under my hair, and that sobers me.

He can't go with me.

He shouldn't be anywhere near me. How long could I possibly go without hurting him? Without killing him? Sure, he seems immune now, but what happens when I lose it again? I know I'm just a time bomb, ticking down to my eventual end. The best I can hope for is to reduce the collateral damage.

No, he can't come, but I nod, anyway. Lying with my body so I don't have to with my mouth, praying that when I leave this world, he forgives me for my dishonesty.

When I return to the safety of my room, I pull off my clothes for another shower—the fear and bitter stain at the thought of Iva making me itch. I need to wash her away. I step under the still-warming spray, and my mind drifts away to my time in that cell.

"MENA." I HEAR MY VOICE WHISPERED IN THE BLACKNESS. I HAVE been here so long, hearing my name when no one is there isn't new. I hear lots of things in the dark, and none of them are good.

But this voice is louder than my thoughts and the whispers of the dead that scream in my ears for vengeance. Louder than the echoes of Iva's taunts and my mother's screams of agony as I burned her to ash.

"Mena. I need you to listen to me. I need you to understand," the female voice says. "I have done horrible things. I have neglected you, and for that,

I am sorry. But I will do anything to save this Legion. I will manipulate, and sacrifice, and I will kill to save them. I will sacrifice a few to save many. I will do horrible things for the greater good. And you can hate me for that. I hate me for that. And after all I've done, I will probably go straight to Hell once this life is finished. And I will accept it, because in this life I was given, I did not choose my path, but I accept my destiny. So, you can dislike me, even hate me, all you want. I accept that. But I will save them. I will make sure that they are on the right path."

The female voice pauses, the faint but cultured British accent one I'm familiar with.

"I will bring them back from the darkness. But I need your help. I need you to stay here. I need you to endure this hell, and I will help you when I can. Your sister is coming. Not for a while, but she is. I need you to stay here until she gets you out. And when you get out, I need you to leave her and hide. People will come for you. They will try and steal you and make you a slave to feed their thirst for power. I need you to hide until Evangeline Marie Black has been made the Wraith Queen. When she's made Queen, go to her and help her. She will make sure Iva dies and stays dead. Do whatever you can to help her. And once Iva is gone, make sure you live. Live for all the time we stole from you and all the pain we caused. Stay strong, cousin."

That voice isn't mine, nor is it the tortured screams of my parents.

This one is real. Someone is in this barren room with me, and it is the one person who I thought of as neutral, if not a little evil.

Apparently, my cousin, Nicola, isn't as bad as I thought.

I NEED TO LEAVE.

I have to leave them all. I shouldn't have stayed this long.

And as these thoughts roll unbidden through my head, I allow myself just these few minutes to grieve.

12

SHE'S GOING TO LEAVE ME.

That thought runs on a loop through my head, and I want to rip the house apart in my rage. I should go back to John and Olivia and see how I can help, but losing time with her tears my chest apart worse than anything I can imagine.

I want to do my duty, but I need her more than my next breath.

She's going to leave me.

And I can't remove myself from this hallway. Even when Aidan comes in behind me, I don't move my gaze from the door, separating me from the only woman I could ever want.

"John wants you to get back to the house, Ash," Aidan says gently from behind me, and I close my eyes to the battle waging in my head, resting my forehead on her door.

She's going to leave me. One way or another.

"I'll make sure she stays here, but you have to go," he says, and it takes a moment to realize I spoke my thoughts aloud. When I finally open my eyes and look at the man I've called a friend for so many years, he winces at my expression.

"I swear it, Ash," he promises, and I believe he'll try, but nothing and no one can hold Mena if she doesn't want to be.

"John needs you, Ash."

My gaze lingers on the door a moment longer before I travel to my King, dreading every moment I'm away from Mena. It takes seconds, but it kills me. I can't fathom how John could be away from Olivia for even a minute without losing his fucking mind. How can he stand this? This clawing, gouging ache. It rips at my chest, and I have to focus all my energy on not traveling back to her. I knock on the chamber door, feeling torn in two.

"Enter," John calls, his voice grave, and I open the carved doors for what seems like the last time.

"Sir," I say with a slight bow of my head when I reach the edge of the bed. Olivia is sleeping in John's arms, and her pallor is much better than when I saw her last—a faint rose in her cheeks that has been missing for these last few weeks. Her hair is still white, and that's how I know she's still dying before John says a word.

"Bixbite. Fucking Bixbite," he mutters, tears coating his lashes, running in rivulets down his face.

When Aurelia said poison, she wasn't kidding. Bixbite or Red Beryl is one of the few poisons that can kill a wraith. Sure, many substances can harm us, but never kill. A gemstone in the beryl family can only be found in large enough quantities in one place—the Wah-Wah Mountains in Utah. Bixbite is so rare, the practical usage of it is almost nil. In fact, I've never actually heard of it being used except in cautionary tales told to children to get them to straighten up and act right.

I don't know how to respond, so I don't. I've never been a man to fill the silence when I don't have anything to say, and I'm guessing a "Gee, that sucks," won't be received well.

John sifts his fingers through his mate's hair, the white of her locks a shock of pale against his tanned hands.

"I release you," he whispers, not taking his attention from his mate's face.

Uh, what?

"I will not sentence you to die when you have found your mate," he tells me wearily. "That goes against everything in me, everything I stand for as a leader to betray our most fundamental law. I release you."

If he's releasing me, there is no hope for Olivia, no hope for him, and the pain is like losing a limb—blotting out all my questions of what is going to happen next. My composure breaks and my knees give out on the unforgiving hardwood.

John is a better father than the one I had, and Olivia is... she is the best Queen I could have asked for. These two souls are irreplaceable, and if I weren't mated, I would gladly honor my post and die with them. As it stands, I don't know who could fill their shoes. Evan isn't allowed to succeed to the throne without a mate—archaic, I know—and West has all but refused the mantle.

"How much time?" I choke out, the tears I'm hanging on to clogging my throat.

"A few weeks. Maybe a month. Aurelia wasn't certain, but it's not going to be today. We have some time to figure it out."

A month. So little time? I've lived five lifetimes, and it isn't long enough. Now that I have a mate, a hundred wouldn't cut it, and it angers me that he's so calm.

"Get your mate, Asher," he says. "She needs you more than I do. All this mess can't be helping her, and now that we can guess Iva's involved... she needs you more."

Even though he is giving me something I need, it stings that he doesn't want me here. I give him what he asks for anyway no matter how much pain it causes me.

Old habits die hard.

I stand, bowing to my King, then I travel out of that room and that house back to Mena's door.

Aidan looks up from his book, perched on a barstool that he must have stolen from the kitchen island.

"Back so soon?"

"I've been released," I murmur, and Aidan flinches as if he's in pain.

He knows that means our King doesn't have much time, and he's eliminating collateral damage.

Aidan stands, his book forgotten, falling from his fingers. "How long?"

How long until we lose our leader, until we lose the one man that unites us all? How long until our whole world changes?

"A month at most." I scrub my hand down my face. "Trouble's coming. Can you feel it?"

"Yeah. West isn't going to step up, is he?"

"I don't know. But we need to be prepared for anything. I'm going to take a few days and see if I can get Mena to stay with me. I won't be any good to anyone if I can't get her to do that."

"Do what you have to, man. Just remember that kidnapping is a felony," he says, giving me a backslapping hug before he smokes out with his chair.

My way now clear, I knock on Mena's door. After a few moments of no answer, I try the doorknob. It turns smoothly, and I poke my head in to see if she's okay. When I notice the bed is empty, I lose it, slapping the door open hard enough to make it hit the wall and bounce back, smacking me in the shoulder.

I don't hesitate as I bust through the bathroom door.

When I find her in a heap on the floor of the shower, my mind goes blank, and my body moves on its own. As I open the door, I don't process that she's naked. I don't think about the deep scars gouged into her back. My hands find her shoulders, and I turn her so that I can see her face. It doesn't matter that I'm soaked to the skin, my blue button-up plastered to my arms and chest.

She's breathing. And conscious. And sobbing so hard her body bucks and shudders with them. I pull her onto my lap and just hold her for a moment.

She's alive. She's breathing. She's okay.

But then my brain finally catches up, and I realize she's bleeding from a gash on her brow bone.

"What happened, Princess?" I ask as I cup her cheek, inspecting the cut.

"I-I...can't deal with all of this. I can't...be... here," she says through gritted teeth, trying to stem the flow of her tears. But she's failing. She can't get ahold of herself and her body bucks again.

Right now, I just want to protect her—want her to feel safe.

"Then we'll go. We'll pack a bag, and I'll take you to my place. It's private, and we can get away from everything for a couple of days. What do you say?"

She seems to think about it for a moment, searching my face for an answer before closing her eyes, squeezing fresh tears from her lashes.

"Okay." She nods, her lips pressed so hard between her teeth, the edges turn white.

I pull on her bottom lip with my thumb until she releases the soft skin from the punishment of her teeth.

"But first, we need to take care of this cut," I say as I climb to my feet with her still in my arms, refusing to put her down for even a second.

She slips her slender arms around my shoulders, and I realize she may fear everything else, she may want to escape, but she'll escape *with* me instead of from me.

Progress.

Reaching for a towel hanging from a brushed bronze hook, I wrap the white terry cloth around her before setting her on the granite vanity.

"You never told me what happened," I press, unwilling to let it go.

"I slipped."

"That much I gathered. What made you slip, Princess?" I ask as I pull a first-aid kit from the bottom drawer. Unzipping the bag, I pick a few sterile gauze pads from their wrappings and start cleaning the blood from her face. The cut is already beginning to close, and I wait patiently while she fidgets with the towel to avoid answering me.

"I couldn't breathe," she admits, her lip trembling, "I was trying to figure out a plan. I was going to leave, but every time I thought about going, I couldn't breathe."

Her gaze pleads with me, torn between an apology and begging for help. I can't fault her because she couldn't leave. She feels the same pull I do.

"And how do you feel about leaving with me?"

Mena's lips curve into a shaky smile. "Like it's something I need to do."

"Good," I whisper, relieved. "How does your head feel?" I wipe the last of the blood from her freshly closed cut—the small mountain of blood-stained gauze on the vanity making my stomach drop.

"I've had worse."

I'll bet she has. I take in the exposed skin of her shoulders and arms, the creamy softness interrupted so frequently by the rough rivulets of her scars. I don't want to think about what she's gone through in that hell. If I do, I can't promise I won't stash her in a safe place and then find every person who lived in that house who didn't save her and torture them until they wish they were never born.

"Are your eyes going to turn black every time you look at my scars? Because I'm pretty sure that will put a damper on our relationship."

I feel like an asshole. My innate sense of justice is fucking things up all over the place. I'd hate it if she felt self-conscious about them, so I go about distracting her in the only way I know that has a chance in hell of working.

"My eyes are tied to my emotions just like yours," I say as my hands find their way to her knees, parting them to situate myself in between her bare legs. I can feel her answering gasp in my dick.

"They change when I'm angry or frustrated, or aroused," I murmur in her ear. "My eyes turning black doesn't always have to mean bad things."

When I run my lips along the soft skin at the column of her throat, she grips my wet shirt in her fingers and pulls me closer. At this point, I'm cursing the godforsaken towel covering her and the roughness of my wet jeans against my stiff dick. But then her warmth filters in through the denim, and I'm finding it hard to think about anything but getting her mouth on mine. When our tongues finally collide, my fingers find that fucking towel, ripping it from her wet skin.

Her moan in response is almost more than I can take.

The rip of my shirt in her greedy fingers barely registers in my ears, but when the warm skin of her breasts hit my cool flesh, the very last vestiges of my control go up in smoke. Our hands tangle at my belt, and I'm so fucking turned on, I let her work the leather while I run my hands up her legs to find her slick, wet heat with the pads of my thumbs.

Wanting to taste her, I drop to my knees right there, grabbing her ass in my palms and dragging her to the edge of the vanity. Her palms smack the granite, bracing herself, and I can't fathom why that one little sound makes my whole body clench. Before I'm overcome just from the smell of her, I look up, checking her face. Eyes heavy-lidded, her mouth is open slightly as she sucks in panting breaths.

I was her first kiss. I'll be the first man to touch her this way, and while I want to take, I only want to take what she wants to give me.

"Say yes," I growl. "Tell me I can give you this."

Mena's eyes blaze amber as she nods. "Yes. I want you."

My mouth makes contact and the taste of her... fucking hell. Her sweetness on my tongue, the moans vibrating from her throat. All I want is to make her scream, make her lose herself, make her fucking come. I slip a single finger into her, and her back bows hard enough to snap a vertebra.

Nibbling at the lips of her sex, I work my finger in and out of her before giving her a long slow lick. Fuck, she tastes good. I slip in another finger, curling them as I concentrate the efforts of my tongue on her swollen clit. It doesn't take another second before she comes all over my face, wet and screaming.

After I work her through all her aftershocks, she's the consistency of wet spaghetti. Her damp hair is matted against her face and the mirror behind her head, clinging to the glass like a frog on a leaf. Her chest is flushed from her neck, past her breasts all the way down her stomach.

I have never seen a woman as beautiful as Mena in my whole fucking life.

I want to ask her if she's okay, but I'm not sure she's capable of coherent speech at this point, not to mention I hear the heavy *thud* of footsteps in the hallway, doing their damnedest to kill my hard-on. It doesn't quite work, because I just watched the love of my life come for the first time, and I have plans for her for the foreseeable future. And most of them require zero clothes and whatever sweet condiment I have in the fridge of my cabin.

I wonder if I have strawberry preserves in my refrigerator.

"I'd ask what that smile is for, but I have a feeling you'll show me when we don't have a herd of freaking elephants stomping outside our door," she rasps, and I realize she must have screamed loud enough to wake the whole house. Good thing the vast majority of the residents aren't here.

Shit.

My mind focuses on where everyone else is, and the bitter sadness comes rushing back, choking me. I rest my forehead on her thigh and force it to the back of my mind. My mission is to make sure Mena is okay. Screw everything else.

I stand, plucking her from the counter and carrying her back to the bedroom. I give her a swift kiss on her rosy lips and set her on the bed. I cup her cheeks and dive in for another quick kiss.

"Get dressed and pack a bag. We're going on a trip," I murmur against her lips and promptly travel from the room.

No more interruptions, no more drama. Just me and Mena and a chance for her to heal.

13

MENA

IT TAKES A FEW MINUTES TO GET MYSELF TOGETHER BEFORE I can A—stand up and B—focus enough to pack a bag. I've heard women talking about orgasms, but *holy shit*... I've obviously never had one. My sexual experience is limited to fade-to-black romance novels from the 1950s and '60s and some naughty translations of Shakespeare.

Well, that, and my first week under Iva's care.

I was only raped the once, and it kills me that my mind drifts back there after the beauty Asher showed me. It makes me feel dirty and soiled for an awful moment before I manage to shove it back.

In my soul, I know the difference between what that guard took from me and what Asher gave. I was a participant with Asher. I wanted it—more, I needed it. Fifty years is a long time to come to grips with sexual assault, and even though I didn't have anyone to talk it out with, I was taught enough about love to know what was taken from me wasn't my fault.

I didn't ask for it, and I didn't deserve it.

If I'd venture a guess, Iva probably coerced or brainwashed that guard to rape me—not that it stopped me from killing him when he tried to do it again or his friends when they attempted it. Even if they were coerced, I still don't feel a single iota of guilt for killing them, and I don't care if that makes me a bloodthirsty devil. I'm allowed to save myself from going through that again.

Heaven and Hell be damned.

What I do blame myself for are my parents' deaths. If I'd had more control, if I hadn't had to hide my abilities for so much of my life, I might have been able to save them. I might have been able to stop myself.

But when I cast my mind back to the deep pulsing agony of the aftermath of my assault, I'm unsure of any control I could have obtained in my long life that would have made even a little bit of difference. That scenario was orchestrated with only one inevitable outcome. Iva made sure she did the most horrible thing right out of the gate. She was just pleased she only had to do it once to get what she wanted.

At some point, I'm going to have to tell Aurelia, but I dread it. She's been estranged from them for so long, I'm not sure how she'll react when I tell her they've been gone from this earth for a very long time.

Will she hate me? Will she even care?

I dress in a sapphire-blue tank top, dark jeans that have a slight flare to the hem, silver T-strap sandals, and a thin, pale-blue, floral print cardigan. I'm not sure I'll ever be comfortable dressing in anything that doesn't cover my arms and back. The more I think about it, the more I want them covered with tattoos.

My sister had a good idea to take her pain and make it beautiful.

I find a brown leather weekender bag on a shelf in the walk-in closet, and pack enough clothes for at least three days, stuffing them into the bag haphazardly. On my way back from the bathroom with a full-to-bursting toiletry bag, the door bursts open. My sister looks fit to be tied, standing in the doorway.

"Is there something I can help you with, Aurelia? Or do you enter every room like a battering ram?" I ask as I stuff the toiletries in the weekender and zip it shut.

"You're leaving?" she half-yells, her chest heaving in a way that looks supremely unhealthy. Out of the two of us, she should be the most adjusted, but right now, I seriously doubt it.

"I'm taking a few days with Asher to get my head on straight."

"And what happens when the king dies, Mena? Because he will.

Asher is the king's guardian and will die right along with him! I can't let you tie yourself to him only to lose him, Mena-girl," she says through tears, but I feel like she just shot me in the chest.

Staggering, I grip the bedpost to stay standing.

"Asher is going to die?" I breathe in a daze as I stumble back, my knees hitting the mattress as I plop down. A loud buzzing in my ears blots out her voice, but I don't need her to speak to know my decision.

"Yes," I say, my voice cracking.

"Yes, what?" she asks.

"Yes, I'd go with him, even if he was sentenced to die," I tell her, my voice barely audible. "Yes, I'd tie myself to him even if our days are numbered."

She looks dumbfounded for a moment before her voice goes soft, and she asks, "And how many of those numbered days are you going to deal with the fact that you were raped under Iva's care?"

"How do you know that? Did Rhys tell you?" I ask accusingly through tears, as I shove myself back to standing and take a threatening step toward her.

"Rhys knew?"

"He guessed. He wasn't with me for more than five minutes before he figured it out. If he didn't tell you, how did you know?"

"I'm not stupid, maybe?" she says, throwing her hands up before slapping them back down on her thighs.

"You shocked Rhys when he tried to touch you." She counts on a finger. "You wouldn't let Ian examine you without a serious pep talk, even though you had a major injury. Cam scares the shit out of you, but you don't fear Evan or me. You don't fear Asher either, which freaks me out. I don't know if it's the bond or him or you. I don't know if it's a good idea for you to be so intimate with him so early."

She heaves a sigh, dropping the hand that counted all her very good yet invasive points. "But none of that tells me how you're going to deal with it. I don't want you to go through any more pain than you already have. It's not fair to you."

"With Asher, I feel a warmth in my chest that has been missing my whole life. I feel... happy. I can see he cares for me. I can see it in his eyes and hear it in the hum of his voice. I *know* because he puts himself in front of me, protects me...he jumped off a damn cliff after me. So, I don't care if he has days or weeks or millennium. I'll spend that time with him and deal with the fallout later."

Her dubious expression informs me she's unconvinced.

"What would you say if I told you I killed my rapist? And the fifteen other men that tried after him? That I'm more afraid of Iva than I am of any man?"

"I'd say that you were well within your right to do so and that you were smart," she says without blinking, and if there were ever a time to not bring this up, it would be now, but I have to tell her. If I wait, she will hate me for it.

"And what would you say if I told you I killed our parents by accident after I was raped? That I am more scarred by that than I am of the single element of torture that Iva used as a catalyst?"

Aurelia blinks once and hard.

"I'd say there are some things you can't take back, some things where a hypothetical just won't work. I'd say I need the facts," she says, and the shock and agony on her face makes me flinch.

Well, I opened this can of worms, I might as well tell her. Even if this is going to rip me to shreds.

"I was taken in 1965. I'd been working as a gentry at a funeral home. One night after my shift, I was walking home, and someone came up behind me and snapped my neck. I couldn't tell you how many days I was stuck in the dark, alone in my cell, before a soldier brought Mama and Papa in and chained them to the floor. It took days before they were awake, and we knew pretty early on it was because of me that we were there. Why else would they put an Aegis in the same room with Papa, if they didn't want to make sure that he wouldn't see a way out?"

Swallowing hard to dislodge the lump in my throat, I manage to continue.

"They tried to make plans to escape, but I think we all knew that we weren't making it out of there." I pause, taking a deep breath through the choking ache in my chest.

"T-then a soldier came in," I rasp, "and he r-raped me right in front of our parents on the dirty stone floor. And h-he made sure it *hurt*. Afterward, I t-tried to hold it in, but I couldn't—I couldn't hold it. When I woke up, Mama and Papa were ash, and Iva was sitting there clapping, congratulating me on a job well done." My short laugh is bitter through my tears. "Are those enough facts for you?"

Aurelia appears angry and lost, like I just took something from her, and I suppose I have. But I have enough guilt on my shoulders. I don't need hers, too.

She doesn't speak. She doesn't even blink.

"I'd say you've given her enough," Asher rumbles from the doorway, his growl a threat. He looks murderous, fully phased, and if I didn't know better, he seems to be ready to rip my sister limb from limb.

She shakes from her stupor and meets his hard stare.

He doesn't move his black eyes from hers when he asks, "Are you packed?"

"Anything else I need, we can buy," I say, ready to get out of this room and this house. I've done all I came here to do. I don't need to come back for anything.

He holds out his hand for mine, saying, "Then, let's get out of here."

I nod, stopping in front of Aurelia. "I love you, twin. Even if I didn't show it. I kept secrets to protect you and our family, and it kills me that you were mistreated because of them. I will regret my abilities and my part in our parents' death until the day I die. And I will love you even if you can't forgive me."

Moving around her, I snatch my bag, taking Asher's hand with my free one. As my freezing fingers make contact with his smoking taloned ones, a sharp tendril of dread snakes down my spine. Not from his phase or his anger, but the realization that is just dawning on me.

He heard every word.

The tears I tried to hold back crest the dam of my eyelids and fall unbidden down my cheeks. While he may be my safe place for now, our bond and our relationship will be scarred by this. I never wanted to tell him.

Other than informing Aurelia about our parents, I never wanted to divulge my shame to anyone else. Not that I thought I would be around people. I'd planned on going away in seclusion, avoiding relationships and anyone else who I could possibly hurt or kill. If Ash can't forgive my past, that plan might still be on the table.

He meets my gaze, his ink-like orbs piercing my thoughts and my heart, and we travel together, smoking out of the room in a swirl of black. The trip is short, and he releases my hand once we're outside to open the passenger door of a large coal-black vehicle with the word "Sahara" on the side.

"Get in, Princess, and let's get the fuck out of here," he rasps, his voice low, sending a surge of hope through me as I climb into the vehicle using the steel runner board to hoist myself onto the black leather seat.

Maybe I don't have to worry about him not wanting me. Maybe I don't have to let him go. If he only has so few days left, I'll spend every single second I can with him before I lose what's left of my heart when he goes.

14

ASHER

Focusing on the pavement in front of me, I carefully make sure the large all-terrain tires of my Sahara stay between the perforated yellow lines of the winding mountain road. I haven't said a word since I started the SUV, directing the tires away from the cabin and toward my house on the outskirts of Fraser. I'm holding onto my rage by a fragile, fraying thread.

I want to hate Aurelia for making Mena tell her what is most likely the worst sin on her soul, but I can't. I have this needling suspicion that if Mena could have, she would have kept that horror from me, she would have never told me a single shred of the terror she lived through. It makes me simultaneously need to hide her away to keep her safe and let her fly free. She has been cooped up in a cage for so long, I don't want to suffocate her.

I don't want to be another cage.

But I also want to go to the depths of Hell just to rip the flesh from the bones of the bastards who touched her and then kill them all over again. Slowly. Painfully. In ways that would haunt them and make the Devil himself shudder in horror. It scares me that I have that much depravity in my soul, but then again, it doesn't. John has done the same for Olivia, and for better or worse, he taught me how to be a man.

"How much did you hear?" she asks, her voice a quiet rasp in the silence of the cab.

"I came in at 'What would you say if I told you I killed my rapist?' and it was a fight to stay sane after that. I didn't want to eavesdrop, but I couldn't make myself leave," I admit, shifting my stare from the road for the first time since I turned over the ignition.

She's stopped crying, but her cheeks are still damp. I take my hand off the gearshift and reach for one of the hands trapped in between her knees. She weaves her slender fingers with mine, and I breathe a sigh of relief.

"Are you angry I heard?" I ask, hoping if she is, she forgives me soon.

"No. If the tables were turned, and I heard something so horrible happened to you, I wouldn't have been able to leave. You and I do our best to protect one another. I can't explain it, but I can't stand to see you hurt, and I know you can't live with seeing me in pain, either."

"I'm sorry you had to tell her that. I'm sorry it happened to you. I don't know how much guilt you have weighing you down, but I know you don't deserve to carry it."

"Maybe."

"No maybe. You were put in a situation where there was zero chance of a happy ending. You were put there on purpose by a woman who wanted to punish you for some dreamed-up infraction that had nothing to do with who you are as a person and everything to do with what you are. If the shoe were on the other foot, Aurelia would have been in the same boat as you in that cell."

"Maybe," she whispers, her brow puckered in a deep frown, and she is silent for a long while.

"You hungry?" I ask, trying to get her mind off all that has happened in just a few short hours since the sun came up. It's not too far past lunch, and I can't remember the last time I ate.

"Yeah," she mutters, sounding aloof, but she still rubs her thumb against my forefinger.

"We can stop in Granby to pick up some supplies before heading to the house."

"I'm not sure how good I'm going to be in public."

"Things have changed quite a bit since the last time you've been around other people. If you don't want to go in, you can stay in the car while I get what we need," I suggest, "and I can get something quick to make at the house."

Her mouth twists as if she's tasted something rancid, and she shakes her head no. I don't blame her. Leaving her in the car would sting, but I would have if she needed me to. I'm glad she doesn't want to be without me, as conceited as that sounds in my head. The shortcut to Granby is open for the next month or two until the snow moves over the mountain and this pass closes for the winter months.

I pull into one of the few grocery stores in this small mountain town and thrust the gear shift to "Neutral" before setting the emergency brake. Mena is practically plastered to the window, taking in the cars and signs and people.

Granby is a small ski town, with only about two thousand people in permanent residence with plenty of transient tourists in the winter months.

When I get out of the SUV and round the hood, she is still staring out the glass, slack-jawed. I try to cast my mind back to the 1960s to what this town might have looked like then. So many decades have passed in my lifetime that I have trouble singling out just one, and it makes me want to ask what her life was like before her capture—before her life went to hell.

"You coming?" I ask as I open her door.

"Yeah," she says, shaking her head and jumping down from the cab.

She shivers a bit in the brisk mountain air, and I wrap an arm around her shoulders. Our steps fall in sync, her long legs matching my pace with ease. I grab a cart at the entrance and start at the nonperishables, picking up paper products, a pack of extra light bulbs, replacement batteries for the flashlights and alcohol.

"What did you do before?" I ask, not elaborating on what "before" means.

"I was a gentry," she says absently as she inspects a package of disposable lighters as if they are the strangest thing in the whole world. "I worked in funeral homes or hospitals—though it is much harder to phase at a hospital—and ferried souls. I lived quietly, moving every five years or so."

We weave through the entire store, mostly to let Mena inspect each item that catches her eye, and I ask her questions when she's semi-distracted, learning little snippets of her life. The flu pandemic she lived through in 1918 New Orleans, the consumption outbreaks in 1880 and 1890. Most of her stories are about the work she did, but not much about her or her family.

Even peppering her with questions, Mena is still a mystery to me.

We load up with everything we'll need for at least a week at the house. Mena can't believe how many choices there are in products, from the different kinds of toilet paper to the fact that there is more than one brand of light bulb. When the store starts to get busy, her questions dry up, and she sticks even closer to me, wedging herself between the cart and the shelves, avoiding people as much as she can. I pick up the pace, grabbing the things I think we'll need and skipping the crap I know we won't.

The checkout process mystifies her, I can tell by her wide eyes and the eyebrows that have practically crept into her hairline, but she doesn't ask any questions. We leave after paying a sum that makes her eyes nearly pop out of their sockets, and load the Jeep to the brim before driving the last twenty-five minutes to my secluded home on the banks of the Fraser River.

I escape here every chance I can get, which isn't much. I come here so rarely, but having a house separate from John and Olivia was important to me. Maybe it's because I feel like myself here. I feel like this place is mine. It is a modest home in comparison to the Grand Lake cabin, with four bedrooms, four bathrooms, and a nice two-car garage to house my cars and toys. It is peaceful, my closest neighbor is maybe a few football fields away—a small foothill separating us from view. The river is low here, practically a creek in some places, but this year the snow melted late, and the waters rose higher than I've seen them in the last five years.

Mena assesses the house, a gentle upturn of her mouth letting me know she likes the look of my home. But she stops herself from crossing the threshold, stepping back off the porch and retreating to the open space near the Jeep.

"What's wrong?" I ask, worried.

"I need to bleed my power. I used to do it daily before I was captured.

It helps me keep myself under control. I'd hate to blow up your beautiful house," she says with a self-deprecating twist to her mouth. "Where can I go?"

"Any place is good, there isn't anyone with a line of sight to this house. Just not too close to the Jeep, if you don't mind. Cars nowadays are mostly run on electronics."

"Duly noted," she says as she walks beyond the Sahara, putting about a hundred yards between herself and the SUV. She seems to consider it for another moment before walking just a bit farther and then she stops. I unload the groceries as she paces back and forth in the tall grass near the bank of the river. I put the milk, eggs, ice cream, and butter in the fridge and abandon the rest to go back out to watch her. She finally stops pacing and picks a spot a little farther from the water.

Then the light show begins, and I'm glad she's doing this during the day, so her Aegis is masked by the sunlight, scorching through the fat cumulus clouds. Her light strobes like a beacon, bolting from her in great wide arcs of electricity, reaching like fat fingers to the sky. They coalesce into a sphere around her body. It gets brighter and brighter, a jarring buzz coming from the beams before exploding in a sea of fragmented shards of light.

She stumbles, crumpling to the scorched grass like a puppet cut from its strings. The ground is blackened in a fifty-foot circle of ash around her, some of the gritty sand on the banks of the stream melted into a crackled glass. I don't think, I just travel to her, my feet burning from the residual heat coming up from the earth. I snatch her from the ground and move back to the porch before my shoes start to melt.

"I'm okay," she mumbles, her eyes closed, her head listing to the side enough for me to notice the bright-red blood coming from her nose and ears. She's breathing and talking at least, but it makes me wonder how much power she drained if she can't even stand.

"Princess, I need you to open your eyes for me," I murmur against her forehead, my fingers buried in her hair, clutching her to my chest.

"Gimme a minute. I'll be good in a minute," she haltingly mumbles, her eyes cracking open. "That was harder than I remember."

"I fucking hope so," I rumble. "Jesus Christ, you scared the shit out of me. Don't do that again. Fuck the house, and the truck and anything else that you could blow up. I only give a shit about you. The rest is just stuff. Never hurt yourself like that again, do you hear me?" I growl, my voice pitched low so I don't yell, but fuck, I want to.

She nods against my shoulder, but that just isn't good enough.

"Promise me. Promise me you will never hurt yourself like that again."

"I wasn't trying to this time. It's been a long time since I've drained myself. I've spent the last fifty years having Iva leach my power from me, sorry if I'm a little rusty," she grumbles back, sassy.

Iva drained her like this… My mind blanks. She's had to do that over and over again for the last fifty years? I can't stand it. I can't fathom the pain she's gone through. I can't imagine the agony of it.

I can't…

I cup her face and kiss her, rubbing my tongue against hers, hoping my kisses and my touch is enough to heal the weight of her scars.

15

MENA

I LOVE THE MINDLESS FEELING OF KISSING HIM, NOT HAVING TO think or plan or concentrate on controlling myself. In fact, he seems to want me more when I don't rein in my reactions. His response when my brittle control snaps makes me burn hotter, brighter. His groans and growls do something to me, giving me this pulsing ache in my lower belly.

I know we started the kiss off with me in his arms, but somehow, I'm now straddling him. I don't know if I moved or if he moved me, but I love the way my center lines up perfectly with the hard ridge in his jeans, pressing just right on my throbbing sex. I feel wild and out of control, and I love it without the fear or trepidation I thought I would.

The brisk outside air kisses my skin, lighting up every wet place on my flesh where his tongue has touched—the space just underneath my ear, my collarbone, the top of my breasts. I love that cold bite mixed with the hot lash of his mouth on my nipples, the texture of his tongue as it curls around the sharp points.

I can't hold in my growling moan—not that I'd want to.

He rests his head in the center of my chest for a moment, his heaving breath washing over my skin before looking up at me. His eyes bleed from their phased black back to his natural ice blue. He opens his mouth to speak but hesitates and snaps his jaw shut. I can feel the questions rising in him. I can feel his need to make sure I'm okay.

"I'm okay, Ash. I'm not afraid of you or this pull between us. I'll tell you if I'm not okay," I breathe across his lips, trying to dissolve the puckered line of his brow.

"Promise," he rumbles. It's not a question, it's an order, and if it were about anything else or from anyone else, I would balk. But about this? I only nod.

"I promise," I reassure him.

"Not just that. Promise me that you'll stay with me—that you won't run. Promise," he orders again, but my response is less swift this time.

It isn't because I want to run from him, it's because I know his time is so scarce. I grip his face in my hands, stare into his worried face and give him the answer he needs.

"I swear, Ash. I'm not going anywhere," I say, and it feels truer now than it did when I said it this morning. It's not a lie anymore. Dropping my lips to his, we catch fire all over again.

My shirt hangs in tattered strips from my arms, and even though my clothing options are limited, I couldn't care less about the ruined cardigan or the tank top that seems to have disappeared or the bra that I heard rip just before his mouth made contact with my chest. I'm worried more about how I'm going to get his jeans off and how I can get myself naked without losing the hard press of him against my sensitive center.

My question is answered when he moves us, the hard, cold planks of the porch hitting my back, and I lose him for a moment before the crisp air meets my bare legs. I'm naked, my panties following the jeans as if they knew they weren't needed. The moment goes on longer, and I realize he is staring hungrily at my breasts, my stomach, my sex, my legs —his black gaze feeling like another caress on my skin.

Scars be damned, Asher wants me.

His expression says he doesn't even see them, but he gives me more when his voice rumbles a whisper, "Beautiful. So fucking beautiful."

Just that little bit makes me want to have him fill me right here. I don't need a bed or walls.

I just need him.

He still has his shirt on, and I need to know what his body looks like.

I sit up, pulling and yanking the fabric until he gets the hint and reaches behind his neck to tug his shirt off.

His smooth skin is an unlined, perfect golden color as far as the eye can see. Built, thick-muscled, and solid. I've never felt small, being five-foot-ten, I've towered over men my entire life, but Ash makes me feel tiny, diminutive, feminine. I suppose I could feel fear, but I don't. It doesn't matter that he could probably toss me into the next county. I know he won't. I trust him.

I run the tips of my fingers over his chest, the hard ridges of his abdomen. My eyes must look hungry—he looks like a buffet—I only want him. Finding his nipple with my mouth, I torture a groan from his chest, which makes my sex clench. My teeth tighten on the flesh, and he grabs my face with his rough hands, and he kisses me, hard and hot, all tongues and teeth.

Suddenly, I'm not even a little cold. It was brisk on the porch, but we've somehow moved. In the back of my mind, I figure he must have made us travel to a bedroom if the soft mattress beneath my back is any indication. *Handy.* I smile against his mouth and flip us, moving my lips from his to taste the cords of his neck, biting the pulse point like I've longed to.

I never expected I would have sex in the first place, let alone have it be so easy. And it is. I kiss and touch the places I think will bring him pleasure, and he does the same to me.

"Fuck," he groans, drawing out the word until its rumble meets my lips against his skin, pulling a smile from me.

He tastes so good. I wonder what else I can nibble that will make him make that noise. My nipples brush against the dusting of light-brown chest hair across his pecs, leading down the center of his abs, interrupted by the waistband of his jeans, and it sends a surge of wetness between my legs.

His pants need to be off. Now.

He must read my thoughts because his hands move from my hair to his belt, pulling the stiff leather from the buckle and moving to the buttons of his fly. I want to help him, but I am struck dumb at the sight of the denim popping open with each buttonhole, exposing the root of his cock. He's not wearing any underwear, and two thoughts run through my head. I wonder what he tastes like, and in the back of my mind, I wonder if it will hurt. But that last thought is fleeting.

God, I want to taste him, comes back through my brain, and I reach for him.

Our hands tangle at his waistband, pulling, yanking the denim from his legs. I'm not sure when his boots came off, but I'm not complaining. I take in the perfect, tanned flesh, the striations of muscles creating peaks and valleys of his broad chest, the abs and thick cock jutting up from between his legs toward his belly button.

I'm nearly coming out of my skin.

My inspection must go on too long because he's moving, picking me up by the cheeks of my ass and flipping me and then he's over me, dragging us up the mattress, moving in between my legs and I can't wait anymore. I meet his gaze as I reach between us, guiding him to my entrance, notching the head of his dick at my opening. Asher hesitates, his fingers winding their way into my hair, his coal-black eyes holding mine as his thick shaft presses slowly into me.

Making love to Asher is like I always knew it should be. It doesn't hurt, it doesn't feel wrong, and when his voice reaches my ears, I know.

"Mena," he whispers, and I watch his mouth as he says my name, his full lower lip begging for my teeth and I oblige, nibbling it before kissing him for real.

He growls in my mouth as he moves, my hips rocking to match the rhythm of his, and I can't hold in the moan erupting from my throat, even if I wanted to. My legs wrap around his back, sliding him in even farther, touching a place in me I didn't know I had and didn't know I needed to be stroked until that very second. His dark eyes never look away from mine, and I feel them like a caress on my skin. He makes me feel beautiful and sexy, and the love and adoration in them touches an undiscovered broken part of my soul and heals it.

"More. There. Please," I beg, but I don't have to.

He felt me squeeze him, and he knows just where to stroke, he knows just how I need him to move. He sits up, bringing me with him and he gets even deeper somehow, his hands gripping my ass as he moves me, guiding me up and down his thick cock. My back bows with the feel of him, my breasts pressing against his chest, and then I'm coming, my orgasm hitting me so fast it's like a surprise, pulling a scream from my mouth before I can stop it. He moves us again, flipping me on my back, and he thrusts so deep I can feel him everywhere.

I need to kiss him. I need his mouth on mine.

Not want. Need.

My fingers find his hair and I bring his mouth to mine, kissing him through the build of another orgasm, this one bigger, longer. This one feels like it will break me in half, and all the while he's whispering against my mouth, "Jesus, Mena. Fuck, baby, that's so good, so good. You going to come for me?"

The question hits something in my chest because I have to answer him.

"Yessss," I hiss right before it hits me so hard I can't breathe.

I can't think. I can only follow the rhythm of his hips as his orgasm rolls through him, ripping a groan from his throat as his sharp fangs break the skin of my shoulder, but they don't hurt like I thought they would. Instead, they tear another orgasm from me, faster and harder than the rest, wrenching a scream from my throat.

When it finishes pulsing through me, I sag in his arms, spent, melting into the bedding. My eyes close on their own, sleep pulling me under before I can tell him something that I haven't been able to until this very second.

Before I can tell him that I love him.

I WAKE UP ALONE IN THE DARK, FEELING AS IF I'VE SLEPT FOR years instead of what I'm assuming is just a few hours. The moonlight filters in through an east-facing window, and I can make out a bedside table with a lamp perched on top. I hesitate before reaching for the light, wincing as I turn the switch. The bulb blazes to life, illuminating the room with a soft glow.

The bed I neglected to inspect earlier in our haste is an expertly carved sleigh-style, covered in a thick navy down duvet and crisp slate-gray sheets. The bed is decidedly rumpled, the covers mussed from our lovemaking and sleep. I love that I'm in the middle of the bed, not relegated to one side, the pillow I woke up with seeming to have been shared by the both of us.

The side table has a healthy stack of books on top. The rest of the room is clean and tidy, at odds with my thoughts of what a bachelor would be. Across the room, a comfy-looking reading chair has a soft flannel shirt hanging over the back, and I slip it on as I leave the bedroom to search the house for Asher.

"Ash?" I call, moving down a short hallway that leads to an open landing furnished with bookshelves and another reading chair. The dark wood of the stairs is bisected by a soft printed carpet, the pattern nearly indiscernible in the dim. The vaulted ceilings crest over a dark living room, windows spanning nearly floor to ceiling, silver moonlight filtering in through the glass.

I follow the sounds of pans clanging and make my way through the living and dining rooms to a brightly lit kitchen. Ash is shirtless, his bottom half only covered in loose-fitting flannel pajama bottoms and his feet are bare. He's stirring a wonderful-smelling concoction in a saucepan.

"You hungry, Princess?" he asks without turning, stirring the wooden spoon once more before switching the fire off, pulling the cast iron pan from the monster of a stove and resting it on a potholder on the concrete countertop.

"Yeah. How long was I out? I'm starving," I say as he moves to me, trapping me in the circle of his arms against the counter. My lips find his, and he kisses me long enough to reduce my IQ by at least ten points, only breaking the kiss when my belly lets out a roar for the steaming food on the counter. He chuckles and releases me, pulling down two dinner plates from the cupboard.

"I just got up a half-hour ago, but I think we were out for five or six hours." He shrugs. "How do you feel about breakfast for dinner?"

"I think that sounds excellent." I offer a genuine, happy smile. "What did you make?"

"Sunnyside-up eggs and my super-special sweet potatoes," he says, but I know the expression that's now on my face reveals my skepticism.

"Just taste it. If you hate it, I'll make whatever your heart desires," he says as he crosses his heart with his finger and holds up his right hand like he's swearing on a Bible.

He fills our plates and guides us to the wrought-iron barstools at the high counter of the island. Two eggs for me, four eggs for him, and the rest of the available space on his plate is piled high with dark orange sweet potatoes, diced red bell peppers and golden-brown chunks of bacon. He gives me a healthy portion, and after the first bite, I eye his plate, knowing I'm likely going to steal some of his after I fill my belly with every single morsel on my own.

"Okay, you can cook," I admit after my tenth bite. "What other talents do you have hiding under your hat, Mr. Crane?"

He smiles at me, and I can't recall his lips ever curving so far or him looking this at ease in my presence. I want so much for us to stay here, in this moment, in this house, away from the coming heartache. Just stay in this warm little bubble of happiness, away from the pain heading toward us faster than a freight train.

16

ASHER

Mena's giggle is the best sound I have ever heard, only second to her moan. She's laughing at my stories of Aidan and Ian's antics—the brothers are always good for comedic relief. Their stories were needed after Mena explained why she couldn't tell me more about herself.

I'd started asking about her, about who Mena was apart from her captivity, and she couldn't tell me. Her answer when I pressed broke my heart wide open, and I couldn't fathom a life lived in such secrecy.

"I don't know who I am, Ash," she'd said, "Every memory I have has been a lie. Every single day was 'Don't run, don't yell, don't make waves.' I never had an honest reaction to anything before my capture. Every thought filtered through three layers of my parents' rhetoric, and the usual response was 'Don't speak and don't blink.' I don't even know what my favorite color is or what I like to do for fun."

I was speechless for a moment before I told her a story about how Aidan wanted to learn how to crochet and didn't want Ian to know so he tried learning it on YouTube in secret. He ended up getting his fingers trapped in the yarn and Ian had to cut him out of it, and then Ian taught him how to do it right. She giggled from start to finish, peppering me with questions about what YouTube, computers, and the Internet were. Then I told another about how Ian bet Aidan he could out drink him at a TGI Fridays in Denver. Somehow the bartender got roped into it, and she drank them both under the table, and they almost got arrested.

"How'd they get out of it?" she asks, as she leans toward me practically out of her seat. Her legs are trapped between mine, her bare knees brushing against the flannel of my pajama pants. Mena's willowy limbs have filled out a bit in such a brief time. Her cheekbones have lost some of their sharpness, her joints less prominent. Her skin is rosy, flushed with laughter and good food, and I give into the temptation of her smooth skin and run my fingertips up her thighs.

"Ash?" she calls, but I can't take my eyes off my tan hands against her creamy skin. The tails of my blue flannel shirt cover the top of her thighs, and I know there isn't a stitch of clothing underneath the soft cotton. The thought of her bare skin rubbing against the fabric of my shirt makes me want to bite her.

Just a little. Just a little nibble, maybe on the soft skin of her long neck, or maybe on the dark, dusky pink of her nipples. Maybe on the milky skin on the inside of her knee.

The thought of biting her reminds me that I completed our bond and didn't tell her what I was doing or what it means. I didn't tell her that my bite tied her life to mine just as John's is tied to Olivia's. I didn't tell her that my bite made her my mate. Made it so I could feel her heartbeat in my chest, feel her breaths in my lungs. I made it so if she ran I could find her anywhere. I should feel guilty, but I don't. What I did goes against everything I've been taught, and every bit of advice John gave me. But I don't give a shit. I felt it. She was holding a piece of herself back like she was staying with me for a little while and then she was going to go off on her own.

And I just couldn't let her go. But I have to tell her.

"I did something that is most likely going to piss you off," I say, directing my gaze on my hands resting on her thighs.

"How do you know it's going to make me angry?" she asks as she rubs circles along my knuckles and fingers.

"Because I should have asked you first," I admit. "I should have told you what it meant before I did it."

"Okay," she says evenly. "What did you do?"

"I-I bit you," I say, finally meeting her eyes, reaching to the open neckline of *my* shirt, exposing the already-healed scar of my teeth marks on the meat of her shoulder. "I cemented the bond. I-I mated you, tied you to me. I knew what I was doing when I did it. I should have asked you, explained what it meant, but—" I pause, and I can't say any more.

"You were afraid I would say no?" she asks, tilting her head to the side, her eyes unreadable, and a cold finger of dread slices through me.

"I didn't want you to run and me not be able to find you. I didn't want to spend another day without you as mine. I didn't—" I break off.

"And there is no going back, is there? You made the biggest decision of my life for me, just like every single person has done my entire existence," she chastises, and I feel the guilt now. I didn't feel it before, and just like I vowed not to, I put her in a cage.

"I'm sorry I didn't ask," I admit, "but I'm not sorry I did it. I just... I just didn't want you to leave," I confess and pray—just pray—she doesn't leave my sorry ass.

"You should have asked. I would have said yes. Even though you are going to die soon. Even if I only got a few weeks of being yours, I still would have said yes," she says haltingly, her eyes filling.

"Only a few weeks? Do you know something I don't?" I ask, cupping her face in my palms, rubbing the tears away with the pads of my thumbs.

"The king is dying, Ash. That hasn't escaped your attention," she hisses, all pretense of calmness gone. Her eyes are flashing amber, but she holds onto her Aegis for now.

"And he released me from my post before I ever came to you, Mena. I would *never* have tied myself to you if I knew I was going to die. That would make me the worst kind of man. I would never sentence you to death just so I didn't die alone," I murmur, hating that she would think that of me, but knowing I deserve it for my high-handedness.

"You're not dying?" she asks, her body vibrating with either anxiety or fear or relief, and I can't believe she has been with me for this long without asking. Then it dawns on me. She thought I was going to die, and she still would have said yes.

"No, Princess. I'm not dying," I murmur against her lips and then kiss her for all I'm worth, cupping her ass in my palms and pulling her onto my lap. She doesn't hesitate to kiss me back, her tongue meeting mine in a not-so-gentle glide. Her teeth nip at my bottom lip as she digs her fingers in my close-cropped hair. I almost wish it were longer so I could feel her pull it. She's shivering still, but I know it is her need for me making her vibrate. I fucking love it, and I love her, and if I were to die in the next five minutes, she needs to know how I feel.

"I love you, Mena. I wouldn't have done it if I didn't love you. I just want you to stay, please just stay with me," I whisper, my voice clogged with worry and fear and love for this woman.

"I love you, Ash, and I'll stay with you," she vows, looking me right in the eye as she gives me the best gift I've ever received.

I couldn't stop kissing her if I wanted to—which I don't. I don't ever want to stop kissing her. I band one arm under her ass and the other around her back and hoist her tighter to me before standing from my barstool in search of a flat surface—any flat surface. The bar is too tall, but the dining room table—now, that'll do just fine.

Setting her on the dark walnut wood, I love that my bride is sitting her bare ass on a table I hand carved. I pluck open the buttons of her shirt—my shirt—watching as each inch of her skin is exposed. I spread the fabric, revealing Mena's beautiful body, her natural curves finally filling out now that she is properly fed.

I trail my hands up her thighs, circle her waist and ribs in my palms, and then thumb her taut nipples. Her shiver brings a feral growl from my lips, and I pull the shirt off her shoulders, loving the look of my mark on her. I tug the shirt from her arms, and then she's done. With a ghost of a shy smile across her lips, she reaches in, and my cock is no longer trapped in my pajama bottoms. It is free, and in her warm hand, she's stroking me like she knows my dick belongs to her. I suppose it does.

I kiss her, pressing my tongue into her mouth, meeting hers before nipping her lips and moving down her neck over that lightning of a scar, over the crown of her shoulder. Tasting her mouth, her skin, moving to her nipples and her belly, gently pressing her so her back meets the cool, smooth wood. Her ragged pants just spur me on as I pull her ass to the edge of the table, notch my dick at her opening and slowly drive in to the root.

My pants are still half on my ass, but all I care about is the soaking wet warmth on my cock and her pleading moans. She scrabbles for a hold on the edge of the table for a moment before abandoning it to sit up, gripping my chin and moving it out of her way to kiss and lick and bite with those perfect blunt teeth on my neck and shoulder.

I pick her up and turn us, pressing her to the closest wall, ramming into her hard enough to knock the painting or frame or whatever-the-fuck off the wall. The sharp crack of the glass breaking barely filters into my consciousness before I'm pulled under again, lost in her moans and warmth and touch. I wanted to go slow, take my time, but I'm unbidden and unleashed, fucking her, stealing her breath.

She moans into my ear, "Please, God, please don't stop. Don't ever stop." And her words are my undoing. I reach between us, bowing my back just a little to make room for my hand, and I thumb her clit with firm pressing circles. Her body squeezes me, tight enough to almost hurt, and then she's screaming my name.

Before I come, I do what I should have done the first time we made love.

"Mena, I want you to be my wife, my mate, my life. Do you accept me as yours?" I growl my question into her ear, making her shiver in aftershocks.

"Yes," she whispers, and that is all I need to hear. My fangs lengthen just a bit before I strike, piercing her fragile flesh with my cutting teeth as I come unbidden of any guilt, harder than I ever have in my life.

She's mine. All mine, I think as a smile stretches across my face. I am —for the first time in my life—at peace.

17

ASHER

HER MOUTH FINDS ME IN THE NIGHT, WARM AND WET ON MY dick, waking me from a dead sleep. I let her play for a few minutes, loving her gentle sucks mixed with harder, longer ones, groaning at her long licks until I'm about to lose it. I haul her up my body, flipping us until she's pinned under me, and then I make her squirm.

I kiss all the spots I think could possibly elicit a moan from her, the delicate skin of her neck, the crown of her shoulder, the bottom of her breasts, her ribs, her hip bone, before flipping her over to her belly and making my way up her back. I nibble at the gentle swell of her ass before running my tongue up her spine, starting at the small of her back and ending at her hairline. Mena's hips roll, fitting her perfect ass right up against my dick, and then I begin my slow torture as she does her best to break my concentration.

I rake my fangs against the delicate skin of her neck, pinning her to the mattress and winding my arm around her middle and down to find her wet and ready. Her legs spread on their own, and I guide my cock to her opening, sliding into the slickness. I move slowly and stay close against her beautiful back, gently fucking her from behind as our breaths mix and mingle in the quiet of the night.

We never do get very much sleep.

The morning light streaming through the picture window brings me a slumbering Mena, hair wild with sex and sleep, her back cuddled to my front. She is completely naked, and even though I could wake her up again as I did many times last night, I don't. Instead, I opt to slip from the warmth of the sheets and make my way to the master bath to take care of business, brush my teeth, and take a quick shower.

I walk back into the bedroom with a wide white towel wrapped around my waist to find Mena sitting up in bed, the gray sheets clutched to her chest. Half of her face is creased from where she was lying on the rumpled sheet, hair shooting in every available direction, and she only has one eye open. And she is the most beautiful woman on the planet.

"Not a fan of mornings, Princess?" I chuckle.

"Nuh-uh," she grumbles, then yawns wide enough for her jaw to give a little *pop*. Her arms stretch high above her head, causing the sheet to drop, exposing her perfect pert breasts.

"I need a shower. I'm all... sticky. And I need coffee. And... hey! You already took a shower," she accuses with a pout once both her eyes finally open.

"Yes, well, one of us should make the coffee, Princess," I quip and her pout dissolves into a half-smile just before I kiss her.

"That sounds terrific, Ash," she says as she gives me a lingering kiss and slips from the bed to get cleaned up. Her ass gives a gentle sway as if she knows my eyes are glued to her backside, and it takes an enormous amount of willpower to not follow her. Throwing on some jeans, I half-button them in my laziness, setting out to give her another awesome meal.

After a day of lazy fucking on every single available surface—flat or not, horizontal or not—I get to the heart of her. How scared she was of exposure when she was a gentry, how much she hated shunning Aurelia. How her father taught her how to hotwire cars "just in case." How she wishes she had more medical knowledge because "The medicine in the 1800s was atrocious." But mostly, I got to see her smile, hear her laugh, and fall more in love with my mate.

"You made all these pieces?" Mena asks, amazed as she takes in my workshop nestled in the finished basement. I look at the sawdust-laden tables and the curls of shaved wood littering the floor beneath the carving table. The space is considerably less tidy than I normally keep it, but I left in a hurry the last time I was here. I've carved furniture for as long as I can remember. What started as a hobby as a child—anything to be outside—turned into my solace when my world went straight down the proverbial toilet.

Mena is staring at my most recent creation, a circular dining table with a tree of life carved into the walnut wood. The variation in the veining of the wood compliments the carved leaves, making them look like they are being ruffled by a soft breeze. I started it before Olivia fell ill, and it still sits unfinished.

"This reminds me of that gorgeous tree of life carving on the doors of the royal suite," she says in awe, and I can't hold back my chuckle as understanding dawns on her face. "You did the doors?" she asks in admiration.

"Yeah. Before life as I knew it shit the bed, I did much of the furniture for different wraith families. Olivia likes my work, so she had me make the doors. This table was supposed to be a present from John for her breakfast nook," I tell her, and a wave of sadness washes over me.

Olivia and John have been such a big part of my life, I'm unsure of how I'm supposed to move on without them. Having Mena helps, and as if she can sense my swift change in mood, she wraps her arms around my waist and kisses the underside of my jaw.

Today has been one of the best days of my life. Just talking to her, getting to know her responses to the smallest of things, eases the burn in my chest at all the things she has been denied. Mena may not know what she used to like, but she seems to be making up her mind about things as she goes along. Cream and no sugar in her coffee, enough salt to start her own mine on her French fries, and an unwavering thirst for orange juice. I can't wait to see what she discovers she'll like next.

Her kisses are turning sensual, the gentle brush of her tongue against my pulse point sending all the blood to my dick, when the lights abruptly go out. The once-well-lit basement is black as pitch, the evening sky offering only slivers of moonlight through the narrow basement windows. Mena freezes, clutching my waist tighter before she tells me to hush. While a phoenix can't see in the blackness as a wraith can, her ears are much better than mine.

"I think the power was cut," she murmurs against my neck. The hair on the back of my neck stands on end as I phase without thought. I grab her close, ready to travel out of here when she stops me.

"Nicola told me this would happen," she furiously whispers in my ear. "She told me that people would come for me. They would come for my power, ready to drain it as Iva did. Make me a slave all over again. It's why I was going to run—on my own—to spare everyone, but if we run now, they will follow. I am too easy to find." This information would have been good to know before assholes started storming my house, but I can't yell at her. I really want to, though.

I would have run with her. Doesn't she know that?

Through the slight green cast of my night vision, her face is pained—beseeching—begging me to understand.

"Do you suggest we fight in this blackness? I can, but how are you supposed to see? And how will you fight? Do you have any training? Or are you going to rely on the power they crave?" My questions pepper her, rapid fire. I am so pissed at her, but I need the facts.

"I've spent the last fifty years in the dark, I can see just fine. And if you think my father didn't teach me to fight, you are sorely mistaken. The only reason they captured me the first time is because they caught me off guard. If they want me, they're going to have to fight to get me this time," she informs me, her spine straight, her eyes glowing in the dim.

This is the strongest I've ever seen her, the fire that she has had banked for so long finally coming out to play, and fuck if it doesn't make me love her more.

"Weapons?" she asks, and I walk to the west wall, pressing on the shelving just so to release the lock on the false wall, revealing a small weapons cache.

She immediately reaches for a katana, snatching it from its pegs and unsheathing it to check the blade. Satisfied, she sheaths it and unravels the attached back strap to throw it over her head before tightening the strap over the middle of her breasts.

"Got any handguns? I'm shit with a rifle."

Who is this woman? I knew she was strong, but I did not know she was this much of a badass.

I hand her a Sig and watch as she mutters, "Those bastards are ruining my honeymoon," while she checks the magazine and chambers a round. She grabs an extra magazine and tucks it into her bra. She's not wearing much, just a thin, buttoned-up Henley and short pajama shorts, feet bare. I didn't even want her in my workshop with bare feet, and now she has to fight that way. *Fuck.*

I grab a Glock, check the mag, and stuff it in the back of my jeans as a backup. I'm not wearing much either, just jeans and a flannel shirt and no shoes. *Shit.* I grab a pair of Kukris, testing the weight of the blades before stealing a quick kiss from her.

"You stay behind me and stay close," I order, but I can tell she's only staying at my back to humor me if the eye roll is any indication. We move together, up the hardwood stairs to the first floor. I notice that Mena barely makes a sound, the only noise I hear is her soft, steady breaths, and I only hear those because she is barely an inch from me. Her footsteps are silent, her movements economical, and she seems to know to step just where I do to avoid the creaks in the stairs.

The first strike comes when we reach the top of the stairs leading into the kitchen. A wraith I've never met nearly takes my head off with a saw-blade machete. I duck back just in time, and the blade gets stuck in the molding of the doorframe. I take his head quietly with one of my Kukris and Mena catches his body as it drops, gently laying him down out of our way.

"This is a bad man," she whispers shuddering, and it takes me a moment to realize she is talking about his soul. I feel it, too. This is not someone who has been brainwashed or coerced into this. This is a man who would relish the kidnapping and torture of an innocent woman.

The hunger in me rises, the thirst to consume his soul. It's been too long since I feasted on the essence of an evil man, the fatigue in my body screaming at me to take it for myself. My mouth waters.

"Look away," I growl, not waiting to see if she complies as I grab the now-headless corpse, and my fangs lengthen and my jaw unhinges as I consume his soul, breathing it in, siphoning it from what's left of his body. Taking his blackness into me in a swirl of tar-like smoke, his body shrivels to a husk before disintegrating to dust in my fingers.

I look back, and Mena's eyes meet mine. I can tell she saw everything, even though I told her not to look. Her face gives away nothing, and real fear slams into me.

What if she is disgusted? What if she hates me?

"That was gross in an awesomely badass kind of way," she quips, and I breathe a sigh of relief. If I didn't need the strength, I wouldn't have done it in front of her.

"I needed the juice." I shrug, and she nods as we move on. We clear the kitchen, the dining room and have just entered the living room when the gunshots start, exploding a glass-bowled lamp right in front of me. Mena doesn't even flinch and pops off three rounds at the shooter on the stairs like she's playing a fucking video game. All three shots hit their mark: two hitting his chest and one hitting him right between the eyes, and he goes down instantly.

"They're wearing body armor. I can hear it," she murmurs distractedly. Her head cocks to the side as if she's listening to the house.

"There are more. I can't tell how many, but 'a lot' would be my guess," she whispers, and then hell starts. It's moments before we are pinned down behind the couch, caught between the freedom of the front door and certain oblivion by a veritable rain shower of bullets. I try to lay down cover fire, but I'm immediately clipped in the meat of my shoulder close to my neck.

"Fuck, fuck, *fuck,*" I mutter, grabbing at the wound, trying to staunch the flow of blood. I know I have to get us out of here before I can't travel anymore. I reach a bloody hand toward her when she scoots out of my grasp, staying under cover, but out of my reach.

"I need you to get out of this house, Asher," she orders me, eyes blazing gold as her Aegis flashes blue across her skin. Her voice has gone guttural, and I can tell by the curl of her fingers and the clench of her jaw, she has lost all ability to hold it in.

"Leave. Now. I'll come for you."

It kills me to have to leave, and as much as my protective instincts are screaming at me, I know she wouldn't do this if she had any other choice.

"Kiss me, Princess," I growl, and she does.

It's a kiss that says she's coming back to me, and it is the only reason I'm able to travel from that room, leaving her to take care of that hell on her own.

I make it to the truck but just barely. In my last seconds of consciousness, I see the house disintegrate in shards of blue light.

I8

MENA

Seeing the red of Asher's blood in the darkness makes me lose a bit of myself. The part of me that cared but could still leave the people I love behind crumbles to dust in my chest. There is no way I will stand and let these vile men take him away from me. Take away the happiness I've been denied my whole life.

Ash's bloody hand reaches for me, and it takes everything in me to slide across the hardwood away from his fingers. I know what he's thinking. He wants to travel from the raining hail of bullets and get me to safety.

But I don't need saving.

He does.

"I need you to get out of this house, Asher," I tell him, and it kills me to do it. I want to keep him near me. Dress the wound. Make him safe. But I can't do that right now. I feel it rising: the heat, the flames, the energy. My Aegis is pricking along my flesh, begging to be set free.

"Leave. Now. I'll come for you," I growl, my voice a guttural order, one he has to follow. My life is tied to his now, and he has to do this for both of us. Black smoke coats his skin and then he slides away from me into the night. I wait for a few moments, letting him get as far away as possible before I loosen the reins and let my Aegis free.

I stand in the middle of the living room, letting the bullets pepper my shield. Nothing can get in, not unless I let it. I shrug off the katana, marginally upset that I didn't get to use it, and watch the wraiths, the men who stormed this house trying to steal my life, my mate, my happiness away from me. There are less than I thought. Only about ten or so. They stand on the upstairs landing, and on the steps of the staircase, lined up like a firing squad.

My light crawls up my bare feet, warming me, healing my aches, clearing my head. A smile stretches across my lips when it finally crests from my flesh and spills from my body. And I watch their surprised faces when they realize that they made the worst mistake.

With more power than I have ever felt surging from my skin, I let myself go free.

I wake up in a crater where Asher's living room used to be. If I keep blowing up houses, I'm going to run out of places to live real quick.

There is nothing left of the first and second floors, just smoldering timber of the ruined studs, broken and splintered, jutting up from what's left of the walls. The foundation is practically a bowl, the rubble raining all around me, burning to ash where it got too close to my shield. I feel the souls of the wraiths who have perished by my light, and each and every one of them was the worst kind of men. I feel no guilt for ending them. That might make me evil, too, but I don't care.

My only guilt is that I didn't leave Ash before I got too close. I shouldn't have let myself keep him. And now I can't let him go. I need to find Ash and get the hell out of here before the cops or the fire department or more wraiths come.

Tiptoeing through the rubble, I curse my lack of shoes as a piece of glass slices into my foot. I pluck the glass from my arch, blood welling instantly from the cut, but I keep going, making it to the driveway to see Ash slumped against the front passenger tire of the Jeep, eyes closed. His green flannel shirt is stained red, and my knees buckle a bit.

No. No, no, no, no, no, no.

Breaking into a run, I skid on the gravel as I come to a stop inches from him, my knees scraped raw in the slide. I barely feel it. My hands flutter for a moment, my brain blanking.

Blood. There is so much blood. Please don't let me lose him, too.

With shaking hands, I check his pulse and breathe my first sigh of relief at the fluttering beat—my ancient nursing skills finally being of some use. His heart is actually beating. Plus. But the rapid fluttering means he's going into shock—a definite tick in the minus column. I rip the sleeve from his shirt, yanking it off his good arm and wrapping it under his armpit and over the hole in his flesh. I pull it into a knot right over the wound, tightening it as much as I can, without ripping the fabric. It is a testament to how grave his injuries are that he doesn't make a sound, not even a moan of pain at the pressure of the dressing. I need a blanket to keep him warm, and he needs a healer. I can't take him to a hospital. I'm pretty sure they don't stock wraith type O.

Unbidden of my brain, I mutter expletives while I work, searching the wheel wells of the Jeep for a spare key, hitting pay dirt on the third wheel I check.

Thank the freaking Fates.

There is no way I was going to be able to hotwire his Jeep. The last car I hotwired was a 1962 Chevy Impala under my father's intense scrutiny, and that was by the skin of my teeth.

You'd think I'd just be able to zap it started, right? Wrong. I have to tamp down every electrical impulse my body has just so I don't fry a car.

Okay. Breathe. Plan. What is the plan?

First up, getting him in the truck. Now, Ash is a big man, at least two hundred and thirty pounds, and I have to get him into this jacked-up truck without disturbing his shoulder or killing myself in the process.

Super.

I hit the "Unlock" button like I watched Ash do at the store and open the door. I search for the seat release and ratchet the seat back as far as it'll go. Jumping back down to the dirt, I have a mini logistics session in my brain, but quit when I realize I have to hurry. Ash is still losing blood, and I have no freaking clue what I'm supposed to do once I get him in the Jeep. Kneeling on the gravel, I grab his good arm and pull it over my back, easing most of his weight on my shoulders and back. It takes me five tries to stand up and eight tries to actually get him halfway into the seat. I curse my weak muscles as I push-shove him the rest of the way, making sure his feet are clear before slamming the shit out of his door, pissed at this whole situation.

Okay, step two: get him warm. I go to the back of the Jeep and search for a first-aid kit or a blanket or jacket or anything I can use. I find a thick fleece blanket, a first-aid kit, a gallon jug of water, a tool kit, and a jacket.

Grabbing the kit, blanket, water, and jacket, I then climb into the driver's side seat. I open the kit and see more crap than I know what to do with, and ninety-eight percent of it I have no idea how to use. I look for a cauterizing agent, but I'm out of luck. I zip the kit and fling it in the back, throw on the jacket, buckle him in, cover him with the blanket, and start chugging the water. It tastes musty, but I need to keep my wits about me and shock for me isn't an option right now.

On to step three, getting the hell out of here. Putting the key in the ignition, I pop the gear in "Neutral" and stomp the clutch, turning the engine over without stalling. Then, I thrust the truck in gear and promptly stall out. I start the engine again and pull out of the driveway, trying to remember the way back to the cabin in—what was that town called?

Grand Lake.

Okay.

Get back to Aurelia.

I can do this. I can remember the way. I can.

In the dead of night, there is no one on the roads, only the emergency response vehicles barreling past us once I finally make it to Highway 40. I shakily put the truck through the proper gears, trying to remember the other highway we turned off of when we hit Granby. I could try and use Ash's phone to call my sister, but honestly, I have no idea how to work it, whether or not I would fry it, or even if Aurelia would answer my call.

I hope they don't turn us away. I reach across the gearshift to check Ash's pulse. No better, no worse. I'll take it.

There weren't very many turns to get to Ash's house, and even though I studied the way as we went, I'm uneasy about my navigational skills. Papa told me to always know where I was, so I made sure I paid attention to road signs. I notice a black-and-white sign for Highway 34 and downshift with only minor sputtering to make the turn. Asher is going to kill me for hurting his tranny and probably his flywheel. I am awful at manual transmissions.

Only one more turn left, and that is the street for the house. I pass it twice before I finally get the right one, and once I get to the fortress-style wrought-iron gate, I know I'm in the right place. The seriously high-tech keypad has a "Call" button on it, and I gently press it about eight million times before someone answers.

"Do you have any fucking idea what time it is?" A rough voice squawks through the speaker, and my temper snaps.

"We were attacked, and Ash is hurt. Open the gate!" I scream into the speaker, and the buzzer sounds, the iron starting to move, much too slow for my liking. It takes every shred of willpower I possess to not ram the fucking thing. Once it's finally open, I haul ass up the long drive, screeching to a stop near the front door, parking be damned. The engine shudders to a stop, and I slam the emergency brake into place before hopping out onto the pavement.

I take a huge breath to scream for help, but I release it with a relieved sigh when I see Aidan, West and Cam smoking in the space just in front of me. Ian and Rhys burst from the front door, Ian carrying his notorious black medical bag.

"What happened?" Ian barks at me, and I tell him, leaving out the majority of the particulars, only telling him that Ash was shot in the shoulder.

"Get him to the dining room table," he orders, and the guys take him with them when they travel back to the house. Ian follows them, and I wobble, stumbling to my knees on the driveway when I try to take a step toward the door. I plop to my ass on the pavement, praying to everything I know in this universe that I can see those beautiful blue eyes again.

"Mena?" Rhys says as he kneels in front of me, but I don't see him, I'm still watching the door.

"Hmm?" I say, but I don't mean to. My brain is candy floss, and I am floating away. I feel the jacket jerk on my shoulder and hear my sister's voice rise with agony, but her voice sounds like it's in a tunnel.

"They're mated, Rhys. Her life is tied with his."

I don't get my wish. The last thing I see aren't Asher's winter blue eyes, but my sister's pale jade ones.

19

ASHER

WHEN I ROUSE FROM A DECIDEDLY RESTLESS SLEEP IN A BED that I know is not mine, in a room that is not in my house, and my mate nowhere to be found, pissed off is not even close to the emotion I'm feeling.

"Mena!" I thunder into the stillness of the room, worried and weak, my strength slowly coming back after healing such a lethal wound.

If I had gotten hit on the right side, it wouldn't have been too bad, but the left side—not so much. I'm kicking off the covers and about to stand when my beautiful mate comes walking in the door looking like she's been put through the wringer. She's still in the clothes she was wearing when the house was attacked, blood-soaked and soot-covered. Her hair is up in a haphazard ponytail.

Trailing her, is Ian and Aurelia. Her twin is on her like white on rice, riding her ass about something, when Mena explodes—figuratively, this time.

"Jesus fucking Christ, Aurelia!" she shouts as she whirls to face her sister. "I'll take a shower when I'm damn good and ready. If I wanted your opinion, I would ask for the motherfucker. Leave. Me. Alone. I want to check on my mate," she ends with a growl through gritted teeth.

Aurelia looks stunned for a moment before firing back, "You cuss too much." Her arms cross as if she's getting ready to deliver another lecture, but Ian cuts her off.

"Shut up, Half-Pint." Ian breaks in, shouldering Aurelia out of the way before Mena decides to tackle her and start the ass kicking she is dying to give. Mena uses Ian's distraction to come to me, standing in between my pajama-clad legs.

"Hello, my darling," she says as she cups my face and gives me a relieved kiss. Her knees buckle, and Mena's arms wind around my waist as her head hits my chest.

"How long have I been out?" I murmur against her hair, cupping the back of her head, massaging her scalp.

"Three days," she whispers, looking back up at my face, lips trembling as tears well in her eyes. She's breaking down, and by my guess, this is the first time in three days she's cried.

"Okay, you're up. Super. Asher, I'm glad you're alive. Can you get your mate to take a shower, eat something, and go to sleep?" Aurelia gripes from her position at the foot of the bed, eyes flashing in concerned anger. "Because she hasn't done any of that in the last three freaking days, and I'm ready to drug her ass."

The argument makes sense now, and I have trouble faulting her for it.

"And I keep telling you, I've gone months without any of that, and I survived just fine," Mena bites back, voice clogged with the emotions she's trying so desperately to tamp down.

"Great. Fabulous. You're a badass. You've proved it. Now, for God's sake, eat something, take a shower and. Go. To. Sleep!" Aurelia yells, throwing her arms up in exasperation.

"Princess," I murmur, my tone half-scolding and half-sorry. I did this to her, put her through hell.

"I blew up the house," she confesses and then she breaks, chest heaving with sobs as she squeezes my middle. I haul her up, tuck her in the bed, and follow her in, propping myself up on the pillows so I can cradle her in my arms as she finally loses it.

When I look up, Ian is still standing there, brow creased, patiently waiting for Mena to either stop crying, quiet down, or it's entirely possible he's trying to figure out how big a dose of sedative she'll need.

Aurelia shoulders the door open, carrying a tray piled with food. Two huge bowls of chicken and dumplings, crusty French baguettes, and two bottles of water fill the tray, and by the determined twist to Aurelia's mouth, she'll force-feed Mena if she has to. Mena's sobs have quieted even though her tears keep flowing, and Aurelia plops the tray on her lap.

"Now, I made the bread and dumplings from scratch, so you're going to eat all of it."

"I thought you couldn't cook," Mena croaks from my chest.

"I said 'don't' not 'can't.' I hate cooking and kitchens in general, dishes most definitely, but I pull out the big guns for a crisis. You not eating is a fucking crisis. Eat," she says, brandishing the spoon like a weapon.

Mena reaches for the utensil, slipping it from Aurelia's fingers, and sits up, taking her bowl from the tray. Before I know it, she's devouring the hearty soup like a frat boy with the munchies. She rips into one of the baguettes and dabs the rest of the bread in the soup, sopping up some of the broth before shoving the hunk in her mouth again.

I take my bowl, but before I tuck into my food, I ask, "How bad was it?"

"You or her?" Ian murmurs, eyeing Mena, and it occurs to me that she could have been hurt after I left, and I wouldn't have been able to do a thing to help her.

"Her first," I insist.

"Minor injuries. Cuts, bumps, and bruises mostly. My biggest worry was the shock, despite her efforts to keep it at bay. But she did good. Mena got you here, tried to take care of herself so she could do what she needed to, didn't wreck your Jeep, and didn't pass out until we got you inside. It would have been better if she called us, but given what she had to work with, she did good. Teach her how to use a cell phone, would ya?"

I can't believe I didn't take the time to teach her something so simple. "And me?"

"I need to check some things, but my guess is you're fully healed, which is markedly faster than expected, given your injuries. The shot was a through and through, but the bullet broke your clavicle and nicked your subclavian artery. Average bleed out for that is anywhere between two to twenty minutes and it's usually fatal. Now, I know I don't have to tell you that we do not regenerate at the same speed as phoenixes. You don't, and I sure as shit do not."

Ian pauses, trying to make a point, but I'm lost.

"He's attempting to tell you that mating me saved your life." Mena breaks in, talking around a hunk of bread. "I guess a mating shares the strongest traits between the spouses. So, congratulations, it's really hard to kill you now."

"Uh... what?" I sputter, almost choking on my food.

"You are organically drawing on my Aegis, so in life-threatening situations, I protect you," she garbles matter-of-factly around her food. "No spell, no pain, and apparently, you keep me from blowing shit up— your house excluded. Sorry about that one. I don't know if it's temporary or permanent, but I'm calling it a bonus."

"And you swear I'm not hurting you?" I ask as I turn to Mena.

"I promise, Ash," she assures me. "I wouldn't lie to you. Especially not about that."

Taking a deep breath, I try to wrap my mind around shared abilities between mates. I've never heard of a phoenix and a wraith mating in the first place, so I'm at a loss. Is this just because of Mena's Aegis or is this something else? Will she be harder for our enemies to find now that I've drawn from her?

Mena's spoon clatters in her bowl and she lets out a giant yawn.

"Okay, Princess, why don't you grab a shower, Ian can examine me, and then we can get some more rest? Sound like a plan?"

"Yeah," she says sleepily, slowly moving from the bed and padding sluggishly to the en suite bath. She doesn't take any clothes with her, and Aurelia rolls her eyes as she snatches Mena's bag from a leather armchair and trails after her.

"Did anyone ask John about it?" I ask, and I wish I hadn't. Ian's face falls, and I know it's bad.

"He's not doing so great, Ash," he says as he opens his med kit and takes out a stethoscope, fitting it in his ears before placing the cold metal over my heart. He listens in several locations and then switches to my back.

"Deep breath," he instructs, and I comply.

"Your heart sounds good, and your lungs are clear. I'm pretty sure you're completely healed. You don't even have a scar."

"How bad is he?" I murmur, ignoring my clean bill of health, and Ian shrugs, swallowing hard as he grits his teeth.

"He's got maybe a week," he croaks, "and Voyt is coming here to talk about succession. Since he's the next male in the bloodline—however slight his claim to that bloodline might be. He wants to speak to John about handing over the reins early. He says there is a call for war with the phoenixes, and he's been recruiting. Evan is beside herself she's so pissed, and West can't calm her down."

Like he could if she decided she didn't want to be calm. Evan isn't one to just sit there and take some distant third cousin twice removed stealing her father's throne. Not to mention, we all know that if wraiths are behind Olivia's poisoning, Voyt is at the top of the list of suspects.

"Voyt—that fucking douchebag," I growl. "He makes Cam look like Mr. Congeniality. I haven't had a single conversation with that asshole that didn't make me want to punch him in his smarmy fucking face."

"West is going to bail, isn't he?" I ask, less like a question and more like a statement. I know how this is going to go. Bad.

"Probably. You know how he feels about being a leader," Ian grouses.

"It's bullshit, is what it is. He's been the only one John has truly trusted. West knows everything. Every family, every transgression. He knows who to trust and who to kill. Hell, ninety-eight percent of the people who needed killing, West is the one who killed them."

"And that's the problem," Ian whispers, and it occurs to me that West might hate himself more than he hates the throne.

20

NO ONE NEEDS THIS RIGHT NOW. NOT ME. NOT ASH. CERTAINLY not John, and especially not Evan.

"This is such a waste of time," Aurelia grouses as she shrugs into a black suit jacket to cover the loaded shoulder holster under her right arm and spine holster at her back. "You know how this is going to go," she complains as she adjusts her black silk tank to cover a bit more of her generous bosom.

She fiddles with the jacket at the point of her shoulder and the pin-tucked ruffle at her back. Aurelia's long, black hair is pulled up off her neck and secured in a full topknot with several deadly-looking metal spikes, and her makeup is done up to full smoke, highlighting the paleness of her pupilless eyes and the sharpness of her cheekbones.

She moves to re-secure the throwing knives in her boot and then flips the wide leg of her black trousers over the holster. This is the third time she's checked her weapons, and if I didn't know better, I'd think she was nervous.

But I do know better.

She's not the least bit nervous—she's pissed. She'd rather go on an assassination mission than sit and play politics with someone she plans on killing, anyway.

"You know the last time I wore a suit around you, shit went awry," she grumbles to Evan. "This time will be no fucking different. Bad shit is coming, Evan. Bad, bad shit."

"And that is why I need you armed, but you need to look professional, and your weapons need to be concealed. You have to represent your people. I can't find Nicola, and headquarters has gone silent," Evan explains, and her voice has taken a lively quality that I haven't heard from her in the last week. "I can't find Kyle anywhere, and I haven't seen him since he left with her before the house was attacked. We are on the brink of a major shitstorm. I need to feel Voyt out. Dad needs to know what we're dealing with to buy us some time to defuse the situation. I can't just lop his head off and say 'nanny-nanny-foo-foo.' I need to be diplomatic—until diplomacy shits the bed and then I can make him die slowly."

She dusts imaginary lint from her dark wine-colored evening gown and adjusts the beaded sleeve. I admire the design of the dress: the bodice is a high crew neck, but mostly see-through mesh with slashes of beading that protects her modesty. One sleeve is the same fabric as her long flowing skirt, but the other is the mesh and beaded design of the bodice. What tips the sexy scale is the hip-height slit that exposes one shapely leg and one of the five-inch, suede, platform peep-toes adorning her dainty feet.

We abandoned the cabin in Grand Lake for the cliff-top house two days ago. In that time, I procured funeral clothing, an extra black tailored suit, and an evening dress that remarkably covers me from neck to wrists to toes and still makes me feel beautiful. Today, I get to wear the suit. Evan and Aurelia said these clothes were necessary for the coming meetings. Other than the one today, I'm unsure of what other meetings I'll need to attend and don't know why I even need to go to this one.

"And I have to be there because?" I ask for maybe the hundredth time in the last six hours. I don't think I need to be here. I have already helped as much as I am able.

After Ash awoke, I did what I needed to. After a full twenty-four hours of sleep, I gave some of my energy to Olivia and John. I didn't even need a spell—not that I couldn't cast one. I've heard the spell roughly a million times in the last fifty years. All I had to do was touch their hands, and their bodies hungrily pulled the excess from my bones without the agony of draining me dry. It felt organic, and I relished the use for my Aegis besides destruction. Olivia's eyes opened for the first time in a week and John's color came back. It won't sustain them, and I didn't cure them, but it will stave off death for a little while.

I just wish I could do more.

"We need you as a show of strength," Aurelia says as she adjusts the jacket of my suit. "You and I both know that it's likely that Voyt's men are the ones who attacked Asher's house."

While her suit has a bit more coverage so she can conceal her weapons, my jacket has a deep V-neckline, prominently displaying the lightning bolt Aegis marking on my neck. I think showing my mark would be like waving a red flag in front of a bull, but what do I know?

The suit also displays the relatively minor scarring on my chest, but I don't mind it, mostly because of the nude beaded camisole I'm wearing underneath. I feel sexy in this outfit. My jacket is a slim cut with exposed velvet pockets on the front, and the ankle-length trousers showing off my height and the four-inch, thin-heeled, pointed-toe pumps.

"We want him to know you are alive, and you're strong, and you support us. You do support us, right?" Evan asks as she fidgets and then masks it by smoothing her already-meticulously coiffed hair, styled in a delicately messy chignon.

"You know I support you. You know Ash does, too. Don't ask dumb questions. You may not know me as well as my twin, but on the real stuff, our beliefs have always been the same."

Evan looks from me to Aurelia, and Aurelia nods in agreement.

"What she said. Quit being dumb. Okay, I'm ready. I'm going to find my mate, kiss him and see if there is any other prep we need to do," Aurelia says as she opens the bathroom door and flounces out.

Evan goes to follow her, but I gently clutch her elbow. I'm not shocking people anymore, and that scares me as much as it makes me smile. I worry I won't have enough in me to be an offensive weapon.

That I cannot protect them.

"A little red-haired birdie told me a very long time ago that you would be instrumental in taking Iva out. That you would be Queen. She told me I had to do whatever I could to help you. So that's what I'm doing."

Evan nods, raising her eyebrows and asks, "Nicola?"

"Yep. So if she can't be reached it's either because she has a reason, or they have done something to her. You will be Queen, she told me herself."

Evan inhales a deep breath, letting it out slowly. By sheer force of will, the tears pooling in her eyes don't fall.

"How are you doing?" I press.

"I've been better, but I'm standing, right? I'm doing better than my dad and a fuck-ton better than my mom. And I love a man who will not keep me. Even if marrying me—a woman he claims to love—means saving our race from that evil, twisted, murdering son of a bitch. So, I'm *super*," she says sarcastically with a half-shrug and a bitter smile.

"I have no advice to give you, Evan, but I can say this: you are a survivor. It may be the worst time in your life, but you will survive this. I promise. Even if I have to kill everyone in that room myself," I say waggling my eyebrows at the last bit.

Evan huffs out a laugh and gives me a wan smile.

"Let's go, Short Stuff." We link arms and head from Evan's opulent bathroom through an equally sumptuous bedroom down a posh and regal hallway all the way to a sitting area filled with heavy furniture, crystal lamps, and priceless Ming vases. It is also filled with large men in very sharp suits. My eyes immediately move to Asher, and I release Evan to go to my mate.

Mate.

Who would have thought I could have this much, this quickly? Ash is everything I ever wanted for myself, and I need to keep him safe. To keep him safe, I need to present a front of a leader, even if that is the last thing I am.

"You look beautiful, Princess," Ash murmurs as he dips his head to kiss the tender spot right underneath my ear.

With my heels on, I'm eye to eye with him, and I love it. Running my hands over the arms of his suit jacket, I admire the way it clings to his broad shoulders and highlights his slim waist. I want to peel him out of it but refrain from doing so by a very thin margin.

"I love this suit. I'm going to have a grand time taking it off you later," he murmurs against my skin, inciting a shiver from me.

The ring of the doorbell sounds before I'm ready, and I feel a horrible chill steal its way down my spine. John steps into the room before the door opens for our guests and takes his place, sitting on a large, cream linen wingback chair. Evan positions herself on the seat at her father's right, Asher leaves me to stand behind John's chair, and Cam joins him. Aurelia and I take the love seat to John's left, with me sitting closest to Ash. Rhys stands behind Aurelia and West behind Evan, despite the irritated purse to her lips.

Ian moves to the shadows and Aidan answers the door.

Here we go.

Three men stalk into the sitting room behind Aidan, and I can tell already how this will unfold. One man is leading the trio of newcomers. His perfectly coiffed dark hair is swept back from his angular face. He has the features of a model, all sharp cheekbones and full lips, thick slashes of eyebrows highlighting pale eyes. He's tall, taller than Ash, and I dislike him on sight.

It's not just the horrible timing of his visit or the almost-forced politeness I notice on his face—it is the underlying expression, the one behind the fake remorse and false loyalty.

It's the hunger. Either for the throne or power—it's there.

The two men trailing behind him are both dark-haired and dark-eyed, looking similar enough in features that they could be brothers or close cousins. They share the angle of their cheekbones and square of their jaws. Both dressed in dark suits, the one on the left is only marginally distinguished from his counterpart by the long hair pulled back from his face into a low ponytail.

Asher told me that news of John and Olivia's condition started filtering through the wraith community about a month ago. Just whispers at first, and that is how John knew there had to be either eyes in the house or on it. That's when they started to move, and he hid Olivia away in a house, even Asher had no idea of its location. Her guardians were left in the dark, sent to the far reaches of the earth to find a cure for their mistress.

After Javier had taken Aurelia, it was clear who the eyes belonged to but unclear how far his reach was.

John stands to greet Voyt, reaching to shake his guest's hand before retaking his seat. Voyt sits on the wingback opposite John, his minions standing at his back, mirroring Asher and Cam. Even though the room is tense, every person seems to be lounging on their seats or standing, idly waiting for this farce to begin.

"Voyt, I have some people I need to introduce you to before we begin our discussion of succession." He gestures to me first. "This is Mena Constantine, the last living full-blooded Aegis and rightful leader of the phoenixes." I let my Aegis free for a moment, waggling my sparking fingers at our guests. He then gestures to my sister. "And this is Aurelia Constantine, the last living seer, the only Aegis hybrid, and the woman who turned Iva to ash."

Then, John stands.

"And I'm sure you've met my mate," he says as Olivia strides into the room.

21

MENA

The click of Olivia's heels echo through the room. She's a small woman, not much taller than her daughter. Impeccably dressed in a blood-red chiffon evening gown, her stark-white, once-blonde hair pulled back from her face in a delicate twist. The dress is a Grecian, one-shoulder design with a fitted bodice and thigh-high slit. She's beautiful and elegant and regal, and I think I love her a little bit more—she has pulled off such a coup, without looking the least bit ruffled.

Glancing back at our guests, their expressions are not what I expected. I anticipated Voyt to be angry, to reveal a sign of distress that Olivia is not quite on her deathbed, but he's not. He seems pleased that his Queen appears to be on the mend.

His guardians, however, both look like they're ready to tear the room apart.

Interesting.

"Olivia, my Queen, I am so happy to see you," Voyt says as he stands, reaching for her hand and bringing his mouth to her fingers in a full bow. He rises from his position saying, "I am delighted to see that you are feeling better. When I received word that you were ill, I wanted to take a meeting to show my support and propose a few ideas to you and your mate."

No one in this room misses the fact he said "mate" instead of "King," or that he is deferring to Olivia instead of John. The insult may not be intended, but it's taken all the same. Voyt releases Olivia's hand and returns to his seat, and she takes the open spot on the love seat next to Evan.

"I am happy to see you as well, Voyt. How is your mother? I haven't spoken to Madeline in ages," she croons, her upturned midnight eyes turning soft.

Voyt's lips curve into a polite smile. "She is wonderful, ma'am. She speaks of you often."

"Oh, that is wonderful. We appreciate you taking the time to come to see us. Especially given the circumstances in the community," Olivia says, her voice and expression like butter wouldn't melt in her mouth.

"Yes, ma'am. It is a dark time. I wanted to discuss plans for the future. While I am technically the rightful male heir, I do not wish to step on anyone's toes." Voyt shifts in his seat. "I want to make sure a leader is chosen and appropriately trained, but now that I see you are both so healthy, I would rather talk about your intentions to settle the unrest in our community."

John reaches out and takes Evan's hand. "We do, in fact, have a plan to quell the unrest. Iva has been eliminated. Given her ability to control the phoenixes in her retinue, we believe the attacks on us were her doing alone. Their hierarchy is in tumult at the present, but Mena, here, should be the leader of the phoenixes. As she is now mated to a wraith, I am certain, once she takes her rightful position, Phoenix-Wraith relations should heal rather quickly. And as far as succession, I'm not sure if you've met my daughter, Evangeline."

"I have seen her in passing, but we have not been formally introduced," he says to John before addressing Evan, "And I am pleased to make your acquaintance, Evangeline."

His voice isn't quite a purr but almost, and his expression is hungry.

I realize that his hunger before wasn't necessarily for the throne or power, but maybe for the tiny blonde pixie. Voyt smiles earnestly at her, almost sheepish, the exchange earning him a menacing growl from West.

West looks three seconds away from losing his ever-loving mind, and his phase is almost immediate. His sharp talons rip into the upholstery of the couch, creating gaping gashes in the fabric.

If Voyt weren't already sitting, he would have taken a few steps back.

"Oh! My apologies. I had no idea you were mated," Voyt says, clearly abashed, and his face transforms immediately from hopeful to crestfallen.

"I'm not," Evan insists, glancing back at West with enough venom in her gaze to melt him on sight.

Something passes between them, and I realize that Voyt—if he's not a plotting, treasonous murderer—could be a viable option for Evan. West has not claimed her, has no plans to, and from what I'm guessing, this has been going on for a very long time.

Asher waited approximately two days to claim me. I could not imagine waiting for someone to deign to accept me. That would burn my soul so badly, I'm not sure I would recover.

"He is my guardian," she accuses, not taking her eyes away from West, and his face seems to turn to stone.

Before the shutters fall, I glimpse the agony for a moment, and then it's gone.

"Evangeline is not mated," John cuts in, "nor does she have any plans to change that fact. As my only living heir, it was against the covenant for her to take the position of Queen without a mate—a rather archaic custom now that we are in the twenty-first century. However, I have written amendments to certain rules of the covenant, which have been approved by the Council. When I pass, she will be Queen. With or without a mate."

"While this is most irregular, I can see why you would choose that path," Voyt responds.

Since he seems one of the most diplomatic people I've ever met, I almost don't notice he did not give his opinion one way or the other regarding John's pronouncement. Instead, Voyt, who seems to be an expert at avoiding thorny topics, moves to continue the introductions.

"Please allow me to introduce my guardians, Segundo," Voyt points to ponytail guy, "and Guillermo," He gestures to the gentleman with shorter hair. "They are brothers to your Javier. They haven't spoken to him in weeks. Is he here? We would love to see him and Carver as well."

Unease falls over the room in a crushing wave. During my crash course in all things wraith, Asher explained what Revenants were. He also brought me up to speed on what happened in the weeks prior to my release. The attack on the cabin in Grand Lake, how Javier had likely been working for Iva the whole time.

How he attacked and nearly killed his mate. How he ate the hearts of some of the phoenixes who attacked. And how he stabbed and kidnapped Aurelia, bringing her like a present for Iva.

And these were his brothers.

John clears his throat. "Javier isn't here, Voyt. With Carver so injured, we had no idea that Javier had any living family. He did not speak of himself very often," John says, and he seems to be bracing himself for the next blow he has to deliver.

"Javier injured and kidnapped a woman in my care and tried to murder Carver. In fact, Carver is still healing from his wounds and has not regained consciousness. We discovered Javier was in league with Iva, divulging secrets. He also consumed the hearts of several combatants in battle. I hate to tell you this, but he had turned Revenant, and he was dispatched," John says, trying to gently break the news of Javier's passing to the two stone-faced men at Voyt's back.

The silence stretches thin for a long moment.

"Are... are you sure of this?" Voyt asks, seeming incredulous.

"Yes, I am afraid I am."

"Did you dispatch him?" Ponytail—err—Segundo asks, looking murderous.

John opens his mouth to answer, but he's interrupted by my big mouth of a sister.

"No, he did not. I did. I am also the woman he stabbed and delivered to Iva," Aurelia says, her voice even, her eyes unwavering.

She does not feel remorse, nor should she, but she also doesn't show weakness. I admire her and want to kick her right in her fool shin. Especially when Segundo and Guillermo exchange a look and go silent.

"I understand why you might be angry with me, but make no mistake, I do not relish killing, no matter how good at it I might be. My sister is mated to a wraith. My best friend is a wraith. I have been a part of the Black family for more years than I was ever a part of my own. They have sheltered me, protected me, and helped me for most of my life. Iva's assassination of so many is appalling, and it hurts my heart that so many wraiths have been lost. I am sorry for the loss of your brother, but he was working for Iva. He brought me to her to be tortured, and I will not apologize for saving my own life or the lives of those I prevented him from taking," she says, her voice calm and empathetic.

Segundo and Guillermo appear less than appeased, but they both nod all the same. I have a feeling we'll see them later. I'll be sure not to take any strolls in any dark alleys in the near future.

Voyt—to his credit—notices this and his face goes from surprised to what I can only describe as "damage-control mode."

"This news is… upsetting. I wish to postpone our discussion until my guardians can digest this information. Thank you for meeting with me. We will see ourselves out," he says hurriedly.

Voyt rises and walks to the door in a swift clip, and Aidan follows, showing him out. The room is tense for a few more moments before my sister breaks the silence.

"Well, that was less than helpful," Aurelia says.

"Oh, I don't know. Voyt is smarmy, but less of the antagonistic asshole you all made him out to be. And he has no clue that his guardians are piles of shit," I say, and Asher busts out laughing.

"It is so funny when you cuss, Princess," Ash says, chuckling.

"I agree. Both with the funny cussing and the guardian's assessment. I still don't quite trust him, though," Olivia says, her smile broad and teasing, and I realize I have gained more approval from her. "You need to be careful, Ari-darling. I've heard stories of Segundo and Guillermo Cabal. They are not good men. I didn't realize Javier was related to those two jackals. I wish Carver had told us about his family. From what I knew, Javier did not speak to them after he took Carver as his mate. Silly prejudice, I know, but some people believe in the old ways. Those are the same people who will have issues with my Evangeline claiming the throne without a mate." Olivia cups Evan's cheek and looks into her eyes. "But we will change their minds, won't we, my love?"

"Yes, Mama," Evan croaks.

I get the distinct feeling in my gut that Olivia is telling her goodbye, giving one last piece of advice, one last message to her precious daughter. Olivia's face falls for a moment, but her smile returns, even if it trembles a bit.

I can feel it. My power was merely a Band-Aid for Olivia, and she has used it all up.

"I'm suddenly very tired. It has been an eventful and exhausting day," Olivia softly says, and then shakily stands to leave. Her color has gone from lively to gray in an instant.

"I'll go with you, Love," John murmurs and stands, taking her hand and gently wrapping it around his crooked arm.

They walk together out of the sitting room, and down the white, marble-floored hallway.

I feel it then, the overwhelming loss creeping into my soul, and I turn to look at my sister. Her eyes are glowing bright, tears dripping from her face, silent sobs choking her staggered breaths. Rhys kneels in front of her, holding her hands and coaxing her out of what is likely one of the worst things to see.

Olivia has been a mother to Aurelia—the only real mother she's ever had.

My tears come then, for the loss these people feel and what was denied my sister from our family. For Asher, for Cam, and Evan. For every life this delightful woman touched. For the loss these people feel, and my own. I barely met her, but there is no doubt Olivia was a wonderful woman, that I will never, ever get to know.

Asher's hands find me through the darkness of my tears, pulling me from the couch, wrapping me in a hug. We cling to each other in our shared grief.

Evan's gaze darts from her best friend to me, but she doesn't seem to understand that a phoenix can feel when a body is at its end. That we know when death is near, when a thread is drawn for cutting.

She had so much hope that I'd helped them, and this hits her like a sledgehammer. The dawning understanding on her face when she sees Aurelia crying...

She knows.

She doesn't wait to ask—she just smokes out of the room. When we hear her agonized wail a moment later, we know.

Olivia is gone.

22

ASHER

I HAVE NO IDEA WHAT TO DO. I'M NOT SURE ANYONE DOES.

I follow West on his quest to find Evan with Cam trailing reluctantly behind me. It wasn't far, just past the tree of life doors of the royal suite, but I hesitate before passing through them, trying to steel myself for what I know is just beyond.

But I know there is no real preparation for death. It comes as a surprise to us all, whether we want it to or not. When Mena's hand finds mine, I feel a small margin of relief before gathering the courage to walk into that room.

I wish I hadn't. I wish I could never see what will be burned into my brain for the rest of my life.

Evan is crying—no, crying isn't the right word. She is keening, great mutilated sobs filled with enough pain to burn us all. John has plopped on the chaise, Olivia draped, unmoving across his lap. Evan is kneeling at John's feet, clutching her mother's still hand. She's begging, pleading, promising everything in the world to get her to wake up.

This burns my soul with enough fire to consume me completely if I didn't need to stay alive for Mena. Mena's hand squeezes mine again, and she wraps those beautiful, strong arms around me because she knows.

Evan might be losing her blood, but John and Olivia are surrogate parents for every single person in this room. They took us in when we needed saving, or were cast out, or were unloved.

They saved us all.

Tugging Mena into my arms tighter, I rub my tear-stained face into her hair.

"Please, Mama. Please… don't leave me," Evan haltingly pleads, but Olivia doesn't answer her. That's when John reaches down, and rubs a thumb under Evan's eye, cupping her face with his free palm.

"Daddy. Please don't go. Please," Evan begs.

"Evangeline, my beautiful, strong, girl. We need to leave you now," he says, his voice barely above a whisper, thready with death breathing down his neck. "Stay strong. You can lead our people back into the light. You can do this, my dear. We love you, and we trust you. You are the best gift we have ever been given."

When his hand falls from her face, Evan loses it. We all feel the loss as soon as his last breath leaves his lips, but Evan can't deal with the horrible agony bubbling up in her.

"No. No, no, no!" she screams, moving from one parent to the next, grabbing their faces to check for life.

She finds none. Evan can't hold in her phase anymore, and that's when all hell breaks loose. When Evan can't hold in her anger or fear or agony, things around her turn to dust. And this… this loss is the worst kind of hurt.

The floor beneath her feet abrades away, a swirl of dust and smoke surrounding her like a tornado. Her coal-black eyes turn vacant, and the floor and furniture near her begin to crumble.

West takes action, the only one of us brave enough to go toe-to-toe with Evan when she's lost it.

"Evan. Evangeline! You have to stop! You'll send them to Hell without meaning to. They don't deserve to go!" he screams in her face, latching onto her arm and shaking her hard enough to snap her neck.

She does a long, slow blink before her eyes regain their life, and then she rips her arm from his grasp and shoves him away with one small palm. No matter how tiny Evan is, she still made that one little shove count, because not only has West gone back at least five feet, the place on his shirt where her hand touched is now bare, bleeding skin.

The debris swirling around her slows, settling in a pile of dust at her feet.

"I release you," she whispers, and the occupants of the room, myself included, pull in a collective gasp.

"You may stay for the funeral, but afterward, you will leave this house. I *never* want to see your face again. If you ever truly cared for me at all, you will honor this," her command never rising above a murmur.

West hears every word, and he nods. Even when her eyes go dead, he still nods and leaves the room.

MENA TELLS ME FUNERALS ARE AWFUL FOR EVERYONE, AND they are never really for the dead. "Funerals are for the living," she says.

I guess that's true, but I still hate them.

The preparation for the service has been exhausting over the last twenty-four hours, and Mena, Aurelia, Rhys, and myself have been handling the bulk of it. Many families needed to be called, and since Olivia and John were actually good souls, security required a little amping up since phoenixes would be in attendance.

With the unrest, with so many wraith families slaughtered in the last few months, the likelihood that this could turn into a bloodbath is pretty high.

Evan asked both Aidan and Cam to be her new guardians. They accepted immediately, Cam faster than I thought he would, his tie to Olivia transferring to Evan now.

Wraiths from every corner of the earth have come, and as soon as the sun begins to set on this very long day, we can send Olivia and John to their rest.

So many have gathered in the gorge at the base of the cliff, where we can stay concealed from human eyes, and all be in one place at one time. A witch Aurelia knows offered to do a concealment spell for the event, but Mena nixed it, saying the magic could interfere with the passage of the souls.

She would know. Mena worked as a gentry for nearly a century before her capture, working with humans as either a nurse or a mortician, helping the neutral and good pass on.

Twenty-four straight hours of contacting families, making sure Evan was safe and ensuring that my mate and her family wouldn't be murdered, led us here, to the bottom of the gorge, in front of so many wraith families. They stand shoulder to shoulder, women in elegant evening dresses and men in suits, the river rushing around their legs, their gowns sweeping behind them in the water. The rest fill the shore, in the sand, on the rocks, filling the ravine to the brim.

Aurelia and Mena are in phoenix ceremonial funeral garb. Snow-white, one-shoulder, Grecian-style gowns, the fabric pools low on their backs, allowing enough clearance for their wings. Rhys, however, is not in anything that would be considered formal. Instead, he is dressed—like me—in full tactical assault gear. Black shirt under a bulletproof vest, black pants and boots, and every single weapon we can carry. Rhys' only concession in his vest is a missing back plate so his wings can burst free if needed.

We follow our wives, staying close, but assessing threats from the crowd. It also helps that Ian is at the top of the cliff concealing himself to the shadows with a sniper rifle.

One can't be too careful.

Aurelia and Mena phase at the same time, the twins igniting as one, blood-red and bright-blue wings rising in sync from their backs. Aurelia's are remarkably smaller than Mena's, and it takes me a minute to remember that the feathers of Aurelia's wings have been clipped.

I try to keep the horror off my face at the mutilation—something I have heard of, but never actually seen—and avert my eyes back to the crowd before looking at my mate again. Phasing is agony for Mena, but not a single peep falls from her lips. The twins move in unison to the bodies of the dead at the funeral pyre, Aurelia at John's side, and Mena at Olivia's. Evan smokes in at the head of the pyre with Aidan and Cam at her back and raises her hands to speak.

She asked me for help with the eulogy, but I directed her to Ian instead. Ian, while usually the joker, gives some of the best advice for someone so young.

"My mother gave me valuable advice over the years. She told me to never settle for a horrible haircut. She said if you could get away with wearing a higher heel, do it, but never be afraid of going barefoot." Evan chuckles before her voice breaks. "She said when I have my own ch-children, to give them twenty percent more hugs than they request and twice as many as I think they'll need. She also taught me how to be a strong woman. She taught me how to lead, how to be diplomatic, and instructed me when not to be. She is the voice in my head, my guiding star, and my conscience."

Evangeline pauses, gathering herself before she can continue.

"My father, in turn, taught me to be a strong leader. He taught me when to fight and when not to. He taught me how to think and how to breathe. He, along with my mother, will live in my heart for the rest of my days."

Evan nods and then bends to kiss the wrapped foreheads of her parents, tears wetting the white, gauzy fabric before she backs away. I do my best to turn off my emotions, but I feel a heaviness when I swallow, and when I see my mate barely holding herself together, the lump in my throat grows.

I allow myself one lone moment to grieve before swallowing it back. Evan signals to Aurelia and Mena, and they begin the funeral rites, murmuring the ancient language that guides the souls on. They then run their fingers over their charges' heads to their feet, igniting the silk wrappings and stacked wood of the pyre. The twins sweep their hands over the hearts of the dead, plucking glowing white ash from their still-flaming chests, take a deep breath and blow the ashes, scattering them to the beyond.

The whole of the assembly bows as one to Evan, and then all but five, travel from the gorge back to their homes. Wraiths do not believe in congregating after a funeral, they believe in solitude and reflection and mourning.

Of the five that stayed, three are known to me. Voyt, Segundo, and Guillermo.

Here we go.

The two I do not know—a man and woman—assess the threat of the seven of us from their positions in the water and travel hurriedly from the gorge.

Voyt approaches Evan, bowing low, seemingly oblivious to the turmoil behind him. His guardians do not mirror him, and the slight to

Evan makes both Cam and Aidan growl through their fangs. Voyt rises and gazes back at his guardians, seeming confused and more than a little embarrassed.

"Did you know, Voyt, that my mother was being poisoned?" Evan begins, her head tilted to the side as if she's playing a stupid blonde when she is anything but. By his expression when he whips his head back to her, the answer is no.

"No. I did not. Olivia was beloved. I cannot imagine who would do something like that."

Evan rights the tilt to her head, leveling Voyt with a searing glare. "I can. Because I know who poisoned her," she snarls before she smokes out, traveling to the backs of Segundo and Guillermo.

Her tiny hands hit their backs between their shoulder blades. Both men stand stock-still, eyes wide—frozen in pain.

"Oh, Voyt," Evan calls, and he spins, nearly slipping in the sand of the river.

"Your guardians had a hand in it, along with their brother, Javier."

"And who told you that?" Voyt sputters, his tone incredulous.

"I did," a deep male voice calls from behind Evan, and Carver walks slowly into the glow of the flames.

23

MENA

Carver saunters toward us as much as he's able. Dressed in a sharp black suit, he ambles slowly, his cane on the uneven ground making for slow going. A dark eye patch covers his right eye, barely visible underneath the heavy fall of his hair.

Ian said he was still healing from the injuries Javier slashed into his flesh, and it shows. Carver leans heavily on the wood and silver cane. The silver knobbed handle intricately carved into a lion's face, and the wooden shank a silky mahogany with a smooth ferrule.

"Javier was committed to his cause, I'll give you that. I mean, who else but a sociopath would fake being gay, stage a falling out with his family, and cut himself off from his friends just for a coup? A twenty-year-long coup. Commitment. Yeah, I'll give him that," Carver says bitterly, moving closer to this tense circle of frozen combatants.

"Like anyone should believe anything you say, *viado*," Segundo spits, but he remains unmoving, seemingly afraid of what will happen when Evangeline decides to flex her power.

"Yes, because being gay makes me a liar. So you're saying your brother wasn't a *viado*?" Carver asks tilting his head, the Portuguese slur flung back in Segundo's face.

Segundo grits his teeth saying nothing more.

"It really doesn't matter what you say or what lie you try to tell. I wouldn't believe you, anyway. Javier told me everything right before he attempted to rip my heart out and fucking eat it," Carver informs them.

"So my question, Voyt," Evan continues as if she were talking about her nail color and Carver hadn't just dropped the mother of all bombs, "is whether you were a part of it. Your face says no, but Javier had me fooled, so I'm not so sure."

"But I didn't! I didn't know. I was just going to talk to your mother about introducing us because you were unmated, and I saw you at an art gala in Denver months ago. I swear. Segundo and Guillermo have only been my guardians for less than a year," he pleads, hands raised in surrender.

"I'll take that into consideration, but the rumor was that you were recruiting for a war. What war were you planning to start now that Iva has been taken out, Voyt?"

At the accusation, Voyt straightens, his gaze turning sharp.

"I was not recruiting to start a war. I was sending aid to families and preparing for the eventuality of further attacks. That is not recruiting, that is being a competent leader. It is making sure our people are taken care of."

"So noted. I'll remember that while someone is trying to behead me in battle," she snarks. "You have no idea what it means to be a true leader. If you think shelling out more money to already-filthy-rich people who could just as easily provide for themselves makes you a leader, you are sorely mistaken. Since you've been so benevolent to our people, I'll let you live, but I want you to remember who your Queen is so you will watch as I turn your guardians to dust," Evan snarls, and then the screaming starts.

Javier's brothers do not die quickly. Their skin abrades away slowly, showing muscle and sinew and then bone, before the bone chips away to reveal their organs and blood. So much blood. Before that, too, withers away to dust. All the while, Evan watches as Voyt's face morphs from surprise to disgust to fear.

It's the fear she is going for.

After Evan is through with them, she delicately dusts off her hands, and walks to Voyt, grabbing him by the front of his shirt and raising him as high as her limited height allows, showing him that she is no wilting little flower.

"Mr. Voyt, I am letting you live so you can send a message to all your followers. My father made me Queen, and I will hold this position without a mate. Tell them what I do to traitors. What I did to the men who took my parents from me. If anyone tries to come and take my throne, I'll be sure to remind you of my message. Personally. After I kill every single person you hold dear. Have I made myself clear, Voyt?"

"Y-yes. You have, my Queen."

"Good. Oh, one more thing. Tell the leaders of each of the remaining head families that I will be meeting with them in one week's time. Tell them to be ready for my call," Evan murmurs and releases him so he *thumps* to the ground. Voyt wastes no time traveling from the gorge, leaving in a swath of smoke before he even regains his balance.

Then I feel it, the prickle of unease just as Aurelia screams, "Get down!"

We scatter: Cam and Aidan covering Evan, Rhys phasing on the fly and yanking Aurelia behind him, Carver wrenching a rapier from the head of his cane.

I try to move, to get in front of everyone so they can use the cover of my Aegis, but Ash bands an arm around my waist and hauls me to the slim cover of the brush line against the cliff face. I struggle against him, and his arm tightens before I feel his lips at my ear.

"Shh. We don't want to reveal your abilities just yet. These could be the same people who tried to get you in Fraser," he whispers in my ear, and I have to give it to him.

I didn't leave anyone alive in Fraser, so these guys wouldn't know the extent of my abilities. I can't just tip my hand now.

I need them closer, in a group, so I can fry them all at once.

Ash pulls me behind him, but I smack his arm and hold my hand out for a weapon. He rolls his eyes and brandishes a handgun from his left thigh holster, slapping it onto my palm as he raises his compact assault rifle and we both start firing back into the dark.

Then, I hear the sweetest sound, the thunder of the fifty-cal.

Thank the Fates.

It seems I praised the heavens too soon, though, because wraiths smoke in on all sides, advancing on us like a plague. But they aren't strategic, they are either untrained or disposable or both. I go for headshots, taking out five before my clip runs out.

Reaching for Ash, I rip the katana from its scabbard on his back, protecting his front as he drops his empty rifle and draws his kukri.

Aurelia and Rhys fight on my left as one, but Evan is having trouble with her guardians doing their job a little too well, refusing to let her fight at all. Carver ends up on my right, slashing two men down before lifting his apparently decorative eye patch and giving me a wink with his right eye before popping it back down.

He's not as injured as he pretended, and Carver spins and twirls with ease over the rocks and bracken, taking heads of three more men as he goes. The rest of the combatants left alive leave, realizing that they are being mowed down like grass, and then the firing from the cliff intensifies, and it's so much worse than before.

"Son of a bitch," Evan screams when she's grazed at the top of her arm, and Aurelia and I yell for Cam and Asher to get her the fuck out of here. They can't, though, because as soon as Cam touches her uninjured arm, she gives him a feral growl, and he rips his hand away as if burned.

Hell, he probably was.

Growling low in my throat, I catch Aurelia's attention as I notice three men and two women stalking toward us in the dim. They form a loose semi-circle, tightening the noose as they stalk closer. Other than the lit pyre and the Fireskin of Aurelia, Rhys and myself, there is no other light. I discreetly motion to the advancing group and give her a cutting signal. She nudges Rhys, and as one, we phase back, cutting off our light in the now-pitch-black gorge.

My vision is just fine in the shadows, so it's easy to stalk on my bare feet, closer to the rapidly advancing group of bastards, trying to kill my family.

And that's what they've become. This ragtag bunch of misfits are my people. Wraiths. Phoenixes. Doesn't matter. They are mine, and I will protect them.

I don't quite know what I'm capable of until it happens. My phase comes without thought and draws the fire of the five in the water and several from the opposite cliff top. I don't worry about the ones up high —their muzzle fire makes it easier for Ian to find them and take them out. The ones in the river, the ones dumb enough to get so close and not take the lead of their brethren, I make sure they pay. Their bullets ricochet off my shield, and bolts of lightning erupt from the tips of my fingers, snaking like ropes to wrap around their throats.

Their eyes bulge, but I don't hear screams.

Not that they'd be able to even if they tried.

The gunfire is gone, too. But I do smell cooked flesh and hear the muffled keening of their agony over the rush of the river. My power rises in me, tethering their bodies like a lash, raising them up from the water. The tips of their toes don't even touch the surface as I yank them higher and higher, their trousers and dresses dripping over the surface of the rushing water.

"Do you see? Do you see your friends? Do you see them burning?" I scream into the night, and then I take one long beat of my wings, rising from the riverbank, dragging them with me.

"Can you see them? Watch them die," I order into the dark, concentrating all my power into these would-be murderers.

I watch their bodies fill with blue light, their skin burning, cracking, failing to hold it in. Then they explode in a shower of ashes to the water and ground below. Beating my wings, I rise higher into the sky, making sure they hear me.

Making sure they can see what I am capable of. Making sure they know.

"They burned for their crimes. They burned for their defiance of your Queen. If any of you come after me or my family again, I'll do the same to you," I growl into the stillness.

Silence is my only answer.

EPILOGUE

I ROLL OVER IN THE WARMTH OF THE BED AND FEEL COLD sheets where my mate should be. Slowly opening one lone eyelid, I'm irritated until I smell the coffee. The other eyelid finally decides it's okay to open. Asher is sitting shirtless, just in his gray pajama bottoms, in his new reading chair, bare feet crossed on the ottoman I made him get.

"Got any of that for me?" I croak, sleep clogging my throat.

"Me, the book, or the coffee?" he asks, his eyebrow raised, not looking away from the page until he can blindly locate the bookmark on his left armrest.

"The coffee. Duh," I quip as I roll mostly naked from the bed and pad over the hardwood to sit in his lap. I kiss him on the lips before reaching across him and bring the sweet nectar of life to my lips, the large diamond of my four-carat, cushion-cut, pink diamond wedding ring winking at me in the morning light.

"Well, at least you paid the toll," he murmurs against the sensitive skin of my neck, and the beginnings of an exquisite make-out session that will most definitely lead to more sex is interrupted by the doorbell.

Grumbling, Asher presses one last kiss against my lips before setting me off his lap and padding out of the room to answer the door of our new house on the outskirts of Denver. It serves as a phoenix headquarters of sorts with the new wraith hub just forty-five minutes away in a high-rise downtown. It has been a month, and since Nicola still hasn't resurfaced, Aurelia and I took the mantle as leaders.

We have had feelers out almost everywhere looking for her, but when an Oracle doesn't want to be found, she doesn't get found.

I refused to set a single foot in Iva's house in Oregon. Aurelia said since we'd both been tortured there, setting the motherfucker on fire was a viable option. We didn't, but it was tempting.

We're still working out the kinks, mostly with the Oracles, but it is getting better. Or it would if I could get Aurelia's head out of the toilet.

For a woman who claims to be psychic, she sure doesn't realize when she's pregnant very quickly. Rhys and I are still trying to persuade her to take a test, but she's stubborn. She can be stubborn all she wants —I'll get Ian to take blood on her tomorrow.

We'll just see who combat trains while pregnant.

Throwing on a bra, a tank, a fuzzy grandpa sweater, and a pair of jeans, I pop in the bathroom to tame the sex hair and brush my teeth before heading for the stairs.

"Mena!" Asher yells for me as I hit the landing.

The alarm in his voice has me running for my mate before I can blink.

Asher kneels next to a large man lying on the cold tiles of the foyer. He's bloody and dirty and enormous. He lays there nearly naked, only wearing tattered jeans, no shoes or shirt at the start of a Colorado winter. His hair and beard are wild and dirty, as if he's been inside the walls of a cell for a while.

The part that concerns me is, he keeps repeating a name—the name of a woman I owe my life to. The woman we've been searching for.

"Nicola... They took her from me. They took her over... They put Iva in her. They took her over... Nicola..." he rasps before he loses consciousness right there on the cold tile floor. I look up to Ash, but he's already answering my question.

"This is Kyle, Nicola's mate."

Son of a bitch.

FATE KISSED

PHOENIX RISING BOOK THREE

ANNIE ANDERSON

PROLOGUE

EVAN—1906—SAN FRANCISCO

IN THIS SEA OF RUBBLE AND FLAMES, I WISH I COULD REMEMBER why I was so angry, but I seem to have forgotten. I vaguely remember the danger and rage that provoked me, but at this very moment, I cannot fathom how I let it get this far.

What I do know is that I caused this mess, and the longer I look around, the longer I hear the screams of the trapped and dying over the ringing in my ears; the more I know I should let the flames consume me.

I feel the souls, so many souls out there, and most of them were good people.

And I killed them all.

My gaze focuses on a broken baby doll, the pale china face half gone, crumbled to dust in the melee of toppling buildings and shaking earth. A lone child's slipper rests in the middle of the cracked street, teetering on the edge of the broken brick, waffling between the coming fire and oblivion.

The flames creep lazily toward me, tip-toeing their way across the buildings as if they have all the time in the world to put me out of my misery, to dole out my punishment.

I deserve this. I deserve to burn.

I have failed my parents, my race, and for the life of me, I cannot remember why. How could I do this?

Suddenly, it all comes rushing through the fog of shock and the thick ringing in my ears.

Men came in the night. They came for me—for my head—and the poor souls who called themselves my Guardians lost theirs instead. I can still see the shocked look on Devereux's face when the blade pierced his neck, his wide eyes are burned into my brain as if with a hot iron.

I don't think he ever expected them to get this far. To follow us all the way across the country to the bustling port of San Francisco. He thought we were safe in the throng of people coming and going.

He was wrong.

Now, Devereux and Sam are both gone, cut down like wheat against the scythe, and I have no idea what to do. Guilt claws at me, sharp and bleeding.

I didn't mean to lose my mind. I didn't mean to reap this much death.

But I had no idea I was this powerful. I had no idea I could cause so much destruction.

The city is in ruins, like a dollhouse thrown by a toddler in a fit of rage. And what is worse is I am so hungry, starving for the stained souls calling for me to send them to Hell. My fangs descend, cutting into my lips and bringing the coppery taste of blood to my tongue. It only makes me hungrier, and I fight my body's urge to travel to them, to glut myself on the souls of the evil.

I can't do it. I can't send them to Hell when I deserve to go myself. Closing my eyes to the mayhem, I wait for the flames to do their duty.

"Are you going to get out of the way or are you planning on burning to death?" a husky female's voice calls to me.

I blink through my haze of shock to see a woman not much bigger than my own meager height eyeing me like I was a bug on her boot. And her eyes... No pupil and such a pale milky green, she shouldn't be able to see me, but by the expression on her face, she most certainly does.

Dressed as a man in trousers and a waistcoat, she has to be the oddest person I've ever encountered. And for a Wraith in the middle of a ruined city, that's saying something.

"No offense, girlie, but Wraiths like you tend to fry when exposed to open flame. You might want to move," she says matter-of-factly, and that's when I lose it.

"I-I...did this. C-caused all this," I stutter as my breaths come in great gasping heaves, and I break right there in the middle of the cracked street.

Then, the bricks start abrading away underneath my feet, and I feel the pull of the silence, the deadness in my own head calling for me to put it all away. The guilt, the fear, the pain of losing my closest friends— all of it.

I don't see the fist coming for my face until it's too late, and before I know what hits me, blackness clouds my mind.

I wanted oblivion, I think as the lights fade out. It might not be the death I asked for, but a nice sleep will do.

Yes, it will do just fine.

I

WEST

ONE WOULD THINK PEOPLE WOULD KNOW BY NOW, BUT THEY don't. People as a whole are dumb, lazy bastards only out for themselves. Plenty would like to think they're different, but having nearly six hundred years of experience in the selfishness of people, I can attest they're all the same.

Maybe it's just Wraiths that are like this. Perhaps the other factions see us as the cockroaches of the Ethereal because of the way we act. Or maybe it's because of who we are as the gateways to Hell, the soul-eaters of the damned...

It's probably a bit of both.

Welcome to the Ethereal! Where we don't give a shit what color you are, but if you have powers we don't like, well, then fuck you.

I silently chuckle a little to myself. Yep, the game show host in my head has definitely lost his nut. It's easier to stave off the grief if I make myself laugh, but I know my good humor won't last for long.

My King is dead, my Queen along with him. And the mantle I've kept—the vow I took—is a hard thing to let go of.

Even if I have been released. Dismissed. Fired. Whatever.

The job isn't finished and fired or not, I'm still going to make sure it gets done.

Staying in the shadows—not too hard up here on the cliff top across the gorge from John and Olivia's home—I crouch in the darkness of a yawning crevasse. But it isn't their home any longer, is it? They're gone now, death taking them one after the other and all too soon.

I spy the Wraiths in fancy funeral dresses and tuxes prepare to fight a battle they can't win, a few hauling long-range precision rifles from narrow, padded gun cases.

I guess they aren't messing around anymore, but what I really want to know is who in the hell starts a fight at a funeral?

The group is dressed very differently from me. While they look refined and out of place as they spoil for a fight, I look right at home with the prospect of a good, old fashioned blood bath in my black fighting leathers and body armor.

Luck favors the prepared, so the saying goes, and I am very, very lucky.

Smoking out from the cliff top, I travel to a nook on the roof of the house overlooking the gorge where I think Ian might be hiding. Ian possesses an innate ability, making him almost impossible to find if he decides to cloak himself. It pisses me off that I've never been able to find him.

"You looking for me?" Ian asks as he appears in front of me as if from thin air. One second there was nothing, and the next he's lying prone on the rooftop looking through the scope of a fifty-caliber sniper rifle, his dark skin midnight in the moonlight.

I've been looking all over this roof for the last ten minutes, and he's been there the whole damn time. *Dick.*

"Are sure you're not half-witch instead of half-human?" I ask, my voice gruff from disuse. I haven't spoken in the last day—not that I speak much to anyone but Evan...

Or, at least, I did. My girl could talk your ear off, and I'd never tell her, but I love her chatter, her life. She kept me from sliding into the darkness.

Now I have nothing to keep me from darkest parts of my soul.

She is air and light... I miss my light. I miss my Angel.

"Who knows? Dad got around," he quips as he adjusts the elevation dial on his scope.

It pulls me back into the moment, his tone laced with just a hint of derision, and it dawns on me that the circumstances of his birth might be a sore subject.

Oops.

I study his rifle with dubious interest. I have an issue with long-range weapons as a whole. If I'm doing the job, I'm doing it right, and it's too hard to do a dead check from a thousand yards away. None of this 'from afar' bullshit. But it's harder to kill me than it is Ian.

I suppose we must go with our strengths, and the up-close kill is mine.

"Are you going to be able to stay cloaked and fire at the same time?" I ask because he's no good here if he can't.

"Yep. The only thing I can't hide is the sound, but the echo from the mountains will cover it for me. No one will know where I am unless they're right next to me, and even then, they won't live long enough to do anything about it," he murmurs as he adjusts the elevation dial again.

"Good. I'll handle the shitheads on the cliff. You handle any that get too close to the family," I order, and I want to kick myself.

Again.

I don't lead him anymore. I'm not in charge of anyone's security, let alone Evangeline's. My chest aches from her loss. Well, and the fact that my skin is still growing back from her blistering shove. I rub my hand over my sternum, only hurting myself more when I hit body armor.

Pissing her off wasn't part of the plan. Hurting her is the absolute last thing I ever wanted to do. Guess I should have told her why. Why I was waiting to claim her. Not because of her—never because of her.

But who really accepts the 'it's not you, it's me' shit? That's right. No one.

I should have told her all of it, should have made her understand. I hope I'll live long enough to do just that.

"Will do," he says as he pulls his eye from the scope and grins at my gaff.

Ian has hope. Hope I'll come back and everything will be as it was. I guess I still have hope, too.

"You think they'll actually do it? Start this fight?" he asks, showing his youth.

He's been on the right side for so long, he's forgotten how the other side thinks. I give him a long look telling him everything he needs to know. Yes. They will start this war, maybe not today or tomorrow, but...

War is coming.

I don't want this for her, don't want this darkness in her light.

Feeling it clawing at my back, the worry chokes my throat. The worry for Evangeline. The burden for all we have built and the peace we have so tentatively held onto. It is coming to an end, and I can kill and slash and fight, but I can't protect her like I used to. I can't be there every second.

And it's my own fault.

Trying and failing to swallow against the lump of bitter guilt, I escaping the roof, traveling back to a hidden crevasse. Waiting for the beginning of this little war.

It is almost unbearable to watch Evangeline tear up as she sent her parents on, and even worse, I can't hear her voice from up here. More so, I wasn't there with them to send my friends—my family—to their peace.

My chest burns again, but I refuse to rub away the ache. Instead, I ball my fists, cracking my knuckles in the process, and get ready for the shit to hit the fan.

I've tested my weapons more than once, making sure the blades are sharp, my armor is secure. I don't need to go through it all again, but my hands ache to do something. I can't stand another moment of inaction. I adjust my favorite ivory-hilted Kukris, the blades secured in an inverted holster crisscrossed behind my back.

I have never been one to lie in wait. Usually, when people are sent to me, it is because they needed killing. More often than not, the people who needed killing, needed it done to send a message. As the King's assassin, I kept the peace. Killing here and there with almost surgical precision to stamp out threats. But delicacy is not my forte.

I understand why I need to wait for them to make the first move—sniper rifles and all—even if I don't like it. If this group of stupid soon-to-be-dead fucks decides the fight's not worth it, I can't just rip into them—no matter how much I want to. I have to have a reason... even if that reason might blow my whole plan to Hell and back.

It isn't long before they give me one.

Three men ruin their fancy tuxes as they lie in the dirt to line up their shots. Time to move. Using the skills I honed early in my childhood, I make my way slowly but surely through the throng, picking off the outliers like a big cat stalking prey.

To call my past dysfunctional is like slapping a coat of paint on a condemned house. Using a pretty word won't make it any better.

Hell, dysfunctional would be a step up. Then again, anything would be a step up from where I came from.

The first ones give me no trouble, quickly snuffing out the flames of their lives with my knife. I suppose it's hard to hear me over the sound of the rifle or, perhaps, no one expected there to be a real fight at a funeral.

No one notices when the early ones go, poor bastards, and I move on to the shitheads that are doing the actual harm. Popping in and out like a ghost, I steal them away before their buddies even know what hit them. I don't bother to consume them now; I'll wait until I'm done for that. I'll glut myself on their souls, but only when I'm done.

The next round is slightly more tiresome than the first. I guess when most of your friends are missing, you start to notice, but really, how effective can you be in a tuxedo?

My cockiness bites me in the ass, then, when a little weasel in an expensive suit stabs me in the back. He misjudges my armor and hits Kevlar instead of the lung he was aiming for, the bastard. Slashing again, he hits my forearm as I go to block him, but he doesn't get to keep his weapon. I snatch it from him as easily as if I was taking it from a child.

He appears apologetic, and he's so young, I'd probably let him live if it weren't for the blood running down my back.

The dark side starts their recruiting early, I see.

I kill him quickly, painlessly, and it hurts me to do so. I hate killing the young ones—the ones just barely past maturity. While not the worst soul I've ever seen, he still had time to turn it around. If he weren't on the wrong side of a war, he would have had all the time in the world.

This will just have to be another score on my soul added to the mountain of scars from a past I can't change. Really, what's one more?

In that second of self-pity, I lose my grip on the upper hand. Three men attack me at once, stabbing and slicing with their talons like a pack of raptors. Fear trickles into my brain, and I try to beat it back, but...

It's funny, but I'm not afraid of death. Not for death or Hell. In this life, I did what I did, and I can't change it. I always did what I thought was right, and if it makes me evil, then so be it.

No, the fear I feel is for her, my Angel. My Evangeline. Because she deserves so much better in this life than this. Than me.

It is not to say I don't fight back. I do.

With every breath in me, I fight.

For her. For her smile and laugh and light. I fight. To my very last breath, I will, and even when I die, I'll fight some more.

As I dirty my soul, taking more and more life, killing the men who try to snuff out my flame, the thunder of the fifty-cal makes its presence known, earning me precious seconds that will save my hide.

I stab. I slash. I kill, and as I rip my blade against the last throat of the last of what is left of the Wraiths on top of the cliff, I feel a warring sense of disgust for myself and a little satisfaction at a job well done.

No one saw me. I was sure of it. Well, no one who could live to tell the tale, anyway. It is the satisfaction that kills me a little more each day. I shouldn't be proud of this. I shouldn't feel a sense of accomplishment at stomping out life.

Even if the souls I took were on the expressway straight to Hell. And they were, believe me. I don't kill innocents.

Never again, you mean, my mind snidely whispers, reminding me of mistakes from a previous life.

I look over the edge of the cliff at the gritty, rocky shore of the river, and feel the cold slap of regret.

I'm an asshole. A lousy good-for-nothing steaming pile of shit.

I know this.

But I didn't think she did until I see her face scanning the blackness for me in the dark of the gorge.

I should have shown my face, should have fought beside her instead of taking out the men from the shadows.

But it would blow my cover, and before I can fix what I broke by eliminating the threat to her life, I'll have to walk right into the snake pit.

And those slimy bastards don't need to know my only weakness.
Her.

2

EVAN

I'M LIVID. THIS ISN'T A NEW THING FOR ME. LATELY, I GET angry at the drop of a hat. It's no surprise, I mean come on. Who wouldn't be mad? I'd figure today of all days I would get to just be sad.

I put my parents to rest today. I should be crying into a big glass of bourbon right about now.

Nope, not me.

Instead, on the first day of my rule, I not only had to fight for my life, but I also had to *fight to fight* for my life. I was treated like a child by the very men I'm supposed to lead. Sure, I killed the men who conspired to murder my parents in probably the worst way I can think of, but in the grand scheme, I didn't get the head of the snake. I don't even know who the snake *is*.

That will have to come later.

And then I have Idiot One and Idiot Two trying to keep me from fighting alongside my family.

I don't think so.

I take a look around at the aftermath of the gorge. Other than some scorched rock, one would never know so many lost their lives here. In the silence, now that the guns have spent their rounds and the weapons have all been sheathed, the only sound apart from the rush of the water over the rock is the faint beat of Mena's wings as she searches for another threat.

She won't find one.

Wraiths rarely fight if they think they can't win. This is why we've lived in 'peace' for so many years. Why start a war when you can just kill someone in the dead of night and blame somebody else?

Wraith logic. We are a sunny bunch, aren't we?

Mena circles once, twice, and then finally lands on a large boulder jutting into the water from the shore. Phasing almost immediately, she jumps from the rock into Asher's arms, and a new ache wrenches in my chest. *West.*

He didn't come, didn't stay. He didn't help.

The ragged edges of my heart start bleeding once again. I know I released him. I know I told him I never wanted to see him again, and it's true—I don't. Not really, despite the pitiful whining of my heart. I couldn't keep relying on someone who was never going to choose me— who was never going to stay with me.

I can barely wrap my mind around the fact that he *knew* we were mates, knew that the Fates chose us to be together. He felt it with me and decided to deny me. For one hundred and nine years he's denied me. Turning his nose up at all we could be.

You'd think I'd know better by now.

I finally wised up, but only a little, because I was still shocked when he didn't come to the funeral. *Shocked.* How stupid can I be?

A lot, apparently, because I'm still stinging with jealousy from watching Mena and Asher, and as each beat of my heart begins to ache in my chest, I realize I just can't take one more thing today. Before I can leave, my best friend in the entire universe grabs my hand. I'm not looking at her, but I know it's Aurelia. The pain in my chest eases for a moment, and I have never been more glad she is here with me.

Saving me from the fire from the very first day we met, Aurelia knows me better than anyone—even if I've been keeping huge secrets from her.

Pulling me close, she wraps her arms around me, the natural heat of her skin warming me.

"I'll only be able to stall them for a few minutes so you can get your shit together, but *only* a few minutes. The house is empty, so use your time wisely," she whispers into my ear before giving me another squeeze.

I can work with a few minutes. That is just enough time to sling back a shot of bourbon and get out of this stupid gown. Who decided to make funerals formal attire only, for pity's sake?

Not taking the time to ponder the origins of Wraith customs, I travel from the multicolored rock floor of the gorge to my room in the cliff house.

It is an opulent room—far too rich for my taste—but Mama decorated it for me, and I didn't have the heart to tell her it wasn't me. Now, that she's gone, I can't imagine changing it.

The walls are papered in a lightly textured, luminescent cream. In fact, most of the room is in shades of white and silver from the wallpaper to the mirrored side tables. The only color—and my only contribution to the design of the room—is from a plush magenta area rug that is begging me to walk on it. I detour around the white leather sitting chairs just so I can walk across the soft shag on my way to the liquor nook hidden away by an antique-white paneled cabinet.

My mother and the white. *I'm not a virgin, Mama. That ship sailed a long time ago.*

I pull a squat tumbler from the lowest shelf and splash a healthy measure in the glass. I only get a single swallow in before Cam and Aidan bust my door open like an episode of Cops. They file in my room like they are my wardens, and I realize now, letting them get away with the shit they pulled in the gorge was a mistake on my part.

"Well, that was unnecessary," I say before I can stop myself, and I'm happy it comes out calm as you please instead of the seething rage bubbling in my chest.

"What the hell do you think you're doing, Evangeline?" Cam thunders, his hulking form fills the doorway, the black of his clothes making him look only more ominous.

He is chastising me like a naughty toddler.

Yep, big mistake on my part. *Sorry, Papa, I've failed you already.*

Taking another swallow of my bourbon, I carelessly fling the glass back in the cabinet. Before the tumbler can stop spinning on the bar top,

I've traveled to the pair of them and have Cam face first on the tile with his hand pinned behind his back.

First my parents, then West, now this. I am already shitting the bed at this whole leader thing. I am done failing, and if there is anything I learned from my father, it was sometimes lessons need to be taught the hard way.

As my talons gouge into Cam's face, I turn my black eyes to Aidan, and by his expression, I can tell he didn't expect me to know how to fight nor did he know I could take someone much bigger than myself down.

We've fought together. He should know better.

"I assume this tantrum is because I left the gorge?" I ask, and Aidan hesitantly nods.

Cam doesn't move an inch, and I don't blame him. One wrong move and his eye is going bye-bye.

"I have some issues with your behavior at the funeral. First and foremost, you held me back from fighting," I say calmly.

"We did our job. We were keeping you safe," Aidan gently pleads and while I appreciate the sentiment, I can't abide by it.

"Would you have refused to let my father fight? Would you have tried to take that away from him?" I ask, and I can tell my question hits home.

He has undermined me without meaning to, and at the realization, Aidan's face goes white.

Aidan and Cam have been with my family long before I was born. They see me as a child, a little sister, and while I trust them with my life, I can't trust them to guard me against the dangers of this reign for another second without this lesson.

"No. You wouldn't," I scold, answering for him.

"But you..." Cam begins.

"Do. Not. Presume to tell me what I can and cannot do. I am your Queen, your leader, and you will treat me as such or I will make you regret it." I say through gritted teeth, and while I feel slightly guilty for smashing his face on the hardwood floor, it has to be done.

I love Cam, he is the big brother I never had. He has tended to more scraped knees than any grown man should, but family or not, he cannot keep playing big brother.

It will get us both killed.

"I love you both, but I will release you and get someone else if you can't get it through your thick skulls that I'm not a delicate little flower. I know how to handle myself. And if you undermine me again, I will make your release the permanent kind. Do you understand me?" I question as I retract my talons from his face and travel to my feet.

I get a reluctant nod from Cam as blood wells from the cuts in his cheek. Cam and Aidan both take a knee of supplication, and when they rise, five little ribbons of red have made their way down Cam's face.

"Good. If it makes you any feel better, I will continue my sparring sessions with Aurelia to keep my skills sharp. She's been training me for a decade already, I see no reason to change things up now," I admit to a stunned Aidan.

"West let you..." Aidan says, and his eyes widen as he trails off realizing his mistake.

Just the sound of his name slices into my chest, and I steady myself against the blow.

"West was not aware. He was my Guardian, not my father. I don't want to hear his name again. Now, no offense guys, but I need some alone time. I'm going to go drown my sorrows in some bourbon and take a bath. I want the door fixed before I get out. Oh, and if you bust in my room again, I'll cut something off of that you need. Understood?" I ask, but it isn't really a question.

They both got a freebie pass for pulling that bullshit in the gorge. I can't be that lenient again.

Walking back to the cabinet, I snag the bourbon and my glass from the bar top and head to the en suite bathroom, gently closing the door when I want to slam it. Flipping on the taps before moving to the walk-in, I pull the zipper down on my dress and slip it from my shoulders. Carefully putting it on the thick, wooden hanger, my mind finally catches up with me. Black gauzy fabric, heavy, black beading, I hate this dress. I want to burn it. I want to rip it to shreds. This is the last thing I wore when I saw my parents for the final time.

It's tainted, infected with the bitter loss I'm trying so hard to stomp down into nothing. It's then that I let myself break a little and hug the now-cold dress to me as I crumple to the plush carpet.

I allow myself three minutes. Just three to vent some of this agony. I have to let it out now—where no one can see. I can't be weak, can't break.

Stemming the flow of the pain leaking from me, I climb to my feet and hang the dress on the rung. I can't let it go now. It was the last thing my mother picked out for me, the last thing we ever shopped for. Had I known at the time it was going to be my funeral dress, I wouldn't have ever bought it.

I reach up and straighten the strap on the hanger before running my fingers down the bodice.

Miss you, Mama.

I suck in a huge breath and let it out in a gust, shoring up my walls again and turn from the closet to turn the taps of the large clawfoot tub off. Filling the tumbler to the brim, I set it in the fancy teak bath tray spanning the width of the tub, and before I can think better of it, I plop the bottle of bourbon right next to it.

One night to grieve.

I need this time to deal with losing my parents. Time to put on my big girl panties and rule as good or better than my father did. My father had to worry about his mate, and that guided his decisions. Some of those, I hate to say, treaded the safe path rather than the right one. He stayed safe to keep his mate alive.

I don't have one of those, and I probably never will.

Nope.

Safe is not for me.

I'll do the right thing instead.

3

WEST

I HATE WAITING, ESPECIALLY WHEN IT'S FOR A POMPOUS wanker like Voyt Garrison. I wouldn't even talk to the smarmy prick, but unfortunately, I need his help.

Perched on a stool in my garage in front of the most beautifully beat-up wreck of a motorcycle—a newer model Triumph Bonneville some idiot decided to neglect—I should feel at home. This is my place—my safe haven. The fact that my garage is twice the size of the cabin in front of it that I tenuously call home is a testament to how much I love it here.

It makes me wonder why I even have a house. I don't sleep there. I don't eat there. And I'm thoroughly afraid of opening the refrigerator, because who knows what's growing in it.

My cabin is just a place; my garage is home.

Two stories tall and four bays wide, the garage is a car lover's dream —slate gray epoxy floors, vaulted ceilings with pendant shop lights hanging from steel cables, coal black 24-gauge steel cabinets lining both the north and south walls, and the best car lift money can buy in the south bay. I even have a bed and a shower in the back room—everything I need under one roof.

Turning a wrench is the only time I feel at peace, but the waiting has yanked my attention so much I've lost the skin of three knuckles already. Yeah, I'll blame waiting instead of what I'm really doing—thinking of Evangeline.

Damn that woman.

I've been dancing around her forever, fighting my baser instincts to avoid tearing my fangs into the delicate column of her porcelain neck. Just thinking about that line of soft skin makes me fight against my dick getting hard. The way that line follows her slim shoulders and petite body, the full curve of her breasts and the gentle swell of her hips that I just so recently got a glimpse of.

A tiny glimpse. Then again, any time looking at her would be too short. I could look at her for the rest of my life, and it wouldn't be enough time. And those eyes—clearer than a Colorado sky and twice as blue. The way her nose scrunches into this adorable little frown when she's irritated. That mass of curly hair that my fingers ache to get tangled in.

It isn't just her body; it's also the sounds she makes. When she's eating her favorite dessert, she makes this little humming noise with every bite that goes straight to my dick. When she knows I'm getting lost in my own head, she tells a joke or tells me a crazy story about some trouble her and Aurelia have gotten into. And the singing. Her voice turns rough when she sings, all bluesy in a way I'd never think her normally soprano vocal cords could go.

Damn, I miss her.

Just as I think that thought, the wrench in my hands slips off the bolt, and I have another skinned knuckle. I can't keep getting distracted like this, or my own brain is going to get me killed.

And with that pleasant thought, the wrench slips again.

Motherfucking, son of a whore.

"Nice mouth, Carmichael," a voice calls drolly from the shadows of my garage.

Voyt.

Took him long enough. I had no idea I was speaking aloud, but trust Voyt Garrison to point it out. He saunters into the light of my shop lamp, running a reverent finger over the fender of my fully restored 1950

Chevy ICON Thriftmaster. I did everything on the pickup except for the painting. The fact that he's touching it makes my lips pull into a snarl. First my girl, now my truck. If he keeps thirsting after what's mine, I'm going to rip his arms off.

"What took you so long? Needed to change your shorts after Evangeline got through with you?" I taunt, and I'm asshole enough to enjoy the uncomfortable twist to his face before he can mask it.

"Wouldn't you have?" he asks, and it is so self-deprecating, I have to give him that point.

"Eh... Probably," I chuckle tossing the wrench close to its proper spot.

Evangeline organized them all years ago, labeling the spots with her trusty label maker. She used specialty glue so the labels would stick to the foam insert. I can't even look at my own tools without missing her.

"So you wanted me here, and against my better judgment, I agreed. What do you need, West? Because this cloak and dagger crap isn't really my forte," he grumbles pulling my gaze from the stupid foam back to him.

"There was an attempt on Evangeline's life tonight," I say dropping a massive bomb on the likely clueless Voyt.

"What?" he growls his eyes going from green to the black of a phase so quick, even I'm surprised.

"Don't you worry your gelled little locks about it, I made sure none of the bastards lived. But they didn't think this shit up on their own. They looked more like pawns. I think some of the head families are behind it—it is the only thing that makes sense to me. They have to be responsible for John and Olivia's deaths, and that cannot stand," I inform him, and if anything it just brings an even more crazed look to his eyes.

His fingers rip through his perfectly coiffed, expertly gelled hair as a snarl erupts from his throat.

"You're telling me after I watched my two best men get liquefied right in front of my eyes, more death happened?" he asks on a demand as he starts pacing in front of the truck.

"What you mean to say is, after Evangeline's parents were poisoned and killed, several members of our community tried to murder her.

Because if you say that you are upset you lost those two assholes, I'm going to rip your dick off," I growl, barely staving off the right hook I so desperately want to plant in his temple.

"No, I do not lament the loss of two duplicitous men whom I obviously had no idea could... Our species as a whole is dwindling into nothing, you idiot. We had maybe ten thousand Wraiths left in the *world* after the Phoenix attacks, and now... There should be millions of us to keep the balance. To send the souls to Hell for good instead of them just sitting in rotting corpses waiting for some witch or warlock or shapeshifter to steal the energy and start some real trouble. There are too many souls for us to reap and not enough of us to go around. And we just lost more," he rants, still pacing in a jerky clip.

"So, you're worried about the hypothetical instead of the shit we're swimming in now?"

"No. I'm worried about how many I'm going to have to kill to keep her alive. I am well aware you don't care how many you kill, but *I* do," he insists pointing to his chest as he does so.

Trust Voyt to know where to hit to cause the most damage. The scars of the people I've killed are not healed on my soul. Rather, they are big gaping wounds that refuse to mend. But I don't kill without reason, and I don't kill the innocent.

Never again.

"I don't kill innocents, Voyt. Even the King's assassin has scruples," I growl.

"Of course not," he mutters, his tone scathing. "What exactly do you need from me?"

"I need an in with the Emerson family. If there were a head family that had anything to do with this, it would be them."

They are also the only head family that was conspicuously absent from the funeral, but I don't say that.

"And why is that? The Emersons have been one of the most upstanding families—they have helped so much with the aftermath of the attacks," Voyt says in disbelief.

Helped, my ass. I've never seen a family more two-faced.

"Devereux and Sampson Emerson were Evangeline's Guardians before me. They were killed in their service. If there is any family that has a serious grudge against her, it would be them," I inform him, and the hope on his face dies replaced with dawning horror.

"*Fates*," he mutters like a curse, and it is the first time Voyt and I have ever agreed on anything.

"I'm not going to attack anyone, but it would be much easier to suss out who the culprits are if I have an in with them. I may not be Evangeline's Guardian anymore, but that doesn't mean my job is done."

Voyt's eyes go wide in shock as he takes a step back. "She released you?"

"Don't sound so broken up about it, asshole. She's my mate, and I love her more than anything. But I... I can't bind her. Not yet. Not until I know she's safe. I'm trying to keep her safe," I admit, and it burns me to do so.

This isn't about avoiding the monarchy, it is about keeping her alive. As the King's Assassin, I made enemies. There are people out there who would rather see me as maggot food than to take another breath. I can't tie her life to mine for so many reasons, but the fact that I have a huge target on my back is at the top of the list.

"And she released you because you won't bind her," he guesses offhandedly.

"Got it in one."

"I assume you have a good reason for not binding her," he whispers, his voice has turned deadly.

He cares for her, and as much as it kills me to ask him for a favor, he is probably the only person I can trust to help me and keep her safe. Granted his reasons make me want to rip his arms off, but... if he keeps her safe, I have to respect him.

Voyt's face closes down, and I can no longer get a bead on him. From a man with my considerable people-reading skills, the thought of not being able to gauge him freaks me a bit. He is silent for a few moments but continues his pacing before he stops suddenly, breathes a huge sigh of resignation, and turns back to me.

"Yeah. I'll help," he says, his voice like sandpaper. "Give me a day. I'll grease the wheels and get you a meeting. I can't promise anything will come of it, but I'll do what I can."

"Even after I told you we are mates, you'll still help me?"

"I want her to be happy. I don't care if it's me who brings her happiness, as long as she's actually happy."

"I hope you mean that, Voyt. I really, really do."

Because when this goes south, at least Evangeline will have someone who loves her that much.

I can do what I need to, knowing that.

4

EVAN

I HAVE A STRONG URGE TO WEAR YOGA PANTS AND NOT GET OUT of bed for a week. Or maybe I'll just eat enough ice cream to give myself a sugar coma and sleep for the next fifty years.

Yeah. That could work.

The funeral was last night, and I haven't left this room for approximately twenty-four hours. By my count, I have less than five minutes left before Aurelia either busts down the door or figures out how to jerry-rig an incendiary device and blow it off its hinges.

The new raw wood door the idiot twins installed is substantial enough, but nothing stops my bestie. Solid oak be damned.

I'm proved right not two minutes later when Asher ferries Aurelia and Mena into the room with him in a swath of black smoke, totally bypassing the door altogether.

Right. I should have thought of that.

"Are you getting subtle in your old age?" I croak from underneath my veritable cocoon of down blankets and pillows.

She doesn't answer me, she simply holds up a finger and covers her mouth with her other hand, swiftly but calmly walking to the bathroom. The retching that quickly bites at her heels tells me all I need to know.

"You think she'll figure it out on her own or should we tell her?" Mena asks me, but I have no freaking clue what she's talking about.

Whatever. I don't have the energy for this.

"Figure out what, Princess?" Asher inquires, but Mena doesn't answer him.

She just gives him a sweet look that from this angle tells me she thinks he's a silly, stupid man. He doesn't catch it, though, because he's too busy looking at her lips to notice anything else.

Barf.

"If I wanted to see the newbie lovers in action, I would have gone outside my room," I gripe, and for an extra barrier against love-sick assholes, I throw a pillow over my head.

Two smarmy doe-eyed lovers and one pukey best friend. If this is the cheer-up crew, I am so screwed.

A flush and the tap sounding from the open bathroom door is a relief. That is until I hear her brushing her teeth. With what has to be my toothbrush.

Umm. No, she did not. The gargle and spit that follows just pisses me off more.

"You're going to need a new toothbrush," Aurelia croaks from the doorway still looking green.

"Are you kidding me?" I screech from my fortress of pillows.

If she thinks this is getting me out of bed, she is sorely mistaken.

"Nope," she groans, shuffling over to the bed and shoving me over to lay down beside me.

She barely has her head on a stolen pillow when there is frantic banging on the new door.

"Aurelia?" Rhys frantically calls through the wood. "You okay, Gorgeous? Open this damn door!"

Mena stifles a snicker as she unlocks it for him, and he damn near bowls her over getting through the door to get to his wife. Before I can blink, he's on his knees next to her side of the bed, checking her forehead for fever.

I have no idea why. As far as I know, I have never heard of Phoenix getting sick. Ever. I look from them to Mena and Asher, who are cuddling in a single white leather slipper chair. I think I would rather be on the moon than see every single one of my friends right now. And it sucks.

I don't want to see people. I don't want to talk. I don't want to bear witness to a cute kiss or nuzzled hug. I want my Mom and Dad. I want to rip out the guts of whoever conspired to take them from me, and if I can't have that, then... I don't know what. I'm not sure I'll let myself want anything else.

Soon, the room is filled with my family. Ian, his face somber for probably the first time in his life, and then Aidan filing in behind him. Even Cam and Carver show up. Carver's superfluous eyepatch is jauntily flipped up showing a perfectly working eye. I think it is supposed to make me laugh, and in normal circumstances, it probably would.

And even though this room is filled with all the people I love, I feel more alone than ever. Their voices practically grate on my skin. They all want to know if I'm okay. They want to know what's next, why I sent West away. The questions aren't asked, but I know they're there. I feel them closing in on me.

But I don't have the answers. I don't know what's next. I don't know if I'm okay. I'd venture a guess as to no—I'm not.

And West...

I sent him away because he would never choose me. I've been waiting for him to pick me—bind me—forever. He had all the time in the world, and he left me alone. And watching how quickly Mena and Asher succumbed to the bond. How little time it took... it just makes the century I've been waiting seem so much longer.

And Mama, Papa. My heart couldn't take much more. I needed to cut the dead weight, so he had to go.

"Hey," Aurelia whispers, pulling me out of the stirrings of a top-notch panic attack. "Want to go beat the shit out of something? I'll even hold the heavy bag for you," she offers, her voice soft in the newly loud room.

It is a kindness she's offering me, a reason to leave without a fuss, and I appreciate it more than I can say.

"Get dressed. I'll kick these assholes out," she assures me, and I feel my lips pull into a pathetic attempt at a smile.

I think I'm at a point in my life where I don't want to have to be grateful, but I am.

Aurelia ushers everyone from my room, allowing me a few moments to collect myself before I go kick the crap out of a heavy bag. But I don't dawdle. Instead, I move as quickly as I can through the motions of opening a brand new toothbrush and attacking my teeth with it, throwing on some clothes and heading out the door to the gym. At this point, I don't even know if my socks match, but I don't really give a crap.

I have the single-minded focus of a woman who is systematically avoiding her problems. No thinking, just doing.

Instead of walking, I travel to the gym located on the top floor of the cliff house and watch Aurelia string up the hundred-and-fifty-pound heavy bag on a wall-mounted L-bracket like she's tying her freaking shoelaces. After she hooks the bag, she doesn't look at me expectantly, she just moves on, wrapping her hands, waiting for me to be ready.

The space is mostly open, the weights and lifting platforms closer to the edges, and the center left open for sparring. I love this room, and if it weren't for the three full walls of floor to ceiling windows, I would have claimed it for myself.

Papa said it wasn't safe for me—it had too many points of entry. It couldn't be fortified. My suite on the second floor doesn't have any windows. As an interior room, I'm boxed in. I hate it. I see these windows, and I realize how naive and sheltered I've been. Skipping along happy when others were keeping me safe.

It's San Francisco all over again—me thinking I know better when everyone else had to watch my back, had to worry for me. I should know better.

"You about done wallowing?" she asks bracing herself behind the bag, and her dumb question is like a red flag in front of a bull.

"Wallowing? Really? You want to know if I'm done wallowing?" I roar, throwing a solid haymaker into the bag—my hands still unwrapped.

I don't move her an inch, and it just pisses me off. The stain of the blood on the canvas makes it worse.

"Pfft. Weak sauce. You've done better in your sleep," she needles me with a sneering little smile on her face.

The feral scream ripping up my throat surprises me, but not Aurelia.

She looks bored, unruffled. My next punch doesn't hit the bag—it doesn't hit anything at all. I clutch at nothing but air as Aurelia moves blindingly fast avoiding my fists at every turn. I can't make myself stop the advance on her, and with every single failed hit, my anger grows.

The phase comes against my will, my fangs ripping through my lips, my talons erupting from my fingertips. I can't stop. I try to rush her, herd her into the corner, but I can't seem to close in on her the way I want to. She's always one step ahead, and with every failed strike, the single-minded pain in my chest chips away. But in its place, the anger grows—the fury and regret and wrath.

I know what to do now. I know how I'm going to fix this mess. And with my last punch, I stop mere millimeters in front of her nose, pulling back just enough so Aurelia knows I could have hit her square in the face if I wanted to.

"Feel better?" she asks, and I realize she meant for me to lose it. She wanted me to vent this noxious poison brewing in my gut.

"A bit, but more importantly, I know what to do now," I say, my breaths coming out ragged.

She nods at me and strolls over to a tucked away mini-fridge filled with water and tosses me a bottle. I chug it down in three large swallows.

"I think Voyt had a good idea. I think if I gain support from the lower echelon of the Wraith community, I can face the head families with more than just my father's word at my back. Vengeance can't be the only goal here. If it is, then I will have nothing left when this is all over."

And I won't give those bastards the satisfaction of beating me after I burn them to the ground.

5

WEST

The Emerson's house makes me uncomfortable, like having an arm lopped off in shark-infested waters uncomfortable. It isn't just that the house—no, this structure could only be described as a mansion—is bigger than any home John and Olivia ever owned. What looks to be three stories with an additional stone-faced basement level tucked into a man-made hill, the only word I can use to describe it is vast.

And white. White paint, white stone, white columns.

The ground level is ensconced in a true southern-style wrap around porch with open slotted railings, complete with ceiling fans and chaise loungers. The second story has more of the same, only with an open-air balcony. The abundance of white is intermittently broken up by tall cobalt planters spilling riots of flowers down their sides. It's like a home and garden show vomited all over this place.

It isn't the lawn trimmed within an inch of its life, or that there isn't a single out of place leaf, twig, or weed to be found on the sprawling expanse of turf butting up against a forest so dense the waning sunlight refuses to filter through the leaves.

No.

The source of the pit in my stomach is the level of security and personnel surrounding the sprawling expanse of land butting the shore of Heritage Lake. Men lounging on chaises appear to be enjoying the sunset, but I know for certain they're covert security by their body language. None of the men are relaxed in their posture. Backs straight as an arrow, their heads move on a continuous scan of their sections, ready and waiting for a threat. Add that to the boats in the lake that only seem to pass to and fro in front of the property and nowhere else.

But these men don't see me yet—at least I don't think they do.

I traveled into the dense forest cradling the estate a football field away from the property line so I could assess the property without an audience. Too bad I'm one hundred percent sure I'm being watched. Either by cameras or people, I can't tell yet, but a finger of apprehension rakes its sharp claw down my back, and I know for certain I have eyes on me.

I suppose it's possible there's someone else out here, but I don't think so.

I've been on this earth for over six hundred years, and I haven't lived this long without learning a few things.

One of those things is how to spot surveillance.

I notice at least three black bullet cameras hidden strategically in the branches of a few southern red oak trees. That should be enough this far from the house, but the most worrisome—and definitely the most dangerous—are the five proximity sensors embedded into the bark of the Virginia pine and white birch trees to my left and right.

Proximity sensors that at this very moment are blinking red.

Okay. Stay calm. You were invited here. Invited... right.

I put my hands in the pockets of my jeans, cease my subversive study of their equipment, and start walking on my booted feet toward the house. Manners dictate that popping into someone's living room is considered bad form, so I mosey on, strolling as if I'm supposed to be here. Technically, I am.

As soon as Voyt told Walter Emerson—the patriarch of the Emerson family—that I had been released from my charge as Evangeline's Guardian, he wasted no time inviting me to his home for a meeting. I believe the word Voyt used was '*clamored.*'

While I'm not sure why old Walter thought it would be the best plan to have Voyt be the go-between, who am I to argue with a man nearly twice my age?

Feeling the thinning of the dense, humid air in front of me heralding the traveling of a Wraith, I have never been happier I don't have a single weapon on me as I am at this moment. If I came here armed I have no idea what would happen.

I don't know my place here with these people. By the looks of this house, they are going to take one look at the exposed ink on my arms, my gauges, my long hair, and they're going to make up their minds.

With John, at least I knew he gave a shit. With these people? Who knows.

Raising my hands in surrender, I try to appear as non-threatening as I can manage—which is difficult for someone six and a half feet tall—and wait. Before I can blink, five Wraiths travel into the space in front of me, all drawing down on my head. They look nothing like the guards on the decks and on the lawn of the house. These men are dressed in head-to-toe black suits, have a '*don't fuck with me, or I'll end you*' look to their faces, and an overt demeanor that screams Guardian.

Even their hair is the same. The lot of them have close-cropped, almost buzz-cuts. The only thing differentiating them is the color of their hair.

Well, hello to you too.

The men don't move—hell, they don't even blink—and we stand in this putridly tense silence waiting for each other to make a move. It might as well be me.

"If this is how you welcome invited guests, you all need some serious hospitality training," I droll, calm on the outside while I curse myself for not bringing at least one blade with me.

"West Carmichael?" the one in the front asks.

He might be the leader, but then again, he might not. He is barely distinguishable from the rest, and the level of uniformity makes me very uneasy.

As if I wasn't already coming out of my skin.

"Yep, that's me. I have a meeting with Walter Emerson in five minutes. May I ask you lower your weapons? Scooter there on the end is looking a little twitchy."

And he is. The poor, young Guardian at the back left looks barely a century old—if that—and it shows. It isn't that he's smaller than the rest —he's not, he's just as tall and broad as his brethren—it is more he seems to be the only uneasy one.

Someone has heard of me.

But when I look into his eyes, it isn't the spark of recognition I expect.

No.

This young one has seen things. Terrible things. And I don't know what he's witnessed, but I remember that look. It is one I used to see in the mirror every day before I got away from the people who made me. Before I changed my name. Before John got me out of the gutter.

Masking my reaction, I still feel my teeth clench. I'm an idiot for not bringing weapons.

The leader nods and all five firearms lower at once. He about-faces turning his back to me like a damn robot and marches toward the house, the other four men following suit.

"Follow us," he orders over his shoulder, and I have never wanted to do something less in my whole life than I want to walk into whatever is in that pretty house.

But I will. For my Angel.

The trek seems to take ages, even at the fast clip of the Guardians that appear to have a serious sticks up their asses. When we finally reach the sprawling porch, I'm told to wait. The house is even more perfect up close. No filth from pollen or weather mars the pristine white-planked porch. The chaises are perfectly fluffed, not a pillow or cushion out of place. The flowering pots are deadheaded—not a single wilted flower to be found.

This place creeps me the hell out.

"Someone will be right with you," the leader says, breaking me from my inspection, and four of the five travel from the porch as one. The fifth—the youngest—catches my eye and gives a slight shake of his head before traveling himself.

My gut clenches, the pit in my stomach growing larger. I want to get out of here. I want to travel from this picture perfect hell and go back to my Angel.

But I can't. I can't leave without making sure she stays alive. Rock, meet hard place.

Before I can change my mind and get the fuck out of here, the ornate front door opens. The tall, blonde woman behind it, looks to be no more than twenty-five human years old. But with our kind, she could be anywhere from twenty-five to twelve hundred and nine for all I know. The hardened cast to her honey-brown eyes tells me she's either very old or has lived through Hell.

My guess is the latter.

She's dressed to match the house. Prim, proper, and white—white dress, white shoes, white pearls. What is with these people and the white? Her makeup is tasteful but subdued, and her hair is pulled back into a bun at the nape of her neck like Evangeline does when she wants to look classy.

I hate it when my Angel pulls her riot of curls back.

Focus, dipshit.

"Mr. Carmichael?" she asks as if she isn't sure.

I'm a big man and the ink puts people off, but this lady looks like she's ready to bolt. Based on the pit in my gut, the young Guardian's response and this woman's face, I'm thinking this is probably the worst fucking idea I've ever had.

But intuition tells me this is the family. This is the place. These are the people behind so much unneeded death. And as much as I want to leave, as much as I want to travel from this place and never darken their door again, Evangeline comes first. I tip my chin up in the affirmative and wait for her to either open the door or tell me to go to hell.

"Please, come in," she says as she opens the door wider for me to enter displaying more and more of the opulence.

But I don't really see it. What I do see is the way her eyes flit down to the floor. The way her shoulders turn inward like a wounded little bird.

She's either seriously afraid of me, or she's been abused.

I'm getting real tired of this shit. Who hurts women? Aurelia. Mena. Two females that didn't deserve the hell they've lived with. Now this poor girl. What kind of sick bastard does this?

As I take a step to pass her, she whispers. The word doesn't register at first, but when the same five Guardians travel into the room accompanied by several more men, what she said makes sense.

She was trying to save me. Just like that young Guardian tried to warn me.

She was telling me to *run*.

6

EVAN

"YOU WANT TO DO WHAT NOW?"

I studied the plum polish on my fingernails, in an attempt not to maim one of my oldest confidants. There was no *want* about it. I was going to do this whether Aidan and Cam liked it or not.

Once I was confident I wouldn't launch myself across the room to punch Cam in the face, I lifted my gaze.

"What is so difficult to understand? Papa did not address the concerns of our people for almost a year, Cam. Support for the Black family is likely in the toilet, half of our species has been slaughtered, and the ones that weren't already in hiding, are wishing they'd found a good rock to retire under. If I want to actually be a Queen, it's high time I started acting like one."

Cam sputters, huffs, and then mashes his lips together in indignation. I'm right, and he knows it.

"I'm not talking about gracing the high and mighty with my presence. I'm talking about the regular folk, the people who are just trying to live their lives without a target on their backs. I'm talking about organized, methodical ways of obtaining souls, keeping Wraiths fed and healthy before they lose their minds."

Uncrossing my legs, I lean forward on the couch, pinning Cam with the truth.

"I need support, Cam, and I'm not going to get it from those stuffy bastards who sit up on high no matter what the Council says. If I'm going to be their Queen, I need to earn it."

Cam shoves to his feet and starts pacing the length of the living room, pausing at every revolution to eye the liquor cabinet like he would love a bourbon.

"I really hate it when you're right," he grumbles. "But right or not, how in the Fates are we supposed to keep you safe?"

"We can bring a team of security," Aidan offers from his formerly silent section of the couch.

Yeah, that would go over well. *Hi! I'm your Queen, but obviously, I can't defend myself so here's a bunch of huge men. You don't mind if they come in your house too, right?*

"Absolutely not. Just you two. This is a peacekeeping goodwill mission, not an invasion."

Cam's face goes beet red, and I can see him grinding his teeth from here.

"I don't know why you two are pissing and moaning. At least your charge doesn't have to go back into a society that has practiced mass genocide on their own people," Asher pipes up from the door to the office.

He's spent the last twenty-four hours trying to talk Mena and Aurelia out of their current plan to help restructure the power vacuum left with Iva's death and Nicola's absence. He isn't having any more luck than my Guardians.

Mena hugs her husband from behind, resting her chin on his shoulder. "We're doing this. You're just going to have to get over it."

Nodding, I speared Cam and Aidan with a hard look.

"We're doing this," I insist.

I just hope it doesn't come to bite me in the ass.

AURELIA, RHYS, MENA, AND ASHER LEFT THE CLIFF HOUSE THE same time I left to go on my pilgrimage to meet Wraiths that were anything but the filth of the head families. They needed to get back to their people, and with Nicola missing, who knew what kind of chaos they were walking into. I wasn't a huge fan of the division—and I'm still not—but letting your people hang in the wind is the reason both our factions were imploding.

The first family on my list were the Webers. A modest family with a small homestead in the foothills of the Canadian Rockies. We traveled to the edge of their property, ambling up the driveway at a sedate pace.

I wanted to give them plenty of time to prepare themselves for my visit, just not as much time as a phone call would provide.

This far away from a large populace, I wonder how they stay fed. It wasn't like people died out here in the country every day or even every week. I pause my pondering when a large man exits the home, waiting for us on the porch. Mocha-skinned and roughly a billion feet tall— okay, probably close to seven, but still—he waits patiently for us to traverse the driveway, parking himself in one of the several wooden rocking chairs peppered on the covered porch.

The three of us stop at the steps leading up to the house, waiting for the man to acknowledge us. After about thirty seconds, I had enough with the waiting bit.

"Mr. Weber?" I call. "Are you Xavier Weber, sir?"

He nods, still rocking, looking off into the distance.

"You that new Queen everyone's going on about?"

I worry about the level of talk and what they're probably saying, but I don't tell him that.

"I am. Would you be willing to speak to me?"

The man stops his rocking and turns to eye me up and down. Not in a rude way but in an assessing one.

"I suppose that would be alright. Your guard dogs can even come in too, but they'll leave their weapons outside. I don't allow weapons of any kind in my home."

"Absolutely fucking not," Cam growls under his breath, stepping in front of me, putting himself in between this behemoth of a man.

But his words weren't said quietly enough so Xavier doesn't hear him, and it's all I can do not to punch him in his fool face. Tapping Cam on the shoulder, I wait for him to turn his head.

"Your asshole, uber-protective ways are only hurting my chances of looking like a competent leader," I hiss between gritted teeth. "Knock it the fuck off, or I'm going to have to behead your ass right here."

Cam's eyes widen a fraction before he steps aside, allowing me to address Xavier once again.

"I apologize for any insult. Cameron has been with my family since before I was born. He has trouble letting me participate in things he deems as a detriment to my safety. There have been a few threats to my life in these last few days, so my Guardians are a little twitchy. Are you or your family a detriment to my safety, Mr. Weber?"

"No, your highness."

"Do you mind if we talk on your porch? That way you and I can talk freely, and my Guardians aren't overly concerned with my safety. How'd that be?"

"That would be just fine."

It takes less than five minutes to realize that Xavier Weber is a friendly mountain of a man. Of Dominican and German ancestry, he and his family relocated to this property to avoid being exterminated by Iva. But they miss their home and the ease of obtaining food. They miss the warm weather.

And they want to know if it's safe to return.

"A good politician would tell you what you want to hear, but I've never been a politician, and I don't plan to be. The truth is, I don't know. Iva is ashes, but I'm not sure if that's permanent. The newest Phoenix leader is mated to a Wraith, so relations between our species should smooth out, but I can't promise no one will act like a jackass and ruin it. My goal is to get you home, to make sure you're fed, and to keep you and your family safe."

Xavier gave me another one of his assessing looks. "I like your plan, highness, but you know I'm not the man you need to convince."

I'd known that tidbit, but I'd hoped it wasn't true. My sources told me that Xavier was one of the most respected Wraiths in the community. The problem was, his veneration was second to a man that pretty much hated my father.

"The man you need to convince is Trenton Price."

Figures.

EVAN—1928—LOS ANGELES, CA

The first time I met West Carmichael, I was singing at a speakeasy in Los Angeles. My parents didn't know where I was, and for the first time in a long time, neither did Aurelia. Hiding from a Seer is probably the hardest thing I've ever done, but a special cloaking amulet from a witch friend worked wonders.

It was pretty. A sapphire the size of my thumbnail set in a silver filigree setting hanging from a thin chain that rests just below my collarbone. It wasn't the nicest piece of jewelry I owned, but it was my favorite.

Maybe because it granted me my freedom.

Or maybe because it matched my royal blue silk charmeuse gown to perfection. I used to hate dressing up, but this lone frock made me feel like a woman. It was an off the shoulder number with a daring sweetheart neckline—far ahead of its time. It fit like a second skin until it hit my thighs then flared out like a calla lily into a delicate but short train. It may not have been the most comfortable dress I owned, but it made me feel like a sexy siren. Something that with my diminutive height, I rarely felt.

I was alone—finally alone even in this sea of people—after so much time with the ones I loved breathing down my neck. It was like a vacation. I needed something of my own. A secret, a life, something to break away from my family. Something that didn't say princess or royalty.

Something that let me just be me. Singing was it for me.

I was ending my five-song set with a favorite of mine, an old Jane Greene song when I saw him. I'd glimpsed him around town a few times, when I was shopping by myself or when I watched a boxing match at the Olympic Auditorium, a scandalous activity for an unchaperoned young lady.

But we'd never met.

He was handsome, I even daresay beautiful. If you can call a man like that beautiful. Tall—taller than anyone in the room by nearly a whole head—and built so powerfully he made the other men look like pitiful adolescents dressed up in their daddy's clothes. It was difficult to tell if his hair was as dark as it seemed in the low light of the secret club, but it appeared so in the dim.

Dressed to the nines in a brilliant black suit, he moved with grace through the crowd until he found his seat at the only open table in the joint, folding his huge frame into the chair with the grace of a jaguar.

Papa had taken me to Brazil when I was just a little girl, and we saw the big cats roam the rainforests. He moved just like one of those jungle cats, scanning the room for prey and threats, watching everything with casual disinterest, as if he could take or leave the sights and sounds and people. As if he were bored in this raucous party that seemed to never end.

But when his eyes hit mine... I was struck dumb, and I nearly flubbed the last three words of the chorus. His eyes were green, the color somewhere between jade and emerald, and framed in lashes so thick it was a wonder his eyelids could carry the weight of them.

I could tell he was like me—a Wraith—but despite his rather comely appearance, I wanted nothing to do with him. Better he think I was just some boozy siren losing her morals in the backroom of some secret gin joint than to know what I really was.

A prim and proper princess hiding out as if I wasn't of age, as if I was a young one. As if I wasn't more than a child. And maybe... maybe, compared to the rest of them, I might be.

Hell, I was only in my forties. To everyone else, I was practically a baby.

But I didn't feel like a baby. I didn't feel like I was some wayward child, but after San Francisco... it would be a long time before anyone trusted me with anything ever again.

On that troubled thought, I finished my song, made my way to the coat room, snatched my deep pile cranberry red velvet coat from its hanger despite the ire of the rather irritated coat check clerk and made my way through a group of slightly handsy revelers out the back entrance of the club.

This particular door led to a deserted alleyway, but I paid it no mind. I wasn't afraid. Sure, I was a woman alone at night, but I only needed to get out of sight of potential on-lookers before traveling back home.

But I didn't see them until they were within touching distance, and for this lot, was more than too close.

They were three steps past drunk and five steps past evil. I could smell it. Both the musty perfume of cheap alcohol and the mouthwatering scent of a filthy soul. I felt my fangs lengthen behind my lips as their souls called to me, and I fought not to phase on the spot.

Their clothes were in disarray, shirts half untucked, shoes scuffed, hair rumpled, and taking them in, I felt a little fear as my hunger grew.

I'd heard stories. Whispers of what could happen to women out alone. But I wasn't some weak human woman, and I wasn't helpless. I may abhor killing humans, but if it came down to them or me, I'd pick me ten times out of ten.

At their leers and snide little jeers, I felt my talons start to grow—my phase roiling under my skin, spoiling for a fight when I wanted anything but one.

But they never laid a finger on me.

Like an avenging angel, a large shadow loomed over my shoulder, blocking the light of the electric street lamp just thirty feet away at the mouth of the alley.

The men didn't have time to run. Or scream. Or fight. They were dead before they took their next breath. And standing before me was the Wraith from before. His hair was slightly mussed, but not one other thing was out of place.

I'd known I'd seen him before. But the way he'd intervened... The way he'd stood, breaths heaving, shoulders set, jaw clenched, eyeing me with censure and disdain, I knew. I'd thought since I'd been home so much, they would forgo assigning me a Guardian. A babysitter.

After twenty-two years, I thought I had slipped my leash. I was wrong.

I wanted to cry, but that was a luxury I wouldn't allow myself. Not in front of this beautiful man who seemed to despise me so much.

"Guardian?" I asked, my voice clogged with the tears I held onto by the skin of my teeth, but I already knew the answer.

Averting my eyes, I refused to watch his face shame me more. But because I was looking at my sapphire silk shoes, I missed his eyes dilating. I missed his breath go from labored to non-existent.

I missed seeing him realize I was his mate.

"Are you going to tell my father?" I asked, still looking at my shoes, but I never got an answer.

When I looked up again, the large Wraith and the three men were gone.

And I'd never even got his name.

EVAN

West has been on my mind more not less since I released him. Maybe I just need something to obsess about instead of thinking about my parents. Really? Who wouldn't? But the more I ponder it, the more I think maybe I just miss him.

After the first day he intervened outside that speakeasy, West has been a fixture in my life. My own personal hulking shadow saving me from myself. I want him—more than I'm willing to admit out loud—and it just pisses me off. I snap my eyes open as my feet touch the pavement.

This is how the bulk of our people live? Here? In Mayberry?

I think this as I walk up the brick-paved drive of a pretty, middle-class house, in a middle-class neighborhood, in a nice, quiet, small town. This is the seventh family I've called on, and it shocks me every time. This house is no different than the others I've visited—a different style of decorating and cars, maybe—but the theme is the same.

These are normal people. Normal folk who live regular lives in ordinary neighborhoods. Just living their lives. Two point five kids and a labradoodle, having brunch on Sundays, fucking normal. Not rich, not having more money than they can use in ten lifetimes, not evil or hungry for power. Real people with jobs and lives, on the PTA and neighborhood watch.

They just also happen to eat the souls of the damned on the weekends.

Here I thought all Wraiths—my own people—were greedy, scheming, shitty individuals, but the families I've met over the last week are decidedly not. They are friendly and hospitable and humble.

I have never felt at ease with a single member of the head families. Fearing the use of the wrong fork at dinner or tripping over my own feet —which happens more than one would think. I have never wanted to get to know them or speak casually with them or even give them the time of day. Too many chances to fuck up in front of them and have whispers about some random slip-up filter back to my parents. Not that they would mind. But these people... these are the people I would protect. And if these are the people Voyt has been helping, my respect for him has shot up by about three hundred percent.

I've avoided this house and this man for as long as I could.

My heels click on the pale gray brick paver pathway leading to the front porch of an elegant-but-simple craftsman-style home in the small town of Warrenton, Virginia. Cam and Aidan are at my back, looking less menacing than they have been over the last week. After each dismissal, each refusal, I knew exactly where I needed to go.

But this family, this house, was the one I was dreading. Their support—or dissention—would determine which way the domino would fall.

The Price clan was not among my father's biggest supporters. In fact, I'm fairly certain Trenton Price didn't even like my father. While they might not have been friends, Papa respected him. I remember them having heated debates about the problems in our society. Usually, it would end up in a sparring match, but Trenton and my father would end up coming to an agreement about whatever had them stirred up after they tried to kick each other's asses.

Things were going fine—or at least semi-amiable—up until about a year ago. I think this was when Mama was starting to get sick. Trenton and Papa's usually good-natured arguments went from fine to not fine pretty quickly.

Before I can take the first step up the porch stairs, Trenton whips open the door. He isn't a small man, well over six feet and solidly built. Sable brown hair clipped tight around his ears and long on top, clear blue eyes and a rocking beard.

I always thought Trenton was a level-headed man. I admired him. Usually the issues he brought to my father, I agreed with. Maybe not his proposed execution of them, but still.

Right now, though, I'm not certain old Trent has all his marbles. Especially since he has a double barreled shotgun aimed right at my chest.

7

WELL, THIS IS A FINE MESS I'VE PUT MYSELF IN.

The trek to my current accommodations was long and arduous. Through the bottom floor of the pristine, white house, down two flights of stairs—one of them so old and rickety I was sure they would break under the weight of my left boot—and along a lengthy stone hallway passing cell after cell, to my new abode. All the while, I have to fight my natural instincts to not maim, murder, and kill because I had the barrel of a gun jammed against the back of my head, and the shithead holding the weapon wasn't nice about it either.

This isn't the first time I've been held at gunpoint, nor is it the first time I've been held captive. My life up to this point hasn't been sunshine and roses, but for the years I was Evangeline's Guardian, it was pretty close. I was a part of something. I had a family—better than the one I was born into.

I should have known I wouldn't get to keep it. I should have known it would all go to hell some time. *And that some time is right about now.*

My new home is a small, ten-by-six stone cell with a stainless steel cot bolted to the right wall and matching toilet on the left. The stone appears ancient, and I would venture a guess I'm in some not-so-forgotten cellar or dungeon, or possibly, given the location and style of the house, the long-abandoned slave quarters. Just thinking that gives me the willies.

The burgundy-black of long dried bloodstains on the floor and walls does nothing to help matters, either.

I suppose the man-made hill the house sits on makes much more sense now, but the water table must have risen since the structure was initially dug because the walls and floor are practically weeping with moisture. The smell of mold, mildew, and the stench of torture and pain are all rank within the dungeon.

All I've had for the last hour is the bare metal cot, the toilet of doom, the wet stone walls, and the solid steel door that could substitute for a bank vault.

Oh, and silence. I've had a fair bit of that.

The first thing I tried as soon as they slammed my cell's door was traveling, but I got nothing and nowhere—just a black mist ping-ponging against the walls. I'm guessing some witchy juju is at play here.

Fabulous.

I want to pace, but I can't make it more than two strides before hitting a wall. I want to punch through the stone, but I have a feeling I'm going to have to avoid injury as much as possible. I have a feeling some serious pain is coming my way.

I have a feeling I've been betrayed.

I cannot believe I trusted that fucker. My gut lied to me. It told me I could trust him. It said he was the in for me here. If I ever see Voyt Garrison again, I'm going to rip his fucking head off.

When the cell door groans open, I tense like a coiled snake, ready to blow through whoever stands between me and freedom. I'm not thinking of what's beyond the door. I'm not thinking of anything but not dying in this little slice of hell. So when Voyt's head comes into view, I feel the beginnings of a sadistic smile stretch across my face before I can stop it.

Just the man I wanted to see, I think as I strike. Lunging across the last few steps to grab him by his perfectly ironed shirtfront, slamming him into the closest wall. I take the extreme pleasure in watching his head bounce off the rough stone. He's only stunned for a second before the phase comes over him, and even though he tries to speak, I wrench him back and slam him again. He's ready for it this time, and the strike to my forearms is hard enough that I nearly lose my grip on him.

Nearly, but not quite. Then, I start hitting him in every soft-tissue spot I can reach. Abdomen, kidneys, solar plexus, are all hammered by my fists before he breaks my hold. He doesn't attack while I recover, only throws his hands up to block my next blow. If I weren't so enraged, I would have picked up on it. I would have noticed he never attacked me back, only blocked me, punch for punch, strike for strike.

I don't notice this until it is almost too late. Then, my brain catches up with my body, and I stifle the blow I was aiming to his throat. One more inch, and he would be dead.

"Is there a reason you're neglecting to fight back, Voyt? Because unless you give me a good reason, I'm ripping your fucking throat out," I growl through my fangs.

"Yes, and if you could manage to calm down, I'll tell you," he says with a sardonic yet relieved expression on his face.

He gets a reluctant nod from me, but he barely pauses to wait for my response.

"I have too much to get out and limited amount of time to do it. I didn't betray you. I swear. As far as I know, Walter is not going to keep you here. He is going to interrogate you, though, and this is what I'm twitchy about. I think he has other people down here. He has some freaky shit going on in this house, and Claire looks like a damn POW," he whispers furiously as he rips his hands through his hair.

"Who is Claire?"

"Claire Emerson. The woman who answered the door? She's Walter's daughter," he informs me.

This bit of info is shocking. She tried to warn me. If she's Walter's daughter, why would she stick her neck out like that? Who knows what is really going on here. Without a good reason, I trust this Claire. She tried to help me, I think, and I even though I can't decide if it is a ruse, I trust those wounded-looking shoulders before I'd trust a smile. Those shoulders said victim, they said pain. Those shoulders told the truth.

"She told me to run, and one of his Guardians signaled for me to leave. I don't think you know what's going on here anymore than I do," I tell him, regretful I asked him to help me.

"Probably not. I'm flying blind here, man. I had no idea... I'm used to petty stuff, West, not this duplicitous horse shit. I have no idea what I'm supposed to do," he admits, and I feel bad for the guy, I do, but not enough to let him off the hook.

I need him to do one thing for me, and I need him to keep his head.

"Just keep calm. I think I can talk my way out of this. Maybe. But if you get out of here, and I don't, you tell Evangeline everything, okay? You tell her I was right. She'll know what you mean," I instruct him, my tone pleading.

I know what I'm telling him to do, and I don't want her in danger, but she needs to know. She needs to know I didn't forget about her. I didn't abandon her. She needs to know who she can trust.

Voyt takes a deep breath, squares his shoulders and gets his shit together. He gives me a nod and turns to leave before I say the absolute last thing I ever wanted to say.

"Keep her safe, Voyt. Promise," I order, my voice like it's been run over broken glass. I think it is the rawness of my voice that stops him in his tracks.

He never turns back around, but as he pushes that cell door wider to leave, he whispers, "I will."

I'll hold him to that.

In this life or the next.

8

*T*RENT *HAS LOST HIS MIND*, I THINK AS I RAISE MY HANDS IN surrender. The three of us have stopped in our tracks on the immaculate brick paver pathway, waiting for the crazy man to decide if he's going to kill us or not.

I hope not, but with the way my life is going right now, I'm not holding out hope for some miracle.

"Get off my land, Evangeline. Whatever you want, I'm not helping you," Trent growls, stepping across the threshold onto the porch, and I see my opening.

I don't wait for Aidan or Cam who I can tell are still trying to come up with an exit strategy. I love them like brothers, but they will just mess this up for me.

I don't wait for Trent to say another word, either. Who knows what has that man in a twist. Instead of the showdown he probably expects, I travel just to the side of the open door and wrench the gun right out of his hands, tossing it to Cam with one hand and with the other, I grab the top cartilage of his ear and bend his big ass frame to my lips.

"That is no way to treat your Queen. Apologize. Now," I hiss into his ear. When his mouth screws up into a grimace but no apology passes his lips, I decide he needs a lesson. Before he knows what hit him, his nose is bleeding, and he's flat on his back on his own porch with my boot digging into his chest.

"You were saying?" I ask on a growl. I haven't phased, and I don't need to. I can do plenty all on my girly lonesome, *thank you very much.*

The crazed smile that breaks across his face is mildly disturbing and a bit endearing. He looks like a proud papa and his favorite child just learned to walk, or at least in my case, learned how to kick someone's ass.

"Evangeline, my Queen, how nice to see you again. Welcome to my home. Please do come in," he says genially enough that I remove my boot heel from his ribs.

"Trent, good to see you. I have a favor to ask. You up for it?" I ask as I smile sweetly down to him.

His smile is manic, but I pay it no mind. Trent is Mercury personified.

"Absolutely."

My plan—at least to me—seems like common sense, but to the head families, it will be seen as an act of aggression if not an all-out call for war. I don't want much; I just want them to use the manners they failed to learn in kindergarten. Hell, kindergarten wasn't even invented when these people were getting their feet in this world. Maybe their parents neglected to teach them the basics.

I'm sitting on a dainty chaise in a sitting room better suited for a *Gone with the Wind* reenactment rather than the super duper important head family meeting I'm supposed to be leading.

I'd wanted it to be in a conference room.

I'd wanted to pay each of the families a visit.

But Aurelia gave me some impeccable—albeit unwanted—advice.

"You have to make sure they underestimate you. Surprise is your friend here," she'd said, and she's right.

It doesn't matter if I dress the part in a power business suit with my hair pulled back or if I'm in a petticoat and corset, these stodgy old farts aren't going to give me the time of day anyway.

I'll have to make them.

By force if necessary.

The said stodgy bastards are all in attendance, thankfully, and I don't have to send someone to reel them in. Carver wanted that job, and I don't blame him. Twenty years of deceit makes a lot of bitter in one's stomach. I'd want to hunt the bastards down too. Alas, each of the head families has a representative here to listen to me even if they'd rather eat dog shit than hear me talk.

Vincent Stein, a lithe, if aged, gentleman sits to my left, casually reclined in a great leather wingback, his left ankle is coolly resting on his right knee, and he's sipping my father's scotch. He doesn't appear old per se, but rather he looks like a thirty-five-year-old man has gone gray very early in his life. He's likely edging on over a thousand if I could take a guess, and unlike my father, he will probably be around for a few more centuries.

I can feel my lips start to curl at that thought but rein in my ire. I can't start off this way.

To Vincent's right is Walter Emerson, and good-looking guy or not, he gives me bad vibes in a pretty major way. It isn't just that his sons, Devereux and Sampson died trying to save me. Anyone would feel awful for that, but I don't feel awful, exactly, more I feel indifferent.

Devereux could have gotten us out of San Francisco. He could have gone back to my father instead of traipsing us all over the country. He was considerably older than I was, and at twenty-one, I had neither the necessary skills to fight myself nor the understanding of security as I do now. I may have caused the destruction in the aftermath, and I will hate myself until the day I die for taking so many lives, but I did not take theirs. Devereux and Sam died because they were too scared to go back to Papa with men on their heels. It may have taken me nearly a century to get over it, but I don't feel the guilt of their loss like I used to.

Walter's eyes are dead—not like he's masking his emotions—like he doesn't have any in the first place. His face is animated enough, but those eyes... pale gray irises thickly lined with long, black lashes which are at odds with his platinum blonde hair have to be the creepiest things in the known universe. He's handsome—taller than average height, square jaw, trim waist, decent upper body. He's not West by any stretch of the imagination, but he's built solidly enough.

I do not need to be thinking of West right now.

Halting my inspection of Walter, I move to the rest of the men in the room. Each of them handsome in their own right, but they all lack a significant emotional trait that is crucial. They do not give one single ripe shit about anyone or anything but themselves.

And because of that, I will have to be a hypocrite.

Staying in the same lounged position, on my completely unnecessary but decorative piece of furniture with Aidan and Cam at my back, I address the room.

"Wraiths are the most hated faction of the Ethereal. Do you know why they hate us? Because they fear us," I announce, and my saying this pulls a smile or positive gesture from every man in this room except for the men I trust.

This tells me all I need to know.

"Ruling by fear is why we are dwindling into nothing. Other factions won't help us. Witches think we are no better than Demons. The Phoenixes—except for a slight few—have practically stomped us into extinction. Warlocks and Shapeshifters think we are no better than cockroaches because a few have tainted the reputation of us all. Stealing from other factions. Threatening Hell to any that oppose them. Extortion of services and money to avoid getting sent downstairs. Trafficking Witches and Warlocks to the highest bidder for Fates only know what. Murder. Sedition. Mutiny," I accuse, my eyes landing on Walter at the last word. "All these crimes have been committed by a person in this room, their family, someone under their care, an employee—doesn't matter. As of this moment, it will stop. My father may have turned a blind eye, but I won't. We have an alliance with the Phoenixes now. Their newest leader, Mena Constantine, is mated with a Wraith. The Primary is Aurelia Constantine, my closest friend and the woman who took down Iva. As far as I'm concerned, all grievances with the Phoenixes have been squashed. Now, it is up to you to help me in this endeavor."

"And what would you have us do?" Vincent asks, and I can tell by his tone, he actually gives a shit.

He is really asking me because he wants to know. My relief in this is extinguished when Walter cuts in.

"It doesn't matter what she would have us do. This little girl isn't a

Queen. She's barely over a century of unmated pussy," he says with a sneer, and he gets a butter wouldn't melt in my mouth smile in return.

My bland smile must prove something to him because he sits back in his chair and sips from his tumbler of my father's fucking scotch.

He doesn't get a swallow in before I've traveled to him and smashed that glass against his misogynistic face. While he's still stunned, I wrench him from his seat and bounce his head off an end table and then use his hair as a handle and drag him like a broken puppet to his feet. He can't keep them, and I feel the hair start ripping from his scalp as I speak.

"Using fear as a deterrent does not work for most people. Fear breeds unrest, unrest breeds hate, hate breeds war. You, gentlemen, have fucked around and done nothing for so long, we're at the late stage. I want you to stop whatever scams you have going on. Whatever nefarious activities your family, friends, employees, your second cousins twice removed has in the fire. Doesn't matter. Whatever it is, it stops now. You will investigate and eliminate these operations. Eliminate but not kill. You will bring them to me, and I will deal with them. We will be doing things very differently from now on, gentlemen," I inform them, still holding up Walter by his hair.

"Is this you not leading by fear?" Vincent asks, and by his smile, I can tell he's proud.

"I said fear doesn't work for most people. For some, it is the only thing they respond to. They will only respect someone stronger than them," I say with a smile, and unleash some of the power bubbling under my skin.

The thick-pile Persian rug beneath my feet begins to abrade away, tiny particles circling around me and my captive like a tornado. Then I really let it out, and the chaise behind me, and every single stick of furniture not nailed down moves as if pulled by a string, smashing against the closest wall.

"Trust me when I say, gentlemen, I'm stronger than you. Any questions?"

9

I'D ALWAYS THOUGHT MY LIFE UP TO THIS POINT WAS AS BAD AS it could get. I figured nothing could be worse than my childhood and the gutter I crawled my way out of. I thought my father was the worst man I'd ever meet, and the level of his depravity and malice would forever go unsurpassed.

I had no idea.

I never made it out of that cell. Walter had no intention of listening to me or meeting with me for any other reason than to inflict pain. He paid me a visit in my lovely six-by-nine cell for the first time about a month ago.

And every day—every waking moment—is worse than the last.

He told me all about his visit with Evangeline, and I couldn't help but be proud of my Angel. My tiny, little pixie sure showed him. His nose had the obvious slant of a fresh break, and there were anywhere from ten to twenty small slices in the flesh of his cheeks, lips and forehead. I was proud—still am—but I paid the price.

Every single cut and broken bone, every slash and crunch, every single gasp of pain and drop of blood.

I paid.

I'm still paying.

He refuses to kill me, though. No, that would be too easy. It would let me off the hook, and Walter is having far too much fun. I know why I'm here. I'm a tool, a weapon, a chink in Evangeline's armor. They know how much she loves me, and I her. They know so much about her. Not from my own mouth, though. I have suffered absolute agony, and still I haven't said a peep.

But, I'm not the only prisoner here, and those prisoners don't love her like I do. Voyt and Kyle are two that I know of. In fact, their cells are on either side of mine. Voyt tried to get me out, tried to convince Walter that I was an asset to him. He had no idea what he was getting himself into.

My dungeon-mates don't know it yet, but I have a plan to get us out of here. I just need one little sliver of a chance, and we're bouncing out of this hell hole. Really, only one of us needs to get out, but I'm gunning for the three of us.

I refuse to leave a man behind.

My only respite is this cell, and as awful as it is, I'd rather be here. The torture is never inflicted here, only in the main chamber at the end of the corridor. That chamber has all the tools—pokers, blades, vices, racks, presses, manacles—all with the stench of old blood and the sweat of agony. But my respite never lasts very long. I can't remember the last time I ate anything, and it brings back memories of my childhood. The cold hunger in my belly, the wet chill that never seems to go away.

Then, my chance comes. The guards have never tried to get me out of my cell without incapacitating me first. Which is smart of them. Usually, they open a narrow slot in my door, slip the barrel of a gun through the gap in the steel and shoot me with a healthy dose of tranquilizer. It has happened enough, and I've been in this cell long enough, that I know the sounds heralding the shot. Tensing, readying myself for what I have to do, I try to keep my intentions off my face.

When the shot finally comes, I almost fail. The needle barely pricks my flesh before I catch it, stopping the dart from embedding into my belly. From experience, I know it takes a minute or two for the drugs to take effect, so when I pretend to pull the dart from my stomach, I know I have at least two minutes before they'll come in to get me. I relax my body slowly, ignoring the pain in my broken toes and shin, ignoring the slashes and bruises and seeping wounds, faking a drugged sleep better than I thought I'd be able to. I'm tired, and those pharmaceutically enhanced nap times have been the best sleep I've gotten here.

Too bad they're usually followed up by torture.

Two guards file into my cell, each taking an end and carry me down the corridor to the room I'm dreading. I dread, yet am thankful for this room. Whoever did the warding on my cell, failed to do the same level of warding on the torture chamber. I feel the magic in the air, and I have a sneaking suspicion I can travel out of that room. While my cell is damn near impenetrable, the room-of-pain has little pockets of un-warded space—hopefully, big enough for us to travel through.

That is *if* we can travel.

My transportation and I are the last to arrive to the party, and I peek through my eyelashes to survey the room. Voyt, Kyle, and another small form are unconscious and already manacled to wooden racks that look older than I am. A few torches dot the walls of the circular space, highlighting the tools of the torture trade, but keeping most of the area covered in inky shadow. Sharp hooks, dragon's tail rope darts, curved knives, vices with spiked barbs, and more all hang from pegs in the stone.

The guards drop me unceremoniously on the wooden rack, and I notice the four of us are positioned equidistantly apart almost as if we are the four points of a compass.

Not good. Really, really not good.

We have never all been here together, and the fact that we are arranged in such a way... this does not bode well for us.

Just then, a man strides into the room. He's mostly in shadow, staying to the dark edges of the room, but stops at the rack that points south—or what I think is south—where a very small form rests. The flames flicker just right, and I catch a glimpse of copper hair.

Nicola.

Oh. Shit.

No wonder they knew so much about us. I wonder how long she and Kyle have been here. Did they get him first? Her? And how in the hell did they sneak up on an Oracle for fuck's sake? I don't care if she's blind, the woman is a damn psychic.

I have too many questions and no way to get answers—no way to know anything but that we have to get out of here as soon as fucking possible.

The man leans down, whispering in her ear—his voice so low I can't make out a single word. Her unseeing eyes flash open, her head and shoulders rise off the wooden rack, her face so horrified she can't even speak. Nicola shakes her head violently, mouthing the word 'No' over and over again.

The man turns from her and goes to the rack to her left where Kyle is still unconscious. His face is visible now. Blond hair tops sharp and angular features, and his cold smile reminds me of Walter's so much this man must be an Emerson.

He pulls a wicked blade from a sheath at his belt and begins to remove Kyle's shirt. Once Kyle's chest is exposed, the man begins debating where to place the knife, asking Nicola where she would like her mate to be stuck in the sickest sing-song voice I have ever heard. He's beyond deranged and taking great joy in the hypothetical torture of her sleeping mate.

"Come on, Nikki. Tell me. The lung? The heart? Maybe the liver? How do you want your mate to die, Nikki? How painful do you want it to be? Say yes, and I'll let him go. Say no one more time, and I'll make his death last days," he threatens as he runs the knife down Kyle's face. I don't blame her when she breaks down and reluctantly nods.

"No, Nic. Don't do this. Don't let them do that to you," Kyle groggily pleads, the cut of the knife rousing from his drugged slumber. He's yanking at his barbed steel manacles, drawing rivulets of blood with each pull.

"I have to. There's no other way," she rasps as she turns her head to face Kyle, her eyes unseeing, but her face pleading. He struggles to swallow, his head thudding on the rack and his body falters.

"Well, then. That was surprisingly easy," the man remarks, clapping his hands together as he walks to the center of the circle, raising his hands to the heavens and start to chant.

I don't know what's coming, but I need to get us out of here.

Now.

I spied Voyt's body lying untethered at the eastern point of the circle. He's feigning sleep, but I can tell by the rigid set of his shoulders, he's about to move. I cluck my tongue as quietly I can to get his attention, and he slowly turns his head to me. A silent conversation passes between us, and I knew we need to get Kyle and hopefully Nicola out of here before Crazy Ass Emerson can do whatever it is he's planning.

I nod to him to get Kyle while I go for Nicola. All the while Emerson is chanting, and some of the words he's using start to filter in my brain. They're Latin—only some long forgotten bastardized version that I haven't heard since childhood.

The words he's using filter through my poor knowledge of the language. Words like '*summon*' and '*return*' and '*death*'. And then it all comes clear. He's trying to summon a soul from the Otherside.

My head whips to Voyt, and I can tell he just put it together himself because the blood drains from his face. Then Nicola starts thrashing and screaming, her pained cries so loud they reverberate off the stone walls, echoing into a tortured tornado of agony. We don't wait, and travel to our respective charges, him much faster than me and it takes me a second to realize I'm more injured than I thought.

In the next second that passes, as I yell for Voyt to take Kyle and go, realizing all too quickly that I can't carry both Nicola and myself out of here.

And I won't leave her behind to suffer. Not like I suffered.

I don't see or hear the man behind me, but I do feel the sharp sting of the dart embedding its way into my back.

Well, at least they got out, I think as the stone floor rushes up to meet my face.

WEST—1423—SCOTLAND

I woke up in my bed of old thatching before the light ever cracked across the sky. I had chores to do and a limited amount of time to do them. Father wanted things just so, and if I didn't get them done timely enough, I wouldn't be able to walk the next day.

My tunic and breeches were woefully inadequate for the winter weather, and my shoes were three steps past threadbare. The snow seeped into the holes in them as I trudged through it to gather water from the well and give the horses their daily drink. Having no coat, I shivered in the freezing air, but you'd better believe Father had one. I needed shoes and clothes and at the very least a sheepskin to keep me warm at night. At ten years old, I had long since forgotten what warmth felt like. I didn't even have enough food to put a dent in the hunger in my belly.

But Father did.

Father's bed was more than just thatching on the dirt floor of one of the outbuildings. His was in the house proper and was up off the ground in a wooden bedframe. He didn't have a dirt floor—he had slate. His mattress was filled with feathers and fresh straw, and his meals were more than scraps left over that I stole from the dogs and pigs.

I wasn't the only servant—and make no mistake, that's exactly what I was—I was just the only one he had fathered. A bastard child of a sadistic nobleman and the poor dairy maid he took as repayment of a debt—I was only slightly more important than pig shit on his boot heel. The other servants knew my place. I was less than nothing, an inconvenience. The only person who had ever loved me was my mother, but she'd died a rather painful death three winters ago.

I'd promised myself as soon as I could find a way out, I'd take it, but there have been plenty of chances, and I hadn't taken any of them. It felt wrong to leave when I feared humans so. I didn't know how to hide yet. I was a good twenty years until maturity and knew no family who would take me in.

And why would they?

My father ruled over this village of Wraiths. He was known to be an evil man—evil but cunning. No one would dare go against him, and at least here, I knew what to expect.

"Henry!" I heard my father's slurred voice shout, and I froze.

He so rarely called me by name. It was usually 'boy' or whatever horrible name he could come up with on that given day.

I searched my mind and was certain I did everything required of me. I fed and watered the horses, fed the pigs, gathered water for the house and mucked the stable.

But I forgot one crucial detail.

It didn't matter if I completed my chores or if I didn't. Some days, I would receive a beating anyway. Not just beatings. These were the worst forms of punishment. Broken bones, blood drawn. And he did things to me. Things I hope to never think of again. Things I'd never wish on my worst enemy.

I took a deep breath and went to face my father, but staying to the shadows so I could see him first. I peered around a hay cart, and my belly dropped. It was barely past midday, and he was already drunk on mulled wine. Drunk or sober, it didn't matter, he was still mean as a snake, but drunk was invariably worse.

"HENRY!" he roared again, and I knew, I just knew my time on this earth was up.

He held a knife—a shiny silver dagger I'd seen him carry before. Usually, it hung in a small scabbard at his belt, and as far as I knew, he'd only been without it once. He'd lost it in a game of chance, but I'd heard the other servants say he murdered the man who won it from him— rather brutally—to get it back.

"Y-yes, Sir?" I said, the small act of calling him 'sir' instead of 'my lord' was an act of defiance, but I hated how my voice wobbled. I was never permitted to call him Father, even though everyone knew he was mine. We looked just alike—same dark hair, same tall stature, same green eyes. Our noses, our chins, our cheeks—they all matched.

I was my father—just in miniature.

I could tell my face irked him. It was in his expression every time he looked at me.

"Did you take this book?" he said, brandishing the leather-bound journal like a weapon. I'd hidden it in a secret nook in the stable—well, not so secret anymore—and read through it most nights. I'd pilfered it from my mother's things years ago. Father had taken all of her possessions from me when she died. I had nothing from her until I stole that journal back before he could burn it.

My mother—unlike many of the other servants—knew how to read and write, and taught me at a very young age. I knew what was in that journal. I knew every secret and every wrong doing my father had orchestrated over the last ten years. I knew the pain my mother endured. And I knew what she faced before he killed her.

Painfully. He drew out her punishment for days before there was nothing left to her. Before her poor body just couldn't take another moment.

But that journal was my ticket to freedom—as soon as I could muster the courage. And he had my ticket in his filthy, drunkard hands.

"Answer me, boy!" he roared, but he didn't need an answer.

He needed an excuse. An excuse to kill me just like my mother. Now he had one.

I wasn't expecting him to throw the book down and charge me. My only saving grace was his drunken state—it helped me avoid the flashing steel in his hand. Otherwise, the dagger he held just a moment ago would have ended up in my belly instead of in the dirt where it laid between us. He lunged for it first, but stumbled over his own feet, landing on all fours in the muck.

I knew he wasn't going to stop. He was going to keep reaching for that dagger until it made its home in my gut. I debated saving myself until he reached for it again, and then it wasn't in my control whether or not I was going to grab for the knife—I plucked it from the dirt before his awful fingers could close over the carved silver hilt.

"You give my dagger back to me, boy," he ordered as he climbed to his feet.

His face had clarity to it, he was either no longer drunk or had sobered up enough to know I'd protect myself if I had to. Like my mother couldn't.

"No," I whispered.

"Henry Carmichael Weston, you give me the dagger back right now!" he roared as he lunged, staggering at the last possible second and impaling himself on the blade.

My only thought was on the fact that he called me by my full name —the name my mother gave me as a slight to him because it carried a part of him that he refused to acknowledge. The part that named him my father. I hadn't even been sure he knew my full name until then.

Father lurched backward off of the blade, but the damage was already done. Dark red blood flowed from the wound in his chest, pouring down his pale brocade tunic and velvet breeches all the way down to the buckles on his boots. He lost his feet then, his knees hitting the ground first.

In my ten-year-old brain, I was still stuck on the name—my mind refusing to process the death of my tormentor.

His face turned a sick shade of gray, the blood that used to fill it flooded from him in great gushes. Then he fell, face-first into the muck, still and silent as only the dead can be.

"That's not my name anymore," I said to his back, and those were the last words I spoke for a very long time.

IO

VOYT

Traveling injured is not my favorite thing in the world to do. It isn't even in the top ten. Or twenty. Or three million. Traveling injured is taking an already agonizing activity and making it black-out-from-pain awful. Three weeks in Walter's care is probably what Hell feels like. It makes me never ever want to fuck up so royally that I have to go to Hell, because I think I'd rather intentionally set myself on fire.

It's my own fault. I should have been better at the stealth. I should have been able to talk these guys around, and if I couldn't do that, then I had to figure out what the game was and see what I could do to stop it since West was stuck in that cell because of me. I had a week. One single week to try and get as much info as I could to give to Evangeline.

I failed and got myself caught.

Now that I'm out, I have no idea what I am supposed to do other than tell Evangeline everything. And pray she doesn't kill me.

Jesus Christ on a crutch, Kyle is the heaviest person I have ever carried, and I pray I never have to do it again. It took me three tries to get myself and Kyle to Mena and fifteen to reach that doorbell once I got us to her front porch. I'm just lucky I remembered where she was looking to buy a house, or I would be worse than screwed.

I'd be dead.

It's freezing this high up the mountain, and given the fact that I'm wearing a pair of three-weeks-long soiled jeans and nothing else does absolutely zilch in the way of making this any better. The door opens after what seems like an eternity on this damn porch and Asher sees Kyle and immediately drags him inside.

What the am I, chopped liver?

It's hard for me to talk and has been for some time. I'd been screaming quite a bit over the last few weeks, and the last time I screamed it felt like I was swallowing glass. I haven't tried talking, and I don't want to. I've had enough pain thank you very much.

It takes me ten more tries to reach the damn doorbell from my slumped position on rust-colored porch planks. They're half-hearted swats at the freaking thing, but I can't bring myself to try harder. My light is going out, but I need to figure out a way to tell them what happened.

I need to figure out where West went.

I need to... I need to...

When the door opens again, Mena is the one to grab me under my armpits and drag me into the foyer of a modest, but elegant mountain house. But the foyer floor is freezing—still warmer than the frigid temperature outside—and I need to tell her...

When her burning hot hand touches my shoulder, I flinch away from the warmth. My body so cold it can't handle even the slight heat of her hand. But then the warmth floods through me—easing aches I'd long forgotten about, loosening my throat and mending the awful tearing of my vocal chords. Her enormous power is not enough—not right now anyway—to heal all of it, and the ease of so many aches and so long without sleep and nourishment takes its toll, and I speak the first words that have passed my lips in weeks.

"Get Evangeline," I say, my voice odd to my own ears, and that is all I am able to get out before my consciousness dims into nothing and I pass out right there on that cold fucking tile.

MENA

Not one, but two Wraiths passed out in my foyer.

Fuck a damn duck.

"Rally everyone. Bring them here. Can you call Aurelia? She and Rhys can drive over. I don't like her traveling in her condition," I tell Asher before he even has to ask. I love when I don't need him to ask, I can just read the expression on his face. It helps when the shit hits the fan.

Kinda like right about now.

I get a nod and a brief but scorching kiss before he smokes out from the room, off to get the rest of the family here.

I loathe that I am not able to communicate in this modern world. There has to be something I can do that won't A) burn the house down or B) fry every electronic component this side of the Colorado River. Maybe if I bleed enough healing, I could do something... The thought has merit, and it couldn't hurt Kyle or Voyt. By the looks of them, they need it.

Kyle is the better off of the two, but not by very much. The slice in his cheek started closing as soon as I touched him, so the loss of consciousness is probably the dire need for sleep. If there were anyone who knows what prolonged torture is like, it is me.

Both shirtless, it is easy to see that the starvation torture tactic was favored which just pisses me off. I've never met Kyle before, but I can tell he used to be something. His height is probably closer to seven feet than six and by the look at his bare feet, he'd need a shoe the size of a damn boat. Jet black hair and beard that has gone long past mountain-man and straight into hermit in the woods land. For such a large man, he shouldn't be as emaciated as he is. I'll get Aurelia started on that as soon as she gets here.

Voyt, however, is in a bad way. The slight beard on his face and the fact that I just saw him three weeks ago tells me he was interred for a much shorter time than Kyle, but the damage done to him is significant. Voyt had much less meat to lose, and he looks like a skeleton. His already sharp cheekbones have turned knife-edged, and when he spoke, I could tell his time screaming must have been considerable.

I remember screaming. I remember ripping my vocal chords to shit but being unable to stop screaming anyway. I fucking hate evil people.

His skin is nearly freezing, and I need to move them both from the cold tile and get them somewhere warm. I take Voyt first because he has so much less meat on his bones and needs the warmth first. I'm so happy no one is here to see me pick him up and cradle him like a baby in my arms as I carry him to the right side of the sectional in the living room. I would hate for anyone to see him in this state, and I would hate for anyone to make fun of him.

No one knows better than me the power you lose. The shame you feel at not only being caught in a spider's web but all the things you begged for, all the things you promised the Fates you'd do to get out, all the things you swore you'd never do just to be free. Those are the wounds that never heal. Those are the ones that when even the slightest offhand insult can cause a world of hurt.

And I can't have that for these men.

I pick up Kyle next and due to his size and considerable weight— even emaciated as he is—I need to fireman carry him to the couch. Once I have them positioned as comfortably as I can, I scurry to find our thick mink blankets and pillows. Then I start a fire. I'm sweating and the house is nearly sweltering, but they need it. Starting a fire is easy for me, obviously, but it took some time to control my Fireskin enough to not have it run all over my body. Aurelia knew how to control hers before we were even at maturity. Controlling anything other than my Aegis as a child was something I lacked.

Aurelia and Rhys are the first to arrive, and since they live less than ten minutes away, this isn't surprising. She barely bundled up to the elements outside, wearing only black leggings and a thin sapphire, open-weave sweater tunic over a black camisole and I give Rhys my best 'are you kidding me' glare. Mostly because she's not wearing any shoes or socks.

"I know. I tried," he says as he holds up his arm which is laden down with her parka, thick, woolen socks, and boots.

That's it.

"Aurelia Corrine Constantine, I swear to all that is holy if you do not start making sure your health is priority number one, I'm going to make you regret it! You. Are. Pregnant. You know it. Rhys knows it. Everyone knows it. Phoenixes don't get sick. We don't get the flu or food poisoning or car sickness for pity's sake. There is no other reason you'd be throwing up so much. Stop being in denial and accept the fact that you are carrying a child and need to tailor your behaviors accordingly. Now, put on the socks," I yell, finishing my tirade on a scream loud enough to rattle the windows and wake the dead.

Her surprised face tells me she didn't even consider this a possibility, but she holds her hand out to Rhys for the socks, unseeingly sitting on the closest armchair to slip them on her feet.

Mission accomplished.

I go over to her, crouching down in front of her chair to see her face better. I grasp her shoulders until her eyes come to me, and when they finally meet mine they are filled with tears.

"You're sure?" she says in a small voice, and it is a voice laced with hope.

"Yes, big sister. I'm sure. But we can have Ian check if you need him too."

"That would be great," she says nodding.

I feel her body draw on my Aegis a bit, not a lot, just a tiny bit, and it hits me. She's tired and stressed, and this little pull tells me more about her health than any silly blood test or sonogram would.

"And I don't know how to break this to you, but I'm pretty sure you're having twins," I whisper lowly, but not low enough.

"What?" Rhys breathes before his eyes roll back in his head, and he falls out, luckily landing on the plush area rug and barely avoiding the hand-carved solid oak end table Asher carved last week.

Three men down.

Fuck a damn duck.

II

EVAN

I'm going to lose my mind. Nope, I'm sure I've already lost it.

I'm standing in the middle of Mena and Asher's new house with my hands on my hips waiting for someone to start talking sense. Voyt and Kyle are finally awake and propped up on several pillows on the wide-cushioned dark, buttery leather sectional. They are shoveling in heaping spoonfuls of Aurelia's broccoli-cheddar-bacon-chicken soup, and as soon as she sees the bottom of their bowls, she whisks them away before they can ask for a refill. She has gone into full-scale mother hen mode, and I know why.

In this room, I am one of the few who haven't undergone torture. I'm one of the lucky ones and it burns in the back of my throat that these men were treated this way. That they were hurt on my watch. It also makes me wish I would have ripped Walter's throat out when I had the chance.

But the more they try and talk me into going to get West, the more I want to scream. The more I hear why he was doing what he was doing, the more I want to slap the shit out of him. In the back of my mind, I know he did this out of love.

I know this. I do. *Maybe.*

But it just shows how little he valued what I had to say. How little he trusted me to know what was best. How little he believed I could handle this throne on my own.

"He was doing it to keep you safe, Evangeline. That's why he wouldn't mate you," Voyt pleads, his voice a sharp gravel he didn't have before.

"No. He did this because he didn't trust me. He never has," I whisper the painful truth, and it is the most honest thing I've ever said about him. Because if he wanted to wait, why did he just say that? Why didn't he tell me why instead of just changing the subject or putting me off?

It's not like I'm some ring-starved co-ed begging their boyfriend of three months to pop the question. I'm his mate. I'm who the Fates chose for him.

But he didn't trust me with the truth. Not really.

West Carmichael has never trusted me, and that pill is the hardest to swallow. Never. No matter that I gave him everything in me. My thoughts, my dreams, my ideas, my body, my love.

Everything I had to give, and now there's nothing left.

"He did. I swear. He just wanted you safe," Rhys' voice rumbles behind me.

"I didn't need him to keep me safe. I can do that for myself. I just needed him to trust. Just once know that I could do it myself. You can't love someone you don't trust, and this is once again proof that he never loved me."

"Are you just going to let him rot?" Voyt asks incredulously, ripping the blanket off his legs and moving to stand.

Aurelia nips it in the bud before he can put a hand to the cushion to heft himself up, leveling him with a look that could peel the paint off a car. She's not letting him go anywhere.

"No, she isn't going to let him rot. Sit your skinny ass down and eat some bread," she says handing him a chunk of fresh sourdough.

The smell of it must be good because he begrudgingly takes and bite while giving her a petulant look.

"All this bitching about West is not getting me my mate back," Kyle's pissed off growl resonates through the room.

His face is gaunt behind months of beard growth and filth, but his eyes are bright and shining. He has hope for her, and my sad eyes just piss him off.

"She's not dead. My Nicola is a fighter. No way is she going to let that bitch win. We might have disrupted them. He might not have had enough sacrifices for the spell. She might be okay. She has to be. I'd feel it. I would. I'd feel it if she were gone," his voice frantic with blind hope.

He doesn't even believe himself, though, because this big bear of a man breaks—great gasping howls of agony rip up from his throat. Cam puts a comforting hand on his shoulder in a show of support, and it just proves once again that Cam is someone who knows loss.

"She did it for me, you know? That slimy fucker said he was going to kill me, and she knew. She knew he meant it. That's the only reason she'd do that. The only reason she'd allow it. She's been watching them torture me for months. But I told her. I told her I would take it. I would take it to my end if it meant she didn't let them put that fucking monster in her. But they were going to kill me... I told her no. I told her no. Why did she do that?" he asks, and I know the answer.

Because she loved him.

If Nicola didn't survive it, how could West? They said he was the worst off of the lot. He could be gone...

The thought runs through my brain, and the stab of fiery pain rips through my chest. He may have never loved me, but I still love him despite my best efforts. No, I won't let him rot. Whether he loves me or not, I still love him. That will just have to be enough to pull his ass out of the flames.

"We'll get them back, Kyle. I'll do everything in my power to get them back. I swear to you. I will," I promise as I kneel down in front of his perch on the couch.

"This might make me the pragmatic asshole of the group, but the question has to be asked. Have they passed? Because I'm not risking the Queen's life for a dead man, I don't care if I have to hog tie you and stuff you in a closet," Aidan says, his eyes boring into mine with enough force that I know he means it.

It doesn't matter if he means it or not, and it doesn't matter if West is alive or dead. Walter Emerson is going to die tonight, that is for damn certain. I flash my fangs at Aidan, so he knows I don't take kindly to his threat. To help stave off the fight that is about to break out in the middle of the living room, Aurelia butts in.

"I haven't seen them pass if that helps," she says.

"Good. We're going. Get your shit and let's go," I order and almost everyone starts moving—including Kyle.

"Whoa, whoa, whoa there, hoss. You're going nowhere. Sit your big ass down," Aurelia tells him, crossing the room to put a hand on his shoulder, holding him down and he's having a hard time not throwing it off of him and leaving. His face isn't petulant—it is lethal.

A feral growl rips up Rhys' throat, but Aurelia lays a calming hand on his chest holding him off as she turns back to Kyle.

"Don't look at me like that, mister. I can't go either."

"Why can't you go?" I ask, hearing the thread of panic in my own voice. I need her. I need her with me. I need her so much right now.

"I'm knocked up, kiddo. I love you more than anyone, but I'm not risking my children for anyone or anything. Sorry, baby girl," Aurelia explains, her eyes pleading me to understand.

And I do. She wouldn't ever admit it, but losing her child was the worst day of her life. She would have gladly taken torture, death, anything. And now that she...

"Wait, what? Pregnant? Child-*ren*?" I ask baffled.

I knew she was sick, but I just thought... I don't know what I thought, but pregnancy never crossed my mind.

"Evidently, Phoenixes don't get sick. Ever. The only reason I'd be throwing up is if I either broke a bone—which I haven't—or if I'm knocked up. I have it on good authority I am expecting twins. You missed it when Rhys passed out. It was hilarious," she explains, smiling this beaming grin.

Huh. My bestie is having babies. I love it.

"That... makes sense," I say, nodding, a smile stretching across my face so fast I think it might crack and I look to Mena. "We're sharing auntie duties. I don't want to hear any guff, got it?" I inform her pointing so she knows I mean business.

My comment is met with an insolent '*no shit, Sherlock*' look that is similar to Aurelia's, it makes me smile. But it fades as soon as the problem at hand comes back to me. West. Nicola. *Iva.*

"Glad we got that cleared up. Plan B. Who's coming?" Cam says irritably.

"Not me," Rhys pipes up. "If I get a scratch, she gets a scratch. If I die, I lose both her and the babies. I'm not risking it."

Rhys has been her shadow, watching her with more than his usual intensity, and it is starting to make sense. He never thought he would get that with her. Now that the dream is within reach, he'll do anything not to lose it.

I don't blame him, but that leaves us two warriors down. Myself, Aidan, Cam, Carver, Ian, and hopefully Mena and Asher are helping.

"Everyone else besides Voyt, Kyle, Aurelia & Rhys is coming, right? Anyone else bowing out?" I ask looking around the room. Mena meets my eyes, and I didn't realize that her expressions are nearly identical to her twin's. This one says *'I'm ready to fuck shit up.'* Fates, I love these women.

Voyt and Kyle give us a rundown of what they knew of the layout and security measures, and then we load up with the scary amount of blades, firearms, body armor and ammunition stocked in Mena and Asher's basement.

But I don't know if it's enough.

I ALREADY DON'T LIKE THIS PLAN, AND WE'RE FIVE SECONDS into it.

Voyt told us all about the cameras, motion sensors and personnel floating around the Emerson house. He did not, however, tell us about the warding, and this place is sealed up tighter than an alligator's asshole.

We are a mile out from the house, and to a human's eye, there is nothing here. Even I'm having a hard time focusing on the space beyond the ward, and I assume that's the idea. The ward is barely visible, but it doesn't need to be. I'm certain every single member of the Ethereal can feel it. It was like they were either begging to be found or shouting to back off.

Either way, I don't know how we can break it without a Witch, and I don't have one of those in my pocket.

I suppose it is possible he didn't know, and Kyle's input wasn't helpful at this level due to the fact he didn't come here of his own free will, and rather, he was dragged here while unconscious by people he never saw.

"Pfft," Mena scoffs at the barrier. "I could bust this in my damn sleep, but I might as well take out the cameras, motion sensors and electricity while I'm at it, so you need to skedaddle for a minute."

"Nothing doing, Princess. We have no clue who's out here. We're not going anywhere," Asher counters taking the words right out of my mouth.

Good man. Mena looks to me to get another girl's opinion, but I'm already shaking my head.

"Fine, but if you see me start to slip, get the hell out of here. Killing the good guys is not on my list of tonight's activities."

"Sure, thing," I tell her, and I get *'the eyebrow'* in response as she eyes me skeptically. "Seriously," I promise, and the lot of us—at her urging—back up at least a hundred feet.

When the light show begins, I think nothing of it. I'm waiting for the ward to break, waiting to get to him. Waiting to bring him home.

So when Mena screams, it comes as to worst kind of shock.

Because we are surrounded.

Because this was a trap.

And my blind need to get West back may have killed us all.

12

EVAN

IF I MAKE IT OUT OF HERE, IF I EVER SEE WEST CARMICHAEL again, I'm slapping the shit out of him. This thought runs on loop in my brain as I take another head shot, watching my bullet bore through the skull of another Guardian. I hate doing this. I hate taking life, but I hope I'm at least making a dent—cutting out the cancer that is infecting our race. The fact that they're closing in on us like the tightening of a noose does wonders to keep the guilt at bay.

They were silent as the grave when they surrounded us, likely lying in wait and ready for us to arrive. That's the problem with them having an Oracle at their disposal and us having no one. They can see ahead. They can know, plan.

I should have thought to have Aurelia on coms.

Or at least Rhys since she has a bad habit of frying electronics, but I didn't think ahead. I didn't think of anything but getting to West, and that stupid lack of planning got us here. I swear, if I lose anyone, I'll never forgive myself.

And I'll never forgive him.

For Wraiths, it is easy to tell who is evil and who is not. The evil ones make us hungry—ravenous really—so hungry we can barely control it. The more power you possess, the hungrier you get. It is why Revenants are such a problem. Sometimes, anger and hate drives us, and when that happens, the hunger takes over, and it's just a hop, skip and jump to heart-eating crazytown. It turns normal, level-headed, reasonable individuals into flesh-hungry sociopaths. This is why balance is so hard.

Because evil souls are tasty.

The ones that don't feel as appetizing—the ones that maybe, someday, could be saved—I shoot in the kneecap instead of the head. Fighting my urge to consume—the urge to finally feel full—I keep going until I run out of ammo for the Glock and realize I may be just the tiniest bit screwed.

I'm separated from everyone else, and although I can hear them fighting, I can't see them through the trees. What I can see are four Guardians eyeing me with the smug indifference of men who think they've already won.

The eight of us against an army. Who thought that was a good plan? Oh, that's right. Me.

I'm an idiot.

I pull a tri-dagger from its sheath on my right hip and plunge it into the chest of the closest Guardian.

Heal from that, you bastard.

I'd never used the tri-dagger before, and despite its weight, I have to admit, it is handy. Handy and deadly—a triangular, oscillating shank with venting holes bored into the center to prevent suction. I knew I'd only use it if I meant to kill, and as much as I hate taking life, as much as I hate the stain to my soul, I choose to live.

These bastards aren't going to stand between West and me.

As I rip the dagger out of the first Guardian's chest, I pull the small rapier out of my back sheath, adjust to an overhand grip and make an economical slash to the second's neck. The blade slides through his windpipe like melted butter, and I have to give it to Aidan, when he said he made sure it was the sharpest it could get, he was right. The third and fourth Guardians travel to me in rage. I can't blame them per se—I did just take out two of their buddies in less than a second—but their double-teaming isn't convenient, to say the least. When they pop up right in front of me, I get the sinking feeling in my gut that I might be not long for this world.

Two whole months as Queen. That has to be a record.

An arc of lightning passes right in front of my face, simultaneously hitting a Guardian in the chest and blowing me off my feet. I'm not sure if I should be grateful I'm not dead or pissed Mena put me on my ass. I'll go with grateful at the moment because living and flat on my ass is better than dead any day of the week.

I make it to my feet in time to watch Mena grab the last Guardian by the throat and shock him into dust.

Note to self, do not piss this woman off.

"You all right?" she asks as she touches my shoulder, most likely checking for injuries. I've noticed she does this more now that she can control her Aegis better.

"I'm good, just got the wind knocked out of me," I return glancing around to check for threats.

"All the Guardians have been neutralized for the time being. I have to break this ward. I tried to have Ash get Aurelia on coms, and there is so much juju flying around here, I bet you money I couldn't even get a damn compass to work around it. If they have working electricity inside it, I'd be surprised," she informs me.

"What about our guys? Everyone okay?" I ask because ward or not, West or not, I need to know about my people.

"Bumps and bruises. Nothing major. Let's get the ward busted and get your man before they decide to send reinforcements."

"Agreed," I say, sheathing my dagger and grabbing her hand to travel the two hundred or so feet to the ward instead of walking it.

"Thanks for the lift," she says as she bumps me with her hip, half to get me out of the way and half as a thanks. I back up a bit and feel a hand on my shoulder. Cam is right behind my left shoulder, and his face is part apologetic, part proud, and part thankful I'm alive. None of the men in my life are what could be considered talkers—their facial expressions doing the speaking for them—so I've become an expert at reading faces.

I feel someone at my right, and I don't need to look to know it is Aidan, but I do to see what his face has to say. It is easy to read—it says I will be on you like white on rice, so don't try anything funny.

I nod and turn back to Mena, watching as she throws bolt after bolt of lightning from her fingers at the enormous barrier. When that doesn't work, she walks right up to the edge and places her palms on the slightly shimmering dome-like spell—giving it the full dose of her juice. The ward busts in an instant, but Mena wavers a moment before plopping down on her ass in the leaves.

"I just need a minute," she says as Asher cradles her in his arms.

"I'm not sure what kind of time we have, Princess. I need you to try and stand for me, babe," Asher tells her and she struggles to her feet.

"Try to get Rhys on coms. I have a feeling we're going to need a Seer for this shit. There is bad juju going on here."

"I fucking hate Witches," Carver says from behind us as he plugs his earpiece into his phone and dials Rhys.

"You think you could get your wife to look out for us here? I've already almost died once this year, and I have to say, I've lost my taste for it," Carver says by way of greeting before he nearly drops the phone as his eyes go wide. Even in the near blackness of the dim, I can see his caramel face go gray.

"She said she can't see anything. All she sees is blackness," Carver croaks, his eyes filling.

"What?" I breathe, and it feels like someone has ripped the heart from my chest. I can't lose him too. I can't...

Before anyone can stop me, I move, traveling to the front steps of this ostentatious mansion. I lift my foot and kick the flimsy fucking door open. I met with nothing.

No sound. No lights. No people.

Nothing.

My heart wants to drop and soar at the same time. Maybe the blackness Aurelia sees isn't death. Maybe he isn't gone. Maybe the blackness she sees is just the dark.

Please, please, let it just be the dark, I think as I step carefully through the ground level, making my way to the basement dungeon based on the directions Voyt gave me. He only had one request—if I saw a blonde woman named Claire, that I take her with us. He promised she was a good woman, but I'm hesitant to follow his request. I suppose I'll just have to judge her myself. If she's even here.

I make it to the bottom of the ricketiest staircase ever made when I feel a presence to my left. Moving before I think, I stop myself from embedding the tri-dagger in Cam's throat at the absolute last second, earning him a nick to his Adam's apple.

The look I give him tells him I'm not sorry, and I move past him down a moldy stone corridor lined on both sides by vault-like cell doors.

I smell death. So much death it makes my stomach turn. There are no evil souls here, only innocents, and by the twist in my gut, they feel young—not even to maturity.

I can't stand it, the blankness in my brain wants control, so I keep it at bay by turning the doors to dust. The first door to my right contains the remains of a dead Shifter—still in his shifted form, I can't tell his age, but I know he was some sort of big cat. Moving to the left one, I find the remains of a Warlock who couldn't be more than fifteen human years old.

The bile rises, but I won't stop until I find him. I find another Shifter and the body of a Witch child no more than eight. The tears come, and I don't stop them.

When the next two cells turn up empty, it is a relief, but then again, it isn't. Every cell is either empty or full of death. I don't want to check the rest, fearing the death I still feel crawling against my skin. I hesitate before I dissolve the next door.

What if he's gone when I find him? I shouldn't have sent him away. I shouldn't have let him go. *Please. Please, please, please don't let him be dead.*

My hands are shaking when I place them on the door. The solid metal door abrades away bit by bit, slower than the others because I have a feeling I know what is behind this door, and if he's gone I almost don't want to know.

But it isn't West's large form I see on the cold, steel cot, but a crumpled blonde woman—and she's breathing.

"Mena! One of them is alive!" I yell back to the hallway.

She's a Wraith, certainly, and she's unconscious, huddled into a tiny ball on the cot, her arms wrapped tight around her bent legs even in sleep. Her face is bruised so horribly one of her eyes looks as if it would stay closed even if she were awake. Her nose assuredly broken and still dripping blood, and her fingernails are bleeding and jagged.

Mena joins me in the cell and immediately grabs her hand. I watch as the bruises fade from the prisoner's battered face, and the swelling deflates to reveal her beauty. A few more seconds and her eyelids flutter open. When she sees Mena and me, she flinches back.

"Wh-who are you?" she asks, her voice trembling.

"I'm Evangeline Black, your Queen, and this is Mena Constantine, leader of the Phoenixes. Who are you?"

"C-Claire. My name is Claire," she whispers.

"I was hoping you'd say that. Voyt asked us to bring you with us. Is that all right with you?" I ask her gently.

I won't take her if she doesn't want to come, but I don't expect an objection. Her frantic, shaky nod confirms it.

"We're looking for West. Have you seen him?" I ask her, my voice breaking.

She shakes her head no and says, "I haven't seen him today. I'm so sorry, but if he's here, he might be in the chamber at the end of the corridor. But... Be careful," her voice halts as her tears spill over. "Bad things happen in there."

I try to bolt from the room, but Cam stops me.

"Not this time, darling girl. Let one of us go. You've done enough."

"No. It has to be me. I have to see for myself."

Of all the doors in the hallway, this is the only one that is unlocked, and that fact is the scariest of them all. No one wants to go to this room, I know it in my gut.

And after what happens here, no one is able to leave on their own steam. Claire is right.

Bad things do happen here.

Blood is pooled underneath a wooden rack that is one of four set in a circle. And on it is a man... If he weren't the other half of my soul, I'd never be able to recognize what's left of him. Even from here I can barely make out the features of his face. His body emaciated, his skin mottled green and purple.

And the blood. So much blood. I can't...

I travel to him, unable to walk the thirty feet from the door to the northernmost rack.

"West. Baby? Help me! Somebody help me!" I scream searching his neck and wrists for a pulse.

I can't find one.

A pair of hands gently pull me away as Mena and Ian work on him —trying to put Humpty Dumpty back together again.

I don't know if they can.

All I can do is hope.

13

IF I WATCHED ONE MORE HIPPIE ASSHOLE OFFER A SMOKE TO MY woman, I couldn't be held responsible for what I did next. I didn't know when I started thinking of her as my woman. That's a lie. I knew exactly when it was. It was the first time I heard her speak. I'd heard her sing so many times before—a huskily haunting voice so beautiful it would put an angel to shame—but the first time I heard her speak...

I was lost, and I was found all at the same time. It was then that she became my Angel.

But my Angel was a pain in my ass. Of all the places we could be, of all the things could have been doing, we were standing in a field in the midst of hundreds of thousands of shirtless hippies. At least the music was good.

My Angel was in a lacy white dress with wilted daisies woven through her pale, curly locks. Her feet were bare—against my insistence that she put on some damn shoes—and she was dancing to the supreme guitar strains of Santana. It was the second day of the festival, and we had worked out an agreement. If she agreed not to sleep here in this mass of people, I would be happy to let her come back until it ended.

The real story was I couldn't stop her if she wanted to go, but if I didn't hold her too tight, if I didn't try to keep her in a cage, she would always tell me where she was going. Most of the time, she didn't like for me to be too close. She said I was too serious and made her feel like there was a noose around her neck choking the life out of her. That admission damn near broke my heart.

I never wanted to hurt her, never wanted to drown her. But that is what I was doing. Because I couldn't keep her. I couldn't disrespect John that way.

It was a flimsy excuse at best.

John most likely wouldn't mind, and Olivia surely wouldn't. Olivia would love for me to be her daughter's mate if it meant those rich jerks from the head families wouldn't weasel their way into her heart and into being King.

If there were a real noose, those pompous suitors would be it—they would want her to be proper and quiet. My Angel is anything but proper and couldn't be quiet even if you taped her mouth shut. But her constant talking meant I didn't have to talk at all. She did the bulk of it, and if I couldn't get by with grunts and nods, then I used silence.

It's worked for forty years, so why ruin it? If it ain't broke…

I'd do anything to keep her from knowing—from feeling the pull I feel. Anything to keep her from the wanting. There are so many reasons to keep her away from me.

I'm not a good man. It wasn't just my chosen profession, my past, or my lineage—they were all factors, absolutely—it was that I couldn't make myself leave her. I couldn't bring myself to tell John he needed to reassign me. I couldn't leave her in the hands of someone else.

Someone who wouldn't love her like I did. Someone who wouldn't treat her like the precious woman she was. Someone who wouldn't understand that she needed music like she needed breath, or that she had an unhealthy obsession with organizing things, or that she didn't consume nearly as much as she should.

I've followed her every single day for the last sixty-three years—mostly in the shadows and unbeknownst to my charge—making sure she was safe. I know more about her than anyone. I know that underneath all of her frenetic energy, despite the fact that she flits around like a hummingbird of smiles and light, she is probably the saddest person I have ever met.

She feels guilty—over something which is no more her fault than the color of the sky. She wouldn't blame an animal for snapping when wounded, or rain causing a flood, or the lightning causing a fire, so why she blames herself for losing control when she was in imminent danger is beyond me.

San Francisco was an accident. Nothing more or less, and I didn't blame her—not many did—but she still blamed herself. It was easy to see the lengths she went to not to lose control—only consuming little bits here and there so her body stayed tired. Then, she would run herself ragged, flitting about doing things for everyone she knew—helping, giving more and more of herself until there was nothing left.

So, no, I didn't want to cage her. I wanted her free. I wanted her safe. I wanted her to be mine.

But I wasn't going to get what I wanted—I wasn't going to keep her good soul with my tainted one.

Evangeline killed by accident. I killed on purpose.

And as I watched this beautiful pixie shine her light in the throng of concertgoers I vowed to myself she'd never be mine.

WEST—1987—LONDON, ENGLAND

I'd lost her. I never had her in the first place, but I'd lost her all the same. She was tired of waiting for me. Tired of my silence. Tired of feeling the pull and getting nothing in return. Make no mistake—she felt it. It didn't matter that I tried my best to avoid speaking around her. I figured that if I didn't speak, she wouldn't know about the bond, but I failed in that endeavor about a decade ago.

She went on a date tonight.

The first date she's ever been on, at least to my knowledge—and the twist to my heart was unbearable. She wouldn't choose me over him, this pale-headed suitor with the nice clothes and even nicer car. Why would she? I have done nothing in these some eighty years to dissuade her.

Here I stood—in the rain no less—like a pathetic sack of shit waiting to get my heart ripped up a little more. He took her to a decent restaurant, a new Moroccan place that opened up last year. He pulled out her chair, opened her door, he was polite.

I wanted to murder him on sight.

I hated where we were living. I hated that we were so far from John and Olivia. I hated the rain and gray skies and cold weather. But it didn't stop me from agreeing that she needed a change.

My Angel was withering away. I thought keeping my vow would keep her safe, but...

It had been months since the last time she consumed a soul, and it was starting to show. She looked painfully gaunt, her cheeks hollow, her collarbone prominent despite the thick sweaters she wore. But I didn't know what to do, so I agreed to move across the world.

Still, she refused to consume.

Evangeline lived quiet here, managing an art gallery where her best friend's paintings regularly made an appearance. John has received roughly a dozen calls and updates from Aurelia about my Angel. It was good she had Aurelia—someone to talk to when she stopped talking to me. Someone else to care for her. I didn't even have to meet her to know Aurelia Constantine cared deeply for my Angel.

But John was worried, and Olivia was concerned enough that Aurelia kept her updated with daily phone calls.

But me? I was beside myself. Scared out of my mind for so many reasons.

Should I leave her be?

Should I butt into her date and take her away from this place?

Should I just get over myself and kiss her?

Evangeline wasn't getting any better. How much longer could she go before the damage was irreversible?

I watched them dine through the window, the barest hint of a smile passed her lips, quickly marred by a frown when she met my eyes through the glass. Oh, she was mad.

They ate their meals in tense silence and parted ways at the door of the restaurant. She waited impatiently for him to get into the low-slung car parked on the street and drive away before stomping across the street to me.

She was pissed, but I didn't care. There was a life to her that had been missing these last few years. So when she opened her mouth to yell at me for whatever reason she had to do so, I couldn't help myself.

I closed the few feet that separated us, wrapped an arm around her waist, fitted her small, firm body to mine, and kissed her with everything in me. Whatever she was about to say, whatever tirade she planned in those tense minutes while she waited for her date to end, died on her tongue as I met it with mine. I tangled my fingers in the thick curls of her hair and breathed her in—tasting her sweetness, her light—until I couldn't breathe anymore.

"You going out with that fucker again?" I asked, but I knew she wouldn't before she shook her head no.

"Why would I waste my time on anyone who wasn't you?" she asked by way of explanation.

I answered her with my mouth over hers, stealing both of our breaths as the warm, slick slide of her tongue met mine. I couldn't tell if she climbed me or if my hands moved of their own accord, but before I knew it, her pert little bottom was in my palms and her legs were wrapped around my waist.

I was soaked to the skin from the winter downpour, but I wasn't cold —not with this beautiful woman in my arms. Then I no longer felt the pelting of the rain and knew we'd moved. Once again, I wasn't sure if I'd done it or if she did, but we found ourselves in her opulent flat in Knightsbridge. I didn't see it. I didn't need to.

I didn't need anything but my Angel and her breaths on my lips, her moans in my ear, her warm body in my hands.

And then I didn't see anything at all but the backs of my eyelids as her tongue stroked the pulse point on my neck as she clawed at my sodden sweater.

My fingers tugged at the blouse that refused to lose its purchase on her skin, and it pissed me off enough that instead of the delicacy I planned to take with her, I ripped the fabric away from her skin without meaning to.

"Shit, babe. I didn't mean to rip it," I murmured my apology but by her giggle, she didn't care.

Then she returned the favor by ruining my shirt as well as she ran a long black talon down the center of my sweater, parting the wool from my flesh. I couldn't say why that caused such an intense curl of heat in my gut, but I wanted her more than I ever had at that second.

It isn't until her whole body freezes do I snap out of my lust-filled trance.

"What?" I asked cupping her jaw in my palm and tipping her chin so her eyes met mine.

"Your tattoo," she whispered.

"Which one, babe? There isn't much skin that isn't tattooed."

One cool finger traced the large calligraphy 'E' over my heart, and I froze. I'd gotten it one rare night off in the fifties. The green cast to the ink a dead giveaway of the age of the tattoo.

"It's old," she murmured.

"It is," I admitted, but she didn't need to know just how old it was.

She took my non-answer in stride, nodding as if she knew the whole story when I gave her only bits and pieces. I vowed there and then to give her more even if I couldn't give her all of me.

I backed up until my legs hit the soft cushion of her couch, and then I sat with my beautiful prize in my lap, moving my hands from her hips to cup her face, I brought her face to mine. Brushed my lips across her cheekbone, down the delicate column of her neck, nipped at her collarbone, tore the remnants of her shirt away to run my fangs over the crown of her shoulder. That one earned me a shiver so fierce she practically vibrated in my hands, her mewling moans causing my dick to jerk behind my zipper. I ran my nose back up her neck, memorizing the delicate scent of her and wondering if her pussy smelled the same.

My mouth watered, my cock pulsed, and I froze for a moment to collect myself before I lost all reason. Impatient, she quit waiting for me to undress her and reached behind her back to unclasp her bra. When the magenta lace fell away to reveal her creamy swells, my brain quit functioning except for my baser instincts.

My only thought was her scent, her sounds and the pale flesh beneath my rough fingertips.

I stood without preamble and headed for the dark hallway that I hoped held her bedroom. I hit pay dirt on the last room and laid her down on her king size bed. Shifting her to the center of the bed, I luckily had the forethought to drag her jeans and panties down her legs. My brain pressed pause on the moment—freezing it in my mind so I never, ever forgot the slim line of her legs, the dainty patch of blond curls at her center, her hips, her high, firm breasts, her neck, her face, her wild hair splayed all over her pillow. Her cheeks rosy from arousal and her eyes shining bright yet heavy lidded with want.

How did I get so lucky?

"If you don't take off those pants and get up here, I'm going to lose my, West," she grumbled, snapping me out of my reverie. I ripped my boots off my feet and shoved my jeans down my thighs and off, before climbing onto the bed between her legs.

She reached for my face, bringing her mouth to mine and I was done. Decades of wanting, decades of needed her, and now I had my Angel. I ran my blunt fingers through her wet heat, testing her readiness before notching my dick against her, feeling her slick arousal. At her needy moan, I pressed forward, her flesh parting around me, her gasps hitting me straight in my gut.

Hot, wet, tight.

I couldn't think of anything but her sounds—the gasping groans mixed with almost agonized whimpers of need, the smell of her neck, the feel of her desperate pants against my neck as I move in and out of her. And when her whole body tightened like the string of a bow—her arms closing around my shoulders, her legs becoming vices on my hips, her heat tightening on my cock—I lost it.

My fangs descended, the phase taking over before I have a chance to stop it. I had to fight every instinct I have not to rip into the meat of her shoulder as she breaks. Her moans reached my ears, and I was lost, pounding into her until my release came over me, groaning into the skin of her chest through gritted teeth.

Lifting my head, I looked at her smiling mouth, unable to stop the kisses I rained down on her face and neck. And when her lips caught mine I reveled in her warmth. When the kiss ended, her smile was all I needed, and it was easy to coax her to consume again—to live again.

We were happy.

For a time.

WEST—1995—OUTER BANKS, NC

We were sleeping naked and wrapped around each other when I nearly lost her.

It's funny how little we thought of the outside world—how little we thought of the consequences of my life before her. But physics has it right. For every action, there is an equal and opposite reaction.

Even if it's a hundred some odd years late.

I was dreaming—dreaming of her running away from me and me chasing her, a game we used to play. Evangeline loved cat and mouse. She would pop in my workshop, poke me in the belly, say 'You're it!' and pop back out, practically begging for me to chase her—usually when I'd been working on an engine too long. I loved the game and her, mostly because she got me out of my own head. She got me to have fun. She got me to forget. The game usually ended with us wrapped around each other in bed—just like we were right then.

But this dream was so much different than all the others. It didn't feel playful, it felt like she was running from someone or thing. In my dream, she looked frightened, so when I shook myself out of it, I was already on high alert. Had I woken up a second later, we both would have died.

I saw a glint of moonlight coming in through the open French doors, reflecting off the steel of a rather large hunting knife.

Just one second later and her light would be out, and that one second would haunt me for the rest of my life. I didn't wait, I tightened my hold on her still-sleeping form and traveled to the panic room I set up in an interior, windowless room on the bottom floor.

By then, she was awake, and I threw clothes at her as I tried to dress, grab weapons from their assigned pegs and get back to the men who broke into our island house with not so much as a whisper.

"West, wait," she said as she grabbed my elbow, but I couldn't look at her.

I couldn't—I was too guilty.

I left her there in that steel-walled room, and even after I eliminated the threat—a family member of a target I'd ended at John's insistence when he'd murdered four small children—it was a long time before I spoke again.

WEST—A FEW MONTHS AGO—GRAND LAKE, CO

We were in the loft of the lake house, and I'd about had it with this woman. We'd just left Aurelia and Rhys to find the exceedingly romantic room Evangeline decorated. She'd said she was done with these two *dancing around each other.*

"You just can't let it go, can you?" she griped after I'd asked her for the tenth time.

"I know you're going somewhere without me—which in this particular climate is not only scary, it is dumb as shit. Now, where is it?" I demanded.

She was. I'd lose her for hours where she wasn't with Aurelia, and she wasn't home or at the gallery. Where in the blue fuck was she?

"I was with Mom, okay? She's dying, West. The both of them are. Where else would I be?"

"Was that so damn hard? It's my job to keep you safe, but you keep secrets. You're even keeping secrets from Aurelia, and she's your best friend. I've been your Guardian for over a century, and she didn't know who I was until an hour ago. What the fuck, Evangeline? You ashamed of me or something?"

"Shouldn't I ask you that question?"

"You know why I won't. Outer Banks proved it, so don't tell me I'm a paranoid asshole. Look at your mom and dad. Look at them, and tell me you want to watch me die just so you can follow."

I regretted the last sentence as soon as it passed my lips, but the expression on her face was the worst sort of punishment. She looked like I'd just slapped her, and the tears welling in her eyes broke me.

"Dammit," I muttered as I crossed the loft, crowding her space, and cupping her small, delicate face in my rough hands. Her skin was like silk, and it had been so long since I'd felt it against my fingertips.

"I love you. I've always loved you. Do not punish me for wanting to keep you safe, Angel," I said before I ran my lips over her closed, wet eyelids, over the bridge of her nose, over her parted lips.

I stopped there, tasting her, feeling the heat of her that we'd denied ourselves for so long.

"Just don't leave me again," she ordered.

"I swear, Angel. If you want me to go, you're going to have to send me away."

"I'll hold you to that," I said, and if everything had gone to plan, she would have been my mate that night.

But when in my life had things ever gone to plan?

That's right. Never.

14

EVAN

TIME STOOD STILL AS I WATCH MY FRIENDS—MY FAMILY—TRY to breathe life into the man I couldn't live without. It was then that I completely understood why the Fates decided to make mates. Because if you loved someone just that much, when they left this world, you'd want to follow them.

There were so many regrets I had when it came to West, but the single largest thing I regretted was the time we wasted. The time I spent mad at him for doing what he believed in. The time we spent apart.

I was torn. Did I stay and watch Mena and Ian try to put him together? Or did I scour this most likely empty house for the person who hurt him?

So much death. So much pain.

No one should have to endure this, but especially not him. Not my West. It isn't fair or right that he should have to bear so much.

I don't lose it until Ian starts the chest compressions, climbing up on the rack to get the right angle. Until I hear his poor ribs crack with the force of them. Until Mena tells him to move so she can try to restart his heart. All the while, unbreakable arms hold me back as I try to get to him. Clawing, biting, kicking, I can't break them.

In my haze of anger and fear and regret, I barely notice the man hovering just out of the shadows, but when I catch a glimpse of white-blond hair, fury floods me. My power leaks from my skin—enough that the four men holding me so Ian and Mena can work unheeded, go flying outward like rag dolls.

My bonds gone, I stalk across the circular chamber to the place where I saw him, but nothing remains. No clue, nothing to prove the flash of blond was anything other than my imagination conjuring up something to keep my mind busy while I wait to know if the man I love is alive or dead. At first, I thought it was Walter, but the more I think about it, the more I'm sure it wasn't. And I know my mind must be playing tricks on me.

Why else would I see a man who died over a hundred years ago? I watched Devereux Emerson die with my own eyes in 1906.

Didn't I?

"He's breathing!" Mena yells, and I forget the man who was never there in the first place and go to West.

"He's still unconscious, and we need to get to a medical facility right now, but he's alive," Ian informs me, but I can't think about that right now.

All I can do is play *'he's alive'* in my head over and over again.

"You have what you need at the high-rise or do we need to commandeer a surgical suite at the local hospital?" I ask him. Ian has been outfitting the new headquarters into a better facility than we had in Grand Lake, but getting all the things we need takes time.

"I'm going to need the hospital," Ian replies, "And we need to be quick about it. He has some internal bleeding—I'm sure of it."

"I have a contact at the local university hospital. She was going... to help me leave before I got caught trying to get the ch-children out," Claire struggles to say behind us. "I-I could call her if someone has a phone. There are good people there. It is a safe place."

Carver passes over his cell, and he and Claire travel from the chamber to find a place that actually has cell service.

"I don't even know if he should travel," Mena mutters under her breath. "I'm not sure he'd survive the trip. We need a car or an ambulance or something. He's... drawing on me still. I can't let him go or..." She shakes her head.

"We'll do small distances," Asher offers. "There is no way we can make it up those stairs carrying him. I say we take him to the foyer first."

"I can carry West and Mena, but I need you to follow close," I tell Asher and Ian. Turning to Aidan and Cam, "I need you to find a car and get it to the front door. Now."

Carver and Claire pop back in the room. "My friend is setting up the OR now," she informs us.

"How long is the drive?" Ian asks.

"About twenty minutes. Ten if we hurry," Claire says.

"Let's go," I order and smoke out with my hands on Mena and West from this horrible room to the foyer then to the back of the SUV that screeches up to the front door. It's a tight fit, but since all the seats are laid down in the back, we can squeeze in.

"Meet us there," Mena yells through the glass to Asher, Carver and Claire as we speed off through the night hoping we make it in time.

I brush West's long, blood-crusted hair away from his face. If I didn't know him, if I didn't love him, I would never recognize him. His eyes are swollen shut, his nose mangled, his full lower lip split clean through. I don't realize I'm trembling until I see my shaking hand hover over his injuries. I don't know where to touch him so it won't hurt. I don't know what I'm supposed to do.

Doing the only thing I can, I brush his hair back and kiss him on the only uninjured part of his whole body. I press my lips to his forehead and pray with everything in me he stays alive.

It doesn't take us twenty or even ten minutes to get to the hospital.

It takes us eight.

Nurses are waiting for us with a gurney when we screech up to the emergency room entrance, and they help us carefully extract West's limp body from the back of the SUV. I have to give it to Claire, she was right —this is a safe place. The four nurses that met us are made up of a Phoenix, two Witches and some sort of Shifter. I follow them as they haul ass into the hospital through the emergency room entrance straight to an OR elevator. When I try to follow, two sets of hands hold me back.

"Let them work, darling girl," Aurelia says in my ear when I struggle against Cam and Aidan's hold. I turn, spying my best friend. She's here right when I need her, and I can't help but break. I slam into her with a hug so tight it's possible I cracked a rib.

"When did you get here? How?" I question muffled by tears as I burrow my face in the leather of her jacket.

"Voyt and Kyle brought us when Carver gave me a call about the hospital," she says. "He thought you might need me."

"He... he's *hurt,* Ari. Do you... do you know if..."

I can't even finish that sentence. I don't think I want to know if he's leaving me yet.

"I don't know what's going to happen, baby girl. All we can do it wait," she says as she squeezes me tight.

<hr>

EIGHT HOURS.

We waited eight hours in a private operating room lobby on the stiff vinyl benches, picking over fast food remnants and vending machine offerings.

Waiting for word, for hope. Waiting for West.

Well, waiting and trying to calm Kyle down when he found out we didn't find Nicola along with West. It took some doing, but we convinced him we would work together to find her, and while he wasn't appeased, he took one look at my pleading face and sat the fuck down.

The surgeon who emerges from the automatic double doors has carefully masked her features. Why do doctors do that? Any facial expression at all would be better than this.

"Mrs. Carmichael?" she says as she scans the room for me. The name gives me pause, but whatever she needs to call me to give me what I want to know is good with me. It doesn't matter how many times I'd wished for someone to call me by that name, and if it is the last time someone does it, at least I got it once.

"Th-that's me," I croak, struggling to stand under the weight of the unknown.

Aurelia grabs my hand and we stand together. The smile that breaks across her face nearly makes my legs give out in relief.

"He's alive, ma'am, and doing well. There was a severe bleed in his abdomen, and we had to remove his spleen, but we got it under control. We're going to need to watch him for a few days, but given his species, he should make a full recovery. This hospital is a safe zone, so whomever did this cannot enter. It is appropriately warded against it."

"Good," I sob in relief. "Can I see him?"

"Absolutely. Follow me," she says as she leads me to a private recovery room where I see the best thing ever.

West. Safe and warm and alive.

Wasting no time, I rush to his side. His face is still mangled, but his nose has been set and he's breathing on his own, so I don't give one single shit if he has scars or if he's disfigured. He's alive and mine, and if I had half a mind and he were anywhere near able, I'd bite him and cement the bond. Screw this *'the man has to bond the woman'* bullshit.

Damn patriarchal society. Always screwing shit up.

Climbing as carefully as I can into the bed beside him, I curl like a cat into his side and settle in to wait some more.

I can wait forever if he's breathing beside me.

EVAN—1991—SORRENTO, ITALY

We lounged on beach chairs on the black sands of a little inlet in the cliff face. The turquoise water lapped calmly against the beach, and I was finally at peace. One better, West was right beside me, sunning himself. His wide, muscular body exposed to the warm rays of a beautiful Italian summer.

His tattoos were on display for all the world to see, but the one that meant the most to me was the large stylized 'E' tattooed right over his heart. He'd had it long before we got together. I saw it the first time we made love on that cold winter night in England four years ago. I knew right away what it was and what it meant. The ink slightly faded with age, the greenish cast that most older tattoos had, I knew then he'd loved me for much longer than he'd let on. I didn't need any more than that.

He still refused to cement the bond, but I'd wait. I'd wait forever for him.

"You want to go swimming, Angel?" he asked turning to his side to watch me, his voice a quiet rumble in the calm.

"No, babe," I said shaking my head. "I just want to doze. Wake me if I start to burn?"

"Sure, darlin'."

"Love you," I said as I drifted off into a light doze.

So I heard him when he said, "Love you, too, Angel. Love you, too."

And because I heard the gruff timber of his voice, I knew I was safe, and I had sweet dreams.

15

WEST

I can't decide if I'm in Heaven or Hell. I'm warm for the first time in a month, so that's a plus. The fact that my entire body feels like it has been run over twice by a semi-truck is definitely going in the minus column. But the best feeling—the absolute best thing in this world or the next—filters through my consciousness despite the pain.

The warmth and softness of my Angel pressing against my side.

I feel the pull of my answering smile yank at the stitches in my lip, and it all comes filtering back.

The dungeon. Nicola. Emerson... he put a soul in her. A soul summoned from the depths of the worst pit of Hell. I have no idea how he did it or how he knew how to do it. And I have the worst feeling I know exactly who he put in her.

But why? What does he have to gain by putting the woman who damn near exterminated us back into this world?

Evangeline. He wants to kill Evangeline.

My eyes jerk open to reveal the off-white acoustic tiles of a hospital ceiling, and I frown, confused. Hospital? If I'm in a hospital, it must be really bad. I have half a mind to lift the sheet to make sure I still have all my bits and pieces, but I'm having the hardest time moving my arms.

I have to tell her. I have to tell her what they did…

Instead, the pull of sleep—something I'd been missing out on considerably over the last month—yanks at my consciousness, and I succumb to the darkness with my Angel at my side.

I wake again to the sun filtering through the blinds of my hospital room and Evangeline snoring next to me. I always found it hilarious that someone so small was capable of sounding like a freight train when she's really out of it. It's how I know she hasn't been sleeping, she hasn't been taking care of herself. She only snores when she is truly exhausted.

I look down at the mess of curls spilling over my shoulder and bare chest. Her eyes have deep purple shadows underneath them, and the arm gently wrapped around my chest is one step away from skeletal.

How did they let her get this bad? How did they let her go that long without eating? Without consuming?

This is my fault.

I should have made the time to bind her. I should have put away my own bullshit and took care of her. She was losing her parents, and I was stuck in my own head so much I didn't see what I was doing wasn't what she needed. What I was doing was pushing her away.

But it doesn't matter what happened in the past—the fights and disagreements and all the other bullshit. I have her, and that is all that matters now.

She makes a highly indelicate and downright hilarious snort in her sleep, and I can't help but laugh. I regret it instantly. Red hot fire runs through my chest and gut.

Holy shit, that hurts.

Evangeline rouses from her sound sleep at my pained groan.

"West? Baby?" she calls to me, wide awake. "Are you okay? Do I need to call a doctor?"

I shake my head, but just then, the door opens, and Aurelia drags Mena by the hand into the room. Mena's eyes flash, and she reaches for my shoulder placing her healing hand on my skin. The relief I feel is immediate, but it doesn't cure everything. Rhys and Asher file in next.

"Well, that sucked," I groan.

"Yeah, yesterday pretty much sucked all around. Good to have you awake, man," Rhys murmurs, subdued.

"Okay? What did I miss? Why does everyone look like somebody died?"

"Four children were found in the dungeon where you were held," Mena informs me, the only one of the women in the room whose eyes aren't swimming in tears.

"What? Are they okay?" I ask aloud, but even I know it is probably the dumbest question I could ask.

If they were okay—these children—Aurelia wouldn't be shaking her head at me as tears pour down her face. Evangeline wouldn't be holding in her sobs by the skin of her teeth. Mena wouldn't be looking at me with dead eyes. And Rhys and Asher wouldn't be staring at me like they're just glad I'm alive.

I didn't know there were children down there with us, and now all I'd gone through seems trivial, selfish even. Because I made it out. I'm alive. I've lived longer than I ever thought possible, and these kids barely lived at all. Brutality towards children kills me. It brings up so many old ghosts. Ghosts of a long dead father who was the vilest man I'd known of until this moment.

"Do we..." I choke out. "Do we know who the children are? Have we informed their parents?"

"We've called in the faction representatives," Mena answers. "We're doing the hard shit here where it is neutral. This hospital is warded against malevolent activity. Harm can't be done on the grounds. They'll be here soon," Asher says.

"I want to go with you. To tell the families."

"I don't think that's a good idea," Aurelia mutters.

"I don't either," Evan says.

"Those families are going to come here, sit down in a conference room or waiting area or whatever and get the worst news they've ever received. Someone who was there with their children needs to be there when you tell them."

"And what happens when they see your broken but breathing self in that room, and they decide you need to die, too? Huh?" Evan demands. "You can't stay in this hospital forever."

"I think I have given up too much of my life worrying that someone will come after me for the things I've done or the things I couldn't control. If they have that much hate in their hearts for someone who barely made it out, then let them come. But I don't think we need to discount them just yet."

My Angel's answering growl tells me I've won this argument. She hops off the bed and slams out of the room. She returns a few moments later with a wheelchair and Ian, who goes to my left arm and the IV in my hand. He deftly removes it, turns off machines, and shoos everyone out of the room before he helps with the transfer from the bed to the chair.

It sucks that he had to do it, but there is no way in hell I'd make it on my own. Sitting up took pretty much everything I had even with the handy dandy motorized bed helping me out with eighty percent of it. I'm just lucky I'm dressed from the waist down. Ian passes me a scrub top which matches the blue bottoms, and I struggle to get it over my head.

Two small hands help me tug the fabric down the rest of the way over my eyes, and my Angel is there.

I grab one of her delicately fragile hands and turn it over so I can kiss the center of her palm. I move it to the center of my chest, and I say the words I've needed to say since the beginning.

"I'm staying with you, and you're staying with me. I'm not letting you do the hard shit alone anymore. Don't be mad at me for not wanting to abandon you again. Okay?" I murmur, and I watch as her expression goes from pissed to tearful in an instant.

"Do you promise?" she asks.

"I swear," I whisper as I reach up to cup her jaw in my hands and bring her down to me. "I'm never leaving you again, Evangeline. Even if you send me away."

She laughs through a sob at my pronouncement.

"I really wish I could kiss you right now," she grumbles.

"I do, too, Angel," I murmur as I rest her forehead on mine for a moment before she gently kisses the tip of my nose and moves to the back of the chair.

"Let's go do the hard shit," she says as we walk through the door into the hallway and toward another form of Hell.

The room they put us in to break the news is larger than I expected. It has couches and comfy chairs, and even though someone was kind enough to bring platters full of Danish and croissants splayed on the large sideboard at the back of the room, I can't bring myself to eat. It doesn't matter that I can't remember when the last time I ate was.

What matters is Evangeline and Mena have to tell these faction leaders that their young ones have died, and it was at Wraith hands. Here's hoping it doesn't start a war.

Two men and a woman file into the room. The first man is medium height, maybe just under six feet and built with dark hair and pale amber eyes that flash like a cat's in the florescent light. *The Shifter representative.* He's dressed casually in a flannel shirt and jeans, and I expect if he weren't frowning in preparation for the news he's about to receive, he'd be smiling. Laugh lines radiate from his eyes, and he has a peace about him I wish I had.

The second man is abnormally tall, so much so he has to duck considerably at the threshold to get in the room. He's painfully thin, and his thinness is highlighted by the black suit hanging on his frame. *Warlock.* His face is impassive, if a little worried.

The woman is nothing how I would expect a Witch to dress—she's buttoned up to her neck in a black on black pantsuit and heels. She too is gaunt, and her ash blonde hair is pulled back so severely from her face, I half expect to see blood at her scalp. Her face is what gives me pause. If there were one I'd bet on giving us some trouble, it'd be her. Most Witches are neutral, but this one has evil tattooed on her face in the form of a sneer. Plus, she smells like a damn snack, so I know she's the damn devil.

Phoenixes and Wraiths don't hang out much with other factions, but if we did, we'd have the upper hand in most situations because we can smell a double-dealing psychopath a mile away. And this bitch smells like Sunday dinner.

Greetings are said, hands are shook, but when they sit in their seats, I can tell they have a good idea what they're doing here.

The first man, the Shifter, Anthony, pipes up.

"Well, out with it. I have fifteen missing children in my community, I'm assuming you found them?"

Evangeline's face goes gray. "Fif-fifteen?" she asks before shaking her head. "We recovered the bodies of four children in our raid on Walter Emerson's house. Two shifter children, one Warlock, and one Witch. We did not find anyone else in the house except for Claire and West, and had we taken any longer to find him, he would have been among the dead. Claire was caught trying to free the children, and either because he was her father or he just wanted her to die slowly, he left her beaten in a cell with no food, water, or way out. As far as we know, no one else was in the house," she says squeezing my hand tight so her voice doesn't falter again.

I have never been more proud of her than I am right now, and even though I wish I could take this burden from her and shoulder it myself, I won't. She's doing what she needs to do to lead. Even the hard shit. *Especially* the hard shit.

"We didn't send them on yet. We wanted to inform you of their passing so you could help their families put them to rest. We will be more than willing to help you with the funeral rites if you so choose," Mena informs them.

Anthony and the Warlock, Sebastian look stunned, but the Witch, Tessa, does not. Her face doesn't change at all.

"You only found two?" Anthony asks.

"Yes, but are you sure there are fifteen that you are missing? Do you... do you mind if I touch you? I'd see better if I did," Aurelia says from her chair. "I might be able to see if they've passed."

Anthony nods and Aurelia places her hand on his exposed forearm. Her eyes immediately light up with a vision, but by her tears the news is the worst kind. Her eyes dim and when they can focus again, she looks at the three faction leaders.

Her face ravaged, she says, "I know where your missing children are."

"Where are they, child?" Sebastian asks. It is the first time he's spoken, and I had no idea his voice would be as kind as it is.

"They're buried in the woods."

16

EVAN

I NEVER WANTED TO COME BACK TO THIS HOUSE. I DIDN'T WANT West here either. Especially him. I don't know the extent of the hell he lived through as a child, but I know there was abuse. He doesn't have to tell me for me to know there were horrendous things done to him. And bringing him back to this place makes me sick to my stomach.

Mena and Aurelia won't step a single toe on the Oregon property where they were tortured, and if Aurelia had her way, they'd burn it to the ground. So to have West, Voyt, and Kyle here when they so recently endured so much pain, makes me angry, it makes my heart hurt, makes me hate my own kind.

And Claire...

West told me he could tell right away she'd been abused—before he even learned her name, he knew. I hate that he can recognize it so easily in another victim. I cannot fathom the atrocities she's been subjected to, and I can't stand this for them.

But there are children out there that need to be put to rest, and we have a murderer—or murderers—to find. I'd thought I had started to make a difference for my people, but letting Walter run free will haunt me to the day I die.

We're sitting in the SUV we commandeered from Walter's garage, and I'm having the hardest time making myself let go of West's hand so I can step out and deal with the horrors committed here. I want to tell Rhys to just drive on, but Aurelia takes the decision out of my hands as she opens the door and shakily steps down from the front passenger seat. Rhys is with her in a flash, holding her up as she walks on trembling legs not in the direction of the house, but to the trees.

I go to open my door when West squeezes my hand to stop me.

"I want you to stop worrying about me, Angel. I'm alive, and I'll heal. You need to worry about what happened here and watch your back around the Witch. You don't need to worry about anything else. Okay?"

I nod, but the thought that has been running on loop in my head spills out of my mouth.

"Is this my fault? Did changing everything about our community make him do this? Did I cause this?" West pulls my hand and then I'm in his arms, wrapped in his warmth, his strength.

"No, babe. He caused this. He did what he did and was doing it for a long time. Anthony said they've been searching for these kids for months. Not weeks. Months. Walter has been doing this for a while, and nothing you did was going to change it."

"Then why do I feel like it is? Why do I feel like I could have prevented this?"

He shakes his head at me and presses a kiss to my forehead.

"Because you give a shit, Angel," he murmurs into my hair. "But you cannot predict or control the actions of evil men any more than you can change the stars in the sky. So why would you take the blame for them?"

I shrug, giving him a slight squeeze before turning and exiting the SUV. In an instant, Cam and Aidan are at my side.

"We would like to be within arm's reach of you the entire time you are on this property, Evan. It is imperative you stay with us," Aidan says in my ear before I can take another step.

"Please," Cam throws in.

"The Witch?" I ask.

"Someone had to ward the place, and one that big, it had to be a powerful Witch who did it. Plus, she smells... *tasty*. Keep your weapons on you and stay close. I don't know what kind of juju she has under her belt, but I don't want to take any chances," Cam confirms.

I nod and open my emerald cashmere knee-length coat that Aurelia so graciously brought with her, to show Aidan and Cam the under arm holster holding my Glock and the tri-dagger sheathed at the hip of my leather fighting pants.

"I'm good. But if I'm moving, you need to stay with me. Got it?" I order. I have a feeling things are about to go to shit real quick."

"Aurelia rubbing off on you?" Aidan half jokes.

"Maybe."

We walk in the direction Aurelia headed in—the same place we fought so many Guardians—and I feel like an idiot for not seeing it earlier. At the edge of the forest, the ground is disturbed. Not enough that we would have seen it or distinguished it in the night when we raided, but enough that I feel like an imbecile now. The slight mounds of the shallow graves are in a tri-semicircle pattern similar to a Celtic knot, but the mounds are so small, they could easily be confused for varying elevation in the night.

How did we miss the feel of it, though? How did we miss the call of so many souls?

Anthony, Sebastian, and Tessa have followed close behind us, and we all stand in a loose circle around the disturbed earth.

"There are t-twenty ch-children here," Aurelia says, shivering while cradling her middle, protecting her unborn children as she witnesses Hell behind her glowing eyes. To anyone else, she looks like she'll be sick to her stomach—and she might—but I know what she's doing. This is a nightmare for me, but for someone who has already lost one child and is terrified of losing another, she is looking at her own personal version of Hell.

"Some-someone was using them. Stealing their power..." she says as she trails off and her eyes dim again. Rhys holds her up as she sags in his arms. When she can stand again, she doesn't look at anyone but Tessa. Her upper lip curls into a snarl, and she goes from sagging to phased in an instant—wings rip through the thick gray wool sweater as they burst from her back.

West was right—we needed to watch out for Tessa.

"How many did you kill personally? Ten? All twenty?" Aurelia asks Tessa, her eyes glowing white, flames licking up her arms as her wings spread wide. Rhys, spurred by his wife, phases immediately.

Tessa's eyes go wide as she starts to back away from my flaming best friend and her husband. She doesn't make it two steps before she runs into Mena and Asher. Both of them phase in an instant—Mena's blue flames and wings paired with the electricity pulsing like lightning across her skin and Asher's talons and fangs erupting in a swath of black smoke. Tessa edges away from them and runs into a fully phased Ian and Carver; then she runs into Claire. I never expected Claire to be anything even marginally resembling fierce, but phased and pissed off— she is more than terrifying.

Tessa flinches away from her and into Anthony and Sebastian. Anthony's eyes flash gold, and the rumbling growl ripping up his throat sounds similar to a cougar. Sebastian is the only one of us who is completely silent, but his once impassive face is now gone to reveal a look so deadly, if I were Tessa, I'd be terrified. Right now all I can feel is rage.

I sense more than see West's arrival at my back.

"Where is Walter, Tessa?" he growls the question I hadn't thought to ask. I hadn't thought anything past ripping her limb from limb with my talons. "Did you help him raise Iva?"

I'm glad he's asking questions. I'm glad he has his head in the sea of bloodlust, but I would expect nothing less of him. Despite all his protests about worthiness, West is more equipped to be a King than I am to be a Queen.

"Why are you people trying to attack me? I have done nothing wrong!" she insists, her voice frantic, but her face betrays her. I see the cruel twist to her mouth and the cold deadness to her eyes. She doesn't care about the loss of life. She doesn't give one single shit about the lives she stole from these children or the agony their parents will feel or the light she snuffed out.

"Killing innocent children is wrong. Using the deaths of children for your own gain is wrong," his furious voice rumbles, livid that he has to explain this shit.

Aurelia, tired of Tessa's stalling, grabs her forearm with her burning hand and asks again.

"Where is Walter, Tessa?" Aurelia asks through gritted teeth, but all Tessa can do is scream.

Aurelia lets her go, and she drops into a ball of agony on the forest floor.

"I-I didn't k-kill them. I j-just did the s-spell," she sobs. "It was Devereux. He killed the children. F-for the spell. I needed the p-power," she confesses as she cradles her now blackened forearm.

"Devereux Emerson?" I ask, but I know. I could have sworn I saw him in the chamber, but I'd just brushed it off to stress and my guilty mind.

But when she nods...

"He died in 1906. I watched a blade pierce his damn neck," I argue.

Tessa shakes her head. "If you think Iva is the first soul Walter Emerson forced me to bring back, you are sadly mistaken."

"No reason on this earth or the next absolves your hand in this, Tessa. You are complicit in these murders and just as responsible," Sebastian decrees. "You have upset the balance, and as such you. Will. Burn," he snarls as he gives Aurelia a nod.

Aurelia's lips curl back from her teeth in snarl as she grabs Tessa by her throat. Aurelia's fire burns hotter, brighter as she lifts Tessa off of her feet and into the air and coats her body in flames. Tessa's scream quickly trickles off to a gurgle and then to nothing. Her body crumbles to ash and bone, slipping through Aurelia's fingers.

"You need to deport her sorry ass to Hell, Evan," Aurelia practically orders me, and although I agree, I shouldn't be the one to do it. I can't be the one.

"West can. He needs it more," I tell her, but I feel the squeeze of West's fingers at my shoulder.

"You need this, Angel. I'll get the next one," he whispers in my ear.

"I'll lose it. There are too many souls. I'll take the wrong ones. I can't do this here with all of these people. I could hurt someone," I whisper back furiously.

He brings a finger to my chin and turns my head so I meet his eyes. His expression tells me he's digging in. He won't take the soul—even though he needs it. Even though he's hurt and barely healing and in pain.

Stalemate.

17

EVANGELINE HAS LOST HER MIND IF SHE THINKS I'M TAKING this soul when she's so hungry. By her face, she's thinking the same damn thing about me. The stubborn twist to her mouth tells me I'm going to lose this one.

"I'm not going to argue with you about it. This is not the time nor the place to have this discussion. Take the damn soul, West. I will get the next one," she whispers furiously through gritted teeth.

Out of all of us, she is the only one in control.

She always is.

I love it and hate it all at the same time. But then, I see how close to losing it she is. How frightened she is that she will hurt someone. How much pain she's in so she doesn't mess up and take good souls to Hell. Her pale blue eyes beg me for understanding.

So, I concede, phasing as quickly as my battered body will allow, feeling the ache in my jaw as my fangs break free, the bitter sting in my fingertips as my talons grow despite the fact that they'd been ripped out during my torture. I unhinge my jaw the same way a snake would and breathe in the soul.

For so many years I hated what I was, hated that we as Wraiths had to consume so much evil just to survive. I assume my Angel hates herself just as much as I did at her age. I see it differently than I did as a younger man—we are keeping the balance. We are making the world safer and if that brings us nourishment, well then, so be it.

Tessa's soul gives me energy, heals some of the most superficial of my wounds, and eases the ache in my abdomen. But with the good, comes the bad. I can see every single stain on her soul and for a woman less than half my age, she had many. The children she's slaughtered at her own hand for power. The abilities she stole by way of torture. The Witches she shunned—cutting them off from their families so they had nothing and no one. The damned souls she brought back from Hell and the good souls she stole from the heavens at their parent's command.

Including Devereux Emerson.

I have no idea what to do about him or the fact that he and his brother's deaths were the reason Evangeline demolished an entire city. And if I have to venture a guess, he was the man who nearly took my damn life.

I have to tell her, but it can't be right now.

"We need to put these children to rest. Aurelia. Mena. Rhys. Help them identify their dead, and get the souls taken care of. A few of us are going to search the rest of the property. Claire, I need you to show us around the grounds," Evangeline orders, snapping us out of the feral bloodlust.

She's right. We do have a job to do.

Evangeline turns to go but immediately comes back to grab my hand before getting the fuck out of there, marching double time back to the cars. She's shaking, practically vibrating with the strain of holding back. I yank on her hand, pulling her into my arms as she breaks. Aidan, Cam, and Claire stand back for a moment as my Angel tries to get herself under control.

"Th-those children. All those lives. I couldn't do it. I couldn't consume her with them so close. I couldn't... What if I took them with her? What if I consumed too much and hurt people?" she sobs, her breathing picking up to full-blown panic attack hyperventilation.

"Shh, Angel," I murmur into her hair as I wrap her up in my arms. "We'll get you consuming again. We'll start small, and it'll just be you and me."

Her head snaps up at that moment as her nostrils flare. Her eyes bleed from blue to black, her fangs snap down, talons erupting from her fingertips. I realize pretty quickly there is another soul out here. I didn't notice before, but now that I'm not in pain my mind is clearer and I can sense it.

But the Evangeline I know is not here right now. This woman before me is a feral representation of my Angel, and she's three steps past hungry.

She's famished, and there is something to eat, or rather some*one*.

She breaks from my hold, taking off into a sprint. Not for the house or the forest but for the water of the lake. Cam and Aidan rush after her, but I can feel it—the tasty morsel she's heading toward—so I travel there to wait for her because there is no chance in hell I'm running.

I make it to the wooden planking of the path to the boathouse before she does, but that doesn't stop her. Evangeline leaps into the air, plants both hands and feet on my chest, and takes me down to the ground as she uses my body like a fucking springboard to get past me. It would be hot as hell if she didn't just pop some of my staples and knock the breath out of me.

I turn and scramble to my feet, hobbling for a moment until Cam and Aidan come up behind me and grab me by the arms to chase her down.

Shit. Fuck. Motherfucking shit. Holy Fates that hurts.

We bust through the already obliterated boathouse door to see Evangeline stalking around Walter's body. By the looks of him, he's been dead about a day. The pooled blood around his still stiff body is nearly congealed, so I'm not worried that she killed him.

I'm more worried about her ability to discern reason at this point. Oh, and that whole *please-don't-eat-him* thought that seems to be running on a constant loop in my brain. I'm prepared to tackle her, and I'm honestly scared I might have to—popped staples or not.

She circles him like an animal on the hunt, her nostrils flaring. The crack of her jaw audibly unhinging sends a shiver of unease down my spine. I don't know what I would do if she turned Revenant.

"Angel," I rasp, and her eyes snap to mine—clearing for a moment before falling back to her meal.

Her eyes fall closed, and she breathes him in, consuming him and transporting his vile soul to Hell. Immediately, her cheeks fill out, her color coming back. Such a change isn't normal. It had to have been months since her last feed. Fates. She had to be starving.

Evangeline phases back instantly, and her eyes won't meet mine or Aidan's or Cam's. No. She's looking for the exit just behind us. Deciding it isn't worth the footwork, she travels from the room. My mind grays out for a second, and it is then I remember I popped staples in my gut. Looking down, I see my white shirt stained red.

Shit. If I faint, I'll never forgive myself.

I suck it up, hobbling out of the boathouse—away from Walter's ashes and the lingering stench of his corpse—and look for my Angel. It doesn't take too long to find her. She's busy puking her guts up on the grass at the lake's edge.

I make it over to her and plop to my ass, careful not to fall in the water, but just barely.

"Doing okay, Angel," I whisper as I start fading, holding onto my consciousness by a very thin thread.

She wipes her mouth, and brings her tear-filled eyes to mine.

"He hurt you. He hurt Claire. He hurt Devereux and Sam, and so many others. He did things I never want to say out loud. And I could have spared you so much pain if I would have just killed him when I had the chance. My father should have killed him. Someone should have stopped him and no one did. I hate feeling thankful to whomever took his life, but I am."

"You consumed and didn't lose it at least. Can we be happy about that?"

"Sure, I'll get right on that after we send murdered children off to their rest, hunt down a resurrected Guardian, and oh yeah, find the evil bitch they brought back from Hell because she wants to kill me before I kill her. I'll be sure to pencil in my happy time after that, mm-kay? There is no bright side situation in this scenario," she fires back.

"And I popped your staples. Fuck. Cam, can you see if Mena or Ian can do a patch job?" she asks him and he nods before traveling across the property rather than taking the hike.

Aidan looks down at me, and reaches in his back pocket for the clean handkerchief he keeps there, placing it on my open wound.

This day just sucks all around.

Mena was able to patch me up a bit, and Ian fixed me up the rest of the way after they identified and put twenty souls to rest.

Evangeline was right. There was no bright side.

Doing everything they could think of, Aurelia and Mena still couldn't find Nicola or Devereux. Anthony and Sebastian promised to put out every feeler and call in every favor to help find them, and since Claire had no clue her brother was even alive, so she was no help. I'm not sure how much I believe that, but Claire had been through enough without us badgering her. She didn't need more.

Devereux needs to be taken down—that wasn't the question, but Nicola... Her situation was sticky at best and fucking lethal at worst. The horrible question in everyone's mind was what to do when we found her. We didn't know what happened for certain, and without the knowing, there wasn't much we could do.

Kyle left us as soon as he was able. Evangeline didn't want him to go, but she couldn't blame him for wanting to search for his mate.

We all just hoped he didn't regret what he found.

18

I FEEL LIKE I HAVE BEEN WAITING FOR ONE THING OR ANOTHER my whole life. But most of my time has been waiting for West to get his head out of his ass.

Unfortunately, I'm still waiting.

It's been a week—a whole week—and I haven't gotten more than a one-word answer or a grunt in response to any question I've asked. He's lucky he's finally healed up, or I'd pop another staple just to get a reaction from him.

I know why he's pissed.

Well, I should say I know his reason, but not why. Who gives a shit if I saw what Walter did to him? I mean, it isn't like I didn't discover him in that damn chamber. It isn't like I didn't have his blood all over me as I prayed to the Fates not to take him too.

It's not like I didn't see.

But I did. I saw every cut and strike and slice. I saw everything he went through at Walter's hands. I saw what he made Devereux do to him too. Every bad thing, every murder, every single time he beat his children, every time he raped his wife, every underhanded deal and every soul he deported to Hell without reason or cause.

And people wonder why I don't consume. Because I don't want to see this shit.

But now he's all kinds of butt hurt about what I saw.

Does this make him feel vulnerable? Does he think I think less of him? Who fucking knows what is going on in his head. It's not me; that's for sure. It pisses me off to have him so close when he feels miles away.

I feel alone. Again. Even after he said he wouldn't leave, he's done it all the same.

I'm sitting at the dining room table in the high rise condo I purchased a month ago, picking at an omelet Cam shoved in front of me. I couldn't go back to the cliff house where my parents died, and I couldn't even pretend I wanted to go back to Grand Lake. It felt wrong there without them, and I couldn't bring myself to stay there when every wall held my mother's laughter and every single room was missing my father's presence.

Aidan and Cam have made it their mission to make sure I eat and consume. I'd venture a guess this is West's doing, but I can't be sure. Either way, the two of them have taken their Guardian duties to new levels.

Cam scrapes a dining chair back over the slate tiles, eliciting a lovely nails-on-a-chalkboard screech from the wrought iron legs on the stone. Sweet mother, I need a rug underneath this table.

"You going to eat or what?" Cam grumbles.

Appropriately scolded, I use my fork to slice into the fluffy concoction of eggs, bacon, red onion and green bell pepper. It smells wonderful and tastes even better. Who knew Cam could cook?

I inhale the eggs, and I realize I was more than hungry. Especially when I start looking around for more food. Cam rolls his eyes before getting up to warm up a whole slew of leftovers. Creamy sausage-potato-kale soup from Aurelia with crusty French bread, beef medallions topped with seared scallops, roasted asparagus and a mushroom risotto that makes my eyes roll back in my head. I eat enough for four people, and I'm not sorry.

After I finish my buffet of awesomeness, I shuffle off to my bed. I stop by my bathroom to do the whole face washing, teeth brushing, pajama donning deal and flop onto my bed with the last vestiges of my strength, promptly passing out.

Full bellies must be equivalent to tranquilizer darts, is my last thought before I'm dead to the world.

I wake up on my left side and warm for the first time in a week—since the last time I was in West's arms. He's in the bed with me, his delicious heat at my back, his breath and the whiskers of his beard tickling the sensitive skin of my neck. All week he's been sleeping in one of the eight guest rooms in the two-floor penthouse.

But this morning is different.

I am warm and content and so happy to have him next to me that it is a brutal slap to have reality seep into my brain. He's practically ignored me for a week—as if I did something wrong, as if I'm to blame somehow—and it pisses me off. So, despite the warmth, and strength of his massive arm curled around my body and the rough possessive hand he has inside my camisole over my left breast... and the thumb he has rolling over my nipple... and the hard, thick, naked cock against my backside... *mmm...*

Maybe I'm not as mad as I was before. I could totally give him the benefit of the doubt here. Give him a pass just this once.

I roll my hips against him, and the growl I get back sends a shiver down my spine. Okay, I'll be mad at him later. Tomorrow maybe, if he keeps playing with my nipple like that. His fangs graze the skin of my neck, and I freeze.

In all the time we have been together, West has never phased while we were making love. He has always held himself back, always in control. Always.

Because he never wanted me to hope. He never wanted to take the chance of losing control. This is huge. This is the equivalent of a man getting on one knee and showing a woman the rock. My heart swells so big, I want to cry. I'm holding on by a very thin thread as I turn in his arms to look at him.

"You sure? You can't take this back," I whisper, my voice trembling.

This—him—is what I've wanted since the beginning, but I'm torn between pissed off that he dragged his feet, taking his sweet ass time to get here, and so blindingly happy that I'm practically vibrating in his arms.

His gaze bores into me—reaches to the very depths of my soul. I don't need to ask again, and I don't need an answer. His face is his reply, and I feel it like a caress against my skin. His eyes bleed from black back to jade, his fangs retracting back into his jaw and he takes that moment to run lips across my forehead, the softness of lips followed by the gentle scratch of his beard over my cheekbones and down my neck. His hands make quick work of my camisole and sleep shorts, but he doesn't move to do anything else. He just holds my naked body against his, burying his head against my chest as he wraps me up in his arms. I sift my fingers through his shoulder-length hair, missing this closeness we had so long ago.

But the heat of his skin makes me restless, and the throbbing ache between my legs has me shifting and squirming in his arms. My body flashes hot all over and it is as if my blood is answering his call. The quick, hot lash of his tongue on my nipple pulls a moan from me and a growl from him which only gets louder once he pulls my nipple into his mouth and starts torturing me with his blunted teeth.

He rolls us, so I'm on my back with his massive body in between my legs. His lips are on mine then, and his kiss is a promise, a vow. He won't leave me. He won't abandon me. And if one of us leaves this earth, the other will be following close behind. His fingers tangle in my hair, and he gives a soft tug to get my attention. He has it, he so has it.

"I love you, Evangeline. Will you be mine?" his gruff, raspy voice asks.

I've been waiting for those words for a century. I've been waiting so long for them, I can't even speak. I can't do anything but nod, happy tears spilling from the corners of my eyes as I watch his emotions pass like an open book across his face. I see his love, his trust in his expression and I can't fathom how I could have thought he didn't. Then, his lips are on mine again, his tongue sliding into my mouth, and I want him so much. I want him inside of me. I want my blood inside his mouth, my essence in his heart. I want it all.

He gives me everything I want—everything I need—but he makes me wait, he makes me beg. His lips trail down my body, little nips and sucking kisses at my breasts, the luscious heat of his breaths against the skin of my abdomen, the smoldering whip of his tongue against my center, the rasp of his whiskers against my tender flesh. I squirm, my body moving of its own volition. His rough hands hold my hips still as he devours me, licking, kissing, nibbling, and when he thrusts a single finger inside me, I go off.

"Please," the pleading moan erupts from my mouth, and at my plea, West moves up my body.

I steal his lips, his breath, but give it back just as quickly as he slides through my wetness and spears into me. The taste of myself on his tongue sends a curl of heat through me. I'm on fire. I'm burning, and I relish in the flames.

Yes. This is what I wanted. His rough palms burrow underneath me, wrapping me in his arms, caging me in the very best way as he thrusts into me. Rolling my hips, I meet him stroke for furiously delicious stroke, watching his face, watching the way his brow puckers, the way his mouth falls open as the phase comes over me and I rake my fangs up his neck. His eyes flash black again, and his fangs snap down.

"Yessss," I hiss, and he gives me one smoldering kiss before he strikes—the sharp sting of the cutting edge of his teeth biting into the meat of my shoulder is everything.

It's warmth and strength and love. It's home.

I've been missing my home for so long. But now, I have it.

WEST AND I ARE SITTING IN MY ENORMOUS BATHTUB, AND I think it is hilarious that my big, sexy, damn-near-seven-foot-tall mate is taking a bubble bath with me. I can't quit giggling as he runs his fingertips up and down my legs. I feel light, as if a huge boulder of grief has been lifted off my chest.

I miss my parents. It hurts me that they missed out on seeing us bonded, but maybe they sent us the shoves we needed to get our collective heads pulled from our asses. I turn in West's lap, slipping in the suds to face him. I study his face—shoulder-length black hair soaked and dripping tiny rivulets of water down his pecs, strong brow, sexy lumberjack beard over an exceedingly strong jaw. And those eyes—such an indeterminate green, anywhere between jade and emerald with every different shade in between.

I love those eyes. I love how expressive they are, how they tell a story without him ever having to say a word. I open my mouth to tell him how happy I am, and although it is probably unnecessary, I do it anyway.

"I am ridiculously, obnoxiously happy right now," I whisper.

A smile blooms over his face, and the curl of his lips tipping up winds its way around my heart.

"That's good, Angel. I'm happy, too," his gruff murmur vibrates through me, and I can't help but slide up his body to kiss him.

And we were so happy. For a while.

19

THAT'S THE THING ABOUT HAPPINESS—IT BLINDS YOU. IT MAKES you think that everything will be okay, that everything won't eventually go to shit. In my life, I have had very few moments of goodness interspersed with long, dragging years of awful. My few moments of happiness would be the times I've been wrapped around the beautiful Angel currently nestled in my arms.

So, naturally, some asshole has to ruin it.

The ruination comes in the form of a fist pounding on our bedroom door at three-motherfucking-thirty in the morning. Evangeline is straight up dead to the world, and even though the person knocking might actually be using a battering ram instead of a fist, she isn't waking up for anything. A surge of masculine pride hits me as I remember all the dirty things I did to her last night, and I can't help but chuckle as I slide out from underneath her to search for some clothes.

The last four months with Evangeline have been the best of my entire life. While there has always been a niggle of fear in the back of my mind, it isn't for her or us. It is the lingering questions we still have, the fear that Nicola still hasn't been found, and we don't know what really happened there. There is a tense sort of camaraderie we have with the Shifters and Warlocks, but the Witches are less than pleased with us.

And our own kind...

We have many supporters—the working class and regular folk love us because we are cracking down on all of the bullshit from John's reign. Shit I had no idea about. Shit that Walter and a few of his cronies were in on. The head families—except for the Garrison's and Stein's—have been a headache, but nothing we can't handle.

But there is unrest. A sense that something bigger is out there. Something we aren't seeing. Fuck dropping, the proverbial shoe is about to plant itself in our asses. I just know it.

I slip my naked ass into a pair of worn jeans that were slung over a dark purple velvet bench sitting at the end of our bed. The room is decorated in every single color of the rainbow, and is probably the girliest fucking room I've ever been in, but I don't really care. I give Angel shit for it, but only because I love it when she gets riled.

I zip but forego the button because I'm just going to take these damn jeans off as soon as I can get rid of whoever has the death wish beating on our door.

"Are you kidding me?" I whisper to Aidan as I open the bedroom door.

It takes me a second to realize he's not alone, and when I see Kyle a cold pit of dread hits me in the stomach.

"Fates, man," I mutter as give him a quick slap on the back in greeting. "What happened?"

It has been months since I've seen Kyle, and by the look of him, those months were not spent happy. He isn't as gaunt as he was in Walter's dungeon, but Kyle isn't as healthy as he used to be. His beard is trimmed, his hair tamed, but I can tell he hasn't been eating or consuming as he should.

And his eyes... His eyes are haunted.

"We need to wake Evan. I'm not saying this shit twice," his gruff voice orders, and I resist the urge to punch him in his dumbfuck face because I know he has to be going through some shit.

If he were anyone else, his face would be meeting the Carrera marble floor. Yeah, I'm new to this King shit, but still.

Kyle turns and walks woodenly toward the living area, and I look to Aidan. "You know anything?" I ask.

"Not a thing, man. He's been like a ghost trying to find her," Aidan says as he shakes his head.

"Go watch him and call in Mena, at least. If he has info on Nicola, she'll want to know. We can pass on anything pertinent to everyone else."

"You know good and well Aurelia will kick my ass if she finds out I called her sister and not her. It doesn't matter if she's in her third trimester with twins or not."

"Whatever, man. I need to wake up my woman. Go do what you need to."

I slip back into our room to the closet as I button my jeans. Rifling through the drawers, I find a t-shirt and some socks and grab my boots, and head back to my Angel. She hasn't moved a millimeter from where I left her. I brush my fingertips down her spine as I sit in the open space at her hip, loving that she squirms in her sleep at my touch. I lean down to kiss her shoulder blade, and as the rasp of my beard against her skin, her eyes flutter open.

"Mmm... sleepy. You can do naughty things to me later," she mumbles.

"Angel, you need to wake up. Kyle is here."

Her eyes flash open.

"Are you serious?" she asks not waiting for my response before she hauls ass to the closet to get dressed. I have never been more glad that I can see in the dark as I watch her pert bottom race across the room. She comes back moments later hopping as she pulls up a pair of jeans, and I'm treated to the luscious jiggle of her breasts before she shrugs into a bra and tugs a tank top over her head. I follow her into the bathroom where she throws her hair up in a ponytail, and I brush my teeth as she furiously brushes hers.

"Do you know what's going on?" she asks around her toothbrush, foam coating her mouth.

"Nope," I say after I spit.

"It's going to be bad, isn't it?" she replies grimacing.

I rinse and spit, and turn to look at her, wiping my mouth with the hand towel.

"Probably, Angel, but you know what?" I murmur as I walk on my still bare feet across the tile to wrap her up in my arms.

"What?" she whispers back.

"We'll make it through, you and me. No matter what."

"Promise?" she murmurs her question as her eyes fix on my lips.

When the smile hits my mouth, her lips curl up in response. I give her a hot, wet kiss full of promises I intend on keeping as soon as we're alone again and tug her out of our room and down the hallway to a living room full of people.

Curiously, Aurelia is already here and propped up on the couch with every throw pillow at her disposal, ice water in a glass with a straw and every man in the house willing and ready to do her bidding.

None of this surprises me.

Aurelia has a habit of knowing things long before anyone else, and it is standard operating procedure to cater to a woman with child. Pregnant women—at least in Wraith culture—are considered close to deities. It is so rare for Wraith females to conceive, we as a species are hardwired to accommodate our women. And a woman pregnant with multiples? Forget about it. It doesn't matter that Aurelia is a Phoenix or that she's carrying Phoenix babies. She's more one of us than her own kind anyway.

Asher, Carver, Ian, Aidan, Cam and Rhys all stand in her orbit, with Mena holding her left hand. Evan tells me Aurelia has had a relatively easy pregnancy, so I don't know if she's drawing on Mena's power or if she's just cuddling with her sister. Evan leaves me to go to Aurelia's right side, not only kicking Rhys out of his spot but also taking Aurelia's water from her and putting it on the coffee table so she can hold her hand.

I forget that Nicola is Aurelia and Mena's cousin, and although their relationship is tenuous at best, they must care about her.

"Alright, out with it. What are we dealing with here?" Evangeline orders Kyle, and he flinches as if struck.

Oh, shit. It is going to be so much worse than I thought.

"I-I found her," he begins, "She and that guy Devereux have been hopping from one place to another. Hopping all over the damn planet. St-stealing children from families, teenagers, preschoolers, b-babies..."

He pauses then to put a hand over his mouth. "I tried. I tried to get them back. To follow them to keep the children alive. But I lost her so many times, and I... She's holed up in some abandoned mansion in the wilds of Maine or some shit. Th-there are graves." He stops abruptly—choking on his emotion, on his realization that he has to put a stop to a woman that his body is trained to love, that his soul recognizes as his own.

The guilt he must feel bringing this to us, I cannot fathom.

"When you... when you stop her, can you make sure it doesn't hurt? Can you... It isn't her fault. It's the dirty fucking soul they stuck in her. It isn't her. Just don't... Don't make it hurt, okay?" he pleads searching Evangeline's face for sympathy, but it isn't her who speaks up.

It's me.

"Yes. I can make it painless," I admit, and even though I hate bringing up my past, it's true I can do that. Especially for him.

"It can't be you. Nic told me before this happened. She said that the only way for Iva to be killed was if Evangeline did it. It was one of the last things she told me before I was captured. And I-I want your word you'll... you'll..."

Evangeline leaves her perch on the couch to sit next to Kyle and wraps her arms around his shoulders. She whispers in his ear, and tears start falling from the big man's eyes.

"I just have one question. Are you bound?" she asks, the question we've all been hesitant to ask.

No one wants to kill one just to lose another. No one wants to lose Kyle too.

Kyle shakes his head, and I didn't realize I was holding my breath for the answer to that question until a sigh of relief gusts past my parted lips. I've known Kyle Brennan for three centuries. Losing him would be a blow.

"She wouldn't let me. Never said why, but I figure she knew this might happen," he croaks, his face destroyed.

It wouldn't matter if I lost Evangeline before I bound her or not—it would still probably kill me. It would just take longer.

"We'll be humane about it, but it needs to happen. Iva won't stop, and if she hasn't already, she's about to start a war," Evangeline says carefully, looking Kyle right in the eye.

His expression is somewhere between ravaged and dead. He is giving up so much.

"I'll tell you where they are, but you'll have to get in on your own. I can't help you kill her," he responds.

So, we make a plan and pray no one dies.

And I've never been more scared in my whole life.

20

WE COULDN'T JUST WALK UP TO THE FRONT DOOR LIKE A TROOP of girl scouts selling cookies and politely ask, *'Hey will you guys just sit still while we kill you?'*

We needed to prepare. Step one was getting the amulets we needed to keep Iva out of our business and out of our minds. Aurelia, being the only one of us with a Witch in her pocket, offered to be the one to get them. Aurelia's tattoo artist friend, Max, was a very nice Witch who didn't prescribe to the old ways. She did things her way and had a different method of doing magic. And an added plus, she hated Tessa with a fiery passion, so my trust in her increased by at least ten-fold. Aurelia and Rhys left to make the short trip to her studio to procure the amulets while the rest of us got the rundown of the grounds from Kyle.

"From what I saw, there is only two ways into the house," Kyle instructs from his seat at the kitchen island as he points to a rough pen and ink rendering of a rather stately—if dilapidated—mansion. The drawing is dirt-stained and crumpled, but it looks as if he had given great care to it. He'd obviously been watching them for a while. The biggest asset with the 'plan' is the massive cliff the house sits on. Surrounded by a thick alpine terrain, the cover will be easy, and the cliff limits egress. Granted, Devereux can travel away at any time, but I have the distinct feeling he won't want to leave his mistress. That's what she has to be, right? I mean, why else would he summon her from Hell?

The plan feels too easy, too clean, and I'm scared.

What if she knows what we're doing? What if she has control over him? What if this is one huge trap? I startle when a scalding hand closes over my shoulder. I look up and back to Mena, who is watching me with concern.

"You can do this, you know. Nicola said it herself—told me you were the only one of us that could," she says encouragingly, but even she is wary of this plan.

I can see it in her eyes.

"That doesn't mean we won't lose people along the way," I whisper back. "This feels too fucking easy."

And it is. There is no way we're just walking up there and doing what we need to without some serious repercussions.

"And it may very well be harder than he's portraying it to be, and we may lose loved ones. But can you live with yourself if she kills another child? This isn't a wait-and-see situation. We know she is actively killing children, and if it is anything like the Aegis genocide..." she breaks off as she swallows thickly. "She won't stop. Not until we make her stop."

I stop my freak out at the wisdom of her words. No, I can't sit idly by while she kills again. Not while I am possibly in a position to stop it. It would be worse than San Francisco. It would be the worst stain on my soul because neglecting this wouldn't be an accident. Letting these children die would be on purpose. And that is the worst sin—not stepping in when I could help save a life.

I look across the island and catch West's eyes. His face looks like it must match mine—blind fear mixed with resignation. I tip my head to signal for him to follow me and start walking toward the hallway. When we're out of earshot, I ask him, "What do you think?"

"I'm thinking body armor. Lots and lots of body armor. And if I thought it would work, and those bastards wouldn't just travel out of there, a grenade launcher," he says matter-of-factly.

"But you want to go, right?"

"Fuck, yes, I want to go. Not want, Angel, we need to go. And as much as I don't want you to be in harm's way, you have to go too. I know you don't know much about my childhood, but... My father was the Devil himself. The things he did... no one should have to endure. I cannot stand for murder, but when it's kids..." he trails off shaking his head.

I step into his space and wrap my arms around him.

"One of these days, you're going to have to tell me about your life, my love. Not today, but someday, this info would be good to know. I don't even know if you want children of your own."

"Of course I want children. Girls with your beautiful face or little boys with your eyes. I'm not picky. Whether it is one or ten, I don't mind either, but I'd like more than one. We're both only children, and I'd love our kid to have a sibling. I'm actually amazed it took you four months to ask that."

"I didn't want to push. I figured we had time. But the bad stuff—even the not so bad stuff—I'd like to know, my love. You've carried it too long, I think."

I get an affirmative grunt and a squeeze in response. I know it will take some hounding, but I'll get at least some of it from him. West has held that horribly toxic poison in his chest for centuries.

Maybe one of these days he'll let it go.

That thought passes through my brain at the same instant the front door opens, and Aurelia and Rhys walk through it. Well, Aurelia waddles through it, but whatever. Her waddle is slight, but the woman is carrying twins, so naturally I have to give her shit.

"What's up, Mama Duck?" I say with a snicker.

"Fuck you," she replies with a baleful expression on her face.

Touchy, touchy. She adjusts the short jean jacket that covers her arms, and fiddles with the black crepe sundress that flows over her ripe belly.

"Aww, come on, you waddle and have feathers. You're more than halfway there," I giggle.

"Seriously. I will make Rhys kill you. Don't test the limits of my friendship, woman," she says, but I know she's just fucking with me.

Aurelia is warily excited about her pregnancy, and has been taking every precaution so her babies turn out healthy. Sparing, no; katas, yes. Junk food, no; fruit and veg, yes. Over-training, no; resting when needed, yes. In the beginning, she over trained and fought and exposed herself to the elements, but now, she does everything she can to be safe. I think it is because she's scared she'll lose them, and with her history, I don't blame her.

"Fine, Sensitive Sally, I'll quit fucking with you. Max help us out?" I ask.

"Yep. You already have one—Max told me she saw one around your neck the last time you came with me to the shop—which explains so freaking much, BTW. She was in a rush so she didn't make one for me, Mena, Rhys or you because we didn't need them. Rhys, because he's not going with you and me and Mena because our Aegis protects us. Everyone else gets one," she informs me as she raises a censuring eyebrow.

Busted. It's been a century and Aurelia didn't know about my little blue amulet. Well, she knows now.

"What? A girl has to have her secrets," I shrug, unapologetic.

"Yeah, yeah. You say that now. What happens when you're in trouble? Huh? I can't see shit with that fucking thing on. It's annoying."

"Yeah, yeah. I'll be fine."

"Whatever, pass these out, and make sure Kyle gets one. I have a feeling he'll be an easy mark for her to tap into," she says as she hands me the pouch of amulets in her hand.

"Good idea," I say as we walk into the kitchen.

A kitchen that doesn't have a Kyle perched at a barstool.

"Where's Kyle?" West rumbles behind me.

"He just smoked out..." Cam answers bewildered.

"Oh, son of a fucking bitch. He. Did. Not," Aurelia curses as her eyes begin to glow. "He did. That stupid motherfucker!"

"He went to her, didn't he?" West asks.

"Of course he did, the moron. Is he trying to get you killed?" she replies.

"No. He's trying to say goodbye. I would probably do the same," he returns gruffly. "If you only had minutes with Rhys, wouldn't you?"

Her eyes stop glowing, and she takes a good long look at him. "Probably, but that fucks with your timeline. You guys need to go as soon as possible to try and intercept him."

"Alright, everyone. Get your shit squared away and be ready in ten," West orders and they move.

The King has spoken.

FIRST, MID-MARCH IN NORTHERN MAINE IS COLD AS FUCK. Second, the nighttime temperatures make the daytime temps look like summer. I wish I would have brought a parka. I thought Colorado was chilly, but I had no idea.

This is not the excellent Colorado weather. This is windy hell on a stick.

The forest gives adequate cover, but the early morning hours are working against us. I would have preferred to attack under the cover of darkness, but Kyle royally screwed our timeline. I find it hard to be angry with him. If I only had one single day left with West, I couldn't say how rational I'd be.

We traveled in about a mile out from the house, checking for traps, surveillance and the like, but finding none. It's like they want us to come —either that or they think they aren't going to be caught. I don't know which option scares me more.

The trees are dense right up next to the small yard in front of the house, and the bellows of the ocean rushing against the cliffs the only sounds.

No birds. No crickets. No animals.

It is the calm before the storm. I feel it and so does everyone else, this electric charge in the air like just before a lightning strike. The pressure, the oppressive weight of the air sticks to us. I'm just behind West when I feel a stir. I don't think anything of it at first until I catch a glimpse of Mena.

She wasn't phased a moment ago, but she is now, and despite the blue flames that lick her skin and the brilliantly bright blue wings that are spread wide, she is white as a sheet. Her fingertips crackle like tiny lightning rods, and her head is cocked to one side as if she's listening to something only she can hear.

While she's frozen, all hell seems to break out around us. Men file out of the front door of the house while barrels of rifles peek out of the upper floor windows. The world explodes as bullets whiz past us, but I'm not watching them. I'm watching Mena's face because she knows something. Something horrible is happening, and I don't know what it is, but I know it's bad.

Her eyes meet mine.

"Aurelia is in trouble. I have to go," she whispers, and I have no idea how I hear her with the guns firing and men fighting around us.

She pulls a katana from her back in a quick, seamless motion and cuts down the Wraith barreling for her, practically cutting him in two. She cuts down two more before she grabs Asher, and they smoke out of the forest leaving us to this Hell to go to a new one with her sister, my best friend.

Fates, we're too late.

21

I THOUGHT I WAS SAFE, THOUGHT NOT GOING INTO BATTLE WITH them would make it so. While I regretted not going to help, I knew I wasn't going to waddle my seven-and-a-half-months-pregnant ass onto the battlefield and do anything of consequence. I would be in the way, and I would put my babies lives and my husband's life at risk. But while I was worrying about my friends—no, my family—I should have been worrying about my babies, my husband, myself.

I'd wanted to stay at the penthouse. It was Evangeline's headquarters after all, and I figured this would be the place everyone would head to once the dust was settled.

The pregnancy had been easier than I thought it would be. Sure, I was always hot—even in the dead of winter—I couldn't see my feet anymore, and shaving my legs had become a real problem, but my babies were thriving. Only six more weeks to go until they were considered full term and then I would get my lovelies. We have no idea what gender or genders are cooking in there, and since we have no way to know, we did the nursery in neutral colors.

Rhys has been my rock, dealing with my crazy ass while I try to navigate the emotions of guilt and fear. Losing my first child was the worst thing to ever happen to me. More than the torture or losing Lucien or losing my mind to Iva. Losing my first baby was the absolute worst thing, and because of that, I have been either in denial about this pregnancy or running to the end of the spectrum and worrying about every action, morsel of food, and drop of water I've put in my body. I have been a mess, but Rhys... Rhys has been happy—so stinking ecstatic—he's willfully getting every ounce of baby gear set up and ready. It's like he's the one nesting and not me.

But losing the babies is my worst nightmare. Failing to protect my first child has always been my greatest sin. Failing to protect these children would kill me.

"You doing okay, Gorgeous?" Rhys' honey-over-gravel voice calls from my right.

I break my gaze on the lone brilliant sapphire blue amulet sitting on the island to look at him.

"Yeah, why?"

"You stopped in the middle of heading to the bathroom to stare at the amulet, babe," he says as he rubs me between my shoulder blades. His touch is comforting and sets my mind back to rights, but I feel a niggle of fear.

"I... I don't like not being able to see. I don't like not being able to warn them if I can. I don't like those amulets," I mutter.

"Yeah, I know you hate not knowing shit ahead of time, but they need the protection of them, so do your best not to worry. Mena is with them, and she'll help them if not win, then definitely survive."

"You're right. I know you're right, but I can't help but feel... like something is wrong, and I'm not sure if it is them or the babies or us. I feel off, and I want to grab a weapon, and I want to eat my weight in cheesecake. What the hell is wrong with me?" I ask as I turn away from him, but he comes up behind me and wraps one arm around my chest and puts one large hand over my belly.

It might be weird or trite or whatever, but when he puts a hand over the babies it calms me down so fast, he might as well have shot me with a tranq dart. I cover his hand with both of mine, and one of the babies kicks me. Hard.

I should have listened to my gut.

I should have, but I didn't.

So when the five Wraiths smoke into the room, I don't realize my worst nightmare is coming to life until it is.

WEST

Things are going from okay, to not good, to *we're gonna to die* so fast, I don't know what to do. My first thought is how many minions does this woman have? For fuck's sake, is she that good at brainwashing people or is she just that good at bargaining lives she doesn't have to? It isn't just Wraiths fighting for her either—which doesn't make a lick of sense to me at all. She was the one who ordered the mass killings of so many of our families. She was the one who had our houses and lives burned to ashes. Why would they fight for this woman?

I see a few Phoenixes out here, their Fireskin glowing orange in the early morning light. I don't understand that either. How could someone who was destined for sending souls to a better place, hurt and kill so many? Wouldn't they want to go to the same place they sent so many souls to? Wouldn't they fear Hell that much more because they knew what they'd be missing?

I'm between the house and Evangeline, but that doesn't mean a single thing right now. We're surrounded by men and bullets are whizzing by our heads from the open second-floor windows. Evangeline drops to the bracken of the forest floor to return fire, taking out two of the three before she concentrates on the Wraith in front of her. Aidan and Cam are on her like white on rice, guarding her back as they eliminate threat after threat trying to take out my Angel while I'm stuck separated from her.

Good men.

They can't stop them all, though, and I've never been more glad that she'd spent so much time training to fight. She's fluid and beautiful as she spins, and if she weren't beheading a man with a rapier in the middle of a dicey as hell fight, I'd want to kiss her. But for now, I'm stuck in a well-matched battle with a man just as big as I am. Every strike has a parry, every slice has a block, and I can't seem to get the upper hand on him.

When the slice to my back comes, it's a shock. I was so engrossed in my Angel and the man in front of me who I just can't seem to kill, I missed the man behind me. The blow takes me to my knees.

Now I have two Wraiths bearing down on me.

RHYS

I have never been more glad that I never leave the house without at least one weapon than I am right now. Five Wraiths smoke into the penthouse, and I could kick myself for not taking Aurelia seriously before. When has she ever been wrong about her fears?

That's right, never.

I pull my H&K from my spine holster and fire a round as I yank Aurelia behind me. The first one goes down easy, but when I have my whole world behind me, any threat at all is too much. Then, she isn't behind me anymore. Aurelia's hand rips from mine, and she's dragged away by a Witch I didn't see before. The Witch looks so much like Tessa, if I hadn't watched her die with my own eyes, I would have believed it was her. Aurelia jerks from the woman's hold, but she is unbalanced and falls to all fours just missing the coffee table by mere inches. She seems unhurt at the moment, but all I want to do is kill the Witch who took her from me.

I'm torn, but I shouldn't have been. Aurelia isn't helpless despite her delicate condition. She reaches underneath the skirt of her dress to a thigh bandolier filled with throwing knives. She makes short work of the Witch's Achilles tendon, and then to add insult to injury, Aurelia embeds the knife in the Witch's thigh. In the melee of her screams of agony I take out another Wraith, but my good luck soon runs out.

In the next instant, my left shoulder is struck by a bullet. I don't feel it, but Aurelia's shriek of pain sends the worst sort of fear through me.

If I bleed, she bleeds. If I die, she dies. The babies. The babies.

MENA

I didn't know when I started feeling when Aurelia was in trouble—birth maybe—but it was never this acute. Never this visceral. It was more than just knowing. I felt her fear, her pain. I felt it more than my own and I knew—I knew it was her. It had to be. My left shoulder was on fire, and I could barely keep hold of the Glock in my hand, but I hadn't been struck. Ash was right next to me, and since I'd learned how to shield him as well as myself, I knew he wasn't injured.

My gut said it was her, and I knew I couldn't wait. I knew she had no time. So I met Evan's eyes with apology in mine. Because I couldn't do what I said I would do. I couldn't fulfill my promise to Nicola. I had to leave them. I had to go to Aurelia. Because if I didn't, she would die.

"Aurelia is in trouble. I have to go," I whisper as I grab Asher's hand.

"We have to go back. Now," I tell him.

He doesn't question why, he doesn't do anything but grab my waist and travel from the battlefield back to the penthouse, trading one Hell for another. I reinforce the shield around myself and Ash, and when we reform in the middle of the kitchen, I am supremely glad I had the forethought. Otherwise, Ash would have a bullet in his brain right about now.

Splashes of blood and gore litter the kitchen. A body of a Wraith lay just in front of the sink and another in the dining room. A Witch is screaming of revenge and agony in the living room, and Rhys is trying to protect Aurelia with his body as three Wraiths advance on him. I blink, and Ash has taken out one of the men, but the other prove much harder to kill.

These men are not the untrained peons Walter offered up for slaughter. These men are killers.

I catch movement in the living room just as the two Wraiths make their move. The Witch is crawling for Aurelia, her fingertips glowing red with unspent magic. I do the only thing I can think of, I throw a bolt of my Aegis at her, knocking her into the thick floor to ceiling glass window so hard the three-inch pane cracks. The light in her eyes goes out as blood pours from her eyes, nose, ears, and mouth. Her death was too quick for someone who would hurt a pregnant woman, and I wish I'd killed her slower.

Bloodthirsty, perhaps, but I don't give a fuck.

Ash eliminates one of the two Wraiths still left standing, but we have a bigger problem. The last one has dragged Aurelia away from Rhys and has positioned her in front of him like a shield. The worst part isn't that he's using my sister's pregnant body for his own cowardice.

No, the worst part is the loaded gun he has against her temple.

EVAN

I feel it before I see it—the imminent danger West is in. It is a niggle in the back of my mind and swoop to my gut. I turn in time to see a giant of a man slash a thick sword upward, and the way West's back arches, the blade hit its target.

He's down on all fours. He's breathing, but he's not moving. He's not getting to his feet. *He's hurt. Oh, shit.*

My brain blanks for a split second and then regroups. I embed my rapier in the gut of the closest enemy and slash outward, spilling his innards all over the forest floor. The Wraith's eyes turn from smug to shocked, and I watch his expression go slack with a fucking smile on my face. His death will be slow and painful, and it is a slight comfort to me that I make sure the killers of children leave this world screaming.

I smoke out from my spot of relative safety between Cam and Aidan and go to West. I feel my power rise in my chest as I move, and when I travel to the place just before them, the men fly back as if pulled by a puppeteer's string. I move to them and take their heads with my rapier before they even knew what hit them. I move to the next and the next and the next until there are no more lives for me to take outside.

When Nicola steps out on the wide wrap-around porch, I have to remind myself that it isn't her. That the betrayal I feel at the sight of her face isn't real. I have to remind myself that she has Iva's dark soul squatting inside her like a toad. It is easier than I'd thought to separate the two, especially when she drags a bleeding Kyle across the porch planks from behind her like a rag doll.

Nicola wouldn't do that to him. I saw her with Kyle months ago—before all this mess. I saw her expressions. I saw how she felt even before he did. Nicola was taken by the giant man from the start.

She flings Kyle's broken but still breathing body from her fingertips as if he were a piece of errant trash. Kyle lands at my feet, and I feel more than see the rest of my family file in around me. Her expression flickers for a moment, but when this woman talks, Iva's thick, Irish brogue slips from her lips.

"Evangeline, dearie. I've been expecting you."

22

MENA

I DON'T KNOW WHAT TO DO.

I'm stuck here watching my larger than life sister shiver in fear. No, not shiver—she's vibrating, she's so scared. Scared because anything he does to her, he does to her entire family. Her husband, her babies. Aurelia's eyes pale, pupilless eyes are wide and rivulets of tears are falling from them. Her left shoulder is bloody and limp at her side, and her chest is heaving with panicked breaths.

I have to figure out what to do. If I shock him, his muscles could tense, and he could pull the trigger by accident.

Then, out of the corner of my eye I see Aurelia's fingers tiptoe down her right leg as she pulls up the fabric of her dress to reveal her thigh bandolier filled with throwing knives. I make no movement, nothing to give away her actions because the Wraith holding her looks skittish at best. His eyes dart at the three of us—three fully phased predators ready to skin him alive at the first available opportunity.

I glance at Rhys and Ash out of the corner of my eye. It is amazing to me that these two men who couldn't be more different, have matching expressions of wrath on their faces. Rhys' Fireskin paints him in an orange glow, his black and blood-red wings spread wide, his face a promise of retribution. Ash's phase has turned his ice-blue eyes black, talons longer than Aurelia's throwing knives curl from his fingertips, two-inch-long upper and lower fangs give him a macabre smile, and his power sweeps around him in swaths of black smoke.

It's good we look so deadly. It's keeping the Wraith's fearful eyes on us instead of on the woman in his arms. The woman who at this very moment decides it is high time he feels what Fireskin does to people who fuck with us. Bright orange flames skate over Aurelia's skin, burning the Wraith's arms, face and torso. He flinches back, howling in agony and Aurelia shoves her knife into the soft spot just under the man's chin. The blade isn't long enough to kill him, but that doesn't matter. She takes her burning hand and grabs his jaw as she rips out the knife.

She gives him a look that would strike the fear of God into anyone, but at this point, the man shouldn't fear God—he should fear her. With a hideous snarl, she flips the blade to an overhand grip and drives home into his eye. She holds him up until he quits twitching and then drops him like a smoldering sack of potatoes at her feet.

We're all ready to go to her—ready to check her over until she doubles over in pain as she clutches her belly.

The babies.

EVAN

It is the worst trick in the book to take away someone's will—to take away everything that they are and make them a puppet. Iva has been doing it for centuries under the radar, but never this overt, never killing so indiscriminately, never.

Nicola's body is merely a suit that Iva is wearing. Her voice is different, her mannerisms are different, but the most startling, is her eyes. Nicola's eyes are an unseeing cornflower blue, but Aurelia told me that Iva used brown glass eyes in the place of her missing ones. And though Nicola's eyes were never taken from her because she was born blind, the woman before me possesses an odd honey-brown set of peepers.

Her hair is down, flowing around her shoulders and down her back and she's weirdly wearing makeup—something Nicola neither wears nor has to wear. What is she getting ready for, a fucking party?

She's been expecting me.

Sure. I'll bet she has. I look at Kyle who is struggling to his feet, and realize she has beaten him almost senseless. Well, check one item off my list. West reaches out a hand to help him up, and he shakily makes it to his feet.

"Please, Nic. Please make it back to us. Please," Kyle rasps.

Iva's girlish giggle in response turns my stomach.

"And why would she do that when I am here now? Nicola Miller was a poor blind girl who never did anything but try and scheme her way around me. Now that I'm here, there is no need for her to wonder. She is powerless. There is only me now," she says as she smiles.

Her pronouncement sends a chill down my spine. I held out hope that Nicola was still in there. Still fighting. But I don't know if she is. I don't know if there is anything left of Nicola to fight.

It makes me want to break my promise to Kyle. It makes me want to make her suffer like Nicola has, like we all have. I want to, but I won't. I may have taken lives, but I am nothing like this woman. I don't have this level of evil in me. I don't need power or subjugation. I need love and support and friends—and these are things I have already. These are things Iva will never have because as much power as she scrabbles to possess, she will never have it all.

That thought brings a smile to my face, making the smug one on her face droop a bit. I adjust my hold on my rapier and pull my tri-dagger from its sheath.

"Where's your minion, Iva? Doesn't he want to play?" I taunt.

"Oh, don't you worry your pretty head about him, darling. He's doing exactly what he's supposed to do," she counters and then her Fireskin explodes over her flesh and Nicola's brilliant orange wings burst from her back.

As she takes her first step off the porch stair, fire catches in her wake —jumping from plank to plank, setting the house ablaze.

RHYS

The pain on her face.

Fates, please. Please don't do this to us. It's too early, too early for them. There's something wrong.

I'm proved right when a small puddle of blood starts forming at her feet. It happens in slivers of seconds. The agony on her face morphs into shock. Then her Fireskin dies, and Aurelia's face turns white. Then her eyes roll back in her head as she collapses. Asher moves the quickest of us all and catches her before she hits the ground. He is gentle, but there isn't much that can stop the hurt to her poor body.

Mena places a hand on her belly, and already I can tell Aurelia is drawing on her. Drawing so much of her, her fire goes out as well. Then, Mena's face drains of color, blood running from her nose.

Fates, please.

"T-the hos-hospital in Knoxville. With the W-witches. Go, Ash. Now," Mena orders haltingly.

He meets my eyes, and I can see the fear in them. Fear for his wife, fear for mine, and fear for our lives. He gives me a nod and gathers Aurelia in his arms as he smokes out of the room—carrying my whole world in his arms as he goes.

WEST

The large sprawling porch blazes bright as the flames jump from the steps to the external walls and filter down to the dry forest bracken beneath our feet. We have to move. We have to hurry before we burn. But Evangeline doesn't pay any mind to the flames that will surely burn her or the woman in front of her. My Angel's shoulders set, her jaw clenches and the phase she was holding back flows over her like water.

She moves slightly as if she is about to make her away across the flames to Iva, but before she can make it an inch, black smoke of a traveling Wraith comes in behind her. Time moves like molasses. I won't make it in time to stop them, but I go to her anyway.

Please, no. Please, not my Angel.

I may not be in time, but someone else is. Kyle shoves Evangeline out of the way as he takes the blade meant for her back in his gut.

Devereux Emerson looks slightly put out by this turn of events and uses his boot to shove him off his blade.

By the time Kyle's body meets the earth, Devereux is stuck like a hog on a spit by the blades of Cam, Aidan, Carver, Ian, and myself. Ian wrenches out his blade first as he drops to help Kyle, and the rest of us follow suit, but it is only I who raise my blade again. Devereux's body is pouring blood, but he's still breathing, his eyes rolling like a spooked mare.

He is a threat we have to eliminate, and I'm not waiting for this fucker to figure out a way to resurrect himself a second time. No. Fuck that. I take my kukri and remove his head with one quick strike. I don't wait to transport his sorry ass right where it belongs. Opening my jaws, I inhale his soul as quickly as I can, shutting my mind off to the haunting images that filter through my brain of every horrendous sin he's committed.

The scream coming from Nicola's body sends a chill of fear down my spine. My eyes shoot up from the man who almost took my life to the woman trying to take my Angel's.

23

ASHER

I SHOULDN'T BE THE ONE TO DO THIS. I SHOULDN'T BE THE ONE holding this much responsibility. The only thing in my life that hasn't gone to shit is Mena. The only family I have is the one I made for myself, and I can't be the one to ruin it. I shouldn't be the one holding something so precious.

But I am, and there is no one else who could do it. Mena looked like the life was draining out of her, and if she's that bad, I cannot begin to wrap my mind around what Aurelia's body is going through. She is dead weight in my arms, her jacket and dress soaked in blood as I hold her tight to me and travel to the one hospital I know where we would be accepted.

When I make it to the emergency room entrance, a Shifter I recognize from months ago is waiting for me right outside along with three Witches. The Shifter looks to be the leader of this group and asks me questions rapid fire as I set Aurelia's limp body on a gurney, and the three Witches move as if their hair is on fire, booking it to the operating room elevators. All I can focus on are Aurelia's feet, which are shod in thin-soled sandals that used to be tan leather but are now stained black with blood. My eyes well with tears and as the elevator door close on those feet, the first tears of worry and fear fall.

I feel a pull on my elbow, and I glance back to the Shifter female. I notice right away the color of her hair. It is an odd color that danced back and forth between brown and red.

"What's your name, sir?" the Shifter's voice is calm, and that scares me worse than anything.

"Asher. My name is Asher."

"Okay, Asher, I'm Willa. I need you to tell me what's going on," she orders, her no-nonsense voice waking me up a bit.

"They were attacked. She's—Aurelia—is seven and a half months pregnant with twin Phoenixes. She started bleeding from between her legs... There was a Witch, I don't know if she did a spell. Her fingers were glowing red, and then Aurelia was bleeding. I don't know. I don't know," I say, and I notice she's had my arm in hers as she's leading me to the same elevator Aurelia just went to. I yank my arm from hers and take a step back.

"I-I have to get my wife. I have to get her husband. I have to... I'll be back. Is there a place where we can arrive without going through the ER?" I ask because I need to get back to them as soon as I can.

"Sure, just travel to the conference room upstairs. But Asher? Get back quick, okay?" Willa's voice is soft but firm, and I know I don't have much time.

"Thanks, Willa," I say as I realize I may never be able to thank this woman for snapping me out of my freak out.

She nods and I travel back to my wife with fear embedded deep in my heart.

EVAN

The howl of agony coming from Nicola's body isn't Iva's. No, this is Nicola's pain erupting from her breast, creating a maelstrom of fear and grief and rage. Her eyes are trained on Kyle, and her fear is palpable. She drops to her knees, scrambling across the forest floor through fire and dirt and bracken, trying to get to him. I look behind me and order them to get him out of here.

"Get him to a hospital!" I scream rushing to intercept her.

In her shock, her Fireskin has died down, but I don't trust it or her. I strike out with my rapier, putting a thick gash on her cheek, but that doesn't stop her. I restrain her bodily keeping her away from the injured man.

"No! No, don't keep me back from him. Please! Kyle! Please!" she pleads, and the change in her voice from Iva's thick Irish brogue to Nicola's delicate English accent almost make me believe her.

"I'll let you take her soul. I'll hold her back, just please let me say goodbye to him," she begs, her eyes flooded with desperate tears, and I let her go.

She wastes no time with me and shoves past me to get to him. Nicola grabs his face to hurriedly whisper in his ear as Ian tries to staunch the flow of blood pouring from Kyle's stomach. His eyes drift open, and he grasps her wrists.

"Lo-love you, Nic. See you on the other side," Kyle whispers before his eyes roll back in his head, and he loses consciousness.

"Noooooooo!" she shrieks, but Aidan doesn't wait for her to lose it.

He rips Kyle from her arms and travels from the fray so all she's clutching is air. A rumbled shriek erupts from her chest, her eyes blaze and her Fireskin blooms over her flesh. West and I scramble back from Nicola.

Without Kyle here, without her focus pulled to him, something passes over her face, and I know Iva is back controlling her body.

"You should have killed me when you had the chance, little girl," Iva says as she reaches for me with a lone burning hand.

She misses me by inches as West catches me by the waist and swings me out of the way, accepting the agonizing burn of her touch for himself. He growls in pain before tossing me away from her.

But that's my mate she's fucking with, and I phase without thought or volition. Rushing her without care for my hide or my life. She has West in her clutches, and she's not fucking with one more person I care about. My power swarms through me, the cold blankness causing the earth to shake and debris and dirt and leaves to swirl first around my body, but picking up speed and force and growing, growing, growing until it is bigger than her and me.

This is more than just my life or her life or the lives of my family. This is for the Aegis children she damn near murdered into extinction, the Witch and Warlock and Shifter children that she killed for whatever sick reason she had, for the hurt and pain and suffering she's caused. I make it to her, ripping him from her hands and grabbing her arms in my blistering grip.

Her agony is swift, and though I hate hurting Nicola, I cannot let her get away. I can't let her live after all the death she's caused. Iva's scream turning into Nicola's and it brings me so much pain to do this.

"Ju-just do it, Evan. It always had to be this way. Take the soul, dammit! Do it!"

The permission is what I needed, I think. The knowledge that she knew what I was doing, that she allowed it.

I open my mouth and inhale the dark, twisted essence of Iva and fourteen hundred years of condemning deeds filters through my mind. Murder. Torture. Genocide. And more recently the killing of children with extraordinary powers. The ones who had more power than most. The ones who could be her downfall one day.

And now they never would.

That was the worst because they weren't just teenagers, they were babies, barely a fresh breath in this world before their life was snuffed out. I can't take it. I can't take so much evil… I can't…

Blackness clouds my vision, and I hear my howling scream before I hear nothing at all.

MENA

Asher picked us up and took us to this sterile, silent hospital waiting room where we've been sitting for hours now. I haven't eaten, I have barely moved except for the motion of my nervously shifting feet. Rhys looks like he's about to lose his fucking mind, and all he can do is stare out the window at the rapidly fading day.

Has it only been a day? I've lived almost two centuries, and they have flown by without a word or whisper, but this day? This day has lasted decades, millennia, eons. Aurelia isn't the only person we're waiting on word about. Evan, West, Kyle are all severely injured. Aidan came with Kyle first, and then it was Cam bringing Evan and West hanging onto Ian by a very thin thread.

And Nicola.

We don't know who will be there when she wakes up, or if she even does. Right now I can't think about who she'll be.

I can only think about my sister as I sit here waiting to see if her world will explode once again.

A doctor—Asher called her Willa—passes through the OR automatic doors, and I don't know if I should be pleased or scared, and I don't know how I can breathe right now.

"Aurelia?"

Rhys jumps up from his perch on the windowsill to meet her. His body is strung tight like a string about to snap.

"Your wife is in recovery. Your daughter and son are in the NICU for a little while, but given their species, I don't expect they'll be in there for very long."

"A da-daughter and a son?" Rhys breathes. "Can I see her? Can I see them?"

"Yes to both, but her first, and only one at a time."

"Do you have word on Evangeline, West or Kyle?" Cam asks, his voice a quiet, somber rumble.

Willa looks back at him, and though her eyes flash from amber to green back to amber again, she makes no other outward sign other than a small shake of her head.

"N-not yet," she mutters before leading Rhys away back through the double doors.

Three lives accounted for and three more to go.

I hate waiting.

EVAN

My mind is cotton candy and fluffy clouds, but all I want is clarity. I want to wake up. I want to see my West. My eyelids are heavy, but I force them open. My room is dim, but I can make out the orange blinking lights of a vital sign monitor. Right next to it, sleeping upright in an uncomfortable hospital chair is my West.

Tight black t-shirt over dark-wash jeans and motorcycle boots. His wavy hair is pulled back from his face in a topknot, but his beard is scraggly and unkempt, and I can tell he's been sitting there for quite some time.

His large hand engulfs mine and rests on the bed at my side. I squeeze it before drifting off again, happy he is alive and well, and obviously better off than me if he's out of a hospital bed, but I'm so tired.

"Evangeline? Angel?" his wonderful rumble vibrates through my chest.

"Hmm?" I sleepily respond.

"Never mind, baby. Just sleep."

"Mmmm... only if you come sleep with me. I sleep better with you."

"Whatever you want, Angel," he murmurs, and his warm arms close around me as I drift back to sleep.

And I had sweet dreams.

EPILOGUE

EVAN

"WEST! WE'RE GOING TO BE LATE!" I YELL FROM MY PERCH AT
the bathroom vanity. Yes, I might be on hour two of beauty prep, but
dammit it isn't every day your best friend in the entire universe decides
it is high time to have a wedding.

Aurelia had a bad habit of waiting until the dust is settled to let
herself be happy, concentrating on everyone else and solving all the
problems before she could move on to her joy, but since the twins were
born, she has decided to be happy every day. I've never met a woman
more suited for motherhood than my best friend, and as soon as she
figures out how to stop swearing in front of the kiddos, she'll be golden.

"All I have to do is shower and put on a suit. I do not have to do
makeup and hair for two whole hours that looks like you just rolled out
of bed looking that beautiful. Chill, woman," he grumbles as he leans
down to kiss the sensitive spot on my neck, the soft yet rough rasp of his
beard doing all kinds of awesome things to my belly.

I want to argue, but it's true. All he has to do is put on a suit. And if
he doesn't quit it, all my hard work is going to get shot to hell when I
attack him. He meets my eyes in the mirror, gives me a chuckle, and
then runs his fangs along my shoulder inciting a full body shiver. He

turns and walks his naked ass over to the shower. I have to fight all of my instincts so I don't follow him in and ruin my hair. It took me forever to do this damn hair.

When Aurelia said she wanted to be married to Rhys in a meadow, I loved the idea. She said she wanted something simple, nothing too fussy. Just friends and family and Rhys. It sounded good in theory, but Aurelia was the Primary, and she couldn't do something small if she wanted to —too many people would be pissed if they didn't receive an invitation. Mena skated by on her wedding to Asher because she married a Wraith and it is not customary for Wraiths to have wedding ceremonies. Our bindings are rather private, and in our culture, all a person needs to see is the binding mark to know you're taken. That's not to say Mena and Asher didn't have a wedding—they did—but it was a private affair on a secluded beach.

But Aurelia wasn't that lucky. So I took over the planning and flexed my Queen muscle to get shit done. Well, and I had Claire's help. For someone so quiet and reserved, Claire can organize like a boss and scold caterers like it was her job. Ari had her hands full with the babies once they finally came out of the NICU, and is about the least fussy bride I've ever seen in my freaking life. She only cared about her dress and the fact that she was marrying Rhys. Everything else was fair game for me to choose, and I went nuts with the bohemian theme.

My mind drifts to the first time I got to see her after the twins were born. I was up and about before she was, which is a testament to how much childbirth takes you to the edge of death. My body just needed a few days of rest. Aurelia's body needed to heal itself back from the brink of death. Willa never told Rhys how close the doctors were to losing all three of them, and I'm glad they didn't. Rhys was barely hanging on by a thread.

Aurelia was white as a sheet sitting up in her hospital bed. Rhys was in the NICU watching the twins, and she was alone for the first time since they were born. I didn't even get to ask what was wrong.

"I need to ask you a favor," she burst out.

"Of course, anything."

"Can you get West back here? I want to ask you both something."

"Sure thing, darling," I said as I peeked my head out of the room and crooked a finger to West as he rested on the wall just outside the door.

"All present and accounted for, what's up?" I said as I returned.

"I want to run the twins' names past you to get your approval."

"Okay. Shoot," West said, but Ari looked nervous.

"We want our son to be named Henry Alexander Constantine," she said, her eyes on West.

He took a step back in surprise but didn't look angry. I had no idea why the name held significance to him.

"I was born Henry Carmichael Weston, but you knew that already, didn't you?" he rumbled, and I looked at him in surprise.

West didn't talk about his past. He gave me the highlights—enough to know his father was a fucking rat bastard, and his mother, Merina, was one of the strongest women I'd never get to know—but I didn't know what his given name was.

"That I did, and your mother gave you a good first name that I hope you don't mind me borrowing."

"I think that wherever her soul is, she'd love that," he replied, his voice rough with emotion.

"Good," she said taking a deep breath. "We would like to name our daughter Olivia Collette Constantine," she announced, and it was me who took the step back in surprise.

"Yes. Absolutely. Mama would have loved that."

"My babies have names," she whispered to herself. "What do you guys say about taking a field trip to go see them?"

"You allowed to do that, little mama?" West asked.

"Meh, probably not, but I want to tell Rhys the good news, and I want to feed my babies. So I'm going to one way or another. It would just be easier if one of you procured me a wheelchair first."

"Yes, ma'am," he returned as I went to hold her hand.

Aurelia's teary smile made my heart hurt.

"I'll never be able to thank you for all you did for us. You killed the boogeyman, Evangeline, and I'll never be able to tell you how grateful I am. I love you, darling girl," she whispered as she squeezed my hands.

"Love you too. Now let's go see these babies."

And they were the most beautiful babies I'd ever seen. Born at only four pounds, eight ounces for Henry and four pounds, four ounces for Olivia, they were thriving better than I thought they would for being so small. Both babies had a full head of black hair like their momma, but their eyes did not match at all. Baby Livy had her mother's pale, mint-green pupilless eyes, and Henry had his father's dark, coffee-colored ones. It was obvious already that Henry had some Aegis powers. He kept frying the vital sign monitors, so they quit hooking him up to them. Sooner than they thought possible, the twins were cleared to go home.

A smile stretches across my face, and I blink back into the present. I wonder how hard it would be to convince West to knock me up. Meh. I'll wait until I get done christening every room of the penthouse before I do something like that.

I study my hair and makeup in the mirror. My honey blonde and platinum hair was teased out to maximum volume before I braided sections away from my face and then wrapped it all into a delicate chignon at the nape of my neck. My face was done up to full dewy highlighted awesomeness, and while the look mimicked a 'natural' look, I had more makeup on my face than the law should allow.

West stepped from the shower, still dripping rivulets of water down his tattooed eight-pack leading down his happy trail on down to nirvana.

Hmm. I wonder how bad my hair is going to get messed up when I attack him.

Totally worth the risk.

MENA

Aurelia got ready at my massive master bedroom vanity, her tan skin didn't require much makeup but she still gussied herself up for the big day. Her naturally wavy hair got a stern talking to by a very hot curling iron, and decided to submit to her will and behave for the rest of the day after it was wrestled into submission into a complicated but loose bun at the nape of her neck. Instead of a veil, she wore a beautiful gold leaf hairpin that rested just atop her bun.

Her dress, still on the hanger in my closet waiting for her to finish up, is delicate and ethereal. Full belled sleeves lined with scallops of lace matching the deep open 'V' at the back, full silk organza and scalloped lace skirt with a chapel train. Every time I look at it, I smile. It is so her. Complicated but simple, stylish without giving a fuck. Yep, that's my sister.

"Okay, I'm ready. Where is Evan?" Aurelia calls.

"Never mind. She's going to be five more minutes," she yells answering her own question.

At this point I don't even want to know. I slip into my gold silk organza dress with gathered straps and a deep 'V' in both front and back, and I'm thankful I do not have the same boobage problem my sister does. I'm almost positive she required industrial strength glue and a prayer to get a bra that worked.

Not three seconds later, Evan pops in with her hair down in waves.

"Nice sex hair, Squirt."

"Dude. I tried. I really did, but..." she gave me a look that said '*what are ya gonna do.*' I agree. Sex happens when your husband is hot. No harm no foul.

I shrugged and nodded, and then we helped Aurelia into her dress, grabbed our bouquets, and hit the road. Or I should say we traveled to the venue. Man, it's good to have Wraiths around.

The wedding itself was simple and elegant. No random hipster poem readings, no bullshit, no fuss. Just Aurelia and Rhys standing in front of a massive oak tree swathed in thin gauzy fabric and twinkle lights. Aurelia had Henry on her hip, and Rhys had Livy on his and together they held hands and promised each other forever.

KYLE

I spent a rare moment away from my mate when I went to Aurelia and Rhys' wedding. I felt horrible about the shit they'd gone through, but I couldn't exactly call them friends yet. Not when my mate was still laying in a hospital bed refusing to wake up.

I didn't know if Nic would ever open her eyes. I didn't know if there was anything in her that would allow her to come back to me. I missed her. I missed her so much.

I left the wedding just after the ceremony. Just seeing them together with their children after all Iva had put them through made me feel guilty.

There were many things I regretted about the day Aurelia was attacked. I never should have left without the amulet, for one. I never should have let Iva see me, for two. And third, I should have killed

Devereux Emerson with a bullet to the brain long before he touched my woman.

But for now, my regrets are all funneled into one. I wish I would have bound her before all this mess. I wish I would have made her mine.

I think this as I play with her graceful fingers. I've seen those tiny little digits play the piano like it was an extension of her body. I've seen her whip a violin into submission. I've seen those pale hands all over my body, always moving, playing, waving—never stopping even in sleep.

I miss their movement.

Just as I think this, the index finger of her left hand twitches. Then, she sits up in her hospital bed like she's rising from a nightmare.

Thankful, I reach for her, but when she sees me, she flinches back. It's then that I notice some serious problems.

One, the Nicola I know is blind. She was born that way.

Two, the Nicola I know has cornflower blue eyes.

This woman can most assuredly see me, and her eyes are an odd honey brown—the same color Iva's were when she took Nic over. I control my rising panic.

"Nicola, sweetheart, it's okay. You're in the hospital, baby," I try and soothe her, holding her hand even as she tries to back away, but she looks confused.

"Th-that's not my name," she says, and with a feeling of dread, I ask the question I'm not sure I want the answer to.

"What *is* your name then?" I ask calmly as I push the nurse call button.

"It's... Well... I-I don't know," she answers frowning at the white hospital blankets.

Wonderful.

SHADE KISSED

PHOENIX RISING BOOK FOUR

ANNIE ANDERSON

PROLOGUE

NICOLA—BEFORE

I NEVER SAW HIM COMING.

Just my luck, I suppose, I would find my love when I knew I wasn't long for this world.

Getting a mate before my inevitable end seemed like a horrible thing at first, but I couldn't help the slight niggles of happiness which broke through the wall around my heart.

I'd built that wall myself out of the broken promises and lies told to me in my youth. It kept me safe—staved off the loneliness and heartbreak—but it didn't keep him out.

My visions all but dried up nearly a month ago, but I knew from all the ones before Iva worked the forbidden magic which damned my sight I wasn't going to make it. Three centuries seemed so long and so short all at the same time. How could I have had so much time on this earth and wasted it? Is this what humans feel like when approached with a terminal illness? Do they lament the time they spent on trivial matters and wish they'd done more?

Do they have so much regret?

Everything I'd done, every single atrocity and willful neglect—all of the things I could have prevented, the lives I could have saved—made me the worst sort of person. But I did them all knowing I was saving my race. Sure, I had dirt under my nails, but all my toils wouldn't be for nothing.

I hoped.

Time was speeding by, and I wanted to experience everything I'd been denied. I wasn't going to feel the perfection of an evil put to death or the purity of wrongs being righted. I wasn't going to see my greatest sin washed from my soul. But I could have a little bit of happiness before I went, and with my plan in place and the first domino about to fall... Time was a luxury I no longer had.

Then, he came along with his hulking presence and soft, rumbling voice and death seemed like a blessing and a curse. A blessing because I hadn't had much happiness in my life and he seemed like a gift given to me at the very last second. But a curse as well because I wasn't going to get to keep him. I didn't deserve him and I never would, and the burn of losing him—even if it was in my own death—seemed hotter than any flame I could produce.

But he didn't need to know, and since my time was coming to a close, he didn't have to. I could flit in and out of his long life and be no more than a blip. Yes. I could do that. I could love him to distraction, lose myself in the beautiful newness of a fleeting love, and no one would be the wiser. Especially him. It would be the one gift I could give myself —a single bit of happiness in a rather difficult and awful life.

I wasn't as limited as I'd let everyone believe. Sure, I'm blind in the most basic of senses, but the beauty of being an Oracle is it didn't matter. I saw so much more with my mind; I didn't *need* my eyes. But he came after my visions dried up, and of all the things I saw, of all the events I foretold...

I didn't see him. And I should have.

Maybe if I'd have seen him, I would have done things differently.

NICOLA—AFTER

The darkness blanketing me didn't seem safe. There were things lurking here, evil things, horrible things. Things who whispered in my ear about murder and blood and death. They told me horrific tales of slain children and bloodied sacrifices and ripping the very fabric of the afterlife to shreds.

I wanted out of this darkness—out of the blackness and thick, oily dank of the hell imprisoning me. I was scared—lost and detached from reality and my body, and all I wanted was to make it to the light.

I clawed and scratched and screamed, but I couldn't find a way out of the darkness. In the back of my mind, I knew I belonged here. I knew I deserved this prison. I couldn't remember what I'd done, but I knew... I knew it was a price I had to pay.

And I paid—minute after minute, day after day, month after month —until time lost its meaning and I fell asleep in the cold darkness of my own hell.

I

NICOLA—AFTER

I COME BACK TO MYSELF SLOWLY—PAINFULLY—IN FITS AND starts of consciousness. Feeling my heart first, the slow plodding of a body in rest, then the cool stagnant air of a closed room on my skin. The rough but soft bedding surrounding my legs and then the thing that makes my eyes flash open in fear—the warm heat of a hand on mine. I sit up as if I was shot from a cannon, my eyes flashing open for the first time in what feels like a long time.

I can't remember what I'm so afraid of...

My mind trills with the alarm of danger, but I can't place where it's coming from or why. As my eyes scan the dim room, they instantly snag on the form of a man standing next to me. His body is enormous, standing several inches over six feet, his legs encased in dark denim and feet shod in dangerous black boots. His hair, which is trapped beneath the raised hood of his sweater, is not quite black but close enough to be confused for it, matching the thick but groomed beard decorating his jaw. His eyes, which are locked on me, are the color of a decadent milk chocolate. His hands reach for me, and my first feeling is fear—dark and clawing—and I rear back, pressing myself into the pillows of the narrow bed I'm sitting on.

Vaguely, my mind latches onto the fact that this is a hospital, but I'm not sure if I'm right or if this is a dream or if I really am in the danger my heart and mind are screaming at me I'm in.

"Nicola, sweetheart, it's okay. You're in the hospital, baby," his rough voice says soothingly, but I am not soothed. I am nowhere near the realm of soothed. It doesn't matter that this forbidding man has a voice that calls to me. The name he called me doesn't sound right, for one, and as handsome as this man is, I have no idea who he is supposed to be to me. He has to be in the wrong room, right?

Right?

He grabs my hand, gently closing his large fingers over mine, and although the heat of him is nice—almost calming—I don't want this stranger touching me. I don't want him looking at me like this—the wary hesitance on his bearded face is twisting my stomach in knots and the name he called me...

That's not me. That's not my name.

"Th-that's not my name," I tell him as I shake my head. He has it wrong. The wrong room or wrong woman or something. His face is wrong, his expression is hurt mixed with longing and something worse —fear.

Wrong, wrong, wrong.

"What is your name then?" he asks, his voice calm and controlled as he presses the square orange button on the bedrail. I follow the motion of his hand as he stabs the button, trying to think...

"It's... Well..." I pause, concentrating on a fact which should be so easy to remember, but all I come up with is... *nothing.*

"I-I don't know," I stutter frowning at the white coverlet warming my legs.

I want to say I was holding it together. I want to say my brain went right to denial—which would have helped the situation vastly—that I didn't feel a burning ache in my chest from fear and uncertainty, and Fates knew what else.

But I do—I do feel the ache of loss, of confusion, of unbridled fear.

I don't know my name. How can I not know my name? And who is he? Why is he looking at me like this? What happened to me?

I feel the burn of my breaths coming too fast and my heart pounding too hard. The room begins to spin.

I can't get air... No air... I don't want to go back to the darkness. Nonononononononononono...

The man starts yelling—first at me to breathe and then at the closed door, roaring for help. But his voice is fading, and the room's lights dim further, my sight tunneling to pinpoints. For the life of me, I can't figure out why the fact I'm seeing the light sticks in my mind just before I pass out.

I COME TO WITH MUCH LESS FANFARE THAN THE LAST TIME. THE man isn't there, but a tall, auburn-haired woman is folded in the bedside chair, her eyes closed and her breaths coming in the deep pulls of sleep. Her head is at such an odd angle, resting on her bent, scrub-covered knees as she sleeps curled into an awkward ball in the seat.

I don't want to wake her, but there are a few issues I need to worry about. First, I seem to be attached to this bed by a thick padded cuff on each wrist. This is concerning on so many levels, I'm not sure my brain is taking the time to process it. Second, the original problem of not knowing who I am or where I am or why I'm here is still an issue. A major one. I hate not knowing myself, I hate not knowing how I got here. I clear my throat, realizing too late that at some point I must have been screaming because my throat is on fire.

What the hell happened to me?

The woman comes awake with a start, jumping from her curled ball to her feet with a preternatural grace, her eyes flashing a phosphorescent green. It should worry me. It really should, but for some reason, it doesn't.

"You're not human," I hoarsely croak, stating the obvious. Her lips stretch into a sardonic smile, and it takes her beauty up about ten notches. Her large, almost feline eyes have faded to an odd shade of amber, framed by thick, dark lashes, and she doesn't have a stitch of makeup on her face.

"Neither are you," she returns, her voice a husky alto. This information is not shocking—just like her fantastical jump to her feet, I am not moved. I must have known this before.

Before, I internally scoff. I already hate the word, but I think I need to know a bit more about this 'before' because my brain is not supplying anything other than an extreme lack of shock.

"Are you a healer?" I ask on a wince. What the hell happened to my voice? The woman nods as she pours water into a small blue plastic cup on a rolling bedside table. She eyes my wrists for a moment and plops the pitcher back on the surface with an indelicate thunk.

"My name is Willa, I'm your physician. If I remove your restraints, do you promise not to harm yourself?" she asks with a raised eyebrow. Her eyebrow tells me my answer better be yes, and then her question finally starts to make sense in my head.

I hurt myself? On purpose?

I feel my eyes widen in the surprise I should have had for her jump or her non-human statement, and I quickly nod. Her swift, efficient fingers have my wrists free in mere seconds, but better, her voice prattles on with information. Any and all information is helpful at this point.

"I removed your Foley after your first wake-up call," she says as she moves from my wrists to wave a penlight in front of my eyes. "You've been here for about four months. We weren't sure if you'd ever wake up. Normally, someone of your species should have been up and about ages ago—a week at most, but you're not healing as fast as you should."

Her statement stops me. *I have no idea what I am.*

"Species?" I ask.

"You have no idea, do you?"

"I don't even know my own name, so no, I have absolutely no fucking idea what's going on. Care to share with the class?" I snap. I don't want to snap at her, but I just want to know all of the shit I don't know already.

"Snarky. I like it. I can work with snark, just no more screaming, mmm-kay?"

So this explains what happened to my throat.

"Deal," I reply and Willa holds out the cup as I take a healthy swig. The cool water hits my throat, easing the burn.

"Your name is Nicola. The man who was here before? His name is Kyle. He's your husband."

"Don't start off small, Willa. *Jesus,*" a rumbling voice sounds from the doorway.

The man—Kyle—is in the same clothes as the last time, but his hood has been lowered, giving him a slightly less sinister quality and he now has a pair of thick-framed glasses perched on his nose. His hair is a rumpled mess, as if he has run his hands through it, slept on it, electrocuted himself and possibly took a stroll through a hurricane. He is haggard—probably hasn't slept at all in who knows how long, and immediately I want to give him a hug, make him some food and offer the bed to him so he can get some damn rest.

I want to be freaked at the husband comment Willa threw out there like it was no big deal, but I don't think I can be. *Why else would he be here? Why else would he come back? And why do I want to comfort him?*

"Of all the information I need to know, a husband would be at the top of the list, don't you think?" I retort with a shrug.

"You aren't surprised?" Kyle asks.

"I'm finding very few things have surprised me thus far. Can you come in and take a load off? You look like you've been put through the wringer twice."

I get a scowl, a grunted affirmative and a slow shuffle-walk to the bedside chair Willa vacated. In my bones, I know the shuffle is a ruse. He's moving slowly on purpose so I won't freak out. Standing, he has to be closer to seven feet than to six, but I can tell his height and the considerable bulk to his muscles do not hinder his speed in the slightest.

"While all this is well and good, you still haven't told me how I got here or what I am." The question leaves my mouth without thought, and when they exchange a wary glance, I'm not sure I want to know anymore.

NICOLA—NEW ENGLAND 1723

I ran as fast as my little feet could carry me through the brush, stumbling to my hands and knees more times than I could count. Every single day I breathed, I cursed my visions and my sightless eyes, but on days like today, I wished for death more and more.

If I could die—which it seemed I couldn't—I hoped it would be painless, but I had seen death over and over again, and I knew better. Branches whipped my cheeks, stones gouged my feet, but still I ran. Those switches were nothing compared to the danger behind me. He was coming, and he would do horrible things to me when I wouldn't tell him what was to pass.

Didn't he know? I only told death stories, and if death was not to pass, I couldn't tell anyone anything. He'd tried cutting the visions out of me, tried breaking my bones, starving me—but I couldn't tell him what I didn't know.

At first, he called me a devil. Told me I was made of fire and I would bring him death. I'd been drawn to the woman I saw in my vision—not him. She was dying very soon, bound and shackled in a horrific prison where her breaths became more and more labored and her broken body had to fight minute by minute just to keep going. I knew if I were near, she could return to the sky—I could help this good woman start again. I remembered the rites my mother said when papa passed, they were the only good things I remembered about her since she abandoned me in this new place to survive on my own. Every time I saw a good soul die in my visions, I would try to help them move on.

He'd caught me freeing the woman—her body already gone, but her soul was safe now that I'd saved it. He saw my wings, my fire and told me I was of the fallen. When he realized my blindness, he called me Oracle—he said I could tell him his future.

I couldn't. I could only tell him death.

And then the torture started. He must not have had manacles small enough for my eight-year-old wrists—or maybe he did but once he'd starved me for a month, my already thin wrists were able to slip from the irons and I was free.

But not if he caught me.

I felt the air change, the rush of water met my ears just before the fresh, salty smell of the ocean hit my nose. I ran faster until the ground seemed to dip beneath my feet. I tripped again, sliding at breakneck speeds through the rocks toward the sound of crashing waves.

But then cool, slender hands caught me. They weren't his hands—this I knew.

"Do not worry, child. I have come to help you," a woman's voice crooned as she hugged me to her chest. Her accent was Irish and as soft as a cool summer breeze.

The sound of the man's thrashing through the forest filtered through the trees, and I curled into her, frightened. I didn't want any more of his knives or fists. I didn't want his hot, putrid breath on my face as he called me devil, abomination, demon, harlot. I didn't know what harlot meant, but from his tone, I knew it was bad. I wasn't bad. I was a good girl. I knew I wasn't human, but I couldn't help that. I was born to my strangeness just as I'd been born without sight.

"Cover your ears, child, and I'll take care of this filth," she instructed, calmly brushing my matted hair back from my face. I knew she was going to kill him, and I knew killing was bad, but she was saving me. I couldn't find it in me to care for the man who had tortured me and so many others.

"Wait!" I cried as I clutched to her willowy arm. I didn't want her to leave me. What if she didn't succeed? I needed to have a little piece of her.

"Yes, dearie?" she answered, her voice like watered silk.

"What is your name? I never knew his name. I want to know your name," my voice broke—I was so close to breaking myself.

"My name is Iva, dearie, and I've been looking for you."

2

KYLE—BEFORE

THERE ARE QUITE A FEW THINGS I'D FOUND FOR OTHER FOLKS over the years. Lost people, stolen objects, fugitives on the run from the King. It didn't matter how far or how long they ran, I always found them. I was good at my job, working closely with the King—and West when necessary—but also with other members of the Ethereal. Witches, Warlocks, Shapeshifters—it was known far and wide if you wanted someone or something found, you came to me.

But I had scruples. The people who came to me knew my code. I didn't find anything if I didn't know the story behind it. There had to be a damn good reason I went looking for someone. There had been several times over the years where the story I'd been told was nowhere near the truth. An abusive husband looking for his wife and children, a thief wanting me to do his dirty work, a corrupt leader looking for a whistleblower...

Life didn't quite work out so well for those men.

I had plenty of business—enough where I could pick and choose my jobs based on what interested me—and despite the periphery I consistently found myself on, I felt included with my species. So, when my King called me, I came without question.

I never did get to find out why he needed me.

Too much happened. Nicola happened.

I'll never forget the first time I saw her. If I hadn't been the one to open the door that day, who knows what would have happened. But I was. I saw her. I heard her and knew she was mine.

Maybe if I'd never heard her voice—if I hadn't let her flash of brilliant red hair catch my eye—I could have saved us both.

POUNDING CAME FROM THE SOLID OAK FRONT DOOR OF THE Grand Lake cabin. The pounding was proceeded by five, incessant doorbell rings. Both of these actions were completely unnecessary. Visitors were more than just announced—before you could access the property, you had to pass through an eight-foot wrought-iron security gate complete with digital surveillance. To gain entry without someone in this house knowing, you needed either a remote or thumbprint access. The person on the other side of this door had neither. Not to mention, Ian brought her here, and as far as I knew, he was still parking the car. Why she couldn't drive herself, I didn't know.

At first, I had no idea she was blind. I had no idea who she was at all. All I knew was John asked me to greet our guest, and if his tone was derisive to the point of scathing, well, it wasn't my place to judge.

The woman standing at the threshold was a tiny slip of a thing, but at six-foot-seven, everyone is tiny compared to me. She topped out at a respectable five-five with wildly curly, deep red hair and large, cornflower blue eyes that didn't quite meet mine. Her dewy, porcelain skin was flawless without a single stitch of makeup, and I was immediately transfixed by the delicate rose color of her full lips. My eyes took a trip over her body. Her outfit—a royal blue, spaghetti strapped dress under a waspish cardigan—was paired with simple tan flats and hid exactly zero of her curves. Generous bosom, tiny waist, hips and thighs that could make a man weep and short but slim legs. I immediately chided myself for giving her a full head-to-toe and brought my eyes back up to her face. She wore no jewelry, no makeup, and the bulk of her curly hair was wild except for two braids at each temple that pulled a bit of it back from her face. Her lips parted to speak, and my eyes became laser-focused on her plump lower lip.

It wasn't until Ian stomped up the steps behind her did I realize I was just standing there staring, etching each of her features into my brain.

"You couldn't wait the three minutes for me to park the car? Seriously, Nicola?" Ian grumbled. He paused and waited for me, but I was still stuck on her face. "You just going to stand there, man? You're letting all the bought air out," he chided, nudging past the woman— Nicola—and throwing a shoulder into my arm, snapping me out of it.

I stepped back, sweeping my hand wide for her to enter. After a beat of her remaining immobile, I said, "Any day now, sweetheart."

All I got was a scathing raised eyebrow in response. Then, I noticed the white, probing cane in her hand and immediately felt like a first-rate jackass. Well, this explained why she didn't drive herself.

"Your hospitality is impeccable," Nicola said, her faint British accent curling the sarcasm into a less-than-biting comeback. Maybe it was her accent or the husky rasp of her voice or her unearthly beauty, but I was mesmerized. I immediately felt the hit to my man card that the word 'mesmerized' was even in my vocabulary, but the urge to curl around her, to touch her pale, creamy skin, to protect her—to keep her close to me—rose in me faster than I could help.

I want to say I was calm and collected, but I'd be lying. My only saving grace was her blindness. Otherwise, she would've seen my phase, my fangs, my talons, the problematic bulge in my jeans. How lucky was I no one saw my trip into crazy town?

"Is there some reason you have phased, Wraith? Should I worry for my safety or are you going to play nice?" she challenged, alerting me to the fact her blindness did not detract in any way from her perceptiveness. Shit.

"How did you know?" I asked around my fangs, my voice a garbled mess.

"Phoenixes naturally have a keen sense of hearing. My blindness dials that up to eleven. I heard your talons grow, the bones in your face crack, and the infinitesimal flick of your eyes bleeding to black. Now, are you planning on killing me or offering your arm so I don't bang my shin on every stick of furniture in this house trying to find John?"

"I won't hurt you, Shortcake. You just quoted Spinal Tap. That means we have to be friends now."

"Not if you keep calling me Shortcake. Think of something original, will you, or else I might just start calling you Sasquatch," she returned, but our banter was interrupted by a crash of a dish breaking in the kitchen.

I grabbed her without thought, sweeping her up into my arms and striding through the great room to the source of the sound. Honestly, I was afraid for John. His health wasn't what it should be, his hair was turning gray faster and faster, and Olivia was nowhere to be found. He had yet to tell me why he'd called on me, and with each passing day here holed up in this house while our people—our families—were exterminated... the pit in my stomach grew larger and larger.

My hackles were up already, a ripple of unease flashing across my skin as I crossed the threshold of the kitchen to see Evangeline tackle Rhys to the ground before he could reach for Aurelia.

Aurelia and Rhys came to us days ago after a nasty situation at Aurelia's art show in Denver. Evidently, Phoenixes weren't just exterminating Wraiths—they were taking out any and all threats to the Primary, the Phoenixes' leader. Why Aurelia was considered a threat, I had no idea, but if she needed the help, I'd be happy to give it to her. Granted, she didn't need much help. She'd handed me my ass yesterday in the training room without breaking a sweat. I was really trying there at the end and she whooped my ass without even trying.

But right now, she didn't look like she could do anything to help herself. She stood clutching the granite of the center island, the force of her grip cracking the stone as her body bowed in agony. I lowered Nicola to her feet, setting her to my right as we watched Evan try to keep Rhys from reaching his woman.

"Don't touch her! Her Aegis will kill you!" Evangeline shouted in his face, just as John traveled in next to me, with Aidan, Cam, Asher, West and Ian bringing up the rear.

"Aegis? She's a fucking Aegis, and you didn't tell me? Why?" Rhys roared, understandably upset.

I'd heard of the Aegis, a type of Phoenix whose main ability manifested itself into an electrical shield, but no more than whispers, and I sure as shit had never seen an adult one. As far as I knew no one had because young Aegis could not control their abilities—usually ending up blowing themselves to smithereens.

"Because I told her not to," John answered, his voice threaded with a tired exasperation.

"And why's that, John? What reason could you possibly have for not telling me my mate is a fucking time bomb?"

"Because the Primary would have seen," Nicola piped in, her lilting voice a husky whisper in the middle of the rage-fueled room.

"And who the fuck are you?" Rhys snarled as he picked himself up off the floor, his eyes flitting to each person before landing on her.

"My name is Nicola, and I am the Primary's second," she said as she gave him a dainty bow.

"You!" he growled as his confusion turned into recognition, and I didn't think—I just acted. Rhys lunged for Nicola, but before he could close the last few inches, I pulled her behind me and put a fist to his temple.

My phase was instantaneous as I placed my body between the threat and her. I didn't quite understand what the hell was happening to me— why I wanted to protect her with all of me—I just knew this fucker wasn't touching her. Not on my watch.

He took a minute to shake off my hit, and I just knew he was debating on putting a bullet in me, but Fuck. That. He wasn't getting to her. No fucking way.

Then her hand was on my shoulder. I knew it was her—it had to be. I'd never felt the chord of tension in me ease before—the one that curled in my gut, kept me searching for the one thing I'd never found. Tendrils of peace mixed with want and an urge to slice my fangs into the column of her throat hit me all at once, jarring me. My phase bled from me, but I knew the danger wasn't over. I couldn't deal with all of these issues at once—I needed to handle this shit first.

Rhys relaxed, but his hand twitched just the wrong way. He seemed like a good enough guy, but I knew the lengths he would go to protect Aurelia. I knew better now in the five minutes I'd been in Nicola's presence than I ever did before. So when his finger moved, edging toward the Ruger I knew was in his spine holster, I took him to the ground.

No one was getting to her. No matter what.

KYLE—AFTER

I don't trust her. Or this. Any of this. I'd seen her when Iva was squatting like a toad inside her body, and I wasn't sure if I could ever trust her again. Why did she let him do this to her? Didn't she figure it out already? Devereux was never going to let me live. It didn't matter what he promised her—Devereux Emerson was the worst sort of man. Soulless.

If she'd never have said yes to him, at least my sacrifice would have been for something. But she thought I needed saving, and when Nicola Miller thinks someone needs saving, she will sacrifice everything, move heaven and earth to make sure they stay saved. If Aurelia and Mena had even an inkling of what she'd done—what she'd lived through—to keep them alive...

To keep me alive.

And she could remember none of it. Not them, not me, not even her own fucking name. But she wanted to know what happened, and it felt wrong not to tell her. I met her odd amber eyes. I missed her old ones. I missed the old Nicola.

"Look, Nic," I broke off. She flinched every time I said her name. Fine. "Alright, no saying that name, huh?" I ask trying to keep a lid on the surge of anger ready to erupt.

"It feels wrong. Like I'd been called something else," Nicola confesses, staring at her knees instead of looking me in the eye.

"You mean like Iva?" I spit, the anger cresting and spilling over and out of my mouth. As soon as the name passes my lips I regret it. Her already pale face goes a startling shade of gray, and she curls into herself, flinching back from me.

"Do-don't say that name. Th-that's a bad name," she shudders, covering her face with her hands.

I pull myself up and out of my seat, curling myself around her—doing my best to protect her from the aftermath of my words, feeling like the worst sort of prick. I knew what she'd lived through. I knew, and I still sliced at her with my fucking tongue. Fuck.

"I'm sorry, Shortcake. I won't say it again. I'm sorry, baby," I murmur as I put my arms around her and try to gently pull her hands from her face. Giving up when I meet solid resistance, I scoop her up, trading places and settling her cradled in my lap. I didn't realize how much weight she'd lost lying immobile on this bed for months, but she feels too light in my arms. Too light, too fragile, and I hate this for her.

My strong mate suffered no fools. Her blindness did not debilitate her in any way, and her tongue was wielded like a weapon.

I glance up to see Willa giving me a look that tells me if we weren't on ground warded against violence, she would have kicked my ass up and down this hospital.

Get your head out of your ass, she mouths at me and stalks out of the room, but remembering herself at the last second and stops the door before it slams. The quiet snick of the latch the only sound in the room except for Nicola's shuddered breathing.

"Shh, Shortcake. You're alright, you'll be alright," I murmur as I rock her back and forth to try and soothe her.

"That has to be the worst nickname ever. Think of something else, please," she croaks into my chest, and I cannot help my roar of laughter.

Maybe she's my Nic after all.

3

NICOLA—AFTER

HIS DEEP, BOOMING LAUGH SCARES THE CRAP OUT OF ME AT first—I didn't think I'd said anything funny—but the longer he laughs, the more I can't help the giggle that slips out of my mouth. His outburst shaves the worry from him, and his scowl has left the building. It completely transforms his face, it makes me notice how full his lips are, how young he looks when he isn't constantly frowning, scowling or brooding.

"Some things never change," Kyle says chuckling, giving me a little squeeze.

"What do you mean?" I ask, enjoying the thick weight of his arms around me. I don't know exactly when cuddling became our thing, but I prefer it to the standoffishness of earlier. His arms feel wonderful, and I had no idea I was missing them until just this moment.

"You hated the nickname before, too. It's good to see something staying the same is all."

The statement stings. It reminds me I am a shell of the woman he knew, a withered husk of a woman. I don't even know my last name. *How awful is that?*

But then I realize if some things are the same, then maybe I could get my memories back. *Maybe I could get my life back.*

"So you're my husband, huh?" I question as I lay my head back down on his shoulder and am immediately hit with how good he smells. It isn't cologne, but rather the natural scent of citrus and man. I have to fight the urge to stick my nose in his neck and breathe him in.

"Not the way humans see it, but in the way of my people, yes, I'm your husband," he replies.

"Are your people not my people?" I ask because he piqued my interest. Were we not the same?

"We aren't the same species, but it is becoming more common for inter-species unions. It's not frowned upon or anything, just not common."

Well, at least there was that. I'd hate it if people judged us just based on who we chose as a partner. It seems silly to hate someone based solely on whom they choose to love.

"What are you?" I ask. I want to know as much as I could about this man I had forgotten.

"Species or profession?" he rumbles, his voice wary.

"All of the above."

"Professionally, I am a Tracker. Humans would liken it to a bounty hunter, but I can find just about anything—objects included. Species... I am a Wraith. I consume deserving souls to ferry them to hell," he informs me, his voice and body tense.

Something tells me this isn't everything, but I can't put my finger on it. When his body practically vibrates with tension, I meet his eyes.

Whoa. Did Kyle think I would judge him? His seemed a noble profession and purpose. Bringing my hand up to rest on his chest, I tried to tame the wary beast in him. His muscles relaxed a fraction.

"And I am?" I continue, his muscles tensing once again. Am I something bad?

"Species or profession?" he asks again, his body vibrating.

"All of the above," I repeat on a whisper.

"Species, you are a Phoenix. You help deserving souls move on to be reborn." Holy shit. *I was cool.*

"And professionally?" I ask because although he had told me

something good—at least I thought it was good—he is strung tighter than a bow.

"You... you used to be an Oracle, but I don't know if this is something you can still be," he finishes, his voice lowering to a whisper.

"Why?" I ask even though I don't want to.

"You're not blind anymore," he murmurs and then I get why he was so tense. This was the bad. Something happened to me. I was changed somehow. A jagged feeling of dread fills me, and I don't want to ask, but I have to.

"It's bad I'm not blind anymore, isn't it? It isn't like I was healed or anything. Something bad happened to me," I murmur. I knew in my gut it was worse than whatever I could manage to cook up in my head. I was in a hospital, for fuck's sake. It had to be bad.

"Yeah, baby," he whispers, his voice broken. Did something happen to him? Was he hurt? I may be the only one without a memory, but he knew what happened. He knew, and it made it worse.

"Did it happen to you, too?" I ask, tears clogging my already sore throat. I didn't want this for him. I didn't want him hurt or scared or unsafe.

"Not exactly, but we both endured some bad shit. You just got the worst of it," he answers, his arms squeezing me tighter.

At that moment I was glad I got the worst. I'd take anything if it meant he didn't get the short end of the stick, too. But I also didn't think I could take more.

"I don't... I don't think I can know all of it right now. I don't think I can handle it. I feel... *raw*."

"Anytime you want to know, whatever you want to know, just ask."

I didn't know if I would ever get the courage to ask him what happened.

Maybe it was better not knowing.

NICOLA—OREGON 1855

The guilt clawed at me. I knew exactly what would happen. Of course, I did. I knew it as much as I knew my own name. Aurelia Constantine wouldn't heed my warning—she wouldn't leave when I told her to, she wouldn't take the precautions I warned her about. Aurelia would think she had all the time in the world. She would think my warning was nonsense. She wouldn't hold her love close to her, realize I was right and leave her cold mother, her secretive twin, and neglectful father to their own fate as she made her life anew.

No.

She would endure the worst things... torture, pain, loss, death—all because I couldn't make myself clear enough. I couldn't see her with my eyes, but I knew every expression of her face and every silent gesture of her hands and set to her shoulders.

I'd seen them—maybe not with my eyes, but definitely with my mind. I'd seen the luminescent caramel skin of her cheek as her lips twisted in a wry smile and the delicate slope of her neck as she shrugged in indecision. The incandescent light in her eyes which told everyone what she was...

My power had grown more than I ever thought possible in the last century, but the slip of the woman before me? She would surpass me one day—I knew it. So I had to keep her safe from Iva—I had to change her fate. I had to get her out of here one way or another. There were things I couldn't tell her—things if she knew would alter her course. Things that would give me away as well.

My vagueness would cost Aurelia dearly, and I couldn't figure out how to change it. When she left, hot tears fell from my sightless eyes as I stifled my sobs in my fist. I couldn't let the Soldiers know of my pain.

Soldiers.

Might as well call them what they were—jailers. I was as much a prisoner here as I was a leader. Every single step, every decision, every word that passed my lips was watched and cataloged and reported to Iva. The woman who was so long ago my savior was now my warden.

I had to dry my tears, I couldn't let anyone know.

I had to figure out a way to save them—if it was the last thing I did.

HIS SCREAMS REACHED MY EARS LONG BEFORE I MADE IT through the door. I had no idea a man could make that sound, let alone survive what was causing it. Rhys was paying a price I could not afford to pay—he stopped an evil before it could come to pass, and for this, I would always be grateful. He may well have saved us all with his sacrifice.

Julian was Iva's most trusted Soldier. He took the messier and most dubious of jobs. Nothing was off limits for him. He did things even I didn't know about—things I didn't want to know about. He thirsted for it—his necessity to hunt and kill became an aura around him even I could see. There was nothing left of the man he was before Iva got her hooks into him.

Rhys sent Julian to his death—his own brother—because Julian refused to deny our leader and set out to assassinate the Wraith Queen. In a way, I felt complicit in Julian's death and Rhys' torture. I saw it days ago, long before Rhys made the decision himself. I saw Julian's death and his well-deserved trip to hell.

Rhys' screams hit me in the gut again and again. I had to keep my face stony, but inside I was dying—dying for this man and what I would have to do to him. I used my senses to navigate my way to the ceremonial chamber. That's what Iva called it. In my head, I called it what it was—a bloody torture chamber. Ceremony. No one in their right mind would call this anything but torture.

My ears rang from the roar of agony coming from Rhys' mouth. The smell of burnt flesh hit my nose, and I held back a gag by the skin of my teeth. Phoenixes usually couldn't be burned—but if someone were to heat a Morganite blade and press it to our skin... I couldn't hold back the shudder of sympathy pain for Rhys. This was going too far, I had to figure out a way to stop this before she killed him.

"I detest the smell of burning flesh, Iva-dear. Could you desist, please? It is turning my stomach," I complained, my voice laced with a touch of sullen irritation to hide my revulsion.

"I would, but this wee child needs to answer my question first," she purred.

"And what question might that be? Honestly, Iva. Must you resort to burning? It will be weeks before I can eat meat again," I scolded in a bored tone. It's possible I may never eat anything ever again after this.

"I want him to accept the binding, and he is refusing to obey his Primary. He's being a naughty, naughty boy," she cooed.

"Be that as it may, dear, torture only works until your plaything is dead and your toy is close to the veil. Might I give it a go?"

I need to give this man a break. I have to get her away from him and get this hell to stop.

"You think you can break him? He's been here for a week and nothing. You think you have it in you?" she taunted, a smile in her voice knowing I have a strict aversion to torture. Given my past, you'd think she'd be mindful of it, but not Iva. It doesn't really matter how blank my face is or how bored my tone is. She'll still needle me.

"Maybe I don't need to torture him to get him to do what I want. Give me the room, and if I cannot turn his mind, you can continue burning him until you get the outcome you desire," I offered.

I don't see her nod, but I feel her acquiescence.

"Fine, you have one hour. But if you fail, you'll watch me burn him," she tossed back as I heard her voice carry from the room. A few Soldiers stayed put until I shooed them from the room. Only when the room was cleared did I breathe a sigh of relief.

I made my way closer to Rhys, his pained, labored breathing calling to me. He reminded me of the poor woman I'd sent on so long ago as a child. She'd been burned too, and the smell brought back all the pain I'd felt her endure at the hands of a wayward Puritan.

"Rhys?" I whispered and got a grunt in response.

"I don't have much time, but I need your help. You have to live, darling boy. For Aurelia's sake, you have to live. I can't make you take the binding, but if you do, I can stop this torture and maybe—just maybe—save your love's life. I know if I do not bind the two of you, she will die, Rhys, and it will be soon. With what Iva has planned for her, death will not be a relief. I need your help. Will you help me?" I begged.

"S-she'll die? True death?" he croaked.

"Yes. And Iva will not send her on. She'll use her as an example. Her soul will be trapped here."

"Y-you know this? For certain?"

"Yes. Unless you bind her," I swore. I wasn't lying—this wasn't a ploy to change Rhys' mind. Aurelia Constantine's death had run over and over in my mind. Nothing else I'd done had changed it. My vague warning did nothing—my talks with Iva did nothing. This was my last chance to change it.

"Then do it. I accept," Rhys murmured.

By the time Iva came back, his and Aurelia's binding was complete with a minor change I hope one day they'd forgive me for.

"Do I get to burn him then?" she asked as she bustled into the room along with her guards.

"Afraid not, Iva-dear. The binding is complete with a nice little addition I think you'll appreciate," I replied.

"Oh?"

"Oh, yes," I purred, praying my voice didn't betray me. "I made it a dual bond. What happens to one, happens to both. He won't be able to nick himself shaving without her bleeding. I thought you'd like that."

Bragging was the only way prove myself to Iva. It was the only way my plan would even have a chance at working.

"Brava, dearie. I wish I'd thought it up."

"You bitch!" Rhys railed, not realizing I was warning him as much as I was proving my allegiance once more.

"Now, now. Don't be cross, Rhys. There's no changing it now," I scolded him, and it was true.

Their path together was now set in stone.

4

KYLE—AFTER

SOMEHOW, BOTH NICOLA AND I FELL ASLEEP ON THE TINY AS shit torture chamber called a hospital bed. I'm taking up the majority of the bed, and Nicola is tucked into my side, her fiery red hair spread across my chest, her soft snuffling breaths the only sound in the room. It isn't the first time I've woken up this way, and I'd missed it. This is what I'd been dreaming about for months, her warm little body next to mine. It's what got me through the cold nights trapped in my filthy cell in the Emerson's dungeon.

The memory of her pales to reality. I forgot the way her skin smells, the natural cinnamon scent mixed with woman. I forgot how hot her body is when she's sleeping, as if her body temperature notches up ten degrees as soon as her eyelids close. I missed her warmth. Without her in my arms, I've felt colder than I'd ever felt before in my life, even when I'd been tracking down a murderer in the Canadian Rockies. Alberta is not my favorite place to be in the dead of winter, I don't give a shit how good the skiing is.

I damn near lost a toe on that hunt.

But I didn't know what warmth was until I held her all night long. I didn't know how much I would miss it when her heat was gone. Now that I have it back... I don't know what I'd do if I'd lost it again.

Especially now.

Nicola's delicate hand rests on my left pec, just over my heart, and if I could, I'd draw her spot against my body with permanent marker. This is exactly where her body goes—this is the exact spot she used to take. I don't know if I put her here or if she migrated here on her own, but I don't want this to end. I don't want her to wake up without knowing us or me again.

But I know she will. Because the Nicola I knew is gone—maybe forever.

I cover her hand with mine, and I get to enjoy a few moments of my peace before her hand startles under mine. As I look down into her amber eyes, I hate that I wish they were blue.

KYLE—BEFORE

I took her to my safe place—no one knew about the house tucked in the dense forest of the Appalachians foothills of Kentucky. Purchased over seven decades ago under a false name, I suppose the only people who knew about the property were me and the United States government, but this isolated cabin had probably been long forgotten by any humans who'd dealt with it. Most of them were likely dead or in retirement homes by now.

In a location populated sparsely by one-room hunting cabins, my house was on the large side. A single story ranch-style home with a deep wrap-around porch, it was built by my own two hands and retrofitted to accommodate my size. I was proud of every single board, nail, and brick.

I came here often in between hunts to decompress—needing the solitude and isolation so I wouldn't go crazy. I dealt with a bevy of unsavory characters in my line of work, and I needed time to myself so I wouldn't turn into a feral, heart-eating monster. If you were taunted with your favorite steak, you could only smell the meat for so long before pouncing. This cabin kept me away from the scent—away from the knife edge of losing my mind.

I studied the exterior with fresh eyes and wished fervently that she could see it like I could. The tin roof gleamed in spots where the sun filtered in through the trees. The porch, stained a rich cherry, contrasted with the gray-green paint. Each of the planks were in good repair and freshly sealed against the summer rains.

I held Nicola's warm body to me as my feet met the dirt. I'd made sure no one could travel directly into my house, and the grounds were filled with traps to keep unwanted persons away. Given my line of work, I couldn't be too careful.

"The house is warded," Nicola murmured as soon as her feet touched the ground. Her eyes never trailed from my chest. I'd give her shit for it, but I know she's not really looking at me. It took me about three seconds to adjust to her process. I can't call it a limitation or a handicap—because she isn't handicapped and doesn't have many limitations—but her method of doing things is a little different than someone who can see twenty-twenty.

"How do you know?" I asked. I don't know why I didn't think of her being able to tell the house was warded. She had proven to be much more perceptive than a sighted person.

"I feel it. It's like a buzzing against my skin. Quite unpleasant," she said as she rubbed her hands over her arms as if she were cold. It didn't matter it was July in Kentucky and likely well over ninety degrees, she felt the full-tilt chill warning her to stay away.

"It should go away once we get inside," I assured her as I grabbed her hand to lead her inside, but she tugged at my hand.

"You said no one knew about this place. How did you get it warded?" she asked, her face confused.

"Promise not to tell?" I didn't think I'd have to get into my lineage just yet. Fuck.

"I have no one to tell, so, absolutely," she replied with a delicate shrug.

"I did it," I admitted.

"I was unaware Wraiths possessed that ability."

"They don't," I muttered under my breath as I pulled her through the ward and up the porch steps, unlocking the front door.

With my first steps inside, I felt the weight of worry fall off of me. No one could get into this house, and no one could come within five hundred meters of it without me knowing. I led her through the main room—a great room filled with comfy furniture and a television which took up about eighty percent of the eastern wall—and headed toward the kitchen. I led her to a barstool which butted up against the kitchen island and settled in for the inquisition.

"You're not all Wraith, are you?" Nicola murmured, more to herself than to ask me.

"Nope," I answered as I put the island between us, grabbed a beer from the fridge, popped the top with the bottle opener installed in the counter face, and took a deep pull. I didn't need this woman to judge my lineage and if she did—I'd know the attraction I felt for her was off. It had to be, right? Wraiths and Phoenixes didn't mix. Hell, half of my friends were dead because of a Phoenix. I should hate them.

"So loquacious. Sore subject?" Nicola asked, her head tilting in sympathy. Something told me Nicola was no stranger to the oddities of the Ethereal. There was no judgment in her voice, no censure. She either didn't mind it or really didn't give a shit about the major sticking point so many did. Growing up, my oddities made for few friends and a bevy of enemies.

And she didn't give a single fuck.

"It isn't something I talk about. My mother was a Witch. My father was a Wraith. They were bonded, and she died when I was a boy, taking my father with her when she went. I lived with my grandmama—my mama's mother—until I was old enough to be on my own."

"I bet your grandmother taught you everything there was to know about spells, didn't she?" she asked with a slight laugh in her voice.

"She taught me enough to be dangerous—more to myself than to anyone else," I said as I plunked my beer on the counter, rounded the island and invaded her space. Swiveling the barstool so I stood between her legs.

"You don't care, do you?" I asked as I cupped her chin in my palm, staring into those beautiful blues, watching as her face turned from surprise to anger in a flash.

"Of course not! No one can decide the circumstances of their birth. Blaming someone for their lineage is... is... utter *bullshit*," she spat, the curse word sounding hilarious coming out of her mouth.

I couldn't help myself—I swear I couldn't. Nothing could have stopped me from kissing that frown right off her face. Nothing else she could have said would have been a balm to my soul, soothing the bigotry and hate I'd experienced my whole fucking life with a single sentence.

Just one taste of her—that's all it took.

Just that one and I was lost.

KYLE—AFTER

I'm still staring into those amber depths until she face-plants into my chest and mumbles a sleepy "Morning."

Fuck, she's cute. I forgot how cute she was. Of all the things I remembered, this was the one I forgot. I forgot her rumpled mess of hair and the slight scrunch to her nose when she talked with morning breath. As if I gave a single fuck about that. I fought the urge to cup her face and kiss her like I did so many months ago. It seems like years since the first time my lips touched hers and even longer since the last time.

With Nicola's face in my chest, I look over her snarls of curls to see Willa slip into the room. Willa has checked Nicola over about twenty times since she woke for the first time yesterday, and other than the memory loss and some slight muscle atrophy, she has a clean bill of health. Nicola's walk is a little iffy, but the fact that she *can* walk is a major win. She's not at a Phoenix level of health, but she's alive and that is pretty much all I care about. The memories we can deal with.

"I'm going to the restroom," she mumbles into my chest and shakily removes herself from the bed to walk to the bathroom. When the door snicks closed, I notice Willa's face is full-scale freaked the fuck out.

"What?" I bark, my body going rigid and I'm on my feet in an instant.

"We have a huge fucking problem, Kyle," Willa blurts.

Before I can get the story, I hear Nicola screaming blue bloody murder in the bathroom. I try the door, but the handle doesn't turn. I don't think, putting my boot in the door and busting the lock to find Nic at the mirror gripping the sink for all she's worth. She's not looking at me or Willa—who is crowded in the bathroom behind me.

Nicola is staring at the mirror—staring but not actually seeing. I know for a fact now that the visions won't be an issue because I am one hundred percent certain I'm watching her have one right now.

As rivulets of blood fall from her tear ducts, all of me wishes this was the one thing that never came back.

5

NICOLA—AFTER

MY BOOTS POUNDED AGAINST THE PAVEMENT AS I RAN THROUGH A deserted parking lot in the dead of night. The lot might be bereft of cars, but I wasn't alone. Kyle was running just behind me, unable to travel due to the wide open wound in his gut. Kyle should have been able to pass me, he should be able to leave this place altogether—and would have if he hadn't put himself in between me and the monsters chasing us. Kyle took the clawed swipe meant for me and damn near died doing it.

We couldn't stop. I reach back to grab his hand and yank him along as I sprint toward the safe ground of the hospital. We did what we thought was best, but we shouldn't have left the grounds. We should have come up with a better plan.

I easily pick up the snarling breaths of wolves at our back. They were so close, so close. Then, Kyle stumbles just behind me, nearly pulling me down with him. My grip breaks on his hand, and I feel lost without it.

"Go, Nic! Run!" he roars, and I don't know what to do.

They don't want him. They wouldn't have hurt him if it weren't for me. I turn back to see Kyle on his hands and knees on the pavement, a single arm hugging his middle. His eyes plead with me, begging me to listen, and just this once, I do. I turn on my booted foot and sprint for the light.

When his agonized scream slams into me, I stumble, hitting the asphalt quicker than I can blink. The world spins slowly off its axis, and his scream is replaced with a sharp ringing in my ears. They caught us, they caught us.

Oh nononononono...

I look back, praying to everything holy that I'm wrong. But I'm not.

Two of the wolves are still coming for me, yes, but the third? The third has his maw in Kyle's belly, shaking and shredding the muscle and tender tissue. And he's screaming. He's screaming...

My body feels like it is being ripped in half, my heart and my brain are all trying to deny what I'm seeing.

The two wolves coming for me leap, their form fading into a black mist before touching back down on the pavement into their human forms. There is no smile or joy to their faces, just cold, hard wrath.

The beat of my heart—once galloping from exertion—slows farther and farther until it is barely beating at all in my chest. My breaths slow, and I am almost grateful that I'm dying. I feel in my heart, Kyle is gone. I feel lucky to follow him.

Before I take what I know is my last breath, I do it staring into unearthly yellow eyes.

COLD WATER MEETS MY FACE AS I SNAP OUT OF WHAT CAN ONLY be assumed as a vision. Curled on my side into a ball on the floor of the shower, I let the frigid water chase away the images still branded in my mind. My vision blurred, I blink several times before the room comes into focus.

Kyle, who in no way could ever possibly fit in the narrow stall with me, is kneeling on tile lip of the shower, his knees soaked from the spray. His hulking body is strung tight, nearly vibrating, but the tired dip to his eyes behind the thick frames of his glasses tell me he's seen this before. Fates know what I look like, curled up like a damn cat in this puny excuse for a shower. I probably seem like a crazy drowned rat. So far he's seen me hyperventilate myself into passing out, have a panic attack of epic proportions, unconsciously hurt myself, scream like a crazy woman, and now... passing out from the vision from hell. If I were him, I'd run screaming in the other direction.

What man in his right mind would sign up for this kind of mess?

"Are visions always like this?" I croak, shivering in the now biting water. It takes him a few minutes to respond. I can't tell if he's deciding on what to say to me or if he's just trying to find the right temperature for the water as he fiddles with the dial, but his response tells me I've put him through hell.

"No, babe. Not all of them are that bad," Kyle murmurs, his eyes never quite meeting mine. I swear there is a little ding in my brain telling me he's lying—telling me he's seen so much worse. In the very depths of my soul, I hoped I was wrong.

"Liar," I scold gently, earning me a wry smile and a nod as he finally quits with the tap and looks at me. I put a shaky hand to the shower floor and lever myself up to sitting.

"What did you see?" Kyle asks, his voice a rumbling whisper. I don't want to answer him. If I answer him, it might make it come true, and I don't want to watch him die again. I don't want those men or whoever they were to find us.

Not ever.

I don't want him to die because of me. Because the one thing I am absolutely certain of in all of this is that I'm the reason. Whatever happened, whatever brought me here to this hospital is my fault. I know in my gut those wolves were after me and not him. I won't put him in danger—even if it is to save me.

"I-I don't know. Most of it was too dark to see. It doesn't make much sense to me," I offered, hoping my voice doesn't betray me and I'm lucky because he gives me an out.

"That's okay, Shortcake. I wasn't sure you'd get the visions back at all. Maybe your body needs time to adjust."

I really fucking hope not. If these visions got any more detailed, I'd be carted off to the loony bin faster than I could freaking blink. I've more than likely booked my one-way ticket there already.

It was then I noticed how close to naked I was in my now see-through hospital gown—the water soaking the thin material and turning it into a freaking peep-show attraction. Fantastic. My arms fly to cover my exposed chest, and even though I know I'm technically married to this man, I'm not even in the vicinity of comfortable right now.

I don't know him; I don't know anyone, I tell myself.

But his eyes... his eyes say they've seen all of me before and love what they see. They say he's been starved for months and it's Sunday fucking dinner. Those eyes hit a nerve in me, and I don't know if I want him to act on all the promises those eyes are making or if I should still be mortified I'm practically naked in front of him.

"Move it or lose it, big man," Willa orders him, coming to my rescue. She shoves and prods him until he has no choice but to climb to his considerable height and exit the bathroom. Before he does, I get another heated look that is only tempered slightly by concern as he shuts the door with its now busted lock.

Willa says nothing as she helps me to my feet, makes sure I'm steady and passes toiletries through the half-closed curtain to me as I shower. She does, however, give me her dreaded eyebrow. I loathe that expression already, and I've known her for approximately twenty-four hours.

When I think Kyle's finally out of earshot, I whisper, "What?"

Her head tilts just to the side as her eyes flash green for a moment. She seems to consider me for a moment.

"You lied to him," she accuses

"Of course I lied to him!" I furiously whisper before the memory hits me like a slap in the face and it becomes impossible to stop the tears.

"I... I saw him die. I saw us both die. And it's my fault. They weren't coming for him."

"Who wasn't coming for him?" she asks, her body alert and tense.

"W-wolves," I say, my voice barely audible and watch as her eyes begin to glow.

"I need you to tell me exactly what happened in your vision, Nicola."

"We were off the hospital grounds, and they came and they... and they..." I can't finish that sentence before the horror of it hits me.

My chest feels like it's caving in from the weight of the loss of him. But I shouldn't still feel this way, right? He isn't dead. Just because I saw it, doesn't mean it has to happen. Just because I felt his death in every single cell in my body, doesn't mean I can't stop it.

Right?

"I can't let him die, Willa," I murmur, choking back my emotions. I turn off the water, grab the towel to dry my skin. She puts a comforting hand on my shoulder.

"I know. I'm going to get you some dry clothes to wear, and we'll figure this out. Don't lose it just yet, okay?" Willa assures me as she gives me a quick hug and leaves the room.

She doesn't know. She didn't see. There is no way I'm letting what I saw to happen to him. I don't care what it takes.

I'm saving him, and I don't give a shit if I have to die to do it.

6

KYLE—AFTER

PACING THE SHORT LENGTH OF THE HOSPITAL ROOM IS ABOUT all I can do right now. My emotions are all over the place, ranging from the kind of lust that is close to driving me insane and scared as hell because I know she's lying to me.

If I didn't know Nicola, if I didn't know every single inch of her, I would have believed she couldn't remember her vision. But I do. I know every single tell, and my Shortcake is lying her ass off. She might not want to tell me, and that's okay. She's had to withhold her visions from me before, and I understand why. But she's never lied about it. That kind of shit not only pisses me off, it freaks me the fuck out.

Why did she lie to me?

The thought runs on a constant loop in my brain until Willa steps from the bathroom.

"I need to get her some clothes and then the three of us are going to sit down and have a talk," she says, her face a worried mess, her tall, lithe frame on edge.

"I have clothes here for her—what the fuck did you think I was doing when I left? What the hell is happening, Willa? I know she's lying to me," I say, crossing my arms.

"Yeah, she is, and for good fucking reason, too. I don't know everything, but if she doesn't feel safe, she isn't going to tell us shit. This vision is bad, Ky..." she trails off. Her shoulders twitch in her natural feline way.

"People are going to be coming for us, no fucking shit, Willa. I know there are going to be repercussions for Iva's trail of bodies. Now tell me the goddamn problem," I order, not giving a shit if I'm being an asshole. I pull my glasses from their perch on my nose and pinch the bridge between my eyes.

"It has to do with what I was coming here to tell you anyway. There are wolves at the boundary of the grounds. They can't come in because they intend harm, but... the others here are telling me she can't stay. Right now, you both are being asked to leave. The hospital and the grounds are only sanctuary for the ill. Iva won no favors from the coven keeping the ward."

Of course she didn't. Iva. Just that name makes my skin crawl.

"Fucking Witches and their goddamn rules," I mutter realizing the irony of my statement as I say it. *Fucking Witches when I'm part Witch.* If only it were a part of myself I could just cut off like a wart or a cancer, but no, it's me—even if it's the part of me I hate.

"Be that as it may, they will make you leave if they have to. Is there any place for you to go?"

"Yeah," I say, my fingers knifing through my hair and yanking the short strands.

I do have a place where we could go. I don't know if I want to go back there, though. I don't know if I ever want to see that house—my house—again.

It was my safe place.

It was where I kissed her the first time, where I made love to her for the first time. It was the only sanctuary I had.

It was ours—and they took it away from us.

KYLE—BEFORE

I'd never tasted something so good as Nicola's mouth.

Jesus, shit, fuck.

Never in my life had I had this driving need to kiss and consume and take. I wanted her more than I'd wanted anything ever in my whole fucking life. Sure, I'd bedded plenty of women, but this one tiny Phoenix kicked the shit out of every single memory in my head.

When her lips parted and her tongue met mine, the taste of her just got better. Woman and cinnamon.

Jesus, shit, fuck.

My hands threaded through her mass of hair, gently pulling her head back so I could get better access to that mouth. Her answering moan hit me right in the dick, and finally deciding the distance between our bodies was too great, I abandoned her hair for her waist. I ran my hands over her thin sundress, the heat of her body filtering through the fabric.

Hoisting her up so her chest rested against mine, I couldn't help the grin that pulled at my mouth when her arms wrapped around my neck and her legs circled my hips. Soon, her hands started to roam, pulling at clothes, unbuttoning, unzipping, exposing her pale, porcelain skin to my assuredly black gaze. Her dress hung on her waist, all that stopped me from seeing the rest of her upper body was the pale blue lace of a teeny strapless bra. I wanted the rest. I wanted all of her. I wanted her heat against my chest, my mouth, my hands.

I wanted to taste and touch all of her and so I did. I set her right there on the counter of my kitchen island, and my now free hands spanned the soft skin of her waist, my thumbs skating the underside of each breast. Her shudder and moan in response damn near killed me. Her legs widened and I fell between them, cursing the counter for not being a bed. My fingers curled over the top edge of the lace and I tugged at the fabric to expose the most perfect, delicately pink nipple attached to the best fucking breast I'd ever seen in my whole life.

My lips quickly found the peak and the moan that ripped up her throat damn near turned me feral. I fought the urge to bite, to mark that perfect skin to show anyone and everyone she was mine, and no one else could have her.

"Don't," she murmured, her voice a shaky whisper as her hands pulled my face from her breast. I stopped, my body strung tight and ready to break, but I stopped. I needed to cool myself down, but everything that was her called to me.

"Okay, baby. I'll stop," I said as I ran my nose up the column of her neck and rested my forehead against hers. I got a frustrated moan in response that only ignited me further.

"Not, *stop*, stop. Just don't bite," she explained as her hands drifted down my abs to my belt buckle.

Don't bite?

"I don't know how possible that is, Shortcake. In case you hadn't noticed, my response to you is not exactly rational."

She grabbed my face then, and in a rare moment of accuracy, her eyes met mine. At that moment, I felt all her attention on me—every single fiber of her being was centered on this, on us. I took in every fleck of blue in her eyes, and marveled at the red hue to her long eyelashes. I was laser focused on her, so I didn't miss it when her irises lit with a pale blue phosphorescent glow.

"Do your best, then. It's important, Kyle. Don't rush this," she demanded, her soft husky voice binding around my heart.

I thought I was lost before. I thought I'd already fallen down the rabbit hole. I had no idea how far I'd actually plummeted until that very second.

"I promise, Nic. I won't bite you unless I absolutely cannot stop myself. Just know, one day I will, and you'll be mine." She only smiled in response.

I should have known then.

Two weeks. All we got was two measly weeks when we should have gotten forever. Hiding out in my cabin, we kissed, touched, fucked, made love, and talked for hours—only stopping to eat or for me to make a quick run for supplies. The last time—before everything went to hell—I came back to Nicola sitting on at the kitchen table playing the violin I'd procured for her a few days prior.

In getting to know her, I realized how much she missed her instruments—her piano and violin in particular. I couldn't carry a piano through the dense forest, but I could bring her a violin. I'd found one in a music store in Lexington, not realizing she would have preferred a used one to a brand spanking new violin. Nicola hadn't yet played for me, saying it took time to get to know the instrument before she played it. What she really meant was she wanted to break it in before I heard her.

Walking through the front door, I immediately recognized the song she was playing, 'Farewell' by Apocalyptica. Although the song was made for the deep strains of a cello, she did it justice with her expert skill. Each sweep of her bow and finger vibrato just about broke my heart. Somehow, she poured even more emotion into the song, and I was overcome with an intense feeling of loss. It was like she was telling me goodbye.

As beautiful as the song was, I fucking hated it.

Two goddamn weeks had passed and she still hadn't let me bind her. I was frustrated, but with each passing day I feared there was a reason she wouldn't let me. I feared she'd be ripped away from me.

I should have known.

I FELT HER STIR IN THE DEAD OF NIGHT. SHE SHOULD HAVE BEEN exhausted—I knew I was—from our acrobatics a few hours prior, but she slipped from the bed and felt her way to the kitchen.

I followed her silently, as only a Wraith can, to the kitchen table and watched as she sat naked on the dining chair. Her pale skin glowed from the scant moonlight filtering through the window, her hair a rumpled mass of snarls and curls. She seemed to be readying herself for something, and as fascinating as her naked body was, my unease grew with each passing second.

Something was wrong.

Suddenly, she slapped a hand over her mouth and gripped the table for all she was worth. Her body arching with the strain, her eyes flashed open, glowing bright blue. I'd seen Aurelia's eyes glow like that when she was in the middle of a vision—but never Nicola's. She hadn't had a single one since she'd been here, and the force of them scared the shit out of me.

Then she started screaming, the sound barely muffled by her hand as her body convulsed from whatever she was seeing. I couldn't let her go through it alone. Hell, it was why I got up with her in the first place, but I couldn't just stand there watching.

Crossing the room, I grabbed the hand which had been latched to the table and immediately regretted my decision. The force of her grip was tighter than a vice and I felt my bones creak from the pressure.

"Nicola, baby, I need you snap out of it!" I ordered shaking her hand, but Nicola remained in her vision, tears of blood falling from her eyes.

I did the only thing I could.

I scooped her into my arms and held her until it was over. It seemed like hours that her body was a tense wire of agony, but in reality, it was probably only a few more minutes. Finally, her body relaxed and her eyes closed, squeezing out several more blood tears.

"K-Ky?" Nicola croaked when she came back to herself.

"You scared the shit out of me, Shortcake," I murmured in her hair, as I kissed her temple.

"Ky?" she repeated, her body shivering even though the heat of her felt like she would burst into her Fireskin at any given second.

"Yeah, baby," I answered. I didn't know if she couldn't hear me or if my voice just wasn't registering in her brain, but really, she was just trying to get me to pay attention.

"Men are coming... Here... Th-they are coming. Do-don't have m-much time. Ge-get dressed. Run. Th-they will use you against me," she haltingly explained but her words didn't make sense to me.

"Nic, no one can get through the wards without me knowing, and no one knows where we are, baby."

"They have Witches with them. They found you. They can break the ward. They are going to kill you, Ky. Ge-get b-bloody dressed and get out of here!" she shouted.

Then I felt the ward break—a shiver of a burning ripple flashed across my skin.

They were already here.

7

NICOLA—AFTER

SHIVERING IN A TOWEL. NO, SHIVERING IN A *GODDAMN* TOWEL, sitting on a toilet seat in a hospital bathroom when I should be getting as far from Kyle as humanly possible.

Oh, that's right. You're not human, a snide voice in my head reminded me. Not that I had any frame of reference on what being human meant, but I bet my lily-pale ass it didn't mean watching my quasi-husband being gutted by a fucking werewolf. Or having visions about said gutting that made my eyes literally bleed.

I needed clothes. I needed a plan. I needed to not be a brainless fucking idiot and get a damn clue.

Preferably in that order.

A soft knock on the door proceeds Kyle poking his head in, a stack of clothes in his arms. Fabulous, one problem down, five million to go.

"I had clothes here for you just in case you woke up," he says as he offers the small pile of cloth in his hands to me. "You can get other clothes if you don't like these—just say the word."

I try to study the bundle in his arms but can't seem to tear my eyes away from his hands. I don't know what it is about them that catches my interest. Is it the rough but long-fingered grace to them? Is it the way they seem to have seen the sun and wind and earth of this world and yet seem so gentle?

I know what it is. It's the way his hand pressed to his belly in my vision. It's the way the blood oozed in between the gaps in his fingers, staining the webbings red. It's the way they laid lifeless on the pavement as that fucking wolf ripped into him, only moving with the force from the jerks of its teeth tearing his body apart.

It takes effort to tear my eyes from them and grab the bundle from his hands, mumbling a quick thank you as I turn away. I have to take deep breaths to quell the nausea in my stomach and the bile coming up my throat.

I am the reason. It will be my fault. I have to go, I have to go, I have to go...

Before he leaves me to it, he asks, "You okay, Shortcake?"

Am I okay? Did he not see me cry fucking blood not ten minutes ago?

"I'm bloody fucking super, alright?" I snap and immediately feel bad for it. He doesn't know what I saw, and if I have any say at all, he won't know ever.

"I'm sorry," I whisper, "I'm... not dealing very well, okay?"

I wait for him to yell at me and I assume he might or leave me to my bitchy temper tantrum, but he doesn't. Kyle heaves a sigh before his heat meets my back and his lips brush the top of my hair. "I can understand that. Get dressed, babe, and we'll work it out, okay?"

I nod, and after hearing the broken door close, I drop my towel and inspect my body for the first time. My skin is porcelain pale without a single freckle. The only thing marring it that I can see is a double crescent scar on the meat of my hand. If I didn't know better, I would say the scar looked like someone or something took a chunk out of me. My mind drifts back to the wolves, and I shudder.

I examine the clothing Kyle gave me. The soft gray, knit fabric appears to be a shirt. The pants are made of a thick, dark denim. In between the shirt and the pants is a small bundle of dark gray lace and my brain finally supplies the word—undergarments. I thrust my legs into the lace panties, slip into the bra and then try to figure out the shirt. The thin knit feels smooth against my skin, and once I find the tag and figure out how I should put it on, I realize the draping of the fabric is what held me up. The shirt is a slit-neck sweater, the right shoulder ruched and draping diagonally across my body into an asymmetrical hemline. I take a look at it in the mirror and am surprised at the elegance of it. It looked much more complicated than it was. The pants were easier to figure out—I slipped into the skinny jeans with much less confusion.

Sufficiently dressed, I hunted up a hairbrush and began the attack on my curls before giving up and braiding a few sections of hair away from my face. Shrugging since this was the best it was going to get, I emerge from the bathroom barefoot to the ripe tenseness of my hospital room.

Kyle and Willa are facing off like a pair of pissed off lions. In Willa's case, I am almost certain she is a shifter cat of some sort. The deep guttural growl in her throat was in no way human.

I wonder if I can slip out of this room without either of them noticing?

I was able to eye the door for about three seconds before Kyle's voice snaps me back to the room.

"Don't even think about it," his rumbling growl whips at me, paired with the bulging biceps from his crossed arms and a look that is part exasperation and part utter fury.

Shit! How did he know?

"What? I shouldn't look for an exit before the two of you rip each other apart? Please excuse me for have a modicum of self-preservation instincts," I reply, crossing my arms to match his, squaring my shoulders and hips to show him I am in no way cowed.

"No, you should stop acting shifty as fuck," he growls at me, his eyes flashing from chocolate to inky black and back again. I should be scared —I really should—but I'm not. Now, I'm just pissed off.

"Because I looked for the bloody door?" I ask, bewildered.

"No, because you lied to me, searched for the fucking exit *and* won't answer my goddamn questions," he replies, his voice rising and his hold on calm slipping.

"Maybe it's because I don't. Fucking. Know. You. I don't know her," I say gesturing to Willa. "I don't know my own bloody last name. Maybe because I have no idea if I can trust you. Or what put me in this hospital. Or what I like or don't like. When I was born or who I fucking am," I reply honestly. I don't know if I can trust him—I just know I have to save his life.

Trust is not in the equation at all.

"You said you didn't want to know!" he yells in exasperation, his grip on calm lost to his temper.

"Well, I reserve the right to change my bloody mind!" I volley back realizing too late that we have squared off and are nose to nose, him leaning down to my level.

"I swear to the fucking Fates if I didn't love you so goddamn much I would wring your damn neck. What did you see, Nicola? We don't have time for you to weigh the pros and cons of telling me. Forewarning is *always* better. Stop hoarding everything you see. Maybe you can change this one for fuck's sake."

His words hit me right in the gut, and all of a sudden I want to cry. I can't process the love comment. How could he possibly? I can't be the woman he fell in love with.

I don't even know who that woman was.

I meet his eyes, mine burning with unshed tears—tears I refuse to lose my hold on. "I saw you die. You were mauled by what I can only guess is a werewolf. You tried to save me and got yourself killed. Is that what you want to know?" I ask, defeated.

I just wanted him safe. Is that so bad?

Kyle's face shuts down, the black of his eyes—which had bled all the way through his sclera—flick back to chocolate. His nod comes next and then Kyle turns from me and walks right out the door, leaving me and Willa in his wake.

"He's a hothead. Leave him be and he'll calm down on his own," Willa's voice breaks the silence.

"Sure," I murmur, still staring at the door.

"I'm going to ready your discharge papers. Sit tight, okay?"

I nod as she leaves the room, but I have absolutely no intention of staying put. First order of business, find shoes. Second, get the fuck out of here. I start searching the room for anything and everything, starting with the drawers resting just under the dark window ledge.

The first drawer is socks, underwear, bras and sleepwear. Piles of them in my size. Interesting. The second is shirts, pants, skirts—all carefully folded. The third and final drawer is filled with shoes, a slouchy purse and an empty duffle bag.

I yank out the duffle, filling it with the clothes and shoes, dropping a single pair of black leather flats on the floor and slipping into them as I work. Then, I inspect the purse. It is a buttery black leather with large circles connecting the single strap to the bulk of the bag. In it is a matching thin zippered wallet, a tiny paisley printed bag filled with hair stuff, a small bag of makeup—the tubes all still sealed—and a mechanical device of some sort. My brain supplies the word—phone. Weird. There are no number buttons and except for a single button in the bottom middle and a few on the sides, there is nothing else. I have no freaking idea how to work it.

I drop the phone back in the purse, zip it and heft the duffle on my shoulder, finding it much lighter than I thought it would be. I remember the crap in the bathroom and dash to grab it, shoving the tubes of stuff in the bag and getting the hell out of there.

I crack the door and peer out to a well-lit hallway. At the far end of the hall, Willa stands at a counter talking to another woman. I breathe a sigh of relief when Kyle is nowhere to be found. I see a bright red exit sign hanging from the ceiling to my right, so I open the door wider and slip through, letting it quietly snick shut before calmly walking toward the sign.

I follow the arrow to another door labeled 'stairs' and silently press the lever. As soon as the door is open wide enough I slip through and catch it before it slams. I think I'm home free—Willa didn't see me and Kyle is gone to Fates knew where—when suddenly, a hand latches onto my right bicep and yanks me around to face a smiling woman.

She is tall, blue-haired and tattooed on almost every inch of available skin except for her face, neck and hands. Her makeup is freaking flawless with a pretty red pout and eyeliner I couldn't duplicate if my life depended on it.

She's dressed in light-wash cuffed skinny jeans, a black tank top that reads 'Live Fast, Die Pretty' in a circle of words with a skull and crossed lipsticks instead of crossbones in the center. All of this is under a cropped, three-quarter sleeve black leather jacket that I'm sure I'd sell my first-born for.

She makes me look dull and frumpy. And short. Especially when I get a glimpse at her fire engine red, double strap, sky-high Mary Jane pumps.

I can't remember my last name but I know what those shoes are called. That's some priorities right there.

She has to be the most colorfully cool person I have ever seen—not that I've seen many people. She thrusts out her hand to shake and introduces herself.

"Hi, my name is Max. Your cousin called in a favor. I'm here to save your ass."

I have a cousin? That strikes me as information I probably should have been told. Like, *'hey here's your husband and by the way, you have family waiting in the wings you also don't remember.'*

"Cousin? I have family?" I ask because, well, no one else mentioned this.

"Yeah. You do. Aurelia's on her honeymoon with her hunky hubby and their kiddos, otherwise she'd be here herself. She called yesterday and I hauled my ass here from Denver to come get you. She said you had a wolf problem. Do you... Are you okay?" she asks—either because I am *this-close* to either hyperventilating or losing my mind.

Maybe both.

"I really wish people would stop asking me that when they bloody well know the answer. No. No, I am not okay. I have zero memory, I had to figure out how to put on clothes, and my 'husband' is a big jerk whose life I have to save. I am a huge ball of not fucking okay."

"Well, honey, let's get out of here and then you can tell Momma Max all about it," she says as she takes the duffle off my shoulder and puts it on her own, throws an arm around my shoulders and guides me down the stairs.

8

KYLE—AFTER

SHE IS DOING THIS FOR ME—LYING FOR ME, PROTECTING ME. Again. The last time she protected me, she ripped everything I loved away in a single vicious jerk. I don't know what she thinks she's protecting me from this time, well, I do, but I don't understand it.

Wolves. Of the number of factions Iva wronged, the wolves wouldn't have been my guess of the first ones to come after her. I would have thought it would have been the Witches.

Witches were the ones who stormed our house. They were the ones who broke my ward—the ones who brought us to the Wraiths who beat and tortured us.

They were the ones who betrayed one of their own kind. They were the ones who betrayed me and mine.

KYLE—BEFORE

We dressed as fast as we could, arming ourselves with the limited arsenal I had on hand. Breaking three floorboards to get to the cache I'd hidden in my bedroom—a single Glock and three mags.

It wasn't enough.

I never thought anyone would be able to break the ward. I thought we were safe. I thought I could protect her. For only being half-Witch, I am more potent a caster than most. My Wraith side lends power to my spells—the more fed I was, the stronger I would be—and the day before I cast the warding spell, I'd just glutted myself on the fallen souls of a nasty prison riot. I didn't take them all, of course, just the most rancid.

We Wraiths take the term sin-eater seriously.

But I'd put too much confidence in myself and didn't plan ahead—I was a fucking idiot.

Nicola told me Witches were with the men coming for us, told me about Evangeline and Iva, and so many things that didn't seem to register in my fool brain. It didn't even cross my mind that they would hurt one of their own or break the cardinal rule of a Witch's ward. I'm a half-breed, sure, but my grandmama told me I would be accepted—that Witches never hurt their own. Ridicule, demean, and ostracize them maybe, but never physically hurt them.

I suppose their agenda didn't include me or my heritage because they plowed through my ward like it was nothing—like the boundary of my land was as inconsequential as a line in the sand. Wards are sacred—they are never meant to be crossed. These Witches held no honor.

One second the ward broke, and the next, Nicola was screaming at me to run—grabbing my shoulders, her eyes aglow with a new vision, fresh tears of blood falling down her face.

"No, Shortcake. It is my job to protect you," I argued. There was no way I was leaving her there to deal with the lot of them by herself. They would hurt her—hurt my woman, my mate. Bound or not, she was mine and I wouldn't leave her. Never—but especially not to save my own hide. What kind of coward would that make me?

"There is no protecting me, Ky," she whispered, "Get out of here. Please!" Her voice was like molasses over gravel with the way it broke.

What the fuck did she mean there was no protecting her?

"Wha-" I began, but I couldn't finish the question before every single window and door blew in—the shards of wood and glass peppering us like shrapnel. I threw my body over Nic's, absorbing the concussion of the spell, not realizing she didn't need to be protected at all.

Nicola slipped from beneath my heavy, stunned body, ripped the Glock from the back of my pants and started shooting. Blind as she was,

I never thought she could defend herself. Hell, that was why I spirited her away here—because I thought Nicola couldn't fight at all. She said herself she was no good in a fight. I didn't understand how she could shoot with any accuracy, but her aim was true.

Eyes aglow, Nicola's paisley print dress swished around her thighs as she moved around me barefoot to take a few more shots—the bullets finding their homes in the skulls of three men who were unfortunate enough to set one single foot into this house. But she couldn't catch them all, and soon she was down, a bullet in her right shoulder.

Before I could catch my bearings—before I could get to her—two sets of hands hauled me up, and the cold steel of a curved blade pressed into my throat hard enough to draw blood. A woman stood before me holding the blade—severe face, ash-blonde hair, black on black suit, and so painfully gaunt it was a wonder how she was still standing. Her face was impassive, caring not for the situation or the fact that she was holding the blade cutting into me.

I was nothing to her, a tool to be used.

"Stop! Do-don't hurt him!" Nicola screamed, and the woman's face finally cracked a smile, proving the tool theory.

"But of course, darling, I have no intention of hurting him, but you need to do me a favor first," the woman said with a sick twist to her lips.

"What do you want?" Nicola growled through clenched teeth shrugging off the hands that held her to dig her fingers into the gunshot wound in her arm—pulling the bullet out with her fingertips and dropping it on the floor. The wound began to close almost immediately, and Nicola settled in to wait—the woman's eyes riveted on the knitting flesh.

"I need you to do what we say, when we say. Do you think you can do that?" When she received no reply, she added, "We'll be taking your lover with us as insurance, of course."

At those words, I tried to get the hands off of me, but a few whispered words from the blonde woman and my body went lax without my consent. My body may have been slack, but my mind was sharp and focused on Nicola. I wanted to tell her no. I wanted to tell her there was no way this ended happily and to get the hell away from these people—but my mouth refused to work, sealed shut by the same spell that kept me lethargic.

Nicola was silent—either contemplating the woman's request or waiting for her wound to finish closing so she could kill them all—I didn't know which. She stood proudly, head held high, her body straight if a little bloody from the fight, her hair a wild snarl around her shoulders and face. Nicola's blue eyes lit up again, and she met the woman's eyes with surprising accuracy.

"Tessa, is it? I want you to remember something for me. You can kill and maim and torture, but when the end comes, everything burns. Including you. When *your* end comes, remember I told you that."

KYLE—AFTER

Nicola foretold Tessa's death—I could remember that now that Tessa was dead—by fire just as Nicola said she would.

I couldn't remember Tessa's face until after she died—a spell no doubt to make me forget. Clever Witch to make such a spell for a man she had no intention of ever seeing the light of day again. It was a cover your ass spell if I ever saw one. It made sure that I didn't rip her apart as soon as I saw her ugly fucking face.

I clench my fists, and hiss as the bite of my talons gouge my palms. I have to get it together. I am not a help to anyone if I lose my temper. I look out into the night sky from my perch on a lonely wooden bench in the courtyard at the center of the hospital. If I didn't know Witches warded the place, I could have guessed by the herbs, flowers, and trees planted here. The hospital walls reached for the sky, but if I hadn't walked through the sterile corridor to get here, I would never know I was on a hospital's grounds.

The four exterior walls were covered in thick vines. On the north one grew Clematis, the pink summer flowers still blooming at the end of October. Bright purple Wisteria covered the west one, blue Morning Glories the south and tiny white Jasmine flowers populated the east. Raised beds full of blooming flowers lined the walls, trees dotting the corners, and all the while—even in the midst of what should be my people's work—I couldn't help but feel alone.

Nicola sacrificed for me—did things she hated because they needed to be done. Even when she had no memory of us and what we meant to each other, she still tried to protect me. It pisses me off that she is the only one who has to make these sacrifices.

But she is.

Nicola's making these moves because she thinks she has to... *And I just left her there. I'm a fucking idiot.*

I have to get over my own shit. She needs me and I left her there like an asshole.

I check my surroundings to make sure the coast is clear before traveling directly to Nicola's room. It's probably stupid of me. She has absolutely no frame of reference to grasp what she would be seeing when a swath of black smoke fills her room, but honestly, I don't have time to trek through the entire hospital. It's already bad enough that I have to say sorry, to ask me to stand in an elevator with strangers is pushing it.

I expect a gasp from her—or a scream—but I get nothing. I get nothing because the room is empty. I check the bathroom—nothing. And then my eyes snag on the open and suspiciously empty dresser drawers.

Motherfucker. I should have known she would bolt.

Well, it wasn't the first time I needed to find my woman and given the fiery temper that matched her deep red hair, it wouldn't be the last.

At least I'm good at finding things.

9

NICOLA—AFTER

Max and I walk down the stairs—all nine flights of them—to get to the main entrance. With every step I take, I feel colder and colder—my chest twisting the closer we get to the front door. I don't know what was waiting out there for us.

"Did my cousin tell you what the wolf problem was?" I ask Max.

"She sure did. She said Kyle was going to eat it and because he had been very naughty you were going to eat it too, so I had better haul ass to Knoxville so you didn't die."

I didn't even remotely understand that convoluted sentence. *Kyle was naughty? Eat it? What the hell?*

"Is that all she told you?"

"No," she replies simply.

"Care to elaborate?" I press.

"She said I was supposed to punch Kyle in the junk the next time I saw him for her."

Well, alright then.

"Anything else?"

"Nope. That about covers it," she says as we march through the automatic doors toward the parking lot, not stopping or slowing down until we reach a gleaming, cherry red car.

Max snaps her fingers and with a tiny flash of green, the door locks disengage. I feel my eyebrows reach my hairline as I gape at her.

"What? It's more effective than an alarm," she says as she shrugs, opening the driver side door and tossing my bag in the backseat of the low-slung, tough-as-nails car.

"What is this?" I ask pointing at the beauty reverently.

"A 1971 Chevy Chevelle SS," she says with a little grin that tells me she's about to scare the shit out of me driving this car.

I'm not wrong.

"Hold onto your tits, baby girl. I'm about to knock your socks off," Max informs me as we slide in and she turns the key, igniting the demon who lives in the engine. Holy balls.

"Buckle up, buttercup. We need to haul ass," Max says as she glances at the rearview mirror.

I do as instructed and Max peels out of the spot as if her ass is on fire, fishtailing through the narrow-lane parking lot until she reaches the main thoroughfare. Then, Max really opens her up, the demon in the engine growling a guttural song of speed and agility.

Max at the wheel is frightening, but in such a way that I enjoy the thrill—even if I might die at any moment. We pass cars and trucks, merging onto a freeway and cutting off four cars in the process.

"I need to tell you something," Max says, the reluctance in her voice scaring the shit out of me.

"What?"

"We may or may not have a car following us."

"We *may* have a car following us?" I parrot back.

"Okay, okay. We do have a car following us, and I will bet you all the money I own—which is a considerable amount—that it isn't your husband."

Several things occur to me all at once: A—it still irks me to call Kyle my husband, B—I don't have any money, not that I would ever bet against her, C—given that I have no funds, no memory and limited avenues to ask for help, my escape attempt may have been ill-advised, and D—we have people following us and that is a very bad thing.

"And why would you say that?" I ask, my voice surprisingly calm considering the circumstances. I swear, Max is the least forthcoming person I've ever met. Seeing as I know exactly three people, that isn't saying much, but could a woman spell it out?

"Because they've been following us since we left the hospital and you have a wolf problem. Ergo, wolves are more than likely following us."

"We've been driving for fifteen minutes, and you're just now saying something?" I screech.

"I didn't want to worry you," Max says as she shrugs, making a sharp turn to the wheel and cutting off two cars and an enormous truck to get to an exit on the freeway from the far left lane.

"Well, that's fucking comforting!" I yell, my hands scrambling to hold onto the door handle.

Max blows through a red light and makes a sharp left turn that has the back wheels of the car fighting for purchase on the road. Soon, we are traveling down a pitch-black, two-lane road—the lights of the city far behind us.

"Do you think we lost them?" I ask after a solid stretch of no lights behind us.

Max shrugs, flips her headlights off and guns the engine in the darkness, earning a screech from me.

"What are you doing?" I yell, my hands frantically searching for something to hold onto. It didn't matter that I already had a death-grip on the upholstery.

"I'm trying to keep us both breathing. I can see in the dark. Problem is, so can they. I think I lost them back at the freeway, but it won't hurt to go dark for a bit to make su-"

Max doesn't even get to finish her sentence before lights flash on in the oncoming lane—about two seconds before the enormous truck the lights are attached to slams into the front end of our car.

I don't even have time to scream.

NICOLA—OREGON 1855

You can tell a lot by the way a person fulfills a promise. I promised Rhys that Aurelia would live—I bound them on purpose so she would, so she could do the work I couldn't. I found early on, keeping this promise would be the death of me.

I've never had a Soldier—never needed one. In the beginning, Soldiers were a way to help the newly blind Oracles adjust to their circumstances. I had always been blind, and never needed someone to help me to figure out how to cut my food or fetch water or make my way around our village. I didn't need help. It was a rare occasion for me not to know what was in my path or what was coming next.

I wasn't made an Oracle—I was born one. As a child it was harder—I only saw deaths. I never knew what was coming, but as I grew, so did my abilities. I knew much more than my Oracle sisters. Sisters is what Iva called them—I had none by blood. I had no family except for a distant uncle who refused to see me. Kale Constantine was my mother's half-brother, and his two daughters, my cousins—Aurelia and Mena—would be our race's salvation.

I'd seen it.

The trouble was, keeping these two alive was an exercise in patience and would cost me. Dearly.

I stood in the blackness of an alcove—the lanterns I'd snuffed out myself—the only light coming from my illuminated eyes. Their glow was faint, so when the Soldier came—stumbling and floundering through the darkness, it was easy to cut him down. I refused to kill him, so I made sure the blade in my hand was pure silver instead of the Morganite that would rob him of his life completely.

I had to pave the way for Rhys. He would be injured and not at his full strength.

I grabbed ahold of the fallen Soldier, his name I could not recall, and threw him over my shoulder to dispose of him out of the pathway. I had much more work to do.

NICOLA—OREGON 1965

I was the damn Devil—the absolute worst sort of person—someone who did nothing while others were suffering. Biding my time was one thing, but... Iva was hurting her, starving her, draining her. Letting others hurt her.

And I did nothing. I didn't stop Iva, or the guard who stole Mena's innocence. I didn't feed her. I didn't release her. When I died, I would reside in the lowest pit of Hell.

"Mena," I whispered into the pitch that was Mena's cell. I'd been whispering her name over and over, since I slipped in this vile, stinking hovel an hour ago. She'd been catatonic for days now, not eating the meager scraps of food the guards brought, not sleeping, not blinking.

If she weren't breathing, I'd swear she was dead.

"Mena. I need you to listen to me. I need you to understand," I murmured urgently. My time was almost up. Soon, someone would be checking on me and I couldn't afford to be missing. I had to say what I came there to say. I had to give her hope where she had none.

"I have done horrible things. I have neglected you, and for that I am sorry. But I will do anything to save this Legion. I will manipulate, and sacrifice, and I will kill to save them. I will sacrifice a few to save many. I will do horrible things for the greater good," I told her, unsure if she heard me or if none of my words penetrated the haze of guilt and fear that clouded her mind.

"And you can hate me for that. I hate me for that. And after all I've done, I will probably go straight to hell once this life is finished," I admitted, "And I will accept it because in this life I was given, I did not choose my path, but I accept my destiny. So, you can dislike me, even hate me, all you want. I accept that. But I will save them. I will make sure that they are on the right path. I will bring them back from the darkness."

"But I need your help," I pleaded, "I need you to stay here. I need you to endure this hell, and I will help you when I can."

Fates, how could I ask this of her? How could I ask this of anyone? How could I possibly keep her alive?

"Your sister is coming. Not for a while, but she is," I assured her, "I need you to stay here until she gets you out. And when you get out, I need you to leave her and hide. People will come for you. They will try and steal you and make you a slave to feed their thirst for power. I need you to hide until Evangeline Marie Black has been made the Wraith Queen. When she's made Queen, go to her and help her. She will make sure Iva dies and stays dead. Do whatever you can to help her. And once Iva is gone, make sure you live. Live for all the time we stole from you and all the pain we caused."

Tears clogged my throat, but they were as worthless and I was right then. What could I offer her to assuage this pain? A promise? And what good would it be if I failed her.

I will not fail this girl, I promised myself. I won't.

"Stay strong, cousin," I murmured as I pressed a kiss to her forehead, the faint buzz of power tickled my lips.

She would live. I didn't care who I had to kill to make sure of it, but I'd fight an army to keep my fucking promise.

IO

THE CAR CRUMPLES IN SLOW MOTION, THE CONCUSSION OF impact rippling through the cherry-red metal and us like a wave rolling into the shore. The windshield shatters, raining glass down on us, metal fuses to metal, and Max and I are thrown around the cab like pebbles in an empty tin can.

In the aftermath, confused and aching, my first thought is to reach for Max. She is unconscious, her lax body crumpled over the steering wheel, blood dripping from the wide open gash on her forehead. We are lucky we were wearing our seatbelts, and that the heavy construction of the car could stop a tank. I unbuckle my belt and scoot across the bench seat to check her pulse. I feel the steady beat going strong, but she's still in bad shape. I need to stop the bleeding.

My brain—muddled from the impact—finally catches on that we weren't the only ones in the accident. My eyes drift to the truck that hit us and it dawns on me that the only light is coming from the empty cab of their truck, the driver and passenger doors thrown wide.

Weapons. I need weapons. Danger! my mind screams.

I check under my seat only to find nothing. The glove compartment is empty as well. Deciding the only other place the weapons could be hiding is in the trunk, I go to open the door, only to find it harder than it should be. Looking down to inspect myself, I just now notice a twisted shard of metal sticking out of my right shoulder. As thick as marker and just about as long, the blackened piece of metal could have come from the engine or maybe from the crumpled front hood.

I guess it's lucky I'm left-handed. The thought floats through my brain. I don't know where it came from or how I know that, but I'll take it. Being left-handed will be a virtue right about now.

It takes me a while to realize it doesn't hurt. *That's bad. It should really hurt,* I think and deliberate with myself on the merits of pulling it out. The shard is impaled dead-center, and it's deep—going through bone and completely obliterating the joint. Looking down at it, I think I'm glad it doesn't hurt, because when it does, it is going to be awful.

Shock. You are going into shock.

Something catches my eye out of the passenger-side window—a slinking gray shadow flitting through the blackness. Shit. It is enough to snap me out of my stupor.

I look back to Max, praying for some magical back-up, but she's still passed out and bleeding, her face a macabre mask of blood. It's then that my eye snags on the blissfully filled dash holster. My left hand reaches for it, thumbing off the holster snap and pulling the Glock from its home. My fingers move without my brain telling them to, checking the mag and painfully chambering a round.

Feeling like a sitting duck, I turn in my seat plant both feet in the door, shoving it open. It takes too much out of me, and when I climb out, I find myself sagging against the side of the car. My knees are a pitiful show of strength.

Keep Max safe. She can't defend herself. Keep her safe, my brain supplies idiotically, and I try to quiet my mind and breathing to listen for the pad of wolf feet over the incessant dinging coming from the truck's open doors.

The growl that meets my ears sends a chill down my spine but gives me the information I need. My left arm rises and my finger squeezes the trigger an instant too late. My bullet meets nothing but air as the wolf turns from his animal self into incorporeal smoke, landing with his hand around my throat before I can get off another shot.

He's tall, with scraggly blond hair reaching his chin, eyes the color of amber and a scar as thick as a pencil running from his hairline, through his eyebrow, skipping his eye, before continuing down his cheek and curving through his upper lip. His hot, putrid breath skates across my skin as he takes a long sniff up my neck.

"You smell different, but I know it's you," he whispers in my ear with a thick southern drawl as he tightens his hold on my throat, adding a crippling grip on my wrist forcing me to drop the gun.

"She smells much better now. I bet she'll taste real nice," a second man chimes in.

Damn, I was hoping there was only one.

The first thing I notice isn't his features or his clothes, no, the first thing I notice is the thick blade of the hunting knife he's using to clean the dirt from under his filthy fingernails. Then I realize I've seen these men before. These are the men who kill me in my vision.

Oh, God.

"Oh, look. She started the party already," the man with the knife says with a smile as he gestures with the blade toward the shard of metal protruding from my shoulder.

The blond smiles at me, releases my wrist, and viciously rips out the shard. My scream of agony is trapped in my throat as he tightens his grip on my neck. My fingers claw at his hand, but he is too strong. His friend's laugh echoes in my ears—the tinny sound fading with each second without air.

I can't breathe... They're going to kill me... I can't... breathe... I can't...

The world starts fading away and I feel guilty. I shouldn't have left Kyle like that. Jerk or not, he'd stayed with me. I should have waited for him.

Just before I black out, the blond starts screaming, and for the life of me, I cannot understand why until I see his sleeve catch fire. My eyes follow the flames from his sleeve to my hand and my brain can't quite seem to grasp what I'm seeing.

My hand is covered in fire—orange and yellow and blue flames licking up my skin like a caress of a lover. I don't feel pain from the fire, in fact, I feel just the opposite. My right shoulder, which just a moment ago was a ball of pure agony, is knitting back together. I feel the blood slowing—the flesh mending on its own.

And my fingers still grip his hand, the flames blackening his skin from their heat. I feel stronger, healthier, and pissed right the fuck off.

When Kyle said Phoenix, he wasn't lying. If I grow a beak, I'm going to be pissed.

The man with the scar is still screaming and the one with the knife doesn't look so smug right about now. But I have to give him credit, he won't leave his friend. He slashes and stabs with that damn knife trying to get me to let go of his burning friend.

And I do. I let him go because he's stopped screaming and is a ball of burning flesh on the ground.

"Why did you do this? Why attack me?" I yell at knife-man. Because seriously. What the fuck did I ever do to them? Not that I'd remember if I had, but shit.

"Whaddya mean, you damn devil? You shoulda known you'd have a bounty on your head. You can't go round killing kids and have no consequences," he replies.

"What?" I breathe. *Killing kids? No. No, I didn't do that. I would never do that. That wasn't me. NO.*

My brain screams at me—telling me his words aren't true, but knife-boy breaks in. My head shakes of its own accord, denying his words.

"Yes, ma'am. You have a bounty on your pretty little head and I aim to collect," he says as he lunges with the knife, and I'm still so stunned at his words I can't defend myself fast enough. The blade pierces my belly to the hilt.

I can't think of anything but the pain. So, I don't hear his screaming as my fire hits his flesh when I grab his arms for support as my legs give out. I don't notice when his screams die. I don't see when he turns to ash just from touching my skin.

Because I have his hunting knife in my gut—pouring my lifeblood into the dying, autumn grass.

My eyes snag on the sky as I fall to my back in the pile of smoldering ashes and bone. I really hope I didn't kill innocent children. I hope Kyle finds us because Max is hurt.

And I hope I sleep without bad dreams.

I really don't want to go back to the dark.

NICOLA—KENTUCKY BEFORE

I never saw him coming.

Just my luck, I suppose, I would find my love when I knew I wasn't long for this world.

Getting a mate before my inevitable end seemed like a horrible thing at first, but I couldn't help the slight niggles of happiness which broke through the wall around my heart.

I'd built that wall myself out of the broken promises and lies told to me in my youth. It kept me safe—staved off the loneliness and heartbreak—but it didn't keep him out.

My visions all but dried up nearly a month ago, but I knew from all the ones before Iva worked the forbidden magic which damned my sight I wasn't going to make it. Three centuries seemed so long and so short all at the same time. How could I have had so much time on this earth and wasted it? Is this what humans feel like when approached with a terminal illness? Do they lament the time they spent on trivial matters and wish they'd done more?

Do they have so much regret?

Everything I'd done, every single atrocity and willful neglect—all of the things I could have prevented, the lives I could have saved—made me the worst sort of person. But I did them all knowing I was saving my race—sure I had dirt under my nails, but all my toils wouldn't be for nothing.

I hoped.

Time was speeding by, and I wanted to experience everything I'd been denied. I wasn't going to feel the perfection of an evil put to death or the purity of wrongs being righted. I wasn't going to see my greatest sin washed from my soul. But I could have a little bit of happiness before I went, and with my plan in place and the first domino about to fall... Time was a luxury I no longer had.

Then, he came along with his hulking presence and soft, rumbling voice and death seemed like a blessing and a curse. A blessing because I hadn't had much happiness in my life and he seemed like a gift given to me at the very last second. But a curse as well because I wasn't going to get to keep him. I didn't deserve him and I never would, and the burn of losing him—even if it was in my own death—seemed hotter than any flame I could produce.

But he didn't need to know, and since my time was coming to a close, he didn't have to. I could flit in and out of his long life and be no more than a blip. Yes. I could do that. I could love him to distraction, lose myself in the beautiful newness of a fleeting love, and no one would be the wiser. Especially him. It would be the one gift I could give myself —a single bit of happiness in a rather difficult and awful life.

I wasn't as limited as I'd let everyone believe. Sure, I'm blind in the most basic of senses, but the beauty of being an Oracle is it didn't matter. I saw so much more with my mind; I didn't need my eyes. But he came after my visions dried up, and of all the things I saw, of all the events I foretold...

I didn't see him, and I should have.

I laid in this enormous bed listening to his soft breathing, listening to the house and the wind in the trees. It was beautiful here. The sounds here were the best. The low rumble of the TV while he puttered around the kitchen, making lunch. The sound of him chopping wood out back for the fireplace. The sound of Kyle humming to himself as he worked on spells to strengthen the warding around his property.

Any of the million sounds I cherished because they were his.

Just last week, he procured a new violin from somewhere, giving me my very first present ever in my life. At first, I was scared to touch it. What if I busted the strings, or dropped it when I stubbed my toe on furniture?

It had been so long since I had to use my senses instead of my abilities. I was clumsy and inept and I couldn't bear to destroy the only present I'd ever been given. But I played it. For him I played my goodbye. He knew the song for what it was, and he was angry with me, but I had to tell him, had to prepare him for this.

I just wished it hadn't come so soon.

I reached across the tiny space between us, knowing a vision would come at any moment. Brushing back a stray lock from Kyle's sleeping face, I relished his visage in my mind's eye. He was so beautiful. It made me smile so hard knowing his outside matched his inside.

Iva must have died—only her first death, I knew—but there was no other explanation for my visions to so suddenly return to me. I didn't think it all would end so quickly. Didn't think I would love him so swiftly or so much. I didn't think it would all hurt so much.

But it did.

I cupped his face and placed a gentle kiss on his lips before removing myself from our bed. No. His bed. This house wasn't ours, that bed wasn't ours, and soon, even he wouldn't be mine.

Because soon I wouldn't be living. Soon, I would have to endure and hold on like Aurelia did, like Mena did. I would have to endure all the horrors of Iva had in store for me, but unlike my cousins, I wouldn't live to tell the tale.

When the vision hit me, sitting at the kitchen table of the house I loved so much, it was so much worse than I thought it would be.

Because I wasn't the only one who would lose.

II

KYLE—AFTER

NICOLA IS IN DEEP SHIT. FROM ME CERTAINLY, BECAUSE AS SOON as I find her, I'm tanning that lily-pale ass. I cannot believe she left me here. She knows absolutely nothing about the world—either worlds. Not this human one, and sure as shit, not the Ethereal. Not the politics, the dangers, fucking nothing. She has no fucking clue, and I swear to everything holy if she gets hurt I'm going to wring her skinny neck.

Goddammit, Shortcake. Where the fuck are you?

Nicola's speeding heartbeat trips in my chest, her adrenaline and fear mixed with a healthy dose of anger filters through me, and for the first time, I realize that the bonding took. I didn't think it would. When I sliced my fangs into her hand, I had no idea if the Wraith bond would even work for us. I'm only half-Wraith for one, and for two...

I wasn't sure there was a soul left inside her to bond to, wasn't sure there was anything left to Nicola at all. I know the emotions I'm feeling are hers and not mine—don't ask me how, I just do. They feel different, foreign and yet not. I feel her, and when we were so close together, I didn't realize I could.

I'm probably going to hell for thinking this, but I'm glad I had the foresight to do it before she could say no. I'm not sorry—not in the least.

In my defense, I bound my body and soul to hers when I thought she was dying, figuring I'd follow her like my father followed my mother, like John followed Olivia. I knew when I bound her she might never wake up. She was it for me. Nicola Miller was mine, and if she was leaving this earth, I was going with her, no matter how hard she tried to keep me here alone. I knew then—just like I know now—I won't live in a world without her in it.

Even though she didn't wake up the Nicola I knew, I'm still thankful I did it. Probably more right this very second because it will make finding her that much easier. However, if Aurelia or Mena figure out I bound Nic while she was unconscious, I'm going to get my ass kicked three ways to Sunday.

I feel a pull on my chest, guiding me, yanking me from that room and down the stairwell to the front entrance, through the doors, and to the parking lot. Glad that for once I actually had my truck here, I climb in and crank the engine, peeling out from the lot and hauling ass north. I should call West or Ash for help. I should, but I don't. I have to see if I can find her on my own. I can't intrude on my friends every single time I have a problem—they've already done too much for us, and we've hurt them too much already.

I can't ask them for more.

As soon as I make it to the freeway, I'm hit with a wave of bone deep terror—her heart rate is going through the roof. Shit. I stomp on the gas, praying to anything I can that I get there in time. Nausea roils in my gut as her heart runs double-time in my chest. She's scared, she's hurt. Oh, God.

Please, please, please. I can't lose her.

It takes forever for me to get to the exit—it might have only been a minute, but I'm too far away from her. I can't protect her from here. I don't slow down enough as I take a left at the stoplight and damn near roll the truck as I skid back and forth on the narrow two-lane country road far outside the city limits.

I see the wreck almost immediately, but my mind refuses to process it fully. I scramble from the cab after hastily putting it in park, feeling Nicola's pull, knowing she's nearby.

I study the fused, crumpled hoods of the filthy, mud-covered four-by-four and the cherry red Chevelle. Both of the truck's doors are open wide, the incessant dinging of the door alarm grating on my nerves. The Chevelle's windows are busted, and I find a bloody blue-haired woman passed out in the driver's seat. She smells of Witch and a little of something else I can't place. As I inspect her, I notice the passenger door on the Chevelle is thrown open. Then, the smell of blood, wolf, burnt flesh and bone, and gasoline filters through my shock. Oh, God.

She feels so close. Where the fuck is she?

My eyes snag on something red in the dying grass just beyond the open passenger door, and in the time it takes for me to round the trunk, my brain sluggishly trails behind my heart in figuring out what that red is.

Nicola lays flat on her back in a pile of smoldering ash and bone; her crimson curls spread over the blackened earth. Her breaths are shallow and pained, the blood staining her sweater and the fingers that are pitifully trying to pry the thick hunting knife from her belly.

"Baby," I whisper, shock hitting every vital function of my body as I fall to my knees at her side.

Nicola's eyes sluggishly meet mine. I see the apology in them, the regret, and I do the only thing I can. I pull the phone from the back pocket of my jeans and call for help.

"Crane," Asher's low, groggy voice answers on the fourth ring.

"I-I n-need h-help," I stutter, wondering if I should pull the blade out or leave it in.

Willa said Nic wasn't healing like she should. What if I pull it out and she bleeds out before she can regenerate? What if she dies and doesn't come back?

What if we both die?

"Kyle? Hey, man. Are you okay?" Asher replies, his voice more alert. I hear a rustle of fabric and him whispering to his wife, Mena, to wake up and get dressed.

"Not me. It's N-nicola. We need help. Please, she's hurt. Bring Mena and Ian," I plead, not breaking eye contact with Nicola.

"Where are you?" he barks, ready to help us, no questions asked.

I rattle off something about sending him my location and hang up to send him my coordinates, fumbling with the keys until I get it right.

Grabbing Nic's hand, I gently squeeze it saying, "Help is coming, baby. Help is coming."

"Mm... M-max," she murmurs, her voice a pain-clogged whisper.

"What, babe?"

"Max... Wo-woman. In the car. H-help her. She's hurt. Au-Aurelia sent her to he-help me."

I want to look back to check on this Max, but I can't break Nic's stare. I can't look away from the amber eyes I hated so much just twenty-four hours ago. How could I have hated them? Despite their color, they belong to my Nicola—a woman so preoccupied with saving others that she gets herself hurt.

Dammit, baby, why did you run off like that?

Soon, the grass is crowded with seven pairs of feet, and without looking up I know who they belong to. Mena, Asher, Evan, West, Aidan, Ian and Cam, but all I care about are the two sets that spring into action. The faint sizzle of Mena's gentle touch pulls my eyes away from Nicola's.

"Willa said she's not healing like she supposed to. I didn't know what to do. I don't know what to do..." I murmur, unable to bring my voice any higher.

"Let me see what I can do. Okay, big man?" Mena asks, her naturally calming nature oozing through me even when my whole world is falling apart all over again.

Mena is a different kind of being. Classified as a Phoenix, she attained the mantle of their leader due to her natural ability as an Aegis. An Aegis cannot be controlled, cannot be contained, and the sheer power coursing underneath her skin is enough raw electricity to blow a hole in the world. Regal in the most organic way, Mena is nearly six feet of willowy badass. Dark hair pulled back into a fighting queue, revealing sharp cheekbones and piercing eyes, Mena could only be classified as beautiful. Beautiful in the deadliest of ways. The only woman I know who could match her is Aurelia—her fraternal twin.

Mena scoots me out of the way and places her hands on Nicola, sharing the natural energy that flows through her. Nic's eyes flutter shut —either from relief or from the pain I don't know which—and I fight with myself not to lose it. I can't lose it on Mena. Ian settles in opposite her and gets to work trying to remove the knife, and then I go black-eyed, ready to rip him apart. Ian Moran is the best medic we have only surpassed by Mena's natural ability, but when he touches the knife in

Nic's belly... I can't contain the growl that rips up my throat or the phase that whips over my body.

Shit. He's helping her. Stop it, I think, but my body has other ideas. Ideas that involve blood and fire, talons and teeth.

Two sets of hands pull me to my feet and it is a struggle to meet West's and Asher's stares. I feel everyone looking at me, I feel their censure. I can't for the life of me figure out what I did wrong, but fuck it. I did what I thought was right.

Asher says nothing, but Ash doesn't talk much anyway. The burly blond man simply stares at me, waiting for me to explain. West has no such need for silence.

"We couldn't get a call before the shit hit the fan? When did she wake up?" West asks, arms crossed.

West Carmichael is a big man, not quite six and a half feet, and almost as broad as I am. Hair reaching his shoulders when it isn't up in a topknot for fighting, tattoos reaching from neck to ankle and thick gauges in his ears, the only thing we have in common physically is our black hair and beards. But what I have over him in height and muscle mass, he makes up in power. Our newly minted King used to be the former King's assassin, and in his tenure, West has wiped out countless threats to our way of life. He can kill someone faster than I can blink, and he is not pleased.

Sure, he's my oldest friend and technically my King, but honestly, I wasn't sure Nicola would be welcome in my circle of friends. She did have an evil bitch from hell literally inhabiting her body. The things I saw Iva do with Nicola's body still make me shudder.

And I know the difference. Everyone might not be so sympathetic.

"We hit some snags," is all I reply with.

The shrug that accompanies my less-than-forthcoming reply is just asking for an ass-kicking. It comes in the form of a tiny, pixie fist in my gut. No one that small should pack as much power as Evan does.

Evangeline Black (or it could be Carmichael now, for all I know) is five feet tall at a push. With curly pale blonde hair and bright blue eyes, she is deceptively sweet-looking, a fact she uses in her favor. Evangeline is one of the deadliest women I have ever met, and she doesn't need a weapon in her hand—she is a weapon. San Francisco earthquake of 1906 ring a bell? That was her, and she was only twenty-one then.

Evan doesn't even look at me, her eyes only on Nic and I find I'm more worried about what she'll do to Nicola than I should be for my own hide. Her hand resting on the hilt of the lethal tri-dagger sheathed at the belt of her fighting leathers eases my concerns exactly zero.

"What kind of snags?" Cam asks, and I notice the surly man for the first time. Shit. I need to get my fucking head together. Cameron O'Connor is a Guardian to the last Wraith royal family—Evangeline and West to be exact—staking his life against his ability to keep them breathing.

"She has absolutely no idea who she is, who we are, or what happened. She didn't even know what she was," I explain, side-eyeing my Queen so I don't get another sock in the gut.

"I'd say she does now. Is that char-broiled Wolf I smell?" Aidan asks with a semi-suppressed shudder, the Guardian looking visibly ill.

"Yep. Willa said there were wolves at the boundary. We were going to be kicked out when Nic got a vision of us dying. Nic... she left to save me."

"Is there a reason I smell Witch?" Aidan asks, and it reminds me there is an unconscious woman that needs attention.

"Oh! Yeah. There's a woman passed out in the driver's seat. Nic said Aurelia sent her to help."

"Of course she did," Mena pipes in while she finishes up a field dressing.

"She got a name?" Ian asks as he hoists his med bag and rounds the pile of ash and bone to get to the open passenger door.

"Yeah. Nic said it was Max?"

"Max? Aurelia's Max?" Evan asks.

"Guess so," I reply with a shrug.

"Well, assess her injuries and take her with us. We need to move and if Ari sent her we'll need her help," Mena instructs knowing her twin's wishes even though she is across the world. "Kyle, Nicola needs surgery —Ian and I can do it in the med bay in my house, or we can take her back to the Knoxville hospital. I'd rather take her with us, but it's up to you."

It's a no-brainer for me. As much as Willa thinks that hospital is a safe place, I don't trust it. It is solely Witch ran, and to kick us out into a war is a bullshit quality for people who claim to be neutral.

I want to say we'll go with them, but I don't get to answer Mena's question. Nicola's eyes flash open, illuminated with a vision strong enough to bow her broken body off of the ground with the force of it. It takes both Mena and me together to keep her down.

And she's screaming...

The sound coming out of her mouth has its own talons and teeth. It speaks of terror and agony and fear. But I don't need her to tell me what's coming. I can smell it on the cool, autumn Tennessee wind.

Wolves.

12

KYLE—AFTER

ALL I'VE EVER ASKED FOR IN MY LIFE WAS PEACE. AS A CHILD I had it, but after my parents left this world, peace has been hard to come by. I keep to myself. I find things that need to be found. I live a quiet life —or at least I did before Nic came into it.

Now look at us.

The glow of eyes from the wolves surrounding our small circle is enough for me to know we don't have enough weapons. Having Mena here isn't enough. Having Evangeline here isn't enough. We aren't enough.

Aidan and Cam draw heavy swords from the scabbards at their belts.

"No one said wolves. A wolf problem heads up would have been a good thing to give before we came. What the shit, Ky?" Aidan grouches.

He's right. Wolves are—for lack of a better word—a whole other animal. Shifters are neutral—usually benign. Wolves are more times than not, a feral, pissed-off race of hooligans and mountain and swamp people. They steal, they pilfer, and they are fucking shifty. Nothing against mountain or swamp people, but wolves give them a bad name. Every wolf I've ever met has had several screws loose and is half a step shy of full-blown bat-shit crazy.

One is a problem. A whole pack like this?

We are fucked and not in a good way.

Aidan and Cam are ready to fight—the dumb bastards. West and Asher are smarter and look for an exit strategy. Evan is having none of it.

"We've got to go!" Evan orders as she bends to grab Nicola's arm—the black smoke of her travel has her taking my woman from me in an instant.

"Goddammit!" West and I say at the same time. Pissed off she left without them, Cam, Aidan and West follow her.

I turn to grab Max, knowing Ian isn't able to travel due to his particular cocktail of mixed heritage, but his answering growl is more feral than the wolves ready to attack.

And another one bites the dust.

I wish I could tell him to wait—to not pull that thread—but he wouldn't listen to me, so I'll save my breath. He'll have to figure it out on his own just like I did—just like I'm still trying.

I look back to Mena and Asher and nod for them to go. The roar of running feet hits my ears, and I know we have exactly zero time before they are on us.

"We don't have time for this shit. I'll take you both," I mutter, snatching Max's wrist before Ian can take a chunk out of me. Grabbing the back of his neck, I pull them both with me as I get us the fuck out of there.

As soon as the porch steps of Asher and Mena's Colorado mountain home are under my feet, Max's still-unconscious body is ripped from my grasp by a growling Ian.

"What the fuck, man?" I mutter, raising my hands in surrender as I leave him in the dust, climbing the rest of the steps to get to Nicola. I do not have the time or inclination to deal with that bullshit.

I have enough problems.

"You bonded her, didn't you," a voice I didn't expect to hear calls from the living room.

I turn to see Aurelia seated in the corner rocking chair, a dark-haired baby asleep on her chest. I can't tell if it is Henry or Livvy—her four-month-old twins—but it doesn't matter. The child on her chest prevents her from launching herself across the room to kick my ass. Aurelia Constantine—like Mena—has Aegis blood. Classified as a Phoenix and cursed with the sight, Aurelia knows so much more than she lets on, possesses carefully honed fighting abilities and knows what moves you'll make before you decide to make them. Fighting her is just begging to bleed, and she'll make sure you do with a smile on her face.

"You see, I know for certain I asked you when we started this mess if you'd bonded her and you said no. So that means you had to have done it when she couldn't answer you. You had to have done it when she was in a fucking coma, Kyle," her low voice murmurs in the dim. "Please tell me why I shouldn't kick your ass up and down this mountain. Because I'm drawing a blank."

Aurelia's pale, pupilless eyes focus on me—which to this day is fucking frightening—and I see what she won't say. She's scared for Nicola and for me, and no matter what she says, she's scared she'll lose both of us.

"She going to make it?" the question falls brokenly from my lips. I don't want to ask. I don't want to know if she's not.

"Yep. Whether the both of you make it out of this, though..." she says, shrugging a single shoulder so the baby on her chest isn't disturbed. "I could never see as far ahead as Nicola could. Now, go wash your hands and come back to hold Livvy so I can get something to eat."

I know I don't have the option of telling her no. As one of the two living relatives that Nicola has, staying on her good side is pretty much my only choice. I stomp into the kitchen, and flip on the tap, and it is only when I watch the water turn red do I realize how much of Nicola's blood is on my hands.

I feel like I am about to crack—like everything that makes me sane is slowly circling the drain along with Nicola's blood. It is so hard to watch the water run clear, as if I'm losing another piece of us all over again. I finally sack up and turn off the tap, drying my hands on a nearby dish towel. When the rag comes away red again, I notice Nic's blood is on my hoodie as well.

Fuck.

Stripping off the sweatshirt until I'm down to the thin, white t-shirt underneath, I hold onto my phase by the skin of my teeth. Shit, I damn near tear out my own hair trying not to rip the room apart.

All that blood...

Aurelia clears her throat to get my attention, motioning me over to take her seat, putting a sleeping Livvy in my arms once I'm settled in the thick upholstered rocking chair. Livvy doesn't stir—even in the transfer to my awkward arms, her delicate rosebud mouth a perfect little 'o' of a passed out baby.

"You're keeping me from the med bay so I don't rip anyone apart, aren't you?"

"And doubling down with a sleeping baby so you have to stay calm. I'm practically diabolical," she deadpans.

Turning to leave me alone with her daughter, Aurelia stops in her tracks when she crosses the open front door. Arms crossed and mouth pursed in a disapproving pout, she taps her dainty, ballet flat shod foot on the hardwood for a second. I have no idea what she's looking at, but whatever or whoever they are, are about to get it.

That's when I hear it. I didn't notice it before, but I would venture a guess that Max is awake—especially when Aurelia takes a huge step back from the open door just as Ian sails through it. Wrapped in a thick mist of green magic, Ian is thrown over the threshold, landing face-first on the foyer tile with a crash.

Livvy stirs in my arms, but settles down when I start rocking the chair again, patting her baby booty as I lift her to my shoulder. She nuzzles into my neck and I swear I didn't think I could be as protective over this tiny person as I am right this second. It makes me wonder when—or if—Nic and I will have kids. Will they have her fiery red hair? Her pale skin? Will they take after me?

Will Nic ever remember us before all this shit happened? Will she ever want me like that again?

I pat Livvy's back again, gently holding this little beacon of life to me. Max stalks through the door, ready to kick Ian's ass, but my growl stops her. If she wakes this baby up, I'm going to be really fucking pissed off.

Max is a sight with her blue hair unraveled from her carefully pinned victory rolls, blood half covering her face and neck, and green magic sparking from her fingertips. Her cropped leather jacket, blood-stained jeans and bright red heels only highlight how deadly she looks.

"Max, honey. Why are you trying to kill Ian?" Aurelia asks, drawing Max's eye for the first time. The anger on her face fades to confusion and then to chagrin.

"He's not a wolf, is he?" Max says as she points to Ian's sprawled and slightly stunned body.

"Nope," Aurelia answers and I shake my head to confirm when she looks to me.

"Huh. Sorry, dude, I don't know. You caught me rather unawares," she shrugs addressing Ian. "Umm. Speaking of unaware, where am I? Where's my car? And most importantly, what the fuck happened and why am I bleeding?" she says as she looks down at herself.

The magic dies from her fingertips as she inspects her blood-covered hand. The caramel skin of her face turns white in an instant and Ian is up and to her before anyone else can move, catching her as her legs give way. Ian hoists her up into his arms, and stalks out of the room to what I assume is the med bay, leaving Aurelia and I alone in the living room once again.

"Where's Rhys?" I ask.

"Getting Henry to sleep upstairs," Aurelia answers as she stares after Max and Ian, her eyes aglow.

"When did you get back?"

"About fifteen minutes ago. Would have been here sooner, but the plane had to refuel in Houston," she says yawning.

"Sorry you had to come back to this."

"Meh. Taking a honeymoon was a longshot anyway. There's too much shit going on. We had a good day at the beach with the kids. It was good enough for me."

"You didn't need food, did you?"

"Nope. It was a ruse to make you hold my Phoenix spawn," she replies, batting her eyelashes at me.

"You are so weird," I chuckle

"Thank you. Isn't it a rule that your in-laws have to be bat shit crazy? I mean, come on. I'm doing my civic duty here to keep with tradition. You should be thanking me. It's not like any of us have a mother in law to annoy the shit out of us. Cousins will just have to do."

Family who won't leave you hanging even when the world falls apart? If this is the only family we have, family made from friends and blood and loyalty?

I'll take it and be happy.

13

NICOLA—TENNESSEE BEFORE

IF I NEVER HEARD THE SOUND OF KYLE'S SCREAMS IT WOULD'VE been too soon. They floated to me on torn wings of sound from the chamber at the end of the hall. Stuck in this stone tomb of a prison, I knew I wouldn't make it out of here. This was the place I would die—or at least the god forsaken torture room was.

I didn't want this. Not then. Not ever. Had I known Kyle would have been caught up in this mess, I wouldn't have gone with him that day back in July. I would have done anything—sacrificed anything—to keep this from him. I did everything they wanted. I acted like everything was fine. I made excuses... but they hurt him anyway. I'd only been here for a week, but Kyle? He'd been in the god forsaken hell hole this whole fucking time. A month I'd been dodging my cousins, meting out the orders so he wouldn't be hurt, but by the time I got here I saw how much they'd already done to him.

It wasn't fair. I did everything they asked!

Kyle's screams echoed through me again—their awful guttural bellows ripping up my insides as I tried to find the strength to ignore them. I didn't have it. I couldn't do this anymore. I couldn't let this happen anymore. Not to him.

He didn't deserve this. He didn't deserve the pain loving me brought him. He didn't earn this evil.

Kyle was good and right and everything I wasn't. He was worthy of loving. I wasn't worth the dirt on his boot. Not after the cards I'd dealt. Not after what I'd done just to get to this very spot. I had to quit stalling. It was only causing him more pain.

I'd made up my mind by the time he came for me that I would do whatever Devereux asked of me.

Devereux shouldn't be alive. I felt it whenever he came near. There was something wrong with his soul. He felt wrong, shredded—almost as if what made him a person was gone. This didn't surprise me even a little bit. Devereux Emerson died over a century ago keeping Evangeline alive—whatever this thing was—it couldn't really be him.

Could it?

The door to my cell swung wide and Devereux's hard fist made itself at home against my temple, and it was lights out for me for a long while.

Waking up in a new place frightened me. It was so difficult to orient myself in a room I didn't walk first. There were new smells, new sounds, but this wasn't a new place. If my shackles were anything to go by, I knew exactly where we were. I also knew without a shred of doubt that my time was up.

Devereux's footsteps made their way towards me. They sounded so different from anyone else's—not plodding, not heavy, just a whisper soft menace that turned my stomach.

Devereux's breath hit my ear, and if that wasn't enough to incite a full-body shudder, his words surely did the trick. What he wanted I couldn't give him. No one could.

"I'm bringing Iva back, Nikki. And you're going to help me. I'm going to put my mistress into this lush little body of yours, and then we're going to have so much fun."

I tried to get away—to scramble off that table—but my bonds held me close to the scarred wood. I couldn't agree to this—I couldn't let this be it.

Not me. Not this.

So horrified I couldn't possibly utter a single sound, I shook my head—denying his words, denying that this was what was meant for me.

He didn't like my answer and I heard a blade cutting, cutting, cutting and his voice...

No, please don't make me do this.

"Come on, Nikki. Tell me. The lung? The heart? Maybe the liver? How do you want your mate to die, Nikki? How painful do you want it to be? Say yes, and I'll let him go. Say no one more time, and I'll make his death last days."

Devereux wasn't a patient man and before I could do or say anything, he did something to Kyle. Kyle's indrawn breath laced with pain made me change my answer.

If it meant he'd live, if it meant he'd go free, I would do anything, endure anything. For him I would.

"No, Nic. Don't do this. Don't let them do that to you," Kyle pleaded, his voice slurred with a drug or spell, maybe both. The yank at his manacles, his futile tries to break free, slapped at me. He had to live.

He had to.

"I have to. There's no other way," I said as I choked on my tears, begging for him to understand.

This was my last good thing. The only really good thing I would ever do. Because it didn't fall into a caveat of a vision or a plan. It wasn't a chess move. I did this only because I loved him.

I wanted him to live.

Even if I wouldn't be around to see it.

NICOLA—AFTER

I fight for consciousness, clawing my way out of the blackness that holds me so tight. The room I wake up in appears to be a guest room in a homey but elegant house. Walls painted a warm cream, sunlight streams in through the blinds and dances off the sheen of a gilt-framed mirror on an adjacent wall. A tall dresser, stained a rich walnut, rests against the west wall, a pitcher of wildflower resting on top.

I don't wake up in a hospital. Not a dungeon. Not a shanty filled with wolves. Just a comfortable bed, in a beautiful room, on a sunny morning. It feels too good to be true. More so, when Kyle walks in from the adjoining bathroom, shirtless with a towel wrapped around his waist, another towel in his hands rubbing the water from his hair.

Yep. Definitely dreaming.

The honeyed caramel of his skin reaches far and wide over the thick delineated muscles of his chest and abs. This isn't the body of a boy, that's for damn sure. Kyle's chest is only marginally marred by the pale crisscrossing of old scars, but across his stomach is the freshly healed pink of a large new one.

I wonder what did that to him, and I hope whoever it was, died bloody.

Kyle doesn't notice my ogling; he just continues across the room, drying his hair as he pulls open the top drawer of the dresser and fishes out a pair of plain black boxer briefs. I can't make myself turn away as he drops his towel and bends to pull them on.

Now, I'm not exactly sure about the rest of the planet—I feel like I was born yesterday—but his ass has to beat every other one out there. Wide shoulders jam-packed with muscles tapering down to a narrow waist, firm, round globes of the best ass on the planet, and thick corded thighs. I won the lottery, didn't I, I think as my sex clenches. Whoa, this man is potent.

I should feel guilty for staring, right? I don't, but I should. Probably? Maybe? No. I shouldn't feel guilty for admiring a man who is my husband. Isn't that written in the marriage bylaws? Thou shalt ogle your spouse.

I can't help myself, I give him a long wolf whistle. Kyle startles, jumping to standing, unfortunately bringing those boxer briefs up and over his very delectable ass and what I can bet is a substantial piece of equipment.

The laugh that breaks from me feels good—for about three seconds —until the pain finally reaches my brain and I remember I took a knife to the gut.

Holy fucking God. I'm never laughing again.

"Don't say that, Shortcake. You'll heal up in no time, and I'll get you laughing again," Kyle murmurs in my ear as he slips into bed next to me and gathers me close. His warmth seeps through my pain and eases the fire in my poor abused muscles. I feel comfortable there in his arms— like I've been gone too long and am finally heading home.

"Glad to know you like what you see, though," he teases and I feel the skin of my cheeks heat with what I can only guess is a beet-red blush.

"Don't get a big head, I just couldn't believe how bloody big you are. What are you, half-Sasquatch?"

Half something, I could swear he mumbles, and at my confused look, he slips from the bed and pulls on a pair of jeans lying across a plush, pale gray corner chair.

I wish he wouldn't leave.

Now that the pain has fully woken me up, things are coming back to me, and the questions in my head outnumber the things I know. How did he find me? How did I get here? Where am I? Are we safe? Is he safe?

I open my mouth to voice all my concerns but snap it shut again. I can't keep taking. I can't keep being selfish. Never again. When I part my lips for the second time, it is to issue the apology he deserves.

"I'm sorry," I say, my voice clogged with the tears I refuse to shed.

"For what, Shortcake? As far as I know, you didn't do anything wrong," he says frowning.

"I shouldn't have left without you. I don't know how you found us, but I'm glad you did. I'd likely be dead if you hadn't."

Confusion puckers his brow, and I feel like I may have said something wrong.

"Shortcake, that knife wouldn't have been able to kill you. A car wreck can't kill you. Hell, a bomb can't kill you. If I broke your neck right now, you'd wake up in a week ready to kick my ass. Very few things can scar you, and as far as I know, only two things can take your life. Out of the two of us, you are more indestructible than I am."

"So why did it feel like I was dying?"

"Because, in a sense, you were. A Phoenix regenerates perpetually. You don't age and never will. The only thing that can kill you is a Morganite blade or an Aegis. That's it. Now, me on the other hand... Because we are bonded, I'm not sure how exactly it works. I'd have to ask Mena."

Interesting. "Wrapping my brain around all of this might take some time."

"Well, that's one thing you have plenty of, Shortcake."

I guess so.

14

NICOLA—AFTER

BEING LAID UP IN BED IS PROBABLY MY LEAST FAVORITE THING. It's been six hours, and I hate it. The first hour I could have taken it, but being unable to walk to the bathroom by myself or fetch myself something to eat grates on me. I don't like relying on anyone—even if the man I'm relying on is a six foot seven bearded powerhouse who speaks to me in the gentlest of tones.

But I hadn't seen anyone in hours—three to be exact if the old-school alarm clock was anything to go by. Kyle didn't come back to my—our—room and I was getting worried. I swing my pajama-clad legs over the side of the bed. Three hours ago, I couldn't move my legs at all. Mena said it was because the blade nicked my spinal cord.

Mena Constantine. Kyle told me she is my cousin, but I see zero resemblance between us. She towers over me at nearly six feet tall, her skin the color of warm caramel, and her hair almost black for how dark it is. I don't exactly look anything like her with my red hair, pale skin, and amber eyes.

She seemed nice enough, but I felt like I was missing a whole slew of information. I felt as if I should know her, but couldn't quite place her face. I felt at a disadvantage, and after the last few days of not knowing anyone or anything, I felt uncomfortable being here in this house where everyone knew me, and I didn't know them.

Just as I find my feet—something Mena said would be coming along within the next day—my door opens wide. A woman stands in the middle of it, a tray of food in her hands. Raven black hair pulled into a messy bun on top of her head, caramel skin beautifully decorated with vibrantly colored ink beneath her short-sleeved top, and what looks like a baby strapped to her chest in a turquoise baby carrier. But her eyes are what gives me pause—pale, pupilless green with enough zing to them that I know for sure she isn't blind. Even with the apprehension they give me, she's still a woman with her hands full.

"Let me help you," I say as I cross the few feet to her on trembling legs, taking the tray from her and setting it on the cedar chest at the foot of the bed. It is laden down with a grilled cheese sandwich made from two thick slabs of bread and oozing a beautiful orange cheddar. Next to the sandwich is a fragrant bowl of what appears to be chicken tortilla soup, a bottle of water, and a fan of apple slices.

"Thanks. I figured you were hungry," she says, holding out a hand to shake. I take it and feel a minor frisson of electricity snake up my arm from her touch.

"Aurelia?" I guess only because Mena has a more potent version of the same handshake.

"Yep, and this little monster is Henry," she says, pointing to the dark head sleeping on her chest as she drops a kiss to his forehead.

"He's beautiful." And he is. Black eyelashes sweep his beautifully chubby cheeks, his mouth in a tiny baby pout of reluctant sleep.

"He's a menace, but you're right, he is beautiful. The little heathen didn't want to nap and shocked the shit out of Rhys. His toddler years are going to be a fucking joy, that's for sure. Plus, I figured he would make me seem less threatening. Mena says I can be abrasive," she explains.

I can't necessarily say it was a bad call. Small as she may be, her presence is formidable to the point of intimidating.

"I'm happy to meet you and Mr. Henry. I am so sorry to impose on you. Max said it was your honeymoon and I just feel awful bringing this mess to your doorstep. I appreciate everyone's willingness to help us out."

Aurelia looks at me with confusion, a single eyebrow raised.

"What?" I ask.

"I can't recall you ever apologizing for anything ever, Nic. It's weird."

"Why? Was I an asshole before?" I ask, but this doesn't surprise me. The way a few people I've seen look at me, I must have been a first-rate jackass. Either that or I must have done them a great injustice.

"Yes, and I don't think I've ever heard you cuss either."

"Well, Kyle says I'm different now. Considering according to you I was an unapologetic asshole before; I can't say that's a bad thing. Now, I must dig into this delicious spread you brought me. Maybe you can stay and fill me in on yourself. Max said we were family?" I ask, and I do want to know, but my quip about being starved isn't quite on the mark. Standing is taking it out of me faster than I thought it would.

"Of course. Just slip back in bed, and I'll set you up," she says seeing through my claim of hunger.

"Busted, huh?" I ask as I slip back under the covers and she places the tray on my lap.

"Yep. You can't fool a Seer," she says as she moves to sit in the comfy side chair.

"Oh, I don't know about that. I'm getting fooled all the time. I have no clue what's going on."

I pick up the thick sandwich, taking a monster of a bite and groaning at the buttery, cheesy flavor.

"You'll get there. You're still healing, and from what you went through, I'm amazed you're doing as well as you are."

Something tells me she doesn't just mean the wolves. She means before I woke up in the hospital, before I lost my memory and my mind. Before all of this. The newly swallowed bite almost turns sour in my stomach at the thought.

"I don't know what happened to me, so I'll just have to take your word for it. The old noodle isn't exactly what it used to be."

"Didn't anyone—didn't Kyle—tell you?" she asks, her voice a low growl of pissed off woman.

At this point, I decide to be flattered at her ire on my behalf instead of the fear I probably should feel seeing anger on this formidable woman—baby strapped to her chest or not.

"He tried, I think, but I had a mental breakdown when a certain name was said. I believe he's trying to give me time to either get comfortable with my skin or get my memory back, so he doesn't have to. I kind of feel sorry for the guy. Who would want an amnesiac for a wife?" I ask shrugging as my worry burns a hole in my belly and makes the bite in my tummy turn to ash.

I don't know how much Kyle had to sacrifice or what he endured, but I know it was more than I'm worth. It is a debt I cannot repay.

But I will endeavor to try.

With one look at her, I know Aurelia sees my inadequacies, she sees my guilt, and I don't know how to fix what is wrong with me or how to apologize for whatever I did that I don't remember.

"It is awful being the reason someone is in pain, trust me, I know from experience. The best advice I can give you, is to be honest with him. About your fears, your questions, everything. Trust him to want the best for you—because he does."

"I am the reason, aren't I? So much for wanting to save him."

"Sometimes the sacrifices we make don't always pan out like we thought."

Well that is for damn certain.

"No more running off on your own. No matter the reason. You would have wished for death if I hadn't sent Max to you. You don't have to agree with Kyle. Hell, you don't even have to be nice all the time. But be honest, cousin. Because right now, anything you see, anything you feel is important to the people around you. It is important to keep you safe—to keep us all safe. Don't keep it to yourself. I learned that a long time ago."

KYLE DIDN'T COME BACK. NOT AFTER I FORCED MYSELF TO finish the meal Aurelia brought me or once the night finally fell on the mountains.

I stewed, and I worried over his absence, but he didn't come back to me.

Guess this time I should go to him.

15

I wanted to see her one more time before I went to do the one thing I never, ever wanted to do. Before I took everything I loved and threw it away. Before I turned her in.

Tracking has always been my profession. I can find anything and anyone, and with the right spell, I can find them anywhere in this world. Sometimes even in the next.

But finding Nicola's body was harder than it should have been. It took me a long time to heal, a long time before my abilities and my mind cleared enough so my pain didn't taint the spells, and a long time for me to realize that no matter where Nic's body was, this wasn't Nicola.

This was Iva.

Iva was wearing Nic's skin, animating her limbs, and calling the shots. *Iva* was letting that soulless piece of shit Devereux put his hands all over my woman's body. *Iva* was strutting down the streets of the French Quarter with that fucker, letting him touch her skin, letting him put his mouth on her, letting him... I couldn't even finish the thought. And *Iva* was the one doing unthinkable things to innocent children—stealing souls and abilities to fuel her vengeance.

I'd followed her all over this stupid country. To the Oregon wilderness, the barren Arizona desert, the foothills of the Appalachians, and down in the bayous of Louisiana—just missing her in some occasions and others...

Others I just wished I had.

I shouldn't have to see this—no one should have to see someone they love used this way. But I couldn't stay silent and watch anymore. I couldn't let this demon of a woman hurt anyone else. I couldn't let this go on without being a monster myself. Inaction at this point would make me more of a monster than they were.

Not after this. My eyes scanned the once opulent room of a mansion that was now in condemned disrepair. It was tough to tell what filth had been here before, and what was the detritus of spells no one in their right mind would perform.

Wormwood, grave dirt, wolf's bane, pine straw. Nothing but bad things came from those ingredients thrown together.

The black of dried blood mixed with the dirt and silt left over from flood waters that had long since receded was only broken up by the thick white chalk of sigils marked into the crumbling floorboards. Thick wallpaper peeled from the ancient plaster walls, the ceiling missing in some places, and the smell.

Mildew, swamp, fear, death and all the bodily functions that went along with it. I couldn't take it.

I couldn't take the sight of the body I found. A girl—a wolf girl—no more than four years old. Her little body broken well past the repair a phase would give her, her throat mostly torn out, her chest broken open and her heart missing. Blood from her wounds stained her white-blonde hair red and the sight of it reminded me of Nicola's curls so much it physically hurt to look at her.

Wolf females were rare. Hell, wolf children as a whole were rare—so much so it was lucky they hadn't died out centuries ago. What the hell could they want with such a child? Stealing power, I get, but the motives behind this one didn't make any sense. Wolves don't have much power —never had. Of the shifters, wolves have the least political power, and the least territory. One thing—hell the only thing—they had was brute strength, but as crazy as they were, they didn't use it much unless provoked.

There didn't seem to be a rhyme or reason to it, and the brutality. In my long life I'd never seen things like this. Torture, yes, but not mutilation and murder to this level. And children? Never this.

Looking at that house and the poor, broken body of that child brought home all the truths I'd been denying for way too long. I couldn't let Iva squat in Nicola's body. I couldn't let her do this in her skin. I couldn't let Iva's evil taint the body of my woman any more.

I had to be the one to end it. But before I could do that, I had to find her.

For the last time.

KYLE—AFTER

I need to hit something—a face, a wall, anything. I just slipped into bed with her, let her warmth wrap around me and I forgot she doesn't remember me. Her half-Sasquatch comment cemented that fact.

She doesn't remember I'm half-Witch. She doesn't remember the first time we made love. She doesn't remember what she sacrificed or what Iva did while wearing her skin. She doesn't know what Iva herself did to me. She has no idea and I don't want to be the one to tell her.

So I did what I do best. I left her there in that room to heal up while I scoured the house for a dojo or a workout room or something so I didn't start ripping apart furniture. I found myself in the living room wondering how mad Mena would be if I ripped apart an overstuffed armchair with my talons.

"I have a bone to pick with you," Mena calls from the kitchen, her back to me as she kneads bread at the counter. What is with the Constantine women and cooking all the goddamn time?

"What did I do now?" I ask, flippant when I probably shouldn't be.

"You're lucky I have flour all over my hands, dipshit, or I'd illustrate just how pissed off I am. Sit your big ass down," she scolds, her back still to me.

Deciding it was better to sit than risk my hide, I pull a barstool away from the island and plunk down, crossing my arms in defiance.

"I saw the scar on Nicola's hand. Did you or did you not bind her, Ky?" she asks, but it isn't a question so much as a threat. She already knows the answer; she just wants to see if I'll admit it.

I'm not ashamed of what I did. I'd do it again.

"I did."

"Did you actually ask her, or did you just do it on your own? I'd venture a guess you bit her when she couldn't answer you. Why else would she have a bite on her hand instead of her neck?" she asks, finally looking up at me, her eyes flicking back and forth between green and amber.

"I did it while she was unconscious. I did it when I thought she would either die or never wake up. I would have spent the rest of my life sitting in that hospital chair waiting for her. So you can be pissed at me all you like, I'm still not sorry."

Defiance suits me best, so I stick with it, unapologetically staring her down. If I hadn't held her eyes, I wouldn't know how worried she is.

"What happens when she never remembers? What if this Nicola never loves you? What then?" she asks softly.

I hate that she asks this. I hate that she takes the one fucking thing I'm insecure about and needles it until I want to punch a hole in every single wall I can find.

"Then I have the rest of forever to change her mind. Either way, she's still mine," my voice a rumble of possession.

"Good answer. Whether you deliver on it remains to be seen."

"I aim to please," I growl through gritted teeth, rising from the stool and heading for the door. I couldn't take the questions swirling in my head any more than I could take the walls and roof of that house.

I had to get out of there. The guilt of leaving would just have to come with me.

16

THE TREK DOWN THE WIDE, CURVED STAIRCASE WAS TRICKY. MY legs, which were still shaky, wanted nothing more than to give out on me, and my feet kept catching on the plush patterned runner affixed to the middle of the stairs. The house felt empty, but I didn't know if it actually was or if it was my own loneliness and fear coming to bite me in the ass. I clung to the polished walnut handrail for all I was worth, white-knuckling it until my bare feet met the cool hardwood of what I guessed was a great room.

The great room was done up in creams and blues—blues of all shades. A dark cerulean couch mixed with cream and white Moroccan tile patterned throw pillows. A beige, plush armchair sat in the corner with a turquoise throw blanket draped over an arm, and on every single wall not broken up by windows there were shelves and shelves of books filled almost to bursting.

The house was enormous, and the vaulted ceilings and wide windows filled with the blackness of full nightfall only highlighted it. It also highlighted the emptiness in my chest—the fear I felt at being alone again. Call it co-dependent if you want to, but I felt at even more of a disadvantage than anyone rightfully should without Kyle.

I check the kitchen, my gait slow as molasses. No matter how grateful I am that I can actually walk, I'm still irritated with myself.

Sitting at the dining table is a man I haven't met yet.

How many people are in this house?

It isn't until I'm actually faced with another person do I rethink my wardrobe. I glance down at the midnight blue pajama pants and matching camisole top. I feel underdressed and long for an actual bra instead of the shelf thingie Aurelia said was a joke for large breasted women such as ourselves.

She wasn't lying.

The man is tall, not as tall as Kyle, but then not many people are. His skin is a deep tan, and with his Roman nose and dark hair, I feel practically transparent by comparison. His long, lean body is folded into the chair, and hunched over a plate of food, shoveling forkfuls of roast beef and potatoes into his mouth. He gives me a side eye as he goes back to his plate, ignoring me completely. I make it as far as the island barstools before I have to rest, my legs nearly giving out on me.

Silence stretches between us and I feel more and more awkward as I sit waiting for him to say something, anything. I finally give up, breaking the silence.

"What's your name?" I ask, giving him a list of people I've met so far. "I've met Mena, Aurelia and Ian already, but if we've met before, I don't seem to remember."

"We've met," he replies gruffly around his food.

Oh-kay. Obviously I've done something to offend his delicate sensibilities. The delicious smell of spiced meat wafts from the crockpot on the counter. I gingerly slip from the stool and point myself in the direction of filling my belly. The awkwardness not deterring my appetite at all.

"You have some goddamn nerve coming here," his deep voice calls as I grab a plate to dish up the roast.

"I didn't *ask* to come here. No offense, but I have no idea who you are, and since you haven't introduced yourself, I still don't—not that I'd remember you if you did," I reply, turning to face off against the man, plate in hand.

"Like I'd believe a word out of your mouth," he says, pulling himself to standing.

"I'm sorry? Have I offended you in some way?"

"Have you offended me? You've more than fucking offended me. I don't believe you can't remember three hundred some-odd years of chess moves, double dealings, and broken promises, Nicola. Not for one fucking second," he replies, crossing his arms.

I wish I could say I could keep my cool, but I can't.

"You have no idea. You have no idea. You have no fucking idea!" I scream, slamming the porcelain plate down on the stone countertop, smashing it to bits. I'm unable to handle his ire and I lose the tenuous hold I had on my emotions.

"You don't know what it's like to wake up with nothing—no memory, no inkling of anything but the blank space where it used to be. You don't know what it's like to wake up knowing something horrible happened, to know you were the cause, but not know why. To know death is coming for a man you just met, who sat with you every single day you were asleep, who stayed and protected you, and know it's your fault, but can't remember what started it. To have men come after you for a crime you can't remember committing. To hear inklings of how horrible the crime was, and pray to everything holy that it isn't true. You don't know," I growl through gritted teeth, "Don't pretend like you know the first fucking thing about me."

"Iva's sins are hers, but you had sins of your own, Nicola. You may not remember them, but that doesn't erase them," he fires back, and his arrow hits the mark on two fronts.

Just saying that name turns my stomach, causing my breath the speed and my heart to decide it wants to race right on out of my chest. That name makes me want to claw my skin off and douse myself in bleach.

But he's right.

My racing heart gives way to the hollow feeling in my chest—the one I tried to deny—and it hits me threefold. I have the luxury of forgetting. He does not.

"Oh, get the fuck over it, Rhys," Aurelia's voice filters in from the living room, and she stomps into the kitchen in the middle of our standoff.

"It was over a damn century ago, she probably did it to save us, and it has kept me from killing you roughly a thousand times. You should be counting your lucky fucking stars she bound us that way in the first place. Now, Livvy needs a change and Henry is being fussy. You go help Evan deal with the gruesome twosome or I might cut myself on purpose just to teach your dumb ass a lesson," she scolds, hands on her hips, and looking like she is three seconds away from throwing down.

Rhys gives her a decidedly grumpy look, and stalks around the island, getting in her space quick enough to plant a kiss on her lips.

"It really kept you from killing me?" he whispers his question, but it doesn't stop me from hearing it.

"How many times have I actually killed you?"

"It's in the hundreds by now," he replies good naturedly, his voice so much smoother now that he's talking to anyone but me.

"And that was when I knew it would hurt me. What's that tell you, dummy?" she asks and swats him on the butt, effectively shooing him from the room.

Rhys looks back, his expression almost apologetic, but not quite meeting the mark. He still doesn't know what to make of me, and at this point I can't blame him.

What could I have done to him? What was I capable of?

"What did I do to him?" I ask her, sorry for something I have zero memory of. But like Rhys said, I may not remember what I did, but it doesn't erase what was done.

"You saved his life. And mine. You just had to hurt us to do it," she whispers, a trembling smile on her face.

Her smile tells me so much more than her words do. What I did to her must have been unspeakable.

"I don't remember hurting you, and I don't know what kind of person I was before all of this, but I am sorry you and your husband were hurt. I am sorry for whatever part I had to play in your pain. And I am grateful for your kindness and your protection. I hope to repay it someday."

I didn't think I could feel more alone than I did when I noticed Kyle gone.

I was wrong.

I help Aurelia clean up the glass from the plate, and head back up to my room, swearing to myself I would never be another burden on these good people.

It takes me a long time to realize a few things. One, I never did get to eat. Two, she never accepted my apology. And three, Kyle didn't come back.

17

KYLE—BEFORE

It took weeks to find Iva and Devereux again. They must have felt me closing in on them in New Orleans because I'd never had so many problems searching for someone before. They had to have Witch help, and it pissed me off. Even keeping track of the local and national news did nothing to help. You would think missing children would be plastered on every screen and shouted from every rooftop. Unfortunately, that wasn't the case—the stories were either suppressed by a spell or by the human's own indifference.

I kept my ear to the ground, listening for distressed locals and anything at all about kids. It seemed that was what they were after. Ethereal children with a little extra something to them. Ones maybe Iva would need to fight against one day—at least that was my guess. I was in an upstate New York farm town when I heard of a large group of kids missing, and I knew I had to move faster.

I wasn't fast enough, and for that I will always carry that stain on my soul.

In the end, I couldn't find her—I had to find him, and he was much easier to locate. All I had to do was search for someone without a soul. In today's society, you'd be surprised how low the number actually is.

By the time I followed them to Maine and the dilapidated but stately mansion on a clifftop overlooking the north Atlantic, they had claimed another victim—several more victims. Tiny mounds of freshly hewn graves dotted the floor of the forest butting up against the property, the mark of souls tainted the air and the innocence of them tore at me. The horror of it all brought me to my knees, bile forcing its way up my throat.

I could feel the dead. I could feel the savage cries of children that hung on the whipping wind and I could take no more.

Not one more child would die at my inaction.

Not a single one.

It didn't matter that killing Nicola's body would surely kill my heart and stain my soul. Both were already dead from the things I'd seen and felt. The only thing that mattered was stopping this death.

My heart didn't matter at all.

I left the clifftop and traveled to private elevator for the penthouse apartment that housed my King and Queen. And they were mine. I refused to acknowledge the Witch part of me. I refused to pay homage to a species of people who would help do this. Someone was hiding Iva. Someone was covering the deaths up. Someone warded the Emerson's house. Someone brought Devereux back. Someone helped bring Iva back from Hell.

That someone had to be a Witch. There was no other way to hide from me, no other way to suppress this much death. Tessa was gone, but there had to be someone else. She couldn't have worked alone.

My feet touched down on the marble tile inside the closed elevator, and I raised a finger to the stylized 'P' for the penthouse. As the lift carried me up, I forced myself to meet my own dead eyes in the mirrored wall.

I deserved this guilt. I earned it. I waited too long. I should have come here sooner.

But just couldn't bring myself to do it.

When the elevator dinged its arrival at the top floor, I was met with Aidan's blade to my throat as soon as the doors opened.

"Ky?" Aidan asked, startled. I didn't exactly blame him. I hadn't checked in at all since the day I was fit enough to stand on my own two feet.

"Get West. We have a problem," was all I could bring myself to say. I could have gone with an apology or at least asked how he was dealing with the upheaval of his whole freaking life, but I was too focused on my task to be a decent friend.

"Yeah, man, follow me," he replied, no questions asked and I followed him down the hall to a wide bedroom door where he pounded for a good five minutes. The door was finally ripped open by a pissed off West.

"Are you fucking kidding me?" West whispered to Aidan as he opened the door. It takes him a second to realize Aidan isn't alone, but I guess that is my fault for showing up at three o'clock in the morning.

"Jesus, man," he muttered while giving me a quick slap on the back in greeting. "What happened?" he asked getting right to it.

"We need to wake Evan. I'm not saying this shit twice," my voice came out gruffer than I wanted, but the message was the same. I couldn't say it twice. I couldn't order the death of my woman's body and possibly her soul more than once.

Just the once might kill me.

I turned from them and walked woodenly toward the living area, trying not to lose it.

Soon, the room filled with people, the buzz of talking voices grating on my nerves. They didn't know. How could they? It wasn't their world crumbling to nothing.

"Alright, out with it. What are we dealing with here?" Evangeline ordered, and I couldn't contain my flinch.

"I-I found her," I began, "She and that guy Devereux have been hopping from one place to another. Hopping all over the goddamn planet. St-stealing children from families, teenagers, preschoolers, b-babies... I tried. I tried to get them back. To follow them to keep the children alive. But I lost her so many times, and I... She's holed up in some abandoned mansion in the wilds of Maine or some shit. Th-there are graves..."

I stopped then. How could I tell them the scene in Tennessee was nothing? That I'd seen the aftermath when they were moving too fast or were too careless to dispose of the bodies?

"When you... when you stop her, can you make sure it doesn't hurt? Can you... It isn't her fault. It's the dirty fucking soul they stuck in her. It isn't her. Just don't… Don't make it hurt, okay?" I pleaded searching Evangeline's face for sympathy, for mercy, for anything that would tell me Nicola wouldn't suffer.

"Yes. I can make it painless," West said, his gruff voice breaking our stare-down.

If it were him, I could've trusted it, but it couldn't be him to kill her. Nicola told me so herself. If I'd known what she meant I would have left her then. I would have gone far and wide to keep from getting caught. I would have done anything she asked so they wouldn't have used me against her.

I was the only reason she was in this mess in the first place. If it weren't for me, she could have held out longer. I failed her. I didn't listen, and I would regret it until the day I died.

"It can't be you. Nic told me before this happened. She said that the only way for Iva to be killed was if Evangeline did it. It was one of the last things she told me before I was captured. And I-I want your word you'll… you'll…" I couldn't make the words pass my lips. If I spoke them out loud it would be all too real.

Evan came over to me and wraps her tiny arms around my shoulders.

"I know this is hard, Ky. I could see how much you loved Nicola, but she's gone. I'm so sorry, but she's gone," she whispers in my ear, and I couldn't stop the tears from leaking out of me.

"I just have one question. Are you bound?" she asked, and I shook my head.

"She wouldn't let me. Never said why, but I figure she knew this might happen," I croaked.

"We'll be humane about it, but it needs to happen. Iva won't stop, and if she hasn't already, she's about to start a war," Evangeline said carefully, looking me right in the eye.

"I'll tell you where they are, but you'll have to get in on your own. I can't help you kill her," I admitted not saying what I truly meant.

I couldn't help them kill her because I'd likely already be dead. I was going to see my Nicola one last time before it was all over.

KYLE—AFTER

It didn't matter that it was late October in the Rocky Mountains, I was still sweating my ass off climbing this fucking path. As soon I left Mena's front porch I knew I had to get my head on straight.

The memories of everything that we'd been through, the battle, the last time I saw Nicola before Evan worked her mojo and got Iva out of her...

The walls were closing in on me, and I couldn't stay there and pretend I wasn't losing my mind. Nic deserved better than what she got. She deserved better than the shitty life she lead, better than me. It makes me almost wish I hadn't bound her—almost.

I made it to the summit of a substantial trail, still cursing myself that I decided to actually fucking hike this motherfucker of a mountain. Kyle plus thin mountain air plus zero desire to ever do cardio equals one tired bastard.

Maybe it was the lack of oxygen or just me getting over my own shit, but I still had hope. I just needed to get the memory of what was out of my head. Those two weeks might not come back to her. She might not remember the violin I got her or our first kiss or any of the million and one things we talked about in those two weeks, but we had forever to make new memories.

When she first woke up, I wasn't sure it was her. Her eyes were different and she didn't remember me or us. But then so many things that were singular to Nicola alone surfaced and I knew it didn't matter if she could remember us or not.

I did and that was all I needed.

IT WAS FULL NIGHT BY THE TIME I MADE IT DOWN THE TRAIL and back to Asher and Mena's. Yeah, I could have traveled, but getting my head on straight evidently meant physical exertion.

The house is dark save for the porch light and one lone lamp in the living room. I bypass the locked door and travel directly to my Shortcake. I find her sleeping, curled into a tiny ball, huddled under the covers, the dried tracks of tears staining her temples.

I feel like a first-rate asshole.

I'll make it up to you, Shortcake. That's a fucking promise.

18

THE FEATHER-LIGHT TOUCH OF LIPS AGAINST MY TEMPLE filters through the heavy fog of crying-jag-induced exhaustion. The lips trail to each of my eyes, kissing the lids, and I can't help but open them to find Kyle sitting on the bed in the crook of my legs. His face is close to mine, each hand planted in the bed, so his whole big body surrounds me.

"I'm sorry I left you, Shortcake," he murmurs, and his voice is so gentle and so much of what I need, I can't hold the tears back. I want to be mad at him for leaving me here, but I don't think it crossed his mind how much these people would hate me or how much guilt I would feel for things I couldn't remember.

"Shh, baby. I won't leave you again, I swear," his low voice promises as he scoops me up in his huge arms, sitting me on his lap. His wide hands brush the snarl of curls away from my face, his thumbs catching the tears as they fall and wiping them from my skin.

"It isn't that, Kyle. It's just... I must have done horrible things to these people to have them hate me, and I can't remember."

I don't realize my error until I grasp the look on his face. I've seen his gentle face, the one with the quirked smile and subtle creases at the corners of his eyes. I've seen his pissed off face, the one with fire in his gaze and the hard line of his mouth. I've seen his bald terror face, the one with wide eyes and fear stamped on every inch of him. I barely saw that one before I passed out on the side of the road, but I remember it.

I had not, however, seen his enraged face. This expression is about twelve steps up from the pissed off one. His eyes burn hot before the black bleeds from his pupil out, overtaking the iris, and staining the sclera coal-black.

"They were mean to you? Who was it?" he asks, his voice a menacing growl.

"It doesn't matter," I rush to brush my words aside, praying that he doesn't make it a bigger deal of it than it already is.

"Damn fucking straight it does. Who. The fuck. Was it? I leave my woman in their fucking care, and I come back to her huddled in a damn ball in the bed, tear tracks on her fucking face, exhausted. I left you with your people. I left you with family. It may not have been close family, but I expected you to be welcomed and cared for. If you weren't, it's as much on me as it is on them. Now, who the fuck put tears in your eyes?" he orders.

I have two options. One, I tell him about the Rhys and the 'plate of a thousand pieces' incident. About being left alone for hours in a house I don't know, with people I don't know. About how I have the distinct impression there were a bunch of people here who were avoiding me altogether. But I honestly think I'm being a huge baby about it. Or I could shut his mouth for him and do the one thing I've been dying to do for the last three days.

I pick door number two.

I cross the scant six inches between our faces and press my lips to his. I didn't expect his mouth to be as soft as it is, or for the rough rasp of his beard against my cheek to make me so restless, but they are. Kyle's mouth is only inactive for a single second before he is kissing me back.

Holy shit.

He was my husband. I knew he had to have at least kissed me before. How could my brain forget this? Forget him? How could I forget his scent of outside air, citrus, and man? The way his soft lips harden slightly as they capture mine? And when his tongue touches my lip, asking for permission before it invades my mouth, I can't help but melt against him and let him in. I should probably kick my own ass for forgetting him, but I'll do that later. I was busy.

His arms wind around me, one hand tangled in my mass of hair and one around my waist, and he's holding me so tight, I finally feel warm for the first time all day since he left. My hands find their way to his face, his beard so much softer than I expected it to be against my palms. Kyle's hands move to my hips, lifting me, adjusting me somehow so I'm straddling him, and I can't help the way my hips buck on their own against the thick ridge in his jeans.

Oh. *Oh, shit.*

The groan that comes from him hits me everywhere, and soon, I'm pulling at his shirt, yanking it off of him so my fingers can reach all of his golden skin. Somehow my shirt seems to rest at my waist and the heat of him against the bare skin of my breasts, against the now sensitive points of my nipples makes everything in me clench. I didn't know this is what I wanted, but I'm for damn sure taking it.

I direct my lips to his neck, nibbling the strip of sensitive skin just below his beard line. Fates, what is it about that line that drives me insane. If I had fangs, I'd sink them in right there just so I could taste him. My blunt teeth will just have to do because if I go another second without knowing what his skin tastes like I will lose my mind. As my teeth and tongue make contact, a feral growl rumbles from his chest and I squirm at the vibration of it.

I want.

I didn't think I could, didn't know my body required his touch, but now that I have it, I can't get enough. I want more. Twin points of sharpness meet my neck and the press of it drives me into a frenzy.

I ache.

He moves us and presses me into the mattress, his large body between my legs and the weight of him against me is everything. He moves, rasping his beard over my tender flesh, kissing down my neck to my breasts, pulling my nipples into his mouth and sucking them to ridged peaks. He nibbles at the underside of them and a flash of heat scorches its way through me.

I need.

His wide, rough hands run down my body, taking the thin camisole, my pajama pants, and underwear with them, and then I'm naked. I should feel cold or awkward, but I don't. I only feel the scorching heat of his gaze on my skin and his rough palms running back up my legs, gently spreading them so he can fit his big body in the space they just vacated as he kneels at the edge of the bed.

Kyle roughly tugs me closer and the power of him, the presence of his stark need, makes me squirm with want. Soft lips and the silky rough of his beard scratches against my skin as he kisses the hollow where my hip and thigh meet and then the wet heat of his tongue licks closer and closer to where I want him.

Tremors of anticipation hit me and he has to hold my hips still just so I don't vibrate myself off of the bed.

"How am I supposed to eat this sweet pussy if you won't sit still? Hmm?" he asks as his tongue takes a quick lick of my center, earning him a strangled moan.

"If you quit your squirming, I promise I'll make it so good for you, Shortcake," he rumbles, his low gravelly voice hitting me hard. My moan in response earns me another, longer, lick. My body feels like it is ready to combust. Goose bumps skate across my skin, but I feel like I am on fire. I feel restless and unembarrassed and nearly mindless, and he has barely even touched me.

"Just as sweet as I remembered," he murmurs against me and then he fulfills his promise to the letter. The rasp of his beard between my legs, kissing, licking, sucking my clit in between his mouth, devouring me until I can't recognize the sounds coming from my mouth or control what my body is doing.

My hands find their way into his hair, and I am pulling him closer and closer to me, grasping for something I can't name but need more than my next breath.

Pleasepleasepleaseplease.

"Oh, I'm going to give you what you want, Shortcake, but it's good you asked so nicely," he rumbles.

Then, his thick, blunted fingers spear into me and I am lost but I refuse to care because it feels just so fucking good.

"Ky!" I call out as I come, losing myself and my mind in the pleasure of it. I feel obliterated—completely wrecked but I don't want it to end. I want more. I want what's inside those jeans. I want the promise of that bulge. I want all of it.

Kyle grabs his discarded shirt and wipes his mouth and beard with it, cleaning up the mess I made all over his face. Why does that naughty thought just rile me up again?

When he tugs the top button of his jeans free, I'm back to squirming, but I don't stay that way. I move. Sitting up, I take over and rip his jeans open, and reaching in to take my prize.

Holy. Shit.

I underestimated what I was getting. I won the fucking cock lottery with Kyle. I can't measure exactly, but it doesn't really matter. This thing is going to split me in two and I'm going to love every single second of it.

Suddenly, I feel like we are moving too slowly. I want him on top of me, in me, moving with me. I want his sweat on my skin and his mouth on mine. Circling my fingers around him, I give him a single stroke. He gives me a little shudder of want, and I've never felt more powerful.

I did that.

"Fuck, baby," he groans and the feral growl that rips up his throat should make me fearful, but it doesn't. It does the exact opposite, and I reach up to his face and pull him down to my mouth, tasting his lips and my come on his tongue, and the mix of the two just drives my need higher.

One quick lick into his mouth, and I find myself flat on my back again with Kyle climbing up and over me. He fits himself between my legs, notching his cock at my opening and slowly pressing himself into me. I stretch around him, and the ache of it feels so fucking good. It isn't just his cock, it is the groan I pull from him, it's his heat against my body. It is the safety and the pleasure and the pull at my heart. It is the way he stills before planting his elbows in the bed, tangling his hands in my hair and scorching me with a kiss so full of promise, I clench around him—my arms, my pussy, my legs. All of me is pulling him into me wanting to absorb him, love him.

"Are you mine, Shortcake?" he asks me as he runs his lips over my neck, pulling more at my heart that he has to ask. Of course I am. Of course I'm his. I nod to answer, but it isn't what he wants.

"You have to say it. You have to say you're mine. I need to hear the words," he murmurs his plea as his eyes meet mine and he singes his way into my soul.

"I can't remember us and I love you anyway. I'm yours. I'll always be yours," I whisper back, reaching my neck up so my mouth can meet his, our tongues tangling in a delicate dance of promise.

Then we move together, burning each other up, climbing higher and higher. Our kiss breaks and his lips are back at my ear.

"You're mine and I'm yours, Shortcake. Forever," he whispers in my ear. "Say it, Nicola. Tell me."

I want to tell him I'm scared of what's coming. That I don't know what the future brings and I am so scared of what I can't remember. But I don't. I tell him the truth as I know it because in this moment, I know we can beat whatever comes at us.

His thrusts move faster and faster, our release barreling down on us.

"You're mine, Ky. Forever," I murmur on a moan.

When the twin points of his fangs slice into the place where my neck and shoulder meet, I only feel bliss.

19

KYLE—AFTER

IF I WERE TO VENTURE A GUESS, NICOLA ONLY KISSED ME TO shut me up. Other people might have been offended, but I'm not. I've been dying for those pale, rose lips for months.

My eyes latch onto the already healed double crescent scar my fangs left on her shoulder. It is the mark she should have had months ago, and the pride I feel at looking at it should send me into another frenzy of lovemaking, but Nicola is finally sleeping, and I don't want to wake her. Her body needs the rest because I have plans for it for the rest of our lives.

I refuse to sleep, though. I have to find out why my Shortcake was crying, stowed away up here when she had a whole house-full of family downstairs. Pulling on my discarded jeans and searching for a new shirt, I dress and make my way downstairs. The main floor is empty, but I know there is a training center downstairs in the basement.

Mena and Asher's house is the new hub for the Phoenixes. Mena and Aurelia have been teaching the Oracles to defend themselves in a fight as well as making sure the Soldiers are adequately trained. There was a mountain of messes for them to clean up after Iva was taken down. They let anyone who wanted to leave the Legion go without repercussions. They let the Seers choose their own fate, and they banned all ceremonies that included the forced blinding and eye removal of a Seer.

They are still working out the kinks, and Aurelia has still not chosen a Secondary, but they are making strides. I only know this because I've kept an ear to the ground. Plus, you'd be surprised how many people just flap their gums around me because they assume my silence means I'm not listening.

Oh, I am, cupcake. You better fucking believe it.

I open the steel reinforced door masquerading as oak. It matches all of the other doors in the house, but I know this specialty made door is fire-proof, has a bolt-action seal, and can withstand a battering ram, and probably a pound of C-4. I feel the warding of it. No one can get in if they weren't welcomed into the home first. The spell is delicate in its intricacies, but stronger than the steel reinforcing the oak. Whoever cast it is stronger than even I am, and while I'm not proud of my Witch heritage right now, I have to give credit where it is due. The faint crackle of green at the edges makes me think Max is the source of the magic, and I'm impressed.

Something tells me Max is stronger than I thought. *Good to know.*

The room beyond the magic is buzzing with conversation and activity. Ian and Aidan are sparring with bokkens at the center of the space. If Aidan is here, Evan must be as well, but I don't see her.

I do see West and Cam trading punches in the ring, and Asher and Carver in fencing outfits trading blows with shiny rapiers. I wince internally at the sight of Carver. So much had happened while I was gone that I didn't hear for a long time about Carver's husband, Javier. Javier had been a spy for the Emersons, holed up inside the King and Queen's own house, and his machinations had brought the deaths of John and Olivia even after Aurelia took him out. The bastard.

I peel my eyes from Carver to seek out Rhys. I find him having a discussion with Max and another, taller woman I haven't met yet. The unknown woman is gesturing wildly with her hands. I'm confused at her vehemence until I realize she is signing, and Rhys is translating for her to Max.

I owe my hide to almost every single person here, so it sucks that I have to bite the hand that fed me, but fucking hell. It is high time I settle some shit and air out the dirty laundry of familial fucking drama.

If I had to bet money, Rhys—and not Aurelia—is the one I'd have to talk to anyway. I remember how he reacted to her months ago before all of this shit started. If I hadn't gotten in between them, who knows what he would have done.

I travel the scant twenty yards, getting right in Rhys' space. Out of the corner of my eye, I see Max yank the woman out of the way. Towering over him, I let Rhys know just how pissed off I am by the low warning growl that rumbles through my chest.

"I want to know why I found my wife upstairs, alone, crying herself to sleep when I left her with family. Care to explain that to me?" I spit.

Rhys' face morphs from surprised to pissed in an instant.

"Wife? What the fuck, man? You bond her while she was out or what?" He sounds vaguely angry, but I don't have the time or inclination to deal with this topic again. I said my piece already and the story hasn't changed.

"I explained that shit to your wife already. I don't have to explain it to you. And that doesn't answer my fucking question. Why. Was. Nic. Crying?" My growl says I mean business and his face says he feels fucking guilty.

Jackpot on the first try.

"Why are you asking me? I'm not the only one in this house, you know," he evades.

"Oh, I don't know. Deductive fucking reasoning? Of all the people who I've seen interact with her, you've been the only one who has been overtly hostile. I ventured a fucking guess," I deadpan waiting for him to deny it.

"Fine. It was probably me, but you have no idea what Nicola did to us. You have no idea what kind of pain she caused," he counters, defensive.

"Says who? You think I didn't ask her after I watched you try and strike a blind woman? What are you, high? You think I don't know exactly what she did and why she did it? You think that wasn't my first fucking question?" I yell, pissed.

"And she just told you. When has Nicola Miller ever been

forthcoming with information?" he asks, and even though I can see his point, on this issue, he is in the wrong.

"Maybe when she thought she was going to die? Or when she knew she could trust me? Or when she knew I was her mate? Dealer's fucking choice, Rhys."

"So out with it, then. Tell me. Why did Nicola do this to us? Why did she put us through this? I can't get a fucking paper cut without hurting my wife, Kyle. Who would be that cruel?"

I hate that I have to do this. I wish Nic could remember all of the moves she had to make to keep Rhys and the rest of her family alive.

"It wasn't cruelty. It was the only way you and Aurelia would live. Every path she saw had her dying at Iva's hands, but when she tied her life to yours, she had to be careful, she had to stay out of certain battles that would have gotten her killed. It got her to run and hide, and it got you to protect her when you would have given up. Nicola used to be able to see a lot more than just death, Rhys. She used to be able to see so much more. And you can think Nic's an evil bitch all you want to, but she kept you and Aurelia alive. She kept Mena alive even when every single move she made was being watched, and every path she took could have killed you all and herself. You have no fucking clue. Nicola has been abandoned, used, hung out to dry, hated, and vilified all to keep her family alive. And you ungrateful little shit, can't even wrap your head around the fact that she may have done it for a fucking reason."

Rhys' expression is a mix of guilt, devastation, and rage, but his lips stay closed.

"Do you have any idea what she has gone through to keep you breathing? Who do you think nudged your brother into telling you his plan for Olivia when he was supposed to keep it a secret? Do you know how many steps she took just to get Evangeline born? To make sure Iva was destroyed? She sacrificed her body and her soul to make sure I lived. You and I both have no idea how many people she has saved along the way or how many she saved before they were ever born by taking out Iva. So if you can't be a decent fucking person to her, I need to know. Because I'm making sure she doesn't get treated like shit for the rest of her whole goddamn life. That's a fucking promise," I challenge.

A hand clamps down on my shoulder, and I look back to find the hand is attached to West. Aurelia, Mena, and Evangeline are right behind him. Mena is silently crying and semi-shoves West out of the way to wrap her arms around my middle.

"Thank you. I've been trying to tell them, but they didn't get it. Thanks for getting it," she murmurs before giving me a quick squeeze and letting me go.

The woman I don't know shoves two fingers into Rhys' chest and then starts signing, her chocolate brown eyes blazing fire. Furiously moving her hands and mouthing the words that don't seem to pass her lips. I can't read her lips, but I don't want to be on the receiving end of their ire.

"Samara, honey, stop. I get it. I'll do my best to stop being an asshole," Rhys replies to her flurry of movement, but isn't signing back. Either she can hear or her lip reading skills are unparalleled.

Samara gives him a scalding look and huffs as she turns from him to leave the room.

"What did she say?" Max asks.

"She said that Nicola saved her life, and if I didn't quit being an asshole she would figure out how to lift Aurelia's and my bond just so she could snap my neck," Rhys mutters as he rubs a hand down his face.

I can't stop the full belly laugh the bursts from me which starts a chain reaction because Ian is rolling on the ground holding his stomach laughing, Aidan is gasping for breath as he laughs himself sick, and even Rhys, who looks embarrassed as hell, is chuckling.

"Okay, I was an asshole. I'll tell her I'm sorry and try to avoid my dickhead ways in the future. We good?" he asks me.

"We're good, but if you make her cry again, I'm making you bleed and that's a fucking promise," I warn him.

"Duly noted."

20

NICOLA—AFTER

I STRODE TOWARD A DILAPIDATED WHITE MANSION, MY SHOES *kicking up tiny puffs of dust on the dirt drive. The Spanish moss hung from every single tree on the property as well as the wide portico. A blonde man waited for me there, leaning against one of the thick columns, calm as you please.*

His presence annoyed me, but I masked my irritation with a smile. He was so much easier to manipulate if he thought he was making me happy. Like I could be happy with a child. That was all Devereux Emerson was. He was less than that. He was a soulless tool I could wield at my leisure. If he fell, there were plenty more right behind him to do my bidding.

He really was only good for one thing, but even that was lackluster. I guess it was my fault for picking a soulless minion. When the coming battle was won, I would replace him with a newer model. Maybe someone with a little more heft to him.

Maybe Kyle would do, but I would have to work him over first. He was a bit too shiny, a bit too good for my taste.

"I have the perfect one for you, Mistress," Devereux crooned, and I fought rolling my eyes. Yes, he needed replacing post haste.

"Good. Show me your offering. It had better not be like the sad

specimen you found me in the Quarter. I'll not take another charlatan, Devereux."

"But Mistress..."

"I'll not take another one of your excuses, either. Now, show me what you have," I ordered, flicking my fingers to get him to move.

The last one was a child of a so-called Voodoo Queen. The Voodoo Queen herself had been a two-bit hack from New Jersey with a fake Cajun accent. Her child, however, had been the product of a drunken Mardi Gras night with a Warlock, and her teenage son had been powerful—but not nearly enough.

None of them had been thus far. None of them were what I needed— none have been able to sustain me for anything longer than a month.

Devereux led me to the tattered remnants of a once opulent sitting room. Flood waters had ruined most of the mansion but were especially unkind to this room. The hardwoods were bowed, the ceiling crumbling in some places, missing altogether in others, and the patterned wallpaper was falling off the walls. Honestly, could he not find a better place for this? It reeked of mildew and swamp and fear leaking from the child sitting bound in the middle of the room.

Sigils written in bone dust marked the circle around her, holding her stationary until I could arrive. How thoughtful. The girl could be no more than four, and by her scent, she was a wolf. If Devereux had to tether her to that spot with sigils, then she must be powerful. We would see how much.

She was such a little thing, tethering should be unnecessary. I was beginning to doubt his skills at scouting. It wasn't until I touched her did my faith in him come back. He had done well with this one.

Everything about the girl's past and future flashed through me. The girl's name was Mya. If her path had not crossed mine, she would have been an alpha, a pack leader—one of the first female alphas in three centuries. She would lead an uprising against the members of the Ethereal who oppressed the wolves, and she would bear children just as powerful as she. Her line would grow and prosper, and the wolves would be equals with the other shifters.

Such potential in such a little body. Yes. This would sustain me for more than a month. Maybe three. Her body stayed immobile while I looked her over. White-blonde hair, green eyes, and a dainty upturned nose. She would have been a beautiful girl and done important things.

Pity.

Devereux's voice started chanting then. A well-oiled machine of convenience, he was. Maybe I wouldn't get rid of him just yet. It would be so difficult to train a new one. It wasn't as easy to control the minds of others now that my power source had been stripped.

All those Aegis ashes gone to waste...

Devereux's voice broke through my musings, and I recognized the point in the spell where I would need to play my part.

"Vivifica me morti et artis. Det vobis spiritum meum, quod nutrit animam," I murmured the words as I watched her chest bow from the crumbling floor and the life drain from her eyes.

She still breathed, but her soul was mine now. The unease in my stomach that I was so good at hiding lessened some and I wasn't quite as hungry as I had been. Success.

"Do what you will with the girl, but I will need another before the week is up. Don't fail me, Devereux, or I'll have you replaced. Understand?"

I didn't really need a soul so soon, but better he have one ready than have him with me and have to endure his incessant pawing and fawning. I'd rather keep him busy.

"Y-yes, Mistress," Devereux's said, the frown on his face a sweet little pucker. I did so enjoy ruining his fun.

I removed myself from the dank-smelling room, turning from him, and heading back to the road and the waiting town car sitting on the street instead of the drive. I couldn't have the poor lad driving me scared out of his brain if he heard the chanting and spells. New Orleans or not, humans rarely liked it when they witnessed the Ethereal.

As my shoes hit the dirt drive once again, I picked up the faint scream of the girl as Devereux took his fill. Revenants were always doing nasty business, but good help is hard to come by.

The young chap saw me coming and hustled to open my door for me, his mocha skin paling slightly when a last gurgling scream from the girl rent through the air.

"W-what was that?" he asked.

"No idea. Maybe an animal of some sort?" I offered, sliding into the leather seat.

"Yeah. You're right," the driver murmured, but I heard the disbelief in his tone as he tugged at the collar of his chauffeur uniform.

Oh, bother. I was going to have to dispose of this driver, too. Well, only after he got me to where I was going.

"Where to, Miss?" *he asked once he'd shut my door and settled himself into the driver's seat.*

"The airport will do, thank you."

<hr>

MY EYES FLASH OPEN TO A NEARLY PITCH-BLACK ROOM, THE only light coming from the open blinds and the faint shine of moonlight filtering through the pane. Sweat slicks my skin, and my hands won't stop shaking as they yank the covers away from my naked legs. Despite the sweat, I feel chilled to the bone. That wasn't a vision, it was a memory. From before I woke up in Knoxville. It had to be. There wasn't another way to explain it. It wasn't a dream—it felt too real. And that child...

Mya. Her name was Mya.

Oh, God. I stole her soul. I left her to that man. Oh, God. She's dead —I know it—and it's my fault.

Gorge rises in my throat, and I bolt to the bathroom, emptying the meager contents of my stomach into the toilet. My hands clutch the cold porcelain, and I try to block them out but the thoughts that come refuse to be denied.

Mya was a wolf. She was why the wolves wanted me. Why they came for me. They didn't want Kyle. They wanted me. I was right before. It was my fault.

Did he know? Did Kyle know what I'd done? Did the rest of them?

They couldn't know. No one would harbor someone like me. No one good, anyway, and Kyle was good. I knew it deep in my soul that the man I loved wasn't evil or wrong. There was no way he knew what I really was.

My mind snags on something I said. *I will need another before the week is up.*

Oh, God. Oh, no. Nonononononononononono...

How many? How many children did I kill? How many souls did I steal? The tears that come do nothing to wash away the stain on my soul. I am tainted, worse than garbage. I am evil—or at least I was.

Kyle didn't deserve someone like me. He didn't deserve someone who stole life—there was no redeeming my actions. None.

My brain screams at me, hurling insults I don't want to accept. *Killer. Murderer. Thief. Murderer. Murderer. Murderer!*

I shouldn't have woken up in that hospital. I shouldn't be breathing. Not after that. Not after what I've done.

I don't deserve to live.

Steeling my spine, I pick myself up off the floor, wash out my mouth, and go to the dresser where my clothes have been meticulously organized, butting right next to his. I pull one of his shirts from the stack and breath it in before putting it back on top. I dress in the warmest clothes I can find and leave the rest. I won't need them where I'm going.

I find a paper and pen on top of the dresser and write a quick note, leaving it on the bed. Then I pull on a pair of thick socks and pick up my boots, so no one will hear me when I leave the house. With my hand on the door, I look back to the white square of paper resting on his pillow.

I wish I wouldn't have woken up. I wish I wouldn't have given myself over to Kyle or kissed him or hugged him. I wish my taint weren't all over his skin. He deserved better.

I hope he finds it when I'm gone.

21

KYLE—AFTER

BY THE TIME RHYS AND I IRONED OUT OUR SHIT AND HAD A light sparring session, I'd been gone from Nicola for at least two hours, if not more. Staying down here wasn't a choice I made lightly, but if I thought she was doing anything but sleeping, I would've been upstairs in a heartbeat. I hated being away from her, so I made my excuses and headed for the door. I missed her skin and her sleepy smile, and I needed to taste her lips a few million more times before I would be sated.

I was just glad they didn't hate her. Of all the people I would expect to actually loathe Nicola, Aurelia was one of her more vocal supporters. She had first-hand experience of Iva digging around in her brain and sympathized more than anyone. It was good so many were on her side. We'd need their help down the line if the wolf shit started heating up.

As soon as I cross Max's ward, a heavy pit forms in my stomach. All I feel is agony—in my gut, my heart, my head. My gut clenches and my heart feels ripped in two. Something is wrong.

I don't wait to travel from the basement hallway to our room. But she isn't there. I flip on the lights and check the bathroom. Fuck I even check under the damn bed and the closet, but it's empty. My gut is telling me she isn't even in a fifty-mile radius of this house and when my eye catches on a white slip of paper on my pillow I fight the urge to rip this whole fucking house apart.

With trembling fingers, I reach for the paper, not wanting it to be what I already know it is.

> KYLE,
> YOU DESERVE SO MUCH BETTER THAN TO BE LOVED BY SOMEONE LIKE ME. I'VE GONE TO RIGHT MY WRONGS. DON'T LOOK FOR ME. I'M GOING WHERE YOU CANNOT FOLLOW.
> NICOLA

It takes five full minutes for her words to sink in and when they do, my fist closes around the paper, crushing it into a little ball. I tuck it away in my pocket before I lose it completely. In a rage, I rip the lamp from the bedside table and throw it across the room. The bed is next, and the mattress gets flipped into the next wall. The dresser meets my wrath, as well as the walls and curtains. But the chair gets the worst of it when I rip the plush fabric and upholstery in half with my bare hands. A roar breaks from my chest as I fling the pieces hard enough to embed the wooden frame into the wall.

She left. She fucking left me.

KYLE—BEFORE

I didn't put much thought into coming here. All I knew was I had to say goodbye before there was nothing left to her. A part of me envied humans. When their loved ones died, there was a monument to them— there were remains. There was something tangible on this earth to hold onto. When a member of the Ethereal died, all we had were ashes— fragile things that could be blown away by a stiff breeze.

I had to say goodbye before there was no more to her—that was my only thought. I didn't think about my safety or Evangeline's plan of attack or the outcome.

For once, I was selfish. It was what I needed. Not anyone else. I was probably fucking things up, but I didn't really care. I needed this before I died.

My boots crunched in the pine needles as I walked from the tree line toward the two-story, coastal Maine house. I knew I wasn't alone in these woods, but it didn't matter.

None of it did.

When my first boot made contact with the porch steps, the front door whipped open. Standing in the doorway was my Shortcake.

Or what was left of her.

The hair was the same, the curls fanned away from her face in a fiery red mane. Her body was the same, but everything else was different. Her beautiful blue eyes had muddied to amber. The set of her shoulders and the cock to her hip. That wasn't her. That wasn't my Nicola.

Seeing it again killed me—it felt worse than walking through that forest of dead children, worse than watching Devereux's hands on her skin. Worse than losing her the first time. Because I was only getting to say goodbye to her shell. I wouldn't hear her laugh or listen to her hilarious British curses or watch her play the violin. I wouldn't get to kiss her or tell her goodbye.

Nicola—the woman I loved more than my own soul—was gone.

Iva was talking to me, saying something about how she knew I would come, but I ignored her words and thought my final goodbyes.

The first blow seemed to come from nowhere. One second I was on the porch, staring at the body of the woman I loved, and the next punches and kicks rained down on me. I didn't realize at first that they were coming from her or just how strong Iva was. It made sense. With each new soul, she got stronger, with each life she took, she absorbed a little more power.

I didn't fight back. Not when she picked me up by my shirtfront and threw me across the room, or when she drug me by my hair back to the starting point and started all over again.

I should have protected her better, I should have made sure I listened to her when she tried to warn me. Iva was standing there because I failed Nicola, and I accepted my beating for that reason alone.

I felt my lips split and bones break, felt my skin bruise and all the while I never made an attempt to fight back. I didn't come here for that.

But for every second I didn't strike back, Iva lost her cool. Her rage climbed higher and higher.

"What? Did Nicola take your balls when she took your heart, Kyle?" she taunted as she circled me, the heels of her shoes clicking on the hardwood floor.

She didn't realize she was giving me what I wanted, so I kept my mouth shut and gave her a bloody smile.

KYLE—AFTER

I sink to my knees, my eyes scanning the destruction of the room, my brain silent. I can't think. Why would she leave—that is the real question. She had a reason—*I've gone to right my wrongs.*

Where would she go?

I need a direction, Shortcake. Please just give me that.

"Kyle?" Evangeline's voice filters in from the doorway behind me. "Wh-what happened? Where is Nicola?"

"She's gone," I murmur.

What I don't say is I'll find her. And I have an idea where she's gone. As my gut tells me to head southeast, my idea gains wings. I know where she went.

I'm headed to New Orleans.

22

NICOLA—AFTER

STEALING A CAR WAS EASIER THAN I THOUGHT IT WOULD BE. Getting the hang of driving it, however, is a challenge. I found the shiny car keys on the entryway table of Mena's home and snagged them as I walked out of the door. I wasn't sure what part of my brain was running this show, but some autonomous part of me was supplying information.

Put on your boots once you're outside. It will be quieter. See that shiny emblem with the horse on it? Pick those up.

Pressing the tiny unlock button, lights flashed in the driveway. Even in the darkness, the car shone, but the front end was illuminated by the porch lights, and I decided the color was somewhere between red and wine with a flat black double stripe down the center of the hood, roof and back end. It looks mean and beautiful, and I can't help but recognize the color. Max's car was the exact same one. If I were going to ride out to my death, I picked a good car to do it in. I did a quick circle around it, a single finger brushing over the word 'Mustang' before dropping into the driver seat and figuring out the ignition.

Kyle said I was one hundred percent blind before, so it was doubtful I'd ever driven. Even in that single memory, I'd had a driver. But I could see in that memory. It didn't make any sense...

It didn't matter if it made sense or not. I know what I did—there wasn't an excuse or reason I could accept. I had to do this.

A part of me—the part that was selfish and needy—wanted to stop. She wanted to stay here with Kyle. She wanted to forget what she saw in that memory or at least tell Kyle first. She wanted to know if he would still love her. I knew he would not, and even if he did, I didn't deserve to be loved by him. I didn't deserve his warm smile or the rasp from his beard on my cheek when he kissed me.

I didn't earn that kind of love.

My eyes snag on a bright red ignition button, but when I press it, it does nothing. *Press the brake with your foot, then press it again*, the other part of me supplies. The engine roars to life, and I let that part of me that knows where she is going and what to do lead the way. That part of me adjusts the seat and mirrors, throws the car into drive and rockets her way south, leaving me to trail behind her wallowing in my own self-pity.

I hit a speed bump once I cross the New Mexico border. One, I didn't have any money and the gas gauge was reading less than half a tank. Two, it felt like an icepick was digging a significant hole in my brain. I needed to pull off the road before my brain melted and I wrecked the car. And three, I had the distinct impression I was about to have a vision. The part of my brain that knew more than I did told me I would have a tougher time driving it when I was blinded by a vision.

I see an exit coming up boasting lodging so I take it even though I probably won't find money for a motel room anywhere in the car. If all else fails, I can at least park somewhere before I can't see anymore. The motel advertised on the sign is nothing more than a single story row of rooms with a flickering sign and an empty parking lot. I feel unsafe and conspicuous, like I'm just asking to be robbed and stabbed.

I don't have the luxury of finding a safer spot because as soon as I throw the car into park, a vision hits me like a slap.

AN ELDERLY WOMAN STOOD AT HER KITCHEN WINDOW WASHING A sink full of dishes. Beyond the window was her garden and beyond that was a tiny motel.

The white of her hair stood out against the weathered, paper thin skin of her cheek. Her eyes told of thousands of laughs and smiles. Hundreds of thousands of hugs and kissed boo boos, her gnarled but strong hands spoke of countless cooked meals and full bellies. Arthritis was setting in on her wrists, and she could feel snow coming soon. Fall was edging into winter and her garden's flowers were all but spent. It didn't matter anyway because as she got on in years, there was no one to take care of them. It was hard to cultivate the delicate flowers in the desert landscape, but she did her best.

Her family's motel on the other hand, was much too tiresome. The sign was broken, the town had fallen to disrepair, and even being just off the main highway, few people ever stayed longer than the few hours it took to rest up before they were on the road again. Even those guests were few and far between.

The woman shrugged and pondered if she should sell. A developer has been through about a week back and she still had his card. Her and her husband could move to Arizona or Florida or maybe they should move to Texas to be closer to their children and grand babies. She would think on this some more and make a decision before the week was out.

The woman finished washing that last pot in the sink, rinsing it and setting it in the drainer before heading to bed. Her husband had already gone to bed complaining of a stomach ache. The glutton ate too much of her chili is what it really was. He was always putting too many onions on it, too. The old man would never learn, but it was one of the many things she loved about him.

She dressed in a long nightgown, unpinned her curls, kissed her husband's sleeping cheek, and settled into bed. She fell asleep with a smile on her face, thinking of a move to see her grand babies, and seeing them grow into their own people.

Her breaths slowed farther and farther, and then they stopped altogether.

She didn't wake up.

<hr>

OH, THAT JUST SUCKS, IS MY FIRST THOUGHT ONCE I FEEL BACK to myself again. My eyesight hasn't quite returned yet, and I am one hundred percent positive I have blood tears running down my face. I recognize the motel in my vision as the one I'm sitting outside, and I don't know how I feel about that. The icepick in my brain is gone, which is a plus, but now I have a call hitting me square in the chest to go to her —to help her move on.

This plan is less than ideal. I'm ill equipped, not knowing exactly how I'm supposed to send her anywhere let alone on to be reborn, not to mention I only have so much time before Kyle will get my note. I don't know exactly how he found Max and me outside of Knoxville, but I'm willing to bet his Tracker vocation has something to do with it.

Still, the pull of her soul yanks on my limbs, and I climb from the low-slung seat. Skirting the main building, my low-heeled boots crunch through the underbrush as I walk carefully toward the little white house at the back of the property. The pull of the soul guides me around the back to the bedroom window. It is a cute little house with chrysanthemums in the painted window boxes and a wraparound porch, perfect for an elderly couple. I could imagine a grandmother sitting on this porch, grandkids swarming her legs, and for some reason that makes me sadder because I know I won't have that. I won't have children with Kyle. Or grandchildren. I won't get to see him smile or make him laugh. I won't get to do any of that if I continue to do what I'm doing.

I don't want to take her soul. It makes me feel complicit in her death somehow. Like my presence called her to it rather than it happening naturally. But the soul wants to leave and so do I.

The phase rips through me without thought. Fire skates over my skin as a strange tearing sensation rips at my back.

Oh, this hurts. This hurts!

My hands fly to my mouth, muffling the scream that bubbles up from my throat. I hear a distinct rip, and a huge weight hangs from my back.

I have wings. I have fucking wings!

Craning my neck, I try to get a glimpse of them—brilliant orange feathers with dusky black tips. They are so pretty.

I snap back to myself and my purpose here. It isn't to look at my pretty feathers. It is to help a soul. I'm not exactly sure how I am supposed to do it, but I will give it my best shot. The woman I saw was a good woman, and she deserved her rest.

I move closer to the window, trying not to touch the wood of the house, so I don't set it on fire. A piece of me—some intrinsic part of me starts speaking in a language I don't know.

"*Libertatem concede tibi ita regenerationis ultra valeamus,*" I whisper into the blackness of the desert night.

But I know the words. I know what they mean. *I grant you the freedom of rebirth so one day we may meet again.*

It is a prayer. A... funeral rite and a part of me knows it better than I know my own name. This is my purpose, and as I watch trails of light stream from the woman's chest I feel at peace. Her body is still, and her husband will wake up to a loss, but her soul is at peace.

It is then I decide I can't continue on this path. I can't go without talking to Kyle. I did a shitty thing by leaving him. Again. He may not deserve me, but he at least deserves to know why I left, and my vague note probably told him less than nothing.

My fire dies as quickly as it came, the uncomfortable and altogether unpleasant feeling of my wings going back to wherever the hell they came from washes through me, but I make my way back to the car.

My shirt is toast, I feel a little queasy from hunger, but I know I need to go back. I'll talk to Kyle. We'll work it out. Maybe he could explain what happened. Was I spelled into killing that girl? It didn't feel like myself. It felt vile and dark and evil, and I couldn't just throw myself literally to the wolves for something I didn't understand.

Kyle would explain what happened and we would go from there. Nodding, I reach for the door to the car feeling less like I was walking into a death sentence and more like I was making progress.

I hear a shuffle of feet drawing my eyes up to the empty parking lot. Chills skate down my spine and I scan the lot to see what made that sound. When a ball of red sails over the roof of the car and hits me square in the chest, I'm surprised.

Shit, I think as I fall to my back on the dirty asphalt, and my light goes out.

23

KYLE—AFTER

I FLINCH WHEN EVANGELINE'S HAND TOUCHES ME. I LEFT HER to trail after me as I made my way back down here from the room I tore to pieces upstairs. I've been stuffing weapons from the training room into a duffle bag for the last five minutes and ignoring her completely for the last ten. I have a plan—sort of—and I know where I'm going... Maybe. This is the shit I have been worried about since the first time I was able to wheel my ass into her room. Fucking repercussions. Fucking Iva.

Fuck, fuck, motherfucking fuck!

Hadn't we been through enough? I had two weeks with her before everything fell apart. Two weeks before I endured over a month of torture. Then, I had five and a half months of searching for her fucking puppeteer, four months plus a few weeks of her in a coma, and one single night with her back in my arms before I lost her all over again. Seriously? Could we catch a goddamn break already?

It isn't until Evan pinches me on the underside of my arm do I quit overstuffing the duffle.

"What?" I growl, pissed off I have to stop what I'm doing. Hell, I'm pissed off anyway, but this just sprinkles a little bit of extra lighter fluid on top of an already blazing inferno.

"Where are you going, what are you doing, and if you talk to me like that again, I'm going to have your balls as a fucking necklace. Remember who you are talking to, Kyle."

If she weren't a woman, my Queen, and a friend...

"Pardon me, my liege. I have to go stop my wife before she gets herself killed, oh and fun fact, get me killed as well. She's headed southeast—toward the wolves. You know, the wolves that just tried to kill her? I'm sorry if I can't give you more information than that, but it seems my wife was a little lackadaisical with the fucking details. I've got my bond, a shitty ass goodbye note to work with here and fuck all else," I rant turning back to my weapons.

Nicola must have remembered something. I didn't know how I knew she was going to New Orleans, I just did. Sure there were a fuckton of factions in between there and here, but a lot of them didn't make sense. The wolves did.

"You have family here. People who can kinda see the future, a Wraith or two and a Witch with an attitude—total compliment BTW—it isn't like you need to go off to war alone, big man," she replies, ignoring my attitude altogether.

"Where were they? Huh? How did she get out of the house? How did she make it so far away from me that I only have a fucking direction and a sense of dread? Goddamn it!" I roar, tossing the weapons bag onto the floor of the training center.

Max and that damn ward. She's too powerful. She didn't just ward for threats—that working held back bond ties, visions, everything. No one is supposed to be that fucking strong. And she was able to take it down without a single problem.

Wards are complicated magic—they take massive amounts of power to bring up and take down, and she just snapped her fingers and boom. No ward. What the fucking fuck?

"I'm sorry, okay!" Max pipes in from across the room. "I had to make it strong to keep Wraiths from being able to travel in. How was I supposed to know it was going to turn into a magical fucking dead zone?"

"Maybe if you learned from an elder or consulted with another

Witch instead of figuring shit out as you go, you wouldn't fuck something like this up!"

"Well, it isn't like you practice anymore, so it looks like I'm shit out of luck," she fires back before taking a deep breath and pinching the bridge of her nose. "Look, I know you're pissed, but attacking me isn't going to help."

She's right. I haven't practiced since I realized Iva had Witch help. I didn't want to associate with that part of myself. I could be helping Max develop her abilities—from what I gathered, she had been ostracized from her family and had no one to turn to about stuff like this. My comment was dickish in the extreme. Plus, I should have noticed the ward was wrong as soon as I crossed it. It was as much my fault as hers for making it.

"You're right. I'm sorry I was a dick," I apologize, feeling like an asshole. I remember not having a coven to go to for help. It sucks.

"Yeah, well, you've got a reason. If you didn't I would have handed Evan the knife to cut off your balls," she shrugs.

"She took my fucking car!" Ian thunders from the door, his voice booming through the training center like a bomb.

"Your wife took my Mustang, Kyle. Do you know how long it has been since I've gotten a new car? Nineteen eighty motherfucking five, Kyle, and she took my brand fucking new Mustang. I've driven that woman around more times than I could count when she was blind. I know her ass doesn't know how to drive. I swear to everything holy, if there is one goddamn scratch on it, I am taking it out of your hide!"

Max stifles a snicker, and his eyes cut to her, scorching fire.

"It's not funny, *Maxima*," he zings, knowing Max goes by her nickname for a reason. At the utterance of her given name, her face sobers.

"Don't taunt me, *niñito*. I'm older, stronger, and I can snap my fingers and turn your infantile ass to dust," Max threatens, the tip of her finger sparking green magic as she points to him in her ire.

It's funny as hell, but I don't have time to deal with this shit or the obvious shit storm that is brewing between these two. I just hope Nic and I are far, far away when these two explode.

If you can get to her before she does something stupid, you mean, a snotty little voice inside my head snarks.

"Look, this is amusing and all, but I have bigger problems than whatever sexual tension you two are working with. Now, I'm leaving. If you're coming, come the fuck on. I'm running out of time."

I reach down and grab the duffle but stop short when West forms right between me and the door.

"Sorry, brother, but there is no way I'm letting you do this alone. The last time you went off on your own, you damn near got yourself killed."

"Got you killed, you mean," I mumble.

"No. I don't. That battle was coming long before you tossed your hat in, man. I don't blame you for one bit of it. I don't blame Nicola either. The both of you have gotten a raw deal. I just want to make sure everyone comes home safe," West explains, his hands raised in a placating gesture.

"Whatever, man. But we have to go now-ish. If you're coming, let's go. Nic's in pain, and I don't have the time to wait for you."

"Do you know where you're going?" Aurelia asks from behind West. When she and Rhys came in the room, I have no idea.

"Southeast. I'm thinking NOLA, and my gut says wolves. I can't explain why. It's just the worst kill I saw was a wolf girl. It was the most brutal—the most savage. I can see repercussions from that one coming faster than the others. Plus, we already had a wolf problem. It just makes sense to me."

She takes a moment to ponder my answer, but I don't have time for this.

"I'm hopping to her instead of driving, so if you want to come, find someone who can travel and let's go."

"I'm in," Mena says grabbing Asher's hand. "But you're staying here," she orders, pointing to Aurelia and Rhys.

"What?" Aurelia screeches.

"Chain of command, pumpkin pie. Both of us can't be in the shit, and you have babies. You can take the next one, though. Deal?"

"This is bullshit. But fine," Aurelia grumbles.

"We're in," Evan murmurs, which means West, Cam, and Aidan are in too.

"You'll probably need a medic and a sniper, but someone needs to give me a lift," Ian says exasperatedly.

"Aww. Come on, bro. You know you want to hit something. What's more fun than shifter fights?" Aidan cajoles.

Shifter fights? What. The. Fuck? Sometimes the brothers scare the shit out of me.

Ian just gives his brother a baleful glance.

"Shifter fights? I'm in. Those fuckers made me demolish my baby. I rebuilt her from the frame out, and now I have to start all over again, the fuckers. Who brings the cars into it? That's just mean," Max throws her hat in.

"I'm staying. Nothing against you and your lady, Ky, but the last time these two were left unsupervised, they gave us all a heart attack," Carver explains as he gestures to Aurelia and Rhys.

"Fine. Let's go, and stay close," I order.

Traveling without a set destination in mind is hard, and in a group this size, damn near impossible. But hopping from one location to another with a direction in mind makes it easier. Well, it's faster than driving, at least. I keep close to Interstate 25, traveling twenty miles at a time, stopping to feel Nicola's direction and starting all over again. Our only break was to stop to let Max puke, so she didn't soil Cam with her dinner.

We got close to the Colorado-New Mexico border before I couldn't go any farther. Nicola's heart rate sped and then... *nothing.*

I felt nothing. Not her emotions, not her heart in my chest, not her presence. Nothing.

"Fuck! I lost her!" I roar, my feet crunching in the rocks and desert brush in the mountain pass close to the border.

"What do mean you lost her?" West asks, bewildered.

"There's nothing. I can't feel her. What does that mean?" I ask, panic setting in. This hasn't happened to him. He's never lost Evangeline even before they bonded.

"I don't know," West whispers his reply.

"I'm going to New Orleans. Now," I murmur before smoking out from the mountain pass and arriving at the outskirts of the city.

If I can't find her, I'm going to someone who will.

Or else.

24

KYLE—AFTER

THE LOT OF US ARRIVE IN ONE OF THE SEVERAL SWAMPLAND wildlife refuges around Lake Pontchartrain, well outside the New Orleans city limits. This refuge is located on an inlet between Lake Pontchartrain and Lake Borgne, and the land seems to dwindle beneath our feet as marshland encroaches on the solid ground. How people live here, I don't know, but I wouldn't hate on their lifestyle. It wasn't my place to judge.

What I would hate on was their desire for my wife's head.

We walk at a sedate pace into what appears to be a packed campground. I knew it wasn't what it looks to be in the least. This wasn't transitory residences or people on a camping vacation. This was a pack.

In my scouting of Iva's practices, I came across one of several dens of wolves in and around New Orleans. Some had been hastily abandoned —the stench of death lingering in the soil where unlucky ones met their ends—but this one regularly had occupants. Some wolves lived in secret in the Quarter—hell, all over the country—but the majority of surviving wolves lived in packs either here near the swamps or in the Appalachians far away from the majority of the population.

Tents, campers, and a few RV's were positioned in a wide circle around a rather large bonfire. Some were pup tents, some were newer, ten-man Coleman ones. The RV's were old—at least a decade or two past new—but they seemed to be kept-up and in good repair. Several people—men, women, children—surrounded the fire on log benches. They were talking, joking, shooting the shit. No one was keeping watch, no security. This told me more about these people than anything. They didn't fear the outside world or they didn't expect people to actually come here. The land might be protected somehow, but it didn't keep us out, so I doubted it.

This wasn't exactly my best plan, but I knew who I needed to talk to and I knew I had enough backup to level the whole damn state if need be. With the amount of families, I didn't want to start anything that would get innocent people killed or hurt. I smelled no evil here, all I smelled was wolf.

Just as we are about to breach the circle, I'm elbowed out of the way by Max. I try to yank her back, but she snaps her fingers and my fingertips burn when I touch her. Shit. Max is a wildcard in every single sense of the word.

"Excuse me!" Max yells getting everyone's attention.

The yelling wasn't necessary. Max commands attention with the blue hair pinned up in what I'm gathering is her signature victory rolls, the tattoos which cover nearly all of her available skin, the Rockabilly clothes, and the obvious signature of power written all over her. A wave of tension hits me, and I feel the hairs on my arms stand on end. She got their attention all right.

"Hi everybody! My name is Max, and I have a grievance to share with your Alpha. May I speak with him, please?" she says sweetly. I've known her for approximately three seconds and even I know her sweet voice is not a good thing.

A stout man with dark hair, graying at his temples rises from his spot on one of the logs surrounding the fire, meeting us at the break between a twenty-year-old RV and a derelict camper. His eyes are an odd bottle green, and they flick to each of us, studying each person before settling back on Max.

"Hello, Max. My name is Scott. I'm the leader here. How can I help you?" His voice is soft and his manner is polite. Although he senses the aggression coming from us and the double scoop of crazy coming from Max, he doesn't engage. Interesting.

"A pair of wolves used my fully restored Chevelle as a bumper car. I would like to know why," Max says calmly.

Scott's mouth quirks for a moment as he crosses his arms.

"Was this incident just outside of Knoxville?" he asks, his voice full of mirth.

"Got it in one," she replies, crossing her arms to match him.

"Well, Max, those wolves weren't a part of our pack. They were cast out about a year ago for deciding to become a Witch's lapdog doing mercenary tasks for money. We don't allow that sort around here," Scott says stonily.

"Fascinating. If they were cast out, who gave them orders? And why was a pack surrounding the hospital, Scott?" Max counters.

"Those two are among the Nameless. We don't speak of the ones we cast out. We sure as hell don't give them orders. Especially since you and I both know those two boys are dead as a doornail. What I want to know is where is Nicola? Why isn't she with you?"

"How do you know Nicola?" Max asks just as I break in with, "You don't have her?"

"Where is my wife, Scott? She was headed here before I lost her. I know someone took her. I want to know where my fucking wife is. Now," I growl, the phase overtaking me before I can blink. My fangs break free, elongating my jaw. My talons erupt from my fingers.

My phase triggers a chain reaction. The men, women and children who were so benignly sitting around the campfire are not so benign now. Men and women jump to their wolf forms, children scurry away, toddlers and babies carried away by older children. Snarls and snaps of teeth reverberate through the open space.

"I don't mean anyone any harm unless they've hurt her. I just. Want. My. Wife," I growl, trying to calm my voice and avoid an all-out brawl.

"No one here would have hurt Nicola Miller. We owe her our lives. She's kept Iva from exterminating our pack altogether."

Do they not know? I don't want to be the one to tell them but if they don't know I'd rather explain now.

"But... Iva killed a wolf child. She..." I trail off.

"Was wearing Nicola's skin?" Scott finishes my sentence. "Yeah. We know. The benefit of being a wolf is we can smell the difference. We know it wasn't her. Hell, we even moved in to protect her in Knoxville before we realized ya'll were friendlies."

"That pack was you guys? You were there to help her?" Evangeline throws in.

"Yeah, we got there a little late. You two slipped out while one of our younger pups was keeping watch. He didn't recognize you and said you did something to disguise her face. It didn't help ya'll were downwind," Scott explains.

"Whoops. My bad," Max murmurs earning a guttural growl from me.

"So if you don't have Nicola and you wanted to protect her, who the fuck has her?" I mutter to myself.

"I hate to point this out, but I'd venture a guess that Witches have her, don't they?" Cam asks from behind me, and we all—myself included—turn to look at the usually antagonistic man.

"You said the men who attacked Max and Nicola were Witch's lapdogs. You said they were mercenaries. They were probably under Witch orders. Witches were the ones to kick you guys out of the hospital. Witches helped Iva. Witches attacked Aurelia and Rhys. Duh, guys. I'm not that smart and I put it together," Cam says shrugging.

But if Witches have her, how do we get her back?

"Do you want me to try and locate her? I'm pretty sure I can't fuck that up," Max offers shrugging sheepishly.

The horrible part of all this is, Max hasn't really done anything wrong. She disguised her so the wolves couldn't discern her identity. She did exactly what she was supposed to do. How was she supposed to know they were friendlies? And some of them weren't friendly at all.

"Fine. If you can find her where the bond cannot, by all means, go ahead."

"Gimme a second and I can try to get a bead on her. Do you have anything of hers?"

"No, but I'm bonded to her. I'm hers. Will that be enough?" I reply.

"Maybe," she murmurs as she grabs my hand, closes her eyes and begins murmuring in Latin. Her words are ones I've uttered more times than I can count. *"Inveniam quod quaero. Ostende mihi,"* she murmurs on loop, the grip of her hand cutting off the blood supply to my own.

Find me what I seek. Reveal it to me.

When Max's eyes open again I know she has the same result I did when I searched our bond over and over again.

Nothing.

25

NICOLA—AFTER

I FEEL MY BODY LONG BEFORE I CAN ACTUALLY OPEN MY EYES. As it were, my body is slung over a shoulder, blood is rushing to my head, and for as little as I know, I am damn certain I have a concussion. This is proved when my body is slung off of the shoulder and onto the hard ground because I cannot hold in the moan of pain as the landing jars my whole body.

Clutching my head, I desperately try not to vomit as I hear a woman chuckling in the background. When a boot plants itself into my ribs with enough force to knock me into a wall, my moan turns into a scream. I'm pretty sure I heard a rib snap.

"Wakey, wakey!" a shrill woman's voice calls.

Bitch, I'm already awake, I think as I force my heavy lids open. What the hell did I get hit with? A spell?

My eyes try to focus, but either the spell still is affecting me or the concussion is. When I can finally see one room instead of two, I try to inspect my surroundings. The motel room is less than five-star, more like a shabby shithole. A double bed sits right across from me with a tattered bright orange coverlet. The carpet smells like old shoes, mildew and dirt with a side of magic—which to me is reminiscent of ozone and melted pennies—thrown in. The walls are a dirty taupe color are littered with scratches, dents, and other unidentifiable stains.

A blonde woman kneels down to study me. She is beautiful in an odd, off-putting sort of way. Her features are too sharp, her cheekbones could cut glass, and although her eyes are a stunning ice blue, they have a coldness to them that scares the shit out of me.

"Oh, goodie. You're awake," she deadpans as she grabs the front of my ripped sweater and yanks me up from the floor, passing me off to someone else.

It is only then that I realize she has a man with her, and I can tell by his build he's probably the one who kicked me in the ribs. He's blonde, his eyes and features match the woman's as well. They have to be related. The man is only a slightly smaller build than Kyle.

Oh, God. Kyle.

My thoughts turn to my husband. Why did I leave him? Why did I do that without talking to him? Why was I so stupid?

"Put her in a chair and tie her up," the woman orders, the bored tone of her voice sending chills through me.

"What do you want? What did I ever do to you?" I ask on a whisper, struggling against the hands holding me. A quick whisper and my struggles die, my body falling like a rag doll in his arms.

"Gag her while you're at it, will you, Baron?" she mutters as she turns from us to stare at a timeworn book. It is thick with a leather binding and yellowed pages. He whispers again, and it is like a switch has been flipped, and my voice has been turned off.

The man, Baron, wraps my wrists with thin but chafing ropes, tying me tightly to a wooden armchair. He pulls my boots and socks off and lifts my pant legs, wrapping the rope around the skin of my ankles. Methodically making sure when I can move again, I won't want to.

Making sure if I struggle, I will bleed.

"Now, you've never done a single thing to me. But your family? They've hurt mine. Aurelia Constantine in particular, burned our mother alive. I'd consider cutting her directly, but I don't need Aurelia. I do, however, need you. You are going to help me."

Aurelia burned someone alive? That seems... extreme.

I wonder what her mother did to make Aurelia do that. She doesn't seem to be someone who kills without thought. And what the hell can I possibly help this crazy woman with? I'm betting whatever it is, I don't want to do it.

"I see by the confusion on your face, you have no idea what you really are. You aren't just a Phoenix; you aren't just an Oracle. You're a piece of the Veil. You stand on both sides of life and death. Death calls to you. Death can be molded by you, and souls can be resurrected through you. And that part of it is useful to me." I'm going to bring my mother back, Nicola. And you're going to help."

What the hell is she talking about? A part of me wonders if she's crazy, while the other part knows she is but also knows she isn't lying.

"My name is Bella, by the way. You and I are going to become great friends," she says, and another flash of red hits me in the chest.

Lights out. Again.

NICOLA—CUTLER, MAINE 2016

It was dark here, stuffed inside this hole inside my subconscious. I knew what I was getting into when I said yes, knew the consequences of my actions. I knew Iva would be wearing my flesh. What I didn't know was how strong she was. How easily I could be molded into the little hole I found myself in, how easily I could be gagged and tossed aside, rotting away inside my own head.

Iva's had her fun for months. Killing people with my hands, stealing souls of children, letting that filthy, soulless monster touch my skin. I haven't been awake for all of it, but some of it...

It would be a blessing to forget.

I think she enjoys my pain, my revulsion. It is a feather in her cap to finally bring me down. The insurgent she couldn't find—the one she least expected—not after I bonded Rhys to Aurelia, anyway. She never knew all the things I did to thwart her, and hiding in this little hole inside my brain, she won't. She won't find the people I've hidden away or the steps I took to bring us here.

She won't find out until it is too late.

When Kyle comes calling, though, I almost lose my hold on this one piece of refuge. She relished beating him, but when she realized he wouldn't fight back, wouldn't hit my face or body even though it wasn't me running it, she became enraged.

Iva beat him with my fists, broke bones with them, drew blood with them. And all the while he never once defended himself.

She threw him away, tossing him back to the few people who could help him—who could help me. West was kind enough to reach out a hand and help him up. Kyle barely made it to his feet and struggled to even take a breath.

"Please, Nic. Please make it back to us. Please," Kyle rasped.

"And why would she do that when I am here now? Nicola Miller was a poor blind girl who never did anything but try and scheme her way around me. Now that I'm here, there is no need for her to wonder. She is powerless. There is only me now," she said with my mouth, and I wished at that moment I could kill her. That I could help in some way to bring her down.

I could. I could fight back. I could scream and writhe and break free. I'd kept in the hole to keep my secrets—to keep the secrets of so many who couldn't help themselves.

But the cavalry was here now. I didn't need to stay hidden. I didn't need to stay quiet in this little slice of hell. I feel Iva's smile droop on my face.

That's right, bitch. You'll be getting it from all sides, now.

I screamed, I writhed. I scratched at the walls of my mind, but it wasn't until Kyle took the blade meant for Evangeline did I feel the first crack in my prison.

Seeing his blood run, seeing the knife in his belly, changed something in this prison. It let the light in, untethered the bonds around my wrists and ankles.

It let me out, and the scream that ripped from my lungs was, for once, my own. They wanted Kyle to go to a hospital. I did too, but I needed to say goodbye to him first.

I wasn't coming back from this, but he could. He would.

"Get him to a fucking hospital!" Evangeline screamed rushing to intercept me as I tried to get to Kyle. She slashed with her rapier, gouging my skin with the razor sharp blade, but it doesn't stop me. It won't stop me from going to him.

"No! No, don't keep me back from him. Please! Kyle! Please!" I begged, and the look on her face changed from steely determination to unfettered sorrow.

"I'll let you take her soul. I'll hold her back, just please let me say goodbye to him," I pleaded, my eyes flooded with desperate tears, and she let me go.

I scrambled past her, making it to his side faster than I could blink.

Blink... Seeing his face with these new eyes, I realized how beautiful he was, how strong. It didn't matter that his left eye was swollen nearly shut or his lips were split. It didn't matter a single bit because he was mine and I would get this one moment to say goodbye to him. I grabbed his bloodstained cheeks and whispered in his ear.

"I love you. I will always love you. In the next life, in the one after that, on and on until forever. Don't you forget it," I ordered him.

Ian desperately tries to staunch the flow of blood pouring from Kyle's stomach, and I realize I'm hurting him by keeping him here. I moved to let him go, but Kyle's eyes drifted open, and grabs my wrists, holding me to the spot.

"Lo-love you, Nic. See you on the other side," Kyle murmured before his eyes rolled back in his head, and he lost consciousness.

"Noooooooo!" I howl, but Aidan snatched him from me in a swath of black smoke.

Then, I lost my hold on the walls of my prison, and the gates crashed back down on me, stomping me back into my hole.

NICOLA—AFTER

I feel like I've been thrown off a cliff, rolled in acid and then stabbed with the business end of a hot poker. Holy shit, whatever knock-out juice Bella is packing, I want no part of it.

My eyes stay closed partly because if I open them, I may puke, and also to try and assess my situation. By the scent, I'm still in the shitty motel, but something tells me there is another person in the room.

I'm proved right when Bella and another woman begin to argue. I'm only half listening as I mentally check my body. I'm still tied to the chair, but whatever spell Baron hit me with has been lifted.

"I told you and your idiot brothers to fetch her for me. Did you deliver? No. I told you and your idiot brothers not to hurt her. Did you obey me? No. And then you ran off to save your own hide, and you expect payment? No," Bella scolds, her tone scathing.

"I told you what happened. I told you exactly where she would be after I tracked her back to Colorado and followed her down here. I can't control what my brothers did, and the morons got themselves killed. I didn't wreck her car and stab her in the stomach. I stayed on the periphery and assessed the situation while Idiot One and Two made other plans. There was no way I could capture her by myself, so I called you. She still got captured. I deserve at the very least half of the bounty."

This pings in my mind. In my vision, there were three wolves.

Not two.

Three.

She was the third. She was the other wolf. The one who had her maw in Kyle's gut. The bitch.

My eyes flash open, and I assess the two women arguing over payment. I recognize Bella's platinum blonde hair and pale skin, but the other woman I don't know at all. Plus, she's not exactly a woman. She can't be more than fifteen at a push—messy brown hair pulled into a haphazard bun, dirty black skinny jeans, sneakers, and a wearing an odd assortment of shirts. Her white thermal is layered under an open green flannel shirt, under a gray hoodie, all under a denim jacket. How many layers does this girl need? And then her accent registers. She's from the New Orleans pack.

"I would say she deserves at least two-thirds," I mutter and both their eyes swing to me. "I mean, come on. She did spy on me like a fucking creeper and had I not changed my course, her maw would have been in my husband's belly. That's what you meant to do, isn't it? You weren't going to let us go or bring us here. You planned on killing us," I accuse my eyes meeting the gray eyes of the girl's. "So you should give her two-thirds, at least. Give her enough money to run."

26

KYLE—AFTER

THE PACK HAS LEFT US TO OUR OWN DEVICES, GOING BACK TO their bonfire, leaving us newcomers to our problems, but there are still too many people in my space. Too many people comforting me when all the avenues to find Nicola haven't been exhausted. I know they haven't. Even if some of them are things I swore I'd never do again.

"We'll find her," Mena insists as she turns to Asher so he can call Aurelia. Mena still hasn't managed to get around her aversion to electronics—or shall I say, they haven't gotten over their aversion to her. Ash steps away to make the call, and I meet West's eyes. His expression tells me he thinks the worst.

But she can't be dead. I would be too. That is the way the bond works. Right?

"Stop looking at me like that. She's not dead," I growl. I want to get in his face. Fuck, I want to punch him or anything else that will relieve this gnawing ache of fear.

"I don't think she's dead, Ky. I think whatever mojo has the bond blocked might keep Aurelia from finding her. It might keep us all from finding her," he murmurs consolingly.

Might keep me from finding her, he means. But fuck that. Fuck his consolation, fuck his doubt.

"So that means I'm just supposed to give up now? How many years did you follow Evan? How many years did Rhys follow Aurelia? What makes you think I am any different than you? I'll find Nicola. Even if I have to rip this world apart to do it. You got me?" I growl, and if my eyes turn black or my talons grow, well I really don't fucking care.

At this point, I don't give a shit if he's my friend. I don't care if he's my King. No one is keeping me from Nicola.

No one.

But I'm going to have to do the one thing I promised myself I wouldn't do. I'll have to cast a spell. I swore I wouldn't use my magic after the Witches dishonored me—after they broke my ward, bombarded my house and took me from my Nicola. I swore I would never use that part of myself again, but to find Nicola, I would break any promise, deny any oath.

Even to myself.

"Max, we'll have to try together. I'll have to do the working with you. Together... we might be able to reach her," I concede.

Max gives me an appraising look. I think she understands why I have been avoiding that half of myself, why I would choose to deny the part of me that resembles so many dead, so many lost to darkness, so many who have turned into monsters. Finally, she nods.

"Okay," Max murmurs.

"If I add my juice to it, will it help or hurt you? I can't send souls on with a ward working, so I don't know if it will fuck you guys up," Mena offers as she makes it back to our loose circle.

"It can't hurt. If it doesn't work, we'll try it without you," Max answers.

When Mena slips her hand in one of mine and Max the other, the sheer power from both of these women hits me like a sledgehammer.

"*Inveniam quod quaero. Ostende mihi,*" Max begins and I follow, murmuring the words over and over again until they cease to make sense. Nothing happens until Mena grabs for Max's hand, completing the circuit of power between the three of us. It feels as if a barrier has been lifted. Whatever working they had over Nicola has crumbled to dust. With more acuity than ever before, I have found her.

I can see her in my mind's eye. I can feel her. Her heart beats once again in my chest, her breaths fill my lungs, and the torn, jagged piece of my soul where she had been torn out is healed. I feel almost whole again.

Nicola's tied to a chair in a shitty no-tell motel room. There is dried blood crusted around her nose, but her face is fierce with unspent retribution. I want to rip apart whoever made her bleed. I want to tear them apart with my bare hands.

"I know where she is. I can find her," I murmur, my voice clogged with relief and tinged with rage.

"Where we headed?" Evan pipes in.

"New Mexico."

I'm coming, Shortcake. Sit tight.

Faster than I thought possible, we make it to the outskirts of a property in Raton, New Mexico, a mere twenty miles from where I lost her.

But we have an enormous fucking problem. Sure we know where Nicola is, but getting to her is going to be an issue. Scanning the motel's property, I see about thirty witches in the biggest Witch's circle I have ever seen.

Their focus?

The room where my wife is.

NICOLA—AFTER

Bella's smile is feral. I can tell my words have pissed her right the fuck off, and I couldn't give two shits. She can think I'm trapped all she wants to, but she forgets this whole place is flammable.

And I'm not.

"It won't matter one way or the other what I give Talia or what she's done to you. You won't be here. You won't have a say. You won't be you," Bella informs me, smiling.

"What the fuck are you on about?" I ask to give myself a little more time. I'm not strong enough to phase yet. Whatever mojo the devil twins cooked up hasn't left me completely.

"Did no one tell you what my mother was executed for?" she sneers. "She helped Devereux put Iva inside you, silly. Iva wore you like a party dress, too. Killing children up and down the coasts and everywhere in between. There's blood under your fingernails, sweetheart," Bella says through gritted teeth.

Talia's head swings to appraise Bella, her face one of outrage as bile rises in my throat and the room begins to spin. Does that mean I didn't kill that wolf and Iva did? Does it even matter that it was her inside me if my hands were the ones that killed her? Questions run on loop inside my brain as I struggle not to vomit or hyperventilate. She wants to put her mother inside me.

She wants me to be a puppet.

Before I can scream, before I can cry, before I can say anything at all, she is murmuring in a language I don't know—Latin if I had a guess. Her words run together as her eyes burn red before they close. Magic coats her hands, staining them with crimson light, but no matter how many times she says the words—nothing happens.

Her red eyes flash open, her words are silenced as she rushes me knocking Talia out of the way. She rips at my already torn clothes, searching my skin.

"Where is it? I'll fucking burn it off. There is a mark or sigil keeping me out. Someone protected you. Where the fuck is it?" she screams in my face as she grabs my chin in a bruising grip. Then, her eyes flick to the space where my shoulder and neck meet. She stares at the spot for a moment before her eyes fly wide, and a howling scream erupts from her mouth, piercing my eardrums, making my head swim.

"No! No, no, no!" she screeches as she grabs the armrests of my chair and flings it and me along with it across the room.

She is going to kill me. She can't use me, so she's going to kill me.

Fire explodes across my skin, burning my bonds in seconds. Talia and Bella advance on me as I try to scramble out of the remnants of the now burning chair. Talia jumps from her human form, her body flashing from human to mist to the thin, rangy wolf I saw in my vision just a few days ago. But she doesn't do what I expect—which is to rip me to shreds. No, instead she throws her body into Bella knocking her sideways as a blast of red magic shoots from her fingers, missing me by inches.

Bella turns her focus onto Talia, aiming her magic at her instead of me. A wave of red slams into the teenager, slamming the wolf into the wall before she fades back into her human form, coughing and sputtering up blood. Bella raises her hands again to hit Talia while she's down.

I move to intervene, but I'm so focused on the women in front of me that I've forgotten I haven't seen Baron since I woke up. Well, I forgot until I feel a blade at my throat.

"You're not the only one who is fireproof, darlin'. Now, put out those flames, or I'll slit your pretty little throat," he whispers in my ear.

"Bella! Stop fucking around. We have bigger problems, sister," he orders.

"What?" Bella screeches but turns from the unconscious Talia, the magic dying on her fingertips.

"We're surrounded. The coven came for us, Bell. We've gotta go."

Somehow, I don't think this is good news for me.

27

As a child, my grandmama took me once to a coven meeting. I was nine at the time—much too young for such a thing—but she wanted me to see my heritage. She wanted me to see that I had a large family of welcoming people who would embrace me.

Grandmama kept me on the periphery of the circle and told me to watch as they worked a healing spell on a pregnant human from the next town. The human knew her baby was sick, and begged the coven to help. She offered payment, anything, but the coven would not take a single coin. The coven would never take money for healing. Not ever.

Grandmama said they were good people, and they healed the woman as they held hands and danced around in the moonlight. Celebrating life—no matter the species.

There is no dancing here tonight. No healing. This coven does not want to help us or anyone else but themselves. There was a time I believed otherwise.

I shrug off the weapons bag, unzipping it and fishing out what I need. Had I known I would be dealing with Witches, I would have prepared differently. Turning to West, I pass him a short sword and he gives me a look that tells me all I need to know. He heads left as I go right, drifting closer to the circle. Aidan, Evan, and Cam follow him, and Max and Ian follow me—the eight of us moving equidistantly around the green-tinged circle of Witches. I see a place where I can break the working—in between an older and younger woman but as I move to strike, I'm frozen to the spot.

I fight the spell, fight with all I have in me, but all I am able to do is turn my eyes to Max.

"Don't. That's my mother—my family," she orders, her voice hard. I feel the disbelief and betrayal on my face.

Reading me in an instant, she gives me a withering look.

"I didn't know they were here. I froze them, too. I'm seeing what's going on before people get killed. Don't you dare make me feel bad for that," Max replies to my silent censure with gritted teeth.

Max steps carefully close to the circle without crossing it—if she were to cross it in the middle of a working, she could not only kill herself, but everyone else connected to and inside the circle. Smart girl.

"Mama, what are you doing here?" Max asks the older woman. Now that I am really looking at her, I realize I should have recognized the resemblance.

When she doesn't get a response, she rolls her eyes and then taps her mother's forehead with two fingers, more than likely giving her mother the autonomy of her own mouth.

"Maxima Christina Alcado, if you were still in the coven, I would have you sent to the counsel for this. How dare you interrupt a work—" her mother's words break off when Max taps her forehead again—freezing her mouth.

Max turns to the younger woman instead, tapping her forehead to get an answer.

"Talk, Maria," she orders the younger woman.

"Bella and Baron are in there. They want to bring Tessa back. We're stopping them," she says succinctly.

"Bring her back? How?"

"How did they bring Iva back? Nicola is a piece of the veil. They are going to try to use her again. We're. Stopping. Them," Maria replies snottily as if Max is stupid.

The way Maria says it, I don't think she's talking about fuzzy bunnies and fucking lollipops.

"But... Nicola's in there. A working this size, could kill whoever is in the center of it. Not just Bella, not just Baron. It could kill Nicola, too. Phoenix or no, she might not be able to survive it. What are you doing?" Max argues.

"I did not decide," is all Maria replies with, her eyes downcast.

This tells me all I need to know. They don't plan on saving Nicola. They are stopping Bella and Baron without any regard to my wife's life. They would rather destroy Nicola along with these awful people than figure out a way to get her out safely.

Now, I need to figure out how to break this working without killing anyone, pissing off a coven full of kill-happy witches, or letting Baron and Bella go.

Tall order.

NICOLA—AFTER

Baron still has a knife to my throat when Bella's shrill scream of frustration breaks from her lips. She begins pacing the short thoroughfare between the far wall and the double bed.

"Now, I'm not sure if you remember this, but you and I have met before. You were a bit blinder then, though," Baron whispers in my ear when Bella turns her back to us.

I don't know if this statement is supposed to make me feel at ease with him or has the intended and successful purpose of creeping me the fuck out.

"I don't know you," I say through gritted teeth. Part of me doesn't want to piss him off because he still has a knife to my throat. The other part of me wants to tell him to fuck off.

"Oh, you will," he murmurs and then lowers the knife, skirting around me to join his sister. The knife's blade is an odd orangey-pink color, and looks to be made of some sort of crystal.

Morganite, my brain supplies. Kyle said something about it. What did he say? *'The only thing that can kill you is a Morganite blade or an Aegis.'*
Oh shit.

Bella's pacing back and forth next to the inert Talia, and every time she passes her, Bella looks like she's contemplating kicking the young wolf.

I look behind me, irritated there are no back exits to this stupid room. To my left is a tiny bathroom with a narrow window over the shower inset that seems more for show than an actual exit. I could potentially burn the room down, but I have a few problems with that plan of action. One, Baron seems to be fireproof. I have no idea how or why, but that is an issue. Two, Talia just tried to save my ass. Burning her alive would be a full-scale dick move.

"They won't do a working with all of us in here, right? I mean they wouldn't kill her, would they?" Bella asks her brother as she gnaws on her thumbnail. I assume they are referring to me, but hell, Talia could be important. Maybe.

"Bell, I don't think they give a shit one way or the other as long as our mother doesn't come back. You know the coven. Not that I blame them. Killing children is frowned upon," he says as he sidles me with a sidelong glance.

"Well, I'm not dying in a shitty motel room in the middle of nowhere New Mexico, that's for damn certain," Bella replies and shoots past him, snatching the blade from his fingers as she goes.

"It's time to see how well they like hostage situations," Bella says smiling, the business end of the knife pointing right at my face.

KYLE—AFTER

There are times where you feel as if you have been staying still. Times where the past seems to always bite you in the ass. Times where history repeats itself over and over again. But seeing a knife to Nicola's throat, I finally understand why she would go through anything to save the people she loves.

Because watching someone you love hurt, watching them in danger, is the worst sort of torture. It limits your options down to one thing: sacrifice. I would do anything to trade places with her. When three people emerge from the hotel room, we are all still frozen. The working of the circle has stalled as two women and a man walk out into the parking lot.

Nicola comes out first, and the first thing I notice is how her sweater is ripped, dipping off one shoulder exposing the bonding mark and a fair amount of her pale flesh. The second, is the orangey-pink hue of a

Morganite blade against the delicate skin of her neck held by a hand of a woman I can only assume is Bella.

Rage ignites inside of me—a flash fire over my skin and I fight against the hold of Max's freezing spell. Then, I don't have to fight against it anymore because Max has released me. She has released everyone.

Everything seems to go in slow motion. Nicola's face morphs from surprise at the number of people around her to elation when she spots me. Then swift, steely determination passes over her features and I know what she'll do before she does it.

Nicola's phase washes over her, fire blazing over her skin so fast that no one is prepared for it. Nicola brings her burning hands up and clutches Bella's knife arm, ripping the blade away while Bella screams in agony.

But she's not watching her back and the man is reaching for Bella, reaching for Nicola, heedless of her flames.

"Max! Break the circle!" Mena screams, her phase already upon her. Blue flames licking up her arms and legs, the glint of a katana in her hand.

Max isn't fast enough for Evan's liking because one second the Witches are standing, the working stalled but still in play, and the next, every Witch has flown back ten feet and is firmly planted on their ass.

The working dissolves in an instant, and instead of the man staying and fighting, he grabs the injured Bella and the pair of them disappear in a ball of red light.

I rush to Nicola, her flames dying the second she spots me, and then she is in my arms again.

"Holy shit, Shortcake. Holy shit," I murmur into her hair.

"I'm sorry. I'm so sorry," Nicola sobs. "I shouldn't have left. I should have asked you what happened."

"What..." I begin, but I'm cut off by a woman's scream.

"What have you done?" Max's mother screeches. "You let them get away! They'll just try this again until they bring her back! Goddammit!"

"But... Bella couldn't work the spell. She was going to but she said something was blocking her. And she freaked out when she saw this mark on my shoulder," Nicola replies as she points to her bonding mark.

Max's mother stops short eyeing the crescent scar with surprise.

"The bonding mark?" she asks incredulously. "You're telling me that little scar kept her from using your powers?"

"It isn't that much of a stretch," Mena supplies from behind her. Mena's phase is still upon her and it takes me less than a second to realize she thinks the threat is still upon us.

"The bonding mark ties two people body and soul, Teresa. She cannot be used in this way again, so the threat of Tessa is gone. It's time for you to go," Evangeline orders from beside Mena.

West appears behind us, Aidan and Cam at his side. Asher, Ian and Max of all people moving in front of us, creating a circle of their own around Nicola and I. They are protecting us from the Witches, making sure we're safe.

"You would choose them over us, Maxima? How can you be so cold?" Teresa asks her daughter.

Max's hard exterior cracks for a moment as the hurt slips past her guard, but she manages to bring the wall back up before she speaks again.

"You kicked me out of the coven because I was too strong, mama. You made me live a lonely, abandoned existence with no family whatsoever. Why wouldn't I choose people who have cared for me and sheltered me? It's more than you've done," Max replies.

The rage on Teresa's face heralds the green magic sparking on her fingertips.

"Teresa, this is not a war you want," Mena warns, "We are on your side when it comes to bringing Tessa back. We do not want that either, but if you do what my sister says you are contemplating, I will make sure you and anyone who thinks the execution of an innocent woman is just fucking dandy face the full retribution of both the Phoenix faction and the Wraith." Mena's words strike a chord with Teresa because her magic dies and she takes a full step back from us closer to her coven.

"Nicola is blood, a part of both factions. So, the question you need to ask yourself is: do you value your life? Do you value your coven's life?" Evangeline snarls. "We don't want war. But hurting Nicola will start one. Do you understand me?"

Teresa nods, saying nothing to Evan as she calls for her sisters to depart—the lot of them huddling together before disappearing in in a huge ball of green light.

That's not disconcerting or anything.

"Now that the danger is over, where the fuck is my car?" Ian's voice breaks through the fog of lingering adrenaline and I can't help but chuckle.

"Grand theft auto, Shortcake? I like your style," I murmur in Nicola's ear.

"I aim to please."

EPILOGUE

NICOLA—AFTER

"This is where we started, Shortcake," Kyle murmurs in my ear as we touch down on the soft bed of pine needles outside a gorgeous gray-green cabin with a cherry stained wrap around porch.

The metal roof gleams in spots where the sun filters through the trees. The cold almost-winter wind whips through the trees, and for the first time in weeks, I feel like I can breathe.

A week after our brush with the coven, Mena and Evan were sent a missive from Teresa stating in no uncertain terms should Kyle or I ever go looking for Baron or Bella. As far as I knew, the Witch situation was tense at best, and with Max on 'our' side, best was solidly in our rearview.

Bella and Baron were the last people I wanted to find. No offense to the Witches, but I was lucky to escape from them with my head still attached.

How dumb could I be? I choose life, thank you very much.

In the aftermath, we did find Ian's car. It didn't have a scratch on it, but he was still pissed I took it. He softened only marginally when I gave him a hug and a kiss on the cheek, but I didn't foresee any joyrides in my future.

Kyle and I went back to the motel to look for Talia. I wanted to thank her—to get her some medical attention or at least get her a shower and a good meal. But when we went back to the room to help her, she was long gone.

We tried to stay at Mena and Asher's house, but with everyone there and the tension under that roof from the Witch threat looming over us, Kyle felt it was better for us to break out on our own. I agreed, feeling that I drew way too much bad stuff my way with everything that had happened. We did wait to leave until after he told me a heavily redacted version of what Iva did in my body. I felt violated and half insane and the tensions of brewing unrest only made it worse.

Kyle took me away from there and brought me here to his house in the heavily wooded foothills of the Appalachians. We walk hand in hand toward a single story, ranch-style cabin.

As soon as a single toe touches the first wooden porch step, I'm hit with what I can only assume is a memory.

"YOU'RE NOT ALL WRAITH, ARE YOU?" I MURMURED TO MYSELF.

"Nope," he answered as he moved away from me, opened the fridge, grabbed a bottle and popped the top.

A wall descended at his blunt answer. It wasn't a slight. Only a marvel. I had always hated the 'stay within your own kind' rhetoric.

We were just people. We loved who we loved.

"So loquacious. Sore subject?" I asked.

"It isn't something I talk about. My mother was a Witch. My father was a Wraith. They were bonded, and she died when I was a boy, taking my father with her when she went. I lived with my grandmama—my mama's mother—until I was old enough to be on my own."

"I bet your grandmother taught you everything there was to know about spells, didn't she?" I asked, imagining a naughty Kyle casting workings.

"She taught me enough to be dangerous—more to myself than to anyone else," he said as he plunked his beer on the counter. And then he was in my space, swiveling the barstool he so carefully placed me one so he stood between my legs.

"You don't care, do you?" he asked as he cupped my chin in his rough palm.

His question pissed me off.

Why would I care? Because Iva did? Because of my station? He didn't realize I had been slighted my whole life because of my blindness. Put in another category, labeled as 'other' when women in my own faction blinded themselves on purpose.

But I'm other.

Hypocrites.

"Of course not! No one can decide the circumstances of their birth. Blaming someone for their lineage is... is... utter bullshit," I spat, tripping over the audible curse word.

His lips found mine then, and I was lost.

"You kissed me for the first time while I was sitting at a barstool in your kitchen," I murmur, frozen to the spot as I wrap my brain around the fact that I'm remembering my time before—before my body was stolen.

Tears hit my eyes as that memory washes away a bit of the filth that seems to stain me.

"Yeah, Shortcake. Do you want to come inside? You might be able to remember more," Kyle murmurs as he wraps me up in his warm arms.

"Yes. I think I do," I answer him and he sets me back on my feet, grabbing my hand and leading me inside our home.

SIGHT KISSED

PHOENIX RISING BOOK FIVE

ANNIE ANDERSON

PROLOGUE

MAMA WAS CRYING. NO. SHE WAS WAILING.

Great sobs of agony ripped up her throat as she buried her face into what was left of my papa's chest, only then were they muffled by the soft fabric of his shirt. I couldn't see her with my eyes—those were useless anyhow—but I knew exactly what she was doing.

I'd seen her do it all before when I saw my father's death using an ability I wished I'd never been blessed with. I didn't want to see so many of the images that had screamed across my mind's eye. I didn't want my only sight to be the worst horrors in a person's life. I didn't want the only color in my world to be the stain of death.

But especially, I didn't want to see this.

I saw his death as I had for so many others, but unlike those strangers, I knew it was my father. I knew he was a part of me—even though I had never seen his face before in my life. I saw his raven black hair shining in the sun. I saw the beautiful orange wings flutter in the wind as he swooped and soared over the inky blue ocean, the white caps to the waves signaling a coming storm. The inky black of his eyelashes resting on his bronze cheeks. The way his face sought the last lingering light of the setting sun, the way it warmed his face.

Then, the horrible gray mist that seemed to have come from nowhere, plucking the skin from his bones and turned the voice I'd only heard as a quiet rumble of kind words into the worst howling to ever tear at my ears.

And I had to hear it twice. Once in my mind and then again when I was too slow and too stupid to explain what was coming.

But I hadn't understood.

How could a mist of fog move so fast or with such purpose? How could it strip the flesh from his bones?

"Why, Samuel? Why did you do this? How could you leave us?" my mother's wailed words registered in my mind.

But it wasn't Father's fault! I wanted to scream at her, but I knew, as with so many of the left behind, she wouldn't listen to me.

It didn't matter, and it wouldn't change anything.

Father was gone, and we remained.

"Nicola!" Mama's voice broke through my pain, and I gave her my attention.

"Yes, Mama," I whispered through my tears, heaving breath after breath through my chest by force of will alone.

"W-we must send him on to the Otherside. You will say the words with me this time. We will do it together, okay darling? Do you remember the words?" she asked.

Oh, I remembered.

As a family, it was what we did. We moved from village to village, from town to town. Always moving, never staying anywhere until we found this place where I could stay. A place where no one lived, a place where my visions wouldn't draw attention. Even at a young age, I understood how hard it would be to blend in with humans. My family stayed on the edge of humanity.

"Ye-yes Mama. I remember, but... I don't want to do this. Don't make me send him away," I said, losing my fight with my tears. The growing hole in my chest grew wider, deeper with the agony of this loss.

Father was the only one who understood me—knew what I could see and why it was so difficult.

I gripped his fingers tight, my tum roiling at the feeling of his once strong hands reduced to brittle sticks of bone and congealing blood. My digits were sticky with it, but I didn't want to wash the last pieces of my father off my skin.

My mother began the rites, but I couldn't bring myself to say them with her.

I thought them, though, the words that I should remember, the words that would cross my lips until I took my last breath on this earth: *libertatem concede tibi ita regenerationis ultra valeamus.*

I grant you the freedom of rebirth so one day we may meet again.

The brittle bones I held in my hand crumbled and turned to ash— sifting through my fingers faster than I could hold on. The last piece of him I had, swept away on the winds of the coming storm. I hoped, wherever he went, he was at peace.

I knew my peace was long gone.

I

NICOLA

*MY BRAND NEW EYES FLASHED OPEN. IT HAD BEEN SO LONG SINCE
I had eyes, or a body for that matter. I'd been stuck in the middle—not
heaven, not hell—simply a gray formless void where voices called, but I
could not come. Where I did enough calling of my own, but only one
person heard me.*

*Only one person came to my aid, because he'd been there in that misty
gray place once himself.*

*I'd repay him, in time, but first I had to gain my bearings. This body
was smaller than I was used to. My limbs felt fragile and delicate, but I
knew their former owner very well. To say this turn of events made me
practically giddy was a vast understatement.*

*Nicola deserved this. She practically put me here herself with all her
double dealings. You'd think the little wretch would count her lucky stars. I
plucked her from veritable squalor and all I get for my trouble was
machinations and backstabbing.*

Served her right.

*My new eyes scanned the circular chamber, falling first on the pale
blond hair of my rescuer. Devereux Emerson wanted only one thing from
me—a deal with the devil, so to speak—and he would pledge his life in*

exchange for it. What he didn't know was I would have done it for free, but I wouldn't be who I was today if I wasted an opportunity.

"Iva? Is it you?" Devereux murmured reverently while clutching a double-edged Morganite knife in a loose grip. I could understand his caution; this form of Necromancy was forbidden for a reason.

Sometimes you don't exactly get who you asked for.

"It took you long enough," I chided as he helped me to sitting and I glanced around the room. It smelled of fear, blood, and death. Hundreds of men, women, and children had died in this room. I felt their power, and a large part of me thirsted for it—desired the cloying call of a soul that could sustain me.

"I suppose you'll be wanting your payment then?"

He didn't have to say, I already knew exactly what he wanted. The one and only thing Devereux desired was to watch his father die. Walter Emerson earned his son's wrath, and I was all too happy to settle my debt to him in this way.

"If you would be so kind, Mistress. I believe I have done everything asked of me," Devereux murmured as he found his knees.

Bowing already? I could get used to this level of reverence.

"We shall see if you have or have not. Are the children ready?" I asked. "I'm hungry and if you want your favor, you'll need to feed me."

"Y-yes, Mistress," he stumbled over his words, eager to mete out his justice.

I didn't care either way. I merely needed my meal. My stomach was clawing at me in hunger, and I was too new to this body to go without.

Quick as a hiccup, Devereux came back with a tasty morsel of an eight-year-old girl. She wouldn't be enough.

But she was a start.

NIGHTMARES WOULDN'T BE SO BAD IF THEY WERE FAKE.

If they were just made-up pictures in my head, I could deal with whatever my mind cooked up and move on. But I knew the horrors in my brain really happened, and when you know each nightmare is unearthing layer after layer of an evil that wore my skin like a fucking party dress, well... Sleep is no longer my friend. Sleep is currently my enemy.

And that's saying something.

I've been awake, laying here in the protective circle of Kyle's arms for at least twenty minutes trying to calm my heart down. Every single time I close my eyes, I see what Iva did in my skin. I see the lives she took, and it kills me.

I know if I move a single millimeter, Kyle will wake up and I can't handle the look he'll have on his face. I know exactly what it will be—the exhausted pull of his brow, the fear coiling behind his eyes, the firm press of his lips mashing together so he doesn't say the wrong thing. His voice will be calm and sweet, and it will cut at me worse than the dreams do.

I can't handle sweet when I feel so guilty. My hands did horrible things—my hands, my voice, my body—and dreaming about each life these hands took, makes me want to pull a Lady Macbeth and scrape my own skin off to get them clean. I find it funny that I know who Lady Macbeth is but I can't remember if I have a middle name or not. Like I can't remember all of the things she did in my skin, but I know she did them. And I know my hands won't come clean no matter what I do or how many lives I may have saved along the way.

Not that I can remember saving them.

The past is coming back to me in bits and pieces—never enough to complete the wide-open gaps in my brain or fill in the gaping holes in Kyle's redacted version of events. He tells me the good things. The things I can be proud of. But he never tells me how I hurt people—how I hurt my family—for my own ends.

But I know some of what happened. I know some of the worst sins on my soul weren't committed by Iva while she wore my skin.

They were mine alone.

"I know you're awake, Shortcake," Ky whispers in my ear, the rough tickle of his whiskers brushes the soft skin of my shoulder. "Were you planning on getting any sleep tonight or is sitting there stewing your primary objective?"

"How long have you been awake?" I answer his question with one of my own. I'm not sure if deflection is an innate or learned behavior for me, and at this very second, I hate I don't know this about myself.

I hate I'm deflecting at all.

"When you have a nightmare, darlin', you don't exactly sleep quiet. I was awake before you were," Kyle whispers, but I can hear the exhausted thread of worry in his voice, and it kills me.

We're here, in his violated sanctuary of a cabin—violated because of me, no less—because I can't deal with the guilt piled on my shoulders. It was supposed to be a break, a respite from my Phoenix family, but I'm worse here. I don't see the good things between us like I did when we first got here. I don't see the kisses and banter and touches anymore.

I only see glimpses of what Iva did.

"I'm sorry," I say automatically, gritting my teeth at the words I loathe passing my lips. It has been happening more and more often these days.

"You've got to stop saying sorry, Shortcake," Ky murmurs against my skin as he tightens the band of his arms. "You didn't do anything wrong."

But I did. I did several things wrong.

The self-loathing I'd been shoring up inside me for these last few weeks, bursts like a decrepit dam from my chest.

"I hate it when you say that. You and I both know there is a fuck of a lot to be sorry for," my voice cracks like a whip into the silence.

Suddenly, I lose Kyle's arms when he shoves up from the bed and tosses his legs over the side. Knifing up, he snatches his black boxer briefs and steps into them. His back to me, the tight line of his shoulders catches the light from the full moon filtering through the windows. His hands ball into fists, the knuckles turning white with the strain, and I hate I am the cause.

"I don't know what you see when you close your eyes, but I do know the woman I bound myself to."

His words make my heart sink. He loves the woman I was, not the woman I am. He loves a woman that might never come back.

"How could you? I don't even know the woman you bound yourself to. You couldn't possibly know three hundred years of bullshit," I volley back as I sit up, clutching the sheet to my chest.

Fighting naked. Son of a bitch. If I had to count the number of times I desired to be fighting naked, that number would be less than zero.

"I know every machination and plot, I know every single stain you think you could have on your soul, and every single one was for others. You have never done a fucking thing for yourself. You have never—not once—done a damn thing for personal gain. Not. Once. So please, tell me, how you could ever think Iva's actions, Iva's machinations, Iva's endgame were your fault," Kyle rumbles, his voice trembles with the fight to stay calm. He still hasn't turned to face me, and it pisses me off more than his words do.

"It's tough to take you seriously when you won't even look at me when you say it," I murmur as I stand, snatching the rumpled sheet to wrap around my body, but as hard as I yank, I can't get it off one corner.

I should have forgotten the sheet and paid attention to the coiled-tight, six-foot-seven behemoth in the room because suddenly, I get half-tackled, half-thrown back on the bed. My yelp of surprise quickly turns into an oomph now that I have said behemoth laying right on top of me, his normally chocolate-colored eyes are coal-black from pupil to sclera with either lust, rage, or a little bit of both.

I should be scared, but I'm not. I know Kyle won't hurt me. I hate pissing him off, though. The gentle scrape of his talons scratches against my scalp as his hands cradle my face, and I have a hard time being the snotty little shit I've been acting like for the last few weeks.

"Let me try this again," Kyle growls through his fangs, "I know you. I know exactly who my wife is. You play the violin better than I have ever heard in three centuries. You can't cook for shit. You snore like a fucking grizzly bear. You are the most self-sacrificing woman I have ever met, and I think I hate and love that the most. You are not responsible for Iva. You earned your absolution ten times over because she can't terrorize anyone ever again. So stop feeling sorry for yourself, because the Nicola I know doesn't have time for self-pity. Got it?"

I search his face through watery eyes for a moment, trying to get myself under control when a banging at our front door shocks the shit out of both of us. Kyle's body goes from vibrating with pissed-off energy to rock-solid in an instant. He whips off of me grabbing my hand to pull me to standing.

"I thought the property was warded again?" I ask on a fearful whisper, throwing on a bulky sweater over my braless chest and wriggle into skinnies.

No one should be knocking on our door. No one should even be able to see the fucking property. Kyle warded it against everyone. Hell, I don't even get a cell signal in this place. Kyle abandoned his Witch side at the start of our drama almost a year ago. He refused to use any kind of magic at all. He hated that part of himself. A part of me thinks he still might, but warding our home took priority over his ban on his Witch side.

"It was. I didn't feel anyone cross it," Ky replies as he buttons his jeans. "Can you see who it is?" he asks and I give him a look of bewilderment.

Does he expect me to get the door?

Then it dawns on me. He wants me to use the faulty power which doesn't seem to be back to anywhere close to full strength. Trust me, I've tried looking into the future—trying to see anything that could possibly happen. I've tried touching objects, chanting, meditation…

I see a whole lot of fuck all.

I give Kyle a look which expresses the depths of my skepticism before closing my eyes and pressing my mind outward. A needle of sharp agony blasts through my head and I see a flash of a face in my mind before my eyes snap open. I don't wait, I haul ass for the door, plowing into Kyle when he travels to intercept me, smoking out from our bedroom to the spot just before the front door.

"Who is it?" he says while he holds my hands away from the doorknob.

"Open the door, she's hurt!" I protest, wriggling out of his grasp and flipping the catch on the three deadbolts before ripping the door wide.

The tattered husk of a girl who is a bloody mess of rags on our front porch steals the breath from my lungs. She's propped up like a broken doll against a column, her head lolling to the side.

"Talia," I whisper, earning me a weak, watery smile from her before she passes out.

2

KYLE

THERE ARE FEW THINGS I LIKE LESS THAN MY WARD BEING crossed without my knowledge. Like, say, it being crossed by a fifteen-year-old werewolf who looks like she's been beaten within an inch of her life.

There's blood covering every single inch of her body. Her right eye is swollen shut, the left side of her mouth looks like someone has taken a knife to it Joker-style, and the skin of her chest is mottled in bruises and crusted blood. She's been worked over for a while, and even with preternatural healing, she looks like she's an inch away from death.

At this point, I don't really care if Talia started out on the wrong side of whatever fight is brewing between Bella, Baron, and my Nic—and make no mistake, there is a war coming. I feel it like the cold breath of a monster on the back of my neck.

Whoever the fuck would do this to a young girl—I don't give a shit if she's a werewolf or not—is worse than scum. My skin is hot and tight, a phase rippling through me without will. Never in my life have I ever let a child's abuse go unpunished. I won't this time either. Especially not this child—not when she helped my Nicola survive.

I don't understand the evil in people. Even though my life is predicated on the consumption of evil to survive, I cannot fathom why some are built to destroy this way. I've been in her same position, stranded on Asher and Mena's porch, barely alive. But Mena healed me then, and there is no one to heal her now.

"Help her," Nicola pleads, her hands fluttering above Talia's arms, afraid to touch her.

Nicola doesn't want to cause pain, but the near-freezing temperatures on our front porch are doing nothing for Talia's disposition. Neither of us can miss the tortured rattle of breath in Talia's chest—punctured lung, I'd bet. I pull Nic away from the broken girl and pick Talia up. It is then that it dawns on me how young she is because even in her unconscious state, a nearly inaudible whimper breaks from her lips.

"What do we do? Do we take her to the hospital?" Nicola asks, wringing her hands.

I'm not certain we'd be welcome at the one hospital that serves members of the Ethereal. Nicola and I wore out our welcome approximately ten-fold if I had a guess.

The last time we were there, we pretty much got the boot when our problems came resting on the hospital's doorstep. Warded against malicious intent, the Witches who guard the ward, wanted nothing to do with us once the sanctity of the hospital was threatened by a pack of werewolves and whatever else was coming for the newly awakened Nicola. While I'm sure there must be others—other places where people like us could go—I don't know of any.

Our only other option is to go to Mena, and I don't know if I want to do that either. A part of me knows Nic and I are safer with our family, but the other part of me loathes the way Nic's shoulders hunch and she curls into herself when she's around Aurelia and Mena—the way Nicola hates herself for hurting them even if she can't remember doing so.

I could go around and around with her—explain for the hundredth time the cause and effects of her actions—but I don't think she actually listens to me.

"We need to take her to Mena," I finally answer her.

Nicola's mouth twists to the side in chagrin as she nods. "Let me grab you a sweater and some shoes," she mutters before she darts to our bedroom and returns in a few moments with her feet hastily shoved into flats and a backpack thrown over her shoulder.

Nic grabs onto the waistband of my jeans at the small of my back, resting her head against my skin to steel herself for travel. I wait until I feel the exhale of her sigh against my skin before traveling, carrying Talia and Nicola with me.

When we arrive, I immediately regret not putting on shoes. Or a shirt. Or a fucking parka. The Appalachians of Kentucky in late November are in no way comparable to the Colorado Rockies, and I am officially freezing my ass off as I stand in a mound of fresh powder.

"We didn't think this through at all, did we?" Nicola shivers while she skirts around me, kicking snow off her feet as she climbs the porch steps to ring the bell.

No, we didn't, I think, and it dawns on me about five steps too late that this may be a trap. We saw someone hurt and got them aid. We have no idea what Talia's intentions are or if she's even her, or if she's bait.

She made it through my ward without so much as a blip.

"Nic, before you ring that bell, I need you to make sure she's her. She showed up at our house, broke through a ward, and made it to the porch when I don't even know if she can walk on her own steam. We might have just fucked up, Shortcake."

Nic's finger stops before touching the lit circle of the bell and turns to face me, eyes wide.

"I'm such an idiot. I was so worried about hurting her, I didn't think she might be there to hurt us. When I tried the last time—when I saw her at our house, it was like an ice pick in my brain. I thought I was just rusty. I don't want to bring that shit here if it could hurt them," she says, gesturing to the house and then she mutters something else under her breath. Something that sounds a fuck of a lot like *I've done enough of that already.*

Nicola steels her spine as she marches back down the steps and latches onto Talia's bicep. Immediately, her body goes rigid, and Nic's eyes flash open, glowing gold. Her scream is almost instantaneous, catching me by surprise.

Nic hasn't been able to see anything for weeks, and I've been keeping tabs on the local deaths. Nothing, not even a blip from Nicola saying one way or the other if the souls needed to move on, so the fact that she's had two visions in one day catches me off guard.

It hasn't mattered how much we've tried or how many training sessions we've done. She has been flying blind.

Before I can drop Talia, her eyes shed bloody tears, but that's normal for a vision. I should be used to seeing it, but it cuts at me every time.

What isn't normal, is the trail of dark red coming from her nose.

And her ears.

And her mouth.

Nicola's blood-covered lips move, but no sound comes out.

Then, I drop Talia. I do. I drop the battered girl and lunge for my wife as she wilts as soon as their connection is broken. Nicola should come to any second now...

But she doesn't.

She doesn't move, she doesn't speak, she doesn't even breathe. She is frozen, her eyes open and blazing, while I hold her with my knees in the snow screaming for someone, anyone to help me.

The bond—the mating between us—makes itself known when Nicola's heart flutters a terrifying rhythm in my chest. Our lives are tied to each other's, but the rules for us are unclear. Nicola is a Phoenix. She should be able to die a thousand deaths and rise again and again. Her lifespan is infinite. Mine is not. I may live a thousand or two thousand years, but I only get one life. Even though Wraiths are made of death, we do not get to cheat it.

Her heart slows—the lack of oxygen suffocating her. I don't know what this means. I don't know if when I tied her life to mine if she is able to resurrect like a Phoenix should. I don't know if this is it for her or for me. I don't know if my weaknesses will kill us both.

I don't know if this panicked, bloody vision of my wife is the last I'll ever have.

Shit. *Shitshitshitshitshit.*

I've been here before—me holding a bloody and broken Nicola while I scream for help—and the same as the last time, a whole host of people come to our aid. But Mena finds us first.

Her sizzling Aegis touch finds us both, causing Nicola to gasp, sucking in a huge breath right before she turns out of my arms to vomit scarlet blood all over the pristine snow.

I don't know if we are out of the woods or if we are sinking deeper into the blackness of another battle.

I have a feeling, what I don't know is going to get us both killed.

3

KYLE

I don't know how Aurelia knows this, but there are few things in this world that can back a man like me down from a rage. Holding an eight-month-old ball of precious dressed in dainty ruffles is at the tippy-top of that list.

Mena had to pry Nicola out of my arms. Something inside me wouldn't let her go—my brain tried and failed to send the signal to my arms. But with so many to come to our aid, Nicola was all too quickly taken away from me, Asher absconding into the house with Nicola and Mena in a swirl of black smoke.

As soon as her rapidly cooling skin parted from my fingertips, Aurelia and Rhys pulled up in their winter white Range Rover. Within moments, I was hauled inside, Livy was swiftly removed from her car seat and placed in my arms. It doesn't matter that a few seconds ago my fangs were cutting into my lips or my talons could slash through a rhinoceros. My phase takes a hike once Aurelia plops Livy into my arms.

"Are you going to do this every time Nicola is getting worked on, because eventually Livy will be too big to hold and your leverage will be gone," I say once my fangs retract, addressing Aurelia without taking my eyes off of Livy's pale jade ones. This is the first time I've held her while she's awake and I get to inspect her eyes up close. Like her mother, she doesn't have pupils, but the milky consistency of her irises does nothing to take away from the intelligence in them.

"I'm hoping by the time the twins can walk I won't have to worry about it anymore. That or you'll have little ones of your own so you keep your shit."

"Yeah, I don't see that happening anytime soon."

I have too many doubts to have children right now. Too many facets of our life are not fit for starting a family.

"I could have you hold Henry, but the likelihood that he'd shock the ever-loving fuck out of you and you'd drop him is high. He's teething," she says with a shrug as if that explains everything, and I can't help but bust up laughing.

Poor Rhys, I think as he brings up the rear with a car seat hanging from his forearm. Inside the car seat is an adorably mischievous-looking baby who is presently chewing on his gloved fist, baby slobber soaking the gray baby mitten. By the set of Rhys' jaw, he has zero desire to have his children in the middle of this mess, nor does he seem to want me to be holding one of them.

I don't blame him. I wouldn't want my children—if we ever have any—around this either. Nicola and I fucked up huge by bringing this shit to their doorstep.

"I'm sorry for this. We didn't think it through, and by the time we did, it was too late," I apologize, the lump in my throat thickening, choking me. Flashes of Nicola bleeding from her ears, her nose, throwing up all that blood, scream across my mind.

"Do you... do you think she'll be okay?" I manage to grind out, burying my nose in Livy's dark waves, trying to hold onto her sweetness so I can stop thinking about the way Nicola practically bled out in my arms... or the broken doll of Talia's body. The bitter pinch of guilt for caring more about my wife than the battered girl I dropped hits me. The taste of it on my tongue is bitter.

"No, no. It's cool. I'll carry everything all by myself. It's not like I have a patient that's dying in my arms. Keep moaning about your guilt. That will be super helpful," Ian's voice filters in from the doorway, cradling the battered Talia in his arms, his med bag slung over a shoulder.

"What are you doing? Should you even bring her in here?" Rhys asks incredulously as he grabs the handle of his son's car seat and backs up.

"You're right. We should totally leave her to die in the snow. I'm sure that won't alert the sheriff at all to the fact that there are a bunch of supernatural creatures living on this mountain. You never know. He might be into that kinky blood-porn stuff and get off on the rapidly freezing puddles of it out there," Aurelia says, giving him a scathing look that assures he'll pay for that comment later.

Idiot.

"For fuck's sake. I'm just saying that Talia's touch nearly killed Nicola. You had a vision of it. You saw the danger. You packed us up and hauled ass over here to help Nicola and Kyle. We have no idea what was done to her. We don't know if she's a ticking time bomb. We know nothing and I don't want my babies in danger. I don't want my wife in harm's way. Fucking sue me for being protective," Rhys gripes back.

"Well, I have someone in my arms that needs my help, and she's not hurting me, so if you'll excuse me," Ian says, moving around them to head for the med bay, ignoring Rhys' words entirely.

Rhys grinds his teeth as he stares at Ian's back. If he could incinerate the lot of us without consequences, I'm pretty sure he would.

"I take the time to put on a bra and I miss everything. What the fuck happened?" Evan asks, stomping the snow off her boots in the doorway. Some of the snow comes off pink on the welcome mat, and I wonder if I'm going to need to replace it like I did for every stick of furniture in the room Nicola and I stayed in the last time. Probably.

"And why does the front yard look like someone tried to recreate Wounded Knee," West chimes in from right behind her, dwarfing the tiny blonde. Aidan and Cam follow closely behind the couple—as they should since they carry the Guardian mantle—their weapons drawn, assessing the house for threats.

"I fucked up," I reply, only letting the f-bomb fly after I press Livy's head to my chest and covering her other ear with my hand. This gets me an indulgent smile from Aurelia. Out of everyone, she is the least concerned, and I take a small measure of comfort from that.

"How did you fuck up, pray tell?" Evan asks warily. The kind, unassuming quality to her clear blue eyes does nothing to assuage my guilt. If she were smiling, I would know if I should run or not, but the clear expression and sweet voice incite more fear than reassurances.

"I brought a broken and bloody wolf girl who managed to slide right through my ward without a single blip here without checking her first. When Nicola tried to see if Talia was a danger, Nic almost bled out and then started vomiting blood."

Evan and West do a simultaneous slow blink that tells me I'm in deep shit.

Trust me, guys, I know.

"You know, a shit ton of your problems would be solved if you would just. Pick. Up. A. Fucking. Phone. Ring-ring! Hey guys, Nicola's awake. Ring-ring! Hey guys, there is a bloody wolf on my porch," Evan grumbles as an expression passes over her face that tells me if I didn't have a baby in my arms she would totally punch me.

Naturally, I cuddle Livy tighter. Yes, I am scared of the four-foot-eleven blonde, and nothing anyone can say will convince me otherwise. She's a tiny little bloodthirsty demon when she's pissed.

"We may need to call Max in on this. This has Baron and Bella's stink all over it. I hate doing it because Max's mother is a certifiable piece of work, but..." Aurelia trails off giving Evan a look that says this whole situation is about to start some shit that Max will want no part of.

Suddenly, I feel Nicola's heart wrenching in my chest. The beat of it —the swift pumping of blood—rips through me and I'm handing off Livy to someone so I don't pass out with her in my arms. Breath itself seems to clog in my throat, and I wheeze.

If I didn't know better, I would think I were having a heart attack. It takes a minute for my brain to catch up.

She's dying. *We're dying.*

"He-help her. Oh, god, help her," I moan, grabbing at the invisible spear that seems to have lodged itself between my ribs.

Is this what my father felt when my mother died? This sudden, inescapable realization that my life is not my own, that it belongs to the woman I love.

A woman I cannot save.

West's blurry face comes into view. His mouth is moving, but I hear nothing over the roaring realization that if I can't breathe, neither can Nicola. That if I'm in agony, hers must be a thousand times worse. His face twists and I am hauled up, a man under each arm while they half carry, half drag me down the hall and a flight of stairs, through the steel door and ward of the training room.

Once we cross the ward, the pain hits me harder, wrenches in my chest a hundredfold, and my body loses its fight to stay standing—even with the added help of Rhys and West. Without missing a beat, two more come to my aid and I'm carried through another door.

I stay conscious long enough to watch Mena in all her blue-lit glory using her hands like defibrillator paddles on Nicola's chest.

I COME TO WITH A START, SITTING UP IN WHAT I CAN ONLY assume is another guest room. Or maybe the same one I trashed months ago. I don't stop to confirm, preferring to haul ass out of there and back to my Shortcake.

The last thing I remember, Mena's incandescent blue light, flashes of green...

I shake my head, not even trying to make sense of the images floating around in there. I try traveling to Nicola, but that doesn't seem to work. My brain practically dings with the memory of Max's hulked-out ward, so I adjust my course to outside the training room.

Bupkis.

What the fuck kind of juju is this? Can no one travel in here? Fine, I'll walk.

The stairs prove to be tricky bastards, but I make it down them unscathed, stomping to the training center. My limbs are weak and rubbery, my knees having the distinct consistency of gelatin.

I need to see Nicola.

I need to feel the breath in her lungs and the heartbeat thumping against her ribs. I need to see the flush of her lips and the fire in her hair. I need her.

Then, I need answers.

I don't get to see Nicola right away. What I do get is a shit load of hassle and a baby in my arms once again. Every person in the house save Aurelia and Nicola are huddled in the small vestibule with the med bay beyond. The white tiled hall seems too tight of a fit for the cluster of people, the space seeming smaller due to the attitudes being tossed around and the sheer size of the seven men and two women huddled there.

West's deep rumble cuts through the throng of pissed off voices like a knife.

"I swear, someone needs to start talking some sense. I don't need bullshit posturing. What I need are some goddamn answers. Why can't you get the cuff off, Max?" West orders, gesturing to the pretty, blue-haired Witch.

Somehow between when I passed out/attempted to die, Max got here. I don't quite know what cuff they are talking about, but I'm assuming it is Talia's. I have an inkling it may be what is causing all the trouble.

"Like I was trying to say," Max mutters, giving a pointed look at Ian, "The cuff won't come off with magic. I have tried ten different spells even laced with my own special brand of juju. I got nothing. The sigils aren't something I've seen before. I'd need to do research into a form I don't know, and the only fucking kind of magic I don't know by heart is necromancy. No offense, but I'm not going to cross that bridge. I've got enough heat with my family already, I don't need to add that coal to the fire." Max takes a defiant stance, arms crossed, feet planted wide like she thinks West is going to start a fight.

Or maybe she's more worried about the curiously silent Evan at his right.

I know for a fact West would never strike a lady. Evan on the other hand...

"Sweetheart, no one asked you to. No one is going to use your magic without permission and necromancy is a big no-no pretty much across the board," Evan consoles her, unruffling Max's feathers.

"Just an idea, but has anyone thought of a non-magical, non-Ethereal way to get the cuff off? Say, with maybe bolt cutters? Just a thought, but if magic won't work, maybe something non-magical might," Cam offers, and every single eye swivels to him. I don't know when he got so damn smart, but this new side to him is part annoying and part fucking genius.

"I'll grab some," Aidan offers, and races out of the hallway, not waiting for any objections.

"Oh good, you're awake," Mena says from behind me, and I turn to find the tall beauty with baby Henry in one arm and Livy in the other. Henry has a fist in her hair, and Livy is gnawing on a silver chain around Mena's neck. She looks like she could use a break. Since both Henry and Mena are Aegis and I've been warned off his zap-happy self, I reach to take Livy from her. Immediately, my muscles ease.

"Why aren't you with Nicola?" I ask, honestly concerned because no one is talking about my wife and the thought of what happened to us— the horrible wrenching in my chest earlier—fills me with fear.

"Aurelia is with her. Ari has a better connection to this Nicola than I do. She doesn't remember what she did for me. Looking at me now only brings her pain, so..." Mena trails off, shrugging a shoulder as she gently detangles a strand of hair from Henry's robust grip.

"Can I see her? Is she better?"

"Well, she isn't dead, but I had to shock her five times to get her heart to a rhythm I'm comfortable with, so I wouldn't call her well. I think she's close to stable, but she's still throwing up blood, and I have no idea how to get her to stop. Ian and I were thinking it might have to do with the cuff on Talia, so that is what that is all about," she says gesturing to the mass of itchy people in the hallway.

"You didn't answer if I could see her."

Mena's lips press thin as she gives me the 'don't make me tell you no' look.

"Fine, but as soon as that cuff is off, I'm going in there," I bargain, knowing full well Mena could stop me with a pinky finger.

"We'll see, okay? I'm not trying to hurt you. I just want everyone under my roof safe. Deal?" she counters.

"Deal."

Not a moment later, Aidan waltzes back in the room with a set of cutters, the blood red handle in his sure grip. Bypassing the whole group, he veers left to a doorway that doesn't seem to be the med bay but might be where Talia has been stashed and slips inside. Ian and Max both stare for a moment before hauling ass to follow him.

The scream that follows chills me to the bone.

4

NICOLA

TALIA WAS CURLED INTO A BALL OF TERROR, HER ANKLES CUFFED and chained to an eye hook embedded in the stone floor. The chain was long enough to allow her a small circle of freedom, but otherwise, she was stuck. The cuffs were spelled, keeping her in her human form, preventing her from healing, draining every ability she had. Talia had long since tried to mar the sigils in the metal, but her blunt human nails did nothing to the cold steel manacle.

Her nose was bloody, one eye swollen shut, and the other searched frantically around the room for a tool, a rock, fucking anything that could help her out of here. It didn't matter that she'd been here for days or that the close inspection of every inch of the cinderblock room came up fruitless. She searched anyway.

Talia was built to survive.

She longed to change—to transform into what she truly should be. Her wolf called her, and the longer her body was denied the change, the more her skin crawled. The noise in her head—the one screaming at her to move, to run, grew louder and louder, fogging her brain.

Her ribs screamed, too. The brittle bones in her foot where they had an unfortunate run-in with Baron's boot, weren't as loud, but they should be.

The dulling of the pain there meant she would go into shock soon. That, or she was already neck-deep in the middle of it.

She should have run further—put more distance between herself and her careful watch on Nicola. But, she needed answers. Answers that didn't seem so important now that her life was at stake.

How was she to know the questions were likely going to get her killed?

The heavy clunk of her cell door opening snapped her out of her stupor. Baron muscled the thick steel door open, and with a smile. A glint of light bounced off of the knife in his hand, and she knew.

Baron was no longer playing nice.

MY BRAIN IS ON FIRE. I'M NOT SURE IF IT IS A LITERAL OR figurative fire, but nonetheless, I require assistance. The coppery tang of blood coats my tongue, and I gag, my stomach roiling against the taste. Rolling over, my eyes finally open to a powder blue emesis basin. The blue is marred by the bright red lake of blood collected in its depths.

Fucking gross.

But the smell gets to me, and I lose my hold on the contents of my stomach. The contents of which happen to be straight blood.

This is bad, my brain stupidly offers.

"I told you we should have gotten her a bucket. That stupid thing is about to overflow," a voice I recognize filters through my retching. Max.

"For fuck's sake, woman. It is a tool of measurement. I can't tell how much blood she's losing if I can't measure it, now can I? Jesus Christ, just let the medical professional work and save your commentary. Or maybe, you could do something useful. Like figuring out the Witchy juju that's fucking with my patients," Ian growls back.

Ian and Max's voices float in and out of my mind bickering back and forth while my body tries to liquefy itself.

Thanks, guys, I don't need any help or anything.

My body finally quits trying to turn itself inside out and I roll back over onto what I now realize is a hospital bed. I've officially seen too many of those in my limited memory.

Med room. Basement. Mena and Asher's house, my brain supplies. So, on the upside, I know where I am. On the downside, I don't know where

Kyle is, Ian and Max are arguing like idiots, and well, I'm puking blood. I thought Phoenixes were supposed to be self-healing. Self-healing, my ass.

"I think she's actually awake this time," Max's husky voice offers, moving closer.

"Thank you, Captain Obvious, I couldn't tell by the open eyes. Whatever would I have done without you?" Ian bites back, and the pair of them move within my sight line.

Ian is his naturally mocha-skinned handsome. Lines of worry and stress show around his eyes, but nothing can take the compassion and Lokiesque mirth from them. Dressed in a burgundy Henley and jeans, I half expect him to bust out into scrubs at any moment. Max, however, is clad in what I now know is a style called Rockabilly. Cuffed skinny jeans paired with a floaty fuchsia silk sleeveless blouse carefully tucked into her jeans. Buttoned up to her neck, the top boasts a precious tied bow at the collar that plays peek-a-boo through her electric blue expertly coiffed glam waves. The two of them are facing each other, ready to fling another insult, hands on their hips. Max's bared arms are colorful works of art, but the green glow of her magic shines brightly against the inkless skin of her hands.

"Oh, just fuck already and get it over with," Aurelia gripes from beside me, and it is then that I notice she's been next to me the whole time.

I don't know how I feel about that—about her being here with me when Kyle isn't, or the fact that she is sitting five feet away. If the pitch in my gut that has nothing to do with nausea is anything to go by, I'm guessing not good.

"The last time I tried to help hold your hair back, you bared your teeth at me, so I'm offering emotional support from my own little bubble over here," Aurelia says, drawing a circle in the air over her head, her pale pupilless eyes meeting mine.

"I didn't say anything," I croak.

"Your face is much more readable than it used to be," she explains as she fidgets and knocks a thick, black braid off her shoulder.

"So, you're telling me my World Series of Poker ambitions are pointless. Way to kill my dreams, cousin."

"And she grows a sense of humor, too."

"Not really," I murmur, trying to sit up and assess the damage. The sheets are splattered in ribbons of red. My clothes are soaked in sweat & blood, and by the charred holes in my sweater in the shapes of hands, Mena has probably restarted my heart a couple times.

"No way, spark plug. There is no freaking way you are sitting up right now," Ian says, putting a gentle hand on my shoulder to push me back to the bed. Him touching me, though, doesn't go as planned, and I am not soothed in the least. Images fly through my brain as his fingers make contact.

Ian as a boy in Ireland playing hide and seek with an elderly woman. Ian in tattered clothes, running through a filthy alleyway away from the voices of screaming men. In the bowels of a dark room, etching marks on a wall. Meeting his brother, Aidan, for the first time. Ian saving life after life as an ER doctor. Lying prone on a rooftop looking through a rifle's scope. In a throng of people in what appears to be a dance club. Kissing a veiled woman clad in a rainbow dip-dyed wedding dress. Holding his first-born child, teaching a little boy to ride a bike, escorting a young woman down an aisle, holding his grandchildren, his great-grandchildren...

My body moves away from his fingers without thought, and I find myself off the bed, with my back against a wall. Ian advances on me, but Max catches his elbow before he can take another step.

"I don't know what the hell that was but please, for the love of all that is holy, don't touch me," I choke and fight to stay standing. The world spins for a moment before straightening out again, and I realize I've slumped down to my ass on the cold tile floor.

"Your eyes lit up like a freaking Christmas tree," Aurelia comments, crouching down in front of me.

"Yep," I murmur as I clutch my head in my hands trying to ease the brand new ache in my skull.

I felt the flash fire of my eyes glowing, felt the pulse of past, present, and future roll over me.

"Your head hurt?" Aurelia asks like she already knows the answer. She damn well should, I probably look like I'm trying to keep my brain from liquefying out of my ears.

"Yep."

"You gonna pass out again?"

"It is entirely possible. While I'm still conscious, where is Kyle?"

Her eyes flash for a moment as they drift up and to the side.

"He's holding Livy so he can calm the fuck down. I don't know if it's Livy or babies in general, but he turns into a big ball of protective goo around her. He was freaking the hell out."

My lips twist into a wry smile. It's my fault and the guilt of this whole ordeal stings. We shouldn't have brought this to their doorstep.

"Well this isn't the first time I've tried to die in his arms, now is it? Do we know what the hell happened? Is Talia okay?"

"She's better now that we took bolt cutters to a spelled manacle on her ankle. It was preventing her from…"

"It kept her from shifting and healing. Baron and Bella put it on her. Kept her chained in a stone room… Tortured her for information on me. Yeah, I know," I finish for her.

"Uh… that's new information," Max says, her voice catching me off guard once again. I look up to see her eyes as wide as saucers. "This makes so much more sense now!" she exclaims.

"Wanna share with the class?" Ian gripes.

"The cuffs were spelled to keep magic out, or suppress it somehow, right? So, visions are magic. They are a natural form of magic, but every member of the Ethereal has some kind of juju in them. Werewolves shift, Wraiths consume evil, Warlocks bend time, Phoenixes heal and guide souls, Witches cast spells… All of that is magic. Whatever was on that sigil was keeping magic out, it's why I couldn't get them off until we got the cutters. But it didn't keep Nicola out. She could see around it."

"So instead of seeing nothing, like me, she saw what happened, and her body couldn't handle it—it couldn't heal itself from the pressure of the vision," Aurelia finished for her.

"What the hell does that mean?" Ian asks the question we all want to know the answer to.

"It means Nicola is stronger than any of us thought," Kyle answers him from the doorway, his face set in stone.

The vision of Kyle holding a baby shouldn't be as hot as it is. Even stuck on this cold as shit floor trying to Humpty Dumpty my brain back together, my belly still dips when I finally realize there is a baby booty resting on his forearm.

But I still see the grim look in his eyes and wonder if this revelation of my supposed strength is a blessing…

Or a curse.

The first order of business—after I managed to get off the floor—was to wipe that look off of Kyle's face. Death felt too close to us. It seemed to envelop us in its hold and never let go.

Was I cursed to see that look on his face for our small stretch of forever? Could I make it stop?

Leaving him was out. I'd tried that once—tried to spare him from me—but I didn't have the will to make it stick. I didn't have it then, and I had even less now. But how many times could I do this to him?

I watch as he stalks across the room, handing off Livy to her mother and crouching down in front of me.

"You scared the shit out of me, Shortcake," Kyle murmurs, his chocolate eyes burning into me.

Deep grooves of strain have dug their way into his face, radiating out from his eyes. I reach out to touch his cheek, the coarse yet soft whiskers kissing my palm.

"Are you okay?" I ask, my voice a shaky whisper.

"Yeah, babe. Never better," he mumbles into my hair, snaking a hand under my legs and one behind my back, hefting me up into his arms.

He doesn't look me in the eye when he says it, and I can't help the thought that streaks across my mind even as I manage to hold my tongue.

I don't believe you.

5

NICOLA

I can't remember much of my hospital stint in Knoxville, but I imagine it was nothing like this. Kyle brings me up the stairs through a guest room to an ensuite with an enormous, glass-walled shower. Equipped with a bench seat that could house an entire soccer team, the ornate stonework appears handcrafted, mixing rough textures with glass tiles and rustic brushed bronze fixtures.

Within moments, I'm divested of my ruined clothing, set on the bench seat, and Kyle flips on the taps. I watch through the glass as Kyle pulls off his jeans and t-shirt and rejoins me, an act that would be sexy if I could muster up the energy for it.

Kyle reaches for me, lifting me from the seat and maneuvering my body under the spray while he holds me to him. I try to concentrate on the feel of his skin against mine, but a flash of red catches my eye. Even with my clothes gone, I'm still covered in blood. The steam billows as the lava hot water rinses the scarlet gore from my skin. I watch the water run red for a moment before diluting to a wispy pink and then finally running clear.

Watching it run from my skin causes something inside me to break, and I heave a breath before shattering. I feel it all over again, Talia's broken bones, my breath lodging in my throat when all I wanted to do was scream, the dizzying realization that I might be dying, and my heart...

I feel wrong in my own skin, feel like I'm wrong. And if I am the one who is different—if I am the one who caused all this mess—how can Kyle want me this close to him? How can the rest of them? Baron and Bella wanted intel on me. They still need me for something, and even though I told them why she was hurt, I don't think they grasp what Baron and Bella will do to anyone in their way.

Oh, god... I have to go. I have to leave. I can't be here anymore.

"Breathe, Shortcake," Kyle demands in my ear, and it is like he has said the magic words and my lungs begin their torturous slog of hauling air to my bloodstream.

I can't help the shiver of fear that whips across my skin. Kyle hitches me up his body, my feet leaving the tiled shower floor to wrap around his back. He tightens his hold on me, and for a moment, I feel safe. My breath slows, and I make a concerted effort to bury my nose in his neck and inhale his scent. He is warm where I am cold, he is strong where I am weak, he fills in the gaping gaps of my soul.

My lips find the skin of his neck without prompting from my brain. I need him so much—probably more than he needs me, but I don't care.

"I don't think you realize that your life is precious—that the very breath in your lungs and beat of your heart is a relief to me. I don't know what's going on in your head, and I don't know what happened to Talia. Honestly, when it comes to anything but you, I really don't care. You have to start thinking before you act, Nicola."

"I didn't mean to..." I try to break in, but he isn't having it at all.

"It doesn't matter that our lives are tied together. I knew what it meant to be your husband when I bound you. Hell, I never even expected you to wake up at all, so I knew what I was getting into. But you are worth more than my life. You are more important than just me. You have saved more lives than I could ever hope to count. You've done more good than I could ever hope to do."

Whoa, whoa, whoa. Wait a minute.

"What do you mean our lives are tied, Kyle?" I ask, pulling back to look him in the eye and fight against a full-scale panic attack.

"Exactly what I said. My life is tied to your life. If your heart stops beating, my heart stops beating. When you were in the hospital, I bound you to me knowing that I didn't want to have a life at all without you in it. It was reckless of me, but I don't regret it," he replies, his fervent whisper lashing my heart like a whip.

How could he risk himself that way? And for what? A wife who didn't even remember him when she woke up? If I didn't love him so much, I would knock some sense into this man.

"Why would you do that? My God, Kyle! People want to kill me. How could you?" I plead with him, grabbing his face, so he's forced to look at me. The chocolate of his irises bleeds back and forth from black to brown as if he can't decide which form he wants to take.

"I'm not living without you, Nicola," his gruff whisper hits me as his lips brush mine.

That little, gentle brush is all it takes to wake me up and catch me on fire. The heat of him against my breasts, the feel of his powerful back surrounded by my legs, the strength of his forearm under my ass, the gentle tug of his fist in my hair. The way his fingertips dent the skin at my ass, digging into my flesh because he had to hold me that tight.

Our mouths go from gentle brushes to colliding lips and tongues in an instant, my hunger for him hitting me so hard I could hardly breathe. It wasn't new for me to want him all the time. It wasn't new for me to need him as close as I could get him. I craved Kyle more than air.

Suddenly, we're turning, and I'm seated on his lap as he lowers himself to the bench. I lose his forearm under my ass, but that's okay because it's moved between us to his cock so he can bring himself to my opening. One second, I'm empty, my whole body aching with want and frigid emptiness and the next, Kyle has me full of him. It always took me a solid minute to get used to his size, but right now, I need to move.

I need to, but Kyle holds me immobile, his arms banding around my back in a way nothing is going to move me unless he wills it so. I love those arms holding me so tight—just not right this second. I need his hips to thrust. I need his moans in my mouth, and I expressly need him to move. I give up trying to thrust and began rotating my hips, putting that little bit of pressure on my clit. His answering groan is exactly what I want to hear. His fingers tighten in my hair, the bite of the pull making me squirm more.

"Ky," I moan into his mouth. I've never heard my own voice so needy, so pleading, but if anyone could do it, he could.

"You move when I move you, Shortcake," Kyle orders, his voice a gruff, strained murmur. His lips brush mine as he speaks and the drag of them against mine is enough to make me plead again.

"Please, baby. I need..." I trail off into a moan because he has moved his hands from my hair and back to grip my hips. I scramble to hold on as he lifts me up and slams me down onto his cock.

"This what you want, sweetness? This what you need?" he gruffly asks, and the questions alone make my belly curl with heat. God, the way his voice is almost a snarl kills me.

"Yessss," I hiss as I take in the feel of his chest raking against my nipples and the bite of his talons digging into the skin of my ass and hips as he moves me up and down on his cock.

Then, Kyle finds his feet, and my back hits the rough, raw stone tile of the shower wall as he powers up into me, hitting that spot that makes my limbs convulse around him and my pussy spasm. I love the power of him, the animalistic grunts of pleasure he groans into my neck. The way the sharp points of his fangs score the skin of my shoulder.

The first flutter of my orgasm hits me with the force of a sledgehammer as I watch as Kyle's comes over him. I watch as his fangs lengthen and his eyes bleed to black. He should be frightening. He should, but he isn't. I love that he can't control his phase. I love that I'm the one that does this to him—that I make him lose the tight hold he has on his control. Ky loses it completely when his fangs cut into the tender skin of my shoulder—the flutter of my orgasm morphs into a full-body spasm, hitting me so hard my scream is silent.

"Jesus, I think I'm deaf now," Ky grumbles.

Or at least I could have sworn my scream was silent. Whoops.

"I'm not sorry. That was fucking phenomenal. I think I killed brain cells I couldn't afford to lose."

"Happy to oblige, Shortcake," he murmurs as one of his hands runs up and down my body. I love it when he does this—the way he still can't get enough of our connection that he has to touch as much of me as he can even in the afterglow of an orgasm that nearly decimated us both.

Gently he slips out of me and like the complete taker that I am in bed, I practically drape over him—throwing my arms over his shoulders, tightening my legs around him so he can't set me down. I don't want him to let me go. I don't want him any further away than he is right now.

I need him so much.

As usual, he has to coax me out of my vice grip.

"If you let me wash you up, I'll make you come again and then fuck you in that nice big bed in our room," Kyle whispers in my ear as one of his still sharp but retracting fangs nips at the lobe.

"Sold!" I crow as I release him and he sets out to do just that.

6

KYLE

I wish I could say waking up before Nicola was a good thing, but lately, it isn't. Waking up before her usually consisted of a concerted effort not to scream.

It starts the same—the tense ridge of her back, the way she curls in on herself. Then the moaning starts, and it isn't the good kind. No. These are the moans that shake me to my very core, the ones that make me know that even though I endured hell for her, she suffered her own hell, too. Then the thrashing begins, and so she doesn't hurt herself, I band my arms around her.

In the beginning, I didn't. I let her thrash because I thought the dreams would peter out. They didn't. What they did do was allow her to start clawing at her own skin—raking the sharp edges of her fingernails down her cheeks. Ripping chunks of hair right out of her scalp, thrashing hard enough that her arms hit the lamp, the bedposts— bruising and cutting up her lily pale skin. It didn't matter that she healed from the injuries almost as soon as she inflicted them. I hated that she couldn't help hurting herself, so I started holding her immobile.

Like I am right now.

I can tell this dream is different—don't ask me how. What she's dreaming might have actually happened, but I don't think it happened to her. Then she moans painfully a name, and I know she's remembering a vision she's had and not the hell Iva inflicted in her skin.

"Talia," Nic cries right before her eyes flash open, tears pooling in them before flooding the lids and running into her hair. I hate those tears and what they mean—the pain that she endures that is not her own to bear.

"Shortcake, baby," I whisper as I hold her tighter. Her body shakes—great, wracking tremors that make her teeth chatter. I soothe Nicola the best I can, murmuring into her ear that she is safe, that Talia is safe.

I know I have failed her—in so many ways—and this proves it. I was supposed to keep her safe from Iva. I was supposed to keep her whole.

"I want to go talk to her," Nic whispers after her shudders subside, and the largest part of me wants to try and tell her no. After everything we went through—what she just went through—I don't want her anywhere near Talia. But the likelihood that my concerns will be heard is slim. Nicola damn near bled out in my arms. The memory of that will most likely haunt me until the day I die.

"I don't know if we should, Shortcake. The last time you were next to Talia... I almost lost you," I murmur, my voice turning gruff.

"I know. I don't want you to go through that again, but I need answers, and she's the only one who can give them to me. At least we can check to see if she's awake." The determination shining in her eyes —those honey-colored ones that I have come to love as much as I loved the cornflower blue ones—tells me all I need to know.

I'd give her anything she asked of me.

"You know I love you, right?" I ask as I touch my forehead to hers.

"You know I love you, too, right?" she counters, reaching her neck up and kissing me on the nose.

"You're lucky you're cute," I grumble as I release her and we climb out of bed to get dressed.

"I know," she quips with a wry grin as she slips out of a pair of silky, emerald, lace-edged sleep shorts and wriggles into a pair of black skinny jeans, both of which Evan brought by last night.

Evan has been standoffish with Nicola ever since she woke up. I don't know if it is out of guilt or what, but Evan hasn't said more than two words to Nic since we got here or in the weeks we stayed with Mena and Asher.

Maybe bringing these clothes was a peace offering of some kind. Either that or Evan just likes to shop.

I appreciate her efforts when Nic tightens the strap of a very lacy, very hot lavender bra. Nicola catches my hot look and gives me a naughty little grin that is part devious and part 'later, hot stuff.' It's been a long time since I've seen that kind of smile on her face.

I didn't realize how much I missed it.

"You going to get dressed or what? Don't get me wrong, I dig the whole half-naked hot man vibe you've got going on, but I don't want to throw down with anyone just yet."

"I really fucking love you," I reply after I finish laughing my ass off. That earns me a soft look that I wish I could take a picture of and fucking frame.

"I know these last few months have been hard. But I feel like we're finally getting back to us even though I don't really know what that means," she ends in a chagrined shrug. Nicola immediately hides her face as she pulls on a thin, sapphire thermal that hangs down past the swell of her hips and ass in an asymmetrical hemline. She seems embarrassed by telling me this and that thought is only confirmed as she then turns without a word to the bathroom.

I figure I can give her that—that need to hide she most certainly has, but she only gets her escape for as long as it takes for me to throw on a pair of jeans, a thermal, and my socks and shoes. Walking into the bathroom, I rest my shoulder on the door jamb and watch her finish brushing her teeth. She ignores me for a bit as she wipes her mouth and fluffs her hair.

I surround her back, putting a hand on either side of her hips on the vanity, effectively caging her in.

"Still hiding from me, I see."

"I'm not hiding," Nic replies but she still won't look at me in the mirror. I hate that she's ashamed that she can't remember us. What she endured, I'm glad for the block in her brain that mostly saves her from it. Then again, if she could remember the good, it might temper the bad shit that seems to be seeping back into her mind.

"I loved you then, and I love you now. It doesn't matter to me that you're a little different now. You—everything that makes you who you are—is the same. Your smile, your laugh, your sass. All of that is the exact same."

She meets my eyes in the mirror then.

"Promise?" Her voice is soft and insecure. The soft part isn't unusual. The insecure, however, is.

"Promise. Now, let me brush my teeth and then we can get some grub and go see Talia."

"Okay," she breathes, and I move around her to the sink, handle my business, and we make our way downstairs.

After a quick breakfast that consisted of mostly coffee for Nic and a homemade breakfast burrito for me, courtesy of Asher, we head to the training center where Talia should be. What we find is Talia in wolf form prowling back and forth in front of the big blue exercise mat, staring at the door like she has been waiting for us.

Her steel gray fur is matted with dirt, grime, and blood, and she snarls when I open the door and doesn't quit until Nicola comes from behind me, ignoring my outstretched hand and puts herself between me and the pissed-off wolf.

"We fucking talked about this, Shortcake," I growl, ready to phase in a second if I have to.

"She doesn't know you, Ky. She doesn't know anyone in this whole fucking house besides me. You don't know what she's been through. I do. Leave her be," Nicola shoots back without turning to look at me.

I hate that she's talking sense, but I hate even more than she crouches to Talia's level. Talia whines and her form shifts to human again, sobs wracking her small frame as Nicola wraps gentle hands around her shoulders. Talia is still clad in the bloody rags she came to us with, and I'm starting to get pissed. This girl has been through Fates only know what, and she's still in her bloody, tattered clothes. What the fuck?

Before I can voice my anger at this—or find someone to rip into—Aurelia and Mena come into the room from the med bay followed closely by Max. All three of them carry worried expressions—ones that morph into a small measure of relief at seeing Talia in human form.

Max's eyes cut to me, and she slowly shakes her head. She rounds Aurelia and Mena and comes straight to me.

"She wouldn't let us help her," she whispers under her breath, her eyes never leaving the sobbing girl. "She wouldn't let us leave either to come get you. Cell reception is shit down here, and there isn't a land line. I need to fix that or maybe find a loophole in the ward to work around it because it was about to get really fucking dicey down here for a minute. She almost took my head off. It was really hard to not hurt her and also keep my ass alive."

Shit.

"Where is everyone else?"

"Talia took a chunk out of Aidan, so Ian is sewing up his brother, and Cam won't let West or Evan out of his sight while that's going on, so they're in the med bay. Ash is upstairs somewhere, and Carver went with Rhys to take the babies home. With the overbearing way Rhys was acting, Aurelia was going to kick him in the junk, so it was best for him to head home."

"Is Aidan going to be okay?" I murmur.

"Yeah. He got in between West and Talia," Max says with a shrug. "She lashed out. There were too many men in that room. Mena tried to tell them, but they didn't listen. She's so young, Kyle. To endure what she has…" Max broke off shaking her head. Her eyes shine with tears as she screws up her mouth to hold back a sob.

I want to fucking kill Baron and Bella, but especially Baron motherfucking Bishop. There are few reasons why a woman would be afraid in a group of men. I could only guess at the atrocities done to her, but what else could it be?

"Talia? Sweetheart?" Nicola calls softly, ignoring our company and focusing on the battered teenager in her arms. "I want you to meet my cousins, Aurelia and Mena, and my friend Max. Now, I know you have issues with Witches, darling girl, but she won't hurt you. No one in this house will."

And while everything Nicola said was true, I wonder how she'll cope with surviving after her torture.

7

NICOLA

Holding Talia, I wish for the right words to say. I saw some of what she went through, but I don't know everything. What I did know was enough to make me want to bleach my brain. I knew Baron was a piece of shit from our time in New Mexico. What I didn't know was how he could torture and do Fates only knew what with a fifteen-year-old girl.

If I had to venture a guess—with the way she came to us—I wouldn't put rape off the table. I hated that for her. I fought against the vision clawing at my brain and managed to shove it back.

There are some things I simply don't want to know.

"Talia," Mena coos as she crouches down with us. "Sweetheart, I've been where you are. We want to help you if we can."

"I-I bit a man. Drew blood. Is he okay?" Talia says, her breath hitching in the aftermath of her sobs. I knew she was a good kid, but her asking after someone else before even asking for a meal or a shower made me fall in love with this fragile young woman.

"Yes, baby. He's going to be fine. No one is mad at you for that, and no one blames you. When I was first rescued, I shocked a man and blew up an entire medical bay. You only nipped someone. You're doing way better than me," Mena replies, reassuring her with a small smile. This made me love Mena too. She had endured some of the worst atrocities a person could fathom and is still standing. I admired her. If there was anyone who could help Talia deal, it would be Mena.

Talia chuckles, and I appreciate that sound so much more than the sobs.

"Do you think we can get you cleaned up and in some new clothes? Maybe get you some food?" I ask, my voice soft and coaxing because Talia has started trembling again.

I realize why when I feel Kyle place a hand on my back.

"Talia, you don't have to be afraid, baby. This is my husband, Kyle. I told him all about how you helped me in New Mexico, honey. He won't hurt you."

I know she hears my words, but she does nothing for a long moment.

"His eyes are black," she whispers, her voice trembling.

"Yes, baby, but that's because he's mad at the people who did this to you. He's mad for you, not at you. He's really a big teddy bear. I promise," I reassure her, doing my best to dispel her fears of the looming six-foot-seven powerhouse I'm married to.

"A teddy bear that can eviscerate people into teeny tiny chunks, maybe," she mumbles, and it wrenches a chuckle from both me and Kyle as well as Talia.

"Well, that too, but he'll behave," I promise her.

"O-okay. I could use a shower and some food. Clothes wouldn't hurt either," she mumbles sheepishly as she fingers her tattered rags.

"Awesome. Now, can you walk or do you need help?"

"I-I can do it," she insists, but her legs give out almost immediately. It isn't me or Aurelia or Mena who catches her either, even though we are closer. Kyle is the one who makes it to her first, sweeping her up into his arms to carry her to the ladies' locker room situated at the back left corner the open space. Mena and Aurelia exchange a look, and the three of us trail after them. Kyle sets Talia on one of the teak benches and goes to leave the room. I catch him by the bicep.

"Thank you, baby. Can you brief West and Evan about the current situation and get an update on Aidan? I know she'll want to know if he's okay," I murmur as I watch Mena turn on one of the shower taps and Aurelia fish huge white fluffy towels from a wooden cabinet.

"Sure thing, Shortcake. Anything else you need?" Ky asks his lips at my ear.

I shake my head and give him a swift brush of my lips against his before he gets the hell out of here. I can tell he wants to linger, to make sure we're all okay but has to fight himself on it. He's doing what he thinks Talia needs even though he doesn't want to. Fates, I want to kiss that man, but it'll have to wait.

Right now, we have to see to a young woman who I owe my life to.

The showers in the locker room were as fancy yet comfortable as the rest of the house. Large travertine tiles lined the wide shower stalls, brushed bronze fixture, and each stall had a full-sized bench seat, and an inset cubby filled with bottles of bath products.

It took serious work and coaxing to get Talia undressed and clean. When the tattered rags that used to be relatively sturdy clothes were removed, Mena made sure neither Aurelia or I touched them knowing we could possibly get a vision from the blood-soaked fabric. I could kiss that woman for her kindness.

Especially since it was only me who Talia would allow to touch her. Getting her clean took at least four shampoos, two conditioning treatments, and me wrestling the poof away from her when she started rubbing her skin raw. After all she had been through, I didn't blame her, but I hated that she was hurting herself.

When we finally finished, and the dirt, grime, and blood was washed from Talia's skin, Mena checked her over again.

That's when things got a little dicey.

Because if we didn't know before that Baron was the biggest piece of shit known to mankind, we did now. Mena didn't even need to ask her, all she did was touch Talia's skin. Mena's eyes grew wide, she backed up ten paces, and then she started cussing a blue streak. Now I haven't witnessed it firsthand, but I've heard stories about Mena losing her shit. It wouldn't be good for anyone in the general vicinity of the house altogether.

"That motherfucking pedophile better hope I don't catch him first. I swear to the Fates, I'll cut his dick off and fucking feed it to him!" Mena rails until she realizes she is speaking aloud.

"Sorry, Talia. I know you aren't in the mood to hear me spouting shit. It's just... I've been where you are, and it sucks monkey balls and...

I'm not helping at all, so I'm going to shut up now," Mena finished lamely, the sparks on her fingers dying instantly.

Talia breaks the tension, by laughing her head off as she dries her arms with one of the three towels in use. One I wrapped around her torso, one in Aurelia's grasp as she dries Talia's light brown hair, and the last in Talia's hands. I'm pretty sure I'm going to need to pry the cotton from her fingers before she starts rubbing her skin raw again.

"You know, I didn't know much about anything before my brothers were exiled. I was young and naive. I probably still am even though I feel ancient right now. I was born to the pack, but I'd always been on the outside, and I never felt welcome. We moved around a lot, and I didn't have very many friends. I didn't have a mom or a dad. All I had was my brothers who weren't that smart or kind. They were selfish and could be cruel. This is the nicest anyone has treated me ever. So... thank you," Talia whispers, her eyes downcast.

"Well, you came to the right people. This is a house filled with misfits and outcasts," Aurelia quips as she drapes the towel over Talia's shoulders. "I'm going to go get some clothes," she murmurs, and I catch the sheen of tears in her eyes as quickly exits the locker room with Mena trailing after her.

Aurelia knows all about being exiled—about being cast out of her family. From what I've heard—but unfortunately don't remember—is Aurelia went against Iva's wishes and lost her first husband and child in the process. She lost her parents, her twin, and lived on the run from Iva for a century and a half.

Mena, on the other hand, tried to blend in. Only she was caught and imprisoned, drained of energy and even bits of her sanity along the way. She was violated, and the brutalities she endured will mark me forever —because I could have helped her and I chose to follow a vision instead. Mena has tried to dispel my guilt in this—saying that it needed to happen that way so everyone could live. But I don't know if I can forgive myself for that sin. I'm not sure I deserve anyone's forgiveness—let alone hers.

But that was the old Nicola, one who followed her visions with abandon and hang everyone else. That was the one who sat by when Aurelia was hurt, who let Mena rot in that prison, who let innocents die.

I'm not that woman anymore, and I won't let Talia be the next victim in the line. Not her. Not anyone. Not anymore.

"Well, I can sure clear a room," Talia mumbles, adjusting the towel more securely across her shoulders.

Explaining Aurelia and Mena at this juncture is a must. She needs to know that it isn't out of shame or ire that they left—it is out of empathy. My cousins have gone through so much.

"Both Mena and Aurelia were tortured, both of them have lived on the outskirts of their species. They can relate, and the both of them hate this for you—for anyone, really—but for someone so young... No one deserves what you got. No one." I trail off shaking my head. "But you will survive this. You were built to survive, weren't you?"

"I guess," she shrugs, her mouth screwing up in chagrin.

I have questions for Talia, but I don't know if this is the right time to ask them. She needs time to heal. Maybe more time than I can give her. I crouch down to her level once again, stopping the white towel that is slowly turning pink from her rubbing her skin raw.

"You are clean, darling girl. You have done nothing wrong. You did not deserve this," I say sternly as I meet her pale blue eyes with mine.

"You came to us for a reason. You came to us because you knew we would help, and I hate to do this, but I need to ask you some questions. This is going to be awful, but I need to know what they want. I need to know why they took you and what they asked. And then whatever it is they want, I need to stop them from getting it. Because I'm not going to let this lie. They don't get to kidnap, violate, and torture a young woman. They don't get to hurt my friend. They don't get to do this to you without repercussions. I don't give a rotten fuck what anyone says," I vow, boring my gaze into hers—making sure Talia knows I will be sure she's taken care of.

"They want what they've always wanted—a piece of the veil—a way to bring their mother back. Like they helped their mother bring Iva back... And then they want to burn this world to the ground," she whispers, tears pooling in her lids until they spill over to streak down her cheeks.

"You can't stop them. The magic they're using... it will eat us all alive," she warns, her voice a broken whisper.

Not if I could help it.

8

KYLE

THE LOOK ON NICOLA'S FACE WHEN SHE WALKS OUT BEHIND Mena and Aurelia with Talia under her arm makes my gut twist. She is vengeance and wrath, barely holding onto her fire. Nic's eyes are luminescent, not glowing exactly like she does for a vision, but golden glow of a transformation barely held back.

I don't know what Talia said to her, but I know this is full of the things I don't want. I don't want Nicola hurt. I'm tired of watching her nearly die. It has happened too much to us—we've gone through so much in that past year. I refuse to watch her get hurt again.

Talia is dressed in black leggings and a cream, tunic-like sweater. Around her neck is a plaid cashmere chunky scarf, and her hair is up in a messy, top knot. Her feet are shod in knee-high boots the color of good whiskey, and although Talia's appearance is leaps and bounds better than when we started, there is a fear behind her eyes and in the set of her shoulders that I don't like. It isn't skittishness, exactly, but it's a hollow kind of horrible that I never expected a child of her age to live with.

I've killed men for less than this—whatever it is that fucker did to her. I know West and Asher have, too. Living as long as we do, meeting men who define their worth in abuse happens more than we'd like. Meaning at all. There have been many times where I have been called to track an escaped wife or child. Those men—and sometimes women—were dispatched personally or under my King's command. It may sound callous, but when I can smell and taste the evil wafting off of a person, well, it makes decisions about morality much easier.

As much as I hate the look on Nicola's face, I understand it. That wrath is justified. I don't want her in harm's way in her quest to parcel out her justice.

Suddenly, the whole room tenses. Everyone has been milling around the training room waiting for Talia to emerge. I tried telling them that no woman—even as young as she is, she's still a woman—especially after what she'd endured, wants to go into a room filled with men she doesn't know. Does anyone listen to me? No.

The tenseness is intensified when West approaches Talia with his right arm outstretched. Aidan and Cam each wear a face of utter frustration, and Evan looks like she's fit to be tied.

West is a friend, my King, and an ally, but Aurelia, Mena, and my sweet Nicola do not give that first fuck. They close ranks around Talia, and like the family they are, each of them carries a matching snarl. They don't care that Talia may have snapped at him.

"I'm sorry, Talia," West starts, taking back his outstretched hand and placing it on his chest almost like a promise. "We should have read the situation better, and I'm sorry we scared you. We realize that it was our mistake that made you lash out, and as my wife has made very clear, I am an idiot. You won't find harm here, as I'm sure Mena has promised you, but I wanted to make sure you knew that Wraith or Phoenix, no one here is mad at you."

Talia only nods, her arms wrapped tight around herself against a chill that only she seems to feel, a faint ghost of a smile on her face. At that, West nods and strides from the room with Aidan following him. Evan doesn't leave with him, though, and Cam shadows the blonde pixie as she approaches Talia.

"This will be handled; you know that, right? No one does this without retribution," Evangeline hisses, her determined eyes sparking with fury. "No one."

Talia's eyes dart away, and she shrugs and nods in a weird twitchy way that shows how uncomfortable she is.

Evan nods and follows West and Aidan from the training room, and I look at Aurelia before I grab my wife's hand.

"You got her?" I ask, my gaze indicating Talia.

Aurelia's milky eyes take a certain sheen for a moment, and she nods. "We'll be here when you get back," she sighs, and I feel like she knows much more than she's saying. Likely, she does.

"We'll be back, T. Get some rest. Ari will set you up," Nicola assures Talia as I pull her behind me, not stopping until we get to what I like to call our room.

But I don't exactly stop there either. Before she can protest, I have Nicola up in my arms and flat on her back on the bed. Nicola's fingers threaded with mine offer a dual purpose of keeping her right where I want her, and the added bonus of every single stitch of her exposed skin is against mine.

"Whatever it is, no, Shortcake. Please. Whatever has that look on your face, whatever has you itching to run or fight... Please don't do it," I beg. "It hasn't even been twenty-four hours since the last time you almost died. I can't. Please?" I plead shaking my head.

I can't do it. I can't watch her come to me, again and again, bloody and broken. I can't stand to see her hurt. But her eyes are full of the tears she is trying not to shed, and her throat is bobbing in its effort not to cry, and I hate, hate, hate this.

"Talia was tortured and... r-raped because they wanted information on me. Which means they are looking for me or have found me. If we don't go, they'll come here. If we don't stop them, they will keep steamrolling over anyone in their path. Our family is here. There are children here. Do you want them to come here? Because they will. If we don't stop them, they will," Nicola's voice breaks at the end, and as much as I hate it, she has a point.

Why does it have to be us? Why does it have to be our responsibility? We are no one. We don't lead, we follow. We don't rule anything or anyone. Not anymore, and definitely not again. We have our own lives to live and our own burdens to bear.

But if they are searching for Nicola, then they will find her. It wouldn't be the first time.

"What do they want? You?" I growl, the protective hackles I try so hard to stomp down rising in me once again.

"No. They want a piece of the Veil. Someone like me, but without the barrier of our mating. They can't use me because my soul is bonded to yours, so they are looking for someone else to bring their mother back."

I have never been so happy to have bonded her. That is the only thing that stopped them last time—the only thing that kept Nicola out of a bitter hell of possession once again. We can't do nothing, but maybe I have an alternative.

"So how about we look for the piece of the Veil and not Baron and Bella?" I offer.

"Why would we do that?" she asks. Her voice is cautious but hopeful.

She can see how much I hate this, how much I don't want to put her in harm's way again. I have to say the right thing but saying 'As much as I love you, you aren't who you used to be,' isn't going to cut it.

"You can't defend yourself like you used to," I start gently. "Even blind, you could anticipate where someone was, you could shoot with accuracy, you could defend yourself. If we go and do this, if we go alone, I'm worried I won't be able to protect you. I'm worried it is just going to be you bleeding in my arms again."

That gets her. Nicola knows she's different, and I hate telling her how different she is, but it has to be said. The pain that slides through her features before her face goes blank might as well be a knife in my heart.

"We'll look for the pieces of the Veil," she says, her voice hollow. Nicola tries to give me a reassuring smile, but she misses the mark. The way her eyes still cradle the pain inside her is a dead giveaway.

"I know this may feel like a slight, but it isn't—or at least it isn't meant to be. It is me trying to keep you alive and safe. I love you, Nicola, and I want you to live," I whisper as I let go of her hands to cup her face, running my thumb over her cheekbone.

Her lips twist—either in chagrin or to stop herself from crying—and she nods. "We'll look for pieces of the Veil," she repeats. "Where do you want to start looking?"

"New Orleans, maybe? Talia's pack might have some information," I offer. "It's at least a place to start."

Nicola nods, and I drop my mouth to hers, capturing the juicy plumpness of her bottom lip with my teeth. Her answering gasp gives me the opening I was looking for, and I kiss her properly. Tangling my tongue with hers, I try to show her how much I care—how much I need her. I'm almost there—nearly thawing the cold shell she's wrapped herself in—when a light rapping at our door breaks us apart.

I jump up with a groan, adjust the thick ridge of my dick behind my jeans and open the door. On the other side is an awkward-looking Max who appears really uncomfortable that she might have interrupted something.

Serves her right.

Max opens her mouth to speak, but glances down the hallway and thinks better of it. She skirts past me into the room, murmurs a few words of Latin, and then snaps her fingers. If I would venture a guess, she just soundproofed this room.

"Okay, so you have to go and stop Baron and Bella," Max's words rush from her mouth as if she can't hold them back anymore.

"We know," I reply.

"No, I mean you guys are the only ones who can go. Ari can't go, neither can Mena or Asher. Carver volunteered, but it would look bad for him. West and Evan surely can't go, and I don't trust anyone else. My mother and her stupid judgy coven are watching everyone in leadership, but you guys are flying under the radar. You two are literally the only people who can go. Who can find them."

"We know," Nicola says, repeating my earlier words. "But we aren't going to look for them. We will, however, search for what they are looking for. We're leaving as soon as possible."

"You are going to have to cast. No half-assing it," Max orders, leveling me with her laser-sharp gaze. Normally, I would have a tough time taking her seriously. Max is usually so easy going, but right now I see what she should have been—a Coven leader. I have a feeling if she had been able to hide her power longer, she probably would have been.

"I figured I would have to, Max. Tell them we're going, will you? I'm pretty sure Aurelia already figured we're leaving. She'll take care of Talia," I return.

"We don't get to say goodbye?" Nicola breaks in, her face falling even further than before.

"Asher and Mena will talk us out of it, or they'll want to come and they can't. It's easier to ask for forgiveness than permission, right?"

"Let them know we love them, okay? I don't want my cousins thinking this is all I do. I don't want them thinking all I do is run out on them," Nicola murmurs to Max, shrugging. I've noticed that shrug of hers is a huge indicator of how uncomfortable she is, just how much she wants the small amount of family she's got and hates hurting them.

"Of course, Nic. You know Aurelia wouldn't let them think that, anyway," Max assures her, but by the look on Nicola's face, I don't think she really believes it.

Max mouths a few words and snaps her fingers, dropping whatever soundproofing juju she put up.

"I can't drop the ward on the house, so you'll have to go outside to leave. It shouldn't matter. Samara just got here, and shit is going down with her, so I don't think anyone will see you go," Max instructs us.

"What happened with Samara?" Nicola and I ask at the same time. I know for a fact Nicola saved Samara's life once upon a time. She might not remember it, but Samara is important to her. In fact, one of the things Nicola did lose was her grasp of languages. Normally, Rhys or Mena translate for her, but the old Nicola didn't need it. Even blind, she could always understand the mute Samara.

"No idea, I used the commotion to slip up here. But you need to go if you're going. I have a feeling I'm about to be sucked into some drama I want no part of. So, scoot," Max orders as she does a little finger wave and hightails it out of our room.

Nicola starts packing a leather overnight bag that somehow ended up in our room, throwing our clothes into it and zipping it before I can even move to help.

No wonder she was able to duck me at the hospital last time. She can pack faster than anyone I know. I don't say this out loud, though. I know enough about my wife that a comment like that would end badly for me.

My stomach fills with dread at the thought that we're really going—that we're leaving our friends and family behind.

"Done," she announces as I steal the bag from her hand and wind our fingers together. Nicola tips her head up, and I drop a kiss on her lips.

I hope whatever we're walking into isn't the last thing we ever do.

9

NICOLA

ARRIVING IN NEW ORLEANS UNDETECTED IN THE MIDDLE OF the day during whatever-the-hell festival is going on is tricky. We end up traveling in a swath of smoke into a deserted alleyway behind a dumpster, the smell of garbage and urine is enough to make me gag. I've gotten used to the clean mountain air of both Kentucky and Colorado, and this is like a slap in the face. The humidity and heat smack me next, and it is all I can do to not pass out or hurl at the one-two punch. It's practically December, but evidently, the state of Louisiana did not get the memo.

"Sorry, Shortcake," Kyle mumbles as he pulls me by the hand out of the alley and onto a street heavy with foot traffic. The last time I was in a city was Knoxville, and even then I didn't get to see much. The diverse pulse of locals and tourists beats like a frantic heart slowed by molasses. People meander instead of walk, and yet the throng is thick enough to make me twitchy.

I don't know if I've ever been to NOLA before, or if Iva merely wore my skin like a party dress here. The fact that I can't remember digs at me more than it probably should considering I can't change the past. I suppose I'll get right on being well-adjusted when I have a spare moment. Maybe pencil it in two weeks from never going to happen.

My twitchy gets worse when I lose the warmth of Kyle's fingers. It isn't anything major, merely an accidental bump from a passerby—but the organ in my chest doesn't know that, or more than likely it just doesn't give a shit.

When that same rude passerby brushes my shoulder, I see everything I wish I couldn't.

The man, Marcus, as a scrawny boy playing on the banks of the mighty Mississippi River, the sun beating down on his mocha skin.

Marcus in threadbare but clean clothes as he kicked rocks on his way to elementary school, sour at his mother because she made him do extra reading the night before.

Marcus trying to read a book for class aloud, but the other children mock him for his stutter. They don't know that it is simply reading out loud that is the problem, and he would read forever if he could do it in his head.

In the Army recruiter's office signing up to serve his country. It doesn't matter to him which war he has to fight. He sees the steady income after everyone was losing their jobs or moving deeper and deeper into the crime and filth. His momma said he was too smart for that mess. He wants to prove her right.

In a desert, next to a large vehicle on fire trying to help his friend staunch the flow of blood from a stomach wound and ignoring the wound in his leg. He yells and yells, but when the helo comes, his friend Jacob was already gone.

Coming home with a dependence on opiates and a limp to find his childhood home demolished by a hurricane and no money to rebuild. Parents are gone. Family scattered all over, and the insurance doesn't pay out.

Fuzzy in-between times where barely surviving and wanting to die merge and coalesce together in one huge blur. A dirty needle, a hospital bed, and then nothing, nothing, nothing...

The man isn't rude, he's high as a kite on whatever brand of poison he can get for cheap so he can drown out the pain in his head. Soon, he'll be stuck in a coma for years and years while his body slowly dies. I want to hug him or slap him. I want to get him help. I also never want to touch anyone by accident ever again.

A group of laughing women flow like water around me. A young woman bumps me this time, and I nearly scream at her future. She'll die within six months—alcohol poisoning in her sorority house while two men unzip their pants. I learn from the last one and I grab her by the wrist before she can get away, her name coming to me.

"Carmen, stop drinking. If you don't, you'll die within six months in the upstairs blue bathroom while two men rape you," I order, my voice firm but quiet. My eyes are probably blazing gold fire, but I have to stop her.

Her frightened voice trembles as she whispers a frightened, "What?" while she tries to tug her arm back.

"Stop. Drinking. Get better friends. Don't trust Aaron or Ben. They are going to hurt you. Do you understand?" My voice is harsh as are my words, but she has to know.

"What the fuck are you, lady?" her high, thready voice hits my ears, and it is then that I realize I can't see at all. I can't see with my eyes at the moment, but I can with my mind. Her future is already changing for the better.

When her wrist leaves my fingers, I want to throw up. I want to grab the first man I saw—the wounded vet—but I don't know where he is anymore.

I can't see anything at all, and the loss of the sense is more than jarring. My feet move where I think Kyle might be, but I'm lost here in this solitary darkness surrounded by so many strangers.

Another person bumps me. The woman lives a normal life and dies of old age in seventy years surrounded by her children.

A man brushes past—he dies in three years of heart failure while diddling his mistress...

There are too many people here. Too many chances for me to be touched by these strangers. I don't want their memories or lives or future on my soul.

I don't want this. Am I supposed to save them? Should I change their lives? I did with the sorority girl, but was I right to do so? Did I do the wrong thing? What right do I have to change their circumstances? Isn't that what Iva was doing—changing the position of the players on the board until all she could see was how she could move them?

My breaths come fast and shallow. Even though I can't see a single thing, I'm dizzy in a way that I know I'm about to pass out on the pavement.

Panic attack. This is a panic attack.

But I'm saved again when the warm, safe touch of Kyle's fingers thread with mine before another person can steal my sight—before I have to see how awful their deaths will be.

"Jesus. I looked back, and you were gone. What the fuck, Nicola, you started walking the other way," he growls in my ear, but he must sense that I'm hanging on by a thread because he wraps an arm around me, protecting me from the crowd. Even in the heat, his warmth is a balm to my tattered nerves. I claw at him, burrowing into his chest as I grip the fabric of his shirt.

"I can't see, Ky. Too many visions. You have to get me out of here," I whisper, trembling so bad I have trouble getting the words out. I know he hears me fine when he sweeps me up into his arms and moves us. Cool air conditioning caresses my face, the scent changing drastically once we get inside.

"Can I help you? Oh my god, is she okay?" a young yet smoky female voice calls.

"Yeah, it's the heat. We're from up north, so she's not used to it," Kyle replies.

"I have some bottled water in the employee fridge. I'll be right back," the woman offers and her footsteps float away.

Information comes to me faster than I can help. Her name is Grace. She's twenty-nine and single. Her only real companion is a German Shepherd named Joe who hides out in the back room of this boutique until she can close up for the day and moves to her apartment upstairs. She owns this shop, scraping together everything she saved and the inheritance from some long dead grandmother to buy it. Grace is also nearly a full-blooded Witch and has absolutely no idea. She was adopted at birth to a lovely, healthy, close-knit human family.

Fabulous—well, I sort of mean that one. Honestly, believing she's human might be the best thing for her in this climate, but right now that helps us precisely nil. Except for maybe the bottle of water she's holding in her hand as she passes it off to Kyle. I guzzle the cold liquid, letting it cool the burn in my throat—allowing it to quiet the scream brewing there. I hate that I can only see her in my head and not with my eyes.

While I may be happy Grace—as sweet as she is in my mind's eye— isn't mired in the violence that is coming, we came to New Orleans for answers, and she doesn't have them.

Or at least I don't think she does.

"Y'all aren't even close to human. The way she's lighting up like a Christmas tree and the cast of your eyes, I'm gonna go ahead and bet on it. Let me turn my sign to closed, and you can tell me what in the blue hell you think you're doing here in my shop. The coven knows they aren't welcome and if you're here to start trouble, you aren't either," Grace informs us in her smoky southern drawl. The slide of the deadbolt and slither of the sign against the glass door makes me shiver a little.

"We aren't here to cause trouble, but it does seem to follow us around like a magnet. We were getting out of the foot traffic," Kyle assures her, but I do the exact opposite of what I'm supposed to do. I do the exact opposite of what he wants me to do, too.

I cause trouble.

Reaching across the space between us, I grab Grace's forearm—not hard or rough, but not too gentle either. I face her general direction, but I can't guarantee that I'm meeting her eyes—a fact that irks me probably as much as it is unnerving for her. She isn't more or less than I thought she was. She isn't nefarious or evil. Grace is utterly unaware yet aware all at the same time. She sees but doesn't understand. And she's protected, heavily so.

"Why are the Witches not welcome here? What did they do?" I ask, or rather demand as my voice comes out more like an order for answers instead of a request.

"Nic, what the fuck are you doing?" Kyle whispers a growl, the tenseness rolling off of him in waves.

But Grace is smart because she answers me with a single bit of hesitation.

"I see more than I'm supposed to. They don't like that," Grace says, and I can tell by her tone that her defiance is more out of fear than anything else.

Grace doesn't know enough about us or anything really. She doesn't understand at all. She sees through glamours meant for humans in a city filled with supernaturals, yet doesn't understand. Yeah, I'd bet no one likes that.

"Who doesn't like that?" Kyle growls, and I know he already knows the answer like I do.

"Well, he didn't exactly give me a name, and he didn't stick around, but I made sure the coven knew he especially wasn't welcome," Grace hedges, and I let her go, fear for the girl stealing through me.

Oh, no.

"Let me guess, tall, blonde, blue eyes without a single shred of humanity, built like a linebacker, and could pass for fraternity douche. That about cover it?" I offer Baron's description and pray I'm wrong. I'm not.

"Yeah. How'd you know all that?" Grace asks, her voice thread with fear. Baron more than likely earned it.

"Who do you think we're looking for? He hurt one of my friends. Tortured her and other things besides. You see that man on the street, you do not walk, you run away. Got it?" Kyle orders her, and as a fellow Witch—no matter the degrees of separation—he is wired to protect more than anything else. Something feels different about her, though.

"Already planned on it. I didn't get a good feel for the man, to say the least. He came in here about a month ago. Started breaking things in the shop. But he wasn't breaking them with his hands. Thought I was going crazy at the time—which isn't really new—but I could have sworn he was breaking them with his mind. Gave me a card and told me to call the woman on it. Told me to give her a message and he would never darken my door again. He watched me call her and deliver the message and then he left. Told me to tell her 'Bishop takes pawn.' I ventured a guess that I was the pawn in the scenario."

"I would say that's a safe assumption. Who did he have you call?" Kyle asks.

"Marjorie Baxter. The coven leader of the Southeast United States."
Fuck me sideways. Of course, he did.

And that was why no one was stopping them. No one was even trying. The covens knew about Baron and Bella. They had to.

They knew what the Bishop children were doing too. Because it would only take the tiniest bit of conjecture to figure out that Grace was more than likely Marjorie's blood—be she a daughter, niece, cousin, or hell, even granddaughter—and Baron knew it too.

Bishop takes pawn.

Maybe Grace thinking she was human wasn't such a good idea after all.

IO

KYLE

WHEN WE DECIDED ON NEW ORLEANS—OR SHALL I SAY WHEN I offered to go to NOLA to seek out the pieces of the Veil—I suggested it as a throwaway. I never expected to find anything here. I knew we had allies in the Wolfpack—I knew we would have a haven here even with all that Iva had done.

I knew we should have gone directly to the Wolves. We should have waited to get into the city. Why did I think this city would be anything but fucking misery? So far that is all it has brought me.

After getting here, it has been one thing after another. I lost Nicola in the crowd—something that gives me chills merely thinking about—and when I found her, her sightless eyes glowed gold. Never has she done that in public. Showed her Phoenix side to humans. To get her out of the open, I hauled her into the first shop we came to—a shop ten doors down from where I wanted to go—because I didn't have another option.

The plan was to keep her busy and safe—to keep Nicola on a wild goose chase. Yeah, I was a dick. Yeah, I was doing the wrong thing. But I was doing it for the right reasons. Too many times have we stumbled into a fight that wasn't ours. Too many times have we ended up hurt for someone else. And I only wanted to keep her breathing, to keep her alive, to keep her safe.

Not for the first time, my plan blew to shit. Hell, I should be used to that by now.

To learn that Baron had been here so recently, and how much he arranged the chess pieces on the board, so to speak, made me realize that we weren't dealing with amateur Witches. We weren't dealing with the idiot who stupidly used Wolves to fetch Nicola—Wolves with an ax to grind. No, we were dealing with someone with internal knowledge of how the covens worked, knowledge of how the bloodlines had been forged for centuries.

I don't know how they went from a duo I would easily ignore if they hadn't hurt my wife—to formative foes so quickly. The change in them might mean that Baron is driving this train now and if that is the case, my underestimation might come to bite us in the ass.

I examine Grace. She's cute and could be considered by some as beautiful, but her newness, her earnestness shows how much she does not know about this world. Her blue eyes are unguarded and open. She's slender in the way most Witches are, the magic under their skin sucking up fat and calories like a teenage athlete hoovering through an all-you-can-eat buffet. Her dark hair is pulled from her face into a complicated braid that hangs over one shoulder which gives her another mark in the young column.

If I weren't a Wraith, I wouldn't be able to smell the scent of magic on her skin—however faint it might be. I don't think she has ever cast, and if she hasn't—even by accident—then she must not know what she is. And if she doesn't know what she is, and Baron does, then she has more problems than we do.

My thoughts turn from Grace to the name Marjorie Baxter, and my stomach turns a little. There are a few women on this planet who are so outwardly beautiful and good but still end up sneaking up and stabbing you in the back anyway.

Marjorie is one of them.

Not an evil bone in her body—or at least she didn't have any thirty years ago—but she still ended up treating me like I was filth for having mixed heritage. Coven politics are beyond me, and honestly, I don't want to know the ins and outs of what actually went down. But Marjorie used to be a friend—if not more. If my guess is right, Grace is her blood in one way or another.

"Did you know of Marjorie before then? Did you even know Witches existed?" I ask that last one practically under my breath already pissed at Marj for not keeping better eyes on her kin. The woman I knew was better than that at least.

I ask the questions Nicola isn't, figuring she probably already knows the answer, but I need to know them too. Nic feels around, still blind from whatever vision just slammed into her and I hate that I don't have her probing cane with us. I feel like an asshole for not bringing it, not thinking her blindness would ever return. I guide Nicola to a plush armchair and watch her for a moment as she guzzles water from the bottle in her hand.

"Did I know Witches existed? As in the 'I have real magical fucking powers' kind? I had an inkling. The stuff I see leans toward there being something more than the human world, but I'm willing to admit I could probably fill a library with all the shit I don't know. And no, I'd never heard the name Marjorie Baxter in my fucking life. I'm assuming she's heard of me, though, hasn't she?" Grace grouses, her arms crossed over her chest.

"Do you still have that card—the one Baron gave you?" Nic asks, her gaze not quite meeting Grace's.

"Was that his name? He looked like a rich douche. If that isn't a rich douche name, I don't know what is," Grace mutters. "Yes, I have it somewhere upstairs." Grace looks confused, and it hits me that while she might not think Witches are the only supernatural thing out there, she's never seen people like us.

"I need it. It could give me more information. Can you get it for me please?" Nic requests, but I think it might be simply to get Grace out of the room.

When Grace is out of earshot, Nicola whispers, "She has not one clue how to protect herself. It's going to get her killed. I don't know for certain if she'll die in the near future, but she doesn't even know she is a Witch and none of that mixed with Baron fucking Bishop is a good sign. We have to tell her, don't we?"

"Probably. If I were in her shoes, I'd want to know."

"Well, shit. We'll see what the card tells me. And we need a probing cane or something because I can't see fuck all right now. If this keeps happening when we're in crowds I'm going to need a bloody bubble," she gripes, her body shivering with whatever she gleaned from accidentally knocking into people.

"What did you see, Shortcake?"

"Death. It's what I always see."

Grace's footfalls sound above us, and then the half-stomps come down the stairs as she makes her way toward us, brandishing the olive green business card like a weapon.

I gently take the cardstock from Grace before she can give it to Nicola and I look it over. Nothing special, merely dark green linen cardstock with white lettering. It tells me Marjorie currently resides in Savannah, Georgia, and other than her contact info, it doesn't say much else. That makes sense because more than likely, this is spelled so only Witches can read it, and the headquarters for the Southeastern Coven are in Savannah.

Nicola holds out her hand for the card, and since the sky didn't fall in when I touched it, I reluctantly give it to her.

Nicola's eyes glow bright gold when her fingers brush the cardstock, and the gasp that passes her lips isn't pained, thank the fucking Fates. I think it is a good sign until her eyes dim and the expression on her face is part rage, part fear, and a heavy dose of hurt. Blood doesn't weep from her eyes, though, so I'll take it as soon as I find out what caused the look on her face.

"What the hell was that?" Grace whispers, looking at Nicola wide-eyed. I'm lucky the tears on Nicola's face are the saline kind and not the blood kind. But then again, if she's crying, that isn't good at all.

"Nicola has... abilities," I hedge, my gruff response the definition of an understatement. I don't know how much we should tell Grace.

"No shit, Sherlock," Grace shoots back, irritated at my lack of explanation.

Nicola sucks in a trembling breath, and I know deep in my gut something is wrong. It might not be the life and death kind of wrong, but all the same, I feel like I'm about to get screwed.

"Tell her the truth, Ky. She needs to know. She can't protect herself otherwise," Nic's rough voice is half taunting and half pissed the fuck off, and I have absolutely no idea why she could be pissed at me.

But then it dawns on me that if that card came from Marj, then Nic might know about our brief, ill-timed, and catastrophic fling. Fuuuuuccccckkkkk.

"But..." I trail off not quite wanting to broach the subject of me screwing this girl's mom. Like ever.

"Fine. I'll tell her," Nicola snaps, sitting back in the plush chair, her arms crossing tight over her chest.

This is not good.

"Grace, Marjorie is your mother. She is a Witch. That makes you a Witch whether you cast or not. I suggest you learn how because your adoptive family is going to realize you've quit aging in about five years. I would recommend staying away from the Southeastern Coven for the foreseeable future. They are in an uproar ever since their leader was executed for crimes against the Ethereal. AKA murdering small children and using death magics to bring someone back from Hell. Your mother took the former leader's position, and now the former leader's children are trying to overthrow the whole coven. Any questions?"

Grace guppies for a moment, her mouth opening and closing as she tries to digest the mountain of shit Nic just vomited out into the open. Subtle, Nicola is not. I don't know if I should be pissed at her or amazed that she managed to rip the Band-Aid off in a truly remarkable fashion.

"Well, I wondered who my birth parents were, I guess I've got half of the equation now, don't I?"

Grace throws up her hands and moves around me to plop into the purple plush chair that clashes, yet kind of compliments it's blue counterpart where Nicola currently resides. The table between the two chairs is filled with antique-looking jewelry resting on black velvet jewelry stands mixed with more contemporary pieces hanging from paint-splattered sculptures. The whole boutique is like this—mixing trendy clothes and odd things that you'd think wouldn't work but seem to gel together all the same.

Like her seemingly odd outfit. Grace mixes classic and bohemian styles—blending a pair of cuffed jeans with a floaty, gauzy bright white top and a fuchsia lightweight blazer with the sleeves rolled up to her elbows. A tangle of thin gold necklaces hang from her neck—each one different, but working together, and each wrist has the same treatment. Each bracelet with either an odd design or dangling charm.

I don't know why that catches my eye, but I think at this point I'd rather look at girly jewelry than at my wife. I feel ire and rage, and coming from Nicola, I want no part of either.

"Oh, no. We have the whole equation. Grace, meet your father," Nicola gestures to me, "Kyle. Sweetheart, care to share how you would sleep with, not to mention have a child with a woman who would treat you like garbage?"

A brick to the face would have been less of a surprise.

"Say what now?" I squeak. I actually fucking squeak. Holy god, is that my voice? Did my balls shrivel up and fall off my body?

I need to sit down.

I want to say there is no way, but I don't exactly remember putting the goalie into play the handful of times Marj and I got together.

"Are you sure?" I whisper to Nicola, the hope warring with disbelief in my tone. Yeah, I've always wanted kids, but I wanted to raise them, I wanted to be there from day one. Not finding out twenty-odd years later. I don't know anything about this woman before me.

"Oh yeah. Got a thing for redheads, do you?" Nicola fires back with enough ire to shrivel my balls.

Marj isn't a redhead exactly. Maybe a strawberry blonde at a push, and it was thirty years ago. But none of that really matters to Nicola. She is jealous and pissed off and... I don't know what.

"Whoa, whoa, whoa. No freaking way. He can't be more than thirty-five. Unless he hit puberty as a freaking kindergartener, there is no way he supplied half of my genetic material if you know what I'm sayin'," Grace counters and I almost laugh at the utter and complete absurdity of this whole situation.

Almost.

Am I in a soap opera and no one told me? What the fuck? And now I have to explain the supernatural world to Grace... *my daughter.*

Holy shitballs, I have a daughter.

"Yeah... I'm older than I look. Remember when Nicola said your adoptive family would realize you quit aging? You might have missed that tidbit when my lovely wife blasted you with information, but yeah... I'm a lot older than I appear," I try to explain calmly.

"Oh, God. You're not a vampire or some shit, are you? I'm not half vampire, am I? Because honestly, I can deal with the Witch thing, but the 'I vant to suck your blood!' thing is a hard pass for me," Grace rants, her arm making a sweeping motion to emphasize the throwing of vampires off the table. It's cute in a sad sort of way that I have to tell her that there are worse things out there.

Things like her father.

She must see something on my face because she waves her hand in another sweeping motion to wipe her words away.

"I don't really want to know, do I?" Grace asks, her face screwed up into a wince.

"There is no such thing as vampires. Well, not in the traditional movie-version sense. There are Wraiths otherwise known as Soul Eaters who ferry souls to hell in a rather gruesome way, but unless you get hungry every time you meet a rather unsavory person, that gene might have skipped you. You're only a quarter Wraith so those genes might be latent. Plus, you've been on high alert and I don't see any fangs or talons or black eyes, so... I wouldn't worry about it," I shrug as I give my answer, studying her now gray face.

"Oh, that is so not helpful," Grace mutters.

She looks like a crazy beautiful amalgamation of Marj and I. Grace has my tan skin, black hair, and height as she stands just under six feet. But I see Marj in her too—a fact that doesn't pain me as much as it might if I didn't have Nicola in my life. Grace has Marj's tiny nose and clear, blue eyes, and I have no idea how she could give this child up or leave me out of every single decision of her life up until now.

The way we ended—the way Marj shunned me—I could see where having my child might have been the last thing she would have wanted. But I would have wanted Grace. I would have loved her from the beginning. It burns deep in my chest that Grace might have even been unwanted. But I don't really care how Marj treated me. I care that Grace was lost to me until now. That is the only hurt I feel in this—that I missed so much.

I want to help Grace understand, but I'm at a loss.

A whine comes from the back room, and Grace ticks her tongue against her teeth. An exceptionally large, male German Shepherd plods toward our tight circle, not wary of us in the slightest which is odd. Generally, people like Nicola and I freak animals way the hell out.

Maybe because our kind tread between worlds where so many others do not.

I don't have time to ponder it much further because the dog starts barking his head off just as Nicola turns her head toward the windows and gasps.

Nicola only manages to croak out a strangled, "Get down!" before the storefront glass blows in on us, fire coating the antique dress forms and tables of clothing between us and the exit.

Well, this is a fine welcome to the family.

II

KYLE

THE CRUNCH AND BITE OF GLASS BENEATH MY PALMS WAKES ME up in a way I didn't think possible. My hearing is gone—the blast diminishing it to a high-pitched ringing that seems to be only broken by the roar of the flames licking up the brick walls. The concussion of the blast must have done a number on me because it takes me a minute to realize that looks wrong.

Unless the walls of Grace's trendy boutique had been hosed down with accelerant, that shouldn't be possible.

I'm still stuck on the fucking bricks when my hearing comes back, and it is Nicola's muted but pained scream that pierces my ears. Because she was closest to Grace, because she knew when none of us did, because she gave a shit about my daughter even though it tore at her that I had one, because she has been ingrained from a lifetime of doing it, she threw herself in between the blast and my girl.

Even though Grace is much bigger, Nicola has her covered with her smaller body, the glass shrapnel embedded in her back glinting with firelight. Nic's bleeding again, but at least this time she's breathing. I don't count it as a victory yet. If I don't get us out of this fire, we're going to burn. Nicola may be fireproof, but Grace, the dog, and I aren't.

Because of our tie, if I burn, so does Nic, and I don't want my wife to die because of me.

With Nicola in mind, I don't feel the heat of flames that crawl closer and closer to me or the bite of glass against my palms. I don't hear the ring in my ears at all. All I hear is her wounded whimper as she tries to move off of Grace. It's then I realize that Nicola and Grace's big beast of a dog have tried to cover my daughter up as much as possible—shielding her with their bodies. As much as I know none of this is normal, I can't help but be grateful.

When my hands find Nic, her whimper turns into an agonized moan, the glass in her back shifting with each movement. I do the only thing I can. I grasp Grace's face, making sure even if her hearing is gone, she can read my lips.

"Grab your dog and hold onto Nicola. This is going to hurt," I instruct her and Grace clamps onto the scruff of his neck and nods. I wrap my arms around Nicola and feel myself practically rip in half in my attempt to travel out of this hell. I'm injured—not that I can feel it—so my power is drained. Nicola is bleeding, and Grace is screaming, and the dog is barking, and it's so hard to focus. Blackness swirls around us, and I have to grit my teeth against the agony of carrying all of us from this place.

Then the smell of smoke is gone, and the heat of flames doesn't scald my skin. The scent of the alleyway stings my nostrils—the bite of dead fish, vomit, urine, and fried chicken makes me want to gag, but since I can breathe in semi-fresh air instead of smoke, I'm calling it a win.

It seems I didn't get us very far. I look up at the sign above the alleyway door of Grace's store, Rewind. Shit. I must be hurt more than I thought if I didn't make it more than this.

Nicola stirs in my arms, a moan of agony ripping up her throat as she moves and my eyes land on the large shard of tempered glass protruding from her shoulder blade.

"Take it out, please. I can't... breathe," Nicola pleads, but I don't want to do what she asks of me. I don't want to hurt her this way.

Truth is, I don't have another option.

I wrap my fingers around the shard and yank, preferring to do it fast than the gentle way that would take time I don't think we have. The glass cuts into my palm, but it will heal quickly.

Someone blew up Grace's shop—the same shop that's currently smoldering just past this brick wall. The same shop that Nicola and I just so happened to stumble upon when we had no intention of coming here. The same shop that I would bet my left nut was hit with a bomb full of magic.

Someone knows we're here. Someone knows, and if Nicola and I aren't the target, then Grace is.

Bishop takes pawn. That motherfucker.

Nicola's gasp of pain hits me straight in the gut. I know a million facts from that one gasp. She's hurt, she's trying not to scream, she's trying to avoid drawing attention... plus so many other things. I think she feels the danger like I do. The niggle in the back of my mind that tells me we aren't alone—that getting out of the building is the least of our worries.

"Shortcake?" I start, but she cuts me off.

"I'll heal. Don't worry about me," Nicola barks. "We have problems coming. Grace, darling girl, are you okay?" she coos to my daughter, dismissing me as if I were at fault.

What the fuck? I didn't blow up Grace's shop. I didn't hide a daughter from her. I didn't put the glass in her back.

"I-I think so? I don't think I'm cut or anything, but Joe's hurt," Grace practically whimpers, more worried about the dog than herself. I'm not altogether certain 'Joe' is actually a dog at all, but that is a problem for another time.

"I think he's only knocked out. We need to get the hell out of here, though," I answer her concerns with a calm voice even though I am anything but calm. Someone will come if we don't get out of here—if they aren't already on their way.

"Can you stand, Shortcake?" I murmur, keeping my voice quiet.

"You call her Shortcake?" Grace snickers, but the way she does it, it seems my daughter has reached the very edge of her ability to cope.

"Yeah, but I need a little help. Grace, darling girl, I'm going to need you to quit laughing like a mental patient for a minute. I need to listen."

Grace quiets her snickers just in time for Nicola to murmur a pissed off, "Shit!"

"What?" I ask, but I think I already know.

The alleyway opening to our left is obscured by two men. I can't make out their faces, but I know already I'm dealing with Witches. I don't know if it is the black hoodies they're wearing, but simply wearing the thick, black fabric in this heat would be a dead giveaway that these men are not friendlies.

Shit is right.

I whip my head to the left to check the only other way out and breathe a truncated sigh of relief that it isn't blocked. It isn't a full one because I have an injured Nicola who probably cannot remember how to fight at all, a half-crazed daughter who is one stumbling step away from losing it, and a passed out two-hundred-pound dog on our hands. Oh, and the exit is five shops away at the end of the fucking block, and I think my traveling ability might be broken.

Aces.

Murmured words hit my ears, and it doesn't take a genius to tell me shit is about to head south real fucking quick if I can't figure out a way out of here and fast. The smell of ozone and a burning streak of a spell singes past my cheekbone, and I can't decide if that was a warning shot or if they are just that bad at aiming.

Weak as I am, I don't have the juice to get us out of here. If I didn't make it past the alley, this is a certainty. But traveling takes more than just about any spell I can think of, and I might have enough in me to take care of these two fuckers.

Maybe. If I'm lucky.

It doesn't matter what vows I took after the Witches betrayed us. It doesn't matter that I swore I wouldn't cast again. What matters right now is staying alive—protecting my wife, my daughter.

Fuck my vows.

I thrust myself to my feet, getting between the men and Nicola and Grace. The Latin passes my lips in a muttered curse as I breathe the spell onto my fingertips and then snap them together. The snap of my fingers wrenches screams of agony from the men, the pair of them clutching their heads as the spell I cast burst blood vessel after blood vessel in their brains. It's a nasty way to die, but there are Witches who don't exactly stay dead. Witches who practice the dark arts—necromancy and the like. Not only do I not put it past them to be of that lot, I plan on it.

The two men are still writhing on the ground screaming, but I don't trust it. I don't trust that this is all that is coming for us. We were lead here. We were funneled to this alley. Two men I could easily subdue is not the only thing coming for us.

"We need to get the fuck out of here, ladies," I mutter as I pull Nicola to her feet and then reach down for Grace, but she has no intention of going easy.

"We have to bring Joe. We. Have. To," Grace insists as she buries her hands into the dog's fur.

There really isn't any arguing with her so I won't. Plus, Joe put himself between a blast and my daughter. If he really is a dog, he's getting a steak from me. If he isn't, he probably still getting a steak—it just might be cooked. I look in my girl's eyes, realizing in that moment, that I don't mind she shares the color with her mother. I don't mind because despite the burn of what her mother did to me—before and after all of this—I'm glad Grace is here on this earth.

A guttural growl takes me by surprise. When I lift my eyes from Grace to Nicola, I'm taken off guard once again. Nic is half-phased—fire racing over her skin almost faster than my eye can catch. The oranges and reds and blues of her flames lick up her arms before the orange plumes of her wings burst from her back. Nicola's growl morphs into a scream so fast I don't have time to react.

I should have been paying attention.

I should have—but I wasn't—so when three more Witches come from behind us, I am unprepared.

And when fresh agony hits me square in the back, all I can think is *I should have known better.*

12

NICOLA

My vision is not something I have adjusted to living without. So when it leaves me unprepared and helpless, I can't wait to get it back. But seeing Kyle fall in my mind and then watching him crumble with my eyes, it makes me wish I couldn't see at all.

But I can.

I watch in vivid detail as the putrid red light of a spell hits Kyle right between his shoulder blades. An expression of shock crosses his beautiful face before his eyes roll up into his head and he falls to the floor of this filthy alleyway. He's breathing—I know that much—but he isn't moving otherwise and all I can see is red.

I wouldn't call myself a particularly angry person, but at this moment I am the definition of rage. I am wrath personified, and the fire on my skin is my tool of destruction.

Because I will make these men and women pay—even if I have to burn this whole fucking city down to do it. My wings twitch as if they have a mind of their own, and they're itching to jump in with me and kick some ass. I'm pissed that this stupid, dirty, fucking alleyway is too narrow for me to pick us up and get us the hell out of here.

It makes me happy I have a few little surprises from Max tucked away in my boots. I dodge a streak of yellow magic and reach into my low-heeled booties for the three throwing knives and amulet Max slipped me before she headed downstairs to deal with whatever shit hit the fan with Samara.

Just in case, she'd said. Just in case was right.

I slip the leather string of the necklace over my head with my right hand and grab one of the thin knives with my left. Whether it is muscle memory from the thousands of times Kyle forced me to train with him or my body actually remembering what my brain cannot, but my hand is sure as I close it around the steel hilt and I let the blade fly.

My aim is true, hitting one of the three dead center. The slight hooded figure claws at the blade for a few futile seconds before slumping to the pavement. His two buddies are thoroughly displeased and show their ire in the form of red streaks of magic rocketing toward us at lightning speed.

I didn't think I would need Max's care package so early in this quest, nor did I think it would be so insufficient. Three knives and a small shielding amulet are not going to fucking cut it in this chokepoint on an alleyway. I do what I can to shield the loved ones behind me and spread my wings to deflect the spells and absorb whatever blast is coming my way. Feathers don't exactly offer much cover, but it's all I've got.

When their magics hit me, the force of them drives me back on a foot, but other than a faint smell of ozone, I am unharmed. I can't keep the wrathful smile off of my face as I hurtle another knife down the alley. My smile only growing when my knife hits its mark—buried in the chest of another Witch.

I suppose I should feel guilty for killing. I shouldn't relish exacting my wrath on these people. I shouldn't want to kill to survive.

And part of me doesn't.

But there are parts of me—in the deep, dark recesses of my soul—that don't mind killing to keep my loved ones safe. There are parts of me that don't mind killing at all. There are parts of me that hunger to consume the evil of this world, and because of who I am, because of who my husband is, I wonder if this is why there have been so few unions between our species.

I wonder if we became something else entirely—not exactly Phoenix, not exactly Wraith, but something else—when we bonded. At this point, I don't care that I am different or odd or other. I don't care that I relish in death or that I am now dealing death like cards at a casino.

My only care is keeping Kyle and Grace and even Joe alive. That and watching Baron Bishop burn for hurting my friends and family. After that, I'm not exactly certain I give a shit.

The remaining Witch doesn't seem to want to go down without a fight. The hood of her jacket falls as she hits me with another spell. This one, I feel. Its barbed, toxic tendrils rake my skin before sliding off me. I don't know what kind of magic would do that, but I think I'd better kill this woman before I find out. The amulet Max spelled is hot against my skin, and I am positive it will not sustain me for much longer.

I don't have enough time to throw my last knife before she hits me again. This time, I feel the slice of the spell cutting into my skin and wings before it slides off of me. The amulet burns through my shirt, scalding my skin before the smooth jade stone cracks down the middle, and I know I am well and truly fucked if I can't kill this bitch before she hits me again.

I let the last knife fly, but this time, I miss my mark, only getting her in the shoulder.

"Get up!" I scream over my shoulder at Grace knowing we have to move—or at least she has to. If I can't eliminate this Witch, if I can't protect her the way Ky would want me to, then she has to run.

I rush the Witch who is gearing up to hit me again. Catching air as I jump the last ten feet, I plant both my hands and feet in her chest taking her to the pavement and burning through her clothes to her skin. I could kill her now, but I need answers.

I study her face for a single moment—close-cropped platinum blonde hair, wide almond eyes the color of rich coffee, high cheekbones, wide mouth. She's beautiful in a strikingly androgynous way, but I don't recognize her from Max's family coven from New Mexico.

I remove my still burning hands and feet from her skin, close my left hand over the hilt protruding from her shoulder, and give it a hard yank as I twist, opening the wound further. Her screams shut off abruptly once she feels the tip of the knife centered over her heart.

"If I hear a single syllable of Latin, I'm going to turn your heart into a fucking shish kabob, got it?"

I get an enthusiastic nod, her eyes wide with the fear of death.

"Did Baron send you?" I ask, but press the blade into her burnt skin harder when she opens her mouth.

"This is a yes or no question. Speaking is not necessary," I command through gritted teeth.

Her head shakes and then nods. I don't get it for a second, but then it comes to me.

"Bella sent you?" I offer already annoyed with this process, and I hadn't even gotten started, but I get a fevered nod in response.

"Were you supposed to kill us?" I ask as blood from her last curse wells from the wounds in my arms and drip, drip, drips down my fingers. I should be healing, but I'm not, and it pisses me off.

This question gets a firm shake of a no, and I have the distinct feeling she's lying to me—so much so that I ask again, but this time I can see the lie on her face. We had done nothing to this woman. We had committed no crime. She was sent here to kill us for no other reason than Bella willed it so.

This woman had no honor, no scruples. She was a mercenary, and I held no regard for Witches who killed without reason.

"Liar," I murmur and then drive the blade home in her heart, watching as the light dims in her eyes.

A niggling part of me, the part I don't like very much, wants to consume her like I'd watched Kyle do once. I can't figure out why I want this so badly, but I shove it aside once I hear the guttural growl of a dog.

I whip around to find Joe herding Grace back against the brick building, putting himself between her and a stirring Witch. I turn back to wrap my fingers around the bloody hilt of the knife in the now-dead Witch's chest and give it a yank, bringing it with me as I stalk my fiery ass back down the alleyway and eliminate the stirring threat.

I don't actually need the knife I hold, but the last time I burned someone alive, I couldn't get the smell out of my nose for a solid week and honestly, I find it thoroughly repugnant.

Two swift drives of the blade and I have ended the stirring Witch and completed a dead check on his buddy. With that done, my strength decides to take a shit on this gore-covered alley and I fall right on my ass on the pavement. My fire dies, and my wings make their painful trek back to their vestigial hiding place.

"Holy fucking shit. Holy shit," Grace breathes. "You killed all those people."

Her words are like a punch in the gut, slamming me with a guilt I shouldn't feel. Protecting her and her father is not wrong. Fighting to live is not wrong. I won't let her think otherwise.

"Yep. They were sent here to kill us. Would you rather I let them complete their errand or are you happy to be breathing? My life is tied to your father's, and I'll be damned if I sit here and let him die because I didn't stand and fight. You want to judge me? Fine. But do it silently."

Grace gives me a shaky nod, realizing maybe a hair too late that I'm at the edge of my rope. I crawl to Kyle, and turn him on his side, resting my forehead on his. This is it. This all the strength I have left.

"Come on, Ky. I need you to wake up. There is no fucking way I can carry your Sasquatch-sized ass up a fire escape. Please, baby," I murmur into his cheek, letting the whiskers of his beard brush my lips. I am so close to breaking, so close to losing it.

I honestly don't know what I'm going to do if he doesn't wake up.

It isn't like we can stay here in this alley for the rest of forever. Someone will come, someone will see. I expect a fire truck any second now. I fully expect onlookers to round the side of the building at any moment and see five corpses I really didn't give a good explanation for.

"Shortcake?" Kyle groans, his eyes struggling to open as a frown creases his forehead.

"Yeah, baby," I murmur on a relieved whisper. "Come on, Ky. Open those beautiful eyes for me."

Kyle's eyes flutter open, and he stares at me for a moment before he hooks a hand behind my neck and pulls me to him. I meet his lips eagerly with mine, grateful that he is alive and awake, and we are out of danger for the immediate present. Granted this isn't the most romantic of locales, but I'll take Ky any way I can get him.

Kyle breaks the kiss, gives my neck a squeeze, and then he thrusts himself up from the pavement to his ass. His head swivels to take stock of the alley, his eyes lingering on the trio of dead bodies at one end and then the pair at the other. Then he takes stock of me, the slow healing of the open wounds on my arms and face, the gore on my hands. Then he looks at Grace who at this moment appears to be on the verge of a nervous breakdown as she hangs onto Joe.

"We need to go, Shortcake," he murmurs. "I'll grab your weapons. We don't need the problem of fingerprints. I'm going to get full and then we can get out of here. Take Grace and Joe. I don't want her to see."

I hate that he feels he has to hide, but he's probably right. Grace couldn't handle another thing.

"That might be a tall order since she watched me take out a handful of Witches, but I'll see what I can do," I whisper back.

The pair of us struggle to our feet, him going to clean up the bodies by way of consumption and I get the lovely task of trying not to frighten Grace farther.

Yay, me.

"Grace, honey, are you alright?" I say as I crouch in front of her as fire engines scream down the street up ahead.

"No. No, I think I'm as far from alright as I could possibly be," Grace mutters as she rakes a hand through her now frayed braid. She seems to collect herself as she stands up, reaching out a hand to help me to my feet.

"I'm sorry I freaked on you earlier. You saved our lives. You protected me when the glass blew in. You got hurt for me. Thank you," she says meeting my eyes. Her words are sincere, and it feels good that she doesn't look at me like I am the spawn of Satan anymore.

"It's really gone, isn't it?" Grace says as she gestures to the building behind me.

"Yeah, baby. Yeah, it is."

"I have to go with you, don't I?" she asks.

"Yeah, darling. You do."

Grace nods twice and seems to steel herself before her eyes float over my head to her father's approach.

His gait is sure and steady, his wounds gone, having healed from the glut of five souls he consumed. He pauses to give me a kiss on my forehead before he reaches down to grab Joe's scruff.

"Time to go," Kyle mutters as he wraps us in his embrace and gets us the hell out of there.

13

KYLE

At any other time in my life, I have had a plan. A backup to the backup. A contingency laden plot of how I should handle a situation. Call it an occupational hazard, good old-fashioned common sense, whatever. But I do not have a plan for this.

I do not have a plan of action for carrying an adult daughter I had no idea existed until an hour ago, her giant fucking dog, and my wife out of Witch-laden New Orleans. Add in the impending authorities and recent assassination attempt, getting the fuck out of dodge is my only thought.

So that is what I do.

When I take in the Spanish moss hanging from the thick branches of a sprawling oak, I realize my mistake. Like an idiot, I took us to the exact place I did not want to go if I could help it. If we had a Witch problem in New Orleans, then Savannah—the hub of the Southeastern coven—is the last place we should be.

But here we are.

It is dusk, but since it is damn near December, it isn't actually that late. The streetlights are already on and houses are lit with string lights even though Thanksgiving was three days ago. The town has decorated for the winter holidays, which doesn't surprise me in the least.

I recognize the house to our left, a sprawling three-story home built in the late 1800's. It used to belong to Marjorie's father, but after his death twenty years ago, it is more than likely Marjorie's now. The brick and iron fence surrounding the courtyard is shot through with an abundance of white twinkle lights, a feat unheard of when Winston Baxter was the head of this house.

I don't want to be here. I have too many memories of this house that I don't want. Granted, I want to have words with Marjorie but only when the whole of us are all at full strength. Not like this, not when Nicola was barely holding onto consciousness and Grace was one tiny tip-toe away from a total fucking breakdown. Meeting your birth mother on a day like today shouldn't be in the cards.

"Where are we?" Grace asks, hugging her elbows to try and hide her shivering. I don't know if it is the cooler temp or shock that has her quaking, but I'm certain my answer is not going to help.

"Savannah," I murmur and watch her eyes widen in surprise before narrowing to slits. "I'm pretty sure this is Marjorie's house. I didn't plan on taking us here. Did you happen to want to be here because I can't think of a good reason why we ended up in this city. This is the last place we should be."

Grace thinks on it a minute, her bottom lip trembling as she gets herself under control.

"I want to meet her. At the very least, she owes me for the bullshit that just went down."

"You honestly think we are going to walk in there to open arms? Don't get your hopes up, kid. This family practically invented assholes," I inform her, remembering my own time on the outside of this very fence.

SAVANNAH, GA 1986

"You tell that... that filth, you will not see him again, Marjorie Anne," Winston roared at his daughter as she tried to get out of the front door. He had her by the arm, and if it weren't for the ward keeping me on this side of the half brick, half wrought iron courtyard fence, I would have ripped his head off five fucking minutes ago.

I knew I was a punk, but I wasn't filth. Sure, with my clothes and hair, no father would want me dating their daughter, but hell, I had a stable job, and I was wealthy. Maybe more so than they were.

"I'm not a child. I'm a goddamn adult and I will make my own decisions. And he isn't filth!" Marj shoots back.

She's right. Marjorie is close to my age, and I'm edging toward my third century on this earth. She hasn't been a child in a long, long time. But Winston Baxter does not give that first fuck about his daughter. He doesn't give a ripe shit about her wants or needs. He cares about one thing, and one thing alone: status. Blood status and family wealth.

In that order.

My blood status is decidedly murky, and I have no family wealth. Mine has come from hard work and exceptional skill, not sitting on my ass while my parents handed me money.

The Baxter's have a long tradition of coming in second place, but it's a seat they don't want to lose. Second place—at least in a coven—is almost as good as first. Second place offers much of the power of leading with none of the death threats or responsibilities.

And Winston fucking Baxter loves his seat at the table.

"He's half Wraith, Marjorie. Half! Like we wouldn't learn who his father was, the bloody cretin," Winston informed her, spittle running down his chin.

Dammit. I wanted to tell her, but it never seemed to be the right time. How the fuck do I tell my woman that I wasn't all my grandmother said I was? Gran was a good woman, but she lied to keep this exact shit from happening. Now, I wished she hadn't said anything at all.

"What?" Marjorie breathed, as if her father's words were a blow. I never thought she would ever care what I was or who my parents were. But by the look on her face, she did.

"Do you even know who he is? What he does? Kyle Brennan is in no uncertain terms a bounty hunter. A bottom-feeding low life who uses his ill-gotten gifts to find people and blasted treasure. He is nothing more than trash, and I'll be damned if I don't keep him on the curb where he belongs."

Marjorie gently pried her arm from her father's grasp and turned to face me. The look on her face was a mask of revulsion and shame. We had an entire courtyard between us, but I knew. I knew she despised Wraiths as much as her father did. I knew that no matter that I didn't have a choice in how I was born or the power that ran in my veins, she didn't care.

His words hurt, but her not defending me hurt worse. Marjorie Baxter was no better than her bigoted, power hungry father. But at least I got to see it with my own two eyes. Those, at least, I could trust. I sure as shit couldn't trust another Witch.

That was for damn certain.

"You should go, Kyle, and I don't think we should see each other anymore," Marj said in an even tone but with a face that looked like she was tasting something bad. What a bitch. That same mouth twisted in disgust was kissing me two hours ago, was saying my name and telling me she loved me.

She didn't have that first fucking clue what love meant.

"Yeah, you fucking think? Good luck being his lapdog, sugar. I'm sure it will work out just fine for you," I said and then turned my back on her and that house and never looked back.

Good riddance.

KYLE

I don't want to be within three hundred miles of this fucking fence, let alone three feet from it. Nor do I want Grace anywhere near her mother or whatever shit she has going on with Baron. More than likely, Marj did Grace a favor by giving her up. Marj's father was a small-minded, selfish man. If Grace had grown up in this house with his influence—even for such a short time—she might not be the woman she was today.

"I don't care if her arms are open or not. She owes me at least an explanation if nothing else. We're here—whether I brought us here or you did—and I'm going to collect," Grace insists, the steely determination in her shoulders and set of her mouth reminding me of Nicola in a way.

"I don't think we..." I begin, but I am cut off by Nicola losing her fight with consciousness and wilting in my arms. We need a Witch to undo whatever was done to Nicola and fast. Whether Marj will help us is a whole other story.

Grace takes the decision out of my hands when she puts a hand to the wrought iron gate and pushes it open, Joe following her in. I know from experience only a Baxter Witch can open that door—the ward is laced in blood magic; a kind I could never break.

Hell, a whole coven couldn't break it.

Grace holds open the gate for me and I hitch Nicola up in my arms and carry her through. I don't like that she hasn't had much of a say in this situation—that Nicola has been an uneasy bystander to my past taking a shit on our present. But at this point I don't have a choice in the matter.

We scale the moss-covered brick steps which are lined with vibrant pots of poinsettias that point to the wide double door. Pausing, a look of uncertainty passes between us before a quiet, pained moan escapes Nicola's throat. Three sharp knocks from Grace and the porch light comes on, illuminating the carefully restored white planks under our feet and the nineteenth century moldings around the door.

Then, instead of a butler, Marjorie opens the door herself. Dressed casually in a light weight dark blue sweater and light blue jeans. Her feet are bare, the frayed hem of the jeans brushing the polished tips of her toes. Marjorie's eyes go wide at the sight of us all—the daughter she abandoned and her former lover with a dog and a Phoenix in tow. Add in our soot and blood-covered attire and the fact one of us is unconscious, the alarm on Marj's face is more than warranted.

Marj's eyes shift to Grace, and I can tell by the soft way she looks at her that Marj knows exactly who she is. She seems to come back to herself for a moment, studying Nicola for a quick moment and then steps to the side to wave us in.

"Come in, come in," Marj murmurs quickly closing the door and muttering in Latin to re-ward it. Why she thinks she'll need both wards, I don't know, but if I think hard enough on it, I'm pretty sure I can come up with an answer. An answer I won't like one bit. I doubt we are any safer inside these walls than we were standing out in the open.

"What happened?" Marj asks, and that is when Grace finally loses it.

"Are you fucking kidding me?" Grace's voice is as sharp as a whip. "*Bishop takes pawn.* What did I tell you the first time we spoke? I told you I didn't know what this man was doing in my shop, but Witch business was not my business. I told you to keep that man away from me. Not even a month passes and someone blows up my shop. Care to explain, Mother?" Grace asks snidely, her fingers rolling into fists before flexing straight once again.

"Yes, well, things did not go to plan, obviously," Marj mutters eyeing Joe with distaste. Joe, in turn, growls and bares his teeth before letting out a great booming bark.

"If you insist," Marj says, her tone exasperated, but the set of her shoulders tells a different story altogether.

Marj breathes onto her fingertips before running her thumb in a circle over her index and middle fingers, saying the spell I hoped she wouldn't.

"*Quid est quod estis vos*," she whispers. *What you were is what you are.*

"You didn't," I accuse and watch as 'Joe' transforms from a giant German Shepherd to a crouching two-hundred-pound man. His bronze shaved-bald head is bowed before he spears Marj with dark, nearly black eyes. He slowly rises to standing, his stocky build shaking with what appears to be an effort not to launch himself across the room.

"Oh, she did," Joe mutters to me, cracking his neck and glaring at Marjorie with enough hate to singe her soul if she still has one.

At that, Grace takes a long look at Joe, then stalks across the few feet to her mother, and promptly slaps her across the face.

14

KYLE

GRACE ONLY GETS THE ONE HIT IN BEFORE JOE HAS HER BY THE middle and hauls her to him with her back against his front. He doesn't let her go when she quits struggling, either realizing that she would launch herself at her mother as soon as he does, or maybe something else. His touch is familiar in a way I don't really care for, but I think I trust him more than Marj at this point, so I don't say anything. Joe—even as a dog—has put himself in between my girl and danger. That has earned him some leeway in the overbearing parenting stakes.

But despite all this well-earned drama, Nicola is still in my arms unconscious.

"This family reunion is all real fascinating, but my wife is bleeding from a hex or curse of some sort, so can we fucking focus?" I break the staring contest going on between my ex and my daughter. I swear this whole day has been surreal in a way I can't quite process.

My words seem to snap Marj out of it, but she focuses on the wrong shit. "Wife?" she asks incredulously, the tone in her voice leaning far too much toward hurt for my liking.

"Yeah, Marj. Wife. It's been thirty years, and in that time I found my mate. She carries my bonding mark and everything," I shoot back.

"But... but she's a Phoenix," Marjorie sputters in disbelief. The way she was raised, this doesn't surprise me at all, but it does piss me off.

"Yeah... and I'm a Witch Wraith mixed breed. I don't get to choose my mate, Marj. And even if I did, I'd still choose her. I don't care what she is no more than she cares what I am," I murmur, pulling Nicola more into my body as I realize that Marj might not help us. She could be blinded still by the idiotic notion that different is less.

"But her station... She was Secondary," Marj whispers, more to herself than anything, but she's still not getting it.

"Yeah, and the new Primary is mated to a Wraith. No one gives a shit about pure bloodlines except for Witches. As a coven leader, maybe you should think about the old ways not becoming the new way. Prejudice has been going out of style for a while now, maybe you should get with the times. But all of this does not lift the fucking curse on. My. Wife. Help would be real beneficial right about now-ish," I scold, my voice curt.

Marj seems to blink back to herself, realizing whatever trip she was taking down memory lane isn't going to change the present. It won't give her those years she spent at the heels of her father back—it won't change my mind about her prejudice or what she did to Joe.

"Come, the parlor will be better suited for this," she orders, and I have to fight an eye roll.

I'd never been inside this house—the ward on the gate making it nigh impossible—but the sheer fact that there was even a 'parlor' made me want to snicker. Why she couldn't call it a living room, I didn't know, but I followed her anyway, anxious to get Nicola to wake up.

"Put her on the settee," Marj orders, her voice soft but authoritative as I expect the leader of a coven should be. I do as she asks, Joe and Grace following behind. Marj turns from us, plucking ingredients from a built-in mahogany cabinet and setting them on the gray marble counter top that bisects the middle.

The parlor looks like we may have time-warped back to the 1800s. The settee in a dusky rose floral print that would probably break if I sat on it is bookended by a pair of thin tables with spindly legs with Tiffany lamps perched on top of them. Nothing in this room is made for comfort, it is merely for displaying wealth.

I gently place Nicola on the delicate settee, but I have a hard time letting her go. I still don't know if Marj will do all she can to help her.

"You know her life is tied to mine, right? And even if... you don't like me very much, please do-don't hurt her," I plead, unable to meet Marj's eyes. Instead, my gaze is glued to Nicola's closed lids, studying the russet cast to her lashes.

The gentle touch on my shoulder is not one I would expect from Marj.

"Hey. My kind did this, and it is my duty to reverse it. But it's more than that. I want to help. I'm going to help you," Marj reassures soothingly before patting my shoulder one last time and going back to her task.

I watch as she lifts a deep stone basin and rests it on the counter, tossing in ingredients before I can catch what they are. The smell of white sage and hyssop hits my nose and then she strikes a long match, catching the dried herbs on fire before hitting them with a pinch of salt from a squat glass bottle. The salt makes the fire blossom, billowing from the base of the bowl.

"I've seen the work before, but the injuries were much worse than this. I don't know if Nicola had protection or if it's her natural healing process, but I know this spell. *Scissura. To rend.* It rips the flesh from the bone over and over until death. I doubt the Witch who cast it is still alive, so it shouldn't still be active. But *Scissura* is Necromancy, so..." Marj trails off with a shrug, her back to me as she works.

I get what she's alluding to. Necromancy is not bound by the natural laws—death does not dictate the life of a spell. Sometimes, death just intensifies it. This type of curse could kill my Nicola. Why? Why did we ever leave Colorado?

Am I ever going to be able to keep her safe?

"Are you going to be able to help her?" Grace asks, her voice meek in a way I haven't heard it before.

I want to reassure her, but I can't. I want to tell her that Nicola and I will be okay, but right now I'm too scared to do anything but stare at the three dots of blood on Nicola's cheek.

"If your mother can keep me in dog form for two straight years, she can do about anything, can't you Marjorie?" Joe quips, his voice like hate-filled gravel even as he pulls Grace into his arms to comfort her.

"And if you hadn't been sniffing around my daughter and did the protection detail you were assigned to do; I wouldn't have had to. You were supposed to be invisible, which for a pureblooded shapeshifter, shouldn't be a difficult task to manage. But no, you wanted to do meet-cutes in coffee shops. You wanted to 'bump' into her in the jazz clubs. You wanted to ask her opinion on a book at a bookstore. You wanted to try and date her. That was not the agreement you signed, Joseph Gautier. Do not sass me because you broke the accord and I had to get creative," Marjorie whips back, her work for Nicola stopped as she faces off with Joe. Grace's face is white as a sheet, but she doesn't really look surprised. I guess it explains the slap, though.

"But I was dating her, you viper. And then I just dropped off the face of the earth with no word. Only to be replaced by a mangy fucking dog!" Joe rails. "Do you know what it is like to not be in human form for two fucking years? To watch the woman I'm in love with cry herself to sleep because I didn't come back? To watch her suffer because she has no idea where I am? Why the fuck do you think she named me Joe?"

"You knew..." Marj begins but I put a stop to it.

"Yo!" I yell, pissed off they decided to start this now. "Work your shit out later. Nicola doesn't have time for this, and neither do I."

All three of them look contrite—even Grace who has been hanging at the fringes watching her pseudo-boyfriend and mother go at it like cats and dogs.

"Sorry, Kyle."

"Sorry, man."

"What do you need to get this thing lifted?" I ask Marj, pleased we're moving the fuck on from the bullshit.

"I just need energy. The four of us should stand at north, east, south, and west. We need to join hands while the herbs burn. I'll be able to see what I'm working with to unravel it once we're in there," Marj replies as she carries the stone basin to the coffee table in front of Nic. She waves the sweet-smelling smoke toward Nicola, hitting her body from head to foot, smudging her with the protective and cleansing herbs.

"We need to join hands. Kyle, you're at the western point closest to her heart, Grace, you're at east, Joseph, you're at the south. I'm taking the north. Hold hands, shut up, and don't move. This is going to be tricky," Marj orders us and we fall into line.

"Haec femina purgato, et liberate," Marj murmurs over and over again, her murmurs turning to whispers and then to inaudible moving of her lips. *Cleanse and free this woman.*

Marjorie's hand tightens on mine, and then so does Joe's. The green light of her magic coats the five of us as she casts the cleansing spell. But the more Marjorie says the words, the worse I feel.

"Something isn't right. The *Scissura* is lifted but there is something else tainting her. I can't... *Oh, God...*" Marjorie trails off before a pained whimper escapes her lips.

Then the drip, drip, drip of my nose hits me and I take a look around. Grace wobbles where she stands, her skin is so pale, her nose bleeding. Joe's grip on her is loose, but his grip on me might be breaking a few fingers. His bronze skin is ashen, his nose dribbling blood.

Then Nicola starts screaming, the howling wail of a soul wrenching clean scoring through my bones. Her upper body lifts from the settee as if her heart is being ripped from her chest. The burning twist to my heart tells me it might be.

"Marj," I whisper, "St-stop. You're killing us. Stop. Please."

"I can't stop, Kyle. There's a taint on her soul. I can't leave her like that. It haunts her, poisons her. I have to... have to..."

Marjorie screams then, a full-on horror movie scream. One that tells me it isn't pain—it's blind fear. Fear she refuses to let best her because then, it cuts off all at once as she grits her teeth, blood running from her nose, down her neck absorbing into the collar of her sweater. The point of our hands starts to burn, the sizzling pain radiating up my arms.

A wave of power crashes into us all, knocking us on our asses and breaking the connection. Moans sound around the room, so I know everyone is at least alive, allowing me to lay there and recover for a second.

It is a long while before I can even sit up, but probably before my body is ready, I'm crawling to Nicola and brushing an errant curl from her forehead, waiting again for her to wake up.

Nicola's eyes flutter for a moment before stilling.

"Shortcake?" I murmur, my voice pleading. They flutter once more and then her eyes flash open. Nicola's irises are hazy for a moment and then I watch as the amber bleeds away to cornflower blue, a sight I thought I'd never see again.

"Kyle?" Nicola calls her voice trembling.

"Yeah, Shortcake?"

"I remember."

"You remember what, baby?"

"I remember everything."

15

Mama was crying. No. She was wailing. Great sobs of agony ripped up her throat as she buried her face into what was left of my papa's chest, only then were they muffled by the soft fabric of his shirt. I couldn't see her with my eyes—those were useless anyhow—but I knew exactly what she was doing.

I'd seen her do it all before when I saw my father's death using an ability I wished I'd never been blessed with. I didn't want to see so many of the images that had screamed across my mind's eye. I didn't want my only sight to be the worst horrors in a person's life. I didn't want the only color in my world to be the stain of death.

But especially, I didn't want to see this.

I saw his death as I had for so many others, but unlike those strangers, I knew it was my father. I knew he was a part of me—even though I had never seen his face before in my life. I saw his raven black hair shining in the sun. I saw the beautiful orange wings flutter in the wind as he swooped and soared over the inky blue ocean, the white caps to the waves signaling a coming storm. The inky black of his eyelashes resting on his bronze cheeks. The way his face sought the last lingering light of the setting sun, the way it warmed his face.

Then, the horrible gray mist that seemed to have come from nowhere, plucking the skin from his bones and turned the voice I'd only heard as a quiet rumble of kind words into the worst howling to ever tear at my ears.

And I had to hear it twice. Once in my mind and then again when I was too slow and too stupid to explain what was coming.

But I hadn't understood.

How could a mist of fog move so fast or with such purpose? How could it strip the flesh from his bones?

"Why, Samuel? Why did you do this? How could you leave us?" my mother's wailed words registered in my mind.

But it wasn't Father's fault! I wanted to scream at her, but I knew, as with so many of the left behind, she wouldn't listen to me.

It didn't matter, and it wouldn't change anything.

Father was gone, and we remained.

"Nicola!" Mama's voice broke through my pain, and I gave her my attention.

"Yes, Mama," I whispered through my tears, heaving breath after breath through my chest by force of will alone.

"W-we must send him on to the Otherside. You will say the words with me this time. We will do it together, okay darling? Do you remember the words?" she asked.

Oh, I remembered.

As a family, it was what we did. We moved from village to village, from town to town. Always moving, never staying anywhere until we found this place where I could stay. A place where no one lived, a place where my visions wouldn't draw attention. Even at a young age, I understood how hard it would be to blend in with humans. My family stayed on the edge of humanity.

"Ye-yes Mama. I remember, but... I don't want to do this. Don't make me send him away," I said, losing my fight with my tears. The growing hole in my chest grew wider, deeper with the agony of this loss.

Father was the only one who understood me—knew what I could see and why it was so difficult.

I gripped his fingers tight, my tum roiling at the feeling of his once strong hands reduced to brittle sticks of bone and congealing blood. My digits were sticky with it, but I didn't want to wash the last pieces of my father off my skin.

My mother began the rites, but I couldn't bring myself to say them with her.

I thought them, though, the words that I should remember, the words that would cross my lips until I took my last breath on this earth: libertatem concede tibi ita regenerationis ultra valeamus.

I grant you the freedom of rebirth so one day we may meet again.

The brittle bones I held in my hand crumbled and turned to ash sifting through my fingers faster than I could hold on. The last piece of him I had, swept away on the winds of the coming storm. I hoped, wherever he went, he was at peace.

I knew my peace was long gone.

NICOLA—NEW ENGLAND 1722

Waking up all alone in a new place was always a struggle. Before my father's death, my mother would wake me, helping me acclimate to my surroundings before we went about our daily chores. We moved from place to place so often, I couldn't adjust as easily as I should. Now, I often woke up alone, having to find my way to my mother on my own.

Mother rarely slept, and when she did, she cried and cried throughout the night until the morning came again. She wailed for my father and moaned about a veil. She screamed about it, saying we had to protect it.

When I asked her about her nightmares, she said that the two of us were special, and one day, people would come for us. They would hurt us and enslave us. I wasn't to trust anyone—not ever. We could have no real home. We could have no friends. If people knew what we really were, if the leaders of our kind found us, we would die.

But it wasn't long before she forgot she had a child to take care of at all. It wasn't long at all until she forgot all about me. At seven years of age, I often found myself food, fishing from the rocky shores for our dinner from nets I made myself. Force-feeding my mother so she would survive.

But this morning, no matter where I searched, I could not find her. I could not hear her footsteps in the sand or her disturbing rocks at the path to our home. I could not feel her presence. I could not hear her anywhere.

I waited for weeks, waiting for her to come back to me. Refusing to believe that she would leave me alone, blind to all except for the death of others, forever alone in my own darkness.

I knew it was coming, a part of me always simply knew things. Father had told me that one day I would know lots of things like that. That because of who I was, because of who my parents were, I would only get stronger with time.

Mother had become so distant since Father's death, but I never thought she really would do it. As the days turned into weeks and the weeks to months, I realized it was true.

She had abandoned me to survive on my own. At seven, I was more or less an orphan, left to my own devices in the bitter wilds of this cold coastal homestead.

NICOLA—COLORADO BEFORE

I've known John Black for longer than most—except for maybe his wife. He has been my friend and ally for going on two centuries. Normally, my kind do not deal with Wraiths, but I find—especially his lot—are kinder and more honorable than mine.

Phoenixes are supposed to be the light in the darkness. The ember that burns bright when all other lights have gone out. The longer I live, the more I believe we have been tainted by the evil we are fighting against. The longer I live, the more I believe we are the problem.

The deaths that are coming—including my own—will change the face of our species. It will bring us out of the shadows of bureaucracy and greed. But John's death, with its swift approach, will likely wrench my soul in two.

Coming here today was less about the future I could no longer see and more about visiting my good friend for what would be my last time. Sure, I needed to set Aurelia and Rhys back on their path, but it wasn't really the reason I came. At least with all the coming ends, I was more than likely going first. I wouldn't have to watch my friend die, and that was probably the last blessing I would get in this life.

There were so many things that I had wished for and never received.

I never got the love of my own. I never had the children I so wanted. I never got the family that life was so keen on denying me. I knew life was cruel, but as I rapped my probing cane on the thick wooden door of John's family cabin, I hadn't known just how cruel.

Blind from birth, my other senses were more acute than most. From simply the door opening I could decipher a hundred things. I could tell the person on the other side was male based on his footfalls. I knew he was tall by the change in the air around him. I heard the infinitesimal catch in his breath when he took in my appearance, and I didn't want to acknowledge the warmth I felt at knowing he found me pretty. Sure, it was vain, but for some reason I found it thrilling coming from this man even if I didn't know him.

That was where we would begin, and it hurt in a freshly agonizing sort of way that I wasn't going to be able to keep him.

NICOLA—KENTUCKY BEFORE

His lips on mine had me coming out of my skin. The way they were so soft and yet so firm, the way his beard brushed against the skin of my neck, had my breath coming from me in sharp pants. His deft fingers were everywhere, fisting in my curls, pressing into the curve of my ribs, his thumbs brushing the underside of my breasts, pulling one of them free from the now-itchy lace. I needed him closer. I needed his skin on mine.

I widened my legs and he followed me up on the counter to lay between them. The heat of him pressing into me drove me insane. I loved the weight of his body on mine, the way his was so much bigger than my own, the way he surrounded me with his scent and his presence, engulfing me in his arms. My fingertips traced everything they could reach, learning his body the only way I could.

Then, twin points of Kyle's fangs raked the soft skin of my nipple. A moan rippled up my throat in response, but as fabulous as his fangs felt, as wondrous as the pleasure was that seemed to suffuse through my body at the mere brush of them against my skin, I had to stop him.

I wanted his mark—the twin crescents of a visceral bond I knew we shared—but I couldn't have this. I couldn't damn him this way when I knew I my life was coming to a close. I couldn't yank his soul with me when I died.

"Don't," I managed to murmur, my voice a pitifully shaky whisper, my hands reluctantly pulled his face from my breast. He froze where he lay, his body strung tight, ready to break.

"Okay, baby. I'll stop," his voice like honey over gravel, as he ran his nose up the column of my neck and rested his forehead on mine. A frustrated, needy moan broke from my throat.

"Not, stop, stop. Just don't bite," I clarified, my hands raking down his abs to latch onto his belt buckle.

"I don't know how possible that is, Shortcake. In case you hadn't noticed, my response to you is not exactly rational," Ky groaned as he pressed his heavy length against me. Everything in me tightened then. I needed this man. I needed his touch and his kiss, but I couldn't let him go too far.

I couldn't let us go too far.

Grabbing his face, I tried to direct my eyes to where I thought his might be. The lack of my second sight made knowing the exact position difficult, but I did my best. He had to know what he was getting into. He had to be warned off me. No matter that the Fates might urge him to mate to me, I was saving his life.

"Do your best, then. It's important, Kyle. Don't rush this," I demanded.

"I promise, Nic. I won't bite you unless I absolutely cannot stop myself. Just know, one day I will, and you'll be mine."

I only smiled because I knew. As much as I wanted it, I would never really be his. And he should count himself lucky.

Loving me would be a death sentence.

NICOLA—CUTLER, MAINE 2016

I squatted inside the dark hole of my mind and watched—watched as Iva raved to Devereux for the tenth time today as she perfected a wing of eyeliner. I looked decent if you didn't account for the fact that my body was possessed by a she-bitch from Hell or that I looked like a freaking harpy when I screamed. Note to self: the vein in my forehead pops out when I yell. Ugh.

Once again, the offering Dev had brought was unsatisfactory to her, barely filling the void of power she so needed to stay on this plane. Iva's soul would likely be dragged kicking and screaming back to Hell if she couldn't sustain enough power. It was only a matter of time. I knew her secret, and so did Devereux, but he was unlikely to ever disobey her. Just as I was unlikely to get out of the prison of my own head. Who knew what kind of shape my body would be in after a possession.

Or if there would even be a body to come back to...

"Again, you have procured me a child less than what I need, Devereux. How many times must I instruct you? Honestly, with as much power as there is in this world, you should be giving me a bounty, and yet, you still fail me," Iva's Irish lilt coming from my voice still made me mentally shudder even though I couldn't physically do it.

"Yes, Mistress," Devereux whispered, contrite. I didn't know why he would be sorry. It wasn't his fault he was a bumbling fuck-up.

Oh, wait...

"That ungrateful tripe, Tessa, royally fucked us over. She gave you the wrong spell on purpose. As an insurance policy, no doubt. You were the last one she brought over fully. And now that she's dead, I cannot make her give it to me, and her ungrateful children are no help at all. How was I to know Aurelia would burn her alive? She knew better than to get into a room with a Seer. Tessa should have sent an emissary. But no. She didn't, and now we're fucked," Iva continued as she moved onto the other eye. The amber of her irises were the only thing that heralded Iva's presence. I wanted to see my regular blues.

"Again, Mistress, why can't we simply destroy the Veil? If that is what is pulling on you, let us simply take it out of the equation," Dev offered.

I knew enough about my family's legacy that merely killing us would not help the situation one single bit. But Iva, luckily, knew better.

"Destroy the Veil? Are you out of your stupid mind? I want to tap that power source, of course, but destroying the Veil is out of the question. It would eliminate the boundary between this world and the next. Every single person on the Otherside would come back. Every soul sitting in Hell—your father included—would be able to walk freely on this earth. I have enough enemies rotting in Hell that I'd rather skip it, and so do you."

Devereux's face paled at the mention of his father, and I couldn't help but feel a swell of pity... Until every single crime he'd committed filtered through my mind. Still, Devereux couldn't even escape his father with his first death in 1906, no doubt turning him into the monster he was today.

"What do we do now?" he murmured, fear leaching his voice.

"There are only three pieces of the Veil on this plane at any given time. This one," she gestured to my body, "Nicola's mother, Sybil, and Nicola's sadly departed father, Samuel. From what I gathered, Samuel pissed off some Witches in the 1700s, and they called out a hit using a very dark piece of magic. Incidentally, Tessa's mother garnered the Southeastern Coven leader position the very next day. Naughty, naughty.

"You, on the other hand, were brought back to your own body, so Tessa only needed a piece of the Veil as a conduit. If Tessa hadn't lost Sybil after your return, we wouldn't be in the mess we're in now. Those insane Bishop children want to bring Mommy Dearest back to life, and the only way they can do that is if they find Sybil or until a new person is born in Nicola's line. I want to find Sybil before they do, but unfortunately, we'd have to do it the old-fashioned way. She is likely cloaked in magics even I cannot break."

"Don't we want them to find Sybil? Wouldn't they simply bring Tessa back and then you could get the spell from her?"

That was one secret I never wanted them to find. I had an inkling of where my mother might be, but I hadn't been able to get to her safely. Or bucked up enough courage to meet her after her abandonment. Three centuries later, that wound was still wide open and bleeding.

"If it were anyone but those fucking Bishop children, I'd say yes. But if they can't find Sybil, I have an inkling they will try to evict me from this body, and we can't have that. What I need is enough power to anchor me to this plane. An Aegis would be beneficial, but I can't get close to Mena without dying. But..." Iva trailed off pondering her predicament.

"Isn't her twin pregnant? Aegis does run in the bloodline," Devereux offered, making what is left of my consciousness turn cold.

This is the first I'd learned of the pregnancy I'd seen so many years ago. If my vision was correct, then there were two babies. One female Seer, and one male Aegis—exactly what they would need.

My only hope was if they couldn't find Aurelia or if she was guarded enough to keep them away. Either way, I needed to keep myself closed off in my little hole.

Otherwise, my secrets could get someone killed.

16

THREE HUNDRED YEARS OF MEMORIES HITTING ALL AT ONCE can procure one hell of a headache. I was trembling with the force of each one hitting me like a battering ram. But the hardest part of remembering? Knowing every atrocity and double deal, every kiss and touch, and every death and abandonment.

Three centuries of missed opportunities and lives I was unable to save. Three centuries of loss. Less than two years of love.

Looking into Kyle's chocolate brown eyes, every memory, every touch, every single kiss and caress and sacrifice hits me all at once, but my eyes are drawn from his to the blood staining his upper lip.

"Say something, Shortcake," Kyle demands softly, his rough hands cupping my face as I quake on a dainty settee and struggle to get myself under control.

"They hurt you because of me. Iva, Devereux, Tessa. They all hurt you because you loved me. Why did you fall in love with me? Your life would have been so much easier if you'd never answered the door that day. If I hadn't gone to see John..." I trailed off, a sob making its way up my throat.

For a moment, Kyle simply wraps me up in his arms.

"Shortcake, you couldn't have stopped me from meeting you. You sure as shit couldn't have stopped me from loving you. Our souls were meant to be together—meant to be tied in every single way there is. I should have bound you to me sooner. That first day. Then Iva wouldn't have come back, she couldn't have taken you over," Kyle argued.

"Maybe I could have been spared, but she would have found someone else. She knew who to look for," I murmur, trying not to let my voice break, but knowing my effort was futile. "Before I lost my memories, I did too. If she's still alive, Bella and Baron are looking for my mother. That's why they were so interested in me. The Veil is made up of three living members of my line. Me, my mother, and my father. My father is dead, so that only leaves me and Sybil."

The sting of my father's death steals through me. It wasn't the first death I'd seen but it was the first one that was so close to home. Through the years I'd seen many deaths. Ones I could prevent—like Aurelia's and Mena's—and ones I couldn't. The ones I couldn't were too many to count.

"I didn't know your mother was still alive. You've never spoken of her," Kyle whispers as he brushes a hot tear from my cheek.

"She abandoned me when I was seven. She left me blind and alone to fend for myself. Until now, she was dead to me, and when she is safe she will be dead to me once more," I murmur, my voice finally getting stronger as I dash the tears from my cheeks.

Sybil Miller doesn't get to have those tears. I'll find her—or we'll find her—get her out of the mess she will likely attract, and then... I don't know what. We'll move the fuck on with our lives.

"Jesus. I can get that, but Shortcake, you don't have to be strong right now. It's okay to break," he whispers, the quiet rumble of his voice stealing away some of the hurt.

"I think I have been broken for far too long. Let's check on everyone else," I counter, trying to hurdle the mountain of emotions roiling through my brain.

"Whatever you want, babe," Ky rumbles before kissing my forehead and yanking me out of our little bubble to standing. The wounds I sustained in that New Orleans alleyway seem to have healed, but a part of me is still sore, and a solid headache has now cemented itself into my brain. Phoenix healing doesn't fix everything, I guess.

Joe and Grace are surrounding Marj, gently pulling her from the floor and depositing her into a chintz wingback. Marj's nose is bloody, eyes glassy—she looks haggard in a way that tells me she sacrificed a lot of her power to pull whatever hex or curse or whatever off me.

"Thank you. You have done me a great service and I won't ever forget it. I owe you one, Marjorie, and that isn't something I take lightly," I tell her, crouching in front of the chair she's barely sitting in. Sitting isn't the right word. Her body is arranged in such a way her limbs probably feel like some sort of goo.

"You had a taint on your soul. A blackness that was staining you, hurting you. Even after the *Scissura* was gone, it had to be lifted. It was poisoning your mind. I would have done that for anyone who had been hurt by Witch magic. But for you, I would have given every single drop of my power to save your life. Be good to him. He deserves every bit of happiness in this world. You do that for me, and we are even," Marj murmurs, leveling with a look that tells me I'm not the only one who sacrifices for the ones they love. I hold out my hand, and Marj takes it without compunction, even knowing what I am. Knowing that I could see every single thing she had to hide.

I see Marjorie's memories, her trials, and the awful abuse from her father. She loved Kyle completely, the first time she had ever allowed something for herself. But she couldn't keep him—not without hurting him or risking his life after her father found out. They would have been on the run from the Witch counsel, or more accurately her father, for the rest of their lives. Marjorie knew that as soon as her father said he was of mixed heritage, the bigot. She'd heard enough of her father's ravings to know he would go to the ends of the earth and beyond to make her pay for her willfulness.

So, she let him go, and let her father police her life except for the seven months she spent abroad, hiding her pregnancy from everyone. Marjorie kept her baby safe from Witches, gave her child to the best family she could find, and left Grace with a charm that suppressed her magic and kept her cloaked to all except for her. A charm she still wore to this day.

Only one concession was made—when Marjorie discovered her father had found out about Grace and her lineage from one of the Guardians sent to keep Grace a secret. Her father raged and threatened to snuff out Grace, so Marjorie eliminated the threats. First by cursing the Guardian, stopping his heart with a mere snap of her fingers, and then by hexing her father. It was the one and only time she'd used sacrificial magic, and she still regretted the death of the bunny she had to kill to end her father's life. Both men died within an hour, and Marjorie, now gifted with her family's power, cloaked Grace once again.

Since Marjorie came into power, she has kept watch on Grace, guarding her from any who would do her harm. Enlisting Joe to watch out for her. Making him sign an agreement in blood that he would never do anything to harm her—an accord that would end his life if he disobeyed.

Marjorie's life was cold and she often felt alone, but I saw that those days were coming to a close and in the many avenues to come she might find happiness and peace.

"Who is Tobias?" I ask and watch as her eyes widen for a moment before narrowing to slits.

"No one I wish to speak of," Marjorie volleys back. Right. And I'm Miss Cleo.

I smile and nod as I stand, not showing all the cards but trying to give a little nudge in the right direction. Marjorie gives me a questioning look, so I waggle my eyebrows and give her a full-out grin. Understanding hits her features and a very pretty rosy blush slaps her cheeks before her gaze moves away, shyness coloring her expression. I decide not to embarrass her further.

I turn from her to Grace, looking over the black-haired beauty with her Joe-shaped shadow. I knew he wasn't a dog...

"Whoa, Nicola, your eyes changed color. They're blue," Grace marvels, gently grabbing my chin.

"What?" I breathe, pulling my chin from her hand I search the room for a mirror. The closest one is a gilt-framed antique mirror from likely the early 1900s, and I rush it to examine my irises. Iva's amber taint was gone. All that was left was a cornflower iris with a midnight blue limbal ring. It was a sight I'd never seen in a mirror, only in visions of myself. Which brought me to a very worrying fact.

"I can see. I-I'm not blind. I just had a vision and I'm not blind. Iva is gone and I can still see. Did you... did you do this?" I ask Marjorie, my hand pressing into my chest trying to hold in my racing heart. I'm honored and baffled, and awash in so many emotions I feel like my skin can barely hold them all in. When I didn't remember, I thought seeing was normal. I had no idea what being blind even meant. My few brushes with it, were nominal. Now that I my memories are my own again, I've never been more grateful in my life for the gift of sight.

"Even I'm not that good. I have a feeling, though, whatever locks you on this plane might be the culprit," she nods to Kyle who is hovering behind me—either waiting for me to fall out or lose my fucking mind.

I forget everyone in the room and rush him, throwing myself into his arms and promptly burst into tears. He wraps me up once again, surrounding me in his warmth, taking the barbs out of this shit of a day. So much good has come from today—I feel all of it. The good, the bad, the absolutely freaking terrifying. It takes me a minute—okay ten—to pull myself together enough to realize we're on a ticking clock here, and my blubbering is not helping the timeline at all.

"I need to get my shit together," I mumble, wiping my nose on my soot-covered, cut-to-ribbons, blood-soaked sleeve. I look down at myself and wrinkle my nose in disgust. But first I need a shower and a change of clothes. We all probably did. A good night's rest wouldn't hurt either.

"We all do. Holy shit, my shop. My parents. I have to get home," Grace murmurs, aghast at the real life she's neglected while our shit has made a mess of it.

"Yeah, about that..." Joe trails off. "It is unlikely that being anywhere near your parents is not a good idea. I'm pretty sure anywhere in their general vicinity would be a bad plan."

"He's right. You can still call them, but I would tell them that you weren't in the shop and you're staying at a friends out of town for a bit while you plan your next move. At least until this all blows over. You're welcome to stay here," Marjorie offers, her voice quiet and clear, but her manner is almost timid.

Grace looks at her mother

"You're probably right. I don't want this anywhere near them," Grace murmurs, and then looks at her mother—really looks at her. Maybe she's taking my lead with Marjorie, or maybe the sudden brush with death has softened her towards Marjorie.

"I would rather not stay here. *But* when this blows over, I would like to get to know you. You gave me up for a reason, and I'd like to think it was because you were protecting me. Call me naïve if you want, but I want to think the best of you, so I'm keeping that door open. Does that sound good?"

"That sounds great," Marjorie whispers, struggles to standing, and shakily gives Grace a hug.

We all hug Marjorie before we go—all except for Joe—and me last because I have to convince her to call a certain man to come tend to her. She has a seventy-thirty shot at listening to me. I hope she does. I saw good things for her.

"So, hotel or mall first?" I ask, my body moving slowly down the porch steps toward the spelled gate.

This earns me a giggle from Grace, and a groan from the two Y-chromosomes in the bunch.

Smiling, I feel normal probably for the first time in my life.

17

KYLE

Nicola's creamy legs straddle mine as I drive deeper into her heat. The sounds she's making score through me and at this point I'm fighting against coming in five minutes flat if I can't figure out a way to swallow her moans. Nic is torturing me with the sexy as fuck line of her spine, as she pulls her body up and down on me. Her curls piled on her head, I see every smooth inch of her writhing on my dick as she grips the sheet for leverage to drive back on me once again. I yank her back flush against my chest, wrapping a gentle hand around her chin to direct her mouth to mine. Our tongues tangle as she moans down my throat and I swallow the sweet, breathy sound.

With her lips on mine, my hands have so many options to explore. I decide everywhere is the best plan, so one hand cups the heavy swell of a breast, tweaking her nipple just so, and my other hand slides through the slick heat of her sex to her clit. She is so soft and warm and wet, and my eyes roll up into my head when her body squeezes my dick like a vise. The scent of her sleep-warm body coupled with a hint of her arousal pulls at me, add in the wetness dripping from her sex, her sounds, the silk of her skin, and I'm fighting to last as my balls draw up tight against my body.

Racing my own end, I tweak her clit once more, and Nicola stills—her entire body tightening for a single moment—right before she explodes, dragging me along behind her into the best fucking orgasm I've had in my life.

This is a better start to the day than I expected. The night before consisted of a rather brutal shopping trip, scandalized looks from the hotel staff, and a pensive Nicola clipping tags from new clothes, and watching her pace the room. So, phenomenal sex with my wife surpasses the yesterday filled with revelations and death by leaps and bounds. And shopping. I think I'd take a fire fight over shopping any day.

I had never been shopping with Nicola and obviously never with Grace, so I didn't know what I was in for. Both women can locate fifty items to try on within five minutes but then spend roughly the better part of an hour trying on each and every single item in their possession, hemming and hawing over the priority of each before I got pissed and made them take all of whatever the fuck fit. They did this process three fucking times while Joe and I sat and waited. The only plus was Nicola came out to model her favorite finds.

Not too many words were said between Joe and I, but the ones that were made up for it.

"So you're Grace's birth father?" Joe acknowledged, his eyes never leaving Grace's door as we sat on the tufted benches of the second fitting area.

"Yep, I guess so," I clipped, answering his non-question, waiting for the real one. I knew one was coming, I just needed to wait him out. Irritated, he shoved himself back to rest against the wall behind us, and I had to fight a grin.

"You got a problem with Grace and me being together?" he demanded, ready for a fight if he had to. I admired him for asking but had to get some shit clear before I gave him my blessing. It felt odd that he needed my blessing and not the parents who raised her. I was new to Grace's life, but it occurred to me that while I might have just found out about Grace, Joe already knew about me being her father. He was showing me the respect I might not deserve, but he believed was my right all the same.

I might as well do my duty as the father she should have had all along.

"You going to treat her right? Protect her? Teach her?" I knew the answers already, but I needed him to say it.

"Of course."

"You going to throw a fit if she wants to have a relationship with either of her birth parents?"

Joe ground his teeth at that one, likely less at my half of the equation and more Marjorie's, but managed to answer a clipped, "No."

"Then, I have no problem with you. But, any of those promises get broken? I reserve the right to break your neck, got it?" I threatened.

"Sounds about right," he nodded, and we lapsed into silence again for a while.

"Do you know why Marj kept her from me? With everything that was going on, we didn't get into it, and I'm kicking myself for not asking," I admitted.

"Winston," Joe said, his tone scathing, but he didn't have to say anything else. Winston Baxter was enough of an answer.

"Is she the reason he's dead?" I asked, connecting a dot that has been niggling at me for a while now. How often do Witches die of natural causes? Pretty much close to never. Oh, his heart stopped, you say? Yeah, no. Someone made it stop for him, that's a damn promise.

"I can't say for sure, but probably. I'm not the first Guardian Marj put on Grace, but from what I heard, Grace's life was threatened when she was ten. Twenty-four hours later both Grace's Guardian and Winston were dead. I'm pretty sure Winston is the reason for most of the things Marj does," Joe quipped, his mouth turned as if he'd tasted something sour.

Given this information, I figured Joe realized Marj could have easily just killed him instead of turning him into a dog. While I'm pissed at her methods, she was probably doing her best to keep our daughter safe. Without knowing the whole story, I couldn't begin to know if what she did was right or not. Nicola herself has done tons of fucked up shit for the greater good, and I don't blame her for a single bit of it.

I had to cut Marj some slack. I knew I had to, but I was having a hard time reconciling the logic and missing out on everything that is

Grace. Missing seeing her walk her first steps and say her first word. I missed everything and I couldn't help still being pissed.

Joe and I didn't speak much after that, and eventually, the ladies figured out their shit and hauled it to the check out, where I spent an exorbitant amount of money for the third time and we got the hell out of there. I didn't mind. I had more than I could spend in my lifetime, and it was my fault in a way that neither of them had clothes. Joe and I were done already, but picking up jeans, thermals, a coat and boots took the first ten minutes of this four-hour trip.

In fucking Christmas shopping traffic. I cannot count the number of sales ladies I spelled to stay the fuck away from us.

But this morning, Nicola wasn't manic, Grace and Joe were on the other side of the hotel in a warded room so I did not have to hear their reunion, and my wife decided to wake me up with the best blow job of my life before hopping on my dick.

Things were looking up.

I gently lift Nic off me and drag her sex-drunk body to the shower. The pair of us are sticky and sweaty and above all, calm. This is the perfect time to ask what the fuck is our next step.

Last night, Nicola didn't talk much, her manner manic in a way I'd only seen once before in the days leading up to the pair of us being captured. She doesn't want to do whatever it is we have to do to get to Sybil, that is for damn certain. After being abandoned at a young age, I don't blame her one single bit, but wallowing in the sting of it isn't helping anyone.

"Shortcake," I call softly as I massage the shampoo into her scalp. Yeah, I'm the best husband ever, but this is more than watching her eyes roll back in her head when I hit that spot just past her temple.

"Mmm?" she mumbles only half listening.

"What are we doing?"

"Umm... Showering?" she answers, dumbfounded, one eye blearily opening to look at me.

"No, baby, what are we doing today? Are we going to hole up in this hotel room and let Baron and Bella do whatever they're going to do? Or are we going to do the thing you've been avoiding talking or thinking about?" I say gently, knowing how much this hurts her.

Nicola doesn't answer me for a long minute, instead, rinses her hair, and combs a handful of conditioner through her curls with her fingers.

"I've had an idea of where she was for a long time. I kept it secret even with Iva in my head. And then I forgot everything, and with that everything, I lost all that hurt and all the pain that went along with her leaving me. Now that I remember... I'm having a hard time gathering the courage to save her ass from the fire. She never once did that for me," Nicola admits, brushing at the tears on her face, scrubbing them away as if she's pissed they're even there.

"Then don't think of it as saving her. Think of it as taking the bullets out of a gun. You aren't there to figure her out or ask her why she left you. You are there to make sure no one else uses her for their own ends. That's it, and that's all," I offer, trying to help ease this pain, but knowing my words are barely a balm.

Nic nods, "I can do that." Her jaw clenches as she tips her head back into the spray of the showerhead, rinsing her hair of conditioner.

The pair of us lapse into comfortable silence, a quality I have loved in all incarnations of Nicola's personality. She doesn't talk a whole hell of a lot, and the quiet between us contains a calmness I haven't found in anyone else.

Nicola takes longer than I do, so I leave the glass-walled hotel shower to finish getting ready for the day. We will need weapons at some point, but I am hesitant to go back to the cabin in Kentucky after Talia found us there. I'm also really fucking perplexed at what the hell I'm supposed to do with Grace and Joe.

A part of me wants my daughter with me, and the other part would kick my own ass if she got hurt under my care. I can't leave her with Marj, because who the fuck knows what Baron will do then, and Joe—while obviously in love with her—isn't able to ward or hide her appearance. Grace is an untrained Witch, likely with some form of ability-dampening amulet in that mess of necklaces and bracelets she wears. I can't take it off of her without some serious backlash.

I only have two options, neither of which appeal to me at all, but I'm not alone in this shit, so I won't make the decision by myself.

"Is your brain going to melt or is the building on fire?" Nicola's husky breaks into my thoughts.

"What?"

"You're thinking too hard. What's going on in your head?" she murmurs, stepping into my space. Her towel-wrapped hair fits just under my chin as she threads her arms around me.

"I have no idea what's the right way to keep Grace and Joe safe. I don't know..." I trail off.

"We'll ask them what they want to do. We don't need to keep secrets. We can lay it out and let them choose like the adults they are," she offers. "You aren't responsible for every knock and cut that happens to me. Or them. Or anyone. We all make our own decisions. We all make our own mistakes. You must give them the freedom to make them."

"So, what you're saying is you already saw all the ways this can go, and there is a possibility of death in all of them, so you're letting me off the hook with pretty words."

"Pretty much. Everything is fuzzy when I look ahead, so I don't see any one good path. We're going to have to wing it," Nicola says with a sigh.

"Super."

18

NICOLA

I'VE NEVER SEEN THE ROCKY SHORES OF MY CHILDHOOD HOME with my own eyes. Only through visions of death have I witnessed the stark beauty of the outlying Maine island where my father died. Where my mother abandoned me. Where I survived on my own for almost two years as a child. What is now known as Cross Island looks very different than I imagined it would after all this time. The cruel wind whips at us, tossing about the few of my curls that have escaped their braid. I pull my beanie further down over my ears, protecting the delicate skin from the elements.

A part of me thought there might be a town here, people. But there isn't. The razor-sharp cliffs and limited beaches don't lend to a ton of traffic. The whole of the island is a protected wildlife refuge, but even so, the landscape has changed quite a bit in the last three hundred years. What was once one island has split almost in two. A large inlet of water covers an expanse of land where our home used to be, separating the bulk of the forest covered island from a smaller offshoot of primarily steep cliffs. Only a lone strip of rocky beach connects the two land masses, but my home as I knew it is gone.

Rocks shift beneath someone's feet and I turn to look at the faces of my three companions. Each of them have some form of pity in their expression, lines creasing foreheads, mouths turned down. They feel sorry for me. I've only hinted on how it was for me growing up, so the only reason they'd have this level of pity is if Kyle filled them in. It stings and is comforting all at the same time. I've never really had friends. I've had people I've saved, people I've failed to save, and enemies. I don't know how I'm supposed to react to their empathy, so I decide to skip it altogether. There has to be a better time than this to deal with my self-imposed isolation, right?

"You alright, Shortcake?" Ky murmurs in my ear after he sidles up next to me. I give him a trembling smile and half-hearted nod. I suck at pretending at the moment. I used to be so good at it, and I don't know why with him I can't.

"It is so much different than I thought it would be. This cove wasn't here, and where our home was, is now under water. A part of me thought she'd just come back to that house, you know? That she'd be waiting for me for a change," I scoff at my own stupidity, shaking my head. "But, why would she? It's been three hundred years. She could have forgotten all about me..." I trail off, dashing the stupid tears off my cheeks. Sybil doesn't get those. She doesn't get my pain. She only gets my protection until the threat is taken care of.

Then, she gets nothing.

But the tug of a blood bond is harder to ignore than I thought. Especially being this close. So few of my kind still had parents at all—either at Iva's hand or the silent war that had been waging between the species of the Ethereal for centuries. Witches killed my father, Iva killed Wraiths, Warlocks altered timelines to whatever suited them best, Shifters and Wraiths infought within their own lines. There are so few of us left. The world is getting smaller and smaller. But even on this island that can't be more than two square miles, I feel so close and so far from my mother all at the same time.

"Sybil's somewhere on this island. I can feel her. Our presence will likely not be welcome, so keep your eyes peeled. And for the love of all that's holy, do not engage. I don't know what she's capable of," I warn, dead serious, locking eyes with both Grace and Joe.

I know Joe didn't want Grace to come here today. It is written all over him—that bone-deep need to protect. Kyle more than likely didn't either, but refused to say anything, probably feeling like it wasn't his place to dissuade her. With no better alternative and after loading up on enough weapons for a small skirmish, the four of us set out to the last place I felt my mother—a small island off the coast of Maine, near Cutler, where Iva was finally put down. Sybil was right under Iva's nose and she didn't even know it.

I've gotten glimpses of her over the years, but never enough to know if she was okay. That's the hard part about being abandoned. A part of me still gives a shit if she lives or dies. A large chunk of me still worries about her even if she didn't feel the same for me. That niggling doubt about myself—about my failures—only feeds the ache that even Kyle's love can't fill.

Because I'll never feel good enough to deserve it. I'll never feel whole. I'll always feel just slightly wrong because the person who was supposed to love me didn't—or at least not enough to stay.

We move from the cliff face toward the wide-open maw of the forest. We only have a few hours of daylight this far up north, so we need to find Sybil and get the hell out of here.

The farther we get into the trees, the harder the pull on my blood is and I know we're headed in the right direction.

"North," I mutter, my eyes scanning the dim canvas of dense trees. I suppose the visibility could be worse, but since we are in the last vestiges of fall, some of the deciduous trees have dropped their scarlet leaves, letting a bit of late fall sunlight stream through the thick canopy.

The forest is quiet except for us, but there isn't a way to tramp through the underbrush without making a fuck-ton of noise. Leaves crunch, twigs break, feet fall and squelch through the bracken. I don't mind the noise. It lets her know we're coming, and above all, I don't want to sneak up on Sybil. I have a feeling the woman who was edging under a thick blanket of depression in my childhood will be no better these many years later.

Not after Tessa used her.

Not after being hunted by Baron and Bella.

Not after running for so long.

I don't know what we'll find or how we will be received, but the growing knot in my gut is not promising.

"She's out here. I smell her," Joe murmurs, his eyes flashing a phosphorescent blue as he pulls in air through his flared nostrils. "She's hiding somewhere. She's afraid."

"Sybil!" I shout. "Ma-Mama?" I called the word I hadn't spoken in three centuries. "Mama, we're here to help you!" It damn near broke me to use that word—to call her a name she didn't deserve. "Pl-please come out."

Scanning the wealth of trees, I don't see her anywhere, but she feels so close. I expect to see a flash of the red hair we share, but all I see are the scarlet remnants of fallen leaves.

"Shortcake," Kyle murmurs, nudging me, "Look up."

I don't want to, but reluctantly my eyes lead my head and my gaze travels upward. The fire catches my attention first, camouflaged in the foliage she burns but I don't notice her for a good moment. This is before I realize that the flames aren't the fall leaves.

Sybil is perched on a thick branch, her Fireskin ablaze but not touching the bark through either heavy concentration or force of will.

Her bare feet clutch at the branch, her wings hanging down her back. She's dressed in furs of some kind, likely venison if I had to guess. Her face is blank in a way that isn't promising. No recognition. No love. Just blank.

"Who are you people? No one comes to my home. You're not allowed in my home," she scolds, her voice barely above a whisper.

"Mama? It's me, Nicola. Do yo—" I stop my throat catching. This is what I was afraid of. She doesn't know me. But I came here to do a job. I swallow hard and press forward.

"Do you remember me? I'm your daughter."

Sybil says nothing, only jumps off the branch, her body falling in a measured descent aided by a single flap of her powerful scarlet wings. Her landing is flawless, her eyes never breaking contact with mine. Kyle must take this as a threat because he goes from standing at my side to in front of me in an instant. It was so fast I don't know if he stepped there or traveled. I try to move around him, but he throws an arm, stopping me.

And for good reason. Her eyes are no longer blank, but lit with a fire that makes my stomach drop.

"You're lying. My daughter is seven years old. She's playing on the beach making a rock castle. I left her not ten minutes ago. You're not her," Sybil counters, her voice rough with disuse, but mouth twisted into a snarl. "You're trying to trick me. It won't work. I know things," she says, forcefully tapping her temple with a single finger.

Sybil has no idea what year it is. She has no idea how much time has passed. And she's delusional as hell if she thinks I'm still on that beach waiting for her three centuries later.

"No, Mama. I'm not on that beach. It's been a long time since I've seen your face. Almost three hundred years."

Sybil shakes her head the way a child would while throwing a fit. "No. You're lying. She is right there..." she trails off, pointing at a spot in the distance frowning at the trees around her.

It's then that I notice her wrist bears a thick cuff, the metal dull from years of wear, but the burned black sigils are still visible even at thirty feet away. I'm unfamiliar with the spell, but if it is anything like Talia's we're in a world of shit. Her fire dies instantly, scarlet wings folding into her back with a quick little flick.

"Sybil?" I murmur, skirting around Kyle's outstretched hand despite his growl and calmly make my way toward her. Her eyes slowly leave the empty forest behind us to look at me. Her face is clean, her nails void of dirt. The leathers she's wearing are old but in good repair. She has stitched the fawn buckskin into a tunic and breeches, her feet left bare and mud-splattered. Her wild red curls that are so similar to my own have been pulled back from her face into a messy braid with a leather thong.

"My name is Nicola. Do you know me?" I offer not unkindly.

"That's my daughter's name!" she exclaims, her voice bright. "But I'm sorry, I don't know you. Are you lost? Can I help you find your way?" she offers and a heavy lead weight settles over my chest. I blink back the newfound moisture in my eyes, swallowing down the hard lump in my throat.

"That would be wonderful. Do you mind leading us to the shore? We got a little turned around," I offer with a shrug.

"Of course. Follow me," she says pleasantly, walking past me back the way we came. I look at her retreating back for a second.

"Text Asher. We're going to be coming in hot," I murmur, readying myself for a fight.

"Don't," Ky whispers back, clutching my arm. "Let me help. I can help." His urging gives me pause and I look up to meet his concerned gaze. Watching his face, I see nothing but love and the innate need to protect. He wants to take this from me. This barbed pain of seeing my mother like this. Who am I to deny him this when it is within his power?

I can't help but nod.

"*Somnum*," he breathes on his fingers. *Sleep.*

Then he snaps his fingers.

<h1 style="text-align:center">19</h1>

KYLE

"Hello? Is this really the big, bad Kyle Brennan calling me?" Max's sarcasm practically drips from the line as I juggle the sleep-spelled Sybil and the phone.

"We've got a problem," I grumble, my eyes pinned to Nic's grief-ravaged face as she kung-fu death-grips her mother's hand. I've known she was full of shit about her mom since the beginning, but watching her grief is a gut-check I didn't expect.

"It's been thirty-six hours. Nothing could have possibly gone wrong in thirty-six freaking hours that you need to call me. What, did Nicola stub a toe?" Max starts giggling at her own joke, which given the current circumstances kind of makes me want to punch her.

Just a little. I won't, but I want to.

"Stop being an asshole and fucking listen, *Maxima*. We have a boat load of problems, and this sleep spell is only going to work for so long before we have a centuries-old Phoenix with dementia issues wearing a goddamn necromancy cuff waking the fuck up," I growl down the line and pray my words knock some sense into her. "You sent us on this mission, Max. You are obligated to answer the damn phone when I call. This is the fifteenth fucking time I've called you."

"I was in the training center trying to make a loophole in the comm's sitch. Give me a break," she gripes back.

"Yeah, well, rally the troops. We're coming in the next five or so."

"Everyone's already here. Shit was going down with Samara when you left, and that's still not cleared up. Talia is close to losing it without Nicola here, and Mena and Evan are pissed off that you left at all," she warns.

"Shit," I mutter, searching the treeline for Grace and Joe.

"Shit is right. I am not a fan of being dismembered or electrocuted. It fucking stings," she informs me, and it chills my blood to think that she might not be joking.

"Well, that isn't terrifying or anything. We'll be there in a minute," I mutter.

"I shall roll out the red carpet momentarily," she says scathingly and hangs up on me.

Sweet girl. Really. She's a peach.

Joe and Grace make their way out of the trees. Joe had offered to search the island on the off-chance Sybil wasn't as batshit crazy as we all thought. I'm not sure which form he took to search, but he refused to phase in front of me. I don't blame him. Sometimes that shit is personal. He took Grace with him, though, and while I didn't like it, I didn't say anything.

"There isn't another soul on this island, man. Just deer, small rodents, and birds. There are no spells, no warding, no people. I checked the whole island. There is no one here," Joe explains as he adjusts the collar of his jacket.

"How long has she been here? This is worse than a prison," Grace murmurs more to herself than anyone else, shivering in her down jacket and gloves.

I can't help but agree with her, wondering myself how long Sybil has been here. Hell, she imagined her daughter was still seven years old playing on a beach after three hundred years. I wonder how much is the cuff stealing her mind and how much is just the isolation of this island.

"I've circled the wagons. We need to go before she wakes up," I advise, shifting Sybil in my arms.

No one speaks, sobered by Grace's words. Grace and Joe put a hand on me, and I take us from that stark island to what feels like home in Colorado in a swirl of black smoke.

Barely a moment passes, and our feet sink into a fresh snow bank on Mena and Asher's front lawn.

"Aww, come on!" Joe gripes, shaking the snow off his boots. I hitch Sybil up, getting a better hold on her as the front door opens. Max appears in the doorway with her hands on her hips and the five of us—including the sleeping Sybil—make our way up the stairs.

The usually put-together blue-haired Witch looks like she hasn't slept at all in the day and a half we've been gone. Max's face is pale and drawn, bags taking residence under her eyes, her face free of makeup probably for the first time since makeup has been invented. Dressed in yoga pants, a t-shirt, and bare feet, she looks younger than her years.

Vulnerable.

And I'm not the only one who notices.

"Maxima, darling, are you alright?" Nicola asks, concerned.

"You skip eyeliner for one damn day, and everyone wants to know if you're dying," she mutters rolling her eyes. "I'm fine. I've just been researching ancient Greek lore. Have you ever pulled an all-nighter in pedal-pushers? Fucking impossible."

"Darling, I've seen you get pissed your eyeliner was smudged after you almost died in a car wreck. Plus," Nicola says pointing to herself, "Oracle. Who in the bloody hell do you think you're fooling?"

"Whatever. I don't wanna talk about it, okay?" Max mutters, crossing her arms over her chest.

"That, I can oblige," Nicola offers before letting go of her mother's hand to give Max a quick hug as she passes.

"So the gang's all here?" I ask, carrying Sybil into the house, Grace and Joe bringing up the rear.

"Yep. Down in the training center. Who are your friends?" Max asks.

"Not to be rude, and not as a slight to anyone, but I'd rather tell this story just once. And med bay?" I ask gesturing to Sybil's limp body in my arms.

"Yeah, sure. Follow me," Max shrugs, and leads us down the hallway and down the stairs. Through the thick steel door, we cross the ward Max has been tweaking.

Aurelia and Rhys are on the blue sparring mats watching the twins roll around and attempt to crawl. Evan and West are using the peg boards to climb the walls with Cam and Aidan looking on. Mena, Asher, and Talia along with Carver, Ian, and Samara are poring over thick books at a massive table and look like they are running off of just coffee and carbs if the carafe and decimated open box of donuts is anything to go by.

"Has anyone bloody slept since we've been gone?" Nicola scolds, leading me toward the med bay where I can put Sybil down, Max following us.

"Does this lock?" I ask, gesturing to the door when my hands are free.

"Yeah, I think so," Max responds.

"From the outside? Fuck it. I'll do it," I mutter as I usher everyone out of the med bay and breathe on my fingers, saying the Latin word for lock as I snap them.

"Okay, story time, kids. Gather round," I call to the room, but I didn't have to. All eyes are on us. "In case Max didn't tell you, Nicola and I were looking for pieces of the veil. Well, we found it—or I should say her. But first, let me introduce my daughter, Grace and her boyfriend, Joe."

Grace and Joe give half-hearted waves obviously a little intimidated by the bevy of supernaturals in the room.

"Umm. Say what now?" Aurelia pipes up as she comes closer, a slobbery Henry in her arms. Aurelia immediately looks to Nicola for confirmation, and then her eyes go wide.

"Holy shit! Your eyes!" she exclaims.

"Yeah, we'll get there. I promise," I assure her, and then tell the room what we've been up to for the last day and a half. Including, but not limited to, the daughter I didn't know I had, the alleyway fight, Marj lifting Nicola's curse and eliminating the last of Iva, Nicola getting her memories back, and the abduction of Sybil from her maybe-prison island.

"Holy. Shit. Were you really only gone for a couple of days?" Mena asks, aghast.

It doesn't feel like a couple of days. It feels like we've been gone a month, a year even. I don't even know the man I used to be before this. I thought Nicola and I would wait years before having children and I already have one. I thought we would overcome Nicola's memory loss together, and now her memory is back. I thought after the last time, we were safe.

Turns out I'm wrong about everything.

Rhys pipes up, breaking through my thoughts. "Anyone else mildly reluctant to cut that cuff off of her?" he asks, a sleeping Livy on his shoulder as he rubs her back.

It's tough to be mad at him for asking, but damn. Apparently, I'm not the only one, because his wife, and pretty much every other person in the room is giving him the stink eye. Except for maybe Cam and Joe. I have a feeling I'm not the only one who has had that thought cross their mind.

"Yes, I have claimed the mantle of asshole in this group, and I'm thoroughly repulsed at myself for having to ask, but what happens when we do this?" he offers, softening the sting of his question.

"We help that woman," Talia murmurs, her already pale face ashen since we started talking about Baron and his focus on Grace. "We stop her pain. You don't know. You don't know what it's like being in a prison with no one to hear you scream. You don't know what that woman has endured. You have no idea what that family is like. I only met Tessa's children, and they are pure evil. Where do you think they learned it from?" Talia murmurs, tears tracking down her face, a shaking hand covering her mouth to hold in a sob.

Rhys' expression is remorseful but determined.

"Talia, we researched your cuffs. They were for suppression of your Ethereal self. What in the holy hell is that cuff for?" he asks pointing to the steel door of the med bay. "You said she could phase. She had her wings, her Fireskin. I don't want to leave her in pain. I don't want her to suffer. I just want to know what we are bringing to our doorstep before we do it," he pleads, hugging his daughter to his chest once again.

We are all silent for a moment which makes it a huge shock when the pounding starts. Sybil's piercing scream rents through the cavernous room letting everyone in the house know she is not only awake, but she is no saner now than she was a few hours ago.

Sybil isn't even screaming words, just pain-filled howls and screeching.

No one moves for a long moment until Max nods, stalking toward a table and snatching up a set of bolt cutters, tears streaking down her cheeks, her face like stone. I feel my spell on the door break as soon as Max snaps her fingers.

A chorus of, "Max!" and "Wait!" fall on deaf ears because Max isn't stopping and she isn't slowing down.

Max throws open the steel door as if it weighs nothing, letting a fiery Sybil out of her temporary cage. Sybil lunges for the closest person—Max—but never makes it within a foot of her. With another snap of Max's fingers, Sybil goes still and quiet, her flames dying out immediately, her limbs frozen in a pose of attack. Wings tuck away into Sybil's back. Nicola, who was already on the move, is in Max's space in an instant.

"Grab your mother's wrist," Max orders but Nicola doesn't budge.

"What if you're wrong?" Nic asks, fear lacing every word.

"Doesn't matter if I am. No one deserves torture like that. No. One," she growls, and whatever Nicola sees in her expression makes her nod and gently take her mother's hand.

The scream that pierces the air once Max snaps the metal cuff off of Sybil's wrist is enough to chill everyone's blood.

What did we just do?

20

NICOLA

SHIT. *SHITSHITSHITSHIT*.

This is pretty much the whole of my thought process once Max grabs those damn bolt cutters. It only intensifies when the med bay door opens and goes nuclear when my mother in all her fiery glory comes busting out like a goddamn jack in the box.

Yeah.

I thought Sybil's screams in the med bay were bad. I thought after the cuff was off, the worst would be over.

But then the wrenching wail ripped from her throat cuts at me like shattered glass, and I don't know what I'm supposed to do. I thought we were fixing her. I thought we were helping.

We weren't.

"What did you do?" Sybil screeches. "They'll find me. They'll find me again. They'll use me. We were never supposed to be used for this. They'll find me. They will. *Theywilltheywilltheywill*," she raves as she fists her fingers in her hair and yanks.

"No, Mama. Please. Please don't hurt yourself," I plead, my voice brittle, so close to breaking as I do my best to try and still her hands.

Sybil isn't listening and fights me hard when I try to make her stop ripping at her hair. Then, it isn't just my hands on her. Mena's there.

Out of all of us, Sybil's screaming likely affects Mena the most besides me. She has endured more than anyone should have to. More than she ever deserved to. Memories of everything she'd endured sear through my mind, the burn of them just a tally on the long list of my regrets.

Mena's healing touch steals through Sybil, and the tears stop and the cries quiet and her eyes clear. I feel heat at my back, and I know it's Kyle offering his support in the only way he knows how.

Because how does he help with this? How can he do anything but just be there? There isn't a rule book or a how-to manual for how to deal with an estranged parent—especially one with a supernatural onset of dementia. I love his heat at my back. It is the only thing that is keeping me from breaking.

"Mama?" my words are a question more than anything. The likelihood of her knowing who I am is slim.

"Nicola?" she rasps, her voice sounds like she swallowed gravel, but I'll take anything over her screaming.

I can't help the relieved chuckle that escapes my lips or the tears that make tiny rivers down my cheeks. "Yeah, I'm Nicola. I'm your daughter. Do you know me?"

I've asked her this before, but I hope this time her answer is different.

"I-I think so? It's been a long time, hasn't it? You've grown up, and I-and I missed it. Ho-how long has it been? Where am I?" she asks, tears shining in her eyes.

"It's been a while, but you're safe. Hidden from everyone, and we cut that cuff that was hurting you off," I murmur, trying to explain what is probably an impossible concept. But gratitude is not what we get, and the longer the silence stretches between us, the bigger the knot in my stomach grows.

Sybil is silent for long moments, just looks down at her now bare wrist in confusion like she cannot fathom what it is.

"Why is my bracelet gone?" Sybil murmurs accusingly and my gut clenches. This doesn't sound like she thinks that cuff or bracelet or whatever was bad. This doesn't sound like we just freed her from a prison.

"It was hurting you. You didn't know where you were or what year it was. You... Weren't lucid," Kyle offers from behind me not unkindly, and I'm grateful because I'm at a loss. How in the fuck did this day get so turned around? I figured we'd find Sybil, get her safe, and we'd be in the clear.

Well, I didn't think that, really. For once, I had hoped that what we were doing was right—that for once when I tried to save someone, it was just for the saving. Not because of a vision. Not because I knew what was going to happen already. Not because I was altering an already messed up world.

I was just keeping my mother out of harm's way. Isn't that what I was supposed to do?

"But that bracelet kept me safe—kept the Veil safe. You don't know what I had to do or who I had to kill to get that bracelet on. You don't know how hard it was or the sacrifices I made. Please tell me that my sanity wasn't the only reason you cut it off of me," she asks, her hands cupping her elbows in such a way it's more like she's trying not to launch herself at me to slap me silly.

What. The. Fuck. Honestly, what the fuck? Who she had to kill? This is the same woman who couldn't feed herself after my father's death and here she is talking about who she had to kill?

"Ummm... Pretty much?" Max mumbles, her face a mask of disbelief. I'm pretty sure everyone in this room is wearing the exact same one.

"People will look for me," Sybil warns, her voice edging toward shrill.

"They were already looking for you," Aurelia informs her. I catch Aurelia's gaze, and she gives me a subtle shake of her head. She can't see any further ahead than I can which for as much as Sybil is ranting and fucking raving about 'the end is nigh,' I can't see as a good sign.

I try to look forward. I do. But all I see is a great wall of blackness that I thought was just that fucking cuff.

"But they can find me now. That cuff kept me safe from anyone who would use the Veil. That is the only reason you found me at all," Sybil says, her tone panicked.

"Well, fuck," Max mutters. "Maybe we can find a way to keep you hidden without completely wrecking your sanity?"

"Do you think I haven't tried? Do you think I would have done the things I did if it was just about my mind? This is about the world. Do you know what we are capable of?" Sybil implores, and all I see red.

She left me. She abandoned me.

"Of course I have no idea of what we're capable of. Why the fuck would I? You left me alone. You abandoned me on that stupid, lonely island to fend for myself. At seven. You left a blind seven-year-old behind. I didn't know how to fly. It was a year before I braved taking the canoe on the water, and do you know what I found when I made it to the mainland? People who would torture me. People who hated me because all I saw was death. Death, death, and more death. You know what I didn't find? You. But I've been taken over. I know what kind of hell would be in store for you if I left you alone. So I brought you here. You're fucking welcome," I end on a yell.

Yep. I just aired all my family business in a room full of people. *Fabulous.*

"And I thought my mom was a bitch," Max mutters, and I think I might be the only person who hears her because no one else reacts. I want to laugh at the same time I really want to cry. I'm embarrassed and pissed, and I fucking hate her for everything that has happened since she was too goddamn depressed to realize that you don't leave your children behind.

"Want to tell us what you can do? Might as well know what we're in for," Max asks throwing her hands up.

"Sure. Might as well, right? The only reason we ever went to look for you in the first place was because Baron tortured a fifteen-year-old girl for information," Kyle growls, his eyes slits of black fire as he points at Talia. "He's already kidnapped Nicola once, and if she hadn't been bonded to me, he would have tried to raise his mother from Hell. After all of what she's already been through, after surviving you as her mother, they just wanted more. Honestly, I don't give a flying fuck about you. The way you've hurt my wife, I couldn't give two shits if you lived or died. But this Veil is worth protecting, and you're the only accessible piece. So stop scolding, stop bitching, get your shit together, and tell us what the fuck is going on," he orders.

Sybil gives a dry chuckle which turns into a half hysterical laugh. I'm starting to think that cuff wasn't what was making her crazy.

"We were meant to be a conduit, a bridge between the living and the dead. It was an honor bestowed upon the first families. But we are also the Guardians of that bridge. No one comes back, not without being reborn. And no one comes back from Hell. No one. It would tear the very fabric of our world apart. There would be nothing separating our world from the Otherside. There would be nothing but pain and death. Our lives, our line, are the protectors of that bridge. My sanity, my life, is nothing in the face of that."

"People have already come back. Devereux. Iva," Mena murmurs. "You should know you helped with one of them."

"Help is a very loose term, dear," Sybil shoots back.

"But not from Hell, they haven't. Devereux and Iva were never consumed before they came back. Tessa, though. I sent her to Hell personally," West confirms.

"Tessa's dead?" Sybil says, her voice quivering in either relief or pain, I can't tell which.

"Oh, yeah. She was a crispy critter after I was done with her," Aurelia offers, patting a now sleeping Henry's bottom as she does a sort of shuffle-walk to keep him asleep.

"Thank the Fates," Sybil breathes in relief.

"Um... Who in the holy hell do you think they want to bring back? No, not thank the Fates. That woman killed children. She stays the fuck put," Aurelia sasses back.

"Oh, I know she kills children. Trust me. I know," Sybil mutters.

"Alright, this back and forth bullshit isn't getting us anywhere. Let me see if I have this right. Baron, the rapist, and his crackpot sister want to bring back Mommy Dearest from Hell, but doing so will basically bring about Hell on Earth and end life as we know it. Do I have that right?" Evan asks from her perch on West's lap, her curls piled on her head as she massages her temple.

"Yep. That's what I got," West offers.

"In basic, crude terms, yes, you have it right," Sybil answers, her tone scathing. Boy, is she barking up the wrong tree.

"Super. So I'm going to take the asshole mantle from my husband and ask why we can't just kill her? You said only three pieces of the Veil are alive at any given time. Nicola is safe, Samuel is dead, and Sybil is our only dangling thread, no offense," Aurelia offers.

"You know, I don't hate that plan, but it has a flaw. You assume only two pieces of the Veil are left on this Earth. There are three. Nicola, myself, and another. Three families possess the line of Guardians. The Miller's, the Constantine's, and the Oroz'. Now, the Oroz died out a millennium ago, but the Miller's and Constantine's are still alive and kicking. And producing offspring," Sybil says as she nods in Livy's direction as she naps in Rhys' arms. "I don't think you'd be willing to kill every unsafe piece of the Veil, now would you? I suppose since she has a brother, the loss wouldn't be too great," Sybil shrugs as if the killing of an infant was no big deal.

Aurelia nods for a moment, handing off Henry to Mena gently as not to wake him. Then, without a single shred of warning, she launches herself at Sybil and snaps her neck like she was breaking a freaking toothpick.

I suppose I should be aggrieved in some way, but all I can think is, *well done.*

21

NICOLA

It's probably wrong to laugh right now, right? I should be thoroughly repulsed or something. Probably.

I'm not repulsed or pissed, and I cannot help the full-out belly laugh that escapes me. I'm almost positive if Aurelia hadn't broken my mother's neck, any person in this room would have done the job for her.

Myself included.

So, I can't fault a mother for doing her due diligence of giving an actual shit about her child and eliminating some cunt muffin who decided cavalierly talking about murdering an infant was cool. Yes, I called my own mother a cunt muffin.

She fucking deserved it.

"I'm glad you're laughing, Nic. Your mom is a certifiable bitch," Aurelia says, a look of relief on her face as she reclaims Henry from Mena.

"Agreed. If you didn't do it, one of us would have. No one touches my family, and this bitch is not family," I say as I jerk my chin at Sybil's still form. "At least now I can see what the hell is going on without some bullshit hassle," I grouse as I wrap my fingers around Sybil's still forearm.

SYBIL—1721

"We can't keep going like this, Sybil," Samuel hissed as he surreptitiously glanced at a sleeping Nicola. Tonight, we were holed up in a farmer's barn to ward off the freezing temperatures while we made our way farther north. We would have to leave in the morning before the people who owned this land knew we were here. Nicola was huddled in a nest of straw, using a thin cloak as a blanket.

He was right, we couldn't keep moving every few months to keep people off our trail. We were exhausted, Nicola was unable to cope with the constant changes in location due to her blindness and Samuel and I were tired of running.

The three of us were wanted in many circles, and it made sense if we neglected to acknowledge the price the world would have to pay if we gave in. We needed a way out, but not the way Samuel was trying to get it.

"I am aware, Samuel, but there is nothing to be done about it. We can't hide without a heavy cost, and it is a price I am unwilling to pay," I returned his hiss in kind.

I didn't need to be reminded of what we left when we fled the old country. The Americas seemed to be the best bet for our family, but all we had seen so far had been judgment from humans and too many Witches to count. Witches who had so far been heavily persecuted and murdered by rival covens under the guise of human religion.

We were too exposed here without a Legion to protect us, but after the London Primary's assassination, we didn't know who to trust. There were too many eyes and not enough support here in this New World.

"Maybe it is a price I am willing to pay," Samuel murmured and turned his back to me.

"You cannot steal from the Bishop's, Sam. They will kill you."

"That might be, but the two of you would be safe. That is more than I can say right now, isn't it?" Samuel asked, glancing back at me over his shoulder, his anger palpable. He hated this life. He hated hurting our daughter.

But I couldn't dissuade him, and in the end, he did what he wanted to do.

Just like he always did.

I heard Nicola's screams first, and I knew exactly what Samuel had done. The very thing I told him not to do. The very thing that would get him killed.

There was only one reason for Nicola to make that noise. She's seen another death. But we were so far from humans on this tiny, stark island, she hadn't had a vision in months.

I knew Samuel was dead before I ever crested the last rocky dune, but I had to see it for myself. I had to know that the man I loved more than anything was dead. I had to know if all I had in this world was gone. I had to see it with my own eyes.

"Mama!" Nicola screamed again and what I saw when I made it within sight line of the rocky beach knocked the breath right out of me. Samuel was lying there, stiller than I'd ever seen him. And his skin...

He looked nothing like the handsome man I married all those years ago. He was just blood and gore and bones showing through. My sobs broke free without my permission, my keening only muffled by the bloody fabric of Samuel's shirt as I collapsed at his side.

We were safe here. We'd made a home on this secluded island. He didn't need to do what he did. Stealing a grimoire from a Witch was asking for trouble. But taking a grimoire from a Necromancer?

That was a death sentence.

He did it anyway. For Nicola. He had always put her first. Before we sent Samuel to his rest, I plucked the tattered, bloody parchment from the withered husks that once were his fingers.

Samuel was gone, and now I was alone.

SYBIL—1722

The first time I got sick, I thought it was from grief. As it happened more and more, I came to realize Samuel had gifted me with a child before he left this world. I had wanted to be happy about this pregnancy, wanted to rejoice in the fact that I would have a piece of Samuel even after he was gone.

But all I felt was suffocation and fear. Fear because I could not accommodate another child. Fear because I wondered if this child would be blind as well. And suffocation because Nicola would cling to me now that Samuel was gone, and a large part of me blamed this child for our troubles.

We couldn't move as fast or as far. Nicola's blindness called too much attention from strangers. Her visions were too powerful and too sporadic. Her range reached too far. And even if the three of us were pieces of the Veil, she would be the one people sought first because her otherness shone like a beacon. She was our albatross.

She would be the one to sink us.

IN THE DEAD OF NIGHT, I LEFT MY HOME. THE LAST PLACE Samuel was alive, the last place we were happy. Taking a lone satchel filled with limited provisions, I phased on the west coast of the island far from Nicola's bed in the house Samuel had built for us.

I couldn't stay there. I couldn't have my baby near the danger Nicola wrought. I couldn't bring this child into a world that was so closely followed by death. I couldn't look at the face of the reason Samuel was dead every single day and not worry about the safety of the baby in my belly.

I looked down at the burgeoning life in my middle, cradling the last bit of Samuel I had.

Better that Nicola lived alone in the safety of this island than have a woman who couldn't help but hate her as her mother.

I left the rocky shores of my last real home on this earth to have my new baby in peace, and I tried to forget Nicola and Samuel.

I tried to forget the family I left behind.

SYBIL—1906

I had my child in the sweltering heat of summer in a French colony town bustling with people. Time seemed to move slower here and for a while we were safe.

I forgot what we were, and how we'd endured so many years ago. I forgot that we should have been running. Members of the Ethereal flocked to this city where so few noticed our oddities. We were not persecuted here—not like the North, so Lucas and I stayed even when we shouldn't have. For nearly two centuries, we stayed hidden in plain sight until one day we heard of an earthquake in San Francisco.

We heard of it decimating the whole of the city and burning it to the ground. Something of that sort had already happened here many times over throughout the years, but this new disaster felt different.

They came in the night, stealing us right out of our beds while we slept and took Lucas and I to a circular stone room where so many had died before us. I met Tessa there, a Witch who had been tasked with the unthinkable. She was polite—at first—but what she asked of me, I could not do. She tortured me with steel blades, watching as the wounds closed and then cutting me all over again. She broke bones. She had spells that brought a new meaning to the word agony. Then she would enter my mind, taking all the pain away for a short while only to bring it back threefold.

But I never gave in, not to that woman. Until she realized I would not be broken. Then she started on my son. My beautiful son that looked so much like his father.

I lasted three days of watching her torture Lucas before I gave in. She promised she would leave him alone if I agreed to help her.

And in the end, she killed him anyway.

SYBIL—1939

It took me many years to break free from that place. It took me even longer to find someone—a Necromancer specifically—to perform the spell that would keep me safe. The same spell Samuel stole from the Bishops in the first place. The one lone Necromancer I found who was willing to cross the Bishops and the Southeastern coven wasn't the type of man who would do anything out of the kindness of his heart.

He wasn't the type to have a heart at all.

We struck a bargain. I would give him ten years of my life for him to perform that spell to hide me and during that time I was to do anything he asked without question.

It took me ten years of killing women and children, ten years of servitude in every way possible, ten years giving my body, my soul, my sanity. After our bargain was up, he finally fulfilled his end.

He gave me a cuff bearing the spell that would hide me from everyone and everything on this earth. He said it would take the pain away completely, but it had its own price to pay.

I would lose myself.

After everything I had endured, that sounded like bliss. So, I took that cuff to wilds of what was now known as Maine, to that tiny island where no one resided, where Samuel died and Lucas was conceived. I put that beautiful bracelet on.

And I forgot.

NICOLA

I fling Sybil's arm away from me as if the touch of her skin burned my flesh. I've never been burned, but I imagine the barb of her memories is a close estimation of the agony.

There are things a child should never know about a parent. A child should never know how much they were not wanted. They should never learn just how indifferent a parent can be.

Of all the visions I've had in my lifetime, seeing Sybil's life was the worst. Not because she was a self-serving psychopath (she was) or because she'd had a child I knew nothing about (she did). Simply, it was that—for the lack of another person to blame—she laid the whole of my father's death on me.

Had she not abandoned me, maybe my brother would still be alive. Maybe she could have healed from my father's death.

Or maybe it is just wishful thinking on my part.

"Shortcake, you're crying," Kyle murmurs as he brushes a tear off my cheek with the pad of his thumb.

I finally drag my gaze from Sybil's temporarily dead form to my husband's loving eyes. Somehow, just looking at the sun worn creases around his eyes and the odd little bump on his nose, and the way his eyelashes fan almost to his eyebrows in a way that isn't girly but is beautiful all the same, bit by bit the pain leeches away.

Granted, the tears still roll on down my cheeks, but I manage to dislodge the lump in my throat.

"I-I had a brother. His name was Lucas. Tessa murdered him in front of her," I manage to murmur, jerking my chin to Sybil's still form. "Sybil herself has killed women and children at the behest of the Witch who made that cuff. She's done the worst things imaginable—things I didn't think were possible. And never, not for one moment, has she ever cared for me. In fact, I'm pretty positive she hates me. Blames me for my father's death."

"Jesus, babe. It's hard to tell if you weren't better off in Iva's clutches," Kyle murmurs.

"Fucking parents. There's nothing worse than a mother not giving a shit about her kids, is there?" Max mutters at my left. She's not looking at me, but staring at Sybil as if she wished her eyes were lasers and could incinerate her on the spot.

And the award for least popular person in this house goes to...

But she's right. There really isn't.

22

KYLE

THE PROBLEM WITH A CENTURIES-OLD PHOENIX—WHO IS probably older than everyone in this house combined—is containment. It doesn't matter that Sybil should want to stay hidden in this house with as much firepower as she can get behind her. It doesn't matter that she could have an opportunity to reconcile with her daughter. And it certainly doesn't matter to her that Baron could show up here at any moment and kill us all with Sybil no longer under the protection of the cuff. We're all hoping he doesn't, and we're taking steps to rectify this, but I don't hold much hope with the way things have been going.

But Sybil doesn't want to stay here, nor does she want to reconcile with her daughter. Sybil's main focus is to cause as much irritation and pain as possible. She has been the thorn in our collective sides for almost a week now, and I don't know how long Nicola can stand being in her mother's presence before she loses what little patience she has.

Aurelia and Mena both cannot seem to stomach their aunt, and after Sybil's flippant attitude towards killing an infant, well, she won no favors in this house. After everything Aurelia went through to get her babies into this world, the mere suggestion that she should kill one of them is akin to stabbing her in the heart.

Even in a house as big as this one, it still feels too small. I feel stuck and outmaneuvered and each day we're here looking in old grimoires for answers when we should probably be hunting Baron down instead. The more I think on it, the more I realize that Bella and her brother don't seem to be playing the same game. I don't even know if they are on the same board. Bella attacks when she doesn't need to, and Baron threatens.

She enlisted Wolves to take Nicola, only for Nic to eliminate the threat. She kidnapped Nicola only to fail. She blew up Grace's shop and sent Witches to do her dirty work, only for us to get away. I don't know her end game, and I'm not so sure she does either.

Now, Baron seems to be another story altogether. He hurt Talia and set her free. But why? Did he send her to us, and if he did, why? To get us moving? To get us to find Sybil for him? Maybe. He taunted Marj with Grace, but was it just to pave the way for limited retribution for Bella's shit? Or was it something else? And how did we end up in Grace's shop in the first place? Was it coincidence? Fate? Or were we sent there?

I don't regret finding Grace, but after spending months in the New Orleans area last year and never stumbling upon her, it seems too convenient to meet her now when the world seems to be falling in. It puts us all in a rough spot because I don't know what Baron has planned for Marj, but I also feel like a sitting duck with all three pieces of the Veil under one roof. Is Grace safer here with me or with Marj or should I try to stash her someplace and hope for the best?

And Nicola and baby Livy and everyone else. I almost miss the days when the only person I gave a shit about was me because I don't know what I'm going to do if these people—my family—gets hurt. They may not all be blood, but they were family nonetheless.

Now that we knew what Baron and Bella were capable of, it feels like we are in a no-win situation.

I slam the dusty tome I've been translating for the last fucking hour closed. The spells aren't written in the standard Latin but an old form of Creole French that I have a hard time with. It's bad enough that it is a weird mix of French and whatever else, but context clues only go so far when three-hundred-year-old slang is at play, and it pisses me off.

"If you set that book on fire, I won't blame you," Max mutters as she studies her very own dusty tome, her eyes never leaving the page. I hate grimoires—they are basically a Witch's diary, and not all of the information is even in the realm of useful. Sure, there are spells and sometimes there is enough backstory to explain shit, but this one is damn near indecipherable.

"It has some good stuff, just not enough. Plus, it's in goddamn Creole and I'm not good at it. I'd ask Sybil since she lived there, *but...*" I trail off when Sybil's pained screams make themselves known. I'm not quite sure how old Sybil is, but if this is what Phoenix Alzheimer's looks like, I want no part of it.

Aurelia, Mena, Nicola, Samara, and Rhys have been taking turns watching Sybil over the last week. I tried a turn as sentry, but Sybil attempted to set me on fire, so we limited her guard to the only fire-proof people in the house. It took everything Nicola had (and Mena and I holding her back) for her not to kill Sybil on sight. Even five days later, she still isn't over it.

If I didn't think we'd need her for information, or the simple fact that killing her would make Nicola an orphan, I would have taken her out a week ago.

"I don't give a good goddamn if you're mad as a fucking hatter, I will slit your throat and bathe in your blood if you so much as look at him wrong, you hear me?" Nicola's voice carries into the training room just as the door to the med bay opens and she and Sybil walk into the room.

Sybil is walking on her own steam and isn't restrained in any way, but her nose is slightly askew and dripping blood. I'm not certain I want to know.

"Mommy Dearest would like to have a word with you and Max regarding the grimoires you are using. She believes she may help you translate some of the text, and will be happy to assist you in your endeavors," Nicola bites out, her teeth clenched in such a way that she might be doing permanent damage to her teeth.

"And what, pray tell, caused this change of heart? Just yesterday you said you didn't care if this whole world burned down along with you. If I remember right, you said, '*I hope you lose everything you hold dear just like I did. It will serve you right for taking my peace away from me.*' Were those not your exact words?" Max asks, her fingertips sparking green magic as she rubs them together.

Max is having the same problem I am—she'd rather just kill Sybil and get it over with. If she weren't so keen on not dying, everything would be roses. But by her scent, I know exactly where she'd go if she were to die permanently, so her desire to keep breathing isn't so surprising.

"Yes, that is verbatim what I said, but my lovely daughter brought up a very good point. If I helped her and you, she would do her best to put me like I was, back where I was, and keep me there for as long as she lived. Evidently, some Witches owe my daughter a favor and I'd very much like to go home."

Either she was owed a favor or Nicola was going to give one in exchange for help. She knew I wouldn't work the spell for a cuff like that. Especially since I studied it, and there was no way I was working the spell that was etched into the metal of that cuff.

Not even for Nicola.

Sybil's cuff was etched with sigils for a necromancy spell called *occulatatum a dolore—hidden from pain.* It prevented anyone with the intent to do you harm from being able to see you. It also had the side effect of consuming all of your painful memories, and for a woman like Sybil, that was most of her mind. The cuff fed on it like a leech—like a living thing.

The spell itself is the problem—or rather what it requires to perform. Regular, everyday spells simply use the power in our veins. I have more than enough power due to my Wraith genes and can get more when I feed. This spell requires sacrificial magic—meaning I'd have to kill something to make it work. Now, some sacrificial magic will call for a rodent or a snake or something small. The biggest one I've ever seen required the heart of a Gray Wolf which is probably why they were marked as endangered in the 1970's, and that particular casting was for protection. Given the human's war during that time, it wasn't really a shocker that so many people called for whatever means necessary to protect their loved ones.

But a spell like this—something this big, this all-encompassing—requires a life of an innocent. And that is something I have never done and will never do. I catch Nicola's eyes and she gives me a nearly imperceptible shake of her head behind her mother's back which eases the knot in my belly a bit. There is no way Nicola will allow innocent blood to be spilled for this woman either.

"Fine. Help me translate this grimoire," I concede, spinning the heavy tome toward her.

Her fingers skate over the worn leather before she flips open the cover, quickly flipping through pages as if this isn't the first time she's seen the book. It might not be.

"This was Marek's grimoire. He was Tessa's husband until she killed him in 1908. If you look toward the end, you'll see he's talking about the convergence. It is likely the reason Tessa killed him. He wanted to destroy the Veil completely—breaking the barriers between Heaven and Hell and the Otherside. This is why there are three of us. We each represent one of the three barriers—three walls separating this Earth from everywhere else. Killing all three of us will simply close the doors until another member of our line can be activated. But breaching a barrier to reach into Hell will destroy us all, and destroying the barriers will bring the convergence. This is what Marek thought, anyway. I'm not sure how much of it is true, but the Bishop children were raised at their father's knee. I don't doubt this is what they believe as well."

"You've known this whole time that this is what was happening and you said nothing until I broke your bloody nose and promised you your due?" Nicola asks as if she cannot fathom what sort of creature her mother has turned out to be.

"What can I say? I'm an opportunist," Sybil shrugs.

Well, that is for damn certain.

23

MARIA

I miss the hot, sunny days of a Spanish summer.

Living in Idaho for these last few years has made me wish for the land where I and my family was born. Why my mother thought being the leader of the Pacific Northwest coven was a good idea, I may never know. We weren't from here, and even after three centuries, this beautiful, yet cold, city has never felt like home.

I am not built for these winters, I think as I watch the snow fall in thick drives from my bedroom window. Something caught my eye a few minutes ago, but it had to be a trick of the storm.

I'm snuggled in my reading chair, book open at my lap, mug of tea on the side table. I should be reading, but I'm not. I'm lamenting another winter in Coeur d'Alene and shaking off the uneasiness I feel as I stare at the sheets of white falling from the sky.

I don't like wearing thick socks or sweaters and boots and coats. I don't like the way my caramel skin gets pale in the winters or the stupid fuzzy hats I have to wear. I don't like living in my mother's house or sitting at her table when I am old enough to be a grandmother by now— not that I have any children or even a husband to show for it.

I don't want this kind of life where politics and dealings are more important than life and family.

My mother may just love her position more than her children. She would prefer to be a leader than back her own blood. My sister knows enough about that. Mama shunned Maxima when she was only fourteen when she turned out to be even more powerful than any of us thought she would be. I know if I ever go against Mama, I will have the same fate as my sister.

Not that I've been thinking of leaving or anything. Well, maybe. But only these last three hundred years or so. But it is different for me than it was for Maxima. She has her own power. She has more than I ever would.

And if I lose my coven I may have less than none. No better than a human, but left to walk ageless and alone until my mind gives out.

I know enough about loneliness to know I wouldn't last a year by myself with no family, let alone the rest of my long life.

Survival is one hell of a motivator.

Speaking of mother dearest, a near-soundless knock sounds on the thick wood of my bedroom door.

She doesn't wait for me to answer, my mother, Teresa just walks right in. No, that's wrong. She doesn't walk. She barges, swift and hurried through the entry and shoves the door closed behind her with her back to it.

As abruptly as she enters, I notice she made not a single sound except for the faint rap to alert me that she was coming.

"We have to go, Maria. Grab a coat and gloves. And shoes!" she furiously whispers. "Don't forget socks and shoes."

My mother is typically a very put-together sort of woman, always in an appropriate pant suit or stylish outfit, but right now her eyes are wide in fear, her curly hair is frizzed out to maximum volume, and she's haphazardly dressed in jeans and a thick sweater. The jeans themselves could be a red flag, but taking precedence is the bright splatter of blood on her neck and chest.

Mama looks around the room and then snaps her fingers, effectively killing all the lights in the room before she turns and puts her palms flat to the door. She whispers words I don't catch before a green cast of light escapes her fingers, coating the door for a moment before going out.

"Mama, what's going on?" Is that my voice? It sounds so small and childlike. I've prided myself on my strength, but I have never been tested. Is this what I am when times are hard?

"The Bishops. They found us—broke through the ward somehow. Jacob and Corrine are dead. We have to go!" she orders and moves to my dresser, tossing thick socks and a beanie to me before heading to the walk-in and tossing out a parka. She comes out wearing a pair of snow boots and hands me another pair.

When she emerges from my closet, her face is back under control, a stone mask thrown over the fear. This is the mother I know. I'm still reeling from the shock of my friends—my family—losing their life, their blood likely staining my mother's sweater and she looks like she couldn't care less.

But survival and all, so I don't ask questions—not that I ever do— and haul my behind out of my chair, throwing on socks and boots.

She's right. We have to go.

MARJORIE

Who is Tobias?

Nicola's question runs on loop in my brain as I scrabble on my hands and knees on the marble floor of my bathroom, slipping through the thick blood of a Witch I was forced to kill.

I killed him with a pair of shears from my writing desk. I've never used those shears in my life. I bought them because they were pretty. I thought they looked like they belonged at a writing desk in a boudoir of a nice southern woman's home. I thought they made me a little more authentic, a little more appropriate for a position I never wanted but got anyway.

I guess my tacky sense of style served me well because those stupid, gaudy shears were now embedded in the neck of the Witch who tried to kill me in my own bed.

I felt the ward break first, the snapping of the spell breaking against my skin. It was what woke me up. That ward had been in place for four centuries—long before I was ever born—and they broke through it like it was nothing more than tissue paper.

This was the one place where I was truly safe, and they'd taken that from me. Where in the world would I be safe if not here?

I bring the trembling back of my hand to my lips to quiet my breathing. I should be hiding. There are too many in the house—too many men for me to fight and not enough power in my veins to stop them. It took everything I had in me to kill the taint left on Nicola's soul. About all I could possibly do now is throw a glamour, but even then, I might not be able to pull it off. I've never been this weak in my life.

Who is Tobias?

I should have called him when she asked about him. I should have told him I was sorry for pushing him away. I should have done a lot of things I won't be able to do. I didn't realize how much regret I'd feel for not reaching out to him when I had the chance.

But then he would be here with me. He'd be stuck here, trapped in a house full of necromancers bent on killing me and anyone else who supported me.

No.

He was better off. He was better off without me and my title. Me and my fucking politics. Me and my lineage and the heavy weight of the Baxter birthright.

Me and my demons.

Who is Tobias?

The way she said it, like she knew exactly who he was. Like she was a friend asking me about a crush.

But he wasn't a crush.

Kyle was my first foray into rebellion. A way to do something for myself, a way to choose someone that wasn't on my father's short list of acceptable men for me to be with. I didn't know he was anything other than Witch when we were together, not that it mattered to me one bit. I didn't care, but my father despised him and his kind. And even though I killed father myself, his prejudice still stains the way I live my life.

Kyle may have been an undesirable, but he was still part Witch. Tobias was something else altogether, and I hate the way my father's voice echoes in my head when I look at him. When I see how different he is from me.

Who is Tobias?

He is my one regret. He is my one hope that will never be. He is my one and only wish for myself that will never, ever come true.

I know it won't because I hear the footsteps get closer. Thick footfalls of a man's boots sound just outside the open bathroom door. The dead Witch is easily visible even in the dim and the trails of smeared gore will lead whomever it is straight to me as I crouch against my closet door in my blood-soaked silk nightie.

I try to throw up a glamour, but my pitiful attempt is unsuccessful. I don't have even enough power to hide, so I take the coward's way out and close my eyes. I think of Grace and how I wish she could understand how much I missed seeing her grow up. How I wished she knew how proud I am of her, how much I love her, how glad I am that she is with Kyle and thankful that he will protect her.

Who is Tobias?

I think of his face, the way his eyes crinkle when he smiles at me, the lopsided pull of his mouth because he never seems to have a full-out grin. How he makes me feel small, but powerful. The way he makes me feel safe and warm and loved. The way his hands feel on my skin, the way his lips feel against mine.

I should have told him yes when he asked me to leave my coven. I should have said 'I love you, too,' when he confessed how much he cared for me. I should have said so many things I won't get to.

When coarse hands find me I stifle a scream.

My eyes flash open and he's there. Tobias is here.

"Baby, where are you hurt?" His voice is a rough whisper in the quiet as he cradles my face in his hands.

"I... I don't think I am. I'm not... I'm not hurt," I stutter, amazed he is even here. Our last meeting didn't go so well. The last time we were together it ended with Tobias telling me he loved me and that we should go underground for a while. That I wasn't safe in my own coven. That I would be safer with him.

I didn't believe him. On any point. And I was an asshole about it. It's one of my biggest regrets. But here he is saving me when he should hate me.

His eyes flash amber in the dim as his nostrils flare. He's using one of his many abilities to scent me, to make sure I'm not in shock, probably.

"I don't smell any of your blood," he murmurs and then takes a furtive glance at the felled Witch with the shears in his throat. "You did good, sweetheart. You protected yourself. I'm so proud of you. But I need you to rinse off and get dressed," Tobias directs me, using small sentences because it's probably all he thinks I can understand. He's not far wrong.

"What do you mean, rinse off? Don't we need to get out of here now? Aren't there still Witches here?" I ask, not willing to get naked in this house if I'm about to be killed.

"I took care of it," Tobias murmurs, rubbing at my cheek with his thumb. His eyes flash when he says it, and I know he has eliminated every single threat in this house.

For me.

"I love you, Tobias. I should have said it before. That was the thought that ran through my mind when I thought I was never going to see you again. That I didn't tell you that," I whisper as my voice breaks, the tears finally coming when the worst is over.

"You'd better," he replies, his tone and expression disgruntled and as inappropriate as it is, I bust out laughing.

He kisses the laugh off my lips and I think I could do with a bit more inappropriate in my life.

TOBIAS GETS US TO A SAFE PLACE—A TINY MOTEL ON THE Florida-Georgia border just outside of Jacksonville. The drive was chaotic, but it was the best he could do since my magic has decided to take a hike.

When I don't think I'm going to fall off the deep end anymore (or burst into fits of inappropriate laughter) I put a call in to the other coven leaders. I try the New England, Southwest, Pacific Northwest and Mid-West covens all without getting an answer. At first, I thought maybe it was just me—that it was an attack on me because of what happened with Grace.

Grace...

If someone attacked me, then they could have attacked her too. Attacked Kyle.

And I have no idea how to get ahold of him. I can't cast right now, I can't... How do I do this without magic? Then, I shake myself out of it.

The panic at the threat to Grace's safety has made me stupid, I think. I shake my head and dial the first person I can think of that probably has a lead on Kyle and Nicola. If I can't get him through Mena Constantine, then I will do whatever I have to do to find her.

"Constantine residence," a deep, gravelly voice answers on the fifth ring.

"Mena, please. This is Marjorie Baxter of the Southeast Coven." I keep my tone polite, but inside I am beyond scared. I hope he doesn't notice the slight tremble in my voice the way Tobias does.

"Yes, ma'am, Mena is on another call, but I assume you want your daughter and not my wife, right?"

"Yes," I breathe relief slamming through me hard enough to make me stagger a little.

"I'll get her. Were you attacked as well?" he asks, and the relief is tempered with dread.

"Yes, but... How did you know?"

"Mena is on the other line with Teresa Alcado. I'm pretty sure all of the coven leaders were hit tonight."

Tobias' eyes go wide as he hears the man's words.

"We made it out."

"We?"

"Myself and my boyfriend, Tobias." The words are awkward on my tongue. Especially *boyfriend*. What are we, nine? But it gets the job done because Tobias' lips are pulled into a real, honest-to-god grin.

"Good. Here's Grace," he says.

"Umm... sir?" I ask, calling him sir because I don't know his name.

"Asher."

"Asher. Thank you for keeping an eye on my baby girl." He can't know, not unless he has children of his own, what it means to me that she is safe.

"No problem," he murmurs before a harried Grace takes the phone.

"Mama?" Grace's sweet voice filters down the line.

Grace has never called me 'mama' or anything close to similar, and given the circumstances, she might never call me anything close ever again, but I can't help the way the word warms something in me that I thought had died a long time ago.

"Yes, baby. I wanted to call and make sure you're okay." My voice sounds like it has been run over gravel, but I can't quite seem to swallow the lump in my throat.

"I'm okay. Are you okay? Mena said the coven leaders had been attacked."

"Never better, darling girl. I'm catching the first flight to wherever you are, and we are going to figure all this out together. Does that sound okay?"

"I-I think I'm good with that," she says, and for the first time in my life, I feel a smidgen of hope.

24

NICOLA

I'VE BEEN DISGUSTED BY MANY PEOPLE IN MY LIFE. HELL, I SEE people at their worst every single day—it's difficult to be at your best while dying. But none of them have ever been related to me. None have ever had my same blood in their veins.

This last week has made me glad Sybil abandoned me at a young age. Who knows what kind of person I would be if she'd raised me to be like her—to be heartless and cold. I have guarded my heart my whole life, but Sybil seems to not have one at all. I feel sorry for her and hate her all at the same time.

It is difficult to reconcile the woman I wanted her to be with the one she is. Expectations are the heart's worst enemy. But I can't dwell on my broken heart, I cannot harp on what I have lost and what she has tried to take from me. I have to focus on the here and now if I want my real family to survive.

Because the more she talks, the more she shows who she really is. And that isn't an absent mother—it is a woman without a heart.

"Do you know which one of us represents which barrier?" I ask, getting my brain back on target.

"I have a guess, but I could be wrong. I'm pretty sure you are the barrier to the Otherside. You see both good and bad people crossing over. You see all death not just good death like other Oracles do. I am not an Oracle or even a Seer, but I know enough about myself to know how close to Hell I am. And that innocent child took Lucas' place, took Samuel's place. They were good men, better than I've ever witnessed. She would be Heaven. Baron won't want her, but do not leave her unprotected. Any one of us can be used to pluck someone from death. Any one of us can be used to break the barrier into Hell. I am just the optimum conduit," Sybil confesses, her shoulders rigid, jaw tense.

"Are you going to help us? Are you going to help us stop them? I cannot locate them, and I don't give a single shit what my mother's coven says. They have to be stopped," Max insists from her perch on the edge of the wooden table.

"I think I'd rather go to Hell myself than let that woman out of it. I know my son was not the only child she took from this world, but I would rather reside in the depths of Hell than let Tessa Bishop free. So, I guess I'm in," Sybil admits.

"Good. We are going to need all the help we can get," Mena breaks in as she shoves the training room door open. She's followed by Grace, Joe, and Ian. Ian looks like he's ready to tear his hair out. "I just got a call from the leaders of the Pacific Northwest Coven and the Southeastern Coven. They are a bit miffed at the Bishop children right now. Max, your mother was exceptionally colorful with her words. I take it you get your temper from her?"

Max shrugs. "Probably. We're a spirited bunch. I thought she wanted us to stay out of it?"

"Well, I guess she changed her mind since her and your sister were attacked last night by Bella's goons," Mena informs us.

"What!" Max yells as she shoves off the table. I know Max isn't close with her family. In fact, if memory serves, she was exiled from her coven a few hundred years ago.

But family blood runs deep. That is a fact I know all too well.

"They're fine. A little banged up, but fine. Marjorie's house was also attacked. No one but her and a man named Tobias came out alive. They are all on their way here to figure out what the hell to do."

My first thought is of Grace, who is standing behind Mena, white as a sheet. Joe has his arm around her and I know without a shred of doubt, she's rethinking the whole mom-shunning thing. If my mother gave a shit, I'd be in her boat right about now too.

The name Tobias rings a bell too. I'm glad for Marjorie that her man wasn't caught up in the swath of death the Bishops seem to be keen on spreading wide.

"Grace, are you okay? Did you get to talk to your mother?" I ask because I don't want Kyle to feel like an ass for wanting to know. He already feels like an ass for the whole not knowing he had a kid thing. I don't want to add to it. This girl is essentially my step-daughter, and so far, she has seen me kill people, lose my mind, and go through my own mama drama.

"Yeah. She's okay. She'll be at DIA in a few hours," Grace assures me.

"Umm, guys?" Max says, her voice thready in a way I haven't heard from her before—even after nearly dying in a car wreck. I look up from Kyle's face to see Max cradle her head and sway in a way that is not comforting at all. Before she can go down, Ian is there to hold her up.

"Som-someone is trying to break the ward. Someone is trying to get in the house," Max whispers but every single person in this room can hear her.

And like me, I'll bet their stomach drops to the floor.

But unlike me they can't see what's coming. They can't see the death on our doorstep.

KYLE

"Oh, god," Nicola whispers not looking at me anymore, her eyes light up the bright, incandescent blue of an incoming vision. Blood weeps from her tear ducts and I brace, knocking over my chair as I jump up to wrap my arms around her.

Damn Max and this stupid ward.

Damn Baron-fucking-Bishop, and his sister, and his mom roasting in Hell.

Damn that whole fucking family.

I don't need Nicola to tell me what's going on. I don't need her to tell me that she and I and everyone else are in danger yet again. I hold her up as I eye the weapons hanging from their pegs and the cache of weapons hidden behind the false wall. Faintly, I hear Mena screaming for Asher, and soon we are surrounded by so many people—people that I don't really see because all I can do is stare in absolute fear at the slow-moving blood tear that courses its way down Nicola's cheek.

In the back of my mind, I know West and Evan and their Guardians are already there divvying out firearms and blades in an economical fashion.

I need to do that too. I need to prepare for whatever is heading for us. I need to protect her and them and everyone under this roof. But I know I can't do that. I can't protect everyone because that isn't possible. Something is here and I feel it in my gut that this time all of us aren't getting out of here alive.

Half of our crew are loaded down with weapons and ammo in a hot second and are about to investigate when Nicola starts screaming. Not just a little screaming either. Like full-out, horror movie, *I'm dying from disembowelment*, screaming—enough to chill my blood and stop every single person in this room in their tracks.

I look over to Aurelia who is holding her daughter to her chest while she covers her ears, her face awash in a mask of horror and fear as she trembles in her spot.

Aurelia's not having a vision at all. She doesn't see what Nicola does. And that scares the living shit out of her.

It scares the shit out of me too.

Nicola's wails finally quiet as she sucks in a huge breath. Her eye flutter open and they focus almost immediately, boring into me with a single-minded determination that I've only seen on her since she got her memories back.

"We have to get everyone out of here. It's just Bella here now, but Baron is coming and with him..." she shakes her head. "He's using the Eidola. He's using souls of evil humans who were never sent on and, and..." she trails off as if she can't stomach saying the words.

"And what, Nicola?" Mena demands. "What is the Eidola?"

"It kills unmercifully. It consumes everything in its path, no matter what it is. It's what killed my father. It... it eats people alive," Nicola murmurs, her panicked breaths tearing from her chest as she turns to her mother. The pair of them lock eyes and a million words pass between them without them ever speaking. Sybil's face is gray with shock as she grips the wooden table hard enough to make it groan under the strain.

"This is what Voyt was talking about, wasn't he? This is why him and Claire went off to Fates-know-where to try and prevent. Using human souls..." Mena murmurs her fingertips sparking with her stress.

"Yes. This is exactly what he wanted to prevent," West growls, his grip tightening on the hilt of the sword in his hand until the leather creaks.

"Magic is doing this, magic is the only way to undo it. Your swords are of no use. Your bullets will do nothing but abrade away to ash. She will break the ward, and when she does her brother will come and the Eidola will devour us all. Think past your weapons to the power you hold inside you," Sybil commands.

"Well, that may be a problem," Max murmurs as her breaths become heavy. Her face is a startling shade of gray, and if Ian were not holding her up she would be crumpled on the floor.

"You didn't. Please tell me you didn't," Ian begs and gives her a little shake. His face is ravaged, a mask of disbelief and pain so acute he can barely breathe.

I've been where he is right now. I've looked at a woman I could not save and watched her wither away. But Ian's pain is so much more than my own. At least I know when my woman leaves this world, she'll be taking me with her. Ian has no hold on Max, he'll be stuck on this earth without the other half of his soul.

"I can't... do that. Had to make it stronger. Couldn't... leave you unprotected. Had to do my part," she murmurs, her breathing getting shallower and shallower. Max is fading fast.

"What did you do?" Aurelia asks, her voice like broken glass as she watches one of her best friends wither in Ian's arms.

"I reinforced the ward. Tied it to my power. When she breaks it... Well, you're going to be a man down," Max says with a self-depreciating half-smile and a shrug. But Aurelia doesn't want to hear it because she just shakes her head as tears stream down her face.

"I had to keep your babies safe, didn't I? It's better me than them. I've lived longer. Sybil's right, you know. Magic. Use it. Get creative, and get those babies out of here. She's coming. Take them, and be safe," she murmurs, her voice petering out at the end.

Max sucks in one last breath and then her whole body wilts in Ian's arms, her head falling back over his forearm, her arms hanging lifeless at her sides. I feel the ward break, like a rubber band that snaps at my skin and I know she's gone. There is no more life in her, no more magic.

The howl that escapes Ian is enough to shred my insides to nothing. He buries his face into the column of her throat as he hugs her slack body to him as he crumples to his knees.

"We have to get everyone to safety," Mena orders. "Grab someone who cannot go on their own and get the hell out of here."

Evan and West murmur their assent, nodding to their Guardians to grab someone. Aidan grabs Ian and Max's body, Cam grabs Samara. But when the pair of them try to smoke out from the now unwarded training center, they go nowhere.

Max may be gone and her ward may be down, but we're not going anywhere.

25

NICOLA

This isn't supposed to happen. Max isn't supposed to die this way. She isn't.

My friend isn't supposed to leave this world without finding her other half. She isn't supposed to miss out on having babies and grandbabies and great-grandbabies. This world is not supposed to be robbed of her laughter and wit and light. It isn't.

So it takes a while for my brain to comprehend why she isn't breathing, why her half-lidded eyes stare blankly at nothing as Ian clutches her to him. Max is who I saw him marrying in that rainbow dip-dyed wedding dress. Their children were supposed to be beautiful. He was going to get to walk their daughter down the aisle. They were going to raise wonderful children who would have beautiful children of their own.

That is what I saw for her—for them—and it is a knife in the gut to see a life cut short. To see it all torn away.

Then, Ian shakes his head at Aurelia, and stands, lifting Max up in his arms and lays her on the table where we were searching for a way out of this mess. He moves his hands over Max, taking her vitals, assessing her medically. Then he starts CPR, tilting her head and giving her a breath before starting chest compressions.

For some reason, we are all on pause—watching as he beats Max's heart for her, as he breathes for her, as he refuses to let her die. Aidan steps in to rest Ian on compressions, but no one else moves.

Sybil is the one who snaps us all out of it, pulling us from our shock and grief. It makes sense that she'd be the one to do it because out of all of us, she cares the least about Max.

"Okay, guys, get it together. If Bella is keeping us here, we'll have to take her out so her ward will drop," Sybil strategizes. "Is there a crow's nest or something in this house? Tunnels? Anything?"

"No tunnels," Asher replies, "But there are a few concealed portholes in the attic we can get a visual from if they aren't already in the house."

Knowledge slaps me in the face. The walls feel like they are talking to me, the floor whispers in my ear, the air sings across my skin like it has a secret. I feel Bella's spell holding us here, her power sizzles up my body from my toes to my scalp. My eyesight goes wonky for a moment as I see her in my mind.

The last time she was in my presence, she did not feel this strong. I don't know what she's done to gain so much power, and I don't think I want to.

"They aren't in the house. She's waiting—keeping us here like lambs for the slaughter. She wants Baron here before they kill us," I tell them and when my eyes can focus again I train them on Kyle.

Everything this man has gone through, everything he has endured, and he's stuck in this house about to die with me.

"She has friends," Aurelia whispers, her head tilted to the side as her eyes alight with a vision. "They aren't as strong as her. If we wipe them out, she might be weakened. She might be drawing from them," she offers, her phosphorescent light dimming as she blinks back into the now.

"Sounds like a plan. Grace, Aurelia, take the babies and hunker down in the med bay. Kyle can ward the door. Keep the children safe. Carver, Talia, Rhys, Sybil, Joe, I need you to stay here and make sure no one gets through that door. Kyle, ward this room as much as you can. We need as many lines of defense as we can get. Everyone else, weapon up and fan out. Protect all entrances using whatever means necessary," Mena orders.

And we move.

AIDAN

My brother has lost more than most. Like me, he never really knew his mother. Both of our mothers died in childbirth, but whereas I was loved and taken under our father's wing, Ian was not. Ian's mother never informed our father of Ian's existence, so no one really knows who she is. Father has never spoken of her, and to this day neither of us know her name. Ian was raised in an orphanage in Ireland, never knowing his family, never knowing who or what he was. Until it was too late.

I didn't find out about Ian for many years. I didn't know I had a brother until he was captured and tortured by Ethereals masquerading as Christians. Punishing him for mixed heritage and the color of his skin.

He lost his mother at birth. He lost his home as a child. He lost his innocence as a teenager. Now he is losing his other half.

I continue to work on Max with Ian, pumping her heart for her through compressions while Ian gives rescue breaths. I don't know why we haven't moved to the med bay. I don't know why he isn't using the defibrillator paddles and epinephrine and all of the medical goodies he always keeps stocked there. Ian is reduced to base concepts. This is why doctors aren't allowed to work on family, this is why someone else has to make life-saving decisions. Because he isn't coping.

He isn't fixing her. He's burning himself out on the last dregs of hope that his other half will magically wake up on this table when he knows she won't.

But that's Ian. He gives so much of himself but never remembers to ask for it back. He looks on the bright side even when there is none. He has hope even when all of the hope to be had is lost.

So, when I quit compressions and try to get him to stop the rescue breaths, he fights me. A solid left cross that rings my bell but doesn't knock me out and then he goes back to her.

Breathing for her.

Beating her heart for her.

Refusing to acknowledge the reality that Max is not coming back.

RHYS

I've been scared before—when I thought I would lose Aurelia. When I thought the babies would be lost. When I thought our friends and family would be lost.

I've always had hope because I knew if there was a way out, we would find it. If there was a way to live, we would do it.

But right now, I don't know how much hope I've got left in me. My wife, my children, my family are in the crosshairs once again and I don't know if we are going to make it out. I don't know if we'll win this time.

I grab Aurelia by her wrist as she stalks toward the med bay, Livy clinging to her neck as she goes. I'm holding Henry to my chest and I don't want to let either of them go. Her eyes meet mine and the stark terror in them haunts me.

"I'm going to protect you. Do you hear me? This time I won't fuck it up. This time you and our babies will be safe. Believe me?" I ask because I want her to believe in me. I want her to know I will fight to my last breath for us and our children. I will give anything, do anything to keep them breathing.

Aurelia's eyes fill with tears as she nods. I pass her Henry, kissing his head first before moving to Livy's. I hook a hand behind Aurelia's neck and my lips take hers for a quick moment.

"I love you, Handsome," she murmurs against my lips as she bumps her forehead against mine.

"I love you, too, Gorgeous. Keep our babies safe."

She nods as she juggles our children, hugging them to her as she breathes them in, her shoulders setting in a way that lets me know she won't let anyone touch them. She and Grace head down the hall to the med bay and I watch as Kyle seals my whole world in that room.

"No one is getting past us, man. No one," Carver murmurs as he slaps a hand on my shoulder. He passes over my sword which I slid into the back sheath and I move to check my weapons.

Movement catches my eye and I turn to look at Joe and Talia. Talia— even as young as she is—is preparing to fight in the only way she knows how and leaps into her wolf form. One moment she is a pretty but painfully thin young girl and the next she is awash in gray smoke. When it clears, a sleek gray wolf stands in her place. Golden eyes blink up at us with all of Talia's intelligence, and for the millionth time I feel like an asshole for not wanting to help her. For not wanting her in this house. She's no worse than I was when I knocked on the Black's doorstep two hundred years ago. And those poor people saved my bacon.

Joe nods as he watches her phase. "Don't chase me, puppy," he quips before phasing himself. In his spot is the biggest fucking cougar I have ever seen in my life. Joe gives the wolf a plaintive hiss before settling onto his haunches.

Carver and I exchange a loaded glance, and like me, I'd bet he's wondering how these two will react to one another. I suppose we don't really have time to worry about it.

We have bigger fish to fry. Kinda like the freaked the fuck out Phoenix that we've been watching all week. Sybil is pacing behind our furry friends as she mutters to herself.

"Sybil," I call, "You going to fight alongside us or have a nervous breakdown? You know, so I can plan my goddamn day."

My tone snaps her out of whatever is now plaguing her mind and she whips her head back to me.

"What?" Sybil snaps her eyes finally focusing on the world around her.

"Witches surrounding the house? Trying to kill us all and bring about the bloody fucking apocalypse? Care to stay with us and pick up a weapon?"

"Oh. Right. Sorry," she mumbles shaking her head, but her eyes stray to her daughter. She doesn't have the same look in her eyes that Aurelia gets when she looks at our children. It isn't love on her face. But it isn't hate or indifference either. It is a wary sort of duty, and I don't know if it means she has thawed to her daughter or not.

I'm not even sure she has that in her.

But for a moment, I have hope.

26

IAN

"YOU HAVE TO STOP NOW, BROTHER. SHE'S GONE," AIDAN PLEADS with me, and I hear his words.

I do hear him. But he's wrong.

"She isn't. You don't know how strong she is. You don't know what she is capable of. No one does."

Breath, breath. One, two, three, four, five...

"Only necromancers come back, man, and she isn't that. There are seventeen other people in this house that are breathing. Help me help them. Help me keep our family alive. I'm sorry she's gone, Ian. I'm sorry, brother, but you have to stop now."

When he pulls at my elbow, I sock him in the jaw again. Harder this time, harder than I have ever hit anyone. Because he is keeping me from her, he's keeping me from giving her my breath, from giving her a heartbeat, from clinging to that little, tiny sliver of hope I have in my chest.

She needs my help. She needs me to do this for her. Maxima needs me, and I will die before I fail her.

I know she isn't really mine, just like I'm not hers. I know I am second best in every way when it comes to this woman. I know that she will probably never love me or want me. But I'll still want her.

Even when she has another man.

Even when she has a purpose and a life away from the Ethereal.

Even when she has a plan that will probably never include me.

I'll still want her. I'll still remember the one errant night we had dancing in a club, the one time I had her body against mine, the one time I had her lips on my lips. But the next day she didn't remember me —didn't recognize me—and I've been punishing her ever since. I'll still regret the time I wasted, the time we could have had. And I'll love her—even if she doesn't love me—if she would just fucking wake up.

Then everything stops. I hear the thin, thready sound of air being drawn from her lips. Spinning, I turn back to Max to see her eyelids flutter, but not open.

"Max. Baby? Please just open your eyes for me. *Pleasepleaseplease.*"

Regardless of my pleading, she doesn't open her eyes for me. But she's still breathing.

So, I'll take it.

KYLE

I should have kept her on the other side of the ward. I should have shoved Nicola in the med bay or duct taped her to a chair, or fuck, anything. Anything to keep her safe. But I haven't been doing such a great job of that lately—or ever, really.

"Quit it," she scolds, raising one perfect red eyebrow at me as she adjusts the holster under her left arm.

"What?" I look down at myself wondering what the hell I'm doing that she wants me to stop.

"Did you know you get twin lines at the bridge of your nose when you're agitated?" she informs me as she points to her own furrowed forehead. She imitating my frown and it's really fucking cute on her face.

"Do I?" I ask, the side of my mouth pulling up in a sort of wonky half smile.

"Yep. That plus the twitch under your right eye, you grinding your teeth, and the incessant popping of knuckles mean you're probably thinking of keeping me safe and wondering if we're all going to die. Stop flogging yourself, Ky," Nicola murmurs, hitting me with those beautiful blues. She's right, and she's wrong, but I don't tell her that.

"Can you see this in your mind or are you just observant?"

"This time I'm just observant. Well, that and even though my sight doesn't seem to be going away the hearing ability has not diminished even a single iota," she quips, rolling her eyes.

There's a reason Phoenixes typically live in secluded locations. I can't imagine the noise of a bustling city hammering my brain at all hours of the day.

"We will either make it or not. We will keep breathing or we won't. But we are doing this all together as a family."

She shrugs as if that is a given—that this family of our own making will stand together. She's right, though, we will stick together—even if we die in doing it.

"It's the 'won't' and 'not' part of the equation that gets me, Shortcake."

It takes a lot for me to admit this to her. It is what has plagued me since I first met her. We started in the middle of a war, I don't want us to end in one.

"Well, I don't know about you, but I didn't survive three hundred years of misery to lose it all when I just got my taste of happiness. I'm not going down without a fight, I'm not losing everything when I just got it. And when this is all over we'll start a family of our own. We'll have beautiful dark-headed Wraith, Witch, and Phoenix babies and they'll grow up safe and warm and loved. And no one will abandon them, no one will die on them, and no one will leave them. We'll have a house full of children for us to love. With a crazy, hodgepodge family of every kind of Ethereal there is."

I never thought she'd agree to kids. Especially now, but the thought of her heavy with our child, the thought of us swarmed with laughter and mess and all the things that the pair of us have been denied... it eases some of my worry and gives me the thing I've been lacking. Hope.

I pull her to me, my arm banding around her waist as her body fits flush against mine.

"Nah. They'll be gingers. We won't quit until we get at least two redheaded babies. Deal?" I quip, a real smile stretching across my face for the first time in a while.

"Deal," Nicola murmurs and her lips meet mine. When our mouths part we're both breathing heavy.

"Let's go kill some Witches, shall we?"

MENA

The string of curses that wish to escape my lips is varied and vast. I have a bad habit of blowing up houses, so having my entire family trapped under a single roof that I cannot escape is akin to skinning myself alive with a rusty, dull blade.

The shitty part of myself—the one that reminds me that I killed my parents, that I hurt people, that I'm unstable at the best of times—is yelling in my head that I'm going to fuck this up. That I'm going to kill them all. That I am going to hurt everyone I care about. And that isn't something I could survive.

Ash pulls me behind him up the narrow attic staircase, taking the highest spot in the house to get a vantage point. Typically, this would be Ian's job—out of all of us, Ian is the best sniper—but Ash is a close second, and Ian is more than a little occupied.

The finished attic is cozy and warm, decorated in greens and blues of a seriously killer man cave. And no man cave would be complete without a hidden panel concealing a couple of rifles and every single projectile weapon I can think of. Throwing knives, bo shurikens, hand guns, ammo, crossbows, rope darts... The only thing that is missing is a throwing spear and fucking boomerang.

I'm happy for them. I'm happy for every single weapon in this house. I'm also happy the incendiary devices are kept elsewhere. Ash agreed that it was the best course of action after I blew up the TV during a rather fierce hockey game. To my credit, it was the Stanley Cup finals, so I'm not exactly too broken up about it.

Ash is checking the sights on a very fancy sniper rifle, his body and mind laser-focused on the task at hand, but I have to make sure I won't fuck this all up.

"Ash, baby, I need you to make me a promise," I murmur, my voice shaking with the effort to hold myself together as I watch him clear the rifle. His snaps his head up and the winter blue of his eyes focus on me. I know he sees all the things I'm trying to hide. My trembling lip, my fidgeting hands, the thick pools of moisture in my eyes.

Then, I'm in his arms, locked in an embrace that steals away the ragged feeling in my chest.

"Whatever you need, Princess. I'll always do whatever it is you need."

I nod against his neck, but I know my request is a tough ask.

"If it looks like I'm gonna lose it, I need you to remove me from the equation. Snap my neck, shoot me in the head, whatever," I whisper his options for killing me into his skin, wishing I didn't have to say them at all.

"That might take us both out, Princess. You've never died and come back while we've been bonded. We don't know what will happen," Ash reminds me.

"Yeah, that's why it's a big ask. But if I lose it, if I can't pull myself back, then it won't be just me and you. It will be everyone I love lost because of me. Including those two babies. Including my sister and her husband and our friends. I'd lose you, and then we'd both be dead anyway." My tears are falling down my face faster than the soft, thick wool of his sweater can absorb them.

"We all fought together in Maine, and you didn't lose it. Even with Ari in trouble, you didn't hurt anyone but who needed to be hurt," he tries to soothe me, reassure me.

But he has to know, has to prepare for the worst. There has to be a plan because if we just go into this battle without one, we might not ever come out. I pull a bit out of his embrace so I can look him in the eye.

"It was different in Maine. We chose to go there together. We chose to fight, and we could leave at any time. Here, we don't have a choice. We're stuck like rats in a trap, and I don't want to be the one that hurts everyone I love. Please don't make me live through that again."

"You're asking me to do something I swore I would never do. But I get it. If I were a Revenant, I'd want you to do the same thing. So, if you are going to lose it, and if I can't get you to back down, I'll do what I have to do to keep everyone safe. But I will never want it to come to that, and I'll do everything I can to keep us both breathing. You got it?"

I breathe a stilted sigh of relief as I nod.

"Now, kiss me, Princess so I can go shoot a Witch in the melon, okay?"

But he doesn't wait for me to kiss him. He never does. Asher kisses me with a fervor that sings to my very soul, and I kiss him back with everything I have in me.

I just hope this isn't the last kiss we'll ever have.

27

I TOLD KYLE THAT WE WOULD MAKE IT OUT OF THIS. I TOLD HIM we would win and everything would be fine and I'd have his babies. I want all of that. I do. I just hope I wasn't lying when I said we'd make it out of here alive.

I don't know what our future will be. I don't know how we'll die, and for someone who is accustomed to knowing the ins and outs of just about every situation, the lack of knowledge is unsettling to say the least.

But I don't know the answer. I don't know how we're supposed to get out of this.

"Sybil said we needed magic to fight magic, right?" Kyle mumbles to himself more than me as he crouches down to flip through one of the grimoires that fell when Ian started CPR. His question might not have been directed at me, but it's enough to snap me out of my own dreary thoughts and get my head back in the fight.

"Yeah, she did. Do you know of a way to stop them? Or at the very least a way out of this house?"

"Maybe not them but at least the Eidola. There is a casting in here that is advanced magic—bigger than I've ever done. Something that frees trapped souls. I know I saw it…" he trails off as he flips pages looking for the spell. "That's what an Eidola is, right? Trapped souls?" he asks but he isn't really talking to me at all. He's looking through the grimoire as if his life depends on it and it just might.

"There!" he exclaims pointing to the chicken scratch of what I assume is the spell he means. His brows furrow even farther into the rut of his forehead as he studies the nearly illegible text.

"Okay. What do you need?" I ask when his silence stretches past the point of my patience. His mouth opens, ready to give me a list, and before he can get a word out his lips slam shut.

"Angelica root, white sage, wormwood… Most of the stuff I need, Max brought with her, but I don't think you want me to do this spell," Kyle murmurs trailing off.

"Why? What else do you need?"

"A dead body?" Kyle answers, his face screwed up into a wince.

"Yeah… we don't have one of those," I inform him unnecessarily. More worried about the fact that this looks to be sacrificial magic—a kind that Kyle typically refuses to practice.

"I'm aware, but I think we might need to get one," he winces again, in his eyes I see the direness of this whole situation.

I'm frozen because all I can think of is who in the hell we could possibly sacrifice and I'm stuck on one of my family dying. Then West and Evan are there, asking what he needs and I can't help but feel grateful for these people—grateful that they are there to pick up the slack for my weakness.

"You need a dead body? A specific species or will any work?" West asks and it makes sense that he'd be the one to inquire about the specifics. He and Kyle have been friends for hundreds of years and during most of that time, West spent it as the King's assassin.

He may be King now, but that doesn't take away four-hundred plus years as a killer. Not that I'm judging. West's soul is clean despite the blood on his hands.

"It doesn't say, so any might work. You thinking of stealing a Witch from outside?" Kyle offers as his eyes trail to the training center door. We don't actually know if we can get out of this house—not to mention do it undetected.

"He's sure as shit not killing anyone in here," Evan snaps, adjusting the tri-dagger at her hip and checking the bandolier of knives on her thigh. Her tiny body is loaded down with weapons even though her whole body in itself is one.

"Well, we don't have all day, let's go grab a Witch," Evan insists, "I'm sure there are more than a few out there."

West freezes and Cam just looks at her like she has lost her fucking mind. Because they both know just like I do that Evan plans on going herself.

"Yeah, no," Cam objects, shaking his head like he can't believe he has to say whatever is about to fall out of his mouth. "I don't care if I have to hog tie you and stuff you in a closet. You are not going outside. You know why, too."

"It's none of your business, Cam," Evan hisses back.

"Okay. That's cool. I'll just tell your husband that I'm pretty sure you're cooking a bun the oven and we'll just see who's going outside."

"You mother..." Evan fumes but she's cut off by West who grips her shoulders and spins her to look at him.

"Angel. Talk," he orders through gritted teeth. But she doesn't talk. She stands there—all four-foot-eleven of her looking mulish and defiant. She's a Queen, but right now she looks like a petulant toddler.

"I heard her puking in the powder room yesterday. And the day before. And the day before that," Cam interjects when she says nothing, effectively tattling on her.

"I don't know for sure," she mumbles, looking down at her black leather booties.

"Finally a problem I can fix. Gimme your hand," I offer, and when she doesn't move to answer me, I snatch it up to confirm what we all know is true. Oh, she's knocked up alright.

But I get more, too. I get her fear. I get her absolute terror in the possibility of being pregnant in the middle of a war. Evan asking herself how she could bring a child into this—especially since her reign is so new.

But I don't get much more than that. Whatever they are doing outside this house is either scrambling my sight or we won't make it out of here alive. I really hope it's the former because the latter sucks huge monkey balls.

Before I can open my eyes, I hear West's intelligible yell, and when they flash open at the sound, all I see is Cam's retreating back as he bolts out of the training center. West is on his ass rubbing his jaw and I know.

Cam isn't risking either of his charges for what we need.

He's getting the Witch himself.

CAMERON

I'm going to get my ass kicked for what I just did.

Yes, I totally just punched out my King to keep him from following me out the door. If we make it out of this hell alive, I'll take the answering ass whooping with a smile on my face.

I just couldn't take another time where my people got themselves into a situation where they could die. Didn't they know how many counted on them? Didn't they understand how important they were?

Of course, I made it so it was me getting what we needed. Of course, I made it so it was me alone. Aidan has his brother—Ian needs him. Evan and West are important. Mena and Asher are important. Aurelia and Rhys and Kyle and Nicola…

They matter. They have family. They have a purpose.

I don't. I protect people who don't really need my protection. I am Guardian to two of the most lethal Wraiths living or dead. I don't have any living family except for Asher and even he doesn't seem to like me much.

I am superfluous.

I am expendable.

I might as well make myself useful.

Drawing my weapon, I shift the thick drapes aside to see through the basement walk-out door. Since the view is mostly the wide stone steps leading up to the back yard, I can't see shit. That doesn't mean they aren't there, but scenting through the reinforced, bulletproof glass French doors is pretty much impossible. I take one more sweep with my eyes before silently flipping the latch and turning the knob.

Immediately, I realize how much of an idiot I am when a Witch comes into view at the base of the steps as if he is pulling off an invisibility cloak. Fuck. Ian can do that whole 'cloaking' shit too and I should have scented or even used my damn ears before closing the door behind me.

The man before me could be thirty or he could be three hundred. Witches age slowly—some not at all if they use the right spell. His features are somewhere between heroin-chic and 90's small. Either way, he looks like he could use a sandwich or five. Shaved white-blonde hair shines like a beacon against his sallow skin, and the dark brown of his eyes seem to sink into his face, competing too hard with razor-sharp cheekbones and losing rather spectacularly.

The space between us is tight—no more than maybe four feet—but he saw me first and has the time to react long before I do. Trying to smoke out from my unfortunate position turns out to be completely impossible, so when the spell hits me I am utterly unprepared.

It figures. I can't even do this right.

My feet leave the ground from the force of it as if I were a puppet on a string—my body flying back into the closed French doors. My first stroke of luck in this whole mess is the glass is of the two-inch thick, bulletproof variety. The second is the Witch in front of me is weak or weakened significantly by whatever spell is keeping us here. Yay me.

My phase is quick, talons growing, fangs lengthening, the edges of my body becoming wisps of smoke. I'm less than a step from him when I'm knocked into the stone wall of the stairwell.

I would have won—at least against this one Witch—but as my consciousness fades, I'm hit again from the side as another arrives at the mouth of the staircase.

I am superfluous.

I am expendable.

Well, at least I'm right about something.

28

ASHER

LOOKING THROUGH THE SCOPE OF A RIFLE NARROWS YOUR world to a single circle of vision. This is why snipers usually have spotters—someone to tell them the wind speed, the conditions, the other players in the game. Because when you can't see the bigger picture, when you can't see the forest for the trees, you lose a significant chunk of the information you need.

In truth, I could probably do without the scope. My abilities let me see a whole hell of a lot, but having that extra push for accuracy trumps the naked eye any day.

I line up my shot, and honestly, it feels too easy. Bella is standing dead-center of our front yard bold as brass. She might be with a shit-ton of her cronies, formed in a loose circle around the house—probably working the spell that's keeping us here.

The shot is too good to pass up. The ease of squeezing the trigger makes up for the recoil slamming into my shoulder, but the satisfaction of seeing Bella Bishop die never comes. I lined up my shot perfectly, and the bullet should have hit her right in the heart.

But my bullet never made it.

Irritated, I squeeze the trigger again, but this time I actually catch it when my bullet disintegrates mid-air.

Fucking Witches. Goddamn spells.

"This rifle is useless. She's protecting herself somehow," I mutter, pulling back from the scope. Mena shuffles from one foot to the other while looking through a spotting scope on a collapsible tripod, the frenetic energy in her palpable.

"Sybil was right. You have no idea how much that irritates the fuck out of me," she grouses through gritted teeth. This I get. If Sybil were my aunt, I'd hate it if she were right too. "Baron just showed up. Oh god..." Mena trails off.

She's right, Baron has simply appeared on our property and behind him is a dense cloud of slate gray smoke as if he were the charging flag of a dying forest fire. I don't know how I know this, but everything in me turns to ice when I see that cloud behind him. Eidola Nicola had said.

I'd heard stories of it as a small child. So rarely had it been used, the lore of the Eidola was practically fable.

Don't cross a Witch or she will send The Devouring after you. The Eidola will eat you up and turn you to ash.

But the Eidola wouldn't even be here if Wraiths did their jobs. If there were enough Wraiths to go around to send all the evil souls to hell. But there aren't. And that was before Iva's massacres.

Now we are too few.

The inky gray of the smoke tip-toes its way closer and closer to the house skirting around Bella but consuming the Witch right next to her moving to the next and next. Each time it reaches a new person, the smoke grows denser, the red of Bella's magic gets brighter. The Eidola is siphoning magic into her as it kills.

I don't think bullets are gonna work here.

"Shit!" Mena curses, and I look in the direction her scope is pointed.

Cam is outside.

Cam—my idiot fucking cousin—is outside when that mass of evil is swarming us. *Jesus, shit, fuck. Why? What the fucking hell is he thinking?*

I'm frozen as I watch him get hit from the Witch who appears just in front of him and then again from another at the top of the stairs. That isn't to say I don't fire—I do—but whatever juju Bella is working isn't just protecting her, it's protecting all of them until the Eidola consumes them.

I have to go get him. I can't watch the last of my family die right in front of me, but then an odd-colored—for lack of a better word—flame catches my eye in the scope. I pull back from the rubber to get a better look, and I don't quite know what I'm seeing.

I think it's a Phoenix, and I'm almost positive it's Samara, but...

She doesn't look like any Phoenix I've ever seen, and that is saying something. Blue-green flames coat her skin like water. Iridescent green scales run the length of her face, down her neck, and under the three-quarter sleeve of her top, stopping at the peak of her knuckles. The wings bursting from her back appear as if a bird and a fish had a baby because those same scales rise through the rips of her shirt and coat the scapular attachment at her skin diminishing to the teal feathers of the rest of her wings.

I hear Mena's breath catch and evidently, so does Samara because her head whips in our direction for a split second before turning back to the men who hurt Cam.

"Her eyes..." Mena whispers, and she's right. The woman down there has Samara's face and yet doesn't. And her eyes might not be the most shocking of all her features, but they scream different. Her irises have changed from chocolate brown to sea green, but the oddest part is that green fades to the blackness that now coats what used to be the whites of her eyes.

Samara makes the Witches pause too—to their own detriment—and she doesn't waste the opportunity they have given her. She puts her body in between them and Cam, opens her typically silent mouth and screams.

Her shriek is a weapon in and of itself, knocking the Witches on their asses, so she has enough time to grab my idiot cousin by the scruff and drag him inside. The Witches don't get back up, and then the smoke consumes them too, leaving only Baron, Bella, and a fog of death on my snowy front lawn.

What the fuck did we just see?

KYLE

I was too busy looking at a spellbook, trying to find a way out of this house, a way to fight the evil Devourer coming, that I didn't see Cam throw the punch. Then he was gone, and West was rubbing his jaw with his ass planted on the training room floor.

Less than five minutes later, Samara walks back into the training room dragging his unconscious ass behind her like a sack of potatoes. Her signs are furious and fluid, and since so few of us know ASL, we are at a loss until Rhys starts translating.

"The Eidola is here, and the other Witches are dead and gone. There is only Baron and Bella," he tells us.

Fuck.

We needed this win. We needed one of those Witches. We needed this because I don't know what to do without it.

Mena and Asher come barreling in the door next, the pair of them eyeing Samara for a second before telling us what they saw.

"Bella absorbed all the Witches with the Eidola, siphoned the power somehow," Mena blurts.

"Bullets don't touch them. I don't... I don't know how we can fight this," Ash adds, and the heavy pit in my stomach turns to the worst leaden weight.

There is no one to sacrifice, no one I could consider killing to save us. And even if I could, how would I choose?

"Oh, for fuck's sake," Sybil mutters, stomping off to the weapon wall and snatching an ornate Morganite dagger from its pegs. I've always wondered why Mena and Asher would keep Morganite in their house, why they would keep something that could kill them here.

But I don't have time to ponder much further. Sybil stalks to our small circle of confused and frightened family. We brace because at best Sybil is unpredictable and at worst she is a raving fucking lunatic.

The first thing that comes to mind as she makes her way here is she's going to kill Nicola or Mena, and Asher has my same thought because just like me he puts himself in front of his wife, drawing whatever weapon is in easy reach.

"Do you need the blood of the dead or to draw from the essence?" Sybil asks.

Uh, what?

I look down at the book at my feet to find the answer.

"Just the body, but we don't have one."

Sybil meets her daughter's eyes at my side for a long moment before answering me.

"Yes, you do," she whispers before driving the dagger into her own neck.

"Mama, no!" Nicola screeches, shoving past me to catch Sybil before she can go down.

Shock freezes us all as Nicola tries to stem the flow of blood from her rapidly fading mother's neck. They weren't close. They weren't even friendly. I'm pretty sure that they hated each other a little bit. But still. Blood is blood. Family is family. The agony is there even if the love is not.

Sybil's body jerks once, twice, and then stills. Nicola's howl of anguish rips at my heart.

I don't want to do it, but I won't let her sacrifice go to waste. I meet Asher's eyes, and he nods, nudging Mena to help him with Nicola as I take her mother's body from her.

I don't have the time to give Sybil the respect she deserves—the funeral pyre and attire will have to be replaced with a salt circle and desecration. I feel like the Devil himself doing this. I grab what I need from the carved mahogany chest Max brought with her that contains all of her supplies. I pluck the salt, angelica root, wormwood, and white sage from their carefully organized spots and grab the shallow hammered copper bowl too and set about following the spell to the letter.

But I really don't want to.

I position Sybil's body according to the instruction keeping her ankles together and spreading her arms wide. Then, I start the things I don't want to do. I etch the sigils from the book into her forehead with the bloody dagger I plucked from her still hand, and worse still I count three ribs down from the left side of her chest and break the bones to pluck the heart from her chest, depositing it into the bowl with the rest of the herbs. Circling her body in salt, I begin chanting the words on the paper. Hoping I don't fuck this up and waste her sacrifice.

Haec spirituum liberate. Hinc eieci eos. Free these spirits. Banish them from this place.

The heart, pooling blood, and herbs catch fire in the copper bowl, the smoke from the fire coiling like a snake up in the air. The coil turns in on itself, slithering down over the sides and across the ground, funneling under the training room door.

I keep chanting. It's the only thing I know to do.

NICOLA

She did this for me. For us. She might have been an opportunistic bitch, but Sybil was *my* opportunistic bitch. I never expected her to sacrifice herself—not for me, not for anyone. Maybe she did it out of vengeance.

Or spite.

But when I watch the smoke of the spell Ky cast funnel out the door I have to follow it. I have to see my mother's one good thing through. I have to see it banish that evil, liberate those souls. I have to *know* her existence was worth more than a dagger in the neck and a lifetime of toil.

Before I know it, I've left the training center behind, following the wispy tendrils of Kyle's spell up the stairs and out the basement walkout up another flight of stone steps where the inky black smoke forms into a giant snake striking and biting at the dense Eidola.

This is so much larger than what killed my father. This is larger than anything I've seen in my whole life, but Kyle's spell is bigger. It slithers and coils around the Eidola, squeezing and striking and the screams...

Those used to be people. Those souls used to be alive and maybe they weren't good, maybe they weren't decent, but no soul deserves to be used this way, to be desecrated this way. With each strike from the coal black snake, the Eidola gets smaller, another soul freed from the torment of this violation. Soon the only thing standing between me and Baron is Bella.

A gun is too good for them. They need to die slowly, painfully. They need to answer for every wrong they've done and soul they've tainted. They need to answer for my mother, and Talia, and Grace. They need to answer for me and the brother I never met and the father I lost too soon.

The Bishop family has been the architect of so much misery. Fire races over my skin as my wings burst from my back, ripping through my sweater as if it were nothing more than tissue paper. I relish the sweet agony of them exploding from their vestigial hiding place. I love the pain right now. Because it means I can do what they can't. One giant sweep of my wings and I'm airborne, and before the red magics of Bella's answering spell can reach me, I've drawn the throwing knife from my thigh holster and let it fly, planting it in her chest.

Just like her cronies, she scrabbles at the blade for a few moments before realizing too late that she's met her end.

One down. One to go.

But I don't get Baron. No.

As soon as Bella takes her last breath, the spell keeping my family in the house breaks. Kyle is there, and West, and Rhys, and Mena. Joe slinks with his puma grace, and Talia's wolf form follows close behind him, still scared of the man who brutalized her. Max slowly emerges up the stairs, Ian holding her up as she makes each step with a mulish sort of grace. They didn't beat her, she's still breathing, still standing.

"I suppose it's torture for me, right?" Baron sneers. He doesn't appear afraid at all, and that just irritates me.

"Of course. But we'll have to find new and interesting ways to kill you since you're fireproof. How many children did you kill to steal that power?" I find myself asking as my feet touch the ground.

"Plenty," he says with a smile that is more evil than humorous.

"Well, that's good to know. I'd hate to execute an innocent man," West replies. "Did you know I'm rather adept at killing? I've been doing it for quite some time, you see. I'm what you'd call a professional at it. I'm sure we can find a way to make sure you stay dead."

EPILOGUE

KYLE—THREE YEARS LATER

I WAKE UP TO AN EMPTY BED. IT ISN'T THE FIRST TIME AND likely won't be the last. Nicola doesn't sleep as much as she used to these days, but I don't mind it anymore. It has been a very long time since she has woken me with her nightmares.

She sleeps soundly now, which is good since she and I will likely not get much sleep in the near future. Still, I get up to investigate where my lovely wife has gone.

We set up in a house closer to her family, only a mile down the road from Mena's sprawling mansion cabin and three miles from Aurelia's. It took longer than we thought to settle in, to find our place in this new world of fewer enemies. To find our place without turmoil with each other.

Grace and Joe moved from New Orleans to Denver—deciding to live closer to the supernatural side of Grace's family. Sure, she might be farther from her mother, but now that she's been divested of the amulet that suppressed her magic, our lessons are progressing swimmingly.

Grace and Marj have finally broken the ice, though, and now that Marj has a new husband, her rigidness has calmed significantly. Plus, having Grace close gives me a peace I didn't know I was missing. I have a feeling I will be buried under the peace of children for some time.

I have yet to acclimate to the elusive Joseph, but he makes my daughter smile, and for that I cannot fault the man. Even if he is a Shapeshifter.

I make my way downstairs to the kitchen, following the awful smell of Nicola's shoddy attempts at cooking. No matter her keen sense of smell and fierce intellect, she has become no more adept at cooking now than she was three years ago. She tries, though, and I think that is what matters.

Nicola bends awkwardly as she pulls a smoking muffin tin from the oven. The charred remnants of whatever recipe she was trying to concoct bearing no resemblance to actual food. Another one bites the dust.

"I have a feeling when our daughter gets here, I'll be doing most of the cooking," I quip, catching her by surprise.

"Bloody hell, Sasquatch, you damn near gave me a heart attack."

"You can't get a heart attack."

"It's a figure of speech," Nicola says irritably as she rubs the burgeoning swell of her belly. Our daughter only has a few more weeks to cook before we get to meet her, and I can't wait.

"What exactly was that supposed to be?" I inquire, probably to my own detriment. Nicola is a perfectionist and she hates not being able to cook.

"Blueberry muffins. Why can't I do this?" she grouses burying her face in her hands in embarrassment.

I'd hate the sight, but the wide face of the oval sapphire in her wedding ring winks at me in the morning light, and a swell of pride hits me. I love my ring finally on her finger. I love the swell of her belly. I love everything about her. Even her shitty cooking.

"You do realize no one—and I mean no one—actually expects you to bring anything to brunch right? Especially after last year's salmon dip fiasco," I tease, wrapping my arms around her and pressing a kiss to her forehead.

There are some things perpetual healing can't fix. Food poisoning is one of them. The bloody fucking horror. To this day I can't think of salmon without shuddering.

"I just wanted to get it right before she gets here," Nic mumbles, shrugging her shoulders in that defeatist way of hers.

"Shortcake, you're going to have to let it go. You can teach our girl everything else, but I'll take the cooking bit, okay?"

"Fine," she grumbles, her hand making a circular rub over her belly. That wince right there, though, that is new.

"You alright, Shortcake?" I ask but I already know something is a little off.

"Just a cramp. I've had a couple off and on today and..." she trails off, her eyes widening in alarm. The drip, drip, drip I hear is not coming from the faucet.

"She's coming, isn't she?" Nicola's face is a mask of wonder and I love that there are still things on this earth that can surprise her.

Nicola simply nods, and I snatch my phone from the counter. Asher answers on the first ring. I don't even get a hello.

"Hospital?" he asks, two steps ahead of me.

"How the hell did you know?" I grouse as he steals my thunder.

"My sister-in-law is a Seer, you two are thirty minutes late for Little John's birthday pajama brunch, and your wife is thirty-eight weeks pregnant. Please take your pick from the bevy of clues that would tell me that you two are headed to Knoxville."

Only Evan and West would nickname their son Little John. The now two-year-old is anything but little. The kid is built like a Sherman tank.

"Nic's water just broke. See you in a few?"

"Dammit! Aurelia won the pot again!" Carver yells in the background.

"Language!" Ari yells back.

"Yeah right. And Henry's first word wasn't fuck," Max throws in.

"Stop letting the Seer gamble with you, stupid. She cheats," I scold and hang up.

I look into my wife's excited eyes and wonder how we got so lucky.

"Think we'll get a ginger right out of the gate?" I ask trying to keep her calm. I don't really have to try. Nicola is serene in between bouts of wincing in discomfort.

"Maybe," she murmurs, a soft smile on her face as her eyes alight in the iridescent blue of a vision.

She knows already.

And that smile tells me everything is going to be just fine.

Thank you so much for reading Sight Kissed. The Phoenix Rising Series ends here, BUT check out my brand new series which centers around Max and her special brand of shenanigans.

Get Woman of Blood & Bone Today!

Want the skinny on future releases without having to follow me absolutely everywhere on social media?
Text "LEGION" to (844) 311-5791

Grab Woman of Blood & Bone today!

Grab Woman of Blood & Bone today!

BOOKS BY ANNIE ANDERSON

SEVERED FLAMES

Ruined Wings

IMMORTAL VICES & VIRTUES

HER MONSTROUS MATES

Bury Me

SHADOW SHIFTER BONDS

Shadow Me

THE ARCANE SOULS WORLD

GRAVE TALKER SERIES

Dead to Me

Dead & Gone

Dead Calm

Dead Shift

Dead Ahead

Dead Wrong

Dead & Buried

SOUL READER SERIES

Night Watch

Death Watch

Grave Watch

THE WRONG WITCH SERIES

Spells & Slip-ups

Magic & Mayhem

Errors & Exorcisms

The Lost Witch Series

Curses & Chaos

Hexes & Hijinx

THE ETHEREAL WORLD

Phoenix Rising Series

(Formerly the Ashes to Ashes Series)

Flame Kissed

Death Kissed

Fate Kissed

Shade Kissed

Sight Kissed

Rogue Ethereal Series

Woman of Blood & Bone

Daughter of Souls & Silence

Lady of Madness & Moonlight

Sister of Embers & Echoes

Priestess of Storms & Stone

Queen of Fate & Fire

To stay up to date on all things Annie Anderson, get exclusive access to ARCs and giveaways, and be a member of a fun, positive, drama-free space, join The Legion!

facebook.com/groups/ThePhoenixLegion

ABOUT THE AUTHOR

 Annie Anderson is the author of the international bestselling Rogue Ethereal series. A United States Air Force veteran, Annie pens fast-paced Urban Fantasy novels filled with strong, snarky heroines and a boatload of magic. When she takes a break from writing, she can be found binge-watching The Magicians, flirting with her husband, wrangling children, or bribing her cantankerous dogs to go on a walk.

To find out more about Annie and her books, visit
www.annieande.com